SWORDS OF RAEMLLYN
Book 3

Also by Robert E. Vardeman and published by
New English Library

The Demon Crown Trilogy
The Jade Demons Quartet
The Keys to Paradise
Masters of Space
The Weapons of Chaos
The Accursed

By Robert E. Vardeman and Geo. W. Proctor:

Swords of Raemllyn: Book 1
Swords of Raemllyn: Book 2

By Robert E. Vardeman and Victor Milán:

The War of Powers
The War of Powers – Part 2: Istu Awakened

Swords of Raemllyn: Book 3

I: Blade of the Conqueror
II: The Tombs of A'bre
III: The Jewels of Life

Robert E. Vardeman and
Geo. W. Proctor

NEW ENGLISH LIBRARY
Hodder and Stoughton

First published in Great Britain by Hodder and Stoughton
A division of Hodder Headline PLC

A New English Library paperback

British Library Cataloguing in Publication Data

Vardeman, Robert E.
Swords of Raemllyn. – Book 3
I. Title II. Proctor, Geo. W.
813.54 [F]

ISBN 0-340-61774-8

Typeset by
Letterpart Limited, Reigate, Surrey
Printed and bound in Great Britain by
Cox & Wyman, Reading, Berks.

Hodder and Stoughton
A division of Hodder Headline PLC
338 Euston Road, London NW1 3BH

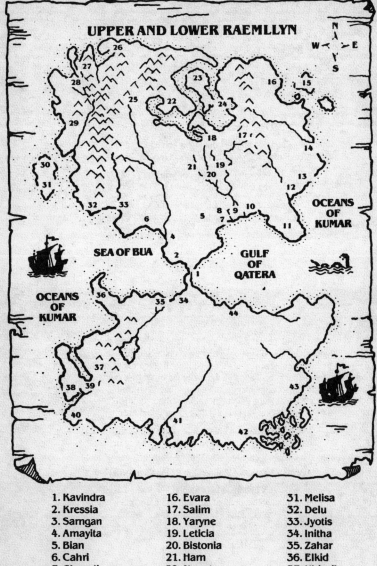

UPPER AND LOWER RAEMLLYN

1. Kavindra
2. Kressia
3. Sarngan
4. Amayita
5. Bian
6. Cahri
7. Chavali
8. Degoolah
9. Garoda
10. Jyn
11. Meakham
12. Parm
13. Qatim
14. Orji
15. Iluska
16. Evara
17. Salim
18. Yaryne
19. Leticia
20. Bistonia
21. Ham
22. Nawat
23. Vatusia
24. Rakell
25. Solana
26. Faldin
27. Weysh
28. Salnal
29. Yow
30. Litonya
31. Melisa
32. Delu
33. Jyotis
34. Initha
35. Zahar
36. Elkid
37. Uhjayib
38. Fayinah
39. Pahl
40. Rattreh
41. Ohnuhn
42. Gatinah
43. Ahvayuh
44. Nayati

BLADE OF THE CONQUEROR

1

Qar, the Black Destroyer, Raemllyn's God of Death, feasted. Unseen by mortals, his shadowy presence enveloped the Isle of Loieter. Here and there a sinewy tendril of mist dipped from the skies. Controlled by the deity's gentle touch, a gray tabby cat leaped from bushy concealment to rob a spring robin of life. Beside a softly gurgling stream a tow-headed boy lifted a stone and abruptly slammed it into the frog with which he played, nudged to act by an invisible finger tapped at the base of his spine.

To the Dark One, these were but tasty tidbits, sweetmeats that provided momentary diversion for the palate. Above the city-state of Rakell and the plain that stretched before the walled metropolis, Qar gorged himself, herself, itself – the Black God's sex adapted to the needs of the moment. There, armies warred.

Qar gave no heed to the fact that the green-uniformed warriors of Raemllyn's rightful liege Prince Felrad routed the armored soldiers of Zarek Yannis, usurper to the Velvet Throne in distant Kavindra. Any life escaping from gutted belly or slashed throat fed the Black Destroyer. Ecstasy as only Death may experience suffused the brume that was the Dark One when Qar's great maw opened to gulp down the rush of agonized souls that rose from the fallen.

Thousands upon thousands died, and Qar supped greedily. Only when the last clash of the battle din died did the Black God's tongue lick over shrouded lips with decided relish. Yet, the Great Destroyer remained unsated; an ever empty stomach rumbled angrily. Such is the nature of Death – eternally to seek prey to feed its unquenchable hunger.

Qar's alert eyes scanned the bloody scene below, sought and found one who had served him well for years.

The sword! Valora trembled, unwilling to believe the fortunate twist of fate the Sitala cast. Her brow furrowed and her dark eyes darted from side to side. Another quiver worked through her slender body. *It can't be this easy.*

Yet, it was!

A blue-robed physician, one of the five tending the ugly gash that ran from Prince Felrad's left shoulder across his chest to his waist, placed the Sword of Kwerin Bloodhawk in her hands. The legendary blade of Raemllyn's first High King – this was the prize that had brought her to Rakell! For this she had allied herself with Prince Felrad and had staved off assault after assault of magicks cast by Zarek Yannis' sorcerers during the day's long battle.

In her wildest flights of fantasy, Valora had envisioned possessing the sword only after weaving a tapestry of subtle spells about the prince and those who surrounded him. Now, without so much as a simple sleeping chant, the Sword of the Bloodhawk lay in her hands.

Her long white fingers closed around the simple unadorned sheath holding the magic-tempered steel. She repressed the urge to clutch the weapon to her breast and run from the hall to which Felrad's litter was borne. A desperate act now would assure failure. Too many eyes were on her.

"Back." Valora waved away those who crowded about the prince as if they were bothersome children. "Let the physicians do their work. He's lost far too much blood. Go, let me get . . ."

"No." Felrad's eyes fluttered open. He glanced over the faces of the men and women around him. "Davin, is that you?"

Unnoticed until now, Valora watched Davin Anane edge beside the litter. Felrad's bastard brother answered, "Yes, my Prince."

A weak smile played across Felrad's lips. "The Sitala like to play with mortals. With the Sword of the Bloodhawk I stood against Yannis' horde of Faceless Ones without serious injury. A soldier armed but with a puny dirk did this. Jumped from an alley, struck, then raced away."

"My Prince," Davin urged, "rest. Save your strength. Valora will see that the physicians attend your wounds."

A soft sigh escaped Valora's lips. She had been wise to stay her flight. Davin Anane, although nothing more than a thief from the realm of Jyotis, was not a man to trifle with. Nor was the fiery-haired giant Goran One-Eye who stood at his side. Goran was no mere man; in truth no man at all, but Challing, a shape-shifting creature drawn to this world through a rent in space and time. As to the frosty-tressed wench to Davin's left, Lijena Farleigh, it was she who first delivered the magic-bound blade into Felrad's hands.

Valora had faced the three in the distant woods of Agda and failed to wrest the fabled weapon from them. That failure had brought her here to Rakell and forged her brief, distasteful alliance with Prince Felrad in his struggle to regain his rightful place as Raemllyn's High King.

"And you attend our wounds, son of Anane," Felrad spoke to the Jyotian. "The others mustn't know of this. Not now, when victory is so sweet. Tend to the dead and wounded, and let it be known that I counsel with Valora to map our strategy for a campaign south to drive Zarek Yannis from the Velvet Throne. Do that for me, my brother."

"Aye." Davin clasped the prince's hand as it rose to him and squeezed tightly. "I will do all that you have commanded."

Valora watched Davin and his two companions turn and stride from the hall. The sorceress's gaze shifted to the prince; she smiled. "Now you must rest and allow these men to heal your wounds."

"Yes, rest would be good." Felrad's eyes drifted closed. "Sleep will renew my strength."

"Go and let the prince sleep." Valora again waved away those who remained around Felrad and his physicians. "And seal your lips. None must know of these wounds until the prince decides the time is right."

As the prince's retinue retreated, Valora leaned to the nearest physician and whispered, "I shall wait in the antechamber should the prince need me."

When the green-robed man nodded, Valora stepped through a door on the left side of the hall. Heart pounding as though attempting to explode from her breast, she hefted the sheathed sword and stared at the weapon. The power to bring Zarek Yannis to his knees – nay, the power to rule all Raemllyn – was hers!

Valora grasped the simple wire-wound hilt intent on wrenching the magic blade free. She hesitated. This was not the time to gloat over her easy victory. Later, when she was free of Rakell and the prince there would be time enough to study the sword first brought to life by the long-dead mage Edan.

A curtain ripped from a window and its drawstring served to bundle and bind the ancient sword. With that bulky parcel tucked beneath an arm, the black-tressed witch walked into the streets of Rakell. Measured strides that disguised the excited race of her pulse carried her along winding avenues to the fortress city's northern gate. There, a single guard stood beside a saddled mount. The rest of Felrad's forces focused their labors to the south where today's battle had been fought.

"Halt." The soldier's right hand dropped to the sword slung from his hip and poised there ready to draw the blade. "No one may pass."

A perplexed frown shadowed the sorceress's face. "Are you certain? I have orders from Prince Felrad himself to deliver this bundle to Vatusia in the north."

Valora's right hand slipped into the folds of her robe as she held out the tightly wrapped sword with her left.

"I know nothing about no packages." The guard shook his head and stepped forward to examine the proffered bundle. "All I know is what Higat, me captain, told me, and that I wasn't to let no one in or out of this . . ."

The soldier's words drowned in a spray of crimson. Valora's right hand snaked from her black robe and struck in a high, wide arc that deftly drew her dirk's honed edge across the guard's neck to open his gullet from ear to ear. Eyes bulging and hands clutched around his throat to stem the flood of red that gushed from the wound with each beat of his heart, the man dropped to his knees.

Valora planted a slippered foot on his side and kicked him away. She paid no heed to his spasmodically jerking body while she hid the dirk beneath her robes again, then lifted a hem to wipe away the blood splattered on the saddle of the guard's mount. Satisfied no trace of red remained on the leather, the sorceress climbed into the saddle and rode north through Rakell's open gates.

High above her floated a black mist stirred by the warm spring breeze. Qar, God of Death, tasted the sweetness of yet another soul.

* * *

High Queen of Raemllyn! In spite of her proximity to danger, Valora could not keep her thoughts from soaring as her fingers caressed the bundle and the key to obtaining that exalted title held within. *I have come far since being apprenticed to that toad Payat'Morve**.

The smell of salt water wafted in the air. Memories of her apprenticeship to Zarek Yannis' former mage edged aside as the future beckoned. She eased the mount to an easy gallop as she scanned the horizon. The ocean still lay beyond the rolling hills, but she was near the coast. Her nose verified that with each deep breath.

Creases furrowed Valora's flawless brow. Her thoughts flew too fast and too high! The Sword of Kwerin *was* the key to destroying the hordes of Faceless Ones Zarek Yannis drew from some demonic realm. Alone, however, it was not enough. She could never hope to defeat Zarek Yannis' army or the remnants of Felrad's legions – if Felrad survived his wounds.

Or whoever else might try to gain the Velvet Throne with arms and troops.

Count Berenicis the Blackheart wedged into the sorceress's mind. The deposed ruler of Jyotia had betrayed Felrad this day, and though his ruse failed, she had heard no reports of her former ally's body being found on the battlefield. If Berenicis had one trait it was the ability to survive when others would have died a hundred times over.

No, she agreed with herself, the ensorcelled blade was only the beginning of her quest for the Velvet Throne. She needed a safe keep to shelter her while she mapped strategies – time to raise an army to ride before her.

Where? She bit at her lower lip and once more surveyed the rolling land before her. Where in all the kingdoms of Upper and Lower Raemllyn could she hide until she grew strong enough to drive toward Kavindra?

An unexpected chill in the breeze sent a shiver through the sorceress's slender body. Her eyes narrowed. Something more than the wind was aplay in the air. A warmth radiated from the

* See *A Yoke of Magic*

bundled Sword of Kwerin Bloodhawk as though the steel sensed the powers that stirred.

Magicks! Valora recognized the presence of unbridled forces rising from an enchanted source as surely as a direwolf's nostrils gather the blood scent of wounded prey. A humorless smile danced at the corners of her mouth when she sat straight in the saddle; her head turned slowly from left to right before steadying directly before her. No magnetic needle pointed with such unerring ability. *North – it flows from the north!*

An uncertain tremble rather than chilly shiver coursed through the witch. Land's end was near. Nothing lay beyond Upper Raemllyn's northern reaches – nothing except sailors' tales, myth and uncharted waters.

Yet, she could not deny the strength of the forces she felt weaving in the air around her. To find the source – to harness those powers – her mind raced. For one seeking to claim the Velvet Throne as her own, such possibilities could not be discarded. *North – to the north I travel!*

Valora allowed her mount to slow to a walk when the animal topped a gentle rise. Below lay a small harbor; fishermen's huts, no more than fifty, nestled near a sandy beach. She tapped the horse's sides with her heels to quicken its pace forward.

Her original intention had been to ride to Vatusia and hire a boat there, but this village would provide all she required. What need of a crew did she have when she could summon the elements to her bidding? Her gaze lifted to the north; her lips moved silently as she recalled the needed spell. Minutes passed before ancient words found form in her voice and burst forth in a sing-song like random notes blown on a reed pipe.

"Milady? Are you well?"

A man's voice shattered the sorceress's concentration. Her head snapped to the right. She blinked. A gray-haired man in hip boots stood staring at her. "What?"

"Is all well with you?" The man asked through snaggled teeth and chapped lips. "You've been standin' and starin' out to sea for nigh on ten minutes."

Valora's jet eyes fixed on the simple fisherman. He clutched a tangled net in one hand and a short iron harpoon in the other. He stank of fish and the sea. His coarsely woven shirt bore the stains of years of use. Valora's lips curled back in a half-smile. "I seek a boat. I would buy the fastest in this village."

"I dunno, milady." The old fisherman scratched at his head. "No one in these parts is much interested in speed. Built 'em for pullin' in the herring and the occasional *surrin* fish. See the fine belt I made from its scaly hide? Biggest *surrin* ever netted, it was."

He thrust out his belly to show a green-scaled cinch holding up heavy canvas britches. Valora waved a hand to dismiss his attempt to launch into fishing stories.

"'Sides, don't know if I can rightly sell you a boat." He cast out an arm toward the clustered huts. "No one here 'cept me. All the others are gone to Rakell to aid Prince Felrad or to Vatusia for safety. Left me here, they did, to watch over everything."

"A boat, fast and able, is all I need." Valora stared past the fisherman to the rickety docks. The largest of the small fishing fleet caught her eye. It had the width of beam and the sturdiness to weather any spring storm she might encounter on a northward journey. She pointed to the double-masted vessel. "That one. I'll take that one."

"Why, that belongs to the town lord, Lord Benzy." The man's eyes widened.

"Lord? In this miserable burrow?" Valora laughed aloud. What airs these rustics assumed! "No matter. You will act as my agent."

Her fingertips danced. Green sparks shot from finger to finger. The fisherman's mud-colored eyes grew wider and his mouth fell open.

"You will give your lord these fine horses," she said, motioning to the exhausted horse that had borne her from Rakell while she dismounted. "All fifty of these thoroughbreds in trade for his pathetic boat."

"Fifty? I see only one." The fisherman's voice trailed off and spittle dribbled down his chin as his mouth became increasingly flaccid. "Fifty, yes, yes, I see them all now. Fine horses."

"Yes," Valora answered impatiently. "Very fine horses. Give them all to your lord after you show me aboard the ship. Tell him what a fine bargain you haggled for this vessel."

"What's a fisherman need with horses?" the weather-beaten

fisherman asked, blinking at the sight of a single horse magically mirrored fifty times.

"Eat them for breakfast, you fool! Qar take your stinking liver!" She shoved past the man and strode toward the dock.

The breeze shifted, blowing from the south. Valora smiled; the elements answered her summoning. Once more her fingers wove patterns in the air. Sail unfurled and lines slithered from pier to deck when she stepped aboard the vessel. The prow of the fishing boat swung away from its rickety berth and nosed northward.

The warmth still radiating from the bundle in her hands drew her attention to the purloined blade forged by the great Edan. What were its powers? Again she sensed the magicked steel, *felt* the forces drawing her northward. She knew the sword could destroy the demon riders called the Faceless Ones. But surely Kwerin's mage Edan had endowed his legendary blade with more potency than that. Her task was to discover the sword's *hidden* powers – then to use those powers.

"High Queen Valora, Ruler of Upper and Lower Raemllyn," she said softly. She savored the sound of it, relished the way it rolled from her tongue.

"Tide's not right, milady. Won't be right 'til sundown." The fisherman called to her from the pier.

"I need no tide." Valora laughed as rising wind filled the sail.

"Storm's rising," the fisherman said, his voice a whisper in the distance.

The man was crazy. Valora shook her head as she studied the cloudless blue sky. The weather was fair with no hint of tempest from horizon to horizon.

The warmth rising from the bundle in her hands demanded attention. Quickly she plucked away the cord knotted about the rolled curtain and then extracted the sheathed weapon. Her right hand closed around the hilt. Slowly Valora withdrew the rune-etched blade.

It was true! The sword sensed magicks! She felt power coursing through the steel that set her hand to tingling. Lifting the blade, she held the Sword of Kwerin high. Valora turned slowly and pointed the tip of the blade toward the mouth of the small harbor.

Her entire body quivered as energy flowed through her. She closed her eyes and reveled in the carnal sensations overwhelming her. No man or woman had ever given her such pleasure. It was as if she were a conduit tapped into an infinite reservoir of power! Power entered her from an unknown realm far beyond the world of mortals.

A startled cry burst from Valora's lips and transformed into a shriek of delight. The ship creaked beneath her feet. The sail now billowed, gravid with wind. The bow sliced through breaking waves.

Harder the wind blew until it howled like an unseen demon. It whipped Valora's long black hair back like a battle pennant. Salt spray filled the air, biting at her cheeks. Valora noticed neither. She focused on the raw energy that streamed through her.

"The sword," she spoke aloud in awe. "The sword is more powerful than I ever imagined."

The faces of all those who had brought her to this moment flashed through her mind – those she had learned from, those she had betrayed – and those she would defeat with this mighty weapon. The path had been crooked and precarious, but this – this – made it all worthwhile.

The ship's speed mounted with each passing moment until it slipped over the waves as if flying. Valora lowered the blade and eased it back into its unadorned sheath. She knew not what she had awakened, but Valora sensed the forces unleashed would suffice for some time to come. Nor did the vessel's speed lessen to prove her wrong.

Smiling at her correct assessment, Valora climbed a trio of steps to the quarterdeck and surveyed her route. Clouds formed on the distant horizon before her, reminding her of the fisherman's warning. But she had no fear of the elements. Within her grasp were magicks surpassing anything naturally occurring in Raemllyn's realms.

Now she had but to learn to control those powers.

2

A ship of the lost. The phrase repeated in David Anane's mind while his gaze played over the deck of the small, cabined fishing boat below. An ironic twist devoid of any hint of humor formed at a corner of his mouth. *A boat lost in the uncharted northern waters of the Oceans of Kumar, manned by three sailors who had lost everything important to their existence in this life on a mission to find a lost sword!*

Davin shifted his grasp on the boat's single mast to ease the cramped muscle in his arms. It would not do to have one of Raemllyn's would-be saviors plunge to his death while perched high above the boat on lookout.

The corner of his mouth twisted higher. The irony of such an ignoble death was not lost on the heir to the house of Anane. To have come this far only to die in a mundane accident was the type of fate the Sitala relished for those whose lives the five gods ruled. Yet, the cosmic tricksters Raemllyn's inhabitants worshiped as the Fates were known for such cruelty. After all, were they not responsible for this fishing boat and its unlikely crew?

Davin scanned the horizon before his attention dipped below for an instant. In a steady stance Lijena Farleigh stood at the rudder, no longer the frail, protected blossom she had been a year ago when Davin had been tricked by Bistonia's emperor of thieves into kidnapping her from her uncle's bodyguards. She held herself like a war-tempered soldier – had proven herself capable of handling the sword slung at her hip when she faced Zarek Yannis' minions at Rakell.

Lijena's frosty blonde hair streamed in the wind while she held the rudder firm. When they last met, she had sworn to take Davin's life when next they crossed paths. Only their common pledge to serve Prince Felrad had stayed her hand in Rakell.

What filled her mind now? Davin could only guess. Did she ponder the names of the men who had used and abused her this past year, those who had killed her father and stolen his fortune, or was it the suffering she had endured while possessed by a demon that had driven her across Raemllyn to Agda's woods? In the space of a single year, Lijena had lost the world and life that had been hers.

Perhaps it was another who stood within her mind, one who had won the young woman's heart, and one she had lost. Although she never spoke a name, Davin had seen the mourning in her face more than once. He felt the magnitude of the loss every time Lijena's thoughts strayed and her gaze grew distant*. Davin shook his head; he could only guess where Lijena's thoughts wove.

Davin's attention shifted to the opposite end of the fishing vessel where Goran One-Eye stood at the bow. The giant of a man, his red mane raked by the wind, stared northward. Never had the Jyotian seen Goran so silent. Since they had ridden from Rakell, Goran had uttered no more than a handful of words, a far cry from the master thief's usual boisterous tales and outrageous claims of his own prowess.

The last son of Anane knew who dwelled at the heart of his long-time companion's thoughts: Kulonna. The royal-born daughter of Duke Tun, liege of the city-stages of Litonya and Melisa, had held Goran's heart since they had rescued her and the other women held captive on the isle of the mage Ah-Banh-Cee.

Goran, too, had lost his lover. Kulonna had been kidnapped by Berenicis called the Blackheart during the Faceless Ones' first attack on Rakell. Goran cared little about returning the Sword of the Bloodhawk to Prince Felrad; he sailed to find Kulonna, in hope that Berenicis again allied himself with the sorceress Valora and Kulonna was held captive on the boat they followed northward.

Like Lijena, Goran had lost his world. Unlike Lijena, the one-eyed giant's world was not Raemllyn but the realm of Gohwohn, another plane of existence. It was no man a mage had brought through a rent in space six years ago, but a Challing, a creature nine parts spirit to each physical. Goran killed the sorcerer with the mage's own dirk, but not before the magician bound him to human form. Although a mage's potion had

* See *Death's Acolyte*

partially restored the Challing's shape-changing abilities, Goran's magicks were unpredictable, controlling him as often as he controlled them.

Awendala! The name almost ripped as a tortured cry from Davin Anane's lips. The Jyotian thief was no different from those with whom he sailed. Pain drove into Davin's heart and twisted there. Among those rescued from Ah-Banh-Cee had been one who sparked love within the Son of Anane – the only woman ever to do so. In their short time together, that love had grown deep.

Berenicis' dirk had stolen the life of Davin's beloved Awendala as the Jyotian duke betrayed Prince Felrad and kidnapped Kulonna. More than the bastard blood of High King Bedrich the Fair that flowed through both their veins bound Davin to the Blackheart. Berenicis' plots had brought about the fall of the House of Anane, the death of Davin's mother, and unjust charges that branded Davin a murderer in his own land.

Davin clamped his eyes shut to stem the tears that welled for Awendala – for himself. *A boat lost in the uncharted northern waters of the Oceans of Kumar, manned by three sailors who had lost everything important to their existence in this life on a mission to find a lost sword!*

"Davin, can you see her ship?" Goran's voice boomed above the rush of the wind. "Surely, the witch is in sight by now!"

Brushing the moisture from his eyes with a sleeve of his blouse, Davin stared northward. "Nothing." He gave an exaggerated shake of his head to ensure his friend saw the gesture. "There's nothing except a squall line of dark clouds in the distance."

"There's no guarantee we follow Valora's course." This from Lijena who looked up at Davin and then stared at Goran. "This is the sea. A ship leaves no trail in the water."

Green sparks of witchfire flared in Goran's good right eye. "But magicks do! Can't you feel the spell plaited into this wind? Do you think it natural to be carried a day's journey in a matter of hours? The wind blows with the force of ten gales, but it merely fills our sail and moves this boat across the water the way a bird might soar on the air currents. Have no doubt that we follow Valora's course. We ride the very wind she summoned for her escape."

Davin could not feel the magicks as did the Challing, but he

believed his friend. No natural wind filled the fishing boat's sail.
The vessel skimmed the waves rather than plowing through them.
Nor did he doubt that Valora's spells had summoned the ghost
wind.

Davin also sensed the truth in Goran's words when he said the
boat traveled a day's journey in a matter of hours. They had lost
sight of land before the sun set last eve. A night and a morning
had passed since then. During that time their course had ever
been north. Where did they sail? What did Valora seek in these
unknown waters?

"Magicks?" Contempt seeped into Lijena's voice. "Are you
certain it's spells you sense and not your own doubts about
leading us on a wild-goose chase?"

"What would a skinny wench like you know of . . ." Goran's
voice trailed into a disgusted growl. He glared up at Davin. "I
told you it was the skinny ones that always give you trouble. But
would you listen to me? I told you she had no business traveling
with us. But your ears were closed!"

"It was Prince Felrad himself who placed this geas on all, not
disgust but our . . ." The chill that ran up Davin's back caused
him to swallow the remainder of his sentence. His right arm lifted
to point to the north. "The clouds – a storm is rising. And it's
rushing at us with the speed of a Faceless One's black steed!"

"The old fisherman who sold us this worm-eaten boat was right
then. There was a storm brewing." Goran turned back to peer
northward. "The mother of all storms, if I be any judge. And it's
we who rush at it, not it at us. We'll be swallowed up in a matter
of minutes!"

"Here, Goran, help me tie down the rudder," Lijena called to
the Challing. "We'd best batten down the boat before the storm
hits."

Goran lost no time. With an alacrity that belied his bulk, he
covered the deck in half a dozen strides, snatched up a length of
rope and began to lash down the rudder.

And I'd best abandon this lofty perch. Carefully lifting one leg,
Davin placed a foot atop the boom on which he sat and pushed
upward. He froze. There, no more than two leagues distant,
rolled another fishing boat. Already in the storm's grasp, it
lurched precariously to port as it crested a mountainous wave.

"Valora!" Davin called out and thrust an arm toward the boat. "I see Valora's ship."

"Where?" Goran twisted about to peer where his friend pointed. "I don't see anything."

"Nor do I," Lijena said. "There's only water."

"And the storm," Goran added.

"It slipped down the backside of a wave," Davin answered, straining to catch sight of the boat again. "The waves hide it now."

"You claim to *feel* magicks, and he claims to *see* phantom boats." Lijena clucked her tongue with decided mockery. "Mayhap Felrad would have been wiser to have kept the pair of you in Rakell."

Damn! Davin's eyes darted from side to side. The boat had been no illusion. He *had* seen it. No more than a moment's glimpse to be certain, but it had been real – as real as the boiling black clouds now blotting out a blue sky – as real as the fist-sized drops of rain that abruptly fell from those clouds.

"Davin, get your arse down here," Goran shouted, his voice nearly lost in the growing wind. "The rain'll have the mast too slick to shinny down in another minute."

"I'll be down in half that . . ."

Davin's assurance was never completed.

Iron-gray water like a clenching fist rose in front of the boat. With bone-jarring force, the wave broke against its battered prow. The small vessel listed to the starboard.

Crouched with one foot under him, Davin hugged the mast and held tight.

His strength would have been enough to ride out the erratic tilt of the boat had not another wave slammed into the fishing vessel. Like a whip flicked by the wrist of a teamster, the boat snapped to the port.

Davin's legs flew out from under him. Hands and arms slipped from around the rain-slicked mast. Like a rock slung from a catapult, the Jyotian hurled through the air toward the roiling sea.

Valora caught herself before she cursed aloud. This was no time to be damning Raemllyn's Gods, not when she needed their strength to aid her. But curse she would have, had she been able.

The sudden onslaught of the storm robbed her of concentration. The simple mist spell she had woven since daybreak crumbled. Her fingers darted in the air to double the strength of the spell binding the wind sprite that filled her vessel's sails.

Only then did Valora open her eyes and release an overly held breath in a shaky sigh. That had been close, too close. To lose the sprite amid the raging storm would have meant certain disaster. She was no sailor, and without her magicks the battering waves would shatter the rickety boat in a matter of seconds.

Her gaze turned toward the south. Again a curse lodged in her throat, choking her. The boat that had followed her all the way from the Isle of Loieter was still there. Without the veiling mist, those who walked the craft's decks could see her as surely as she saw them. Valora needed more than mist now; she needed to remove her pursuers once and for all.

How? The question could not be ignored. Amid the storm, the sprite she had harnessed required her full attention lest it slip its ensorcelling reins. Yet, to succeed, she had to remove those behind her before they muddled her plans with their interference.

The sword!

Fingers tapping the hilt of the Sword of Kwerin, she sucked in a deep breath and closed her eyes. The blade held untapped powers. She would control the sprite and let the ancient weapon deal with those barking at her heels.

Valora cried out in anguish and collapsed to her knees. Magicks ripped at her, not from the sword, but borne within the storm. The wind no longer whipped at her; it slashed her face like an invisible razor. The pounding rain transformed into searing acid that ate into her flesh.

"Nooooooo!" she screamed aloud.

Minima, Goddess of Wind, abandoned her. Valora's pain-riddled brain could not hold the spell binding the sprite. She felt the magic-spawned creature slip away. The fishing boat lurched beneath her as the storm crashed inward to capture the unprotected vessel.

"No, no!" She refused to accept the fate the Sitala cast for her. She had not won the Sword of the Bloodhawk only to drown like some common sailor. "I will not be denied!"

Fighting against the storm-linked magicks, Valora stumbled to her feet and blinked back tears blurring her eyes. Lightning crashed around her, and the decrepit wooden ship creaked and moaned like a thing come alive.

She forced herself to move, staggering through the assault of slashing wind and burning rain. Her arms stretched out for the rudder. Her eyes blinked and only slowly saw truly. Bloody gashes did not crosshatch her bare hands. Her flesh remained whole and unmarred rather than acid-eaten pulp.

Grim determination set her face as Valora locked her arms around the rudder. The storm-borne magic was not real; it was a spell that played in her mind. It was an illusion. Although illusions could kill, recognizing them for what they truly were diminished their power. A smile touched her lips. She had not risen through Raemllyn's ranks of sorcerers without acquiring control. An illusion could be broken.

While she held the fishing boat into the face of the waves that broke against its bow, she willed herself above the slice of the wind, beyond the burn of the rain. The agony of flesh subsided, then faded. Valora's concentration turned to spells of tranquillity, of peace, of soothing.

The storm subsided, humbled. The wind died to a whispered breeze. The waves gentled to lapping water. The rain fell like a soft mist.

For a brief instant!

In the next, control slipped through Valora's mental fingers.

The gale's violence doubled, then redoubled. The ship tossed from side to side, no more than a toy in the hands of a malevolent child set on destruction.

Valora threw her full weight against the rudder, forced to rely on physical strength rather than spells to hold the boat into the face of the storm. The dream of sitting on the Velvet Throne as High Queen of Raemllyn fled before the fear of being swept over the railing into the churning gray-green sea.

Again she forced the pain and the terror to the back of her mind and reached out with the magicks that had served her so well over the years. And failed. Dauntless, she wove again – and failed. Time and again, she tried chant after chant as she strove to exert power over the unbridled elements battering the fishing boat. To deny the possibility of success meant surrender to Dark Qar.

Fail though she did, Valora sensed a seed of unknown knowledge in each futilely cast spell. She felt a *slipping*, a curious sensation as though she struggled not in the world of man called Raemllyn, but drifted beyond space – beyond time.

A wave swelled above the boat and crashed downward. The wall of icy water slammed into the sorceress throwing her to her knees. Still, she clung to the rudder. Valora found untapped willpower deep within herself and forced her legs to push her to her feet. Her stomach, awash with saltwater, churned and threatened to heave. Her head felt as though it would explode from the pressure of casting repeated spells.

Risking loss of complete control over the rocking boat, the mage released one hand from the rudder and drew her cape tightly about her quaking body. The soaked cloth did nothing to keep out the cold or hold in her own body's warmth. Nor did the sizzling lightning flashes that seared the sky just above the ship's masts offer a hint of heat.

Fool! The mistake of her ways penetrated her ragged mind. *Damn me for a fool!*

Conceit had blinded her with the belief she could control the fierce storm. The *slipping* she sensed was real. Magicks weren't braided within the fabric of the storm; they were the storm. The raging tempest howled down from the north, the very direction the awakenings of magic had drawn her. That should have given her a clue to its power.

The *slipping* was real, she mentally repeated, while she assembled the now obvious pieces in her mind. This was no storm – not in the terms of man. She confronted a rent in the fabric of the world. She *was* adrift in a maelstrom beyond space and time!

It has to be! She felt a truth in her realization. No spells found in the grimoires of Raemllyn would ever quell these winds and rains.

Valora shivered anew. The gooseflesh that rippled across her flesh stemmed not from icy water drenching her robes. Fear and excitement coursed through her veins: fear that having entered the rent she was now lost to the world she called her own: excitement because this swirling rent and its unbridled power were what had drawn her blindly northward from the shores of the Isle of Loieter.

To control this unearthly storm – to focus the power! Valora's hopes soared at the prospect of Raemllyn's armies ground to dust beneath the ripping winds of the magic-spawned tempest. In the next instant her spirits plummeted into unyielding reality. No chants, spells or sorcery known to her would bridle the razor-edged winds or the acid-tinged rains.

The sorceress's hand edged to the hilt of the sword hung from her waist. The graceful, pale fingers of her right hand enclosed the hilt and trembled at the touch.

The long dead mage Edan had forged the blade to defeat the hordes of the Faceless Ones – demon warriors drawn to Raemllyn from another dimension. Valora's temples pounded. Had Edan also tapped the power of another dimension and bound it to steel? The mage's heart raced. Was that the secret of the Sword of Kwerin Bloodhawk – fire to fight fire?

Sucking down a steadying breath, Valora's shaking hand tightened about the plainly wound hilt. She raggedly released the air held in her lungs and yanked the blade from its sheath. Deliciously sizzling power rushed along fingers and hand to suffuse her arm before spreading through every cell of her body. Stronger than when she had first freed the sword, its strength filled her like an overflowing chalice.

She was right; she was certain of that. The Sword of the Bloodhawk held other-world magic in its very fabric. Valora lifted the ensorcelled length of steel and bathed in the brilliant white light ignited deep within the blade's heart. Higher she lifted the weapon, thrusting it above her head, tip jabbing at the boiling dark clouds filling the sky.

Lightning streaked, a jagged bolt of raw energy that arced along the bellies of churning clouds, then exploded downward. Valora staggered back and threw her left arm up to protect her eyes from the actinic glare. The lightning struck in sizzling rage, drawn to the sword as though it were a rod of mere steel, and then was deflected.

Valora's arm lowered to reveal saucer-wide eyes. Before she fully comprehended what had occurred, two more bolts of raw energy hurled from the heavens. The Blade of the Bloodhawk turned away the lightning!

Whether she accidentally had stumbled on the secret of Edan's long-lost spells held little importance at the moment. What mattered was her life, and she held in her hand the means of saving it.

Fed by the stark power from the storm, the blade drank deeply and Valora's bone-weariness fled before the surging energies. Once again she chanted spells designed to calm the sea about her. Time upon time lightning lashed from the skies. Like a master swordsman, she parried each thrust, redirecting the bolts into the crashing waves. The wind's fury subsided; the sea's rage quelled; a bubble of serenity enclosed the fishing boat.

It works! A grin of victory spread across the sorceress's face. How or why, she was not certain. But it worked. The Sword of Kwerin Bloodhawk gave her both defense and offense against the other-worldly magicks.

She lowered the blade to study the inner light washing the sword in a glow of white. She had judged the sword correctly. To understand the spells Edan bound within the steel a thousand generations ago would bridle the forces she needed, powers that would bring her to the Velvet Throne in Kavindra.

But Kavindra lay in the future. Between then and now, Valora required time fully to delve the sword's magicks. Her original objective remained unchanged. She required shelter, a secure retreat where she could gather her strength and mount an army. To achieve those ends, she must first find land in these unmapped waters.

Beneath the roiling clouds, lit by the lightning that shot through the sky, a dark line lay on the distant horizon. Land! There could be no doubt. Landfall was within sight.

Valora stepped back to the boat's rudder. She doubted her ability to summon another wind sprite while within the storm's fury, but a breeze, one that would fill the lifeless sail would be enough to bring her to land.

Sails and breezes were forgotten when her eyes lifted. Beyond the still green ocean surrounding the fishing boat, the storm still raged, and locked in that fury sailed another craft. Valora cursed. She had forgotten about those pursuing her.

The serenity she required would be denied as long as Felrad's hounds snapped at her heels. It was time they were thrown off her trail – permanently!

The sorceress settled herself mentally and pointed the magical sword directly at the smaller vessel. Lips moving in a steady chant, Valora drew up a wall of water that crashed over the tiny craft.

Rather than shattering the craft, the pursuers' boat rocked to the right. Furious, Valora summoned another, bigger wave. Again the descending waters failed to crush the craft. It simply rolled violently to the left. A man clinging to the mast flew through the air and disappeared into the water below.

"May squid devour your worthless carcass," Valora vented her frustration. "The rest of your crew will soon join you!"

As her lips began to form the words of another spell, ice flowed through her veins. The surging power from the sword died, as did the blade's inner light. The sorceress felt the storm's returning pressure. The bubble of tranquillity surrounding her boat shrank!

"Away, back, begone!" Valora thrust the Sword of Kwerin Bloodhawk high. The blade's scintillant light refused to ignite again. The storm pressed closer.

The sword and the sheath were one, Valora remembered. Berenicis had explained either was worthless without the other. Perhaps the blade found its source of strength within the sheath? The black-robed sorceress slammed the weapon into its scabbard. Valora waited the space of two hastily gulped breaths and tugged the weapon free again.

Nothing! No surge of renewed energies coursed through her body. No inner light burned within the steel. The Sword of Kwerin Bloodhawk lay dead. Why? Confusion clouded her mind. What had she done? How had the sword drained so quickly?

Time was not hers to ponder the mysteries of the blade. Not now. The deck beneath her feet lifted and fell as the storm reasserted itself.

A breeze – the sail! Valora recited a spell learned as an acolyte.

A simple summoning of magic it was, and it left her as weak as a newborn babe. Her head spun. Dizzying waves washed through her body. But the breeze rose to fill the sail. She staggered to the rudder and held it steady with the weight of her body. Within the dwindling bubble of protection the fishing boat moved toward the distant land.

Hold on, Valora ordered herself as she sucked down three deep breaths to steady herself.

It did not help. The swirling dizziness transformed into a maelstrom that dragged her into the blackness of unconsciousness.

3

A hogshead of wine hurled from the heights splintered when it struck the ground. In a minor tidal wave, wine gushed forth to spill over the sorceress.

"Salt!" Valora sputtered as she spat the wine from her mouth.

Another rush of the salty liquid filled mouth and nostrils.

Valora's head jerked back to escape the new assault. She coughed to clear the ill-tasting wine from her head. Her eyes opened.

Brine, not wine! She glared at her surroundings. No longer lost in a now-forgotten dream, she lay face down on the splintery deck of the fishing boat. Rigging creaked in a gentle breeze somewhere above her.

Shivering, the black-robed mage pushed to her feet and hugged her cape tightly over her breast to fend off biting cold air. Her dark eyes narrowed to slits as she surveyed her situation. That she lived and the Sword of Kwerin Bloodhawk still hung at her waist were the only good things she found.

Guided by magicks or the Sitala themselves, the small craft sat in a tight inlet. Rhythmic waves lapped at the hull and rocked the deck with the gentle touch of a mother's hand on a cradle. Near the prow, a full foot of board lay shattered by an outjut of rock.

The cask and its salty contents, Valora recognized the source of her dream. In spite of the rent wood and the rivulets of water washing the deck with each wave, the fishing vessel appeared in no danger of sinking. *At least, not at this moment*, the mage amended her mental evaluation of the craft. As rickety as the boat was, she held no doubts it might collapse on itself at the slightest provocation.

Worse than the boulder that bit hungrily into the vessel was the ankle-deep snowbank she stood in when she climbed atop the rock to peer about the inlet. Another shiver shot through Valora's body while she studied the frozen desolation around her.

Ice, everywhere was ice and snow! Mountains of ice thrust toward the sky, rising above plains of blinding white snow. No map in all of Raemllyn charted this frozen realm, nor gave it name. Sprite and then storm had carried her beyond the known waters of the Oceans of Kumar.

The realization she had discovered a land unsuspected by all of Raemllyn gave Valora no comfort. How was she to survive in this frigid world? She shuddered; a zephyr indifferent to her plight grew to a fierce howl, cutting through her thin garments. Without shelter she would be as frozen as the icy mountains within an hour, perhaps less.

The ship offered no sanctuary. She scanned her surroundings again. A hundred strides up a beach strewn with snow-capped boulders a spot of dark marred the endless blue-white of snow and ice. A cave? Her eyes narrowed again; she refused to accept what appeared to be a sudden turn of fortune. There was only one way to be certain.

Carefully, she picked her way along the beach, mindful of patches of exposed ice that sought to rob her of her footing. She constantly blinked, fighting the blinding glare that burst from the ice when the sun broke through the thin gray clouds overhead. There was no protection from the mounting wind and the freezing snow carried on its frosty back.

An incline of ice-encrusted talus led up to an opening in the mountain. It *was* a cave. Twice she fell to hands and knees before she stood at the cave's mouth. The entrance was wide and high; beyond a sheet of ice the thickness of a man's stride lay rock. Warmth, like the kiss of spring's first breeze, bathed her face. She cared not from whence the warm air flowed. Shelter awaited within the mountain – that was all that mattered to her frozen limbs.

Valora stepped inside, pushing deep enough to escape the frosty wind outside, then sank down with her back pressed against the rock wall. A heavy sigh escaped her lips as she closed her eyes.

And bolted upright! Her hand darted into her damp robes to close around the hilt of a dagger hidden there.

More than warmth carried on the air blowing from the cave's

interior. The smell of food, roasting meat, wafted through the cavern.

Valora inhaled again. Her nose wrinkled and her eyes narrowed to slits. Her first impression was wrong. She drew the dirk and cautiously stepped deeper into the cave. Not roasting meat, but the odor of burning flesh hung in the air. It was a scent the sorceress knew well. While studying under Payat'Morve, she had witnessed the royal torturer at work, had willingly aided him.

Two hundred feet from the cave mouth, she paused. Her head cocked to one side. A piteous sound like the mewling of a small, frightened animal came from somewhere within the murkiness of the corridor ahead of her.

In a single heartbeat, the pathetic whimper transformed to a full-throated scream followed by choked sobs. No animal made such cries, but did they come from man or woman?

A child? Doubt creased the sorceress's forehead. *Surely not. What child could live in this realm of ice?*

Senses alert for sight or sound, Valora moved deeper along the rock-hewn corridor. Even in the fading light radiating from the cave's mouth, she detected evidence of recent passage through the cave, a large group of men, if she were any judge. The walls were nicked, leaving behind fresh, shiny cuts, and along the walls she found sconces with burned-out torches thrust into them.

An abrupt turn in the corridor brought Valora into a large, light-filled chamber more than a dozen paces in circumference. At the center of the cavern lay a small child – if the malformed thing with matted, greasy hair covering its body could be called a child. It lay atop a flat rock. Leather straps bound it spread-eagled so it could not move.

Valora saw the small creature's captors the same instant they noticed the unexpected intruder.

Larger than their bound prisoner but equally malformed, the five *things* were no more than dwarfs in height. Massive shoulders supported tiny arms. Their waists were impossibly small with hips that flared wide. Their legs bulged from incredible musculature at both calf and thigh. Knotted, filthy hair covered each of those misshapen bodies. From under

heavy bony brow ridges burned dual orbs intent on Valora –
eyes filled with intelligence and hate.

"Back away from the beast-child." Valora summoned all the
bravura she could muster. She knew not what she faced, but
neither did these grotesque creatures. Better to face them as
mistress than craven coward.

Four turned fully to face her. In the hand of a savage near the
child gleamed a steel knife with a wickedly sharp edge. The others
clutched war clubs studded with obsidian spikes. Without so much
as a grunt passing between them, four of the *things* stepped
forward simultaneously. Their short arms jerked about wildly,
waving weapons through the air in ludicrous attack.

Recognizing the futility of a dirk against the four, Valora
resheathed the blade. Immediately the creatures took three quick
strides toward the human intruder.

And halted just as quickly when the mage freed the Sword of
the Bloodhawk.

"Back! Get back or I'll cut you into small pieces and feed you
to one another!" Valora felt warmth moving through the steel.
She risked a glance at the blade.

The magic-forged weapon glowed a faint blue.

Magic? They use magic against me? The thought stunned her.
These were primitive savages, not sophisticated mages. But there
was no denying the response of the sword. It deflected a spell that
Valora had not sensed.

She looked past the foursome and saw that the remaining beast
knelt beside the bound child. The creature had discarded its knife
and stood, hands clasped in front of its breast as if praying. Valora
strained to hear the chant and failed, but there was no denying
that the monster cast a spell against her.

The obscenity of magicks raised against the one destined to
become High Queen of Raemllyn sent rage coursing through
Valora's veins. A curse spewing from her lips like a battle cry, she
lunged forward to slash at the nearest brute.

With a speed that belied its malformed body, the *thing* easily
danced away from the blow intended to cut its muscular legs out
from under it. At the same time, another of the creatures bobbed
forward and awkwardly swung its club.

A cry of pain tore from Valora's lips. The little savage's

movement wasn't *that* awkward. The tip of an obsidian pike ripped through the sleeve of her robe and left a shallow gash in her forearm.

Valora stepped back and suck down a steady breath. Any thoughts of an easily won victory fled her mind. These *things* were more than they appeared.

In the space of two heartbeats, she steeled herself to the discovery of how much more as the foursome advanced on her again while their companion continued to weave primitive magicks.

Icy shock constricted every muscle in Davin Anane's body as he plunged headfirst into the arctic water. He forced arms and legs to move, twisting to fight his way to the surface, and succeeded only in tangling his legs in his battle gear.

An unseen fist of water, stirred by the storm on the surface, slammed into his side and sent him tumbling while his fingers sought to free the belt buckle holding sword and dagger about his waist. The simple task proved impossible; the frigid waters numbed his fingertips. Cloth, leather, metal were all the same to half-frozen nerves.

Legs useless and the cold rapidly robbing his arms of feeling, the Jyotian flailed against the wrenching undercurrents in an attempt to right himself. The storm's lightning bolts provided the orientation he needed. In long, desperate strokes, he pulled toward the flashing light and the dark silhouette of the fishing boat's keel.

His head broke the surface. He gasped as his burning lungs released their overly held burden and gulped down fresh air. He blinked away the bite of brine in his eyes and jerked about to find the boat. Lijena and Goran stood by the rail. "Here! I'm here!"

Whether his companions heard or saw him, he didn't know. A wave crashed over him. Again the undertow dragged him toward the dark depths. Caught in the storm-churned currents, he was like a leaf seized by a hurricane. Beneath the water, he tumbled head over heels, hurled to the left and then to the right by the water's unrelenting force.

Fight as he did with arms and tangled legs, it was no use. The currents tugged him ever downward. Even the flash of lightning above was lost in the ocean's darkness. The pressure in his lungs mounted until it felt as though his chest would explode. In spite of himself, he found his lips parting to release a thin stream of bubbles which were scattered by the swirling currents.

The numbness that filled his body crept into his brain. He died. He sensed Qar's black shadow enfolding him. There was no fear. Death was something that simply occurred. Now the time for it to occur to him had arrived. All he had to do was to open his mouth and—

No!

Anger sparked within the master thief. He had lost all in this world that mattered to him except life itself. He would not lose that, not without a struggle. Davin forced ice-deadened arms to reach out. Cupped hands pulled against the water. Half-bound legs scissored, pushing against the current. If he died this day, it would be fighting for life, not sinking without dispute into the depths.

The barracuda shot forward like a dark arrow released from a longbow. Its powerful, spiked tail sliced the water from side to side as it drove straight toward Davin. Its saw-toothed mouth gaped wide.

Another trickling stream of bubbles burst from the Jyotian's lips as Davin fumbled at his waist and managed to close his right hand around the hilt of his dirk. If the Sitala ordained it, he would drown this day, but Yehseen be damned if he would die in the jaws of a barracuda, no more than fish bait!

Davin slipped the honed blade from its sheath and lashed out with all the strength he could muster. Unyielding steel sank into piscine muscle.

Blood swirled in the roiling water. The barracuda disappeared and in the blink of an eye was replaced by a woman with flowing tresses of rich auburn. Those lengthy strands shortened to a tangled mane of fiery red. A war hammer drove full-force into Davin's gut. His lungs exploded, releasing the precious air they fought to hold. In its place rushed frigid seawater. For the last son of the House of Anane came the blackness of Qar's descending shadow.

* * *

He shuddered, body racking as he vomited out the ocean in his lungs and stomach, then sucked down clean, fresh air.

"He'll live!" Goran's voice boomed above the raging storm. "All he did was drink a mite too much seawater. That won't kill anyone. It's me you should be worrying about. I could bleed to death while you're wasting time with him."

Davin's eyes fluttered. Through a blur of saltwater and tears, he saw Lijena hasten from his side to where Goran One-Eye leaned heavily against the fishing boat's rail. The shaggy, red-haired giant's one good eye peered at the Jyotian with more than a hint of disapproval. The once lush fox-fur patch over his left eye was soaked with saltwater and gave the Challing's face a shrunken, emaciated look. Goran's expression was one of an injured puppy when Lijena edged back his cape to examine a scarlet blossom spreading on Goran's side.

"You're hurt?" Davin managed a sputter that awoke pain in his throat. And chest. And lungs. And sides. And back. Above all, the pealing in his head matched the ceremonial ringing of Kavindra's great bells.

Lijena straightened, stared at the Challing, then at Davin. "It's no more than a scratch. He'll not be dying of his wounds this day. But we all might drown if we don't get this boat under control again." Lijena turned and strode back to the rudder.

"About time you came around, friend Davin." Goran One-Eye walked to his friend and leaned down. "The skinny ones are always the hardest of heart. Not enough room for a drop of tenderness in them, you know."

Strong hands lifted Davin like a child's doll and unceremoniously propped him against the rail.

"This saving you from drowning is getting to be a habit." Goran grinned at his companion. "Must be a full score times since we left Bistonia a lifetime ago."

"You saved me?" Davin vaguely recalled the barracuda attack before he sank into unconsciousness. "You were that fish?"

"One and the same. This storm's magicks have increased my own," Goran answered, then frowned. "And what thanks do you give me? A dagger in my side! I expected a more magnanimous show of gratitude from one royal born."

"Thank the Gods he didn't stab you in the back," Lijena called.

"Now, if you deem your lives worth saving, man the oars. The rudder isn't enough to keep the boat steady without the mast."

Davin's gray eyes turned upward. The ship's mast *was* gone. A splintered stump pushing a foot above the deck was all that remained.

"Lost it when you suddenly decided to take a swim. 'Twas only Jajhana's grace that sent another wave to wash this miserable boat out from under it as it fell," Goran explained.

"The oars, damn you!" Lijena shouted. "If the waves turn us, we're lost!"

"She is right, much as I hate to admit it," Goran said. "Can you handle an oar?"

"If that's what's needed." Davin's words displayed more strength than his body when he pushed from the rail and took his position on the starboard.

"Can you sense rising forces?" The Challing shook himself like a massive dog as he settled on the port and threw his back to the task. Green witchfire bright enough to light the night burned in his right eye.

"It's Valora!" Davin ignored the ringing in his head and forced his chilled, aching muscles to row. "She brought this storm down on us."

"Nay, Davin. Neither Valora nor the Blackheart awoke this storm." Goran's head lifted and stared at the leaden clouds overhead. "I sense my own world here. We've entered a rent between Gohwohn and this miserable ball of clay you call home."

"The beasts!" Davin's own gaze shot to the clouds, searching. The creatures of mists Goran and he had faced when they had rescued Awendala and Kulonna from Ah-Banh-Cee's isle still burned in his mind. Mere steel could not save a man from their rending claws and fangs.

"The beasts are not here." Goran shook his head to assure his friend. "But it's the forces in this storm that have drawn Valora here. I doubt even she realizes what pulls her northward."

For an instant, Davin missed the Challing's meaning, then it struck him. "The sword! The Bloodhawk's Sword is drawn to the magicks in this storm like iron to a lodestone!"

"Aye." Goran grimaced. "This storm and perhaps something

that lies beyond it. I cannot clearly read the energies unleashed
here.''

By Yehseen's potent staff, it all began to make sense. Davin
pulled at his oar in rhythm with Goran's powerful strokes. Why
the sorceress had sailed into uncharted waters had eluded him
until now. Valora stood alone. Even if Berenicis the Blackheart
had allied himself with her, she still was virtually alone. Spells
rather than men and arms were more likely to attract one trained
in the arcane. A single mage could not rally Raemllyn's armies,
but if Valora could discover and control the forces that rent the
fabric between worlds, she could easily win the Velvet Throne for
herself.

"A ship!" Lijena called from the rudder. She pointed ahead. "I
see another boat!"

"It's the she-demon and her lap dog, Berenicis!" Goran
strained to catch a glimpse of the boat. "You were right, Davin.
You *did* see her craft."

The fishing boat crested a swelling wave. For an instant Davin
saw the fishing boat he had first sighted from atop the mast.
Unlike their own boat, the vessel sat amid a great circle of
mirror-smooth water, totally unaffected by the raging storm.

Magicks! Cold fingers that had nothing to do with the icy rain
crept along Davin's spine. Valora had the ability to quell the
energies released in this rent between worlds. He had never
suspected she held such power.

"I see someone on the deck!" This from Goran. "Look near
the rudder. Hold us steady, wench. We'll be on her in a
moment."

"Hold on to yourself," Lijena returned. "The whole ocean is
coming down on us!"

The small craft lifted in the air as if it were nothing more than a
child's toy and was sent flying down the curving face of a wave
rising taller than the towers of Kavindra. From such a wall of
water there could be no escape.

Davin mouthed a silent prayer to Yehseen, Father of the Gods,
as that wall descended. Throwing himself forward, he clasped
hands on his head and bore the full weight of the crashing water
on his back. His prayer was answered. The ocean receded; the
fishing boat remained afloat.

"It comes again!"

He barely heard Lijena's warning before another wall of water collapsed over the boat. Beneath him, Davin felt rather than heard the groan and crack of timbers. The fishing boat came apart at its seams!

There was no time for prayer or warning cry. For the second time that day, cold water rushed in, and Davin Anane was sucked below the ocean's surface.

4

Zarek Yannis stood atop a small rise and stared north toward the distance-hidden Plain of Victory. For him it was the Plain of Desolation. In the space of two days, his dreams of becoming undisputed High King of Raemllyn had faded to nothing on those blood-soaked fields.

His fingers curled tightly, nails pressing deeply into his own flesh. Knuckles cracked as he made a fist and lifted his hand in the direction of Prince Felrad's troops.

"Your victory will be short-lived, dear Prince," snarled Yannis, froth spilling from quivering lips to the chest of his tunic. "When we meet again, you will be mine – for a very long time!"

Yannis relished the vision of Felrad stretched on the torturer's block within the Hall of Screams in Kavindra. It would be a fitting end to Bedrich's son – to die slowly, ever so slowly, mere feet from the Velvet Throne Felrad sought to reclaim.

And Felrad would die slowly. Yannis would see to that task personally. No mage would stand his stead. He would deliver each white-hot iron, each razored blade, each drop of boiling oil to Felrad. The prince was strong; with careful planning Yannis might stretch out his agony for months.

"Majesty?" came a tremulous voice. "We must leave immediately. Felrad's leading units engage our hindmost cavalry. There is little time."

Lonch Porry shifted his slight weight from foot to foot, nervously studying his emperor as Yannis turned to him. Porry had risen rapidly in rank and was all too aware of the reason. His fingers traced over the general's golden sunburst holding his cape closed. Less than a week earlier, he had been a sublieutenant in charge of a small company of sappers recruited from nearby Yaryne.

Zarek Yannis' chain of command had sustained severe casualties during the first engagement with Prince Felrad's troops. When the real battle began, many had deserted rather than face the armed might of Raemllyn's rightful heir. Porry suppressed a shudder, afraid the usurper might notice. The day he had been promoted from lieutenant to colonel, the battle had been the bloodiest ever seen on the continent of Raemllyn.

The next day had been even worse for Yannis' army. Porry had been promoted to general when the Faceless Ones' attack had been turned by Prince Felrad and the damnable Sword of Kwerin Bloodhawk. That magical blade, forged by Edan to battle the demons summoned so long ago by Nnamdi, had glowed and hummed with deadly power when the prince strode forth from the gates of Rakell. While Yannis stood at the flank of his own troops, Felrad led the charge of his own warriors.

And that sword! Porry contained another shiver. The ensorcelled blade had cut through the ranks of the Faceless Ones as though the demons were no more than stalks of wheat beneath the harvest scythe. Without the Faceless Ones, Yannis' forces were mere men fighting for their lives – and losing.

Porry had accepted the rank although he had little training for the position and even less desire to serve directly under Zarek Yannis. The defeat of the Faceless Ones had been a severe setback, but Porry realized Yannis' real loss came in the defection of all his mages. The new general shuddered again, thinking of the long line of mages who failed Yannis and were consigned to the merciless clutches of Black Qar for those failures. Surely Peyneeha must echo with their hellish cries of agony.

"General Porry?" Yannis stared at the soldier as though his mind lay leagues away.

"Majesty, we must leave – now." Porry glanced over his shoulder.

Felrad's cavalry found the fight more difficult than they had anticipated, due in large part to Porry's planning. He had not been a combat engineer long, but he had learned several tricks. Cavalry charges across fields dotted with ankle-deep holes were destined to fail, providing foot soldiers better opportunity for victory over heavily armored riders sprawled on the ground after their mounts fell.

"You, who are you?" Yannis stared at his general. There had been too many commanders for him to remember their names. "What happened to Hamor-Lorn?"

Yannis' pale, watery eyes hardened into chips of polar ice. Porry felt another shudder try to work through his body. He preferred an emperor with distant thought. The here and now were far too close when standing before Zarek Yannis.

"Your mage, Majesty, he – died," Porry said, hoping there was enough diplomacy in his tone.

Rumors of how Yannis had used his scepter to squash the mage's head had passed from soldier to soldier through the ranks like some deadly plague. The emperor's strength lay in magicks; without a mage to cast spells, Yannis' position was tenuous at best. Porry was not certain he put much credence to the wild tales, but the look in his liege's cold eyes told him such a death was easily within Yannis' capability.

"You rescued me. I promoted you to my primary general," Yannis pronounced like a man coming out of a dream. His eyes turned toward Rakell, and he nodded slowly. "I remember so much more now. The war vessel taking me back to Kavindra . . ."

"Driven into the beach by Felrad's navy, Majesty." Porry swallowed hard and began fiddling with the hilt of his sword. They would be surrounded soon unless Yannis retreated. The position on this hill was indefensible and exposed. "My company happened to be nearby and rescued you. The battle against the marines was fierce but . . ."

"Yes, yes," Zarek Yannis said, dismissing the recitation. He had no need of a recounting of the painful memories that were all too vivid in his mind. He had promoted the smallish colonel who rescued him from Felrad's troops, each screaming for the honor of taking his head.

"I've need of a new mage, General." Yannis turned to matters of more import. Hamor-Lorn had been old and frail. His death had provided the needed energies required to draw only a few Faceless Ones from their demon realm. "We must search for sorcerers. The more the better. Have your men scour the land and bring those with any knowledge of spells to me, General. Any, do you understand? Any – man or woman!"

Yannis swept an arm about him as he spoke. The action nearly cost him his footing. He wobbled, knees gone rubbery. He turned ashen and would have fallen had not Porry rushed to support him.

"Majesty, are you injured?"

"No, no. There are magicks aplay. Like a wave they washed over me, robbing my strength for a moment."

"Spells?" Porry glanced around, his eyes narrowing. "Is it the traitor Valora?"

"Nay." Yannis waved the soldier away and stood on his own. "It's the accursed sword. Why, how, I cannot say."

Yannis made no sense, nor was this the time to try to find reason in his words. If they did not leave the Isle of Loieter now, there would be no leaving, Porry realized. "Majesty, please. Look across the plains. An army advances. Look at the sun glint off their armor. Perhaps Felrad himself leads them with the Sword of Kwerin Bloodhawk in his hand. Whether it be Felrad or not, those are reinforcements for the cavalry fighting at the base of this hill."

Porry considered leaving this lunatic and finding his own way home. He wasn't sure what remained of Yarnye, but if need be he would try his luck there rather than die beside Zarek Yannis.

Yannis pushed away from Porry and glared at the short, slight general. He snorted in contempt. "We attack, and we attack now! Felrad cannot rout us, even with the magical blade in his hand. The Faceless Ones are gone. He uses a steel sword against human flesh. The blade's magicks must be depleted. Attack, I say, attack or may Qar take your worm-eaten soul!"

"Sire, your troopers *fear* Felrad and the sword. That makes them all . . . uh . . . tentative. Soldiers who hesitate for even an instant in battle are lost!" Porry inwardly winced at the rage darkening Yannis' thin face. And was that witchfire blazing in the emperor's cold eyes?

Yannis saw only a pitiful handful of men fighting against a superior force. Someone had cleverly ordered holes dug and camouflaged in the path of Felrad's accursed cavalry, snapping leg and ankle of the mighty chargers. Agile-footed soldiers darted among the fallen riders, using dagger and short sword to dispatch quickly an enemy sprawled on the ground like turtles floundering on their backs encumbered by heavy armor. But there were so few of those nimble men. "How many remain?"

"I cannot say." Porry's tone bespoke hundreds rather than the thousands who first moved on Felrad's stronghold. "We retreated from Rakell, many reaching Yarnye and the rest fleeing along the coast. Without a rallying area, the army remains scattered."

"We will return to Kavindra. That is the seat of my power." Yannis' hands drew into tight fists with knuckles turning a tortured white.

The staccato cracking of the emperor's finger joints brought another wince from a less-than-certain general.

"Retreat, General. Order a retreat before all is lost. As we return to Kavindra, assemble as many stragglers as possible. I am not done with Felrad." Zarek Yannis haughtily swirled his cape about his body and stalked off, leaving Porry to deal with the situation.

Not for the first time Lonch Porry considered surrendering to Prince Felrad. But no prisoners were taken on either side. Better to die at Yannis' side than be garroted by a hooded executioner.

"Break off the attack," Prince Felrad ordered the captains who ran at his side.

As the officers darted away to convey their liege's command, Felrad staggered to an uncertain halt. He sucked in a deep breath and almost passed out. The long gash left by a damnable foot soldier's dirk burned like the sun and the stars. Worse, the loss of blood robbed him of strength. Felrad clutched an ersatz sword in his hand and attempted to heft it above his head.

His arm refused to carry the heavy sword higher than his waist. He let arm and sword fall to his side. A grunt of disgust pushed through gritted teeth. *To be hampered so when the situation demands a finish!*

A physician hurried to his side and whispered urgently in his ear. "Enough, my lord. Your strength flows away like a stream. You must rest. No more of this fighting."

"I'm not breaking off the engagement because of weakness," Felrad said, wobbling where he stood.

He thrust the tip of the sword into the ground and leaned his weight against the weapon as another man might use a crutch. His gray eyes shifted from side to side. At least no one but the physician noticed. He wanted his soldiers to keep their distance. Otherwise, they might see his debility, and that the weapon he wielded was only a replica of the Sword of Kwerin Bloodhawk.

He dared not go into battle without *the* sword. Word would spread like wildfire that it was missing.

Such a rumor – such a truth! – would quickly reach Zarek Yannis' ears and give the usurper the rallying point required to counterattack. Felrad had Yannis on the run and had to keep him off balance and outflanked. If Yannis ever rallied his troops for a single thrust through the center of Felrad's army, the tide of victory would flow away for ever and place the usurping fiend permanently on the Velvet Throne.

"But, you must!" protested the physician. He looked to Felrad's advisers for support. He found none among the generals.

"We cannot charge through fields riddled with holes," one officer spoke up. "We should regroup, make our way around the flank, then attack."

"No!"

The chirurgeon's protest went unheeded. Felrad yanked the sword from the ground and, in a two-handed grip, swung it to a shoulder. Teeth gritted and lips drawn taut and thin against the fire in his side, he trudged forward surrounded by his military staff. His eyes blurred for a moment, then focused on the distant hill.

"What's on yon hill?" he asked. "That is where I would conduct my surveillance of the field if I were Yannis."

"His best officers are dead. We think he has promoted an untrained sublieutenant to full command of his army."

Felrad snorted in disgust. "If so, the man does well. He forces our cavalry to break off their attack and makes us go leagues out of our way. We must eliminate as many of Yannis' troops as possible before the usurper flees to his stronghold in Kavindra. We must do more here in Loieterland than win time. We must deal Yannis a crippling blow."

"Please, my lord, rest. I beseech you!" The physician tried again to convince his liege of the danger he brought on himself with each step he took.

"Would you carry me on your own back?" snapped Felrad.

For a moment the chirurgeon stood stock-still, staring in confusion. Then his chin firmed and determination set his eyes. "Climb on, my lord. If I must carry you, let it be from this moment until we both die!"

Felrad had to chuckle at such audacity. "My wound *is* that serious?"

"If you continue, you will not live to see another sunrise, my lord." The determination in the man's eyes remained. "The wound can be healed, but only if you allow your physicians to attend you. Of what value is a victory here if you do not live?"

There was more than a ring of truth in the man's words. Death was a part of Felrad's strategy, but for Zarek Yannis, not himself.

His gaze returned to the distant hill. Those who had stood there but seconds before were gone. Had they deserted the mound in full retreat? Or did they simply pull back to lay more treacherous traps? Were Felrad in the usurper's position, he would choose the latter.

A weary sigh of resignation stoked the fiery pain in the prince's side when he looked back at the purple-robed physician. "Very well, I'll let you perform your job. Summon bearers for me. Until they arrive, let me speak with my staff."

Felrad motioned for the doctor to leave and the officers to attend him. When the generals circled him, Felrad offered but one command, "Keep after Yannis. We must not allow him to reach Kavindra with an army of any size."

"We can capture – or kill – him before he reaches the capital," said Borg-Steede, a thick-chested, towering bull of a man from the port of Chavali along the Gulf of Qatera. "They run like the cravens they are. We defeated them at Rakell and we shall chase them to ground!"

"We cannot afford to lay siege to Kavindra," Felrad spelled out the situation for the generals. "Our numbers are too small and the people are tired to the bone of constant war. We must hasten to assure ourselves of victory."

"I have ordered my troops into full assault," the huge general said. "We cannot fail."

Felrad swallowed a reply when he saw a courier running toward the huddled officers. He motioned the generals to silence and called the messenger to him.

"Majesty," the young boy said, out of breath. "I bring word of the battle."

"Battle?" Felrad glanced at Borg-Steede, who puffed out his barrel-chest even more. Details of a victory must be forthcoming;

Felrad read that on the general's face. He saw something different on the courier's.

The words rushed out, confirming the prince's worst fears.

"It was another trap, Majesty. Their new general is a demon! Our men fell into shallow pits filled with wooden spikes. As others tried to go around the pits, Yannis' soldiers ambushed them. We are in complete rout! Zarek Yannis has escaped!"

5

Lord Berenicis of Jyotis, known as the Blackheart, leaned on the railing and glared at the choppy water that threatened to sink the listing ship. He had spent his life on land, watching ships come and go from the port of Jyotis. Now Berenicis wished he had spent more time studying the vessels to know their capabilities and weaknesses. He had never considered the possibility that his life might one day depend on escape in a wallowing cargo ship.

"We're workin' the bilge pumps, Lord Berenicis," came the captain's voice from below decks. "We can have the ship righted in an hour."

"Time," muttered Berenicis, lifting his attention from the waves to the misty horizon to the south. "Time works against us. Felrad is no fool. He knows who opposed him, and he is a vengeful man."

"How's that, Lord? Can't hear you over the pumps." Captain Pendross thrust his head out of the hatch and peered at Berenicis through one good eye. The left had glazed over with a white film, causing Berenicis to wonder how the captain ever steered with such unerring accuracy past reef and over sea. For all the sailor's failings, Berenicis could not fault Pendross' ability to pilot the *Far Traveler* through the fire laid down by Felrad's unexpectedly effective navy.

"How long until we reach the Isle of Prillae?" Berenicis turned and propped both elbows behind him on the railing, staring at the captain and wondering what the man saw through the bad eye. Berenicis had heard Huata stories that those with the milky veil saw other worlds. Pendross had not mentioned such ability, but it seemed possible, considering how adept the sprightly old sailor had been in eluding Felrad's barques. Only a few flame arrows had struck the *Far Traveler*'s sails and decking, all fires extinguished by the crew as they fled.

"Can't say. If we take on more water, we might be glad to see landfall anywhere." Captain Pendross jumped agilely from the hatch, bent and yelled encouragement to the men toiling at the pumps below, then walked with a rolling gait to stand beside Berenicis. He said nothing for a moment, working on a mouthful of *mylo* weed. The captain spat a black gob of the narcotic plant into the sea, watching intently as it turned over and over in the air before vanishing below the waves.

"We dare not beach too soon," Berenicis pointed out. He turned and looked back into the water, captivated by the hypnotic rise and fall of the waves. He should have spent more time at sea rather than pursuing his destiny in Jyotis. With a decent fleet and a few companies of marines, he could have terrorized the entire western coast of Raemllyn and made himself undisputed ruler.

"Shouldn't have backed that fool Yannis," observed Captain Pendross. "He didn't have the support. Felrad did. Saw that sword of his swingin' in the sunlight. Magicks abound in that steel, mark my words."

Berenicis held down a rising tide of anger. It wasn't the captain's place to tell him how to ally himself. He had betrayed Felrad to curry favor with Zarek Yannis. How was he to know Felrad had regained the Sword of Kwerin Bloodhawk? Yannis had promised a duchy in return for support. Felrad had only hinted at rule once more in Jyotis, a paltry reward for alliance.

Berenicis the Blackheart's ambitions ranged far beyond the city of his birth.

Now all the future held was the executioner's blade should he be so unlucky as to fall into Prince Felrad's hands. An escape from the Isle of Loieter aboard the *Far Traveler* was intended to insure such a capture did not occur. However, with the damage left by the gale that had tossed the vessel for a night and a day, Berenicis doubted the wisdom of his choice.

The Jyotian lord mentally shuffled through the events during the battle and the narrow escape afterward so ably engineered by Pendross. Had he remained on Loieter, Zarek Yannis would have taken his head for the failed ruse that had resulted in the first company of Faceless Ones dying within Rakell's fortified walls. Likewise, Felrad would have his head for planning that attack.

No, 'twas better to take to the sea. Berenicis' dark mood passed and a twisted smile slipped across his lips. To retain one's head on one's shoulders was by far the better choice. Besides, he had no doubt as to his ability to use whatever resources were at hand to their full potential. Aboard the *Far Traveler* was a resource that had not yet been tapped. He chuckled to himself. It was a resource that needed to be fully delved.

"What humor do you find in our situation?" demanded Pendross. He spat another black stream; this time the unsavory juices fell short of the sea and splattered against the edge of the railing.

"From every problem arises opportunity. I might have chosen poorly at Rakell, but we still live. And in my cabin is opportunity, great opportunity for advancement. What if Yannis loses? What if Felrad triumphs? What does any of that matter if I assert myself and become a major power in Litoyna and Melisa?"

"That bitch," grumbled Pendross with a shake of his head, "the one you have drugged. Can she deliver such a plum to you?"

"Ah, yes, Captain, Kulonna can, Kulonna *will*!" His mind exploring the possibilities of new power alliances, Berenicis struggled up the sloping deck to his cabin and went inside. He knelt beside the narrow, hard bed where the young, shapely blonde woman tossed restlessly.

"Goran," she moaned. "Help me. I need you so!" Kulonna reached past the straps restraining her and groped for her absent lover.

Berenicis frowned. Kulonna's moans revealed resistance in her dreams; such resistance, even in dreams, did not suit his purpose. He rose and crossed the cabin to a chest stored in a corner. A brass key opened the lid to reveal an array of glass vials and shiny tins neatly packed within. The former Lord of Jyotis lightly ran his fingertips over the containers, touching one that returned the twisted smile to his lips. He lifted a small box marked *dragonroote*.

"For forgetfulness and to disguise the passage of time," he said aloud to himself when he thumbed open the container's lid, then used the edge of his dagger to shred away a portion of the knotted root within. This he dissolved in a spoonful of wine within a goblet.

Stepping to Kulonna's side, he knelt, lifted the young woman's head and placed the goblet to her ruby lips. She struggled weakly as the first drops entered her mouth, but rather than drown, the drug-dazed woman swallowed.

"Good girl." Berenicis patted her head as if she were a small animal.

Back at the carved wooden chest, Berenicis lifted a vial of pale yellow liquid. "And *calokin* to keep you, my lovely resource, in a stupor until we arrive, whenever that might be."

He poured the liqueur into the goblet and from the goblet into Kulonna's mouth. She choked once, swallowed, and sank back to the bunk. The narcotic took her away to a land beyond dreams of a giant red-bearded Challing and his freebooter friends.

"Think only of me, dear Kulonna," Berenicis said softly, bending low and lightly kissing her cheek. "Think only of Berenicis, your lover!"

Chuckling, the Blackheart stood and tugged off the jacket he wore and tossed it aside. It was time he started delving into the potentials of this resource.

The wave, a mountain of water come to life, swelled above the fishing boat. Lijena Farleigh wrapped her arms around the ship's rudder and steeled herself for what she knew would come next.

The wall of water collapsed onto the small boat. Her steady stance provided the daughter of Bistonia little purchase against the force that slammed into her. The rush of water filling her ears, she felt the rudder give away and her body lifted from the deck and washed overboard.

That rudder formed her salvation. Whether she clutched to the splintered length of wood in panic or with the realization that the rudder's arm would float, she did not know. But float it did. While the currents and undertow tugged and pulled at her, tumbling head over heels through the water, the rudder floated upward.

Lijena's head broke the surface and she gasped for air. She tossed her head to one side and threw back her drenched hair from her face. Brine burned her eyes as she searched the water about her. The sea still churned, stirred by the storm, but gone were the mountainous waves that had assaulted the fishing boat.

Gone, too, was the boat. Shattered boards and beams now rode the rising and falling waves. *Davin? Goran?* She didn't see them! Her heart pounded as she twisted about in the icy water. Had the currents been too powerful for her companions to overcome?

Had these uncharted waters become the thieves' grave?

Chal! Her mind called for one who would never again hear her mental cries, or the sound of her voice. Chal, poet, bard, member of the Elyshah, a race long thought dead among the lands of men, had given comfort when others offered only torment. Chal, a being who took sustenance from the light of the sun, enfolded her in the warmth of love when all those around her felt only hate and greed. Chal, incapable of killing, had given his life so that she might live when they faced Qar's priest in Bistonia.

Chal, you were right. Only life gives life. Death breeds but more death. She had ignored her lover's beliefs and since taking up the Sword of the Bloodhawk and delivering it into the hand of Prince Felrad, she had killed time and again. She had trodden a path of war and death, and now it brought her to this point – her own frozen death in the icy waters of an ocean unexplored by Raemllyn's ships.

Lijena tried to hold back the tears that welled in her eyes; she failed. She cried not for the death that would soon embrace her, but for Chal and the life that might have been theirs had she only listened to his words. If Yehseen's promise of an afterlife was true, she and Chal would soon embrace again.

"Ho!" A voice rolled across the water, booming above the crashing thunder that rebounded among the black clouds overhead. "Lijena! Ho, girl, Nalren's not claimed you yet!"

"Goran!" Lijena scissored her legs and twisted about in the water one-hundred-and-eighty degrees. Her eyes widened, and a grin of relief spread across her face.

Goran One-Eye stood atop the remnants of what had once been the deck of their fishing boat. Beside him was Davin Anane who tossed a coil of rope toward her. Lijena released the broken rudder and caught the rope. Within seconds man and Challing hauled her aboard the makeshift raft.

"How?" Lijena sat on the shattered portion of dry deck, wrapped arms around her legs as she drew her knees beneath her chin and shivered.

"By Jajhana's magnificent grace only," Goran praised the Goddess of Fortune.

"And my fishing him from the water," Davin added with a touch of disgust. "He had swallowed about half the ocean when I managed to grab his collar and pull him onto these boards. He would have drowned in a few more seconds."

"Drown?" A bushy eyebrow arched high over Goran's good right eye. "I've never heard anything more preposterous! Me, a Challing, drown? If the truth be known, I was readying myself to change into a giant squid so that I might have arms enough to rescue you two and still manage to swim. Though, where I would have gone I'm not certain."

"Jajhana didn't happen to provide us with a brazier of fire, did she?" Lijena asked through teeth that refused to stop chattering. "We might be safe from drowning, but we'll still freeze to death."

"Mayhaps there're blankets below?" The jest in Goran's voice faded as he opened a wooden hatch at the center of their makeshift raft. "Jajhana is gracious!"

The Challing leaped forward and disappeared through the hatch.

"What?" Davin hastened across the deck and peered into the opening where his friend had disappeared. A grin spread across his face when he looked back at Lijena. "Goran is right. Jajhana *is* gracious. There's a storage compartment below. Its bulkheads hold, which is why this portion of the deck still floats."

"Better yet," Goran's head popped out of the open hatch, "I've found coats!"

The Challing tossed a crumpled bundle to Davin, who unfolded it to reveal two oiled rain slickers. The Jyotian passed one to Lijena. "Put on the oilskin. It's not fur, but it will cut the chill."

Lijena complied, then huddled back on the deck to conserve her body heat. Whether they survived the cold remained to be seen, but the slickers would give them additional time.

"And there's more." Goran climbed from the hatch wearing a slicker sizes too small for his hulking body. In his hands rested a tin and a bloated wineskin. "Hardtack and wine!"

Goran handed the skin to Davin and crossed to Lijena where he opened the tin and offered it to her. "Brick-hard crackers made of flour, salt, and water lack a certain elegance, but it is food. It will stop your belly from rumbling and provide some strength. Eat."

Lijena accepted two of the biscuits. "The rain lessens and the wind no longer howls."

Goran glanced up at the sky. "I think we near the storm's end. Its magicks weaken." The green witchfire in his eye was a soft glow rather than angry sparks. "Another hour and we'll be free. Until then we can but wait and eat."

Lijena nodded as she placed a cracker in her mouth. The Challing's "brick-hard" description fell short of the granite-like quality of the hardtack. Lijena managed to bite off a portion of a biscuit, but had to let it sit in her mouth for several minutes before it softened enough to chew. Her reward was a favor that rivaled paste mixed from flour and water. She tried not to think about the supplies they had stored in the boat's cabin. Nor did the wine in the skin help the situation; it left a sour aftertaste in her mouth.

However, by the time Lijena worked through the two pieces of hardtack, the rain had stopped and the wind was no more than a bad memory. The black clouds overhead grudgingly gave way to a slate-gray overcast.

"We've ridden out the storm." Davin pushed up from the deck and glanced around. "Now if we only knew where we were."

"Acast in nameless waters, that's where we are," Goran answered, popping another biscuit into his mouth and crunching down on it with relish. "Is there any sign of Valora's boat? She and the Blackheart tally a long list of debts that can only be satisfied with my battle-axe."

"If she remained afloat, Valora gained leagues on us." Lijena stretched muscles that threatened to cramp. She was still chilled to the bone, but the slicker and the wine removed fear of freezing. "We are drifting north, if that still means anything."

"It does!" cried Davin. "Look! There's land ahead. I see land on the horizon!"

6

"We need shelter, fire, a way to dry ourselves." Lijena leaped from the shattered deck to the ice-encrusted shore. "Secure the raft well. The hold may have to serve until we find other shelter."

A puzzled frown wrinkled Davin's brow while he helped tie a line around a boulder on the beach. "Apparently Lijena was promoted to the rank of captain of this venture sometime during the storm. I must have missed the ceremony."

"I saw her against the Faceless Ones in Rakell," Goran answered. "She wears a captain's cloak well."

"I thought she was too skinny to be of any worth."

Davin watched Lijena study the ice-bound terrain that lay before them. Hoarfrost clung to the dark slicker cloaking her. When the sun peeked through the thinning clouds overhead, the rime ignited like myriad jewels asparkle with the colors of the rainbow. Despite her weather-tangled hair and her less than attractive garb, she reminded him of the first day he had seen her riding in the woods outside Harn. Then fine furs cloaked her like some unattainable princess. His act a few days later had totally changed Lijena's life – and his. Now the fate of Raemllyn's realms weighed heavily on their shoulders.

"Skinny? Whoever called Lijena skinny? If I didn't pine for my lost Kulonna, I would be . . ."

"What?" Davin thought himself immune to the Challing's outrageous comments, but this went beyond mere outrage. "For over a year, you've never mentioned Lijena without calling her skinny! It's been 'never trust the skinny ones' this and 'it's always the skinny ones' that!"

"Admittedly, my taste is for a woman with more flesh on her bones," Goran granted to his friend, "but I would never call Lijena skinny. She is fair of face and form. Though, in truth, more your type than mine."

Before Davin could reply, Lijena spoke again. "I fear our

search for the sorceress becomes secondary to simply staying alive. While you two finish here, I will reconnoiter the beach."

"I think it would be best if the three of us stayed . . ."

If Lijena heard Davin, she gave no hint as she strode down the beach. With each step, her slicker creaked and shed ice crystals like a fine mist of jewels.

"Lijena," Davin tried again.

Goran One-Eye placed a meaty hand on the Jyotian's shoulder. "Let her explore for the nonce. She finds our presence a burden too heavy to bear."

Goran laughed and stretched mightily, the cold not affecting him unduly. "Perhaps your scrawny blonde friend would prefer female company? It takes only an instant for me to change to Glylina and . . ."

"No!" Davin flushed at the mention of Goran's feminine form.

He had never forgiven the Challing for trying to seduce him the first time Goran had mastered altering his human manifestation. To the native of Gohwohn, such a transformation was simply a part of his being, a recreation, a new set of emotions and experiences to be savored.

Davin's head cocked to one side. "And did I not hear you just label Lijena scrawny?"

"You are a strange one, Davin Anane. I said scrawny, not skinny. There's a difference. You should know this. After all, this language is yours, not mine." The red-haired giant turned slowly, his one good eye taking in the frigid landscape. "I remember hearing many fanciful tales of a land such as this."

"What? You care little for our legends." Davin bent and picked up two slender pieces of wood, possibly washed ashore from their boat. Worrying thin slits in the wood with his dagger and cutting a piece of fabric from his cloak for a band, he fashioned eyewear to reduce the glare. Peering through the slits limited his vision; it also diminished the blinding reflection from ice and snow.

"Ianya," Goran pronounced with an air of authority. "This is the mythical land of Ianya."

"If we're standing on its shore, it can't be mythical." Davin clenched his teeth, irritated at himself for letting Goran irritate him. The Challing was just being himself. In the same breath he often contradicted himself.

Davin scanned the frozen landscape. He shivered and realized Lijena had spoken the truth. They needed fire to dry their clothing, shelter and, from the grumbling deep in his belly, food.

"Perhaps you have come upon a shred of truth," Davin said slowly. "I remember stories of Ianya told me as a small boy."

"Were you ever *that* small?" laughed Goran. "You pretend you were born grown and swinging your sword. So, tell me of Ianya. I recall stories of it being an entire continent."

"It is a child's tale," Davin replied, trying to recall the fables of his youth. "Ianya was said to lie at the very edge of the world. No man of either Upper or Lower Raemllyn ever saw its shores and lived to tell the tale. Ianya is supposedly a land perpetually locked in winter's frozen grip and inhabited by monsters and demons. There are wizards, too, if I remember correctly. There are always blackhearted mages in children's stories."

"A decent place for a summer's sojourn." Goran began walking, and Davin hastened to his side. The Challing waved an arm about him. "Why endure the ponderous heat offered by Raemllyn's summer when we can enjoy true weather? And there's the added advantage of monsters and demons to keep a man's sword honed."

Davin made no mention of his friend's sudden preference for coldness. He knew nothing of Gohwohn or the climate there. And he placed little weight on the claims Goran made that Gohwohn was a realm of perfection. The Son of Anane had faced a *keedehn*, a dragon escaped from Gohwohn. That twin-tailed creature had a particular taste for Challing.

"Lijena was right, we do need to find fuel for a fire. My boots are soggy and beginning to freeze to my feet." Davin again surveyed the unending snow and frost around them. "Is there no wood on this isle? I've looked for a dry stick or two and found only splinters."

He touched the sun slits he wore, wondering how long the thin pieces would burn. Not long enough, he knew, to make it worthwhile giving them up. And how would they light the fire, even if they found enough wood?

"There is an entire forest." Goran's voice held awe.

Davin's gaze snapped upward. He had to turn his head until the thin slits were filled with the sight. In disbelief, he pulled his sun slits off and squinted at the forest. It was unlike any woodland he had ever seen.

"Ice!" he exclaimed. "The trees are covered in ice!"

"No, friend Davin, not covered with it. They *are* ice. The entire forest is a grove of icicles." Goran crunched his way down the side of a hill toward the peculiar woods and stopped beside a tree towering more than a bowshot in the air. He reached out and grabbed a fragile leaf.

"It turned to water in your hand. Its leaves are nothing more than snowflakes!" Davin placed his own hand against the icy limb and felt the coldness. He drew his sword and swung at the limb. His steel blade skittered along the branch and knocked off a few small twigs. He was treated to a snowy cascade for his efforts.

"They grow like crystals in a cavern." Goran stepped back to avoid a new snowfall as Davin continued to hack at the limb, thinking it possible to cut through it. "Cease your futile labor. There is no reason to destroy such beauty."

"Beauty? You talk of beauty?" This stunned Davin as much as anything else. All Goran ever spoke of was human emotion and experiencing the full spectrum of human vice and depravity. Seldom before had the Challing noticed anything naturally occurring, much less commented on its innate splendor.

"It *is* distinctive," Davin said, trying to keep his teeth from chattering. His toes had turned numb, and he knew frostbite ate away at his flesh. He dropped to one knee and touched the branches he had knocked free. The crystalline leaves might have been green and growing save for their glacial beauty. The branch supporting them was similar to its warmer cousin. Deep ridges ran along the ice limb in mockery of woody bark.

"If only we could find a cold fire to ignite it," Davin said sardonically. He then yawned. The day had been long and hard. He felt bone-weary.

"Would you chew on a root?" Goran rested his boot on a thick protuberance of frozen water and chuckled. "What do the seeds look like for such a monstrous growth? Does a mighty ice behemoth grow from a little drip?"

Davin only shivered the more. His lips were starting to go numb. He felt so tired; if he could nap for a few moments.

"Must keep moving," he said, more to himself than to Goran. "Where's Lijena? We must not become separated."

"Why not? She can take care of herself, as we can take care of ourselves." Goran sauntered off through the forest of ice, whistling a jaunty seafarer's tune.

Davin started after the Challing, then halted. Where *was* Lijena? He recalled her with them when they landed, but a cottony fog floated through his mind making it impossible to remember more.

Sleep.

A gentle voice whispered in his mind. He needed sleep. If he slept, he'd have the strength to fight this damnable cold.

Sleep. Sleep.

Davin blinked, forcing heavy eyelids wide. The distance between him and Goran grew. He had to keep up with his companion. It would not do to lose Goran after he had misplaced Lijena. Would not do at all.

Sleep. Sleep. Sleep.

Davin tried to move and found it difficult to remain standing. His feet were knobs of flesh robbed of all feeling.

Sleep. Sleep. Sleep. Sleep.

He dropped to his knees. Cold, numbing cold, crept upward from his ankles to trickle through calves and thighs. There was no stabbing pain of frostbite. The cold felt comforting.

Sleep. Sleep. Sleep. Sleep. Sleep.

The arctic wave moved up his body inexorably. Davin sat back and abandoned himself to the caress of the cold. His eyes slowly drifted closed. It was so peaceful, quiet, even warm. That surprised him most of all. How warm the cold felt.

Sleep. Sleep. Sleep. Sleep. Sleep. Sleep.

The Jyotian thief drifted to a peaceful sleep.

Davin Anane awoke to needles, heated needles a full league long, stabbing into his arms and legs. There they twisted and turned until every nerve came to life and screamed in abject agony. He could only think of one thing more painful – the fiery needles being thrust into his feet and hands.

"It's about time you came around. I considered leaving you where you sat, but *she* insisted we save you. Covered with ice as you were, you made quite a charming sculpture." Goran squatted beside a low fire that smoldered more than it burned.

"Goran? Lijena?" Davin groaned when he rolled to one side to see the woman rubbing her hands together over a second fire. "You saved me?"

"Goran did it," she said in disgust. "We can't let you out of our sight for a moment."

"I couldn't go on. I felt so sleepy." Davin rubbed a hand over his face. "My mind still moves like treacle. I grew tired and stopped to rest."

"You still don't understand, do you?" Lijena asked in amazement. "That forest is a death trap."

"There are animals throughout the forest frozen into their own glacial husks." Goran pointed to a meaty joint he roasted on his sword over the fire. "I cracked open a few of their ice coffins to fix a small repast. It was easier than hunting."

"Some enchantment draws the animals and then cocoons them in ice?" Davin sat up and fought back the dizziness. He remembered the voice in his mind now, the seductive urging to sleep. "Magicks?"

"Enchantments abound, if Goran is to be believed. I, for one, believe him this time. There is something wrong with this place. It doesn't feel right." An edge crept into Lijena's voice. "Ianya is the sort of place Valora would seek."

"You agree with Goran that this *is* legendary Ianya?" Davin accepted a slice of grease-dripping meat the Challing handed him. The Jyotian's belly offered little complaint.

"If it isn't, it might as well be." Lijena bit into her own portion of the roasted meat as she squatted on her heels by the fire.

Davin studied the woman. A shadow seemed to cover her, darkening her mood. Or was it simply weariness? Either way, there was a sharpness to her words that had not been there since they battled together in Rakell.

The Jyotian turned back to the Challing. "A fire stoked with dung and roasted meat. Do animals abound here?"

"Lijena and I scouted all afternoon while you slept by the fire," Goran said with a shake of his head, "but we saw nothing."

"The dung. What left it?"

Goran shrugged. "A smallish animal, I would say, perhaps half your size. I found nothing larger frozen in the forest."

"A race of mages is supposed to live on Ianya," David said, dredging his memories for any scrap of information that might shed light on their situation. "The tales say they were exiled here after Nnamdi called the Faceless Ones into being."

"Who exiled them?" asked Goran.

"I cannot remember, but . . ."

"Quiet!" Lijena demanded. "Is it too much to ask to be allowed to eat in peace? Do you two have to prattle on constantly?"

A rootless anger flared, pushing Davin to his feet. "Prattle? If this is Ianya, we need to know! It could mean the difference in keeping our lives! Can't you get it through your thick head that . . ."

Davin's tirade fell to meaningless mumbles. The Challing's good eye danced with witchfire. Although Goran One-Eye sat quietly, massive arms resting on knees while he gnawed at the remaining meat, his eye came alive with glowing green.

"Magicks!" he warned. "Someone tries to enthrall us!"

A slight crunch of snow caused by a footfall spun the thief around. Beyond the fire's soft glow a shadow scurried across glistening ice. Davin pulled sword from sheath.

"Spells? What do you know of spells?" Goran idly asked while he tore off another bite of meat. "Do you forget who can read . . ."

"I see them, too." Lijena freed her own sword while she pushed to her feet. "They stay beyond the fire's light."

Davin stepped into the darkness. A shadow moved. He lashed out, slicing through empty air.

"There," Lijena shouted. "To your right!"

Davin dropped to one knee and swung in an arc parallel to the ground. A hideous caterwauling sounded when his blade struck an unseen opponent. The violent thrashing of his victim almost yanked the sword from his grip. Wrenching the blade free, Davin thrust again, uncertain of his target. Once more steel whistled through thin air, although a thick thatch of greasy black hair fell at the thief's feet.

"By Yehseen's jaundiced jewels, what is it?" Davin backed away. In a single beat of his heart something appeared and vanished. He blinked and squinted, attempting to penetrate the darkness shielding the deformed man-thing. "What is it?"

"Never seen anything like it, here or in Gohwohn," Goran replied, staring into the night. "Pretty little thing, isn't it?"

Davin cast a sidelong glance at his friend. The giant Challing's tone lacked its usual sardonic bite.

"Pretty? What is it you see?"

"Why, it is fair of face and long of limb. Such beauty have I seldom seen!" Goran's words were those of one lost in a dream. "It is unlike any creature I have gazed upon. How it promises carnal delights with its every sinuous movement! My kind of wench. She calls to me. And I have no desire to let such a beauty wait for my embraces."

"Bewitched," Davin spat. He watched the Challing step toward the flitting shadows.

"Stop him, Davin," Lijena urged. "He's like a man who's heard the sirens' song."

Did she know what she asked, Davin wondered. Goran was twice his size and thrice as strong. Yet, she was right. The Challing had to be stopped. The shadows gathered closer, waiting to greet Goran. Sucking down a breath, Davin hefted his sword and swung downward, pommel first. He caught the Challing on the back of the head with the full force of the blow.

He might as well have driven his bare fist into a mountain of granite. Goran's head snapped forward, but the Challing did not stop. Goran stumbled into the darkness.

"Davin!" Lijena demanded. "Don't just stand there. Stop him."

Davin dived. His right shoulder slammed into the small of Goran's back. The Challing toppled forward and twisted on the ground.

For his attempt to save his friend, Davin received a boot in his side that sent him rolling. The Jyotian ignored aching ribs and pushed to his knees. As Goran staggered to his feet, Davin swung his sword in a two-handed grip. The flat of the blade hammered into the Challing's knees.

Like a felled oak, Goran crashed facedown in the snow.

Davin did not wait for his friend to regain his feet a second time. The Jyotian jumped up, stepped to the Challing and placed a booted foot on the red-haired giant's throat.

It was not the Challing who held his attention. The shadows took substance. Ten hairy, grotesque man-things stepped from the darkness and advanced toward him.

7

"He is dying," Cor'Mid pronounced with a fatal finality.

Lost in thought, the young mage's yellowed fingers worried his lower lip for several moments, then abruptly darted before his hairless face. Fingertips stained by hours of blending ointments, potions and salves jabbed, dipped, swirled and probed the empty air. A mystical symbol born of nothingness appeared a hand's length from the wizard's thin nose. A wisp of white smoke, the cabalistic rune coiled and uncoiled like a headless serpent before returning to nothingness.

Cor'Mid closed his eyes; his chest heaved heavily as he shook his head. "I cannot help him. My best efforts fail."

"Patience, Cor'Mid. You lack perspective," Tacllyn-lin-Bertam said softly so as not to disturb the sleep of the man whose bed they stood beside.

Motioning the younger wizard to follow, Tacllyn-lin-Bertam eased outside the tent and past two guards. Although only three years separated their ages, Tacllyn-lin-Bertam felt a gulf dividing him from his colleague. The older mage settled his robes and tried to quell the feeling of the land moving beneath his feet. He had served as mate too long on Captain Iuonx's ship and had grown used to the rolling motion of the deck*.

"He is dying," Cor'Mid repeated, his gaze lifting to his taller companion. "Consider his lips. Pale. Bloodless. He needs rest. He needs more than his physicians are offering as treatment. They bleed him to no avail. A fully cast healing spell is required, and Felrad refuses to allow me to lay it. What good am I to him? I wander about muttering to myself and making symbols that do nothing!"

"Prince Felrad is sorely wounded, true, but he does heal, albeit slowly."

Tacllyn-lin-Bertam moved down a line of tents to one of dark

* See *Beasts in the Mist*

blue canvas. The tent served as a makeshift laboratory for Prince Felrad's cadre of mages. He settled into a chair behind a worktable and studied his companion.

The younger man's fingers dexterously wove the air, creating new smoke characters that vanished quickly in the light breeze blowing through the tent's open flap. Mumbling to himself, Cor'Mid walked to the opening and peered outside.

Tacllyn-lin-Bertam leaned back and stared at the acid-burned wooden table where the younger mage had performed some brilliant experiments. An open grimoire showed the results of the innovative spell creations. Never had Bertam seen such ability in one so young. It was not Cor'Mid's affinity for erudite knowledge that lay at the root of his failure.

Experience – practical experience – was what Cor'Mid lacked. For Cor'Mid sorcerous skills were litanies learned from ancient tomes. Knowledge rather than its use was the young mage's goal. Were Raemllyn's political climate different, Cor'Mid would be a rising scholar in one of Kavindra's schools, Bertam thought.

But the politics of would-be kings was not different. Cor'Mid lacked the wisdom experience brought; he fell into spellbound blind alleys that only time would teach him to avoid.

He fails to appreciate the powerful forces at play in Raemllyn, Bertam reflected.

Prince Felrad's condition was important, but Bertam found the presence of the Faceless Ones in Raemllyn a far more weighty matter. The rent in space that allowed the demon riders to pour forth had to be securely stitched closed.

How Zarek Yannis pulled the Faceless Ones back into Raemllyn was the perplexing puzzle. Yannis had scant magical ability of his own, or so it appeared to Bertam. How did the usurper to the Velvet Throne conjure such powerful demons? How did he control them?

Or did he?

The hereto unconsidered possibility sent an icy shiver through the mage. For the usurper to bring forth such potent beings without the ability to bend them to his will would surely result in destruction – destruction of Yannis, Kavindra – all Raemllyn. No human would be safe if Yannis erred and allowed more magical creatures than he could command to rush through the rent in space. Even with those Yannis had arrayed against Felrad in Rakell, Tacllyn-lin-Bertam had sensed a confusion among the demon riders as though the Faceless were uncertain as to who controlled them.

"If Felrad dies, all is lost," Cor'Mid turned from the tent's flap and looked at his colleague.

"Our prince is a symbol, nothing more." Bertam pronounced the harsh reality of the situation. "The common man cares little whose backside is on the Velvet Throne. The less those of royal blood interfere in their lives, the more they love them. To the masses one symbol is as good as the next."

Cor'Mid's eyes widened. "Have you no love for Felrad?"

"I love him as my rightful liege. I respect the inner workings of his mind. He realizes the importance of stopping Yannis completely, not only militarily but politically. But I am not the masses. The citizens of Raemllyn must support Felrad or his mission is impossible."

"And they don't?"

Tacllyn-lin-Bertam shrugged. "The usurper still rallies many around him. Fear is a powerful motive. And Felrad is still untried. His father Bedrich the Fair was loved, but the prince has never sat on the Velvet Throne. Felrad's supporters lend their aid in the hope of regaining a Raemllyn as it was under Bedrich. Should he fall, they will find another of Bedrich's blood to take the prince's place. To them Felrad's death would mean a delay, nothing more."

"And to you?" asked Cor'Mid.

"The prince's death would be the ruin of a Raemllyn I love," Bertam replied. "Yannis is not simply another High King. He is a destroyer. He would turn the continents into realms of slaves. In the time required for those who support the true lineage to find one to take Felrad's place, the usurper would sweep across Upper and Lower Raemllyn and crush all those who stand in his way. After that, there would be no way to unseat him."

"Prince Felrad should realize that," Cor'Mid continued. "He should protect himself from the fray."

"Realize it, he does," Bertam said wearily. "He also realizes that by standing at the head of his forces, he wins the people to him. He walks a path as precarious as any walked by those performers who balance on a tightrope."

"He ought not to go forth as he does. He uses precious energy. He is dying by inches and my best spells avail him naught because he denies them!" Cor'Mid refused to accept the necessity of Felrad endangering his life at the forefront of each battle. "Why keep me here when I can work magicks in Leticia? The people there need me. Disease is rampant."

"They do need you there, but Felrad needs you more. And," the older mage said, holding up his hand to forestall any objection Cor'Mid might make, "Raemllyn needs you most of all. Our mission is greater than putting Felrad on the Velvet Throne."

"What is it?" Cor'Mid walked slowly to his table and idly moved the instruments of his magicks into a more precise alignment. Then he angrily swept them from the table top with his arm. "What can we possibly do that is so vital to Raemllyn?"

Tacllyn-lin-Bertam considered revealing his plans for an expedition to the north. If too many knew, Yannis could thwart his plans. Felrad held much territory, but the remainder of the continent still moaned under the heel of the usurper. Only when Zarek Yannis' head was cut from his shoulders would Bertam's strategy be safe from human circumvention. The loss of the Sword of Kwerin was stunning but not catastrophic.

"Does Fiany share your skepticism?"

Bertam pushed himself straighter in the uncomfortable chair. He glanced beyond Cor'Mid to see a mousy woman shuffling toward the tent. Her brown eyes were fixed on the ground; the wind blew her uncombed brown hair in an even wilder disarray than usual.

Her tiny nervous gestures left Bertam unsettled. He sensed a total lack of dependability in the witch-woman. At times like these, to ally oneself with one such as Fiany was dangerous. Bertam had little choice; the majority of the mages who followed Felrad died in Rakell. Like Cor'Mid, he needed her abilities.

"I doubt she cares for more than her three sisters in Ham. They are all she talks of," Cor'Mid replied, glancing toward the approaching woman.

"But she had great ability." Bertam called out, "Fiany, enter. Join us."

"Sorry, didn't mean to intrude," came the woman's soft voice.

"I wanted to tend Prince Felrad, but he pushed me away. He is so pale and bloodless."

"See?" demanded Cor'Mid. "She shares my concern for our liege. If he refuses our help, if he ignores his own physicians, why should we remain in camp?"

"He no longer has the Sword of Kwerin Bloodhawk," Bertam said softly.

Both mages stared at him as though he pronounced the darkest of heresies.

"I saw it. He waves it about," protested Fiany with a firm shake of her head. "Have you gone mad, Bertam?"

"Madness would be simpler to deal with," Tacllyn-lin-Bertam answered. "While Felrad's physicians first attended him in Rakell, the traitor Valora stole the sword. Felrad sent three of his most trusted deputies to recover it, but they have been gone for long weeks. Nor has there been word from them. I suspect the prince fears they are dead."

"No, not so. I saw Felrad ride into battle swinging the sword only yesterday! He defeated a unit of Yannis' personal guard. In his condition, without the magicks of Edan's sword that would never be possible, but . . ." Fiany sputtered in disbelief.

"It is true," Bertam said. "Yannis will continue retreating as long as he believes Felrad holds the sword. He dares not risk his remaining Faceless Ones unless success is manifest. This makes my scheme all the more urgent."

"Yannis is no one's fool. He must have spies in our camp," muttered Cor'Mid. "I can conjure a spell and root them out!"

"No, nothing of the sort must be done," Bertam said. "The prince follows the proper course, even if it is killing him. He must show no weakness. Yannis will seize upon the slightest hint of hesitation. Instead of retreating toward Kavindra, he will turn and throw his entire army against us. We cannot afford that, not now. Our forces are still too small. We cannot win."

"And each day, Prince Felrad wins more and more of the people to him," Cor'Mid said softly as though he finally grasped the gist of what Bertam had said earlier.

"The prince wins time while denying the same to Zarek Yannis." Bertam stood and motioned to the tent flap. "Come with me. We must speak with Prince Felrad."

"To aid him?" asked Cor'Mid.

"We will aid him in ways you cannot now imagine. But you will."

Bertam edged them outside and to Felrad's quarters. There the prince bid a group of town leaders from Leticia a farewell. As they left, Felrad wiped a sheen of sweat from his forehead with a shaking hand. He glanced at Bertam and shrugged like a child who had been caught stealing sweets from his mother's pantry.

"After you and Cor'Mid left I could not sleep," Felrad explained. "The Letician delegation had been waiting since morning. I had to talk with them."

"Now we must beg a moment of your time, my Prince," Bertam said. "I will try to be brief."

"Yes, of course." Felrad ushered them into the tent and collapsed onto a hard pallet on the ground while the three mages remained standing. "Fiany, what of your promised scrying spell? Have you located Yannis?"

"My scrying does no good, Prince," Fiany answered timidly, her eyes downcast in shame. "Yannis or his mages cloud the air to the south. The usurper's movements are veiled."

"Never mind, it is of no matter. I must worry when you can see him. That will mean he no longer retreats." Felrad's gaze shifted to Tacllyn-lin-Bertam. "What of his new general? Have you learned anything about this Porry?"

"He is of no matter." Bertam brushed aside Felrad's concern. "Lonch Porry has some native ability, but lacks experience of command."

"He makes fools of officers who have trained a lifetime," Felrad pointed out. He lay back, one arm covering his eyes.

Fiany and Cor'Mid exchanged glances, concern in their expressions. Both started a whispered spell to lend energy to their prince.

Bertam ignored his companions. Hasty spells would be of no use. There was but one way to aid this man who pushed himself too far and too fast against powers overwhelming for even a healthy, vital leader. That was why he sought this audience. "I must beg your permission to leave on the mission I outlined earlier."

"So soon?" Felrad opened his eyes and stared at the mage.

"Are you certain it has to be this soon?"

"If the source of Yannis' Faceless Ones is not closed, the usurper will be able to stand successfully against anyone who opposes him," Bertam answered with a nod. "We have discussed this before."

Felrad pursed his lips. "I know, but I didn't realize you meant to leave this soon. I will feel naked without you at my side."

"The more I delay, the stronger Zarek Yannis grows," Bertam replied. "I have located the other two mages needed to close the tear between worlds. With them, I can rob Yannis of his most potent ally."

"Black Qar is his ally, it seems," Felrad said wearily. He rubbed his head, eyes closing.

Fiany's and Cor'Mid's fingers wove the air; their lips moved while they silently intoned spells of comfort and rest.

"Without the Sword of Kwerin, you risk everything. If you fail, who is to stand against Zarek Yannis? No one," Bertam said, answering his own question. "You need never recover the sword if I am successful. You are Raemllyn's rightful ruler. With each passing day, the people flock to you with cries of support. Your army mounts in strength. Remove the Faceless Ones and you can defeat Yannis with soldiers of flesh and blood."

"Flock to me? Support?" Felrad's voice held a distant quality as Cor'Mid's and Fiany's spells began to work. "The people seek to ally themselves with both Yannis *and* me. No loyalty, just hardheaded political maneuvering. They care not who wins, only what the victor can do for them."

"Prince, give me your approval." Bertam dropped to one knee, silently cursing his assistants for calling Ansisian, the God of Sleep, to Felrad's bed before he finished his request. "Free me for my task. The rent must be closed before Yannis summons more demons."

"Yes, Bertam, my friend, go and do what you must. Now, let me sleep. I hear Ansisian calling me. Such a sweet lullaby he sings." Felrad rolled onto his back and began snoring gently.

Tacllyn-lin-Bertam stood and backed away.

"You heard our prince's command. We must leave immediately to recruit the two remaining required to finish our quincunx of power."

Fiany and Cor'Mid exchanged puzzled glances. Bertam saw they had no idea what he meant. That was well. Yannis' spies were everywhere and Bertam dared not risk exposure before he was ready to strike. He thrust directly to the heart of Zarek Yannis' power, even as Felrad's army gnawed at the trailing fringes of the usurper's retreating legions. Of the two battles, one physical and the other magical, Bertam knew which was indispensable to true victory.

8

Valora staggered back as the hairy creatures advanced with their spiked bludgeons flailing the air. For all the clumsiness in their appearance, the misshapen dwarf-things moved with surprising agility. Had the sorceress not struck out in a wide, arcing blow that halted the things, they would have bowled her over with the sheer mass of their well-coordinated attack.

The creatures' hesitancy provided the dark-haired mage with the opportunity to beat a hasty retreat. Valora took only two steps, then the cold stone of the cavern wall bit into her back. She sensed rather than saw victorious grins spread across four faces splotched with tufts of greasy black hair. Or were the yellowed teeth exposed by stretched lips merely in preparation for an unexpected meal? Valora was not sure; in all her travels in Raemllyn's realms she never had encountered entities such as these.

Again the dwarf-things shuffled forward, intent on a quick and easy kill. And again the black-robed mage swung the Sword of Kwerin Bloodhawk. The magic-warmed blade felt lighter in her hand as it struck the nearest of the upraised clubs and sheared it in twain with all the effort of a knife sinking into soft butter.

More than the Faceless Ones fell before Edan's enchanted weapon, Valora realized. The sword reacted to the presence of any magicks. The spell the *thing* wove beside the captive child fed the steel in her hand.

Whether the grotesque creature who blinked at the stub of wood in its hand recognized the sword's power, Valora didn't know. Nor did she care. What she did know was that for an instant she gained an advantage.

She seized that advantage.

With a flick of the wrist, Valora brought the longsword back in a tight quick stroke. The tip of the magic-laden blade sliced across the hairy ice creature's thick chest.

The dwarf-thing dropped the stubby handle of its now useless weapon. Tiny, pathetic arms stretched up and planted hands on each side of the gash in a vain attempt to stem the flow of blood that gushed forth.

Valora used this mistake to end the beast's life. A quick lunge carried the sword through the deformed creature's belly.

Valora twisted and parried an attack from the right. She spun back to block a blow from the left. Her hasty steps moved her from the wall. The remaining three creatures circled her.

Their strategy proved to be a fatal one. The sorceress worked Kwerin's sword like a deadly scythe. With hilt in both hands, she swung the blade in a complete circle. Bludgeon and flesh fell before an edge of steel honed by ancient spells.

Two of the four attackers still stood when she completed her turn, and one of those sported an angry gash on its right arm. A sister gash opened on the beast's throat when Valora easily parried the creature's bludgeon and traced the sword's tip across its hairy neck.

Filled with certain confidence, she swirled about to face the last of the four. A wave of sudden lethargy swept over her. Her eyelids filled with lead and sagged heavily.

Had she not been trained since childhood in the arcane arts, she would have died in that instant. The spell cast against her was a simple, but effective one. Instead of fighting the drowsy sensation, Valora flowed with it. She let her rubbery knees give way. While she slipped to the cavern's floor, she focused every ounce of her strength into her arms. Upward, she swung the Sword of Kwerin Bloodhawk.

The blade found its target. It lashed into the belly of a creature lunging forward with war club hiked high above its head. As the *thing* died, so did the sleep spell. Valora regained her feet and faced the last of the creatures who turned from the child to her.

The sorceress's ears filled with a shrill ringing. A numbness settled into her feet. *A tangle-foot spell!* She instantly recognized the effects of a rudimentary spell she had cast herself hundreds of times. The malformed monster attempted to trip her. What ilk of creatures were these? She had never before encountered mere animals capable of such magicks.

Beneath her breath, Valora muttered a counterspell. When she

moved, it was to thrust forward. No magic hampered her feet or
legs.

The last creature threw up its dagger in a desperate attempt to
parry the longsword. And that was the last action of its life.
Valora brushed aside the knife with the side of the sword and
drove the tip into the dwarf-thing's neck. When she yanked the
blade free, the creature collapsed facedown on the cave's floor.

Heaving a heavy breath, the sorceress slowly turned and
surveyed the five who had fallen beneath the Sword of Kwerin
Bloodhawk. All lay still, deathly still. Wiping the blade on the
exposed back of the last of the *things* to fall, Valora slipped the
ensorcelled weapon back into its sheath.

A pathetic mewling touched her ears, a piteous sound that
transformed into human words!

The Bloodhawk's Sword hissed as Valora yanked it free of its
scabbard once again. The mage spun about, blade leveled and
ready for a renewed attack.

Nothing!

The five creatures remained where they had fallen. Nor did
other dwarf-things storm at her from the chamber's entrance. She
was alone.

Except for the voice which pled: "Help me! Papa, don't let the
Urro kill me. Mama, where are you? Save me from the Urro."

The dead did not speak. Valora turned to the child bound to
the boulder. She stepped forward.

"Please, Papa, save me. I want to go home."

Valora's dark eyes widened. The child was not a grotesquely
misshapen thing. Her original assessment was totally wrong. The
small prisoner was not another of the hirsute creatures. Instead, it
was a human child bundled in a shaggy hide cloak, heavy and
grease-laden with filth. While the mage stared down, imploring,
wide green eyes opened and lifted to her.

"Help me." The words came weak and confused. "I want my
mama."

Abruptly the child's voice wailed to a high-pitched cry of
desperation. "Papa! Save me. Help me. The Urro have me. Don't
let them kill me!"

"Quiet yourself, child." Valora's dislike of children resonated
in the impatience of her tone. Irritation was the wrong approach,

she recognized; gentleness was needed. This child offered a path to other humans in this frozen realm. And humans meant the possibility of rallying an army.

"There is no need to fear, little one." Valora's voice dripped honey. "It is all right now. I have killed these creatures you call the Urro. They'll not bother you any more."

"Did Papa send you?" The child gazed up at the adult towering above her. "You do not look like his other guardsmen."

The girl's words confirmed Valora's hopes. There *were* human beings here. The presence of "guardsmen" meant the existence of a ruler. Valora was experienced in manipulating men of power. After all, for a short time she had bent Zarek Yannis to her will. "Calm yourself, child. I'll see that you are returned to your father."

"Papa should've sent guardsmen. They will be looking . . ." The girl's head snapped to the side and a piercing scream resounded through the cavern's chamber.

Five more Urro pushed into the room.

Valora answered with the Sword of Kwerin Bloodhawk. The blade leaped out in a board, sweeping stroke that opened the throat of the nearest thick-thighed beast. Qar claimed the creature before its brain accepted what had happened.

The remaining four Urro back-pedaled from the room and disappeared down the corridor outside. The sorceress's mind raced. If the four escaped, they would bring others. She could not risk that. She sped after the four, intent on bringing a quick end to their retreat.

"Wait! No! It's a trap!" the girl cried.

Valora glanced over a shoulder. The child struggled against her bonds. The thought of freeing the girl never entered the mage's mind. No reason to risk the girl disappearing in the maze of ice caves never to be seen again. The child's father, whoever he might be or how small his forces were, was the only seed of hope Valora held at the moment.

"They are nothing more than animals," Valora called as she dashed into the corridor.

Not four, but a full twenty Urro awaited outside the chamber. Instead of attacking, they backed away.

Valora did not hesitate. With the Sword of Kwerin Bloodhawk

whistling through the air, she leaped forward. The lashing steel claimed the life of another of the beasts as did the arcing back-slash. Though the Urro's number was four times those whom Valora first encountered, these lacked even a tenth of the courage. No longer did they back-step, but turned and fled in a waddling run. Sword hefted high, the sorceress charged after the misshapen creatures.

Thirty strides beyond a sharp bend in the corridor, the passage-way divided. Half the Urro darted into a low ice tunnel. Ignoring the girl's pleas for her to return, Valora chased down the larger shaft after the remaining Urro.

And instantly regretted her decision.

A heavy sheet of ice fell from the ceiling to block the passage behind her. Valora skidded to a halt. Doubt lined her forehead. The thought that she might have misjudged the deformed Urro's intelligence was confirmed when a grinding sound echoed down the shaft. In the dimness ahead, the mage saw another wall, not of ice, but of wood. The grating sound came from that wall as the Urro pushed it forward.

The realization that the hairy monstrosities intended to crush her between ice and wood barely penetrated Valora's mind when she recognized the Urro's trap was far more insidious.

A series of round holes were cut in the wood. Through these holes the Urro thrust stalactite-sized icicles. The beasts would not be satisfied with crushing her body. They wanted to impale her on frozen spikes!

With the sheet of ice blocking a retreat, Valora advanced. She used the magic sword like an axe. Steel bit into ice, shattering the spikes into a shower of glasslike crystals.

To no avail! The Urro replaced each icicle with a new one the instant Valora's blade did its work. Still, the sorceress struck out to destroy the spears of ice that pressed forward, only to find the holes plugged with longer spikes.

"Qar damn you to his lowest pits!" she cried out in frustration.

Evoking the name of Death did nothing to slow the grinding movement of the barrier.

Nor did a fireball meant to devour the wooden wall in an inferno of flames. Try as she did, Valora's tongue refused to form the needed words of the chant. Instead gibberish spilled from her mouth – utterly meaningless syllables.

Turning from the advancing wooden wall, Valora threw the sword against the sheet of ice behind her. The blade bounced off the barrier as though it were made of adamantine steel.

How?

More than reason-leeching panic ate at her mind. Cold truth penetrated and she was the fool for not seeing it ere now. *The Urro use magic!*

"Aieee!"

Valora sagged. An icicle lance drove into her thigh. She smashed the sword hilt onto the shaft, breaking off the icy length. Valora screamed in pain again as another spike thrust into her side.

No! She found resolve amid the agony. The Sword of the Bloodhawk tingled in her hand; the length of steel glowed to announce the presence of spells. She would not die at the crippled hands of these monsters! Valora lashed out again, shattering the spikes of ice that sought her. Magicks were something she understood. If she could just find what spells the Urro used against her, she could block them.

Valora delved deep into her memories, recalling the grimoires memorized through the years. There on time-yellowed pages were countless mind-muddling spells and their counterchants. But whether she tried to speak or sing the words that would save her, garbled nonsense trickled through her lips.

Tears of rage burned her eyes when she tried to brace the magical sword against the ice fall to hold the spear-laden wall at bay. The blade and hilt were too short by half the distance needed to protect her from the fresh ice spikes the Urro shoved through the holes.

Valora threw herself face down on the corridor's floor in a desperate hope the ice spears would pass above her slender body. For an instant, the dark mage felt a finger of frost trace along her spine. Then it was gone, as was the never ceasing grind of wood. Her head lifted.

Both the walls of ice and wood were gone. She lay in the chamber where she had discovered the child – a child who now stood clinging to the leg of a man dressed in furs.

Valora blinked as she rolled to her back and sat up. A dozen

more men in furs stood to her left. *Illusion*. Reality numbed the
sorceress's mind. The Urro wove illusions to cloud her mind –
illusions that could kill!

"We shall dispatch them. You kept them from killing dear Zizi
until we could arrive." The man tenderly caressed the young girl's
tresses.

Valora pushed to her feet. There was more to this man than
met the eye. He called the child by name and he lovingly touched
her. No mere soldier would dare such with the child of the ruler
he served. Valora bowed. When she straightened, she said
carefully, "It is my pleasure to be of service to such a powerful
lord."

"You know me?" The man frowned, deep lines crossing his
forehead. "Has the fame of Draymo-Vor extended to those from
other lands?" His head canted to one side while he studied
Valora, her dress and the Sword of Kwerin still clutched in her
hand. "You are not of Ianya, are you?"

"A traveler passing through your fair land, King Draymo-
Vor," Valora said. "I am privileged to have come to your
daughter's aid. Now, I must find my way from these caves and
continue my journey."

Draymo-Vor stroked his chin and shook his head. "That
would not be wise. A band of rebel Urro are scattered
throughout these caverns. My men and I will provide protection as you leave these caves. But more, we wish to fête you for
your bravery."

"Who am I to decline such a generous invitation?" Valora
bowed again, barely able to keep a smirk from her face. Draymo-
Vor offered a feast in her honor. And she merely had hoped the
child might lead her to the father.

When she stood straight again, Valora slid the sword back into
its sheath. No longer did the steel hum. Whatever spells the Urro
had used were gone now.

"Come." Draymo-Vor lifted his daughter in his arms and tilted
his head forward.

Valora fell in behind Draymo-Vor while two of his swordsmen
stepped beside her. The rest of the guards moved into the cavern
to pursue the Urro.

Ianya, Valora recalled the king's words. This was Ianya! Not fable or myth but a continent of ice and snow. Of more importance, a continent inhabited by men.

She tried to piece together the legends of Ianya, ones heard or read. Some bespoke a land created by Edan to exile those who stood against Kwerin Bloodhawk; others told of a great upheaval that separated a portion of Raemllyn's land and set it sailing off into the Oceans of Kumar. There was no single thread that ran through all the fables telling of this land.

Not that it mattered, Valora thought. Men dwelled and ruled here was all that mattered – men she would turn to her own purpose.

With sideways glances, she studied the two soldiers escorting her. Like their ruler, she could not judge their size. The thick furs they wore hid their physiques. If the color of their skin, ruddy of cheeks and the brightness of their eyes were any indication, they were healthy and strong.

However, there was something about the trees that bothered the sorceress. When they stepped from the cavern into the arctic air she placed a finger on it.

"No armor, chain or plate," she said to herself.

The guard nearest her turned and smiled wanly. "I fear that is so, milady. Metals are scarce on Ianya."

He opened his fur cloak to reveal a breastplate of leather so hardened that it reflected the wan sunlight.

Valora glanced up. The simple sight of the sun, even through the low overcast, turned it into a thin blue wafer and buoyed her spirits. For a few moments Valora rejoiced, then she frowned. The sun's position in the sky was wrong. Even if she took into account the distance north she had traveled, the sun was not right. It sat too high in the sky for springtime.

A shiver of uncertainty wriggled along her spine. *The storm!* She had judged it correctly. It was a rent in time and space. While she had fought wind and wave for what to her seemed like hours, days, perhaps months had passed in the world of Raemllyn!

Her heart raced, her pulse pounding in her temples. How fared Felrad? Did Yannis still sit on the Velvet Throne? How would these unknown developments affect her own plans?

She nibbled at her lower lip. The answer to the last question was simple: it would not. When the time was right, she would make her move. What happened with Yannis and Felrad now would be of no concern then.

Draymo-Vor led them along a worn path in the snow, avoiding open patches of glasslike ice. They trudged six furlongs then he placed his daughter on the ground and bid her walk on her own. His breath was labored and short. Valora noticed the same shortness of breath from the soldiers at her side. For herself, the hike gave her a chance to reclaim strength lost in the fight against the Urro and their magicks.

As though intent on proving the sorceress's observation correct, the king and his daughter slowed their pace and eventually walked beside Valora.

"From what country do you hail?" Draymo-Vor asked. "We seldom see travelers in Ianya. A few shipwrecks a year give us most of our knowledge of the world, but the crews seldom live long enough for us to rescue."

"The Urro?" Valora guessed at the reason for the castaways' quick demise.

"They are monsters," Zizi said angrily. "They kill us."

The child huddled closer to her father, slipping under his long fur robe. Valora could not tell if the girl was shy or cold or frightened.

"Your courage shines like a bright star in our heavens," Draymo-Vor said, his colorless eyes fixed on Valora. "You fight like ten of my best soldiers. Does your blade hold some power or spell?"

His gaze fell to the sword sheathed at Valora's side. She reached up and rested her hand on its knobbed hilt.

"There's no magic," she lied, "but I wonder at your military's training. These soldiers flag quickly."

She pointed to the two men gasping for breath as they made their way up the gradual slope of the land.

"Our food supplies dwindle during these months. Excuse them, for they are long without a meal large enough to silence their stomachs' complaints."

"Months? When is your growing season?"

"Life in Ianya is different, but you shall find it gracious and giving with its riches. I assure you of that."

Valora boldly looked at Draymo-Vor, hearing more in his tone than simple invitation to hospitality. She favored him with a bright smile. His smile, more a leer, in return convinced Valora that the king lusted after her.

Or was it her body he desired? She had not removed her hand from the hilt of the Sword of Kwerin. King Draymo-Vor had seen its action against the Urro. Valora knew she was a comely woman. She also knew how much an aphrodisiac power was for many men.

Wielder of the fabled Sword of Kwerin Bloodhawk would be a force to be reckoned with, either on or off this frozen lump of mud.

"You are as generous as you are handsome." Valora honed her tone with a husky softness.

She reached up and let her fingertips lightly trace over his bearded cheek. Those fingers artfully darted away before his huge hand could rise and trap her wrist.

"My city and I are yours to command." The fire of desire burned in Draymo-Vor's eyes as he stared at the sorceress. He then proudly swept an arm to the north. "There be it."

Valora squinted against the blinding white of ice and snow for seconds before locating the source of the ruler's pride. A small city lay nestled among three peaks, those barren stony spires giving scant protection from the storms that raged endlessly across Ianya. The mud and stone buildings were hovels, as shabby as anything Valora had seen in the worst slums of Raemllyn's cities. Nothing, not even the largest buildings, rivaled the High King's palace in Kavindra – or even its charnel house. The meandering streets were deep mud ruts, the open markets barren of real food, and the people shuffled about their chores, heads down and backs bent.

"Your city reflects your might, King Draymo-Vor," Valora said, fighting to keep acerbity from her words. "Life in Ianya must be harsh, yet you have led your people to such heights of civilization."

Draymo-Vor's chest swelled. "We are justifiably proud of our hardworking citizens' efforts to create the most sophisticated metropolis in the world!"

"What is it called?" Valora bit her lip to keep from furnishing a long list of potential names, Qar-damned not the least of them.

"Why, it is Draymo-Vor. The capital is always named after the king," Zizi spoke up. She tugged on her father's robe and looked at him with adoring eyes. "Are you going to ask her, Papa?"

"Of course I am, Zizi," the king answered.

Valora tensed. The man's attitude had changed markedly, his huge body straightening and chest puffed out even further. She glanced behind her to see the guardsmen straggling along in no condition to fight. The sorceress considered a spell, then decided her best defense lay in the magical sword. There was no time to conjure properly, nor was it necessary. Valora could outfight these starving peasants with their puny leather armor and hardly break into a sweat if it came to that.

Valora arched a questioning eyebrow when she turned back to the Ianyan ruler. "You have a request for me? How may I assist you further?"

"Never have my eyes beheld one such as you, Valora. Not only is your beauty such as is sung about by bards, but never have I met a woman so strong and *alive*! Ianya would be blessed by your attendance at my left hand as my concubine."

"Concubine?"

Valora caught herself before she burst out laughing at the king's awkwardly abrupt proposition. She had served as mage to the High King of Raemllyn. She had tasted power. She held *real* power in the Sword of Kwerin Bloodhawk. This provincial fool asked her to be his concubine, to be a slave to his lewd cravings!

She glanced around the squalid town and its pathetic citizens. Valora had no trouble in identifying the single large building as Draymo-Vor's palace. She also snorted in contempt. Palace? Shanty! But for the time she spent in Ianya, it was better to live in a pigsty than to be exposed to the elements.

And within Draymo-Vor's court must be some discontent.

If Valora wanted to establish a base, what better place than this? She knew not how distant the rent in space might be, but she had expected to establish a headquarters near it. Draymo-Vor provided the manpower for any expedition Valora might mount.

"Concubine? Royal concubine? I am not worthy of this. You

do me honor beyond my reckoning, King Draymo-Vor. How can a poor wayfarer ever thank you for such charity?"

This time she did not keep the sarcasm from her voice, but it did not matter. The King of Ianya was too pleased at her ready acceptance to notice.

9

"If we can kill enough of them, we'll use their bodies as a barrier around us. Force them to fight over their own dead!" Davin Anane leaped forward, his sword lashing out at the shadows that crept between misshapen mockeries of men and phantoms.

The Jyotian thief found it easier to cut thin air than to slice the malformed monsters attacking him. They moved sluggishly to lure a sure-kill thrust and then adroitly avoided the deadly tip of his blade with a speed that belied their grotesquely proportioned bodies.

"Damn! What are these things?"

"Beauty, my friend. Beauty as mere mortals rarely glimpse." Goran One-Eye sat on his rump and stared about with an idiotic grin stretching from ear to ear.

"Goran, they cloud your mind!" Davin shouted. "Your sword! Draw your blade. Or free your battle-axe! Fight, damn you, fight!"

The red-haired giant managed to stumble to his feet. Like a man in a trance, he tugged the twin-edged axe from his belt. Rather than swing the weapon in a mighty arc, the Challing twirled the axe with his fingers. He laughed aloud. "I please them, friend Davin. They find me amusing, like Huata jugglers. Mayhaps you can cut their purses while I draw their attention?"

"Madness!" Davin pronounced, realizing reason would not penetrate the Challing's spell-bound brain. The Jyotian glanced at Lijena. "We'll have to take them ourselves."

"Wait!" Lijena Farleigh pushed past Goran and stepped to Davin's side. "Sheath your sword. I can parley with them."

"More madness! Are you possessed by a demon again?" Davin's eyes narrowed to suspicious slits. "Or does their spell addle your wits as it does Goran's?"

"Neither." Lijena reached out and took Davin's wrist. "Lower your blade. I can talk with them. I feel it."

Frowning, Davin slowly let his sword dip to the ground. "I travel with fools."

Lijena did not listen. With arms dangling at her side in non-threatening fashion, she took a step toward the shadowy entities. She tilted her head to one side. There were voices, distant to be sure, but they were there the same as Chal's voice had been in her head when he spoke to her with his mind.

"No, Lijena, wait!" Davin stretched out an arm to stop her when she took another step forward.

She sidestepped his hand and walked fearlessly into the night.

Davin started after her, but Goran's huge hand clamped firmly on his friend's shoulder and held him back.

"Let her try," the Challing said. "There is more here than meets the eye, even one as keen as mine." Goran let his war axe swing on its leather thong while he lifted his right hand to touch the matted fox fur patch over his left eye. "Magicks appear in my good eye, and I see much you do not, friend Davin."

"They are monstrosities," Davin protested. "Look at their unkempt fur. Why, they are hardly the size of a *lanka*. No human emotion could reside within such ugly bodies."

"Perhaps not," Goran said, "but is that so bad? Your human emotions are violent, wicked, even depraved. That's how I lost my eye."

Davin stumbled mentally. His attention focused on Lijena who was no more than a shade beyond the campfire's flickering light. "I don't remember hearing about that."

"While I was pearl-diving in the Sea of Bua, not far from Cahri, I found the largest oyster ever seen by man or Challing!" He drew Davin back and shoved him down beside the smoldering fire.

"I didn't know there were pearls to be found off Cahri," Davin said absently. He leaned to one side to get a better view of Lijena. The woman gestured wildly but no cry of fear came from her lips.

"No pearls? You jest! A thief of your wide-ranging skill has not heard of the fist-sized pearls retrieved by the most gorgeous divers in all Raemllyn? The ladies dive naked. It allows them to attain greater depths and return more quickly to the surface with their nacreous booty. Naturally, I was drawn to join such a pearling society, the only male allowed into their ranks, I might add."

"What are you saying, Goran? Is this another of your lies?" The Jyotian only half-listened to his hulking companion.

"Lies? I never lie," Goran said, outraged. "I might embellish to make a dull tale more palatable, but lie? Never!" Goran poked the fire and turned so his good eye fixed firmly on Davin.

"Lady pearlers, naked and ever so lovely – and so eager to please a man such as I! Every day I brought back more pearls than the ladies, I was given my choice among them that night. Seldom did those comely experts ever lack a bed companion." Goran warmed to his tale.

Davin had heard myriad wild stories before; he let the words run in one ear and out the other. Impatiently, his fingers drummed on the hilt of his sword while he strained to see Lijena. It took courage to meet barehanded with the unknown beasts. After all this daughter of Bistonia had suffered, the courage required was tenfold.

"Perhaps that fateful day I was overtired," Goran said, a quality of bittersweet memory weaving through his words. "The previous day, I had brought back more pearls than any *three* of the women, so I claimed them all for my bed. It was a lusty night, I assure you. It taxed even my prodigious powers.

"The next day, though, that was when Jajhana refused to smile at me. I believe even now that the Goddess of Chance and Fortune turned jealous, seeing how I made my own luck with the pearlers and did not need her assistance. Whatever it was, I dived. How I dived! Deeper than ever before, past the shelf where the largest oysters lay waiting for my knife."

How Lijena had changed since that day in Harn's forest when Davin first sighted her, thought Davin. To be certain, her beauty was undiminished by her endless ordeals. But it was not physical attributes that caught the thief's eye of late; it was the way she handled herself. She had developed an uncanny ability to take in a situation at a glance and choose an accurate course. That was the quality of a born leader.

"Down I went, down and down to the bottom of the Sea of Bua until I discovered the king of all oysters. Fully two fathoms across this monster mollusk spanned. It took all my immense strength to lever open the Qar-cursed shell using a rusty ship's anchor I found beside it on the sea floor."

"What? How long were you under water? You only recently learned to assume shapes other than human." Davin shoved to his feet with sword still in hand.

Lijena no longer gestured wildly. She and two of the smaller creatures settled to the ground by a small fire that abruptly burst to life. Davin gave a sideways glance at the smoldering drug serving as their campfire and wistfully yearned for the heat of the distant flames.

"In earlier days, my lung capacity far exceeded what I now possess, and I am still the most powerful of all humans in Raemllyn. I used that rusty ship's anchor to prise open the shell and, by Yehseen's behemoth jewels, I spied the largest pearl ever imagined!" Goran continued without noting he had lost his companion's attention.

"The beasts sway her. I feel it in my gut," Davin said.

"You feel less in your gut than she," Goran growled with obvious irritation at the interruption. "She pukes out her breakfast every morning. My cooking's not that bad. Returning to my tale – my eyes went wide at the sight of a pearl larger than an egotistical man's head."

Davin shifted nervously from one foot to the other. The creatures swayed Lijena; he could feel it in the crisp air. How could she listen to beasts that attacked them? The Jyotian's hand squeezed around the hilt of his sword until his knuckles turned a tortured white. Was it the beasts that worried him or that Lijena had stepped forward and taken charge of the situation? Born of the House of Anane, Davin was not accustomed to being subordinate to anyone. Especially a—

"I swam back and forth, trying to pull it free from the slimy bed where it rested. I was not prepared for what happened."

Davin stiffened. The thought half-formed in his mind held an ugliness he did not realize was within him. Had Lijena not been a woman, would he question her actions? He knew the answer, and it sat uncomfortably on his shoulders. The ability with which Lijena handled herself – the thing he admired – was also the very thing that aroused his suspicions.

The thief stared at Lijena and the beasts with whom she parleyed. What did he truly know about the frosty-haired woman? What did he know about any woman? Until Awendala had awakened love within him, the women in his life had been shallow. He used them, or they used him – in and out of bed. They had been only another adventure like the purloining of jewels from an overly prosperous gem merchant.

"I never knew an oyster squirted ink like a deep-sea squid, but this one did. The inky jet hit me here, squarely in this eye. I went blind, then the entire eye popped out as depleted as a whore's client's . . ."

"She's returning." Davin took two quick steps away from the campfire to assist a woman he realized needed no assistance.

Lijena motioned for him to remain by the fire. There was a grim note in her voice when she spoke. "I have settled affairs. They finally believed that we mean them no harm. Overcoming their suspicion was difficult, but they have reason to mistrust all of us. They are a strange race; they speak with both mind and voice."

"They attacked us, not we them. Are you certain they are to be trusted?" Davin asked, uncertain whether it was the beasts or Lijena who awakened his distrust.

"Trust will serve us better here than your blade," she answered brusquely as she squatted on her heels by the fire. Her arms encircled her belly, and she leaned forward, drawn and pallid. "The Urro – it is the name they give their race – are ancient to the land of Ianya."

"Ianya! I knew it!" Goran smiled smugly. "Where else but that legendary land would be so locked in ice and snow?"

"At some ancient time, probably during the Time of the Called, they were exiled from the mainland. I believe Nnamdi banished them, even as he called forth the Faceless Ones, because of the Urro's magical skills," Lijena continued. "From what the Urro implied, the dark mage feared they would align themselves with Kwerin Bloodhawk."

"They ensorcelled Goran, but then, how difficult is it to cloud his mind? There is hardly anything left of it after being blinded by an ink-squirting oyster at the bottom of the sea." Davin shot a disgusted glance at the Challing.

Lijena frowned and shook her head, dismissing the Jyotian's comments. "The Urro retain a portion of their former skill. Perhaps their spells affect Goran because he is Challing rather than human. I can only guess, but they are a race born of a time when magicks, not logic, ruled Raemllyn's realms. It would seem their ability would more likely touch one whose life is bound with magicks."

"And one who shuns spells?" Davin questioned.

"They employ illusion. They are beings of flesh and blood, not shadow, but we saw them as shades," she replied. "And they can slow our reactions. Remember how easily they evaded your blade?"

Davin's suspicion remained. "How did you know you could talk with them?"

Lijena nibbled the side of her lower lip and frowned. How could she tell Davin of Chal and all he had awakened in her? She could not. The Jyotian was responsible for the year she had spent in hell. Lijena merely shook her head. "I don't know. I sensed the Urro were more than they appeared."

Davin's expression told her he found no comfort in the answer. His comfort was not her concern, completing Prince Felrad's mission was. Lijena turned and beckoned to a pair of Urro standing in the shadows. The two approached with knives held before them as though expecting treachery.

"They mean us no harm." Goran's gaze shifted to Davin. No witchfire burned in his single eye. "No spell-casting moves my tongue, although I can now sense their whispering in my mind. It's as Lijena said. They speak with thought."

Davin pursed his lips and kept his hand on his sword. He heard no whispers or voices, nor was it reassuring that his two companions did. Beyond the campfire's glow, the Jyotian saw other Urro waiting in the darkness. If the creatures sought to beguile them, he would not be able to depend on either Goran's or Lijena's swords.

"Here." Lijena touched the snow beside her.

Davin kept his distance when the pair settled down in a crouch more bestial than human. Their closeness did nothing to improve the Jyotian's first assessment of the Urro's physical form. Tufts of dark, grease-matted hair splotched over skin as pale as the snow covering Ianya. The Urro's bodies were a mismatch of proportions. From the waist down, their legs were ponderously large, thick with cording muscles. The legs hinted at the ability to jump great distances or lift heavy loads. But above their waists, the Urro appeared shriveled. A child could arm-wrestle these smelly beasts and emerge victorious. Such undeveloped limbs were useless for most tasks.

"He is like the others who come to our land," one Urro said, pointing at Davin with his knife. "His mind is closed to us."

"You need not fear him," Lijena reassured the Urro. She cast the thief a reprimanding glance. "Tell my companions what you said before, about the humans in their city."

Davin ignored Lijena and kept his sword ready. Neither she nor the Urro had done anything to dispel the possibility of treachery.

"Draymo-Vor," growled the second Urro.

Davin frowned. The second Urro's words carried a different timbre. Was the speaker female? Through the shaggy fur and hideous disfigurement it was difficult to tell if the creatures had any sex at all.

"The humans came generations after the Urro made their home here." Lijena placed a soothing hand on the female Urro's shoulder.

The Urro returned the gesture in a manner Davin found overly familiar. The Urro reached out and placed her hand on Lijena's belly, making cooing noises like a roosting *kelii* bird.

"Draymo-Vor is the name of both the city and the ruler," Lijena went on, accepting the Urro's touch with a gentle smile. "It might be a hereditary name, though it is difficult for me to tell. King Draymo-Vor is a fiend, a tyrant, intent on eradicating the Urro."

"So they say." Davin arched an eyebrow. "We have only their word for it."

"There is much more." Lijena ignored his pique. "The Urro captured Draymo-Vor's daughter to hold her against new depredations."

"They kidnapped a princess?" The more Davin learned of the Urro, the less comfortable he felt. Where was the wisdom in allying themselves with inhuman creatures who had kidnapped the daughter of the king of this realm?

"What ransom did they claim?" Goran's eye widened with obvious interest. "Jewels? Strongboxes filled with pieces of gold?

What a feat! Would that Davin and I ever had such an opportunity afforded us!"

"They asked for no wealth, nothing but to be left alone. Draymo-Vor captures the Urro and imprisons them in a dungeon beneath his palace. There he tortures them to death for his own pleasure," Lijena answered.

Davin tried to push aside the images of tortures performed by the usurper Zarek Yannis. "A tale calculated to win our sympathy. Is there a coin's weight of truth in it?"

Lijena leaned toward the Urro and spoke in a low voice. She bent forward and traced out lines in the snow by her feet. After a few minutes of conferring, Lijena nodded and looked up.

"I know how to reach Draymo-Vor, the city. There we will find the king, also. And a newcomer."

"Newcomer?" asked Davin.

"The princess was rescued by a woman bearing a sword that glowed a dull blue. She wore robes of black cloth, not the furs that cloak the men of Ianya."

"Valora! It has to be!" Davin momentarily forgot the source of the information. "The glowing blade has to be the Sword of Kwerin Bloodhawk. "We must go to this city and . . ."

"We will go to Draymo-Vor," Lijena said forcefully, "and my two friends will show you the ice prisons. They do not lie."

"Why did the Urro allow the humans to gain a foothold?" asked Goran. "Left to me, I would have slaughtered them as they stepped off their boats, especially if I'd been living here for centuries."

"At first, the Urro welcomed the men because life is harsh on Ianya. They aided the newcomers in building their cities and worked in harmony until a severe winter brought famine."

"Humans stole the Urro's food and used them as slaves." Goran's head tilted to one side as though he listened to voices that were not there. Sympathy filled his voice. "It is always thus with humans. You cannot trust them!"

"Be quiet, you mountain of gristle," Davin quieted his friend. "We've yet to hear this Draymo-Vor's version of the tale. Though, I worry that Valora might have cast a spell on him and . . ."

"The king has taken her as a concubine," Lijena interrupted.

"Valora and Draymo-Vor are of a single mind concerning the Urro."

"Show us the city." Davin stared at the Urro. If this newcomer were Valora, she held the sword they sought.

Lijena spoke softly with the Urro before the pair shot to their feet and vanished into the night. Try as he might, Davin could not tell where they went. Tracking them in this icy wilderness would be a nightmare brought by Yu-Vatruk's cunning. Gathering their sparse belongings, Davin settled his sword in its sheath and kicked snow over the guttering campfires. The instant the weak flames died, he felt the cold intruding once more.

"A brisk spring evening, this." Goran One-Eye threw back his head and sucked in a barrel-chestful of air, then let it out in a single quicksilver-plumed gust. "I already taste the action! All this talking is wearisome. A man yearns for . . ."

The Challing's words faded. His head twisted from side to side as he studied the star-sprinkled sky dominated by Raemllyn's moons. Davin glanced up but saw nothing except a few wisps of clouds that scuttled across the sky.

"Not a spring eve, summer," Goran corrected himself. "Unless my eye deceives me."

"It doesn't." Davin now saw what held his companion's attention. The constellations that rode beside the moons were wrong. They belonged to a summer's night, not the spring. "How can this be?"

"The storm." Goran looked at his fellow thief. "It was as I said – a rent in space and time. While trapped in the storm's rage, mere hours passed for us. But for the rest of this ball of mud, weeks raced by."

"Weeks?" Davin's mind spun in an attempt to reject the Challing's explanation. Yet, the stars remained above him. There was no escaping the truth. "Weeks? Felrad may have fallen in that time!"

"All the more reason to hasten after the Urro." A frown darkened Lijena's face when she stared at the stars. "Prince Felrad's need of the Bloodhawk's sword may be more desperate than when we left the Isle of Loieter."

Without waiting for a reply, Lijena hastened into the night after the Urro. Davin and Goran One-Eye moved at her heels in the darkness.

"Ahoy! Come about and prepare for customs!" a voice hailed.

Captain Pendross sidled closer to Berenicis and pointed at the customs cruiser that sailed under full sail toward the *Far Traveler*.

"No outracin' it, Lord," Pendross said. "We might have enough left in the old ship to reach harbor – and sink there."

The *Far Traveler* had limped along the northern coast of Upper Raemllyn for more than a month, avoiding storms and occasional pirate forays, to reach the Isle of Prillae. The only danger that had not presented itself was a ship from Felrad's navy. Berenicis had outrun the prince's fleet. Now he had to make good on the time purchased by the *Far Traveler*'s erratic but effective escape.

"Give my best wishes to the ship's captain," Berenicis said, "and allow boarding."

"Goes against my principles," Pendross said.

"You have no principles, you old fraud," snapped Berenicis. "Let them have this miserable sliver of wood before it sinks."

"The *Far Traveler*'s been mine for well nigh fifteen years! I won't give it over to any peasant pretendin' to be a sailor. He's not got . . ."

Berenicis grabbed Pendross by the collar and lifted the man's feet from the deck. He was lighter than the Jyotian had thought he would be. To emphasize his intent, Berenicis shook the man. Only when Pendross choked did Berenicis release his hold.

"Surrender your vessel. Do not worry. I will not forget your loyalty. There will be a position for one such as you in my new navy."

"Navy?" Pendross spat but signaled for the *Far Traveler*'s colors to be struck as a signal of surrender. "You're a Qar-damned dreamer, Lord. Qar-damned!"

"Aye," Berenicis said cheerfully, "that I am. And Duke Tun will soon discover that."

"Where is she? Where is my daughter?" Duke Tun bustled into the sleeping chamber, pushing aside retainers. He dropped to one knee beside Kulonna's bed and placed a hand on the young woman's forehead. "She burns with fever."

"We are doing what we can, Duke," the court chirurgeon said nervously. "We feel she had contracted a swamp delirium and are waiting for a mage to . . ."

"She needs no mage," Berenicis interrupted. He weaved through the physicians to stand beside Duke Tun. The portly man eyed the imposing figure of the Lord of Jyotis suspiciously.

"I brought her directly here when I saw her condition, Duke," Berenicis said, bowing low. "I am Berenicis."

"How does Kulonna come to travel with you?" asked Duke Tun. The man's thinning, sandy hair stood out from his head in wild disarray. He had obviously been awakened when word of his daughter's return reached him.

"We are betrothed, my Duke," Berenicis lied without a blink of the eye. "After she was kidnapped, my heart and hers found one another, even in the midst of the fierce war raging across Raemllyn. We had just begun our return to the Isle of Prillae to petition your permission to marry when this malaise befell dear Kulonna."

Berenicis shifted his gray eyes to the drugged woman. Like a well-trained actor, he maintained a worried expression while his heart pumped double time. The duke drank in every word he uttered and accepted it as truth! This was far easier than Berenicis imagined it would be.

"She was kidnapped?" Duke Tun's brow knitted. "How . . ."

"I rescued her," Berenicis said easily. "It was a savage battle, but one I gladly fought for a lady so lovely and loving."

"There is much to learn of Kulonna's travail," Duke Tun said. "But you suggested no mage is required. Do you know the cause of her coma?"

"She will fight off the infections. We tramped through swamps and fought terrible beasts," Berenicis said, warming to his tale.

"Kulonna? She fought beasts?" Duke Tun eyed Berenicis. "I think it was *you*, Lord Berenicis, who fought swamp creatures to bring her home to me. How can I ever thank you?"

"I have spoken of my – our – intent to wed, my Duke. Grant us this wish. Give us your permission."

"Duke Tun, wait," urged an adviser. "Speak with your daughter before . . ."

"I will care for her, as I have these past weeks," Berenicis interrupted, laying his hand on the blonde's burning forehead. Kulonna stirred and moaned something. "I am confident my ability at healing – and our love – will work miracles."

Berenicis turned his cold gray eyes on the court chirurgeon in a silent challenge for the man to gainsay the prescription.

"I should watch over her, Duke," the chirurgeon said timidly. "Lord Berenicis can have no argument with that. We all care deeply for our dear Kulonna."

"So be it," Tun said, "but Berenicis is to have immediate access to her, day or night. And now, Lord Berenicis, let us walk and discuss matters. All this is so sudden. I am overjoyed at the return of my only child, and you hint at great upheaval on the continent. We on the Isle of Prillae are isolated, perhaps too much by choice."

Berenicis accompanied the duke, noting the expressions of the ruler's advisers. One in particular drew Berenicis' notice – a tall, intense brunette woman who appeared to have bitten into a rotted *yalt* fruit. Her brown eyes narrowed every time Berenicis spoke and she stood with arms firmly crossed over her ample breasts.

This one would have to be watched. *And perhaps won over.* The woman's skepticism appealed to the Jyotian ruler. He needed allies who could not be duped.

Too easily duped, he amended. Without the thread of deceit running through the tapestry he wove so expertly, he would have no foundation on which to build the new kingdom he sought. Perhaps a different tale, different promises would win the woman to his side.

"I hardly know where to begin," Berenicis said. "My head spins from weariness. Would it be possible for me to rest before continuing?"

Berenicis looked not at Duke Tun but at the brunette. She straightened in surprise. Their eyes met and held each other. Tall women were drawn to men who equaled their height, Berenicis thought. And this one was comely as well.

"I am a poor host. Excuse me. I am so overwhelmed at seeing my Kulonna again." Duke Tun snapped his fingers at a liveried man trailing a few steps behind. "Major-domo, tend to Lord Berenicis."

The man glided forward and bowed, saying, "This way, milord."

Berenicis looked past the obsequious man to the woman. She heaved a deep breath, causing her breasts to rise and fall delightfully. Berenicis held back a request for her to accompany him to his room. He did not know her status in Duke Tun's court. She would soon spend time in his bed, though. Berenicis felt it as surely as if a mage had ordained it with a premonitory dream. He followed the major-domo, aware of brown eyes burning into his back.

"Your quarters, sire," the servant said, ushering Berenicis into a sumptuous bedchamber. "Food will be prepared and brought to you."

"Wine, also." Berenicis glanced about, wondering where the spyholes were. "My thirst is extreme after our weeks at sea with nothing more than tepid water to drink."

"As you command, milord." The major-domo backed away respectfully, then vanished through the door.

Berenicis sauntered about the room, studying the oil paintings and examining the thick mortar between the stones in the walls. He quickly identified the secret ways and found no fewer than three spyholes. Standing boldly in front of one with a clear view of the large bed in the corner of the room, Berenicis waited. His sharp ears picked up the small scurrying sounds that signaled someone's approach in the secret passage beyond the wall.

When the eyehole opened, Berenicis grinned widely and executed a stately bow.

"Please, it is drafty and cold in those dusty ways. Join me." He motioned to the concealed entry.

Berenicis had no idea how to open the door, nor did he need to. The peephole closed and seconds later a panel swung wide. He smiled even more broadly when he saw the tall brunette step out of the secret passage.

"Wine is coming. May I offer you some?" he asked.

"You are an impostor," the woman snapped. "I recognize *calokin* drugging, even if that fool Summeant cannot."

"*Calokin* – and *dragonroote*," Berenicis answered brazenly. "My interest is less in Kulonna than in her father."

"Her father's realm," the woman said, anger burning brightly.

"Your ambition is apparent to me if not to the rest of Duke Tun's advisers."

"You have an advantage over me." Berenicis sat at a table and leaned back. His right hand rested near the dirk hung from his belt ready to free the weapon should his bold ploy fail.

As much as he needed a trusted coconspirator within the duke's ranks, the woman's corpse would also serve him well. To lay the body of a would-be assassin-traitor at Tun's feet would win him favor. Berenicis' gray eyes watched as the woman paced to and fro, her hands clasped behind her back. The soft folds of her heavy wine-colored velvet dress moved about her in a way he found beguiling. "I do not know the name of the lovely lady who sneaks through the secret passages to spy on me."

"Eliora of Litoyna." Her tone came winter cold, but that she had revealed herself and stood in his room bespoke motives that had nothing to do with her duke's interests.

A smile touched Berenicis' lips. That she had not called for guards or killed him immediately when he revealed the drugs he used to keep Kulonna in a stupor said her hidden motives ran a similar course to his.

"Lady Eliora." Berenicis tilted his head in an imitation of a bow.

"General Eliora," she corrected. "I am Lady Commander of the Realm."

"So?" Berenicis' eyebrows arched. He had not realized the duke employed women in such high positions.

"This surprises you?" Eliora stiffened defensively.

Her movement awakened the soft hiss of cloth on cloth within the folds of her floor-length dress. Beneath that gentle whisper, Berenicis detected a muffled metallic clink. Concealed daggers, he realized. How many daggers did the lady general carry? From the set of her firm chin, he reasoned that she carried only as many as she could use – both hands and possibly two spares. Four deadly weapons at the command of one trained in their use. The path he trod was narrow and precarious.

"I am past surprise," Berenicis chose his words carefully. "I am not even surprised that you come to enlist my aid in your nefarious – enterprise."

The Jyotian found it difficult to keep a pleased smile from his

92   *Robert E. Vardeman & Geo. W. Proctor*

face when Eliora jerked even more rigid. Her hands tucked into the folds of her skirts.

"You know? How? Who told you of our plot?"

Berenicis shrugged, settled back a bit and crossed his legs. All was right with the world – or at least this tin soldier bundled in a feminine package had to believe it was thus. He kept the tremor of excitement from his voice when he spoke: "It is obvious."

He lied. He had cast a stone into the night and struck a solid target. He continued cautiously. "Your face can't mask your contempt when you look upon Duke Tun. You can't see him without seeing his weaknesses. A man with a spine of steel is needed in these times, but Tun's backbone is like a willow branch."

Eliora made no attempt to contradict the words a loyal supporter might find treasonous. However, her hands remained with the daggers hidden in her dress.

"You prowl secret ways to spy upon me. Not for Tun, but for your own purposes. Perhaps you seek to discover if I am truly allying Jyotis with the Isle of Prillae," Berenicis added.

"Not so," Eliora said firmly. "You would never forge such an alliance – and Kulonna would never choose a man such as yourself for a consort."

"Indeed? Ruler of Jyotis is a considerable title," Berenicis said.

"Lord Berenicis the Blackheart," Eliora shot back. "Your infamy precedes you. If Tun had kept his ears open rather than puttering away the hours in his garden, he would know of you."

"The loss of his daughter," Berenicis replied in an offhand manner, as if dismissing Duke Tun's inattention to matters of state.

"She is a bitch." Hitherto concealed passion revealed itself in Eliora's voice. "She deserves you – and you her!"

Tiny spots of angry red flared on the general's china-white cheeks. Whatever had passed between Kulonna and Eliora ran deep. The path Berenicis chose grew narrower with each step he took.

"No." Berenicis shook his head when he pushed to his feet and stood face-to-face with the woman. "I deserve a real woman, one such as the Lady Commander of the Realm."

His arm snaked around Eliora's waist to pull her close. Her face contorted in anger as his mouth covered hers. His arm tightened, drawing her even closer, intimately pressing himself to her.

Berenicis suppressed a wince when the point of a honed blade nicked at his neck dangerously close to the jugular vein. Only when he sensed the tension begin to flow from Eliora's rigidity did he release the woman.

She whirled back, dirks in both hands.

He had read her aright on two counts. She was ambidextrous – and she saw an ally in him. *Else I would be now dead.*

He casually touched a fingertip to his neck. A drop of blood welled there. A thought of poison-dipped steel pushed into his mind and was immediately discarded. Again, had Eliora employed poison he would be dead by now.

"We can proceed, if you wish?" The simple question held a double meaning. Eliora could choose which to answer.

"You arrive at an opportune time. I might have need of a man with your talents." Her answer was as unspecific as the question. However, her hands dipped back into the folds of her dress. The daggers were gone when her fingers resurfaced to smooth over her skirt. "Matters of state are unsettled."

"But soon to be settled – in your favor, I take it." Berenicis' mind raced; pieces fell together to form a delightful picture. He had happened onto the Isle of Prillae at the moment of coup. "Would a firm alliance with Jyotis aid your cause? Or rather the cause of a new duchess?"

"You speak treason," Eliora said, but her expression told Berenicis he had accurately guessed her intentions.

"Duchess Eliora," he said softly. "It sounds right."

"It sounds impossible," Eliora said with new bitterness. "The people would never permit me to assume the title. I am a commoner."

"Ah." Berenicis pressed his index finger against his lips as new elements came into focus. "Perhaps we can work a different sort of alliance, you and I."

"What?"

"Kulonna is drugged. You know that. Even the duke's foolish chirurgeon realizes what has been done."

"He poses no threat. Old Summeant is a fool. An expendable fool," Eliora said.

"Who ascends to the throne of Prillae if Duke Tun meets an unfortunate end? His daughter? Or his daughter's husband, a man of royal blood, a Lord of Jyotis?"

Berenicis saw the light of reason brighten Eliora's brown eyes. He supplied the final piece to her plot. But so many details were hidden to him. He would have to discover them before proceeding further. He no more trusted Eliora than she did him.

"A good solution, Lord Berenicis," the lady general said. "Of course, it would be necessary to declare martial law if Duke Tun should fall prey to an assassin."

"How crude," Berenicis said. "You are new to the ways of court intrigue. A dagger between the ribs is so – obvious. It is better if the duke meets Black Qar in some other, less uncouth fashion."

"What do you propose?" Eliora stepped to him to rest her cool fingertips on his cheek. She leaned against him and let her lips lightly brush over his.

"An accident, soon after Kulonna regains consciousness." Berenicis intended to secure his position as the blonde's husband before proceeding against her father. Anything less than a formal, public marriage would be foolhardy.

"Not before?" Eliora's lips slid seductively to his neck where her tongue flicked over the prick left by her dagger.

"Perhaps sooner is acceptable."

Berenicis enfolded Eliora in his arms, their lips once more meeting as they lowered themselves to his bed.

Duke Tun died that night, slipping on a damp spot along the battlements and plunging to his death on the stakes driven into the bottom of the moat.

10

Goran's massive head twisted from side to side like some great cat surveying its surroundings. He then turned his single good eye to the sky. "There's a new storm brewing. Listen. The wind is picking up."

"We must find cover before it starts to blow." Davin looked up to see a bank of clouds rapidly moving in from the north. "We're ill-dressed to face icy blasts."

"We are almost there," Lijena answered, pointing ahead in the night. "Bonn and Yeeha tell me the city is just over this rocky ridge."

Davin discerned no difference in the terrain. One stretch of the snow and ice appeared similar to any other. However, he kept his opinion to himself and lengthened his stride to keep up with the woman.

There was more than Lijena's sudden assumption of authority niggling in his brain. She had acted strangely since the Battle of Rakell, but exactly what filled him with disquiet failed to be pinned down.

Perhaps it was her inability to keep down food. Davin really hadn't noticed it before, but Goran had been right earlier. Lijena had retched after more than one meal of late. Maybe the weight of their task did more than bend her shoulders.

Her queasy stomach was only part of what bothered him. Pale and drawn, she fell into a distant-eyed stare as if listening to voices only she could hear. Had the demon that had once possessed her found a new foothold in her mind and body?

And she communicated with the Urro – Bonn and Yeeha, she called them, though Davin never heard the names uttered – in a fashion that defied the Jyotian's understanding. Lijena seemed to *know* what the Urro thought. The hairs on the nape of Davin's neck stood on end. Magicks had wrapped around them since sailing from the Isle of Loieter. Was the daughter of Bistonia controlled by some unknown spell?

"Aye, there's the city! And it's rare to find such a well-defended fortress." Goran straightened to his full height at the top of the rise and thrust a finger toward a shallow valley. The Challing laughed sarcastically. "A blind, harelipped halfwit could stroll into such a poorly defended city. The Urro fought well against us. Why do they hesitate to destroy this Draymo-Vor?"

Davin joined his friend and stared ahead. Three crags upsurged to cup the night-darkened city in a valley. Tall ice walls stretched from mountain to mountain to restrict travel – and to keep enemies at bay. A single road meandered across a snowy plain to a city gate. Davin immediately discarded any notion of entering Draymo-Vor by the obvious route. A walled city surely had guards posted at its gates.

"We could melt our way through the walls," he said, suggesting an alternate entrance to the city. "At their thickest, those barriers could be no more than a stride in width."

Goran One-Eye grunted. "That would take fire, something in short supply in Ianya. Perhaps I could toss you atop the wall. If not you, Lijena. Or maybe . . ."

"Would pitch serve instead of flames?" Lijena asked.

"Pitch?" Goran scratched his head. "Sticky, hot tar would do nicely. Finding it amid all this ice is about as likely as stumbling upon enough wood to build a bonfire to melt our way through the ice wall."

"Our friends say there are tar pits nearby – within caverns in that nearest mountain." Lijena turned and spoke quietly to the Urro.

The female creature, the one she called Yeeha, bobbed her shaggy head and vanished into the dim light of predawn. The male, Bonn, trundled after her.

"They'll be back before sunrise can reveal us," Lijena turned back to her companions. "They wonder how you will kill Draymo-Vor."

"He is not our concern." Lijena's focus on the Urro irritated the Jyotian thief. "If he gets in our way, a simple sword thrust will suffice. It's Valora and the Sword of Kwerin we seek."

"Our two missions are complementary," Lijena said simply, apparently unaware of Davin's irritation. "We can recover the sword for Prince Felrad and lift the yoke of slavery from the Urro."

"Your pet beasties have returned." Goran pointed to the city.

Davin squinted against the murk that seemed to be a permanent institution on Ianya. At the base of the ice wall, well concealed from any guards who might stand at the gate, a dozen small, furred beings scurried about. Smoke rising from a heated pot told him the Urro had fetched the pitch more quickly than he would have thought possible.

"We'd best join them." Goran started toward the wall. "If the wind shifts, it will give the guards a good whiff of the pitch. All will be lost before it's begun."

Davin grinned. He saw no evidence of human patrols or guards, though he did not rule them out. Caution atop caution guided the course of a thief who wished to live to dotage. Within the city-state of Draymo-Vor, the king must sleep easily at night, having no fear of the Urro.

In half-step-half-slide strides the trio worked their way down the slope and across a broad sheet of ice stretching before the wall. There the small regiment of Urro worked feverishly. Hissing steam rose with each wooden bucket of pitch they threw against the ice wall.

Goran had been right about the smell; the hot tar stank to Yehseen's own heavens, Davin thought, while he directed the Urro to focus their efforts on a single spot. The stench, like the steam, were whipped away by the rising wind.

Hissing and sizzling, the pitch ran down the wall. Ice transformed to water, ran in rivulets away from the wall only to solidify to ice again. The Jyotian wondered why the Urro had not tried this method of ingress before. Entry to Draymo-Vor afforded them the chance to retrieve those held captive by the human king – if there was a seed of truth in their tale.

The Urro moved back as if frightened when the pitch melted through the ice barrier. Davin turned to Lijena with a questioning eyebrow raised.

"They have been cowed by long centuries of slavery. Even their bravest cannot enter the city. Too many of their people have died here," Lijena answered his unspoken question. "Too many of their race are still in King Draymo-Vor's ice prisons."

"There is no hope of their freedom if they refuse to fight for it."
Davin's mind shifted through the possible courses of action
needed to find Valora. Every minute the sword rode in the dark
mage's hand rather than in Felrad's was another minute the
Faceless Ones ranged across the broad plains of Raemllyn – and it
was another minute that Zarek Yannis sat on the Velvet Throne.

"A city of untold beauty." Sarcasm seeped in Goran's tone
when he ducked his head and entered the ice tunnel melted
through the wall. "Even a master thief such as I would be hard
pressed to scrounge enough crumbs for a decent meal in this
place."

Davin crouched and followed the Challing. Goran did not
exaggerate his verbal portrait of Draymo-Vor. Yet, what else was
to be expected when all Ianya lay glacial and barren? Riches were
surely measured in a cord of wood or a few stones needed for
building a shelter from the cold rather than in jewels and gold.

"Let's find Valora and be done with this miserable place."
Davin stood when he reached the opposite mouth of the hole in
the ice. "Goran speaks true. The only thing worth stealing here is
the sword we seek."

"Silence," Lijena demanded in a whispered hiss when she
pushed through the hole. "We don't have long. A sentry will
surely find the hole. When the alarm goes up, the king will call
out his troops."

"Hmmm, I think you have something there." Goran thoughtfully stroked his thick red beard. "Perhaps that is the best way of
finding the king. If Valora is truly his concubine, the two of them
ought to be together."

It took a moment for Davin to see what the Challing suggested.
On its face, it spoke of sheer madness. So mad that it was
brilliant. If this day was to be won, it would be taken by daring.

"Guard!" The Jyotian yelled without warning. "A breach in the
wall! Someone's breached the wall! King Draymo-Vor must be
alerted! The wall is breached! The wall is breached!"

Lijena tensed for an instant, then the confusion on her face
faded. She turned back to the hole and shooed the Urro off. The
misshapen hairy ice dwellers needed no second urging to vanish
back into the predawn murk.

"This had better work," Lijena said when she looked back at

the Jyotian. "You might have consulted Goran and me before calling out."

Davin shrugged. "It's better to have a guide than to wander these frozen streets for hours hunting for one hovel that is finer than the others." He urged his companions into the shadows of a nearby building. "Now all we need do is wait and – ah, there!"

He nodded to the right.

Three fur-cloaked men rushed along the wall and came to a sliding halt by the hole. After a quick examination of the breach in the ice, one man pronounced. "It's tar. Hot tar was used to melt the ice."

Another added. "The king must be warned!"

With that the three turned and ran back the way they had come.

"Now all we do is follow." Davin stepped from the shadows and moved after the men. Goran and Lijena followed a step behind the Jyotian.

After a twisting dash through streets turned gray with refrozen slush, the three guards entered a distant building whose only noteworthy feature was lamps burning in two upper windows.

"That would be the heart of this puissant kingdom," Goran said, his stride lengthening. "Come. It's time the Blackheart and I met. He has a price to pay for what he's done to my Kulonna."

"We seek the Sword of Kwerin Bloodhawk," Davin warned his friend, "not vengeance – or releasing Urro from their prison cells." He glanced at Lijena.

"I seek my beloved and the whoreson who took her from me." Goran freed his battle-axe and rushed toward the building ahead of them.

Davin's jaw dropped when Goran threw a shoulder against the double doors blocking his entrance. Wood weakened by years of dry rot splintered in a shower of shards and dust. The Jyotian urged Lijena forward. "Come on before he gets himself in trouble!"

A roar like the bellow of a tricorn, the wild bull of Raemllyn's forests, rolled from Goran's throat as he hefted his axe and charged a dozen uniformed guardsmen who ran down a wooden hallway toward the single challenger. Six of the dozen lay dead in their own blood by the time Davin reached his friend's side to add his sword to the fray. Spears of wood provided little defense against blades of fire-forged steel. The remaining Ianyans rushed forward and were served death just as quickly.

Lijena hesitated in the doorway. She tipped her head to one side, then placed her hands on her belly. Nodding, she turned and saw the iron door leading to the dungeons. The Urro prisoners were there awaiting a death of torture for the amusement of a tyrant.

But her steps did not take her in that direction. She edged past Davin and Goran and the last two inept Ianyan soldiers. Should another dozen or three appear to defend their stronghold, she knew the two freebooters could handle them. The soldiers with their stone-tipped spears were no match for Jyotian and Challing.

Lijena stared down a long corridor and the stairway rising to the citadel's second story. With deliberate strides she hastened down the hall, then moved upwards two steps at a time. She knew what lay at the top of the stairs and readied herself to meet it.

Lijena drew her sword and stepped into the upper passageway. Tapestries decorated the walls and a threadbare rug kept her boot heels from meeting the wooden floor. She halted outside an ornately decorated door at the end of the hall. Again she pressed her palms to her belly for a moment before she reached out and pushed the door inward.

As silent as a shadow gliding across another shadow, Lijena entered the sleeping chamber. A large bed dominated the center of the room; its four posts were draped with heavy blankets to provide warmth for those sleeping within. Lijena circled the room, using the tip of her sword to poke into chests and push aside piles of clothing carelessly cast off.

Nothing, she found nothing. But then did she truly expect Valora to leave the fabled sword lying about like the mounds of discarded clothes?

Her attention turned to an armoire that stood in a shadowed corner of the bedchamber. If the sorceress kept the blade close to her, it had to be there, Lijena reasoned. There was no other place in the room large enough to conceal the weapon. Lijena stretched out a hand, twisted a latch and opened its doors. The Sword of Kwerin Bloodhawk, secure in its unadorned sheath, dangled from a hook inside.

A disturbing mixture of relief and dread suffused the daughter of Bistonia as she stared at the blade she had once carried across half of Upper Raemllyn to deliver into Felrad's hands. She hesitated when she reached for the Bloodhawk's sword.

She remembered the feel of the weapon, the life of its own spawned when confronted with magicks. With it she had killed both man and demon. With it Prince Felrad could banish the Faceless Ones from the realms of Raemllyn and drive Zarek Yannis from the Velvet Throne. She knew the ensorcelled steel, had experienced its awesome power.

But the strength of the sword lay in death. That and only that was what it delivered. Chal, born of the Elysian race who worshipped Yehseen, God of Life, had taught her there was more than Qar's embrace. To take up the magic-bound blade again would mean that she betrayed Chal's memory.

"That will be far enough." A cool, deliberate voice came from behind Lijena. "Touch the sword and you will die a thousand deaths before I release your soul to Black Qar."

Lijena turned slowly, knowing whom she would face. "Did you think Felrad would let your treachery go unanswered?" Lijena's eyes locked on Valora who stood beside the bed.

Amusement uplifted the corners of the dark-haired mage's lips. Contempt dripped from her words. "*You*? Felrad sent *you*? That's rich!"

The humorless chuckle that pushed from Valora's throat held less than contempt. It echoed the cold note that the mage felt – that the woman before her was beneath any sentiment at all.

Lijena edged forward in a nervous weight-shifting that gave the appearance of attempting to find a way to escape. The mage's mockery offered no danger. As long as Valora taunted, she uttered no chants. The sorceress's insults bought Lijena time. She had to be within striking distance when the mage made her move. Valora was a magic-weaver of the first water. A simple spell would be all she needed to triumph. If Lijena were to live to see the face of the sun rising outside, she would have to strike before that.

"You were with those on the boat who followed me from the Isle of Loieter? I thought the waves I conjured had sent all of you to the bottom of the sea." Valora moved while she spoke.

Gathering her nightgown about her ankles, the sorceress stepped forward, circling the woman who had disturbed her sleep.

"As you can see, I still live." Lijena's heart pounded, feeling as though it would explode from her chest. Valora's steps allowed Lijena to inch closer to the sorceress. "As do those who sailed with me. Your waves provided us with little more than a needed bath."

"You prove more resilient than a simple merchant's daughter ought to be." Valora halted, her eyes narrowing. "Does a god give you his personal blessing? Black Qar himself? Perhaps the time has come for you to join him!"

Lijena recognized the instant of Valora's attack, but not its direction. With a flick of her wrist, Lijena sent her sword tip arcing upward on a path meant to meet the sorceress's midriff just below the ribs and then drive upward to her heart.

Valora's offense was not a spell. Instead, she leaped toward the cabinet that contained the Sword of Kwerin Bloodhawk. Lijena's sword missed its mark. The edge of steel sliced deeply into the sorceress's forearm as she pivoted toward the armoire. Lijena struck again with a lunging thrust meant to skewer the sorceress.

She missed for a second time.

Valora danced back, clutching her wounded left arm. "Bitch! I had hoped to give you the blade you seek! But I see the kitten has grown to a cat with claws. I will have to amuse myself with you in different ways."

"Bitch, cat – which am I?" Lijena uttered the first words that entered her mind. She attempted to buy time to maneuver close enough for another attack.

"I will enjoy watching you suffer in Draymo-Vor's dungeon. For a savage, he has developed rather sophisticated tortures. Nothing approaching those Yannis employed to make his prisoners regret their last moments in this world, but adequate. Yes, adequate." A smile of wicked delight slid across the sorceress's lips.

In the blink of an eye, Valora moved. She feinted with a jerky swing to the right then reeled back and tried to slide past Lijena's left.

The swordswoman reacted instinctively. Blade held high, she brought it down directly onto Valora's neck.

Steel never met flesh and bone. Lijena's blade rang out as though it struck solid stone and bounced into the air.

"Protective spells!" Lijena glared at the witch. "But no offensive ones. Were your grimoires lost at sea?"

"I need no spell book to deal with you!"

Lijena saw a dark flash of recognition in Valora's eyes the instant her lips uttered the first syllable of conjuration; the sorceress realized her mistake, knew she underestimated her foe who had goaded her into a demonstration of her magicks, accepted the full weight of the price to be exacted for that one faltering moment.

Lijena's sword flashed. Straight and true it leaped forward and sank hilt deep in Valora's stomach. Lijena wrenched back, pulling the blade free.

Valora stiffened, the spell dying on her trembling lips. Her dark eyes widened and blinked with denial. "How? You, a mere merchant's daughter. How?"

The sorceress's face twisted in pain, and she gritted her teeth to hold back a cry of agony that tried to push from her lips. Valora sank to her knees, then toppled sideways to the floor.

Lijena edged to the sorceress's side and rolled her onto her back. Sightless eyes stared up at the crudely hewn wooden ceiling. Lijena's left hand eased to her own belly and lightly rested there. Then she jerked her hand away and shouted defiantly, "No, no, I must be sure!"

She whipped out her dagger and raked it across Valora's throat. Only a thin trickle of blood came forth. The mage's heart had long since stopped pumping. Valora was undeniably dead, ferried to Peyneeha for the rest of eternity.

Lijena Farleigh stood and stared at her dead foe, then turned and reached for the sword of Kwerin Bloodhawk. It glowed brilliantly when she took it from the sheath.

"Destiny," she murmured in answer to Valora's final question. "Destiny for both of us."

11

"A mage! I watched my kingdom crumble for want of a mage!" Zarek Yannis clutched his hands together and twisted them until his knuckles burned bright. "Is it so hard for you to understand that I need a mage? Find one for me, General. Go, find one and bring him to me. Bring *her* to me, if need be. Though I am reluctant to trust any woman after Valora's treachery."

Lonch Porry swallowed hard. Danger lay but a hair's-breadth away when his king began these tirades. As the once mighty army retreated haphazardly across Raemllyn, Porry kept alert for any hint of a mage selling his services, no matter his level of achievement, no matter the cost. Nor had the sex of a magic-wielder concerned the general.

Whether those possessed of arcane knowledge avoided Yannis because of his reputation for butchering mages – and his possible defeat should Prince Felrad prove the stronger – Porry could not say. But something was afoot. Time and again he found the homes of mages emptied of occupants and possessions whenever Yannis' forces entered a city. The realm's wizards fled at the emperor's approach. As did simple country hedge-witches. Like their urban kin, the witches abandoned their hovels and disappeared.

Still Porry sought mages for his liege – and for himself as well. Military campaigns succeeded or failed because of adequate information about terrain, the enemy and his movements, the weather and a dozen other details of war. Porry required a good scrying of Felrad's forces to plan the best retreat across an increasingly hostile Raemllyn.

Of late, the scouts he sent out never returned once they left camp. Whether Felrad's men found and killed them or they simply deserted, he did not know. The results were the same – no intelligence and that many fewer soldiers to fight on.

These were but a symptom of the disease eating away at the troops under his command. In the weeks since falling back from the Isle of Loieter, morale had all but evaporated. To be certain, the usurper still generated a great fear among his troops when he spoke to them directly. Yet that terror faded quickly when Yannis was gone, leaving Porry to maintain discipline over men who no longer knew the meaning of the word. Should desertions increase at their present rate, Yannis would arrive in Kavindra with little more than an honor guard. If Yannis made it back to Kavindra at all.

"I have sent several squads ahead, toward Degoolah, to seek any spell-weaver they can find," Porry answered the usurper. "It might require a week or longer before they report."

"A mage!" Yannis cried, his face darkened with anger. He clenched his fists and shook them at the sky, as if challenging Minima, Goddess of the Winds, to single combat. "I am surrounded by incompetent fools. Find a mage to . . . to . . ."

Froth flecked Yannis' mouth, and his body quaked as though beset by the falling sickness.

Lonch Porry back-pedaled at the onset of the fit, a condition that seemed to grip Yannis more frequently with each passing day. It was not the falling sickness, of that Porry was almost certain. It was as though the ruler fought to contain use of his facilities – as though some unknown force drained away a portion of the man's life.

Porry's right hand dropped to his sword's hilt. As he had done a hundred times before, he considered using the blade. A quick thrust would end it all in a mere instant. What had Yannis brought Raemllyn other than misery and a desolation no one could surmount?

The general's fingers drummed on the wire-wrapped hilt, then fell away. Such defeatist thinking served no one, least of all the people of Raemllyn.

Felrad was no better than Zarek Yannis. No ruler was. Death and slavery were sovereign coinage given out freely by Raemllyn's rulers. Porry had been a young child when Yannis defeated Bedrich the Fair for the throne, and Porry's father had told of the backbreaking taxation levied by Bedrich, how their family had lost farm and home, how Lonch had lost his mother during a plague Bedrich refused to acknowledge.

The fight against Yannis had been foremost in the ruler's mind and he had ignored his citizens. Porry remembered his childish glee at hearing of Yannis' victory and how disappointed he had been that the new High King could not return his mother to life. Indeed, life did not change for the Porry clan, save for father's and son's dual induction into Yannis' army.

The elder Porry died during training, an accident never fully detailed to Lonch Porry. He knew the rigors of good drilling, though, and realized how a man as old and tired as his father might succumb.

Not for a moment had Porry believed the rumors that Zarek Yannis had used the elder Porry's company as practice opponents for his Faceless Ones. Why bother? The demons were invincible – or had been until Prince Felrad retrieved the Sword of Kwerin Bloodhawk.

Porry knew what awaited him if he surrendered to Felrad. He had seen the prince's troops putting prisoners to death. Better to die fighting than to face Black Qar with an executioner's garrote twined around his neck.

He watched while the fit that convulsed every fiber of Zarek Yannis' body ebbed and the king returned to normal – or what passed for normal in these unsettled times. Eyes wide and nostrils flared, Yannis lowered himself cross-legged to the ground and peered up at his lone general through eyes that seemed unable to comprehend what they saw. Then Yannis blinked and shook his head like a man throwing off the veil of sleep.

"What do you do to insure our safety, General Porry?" Yannis spoke as if nothing out of the ordinary had transpired. He wiped spittle from his lips with a sleeve of his cloak.

"I have divided our forces once more, Majesty," Porry replied. "Half lay traps, digging ditches to fill with fuels of any variety we can find."

"Then when Felrad's men ride over the trenches you ignite them!"

"That is so, Majesty," Porry said carefully. Yannis derived great pleasure from descriptions of the holocaust thus brought to Felrad's troops. "Other traps are planted, some fake, but many not. The fake ones require time and effort to examine. Any tactic we can concoct to slow the enemy's pursuit is being used."

"Yes, yes, what of the rest? You said only a few were setting traps. What of the others?"

"Brave men, Majesty," Porry went on, wishing he rode with those cavalrymen rather than providing meaningless reports to a half-crazed king. "Their standing orders are to engage any unit of Felrad's guard that they outnumber. If they do not see clear victory, they retreat and wait for another chance. Hit and run – hit and run. Theirs is to bring maximum damage with as little harm to themselves as possible."

"They ought to attack! Only in attack is there victory!" Zarek Yannis shot to his feet and spun about, sending his cloak flying like a bat's wing. He struck a pose, as if holding the royal scepter at his court. "I hereby promote them all to the rank of captain, if they attack and never retreat!"

"An army of captains is no different from an army of privates," pointed out Porry. Theory of command was not what Yannis desired to hear now, the general abruptly realized. He changed his logic better to meet his liege's concerns. "No matter what their rank or decoration, all fight valiantly for you, King Zarek."

"Yes, of course they do. They fear me. They fear the Faceless Ones!"

Lonch Porry suppressed a snort of derision. How he wished Yannis still commanded those ferocious demons. A few could turn the tide of battle from rout to victory in minutes. Prince Felrad, the Sword of Kwerin in hand, had killed all the Faceless in the span of an hour at the Battle of Rakell.

"How can men fear what is no longer?" Porry asked, returning to his more usual efficient manner. Dwelling on failure availed him nothing. Only by seizing every opportunity presented by the enemy could he hope for any victory.

"They are not all gone!" Zarek Yannis whirled again. "I still command five of the demon riders!"

"Five?"

"Are you a fool? Should I give your liver to them?"

"Majesty, I can use them to good advantage," Porry said, his mind turning over the possibilities. "Just one of the Faceless could do much in distracting Felrad's army from pursuit. We need a few days to rest, then . . ."

"No one but I commands the Faceless Ones," Yannis said

firmly, his eyes narrowing with suspicion. "I brought them into this world and I alone command them."

"How did you bring them forth?" Lonch Porry asked before he realized what he said.

"You are not a mage. You can never know. Why do you ask? Are you a spy for Felrad?" Yannis pointed at his general, fingers arcing with brilliant blue sparks.

Porry gasped when one tiny bolt leaped from Yannis' finger to burn a hole in the general's tunic. He staggered away when pain spread throughout his body from the tiny wound.

"Are you a spy?" roared Yannis. New sparks jumped to Porry's head and face, igniting pain that seared into the core of his brain. He screamed out: "No, no, Majesty, I am loyal. Who else has remained by your side these past weeks?"

"Yes, that is so." Yannis' hand dropped to his side. The blue sparks died. "You are clever and have accounted for the deaths of hundreds of Felrad's swinish soldiers. If you had been at my side during the Battle of Rakell, we would not have lost. I am sure of it. And you promised to find me a mage, many mages. I can use them all – all you can find."

"Why do you need a mage when you are so adept?" asked Porry.

The anger building into Yannis' eyes told Porry he never should have asked that question.

"A Faceless One, Majesty," Lonch Porry said, diverting his liege's attention from the gaffe. "Assign one to me, and I shall report great victories over Felrad's troopers."

Porry remained cautious, although certain he saw the subtle shifts of sanity behind Yannis' eyes. Anger faded and appraisal took over. The king was nothing if not pragmatic about killing his enemies.

"Guarantee five hundred slain and you will receive the use of a Faceless demon."

"Nothing would please me more," Porry said, bowing deeply to cover the surprise on his face. Zarek Yannis had yielded command easily of the most formidable fighter ever to ride across Raemllyn. Porry had never seen the Faceless Ones in battle, but he had heard the tales.

"You will find a rider at the meeting of the River Stane and the

River Faor. Do with it as you will for one week. Then return to me with news of your success."

"I ride immediately, Your Majesty," Porry said, anticipation swelling within him. He finally commanded a real fighter, one no ordinary soldier could best!

Lonch Porry dismounted and approached the Faceless One with trepidation. The demon sat astride a midnight black steed with hooves that set the ground afire wherever they touched. The black, hooded robe did nothing to conceal the rider's other-worldly appearance. From beneath that cowl burned two coal-brilliant eyes. Porry could not determine if the demon stared at him or at something else, farther away – infinitely far away.

The Faceless One's skeletal hand rested on a sword of crystal-line fire; tiny sparks moved ceaselessly along the blade's razored edge. When the demon shifted its weight in the saddle, Porry glimpsed a silver, scaled serpentine tail tucked behind the crea-ture, barely visible under its black robe.

"Zarek Yannis has placed you under my command," Porry said, his mouth drier than the Great Desert of Nayati. He cleared his throat to speak again because the Faceless One showed no sign of having heard. "You are to obey me."

A slight nod was all the reply Lonch Porry received. He backed off, then forced himself to keep from mounting his horse and fleeing like a craven. Not certain he truly commanded this demon, he rode to the east where he had planned an ambush for a company of Felrad's infantry. Several of Porry's most trusted men had prepared the ground with deep pits beset with stakes. This would slow the enemy's advance. Victory over such a large detachment would shake Felrad's confidence. Until now, the prince had pursued Zarek Yannis unhindered.

Porry glanced over his shoulder and saw the Faceless One trotting behind. The demon horse's hooves and their fire left a stench of brimstone in the air. Feathery plumes of smoke gusted from the steed's huge nostrils as if its entrails were aflame. Porry shuddered and turned away, not daring to look longer.

"It will seize my soul and give it to Yu-Vatruk for its dining pleasure." The words came unbidden to his lips. Nothing fright-ened Lonch Porry quite so much as the demon of nightmares. To be for ever trapped in the horrors that roamed his own skull during sleep terrified him more than anything Felrad might do to him.

Porry tapped his heels to his mount's flanks to urge the horse to a greater speed. When he had asked Yannis for one of the Faceless he had never considered the effect of the demon's presence on his own psyche. Now he wondered if his own nerves would hold together for the next week.

The general rejoined his small band of saboteurs a league east of where he had met the Faceless One. Not a single head lifted when he and the demon who rode behind him entered camp. Porry dismounted and walked to a corporal huddled near a fire burning fitfully. The Faceless One remained astride its demon mount.

"Who ordered this fire?" Porry demanded of his subordinate. "Felrad's troops will spy the smoke!"

"Who cares?" the corporal answered with a shrug. "It's summer but the air carries the breath of winter. We're freezing our arses off, and for what? We set the traps as you ordered, but there's no way we can engage more than a few of Felrad's soldiers. There's a full thousand of them!"

"A thousand?" Porry looked to the others sitting with their backs to trees, capes pulled tightly around their bodies to protect against the unseasonable chill borne on the wind.

"He exaggerates, General," spoke a man who had ridden at Porry's side since the general had been a sublieutenant. "Not more 'n a few hundred. Three, possibly four hundred. Black Qar devour the lot of 'em."

"The Black Destroyer just might," Porry replied, fighting the urge to glance over a shoulder at the Faceless One. His soldiers still ignored the rider who had accompanied him to camp. "How long before the rest of our force arrives?"

"How long before we face the Sitala to plead mercy for our sins?" The corporal spat a stream of spittle into the fire with contempt.

Before Porry could reprimand the man, the ground shook and the scent of burning metal reached his nostrils. He spun, hand flying to his sword hilt. The Faceless One trotted up, towering over him. Behind general and demon, soldiers gasped in fear. The

Faceless One raised a bony finger and pointed in the direction of the traps Porry's troop had readied for Prince Felrad's advancing force.

"Now? We fight now?" Inwardly Lonch Porry cursed; his was not to question but to command. Yannis had placed this fiend under his control, not the reverse. However, Porry could not but wonder if this hell-spawned rider realized that?

The Faceless One hefted its blade of crystalline fire and pointed again.

Porry swallowed hard and attempted to reassert himself. "Move the troops into position. We will lead the attack."

"We?" This from the corporal who cowered away from the black-cloaked rider with the burning eyes. The man's expression left no doubt that, given the opportunity, he would have joined the countless others who had deserted Yannis' army.

Porry had no intention of giving any in this meager troop the opportunity to flee. If duty would not spark loyalty in the corporal's breast, then fear would. "The Faceless One and I will lead the attack. Follow, and bring victory this day." Porry paused to let his gaze drift over the faces of his men. "Or stay and I'll let the Faceless One rip out your liver and feed it to Qar!"

With that, Lonch Porry pivoted to face his mount, vaulted into the saddle and drew his sword. Sucking in a deep breath, Yannis' general reined the horse about and drove his heels into its flanks. The animal bolted forward, legs stretching out in an easy gallop. A half-mile from the camp, Porry drew to a halt.

The meadowlands that stretched before Porry had been chosen carefully. Between him and the demon rider at his side lay grasslands sprinkled with camouflaged death – pits lined with wooden stakes tipped in poison. Beyond a stretch of flat, feature-less meadow lay the river Faor. Sandwiched between river and pits stood an advance column of Prince Felrad's force.

Having tasted victory after victory since Rakell, Porry knew the generals commanding the column would never consider retreat, especially when faced with a force they outnumbered three to one. Nor would they merely hold their ground and wait. That left only attack.

It was on that attack Porry staked the day – and his own life. More than battle-weary warriors would face Felrad's troops this day. Today they would die before a demon unleashed from Peyneeha, the deepest level of Hell itself!

"To me!" Porry ordered his command.

Yannis' soldiers moved forward in ragged line that held little hint of military precision. Rather than disgust at the lack of discipline, Porry gave a silent nod of approval. The ragtag appearance of the men would provide added incentive to Felrad's commanders.

Across the field Porry watched the opposing officers huddle. He imagined the hasty exchange of strategies, confirmation of intelligence from scouts and commands for each unit. He saw arms jerk about pointing to locations in the meadow as the officers returned to the ranks. The pits had been discovered and their limits mapped.

Porry denied himself a pleased smile. All went as he had planned, but the battle was yet to be won. The Sitala was devious in the fates they cast for men. Yet, for the first time since the retreat from distant Loieterland, Porry sensed a turning of the tide. The Faceless One and his fire-hooved steed awakened that confidence.

"Forward – double time. Arms level for attack!" Porry raised his sword high above his head, then let it fall, slicing the air in the direction of the enemy.

The advance, too, was part of Porry's plan. A full charge might arouse his opponents' suspicion. He wanted Felrad's troops fired with the blood lust of certain victory before they stared into the face of what confronted them this day.

The charge he hoped for came. War cries ripped through the air as the prince's men abruptly broke into a full run. Screams of death soon mingled with that roar. Porry pursed his lips and gave a silent nod. Felrad's soldiers discovered that the pits they saw earlier were decoys. The treacherous traps with their poisonous stakes had been carefully concealed. They now served their purpose, whittling down the uneven numbers.

Still Felrad's generals urged their warriors on. Porry maintained his steady advance. Sunlight glinted off the steel points when spears lowered to meet Yannis' troops. Porry's nostrils filled with the stink of sweat carried on the soft breeze. He clutched his sword harder and bent low, prepared for the first clash as the enemy swept toward him.

Felrad's ranks bowed slightly in the middle in a blatant attempt to circle and engulf the tattered line of soldiers they attacked. Porry glanced to his side; the demon mount matched his own horse stride for stride.

"Ends advance. Close rank!" The cry echoed through Felrad's troops.

Like a collapsing wave, the prince's soldiers complied.

In a heartbeat, the battle surrounded Porry. The general slashed aside a spear that lanced toward his side and, in a backstroke, hacked into the face of the man who thrust that spear. As easily as the first died, Porry dispatched five more spear carriers. He urged his mount forward to meet three more.

The horse grunted, lurched forward and went down, its forelegs tangled in a rope weighted with two heavy stones.

Kicking free of the stirrups, Porry leaped free of the saddle before the falling horse could trap him beneath its weight. He hit the ground hard on his right shoulder. Shaking his head, he could not push aside the gray blur that fogged his eyes. The din of clashing arms, the screams and cries of battle filled his head. Porry readied himself for the steel he knew waited to steal away his life.

None came. Instead the fog gradually evaporated to reveal puffy white clouds floating across a sky of azure. Slowly, Lonch Porry managed to find his feet and stand. A gasp of horror came unbidden from his lips. Not a battlefield met his wide eyes, but a field of bloody carnage.

Felrad's remaining troops no longer charged but ran for their lives. The Faceless One cut through them like a honed scythe through grain ready for harvest. Porry could not count quickly enough to assess the number killed. Arms and legs and heads lay strewn across the red-stained meadow. Rather than the ring of steel on steel, Porry's ears now filled with piteous cries of terror and dying.

"Father Yehseen, what forces are loosed on Raemllyn?" Porry dropped to his knees. He had won victory this day as he had planned, but he had never imagined the price the enemy would pay.

Lonch Porry doubled over and vomited.

* * *

"My sisters miss me terribly," complained Fiany. "There is no reason for me to hike such long distances away from Ham. The villagers need me more. I can work healing spells for them, no matter how poor they are."

"Quit complaining about your Qar-damned sisters," growled Cor'Mid.

"They need me," Fiany said, pouting. A single tear ran down her cheek, leaving behind a muddy trail.

Tacllyn-lin-Bertam ignored his companions. Since leaving Prince Felrad's camp the two had made travel a ceaseless irritation with their incessant bickering. Cor'Mid wanted to return to his home in Leticia. Bertam suspected the young mage had a lover he missed. And Fiany had formed a tight triad with her two sisters that seemed more than marriage between husband and wife. Yet, those traits were the very ones Bertam needed if he wanted to close magically the demons' doorway into Raemllyn.

Unswerving loyalty: Fiany.

Passion: Cor'Mid.

The remaining pair provided stark power. Wok-Lamol and Wok-Manol, the twin sorcerers plying their magicks outside the seaport of Orji, would complete the quintet Bertam needed for the task.

Bertam had never traveled to this part of Raemllyn, being from antipodally positioned Cahri before joining the crew of the *Twisted Cross*. He shut his ears to Fiany and Cor'Mid and scanned the plains sloping downward to the Oceans of Kumar. The ravages of the war scarring the continent's midsection had yet to touch the eastern coast of Raemllyn. The salt-sharp wind blowing off the ocean was cold, hinting at a rapidly nearing winter although summer was but newly come to the land. Bertam tried to ignore this overwhelming manifestation of the forces loose in the world while he studied the sere grass. Enough for his horses, meager though it was, enough to get them to the small village outside Orji where the twin sorcerers resided.

The older mage blinked and sat straight in the saddle. Magicks were aplay; the hairs on his neck stood on end. He turned slowly until he faced southward, along the coast. The stark power he detected chilled him more than the ocean breeze ever could.

"What is it, Bertam?" Cor'Mid asked, his voice touched by awe.

The mage from Leticia felt it too, Bertam knew. If anything, his companion was more sensitive to the power erupting from the region than was Bertam.

"I don't know." Bertam slowly shook his head. "It is unsettling. I've never felt its like before."

"What are you talking about?" asked Fiany. She stared around in confusion. Nervously, she shifted her weight in the saddle before staring from Bertam to Cor'Mid. A tinge of embarrassed red flushed her grime-smeared cheeks.

"No need for guilt, Fiany," Bertam dismissed the woman's shame over missing the strong magical undercurrents in the air. "Your talents lie elsewhere. There is a might at work yonder unlike anything I have seen conjured – or tried myself."

Bertam drew in a deep breath and composed himself, forcing calmness to quiet his churning doubts. He could not lose the two mages he sought. Only they of all those in Raemllyn possessed the abilities he needed. He feared, though, that Yannis had somehow arrived first.

"Who remains to Yannis?" he asked aloud. "What mage offers his services to a ruler discarding men and women like so many empty wine goblets?"

"There!" cried Cor'Mid, pointing. "I feel it. I feel it. Oh, how it burns my brain!" The young mage jumped from saddle to ground, clutching his bedazzled eyes.

Tacllyn-lin-Bertam swung about and stared into a column of hellfire rising thousands of feet in the air, spearing clouds and blazing far into the sky.

12

Before Bertam comprehended what happened, the fire that beset his companion's brain slashed into his head. He reeled and fell from the back of his mount to the ground. The insidious, invisible magical blade found more than the mage's brain as a target; it drove into his innards and twisted there. Bertam doubled over and tried to force away the torment. He failed.

Beyond his own groans of agony, he heard Fiany softly chanting, spinning magicks into a subtle tapestry. The next instant, Bertam screamed. A chasm opened – a vast crack in the world that stretched all the way to the core of the planet. Lining the impossible shaft hung tortured souls stolen by Black Qar.

And flames! Everywhere he turned, every place his magical senses probed, flared an inferno of death and dying.

Into this pit he was drawn. Fight as he did, he found no solid ground on which to gain purchase. Deeper, Bertam fell, and with each foot he descended, bits of his being ripped away to join the piteous souls shrieking for surcease.

"No! This is not the way I die!" He found strength to shout defiance into the rocky throat that swallowed him.

Join me. Come, join me, weakling!

Tacllyn-lin-Bertam tried to roll into a ball. Instead, the force gripping him stretched his body like rubber, pulling it as thin as a spider's thread.

Above, below, beyond, Bertam spun helplessly, robbed of any sense of time and space. Yet, through the confusion, the wizard felt an indefinable adhesiveness. He reached out to this ineffability and hugged it close. He was not a complete prisoner of the force drawing him to the underworld.

Peyneeha? Did he stare into the maw of Black Qar's netherworld?

No. Beneath the soles of his feet Bertam felt rather than saw firm ground. Closing his eyes, he focused thought and strength on that island of solidity. He coiled the muscles in his legs and thrust upward.

Like a spring suddenly released, he snapped back. He rolled over and over until his side collided with two unyielding columns of—

Bertam's eyes blinked open to stare up at Fiany, her lips moving in a complex spell. Not his strength but her conjuring had snatched him from Qar's maw! His own ability must now mate with hers.

Willing thought above the agony that rippled through his body, Bertam carefully began a spell of his own. Subtlety worked far better than naked force. Nothing could stand long against the stark, raw might of the magical fires that burned so fiercely. Guiding, shaping, urging Fiany different channels allowed Bertam to construct a protective bubble around them. With the burning hellfire held at bay, the mage sat up and looked around.

"Cor'Mid, we must save him." Bertam saw the other mage convulsing like a man caught in a fit a few paces outside the sphere of warding.

"He is in no danger," Fiany answered in her squeaky voice.

Bertam shook himself. For the world she seemed a perfect candidate to change into a mouse sneaking through the night. Everything about her bespoke weakness and a slight will. Yet, she held away the force that had completely overwhelmed Cor'Mid and him.

"What causes the eruption?" Bertam forced himself to stare into the maelstrom of unholy fire in an effort to unravel its mystery. No matter what Fiany said, Cor'Mid stood in peril as long as the hellfire burned. Shuddering, Bertam tried to force away the memory of being sucked into the depths ruled by Black Qar.

"They do it," Fiany said in her thin, meek voice. "They play with powers they cannot – quite – control."

"They?"

For a moment, Bertam missed her meaning. Then it penetrated – Wok-Lamol and Wok-Manol, the twin-born mages they sought. Bertam opened his mind and sought the magical thread controlling the fire, the telltale path of spells and enchantments that would lead back to the mages who summoned the flaming pillar. Nothing. He sensed nothing.

"We can stop it by redirecting the spell," Fiany said.

Her fingers moved in a stately pavane of magic and proficiency. For the first time since they had met, Bertam appreciated the full weight of Fiany's worth. Beneath the woman's mousy exterior dwelled a genius, a worker of wonders! The spells she employed might be considered common, but not the manner in which she used them. Her methods were as unique as those of an artist who carved a masterpiece from a tree trunk with only a paring knife and creativity.

The protective bubble expanded gradually until it encompassed Cor'Mid. The young mage's convulsing subsided immediately, and he lay still, deadly still.

"Give him a moment," Fiany said without a break in the signs her fingers wove. "He'll be all right."

As if drawn to the sound of Fiany's voice, Cor'Mid's eyes slowly opened. His head turned from side to side. Gradually, he pushed up to stare at his fellow magicians.

Shaken but still in one piece, Bertam assessed Cor'Mid's condition. The younger mage's face was drawn taut and his eyes were bloodshot. Tears mingled with the red of blood rolled from those eyes. Bertam re-evaluated his companion, *Mayhaps a few cracks though*.

"They meddle – meddle with no way of controlling the forces they release," Cor'Mid said in a voice that displayed one of those fractures. "We cannot deal with them. They are fools. Dangerous fools!"

"Perhaps so," agreed Bertam, "but they demonstrate the power we lack. Fiany has control. You, Cor'Mid, showed your ability to withstand potent magicks, and I can guide. With the twin mages, we can combine talents into a quincunx of magic and close the rent in space. We can deny the demons access to our world, no matter how Zarek Yannis coaxes them hence."

"How can we deal with the Faceless Ones?" asked Fiany. "They repulse me."

Bertam spun about as if he were a hound that sniffed the air. The column of fire was gone, vanished as though it had never existed. What of those conjuring it?

Bertam turned again, this time with slow precision. He halted when his gaze met the sea. A rocky prominence relentlessly assaulted by waves held his attention. He saw no hint of hewn stone, no thatch of roof, but within that jagged rock dwelled the two they sought. There was no denying the power radiating from the heart of the stone.

"We go there." Bertam started toward the coastline. His lips moved constantly to issue one ward spell after another. He dared not succumb to magical pressures now. Facing the pair and projecting nothing but sureness of purpose – and power – guaranteed success. Less, he knew, would be interpreted as weakness by Wok-Lamol and Wok-Manol.

An hour's hike brought the trio to the edge of the beach. The sudden undulation under their feet halted them. Bertam glanced at his companions. "We tread too close for their comfort. They welcome us – in their fashion."

"They seem well-versed in the social graces," Fiany answered. "They greet us with flowers."

A foot ahead of Bertam a rose bush pushed from the sand. It was not the blood-red blossoms that intrigued the mage but the foot-long thorns the plant sported. In the span of three heartbeats the bush grew from sprout to a height half that of a grown man. Branches became serpentine tendrils that uncoiled and stretched thorny branches to ensnare the wizard.

A pass of Bertam's hand redirected a ward spell straight to the writhing bush. As though struck by a blast of arctic air, blossoms and leaves withered and fell to the ground. Branches abruptly sapless splintered and blew away in the wind.

In reply to his defense, a garden of the deadly roses sprouted from the sand, growing with such speed that the leaves and limbs popped and cracked.

"They seek to pen us like animals!" This from Cor'Mid.

"Do not meet their spells head-on. Sidestep their thrusts and counter with your own magicks. Employ just what is needed to turn their attacks away. There's no need to betray our full power." Bertam forced bravado into his voice to conceal the fear that the two mages they faced had yet to unveil the extent of their might.

As Cor'Mid's and Fiany's spells complemented his own, a path opened in the tangled forest of writhing roses and lashing thorny shoots. Bertam walked deliberately in an attempt to conserve his strength until they reached the base of the rocky pillar.

As quickly as the spike-armed roses appeared, they vanished. A balmy wind blew from the sea. Salt spray snatched from the waves' foam filled the air and showered down on the three mages. In the next instant water was transformed to searing acid!

With a swipe of a hand, Bertam conjured a transparent canopy of magical energy to protect his companions and himself. Angry scarlet colored his cheeks as his ire mounted.

"Enough is enough!" Tacllyn-lin-Bertam's words rolled from his throat in a growl. "I desire solitude as much as any who walks the arcane paths, but these two are like spoiled children. Did I not need the powers of the two who dwell within that rocky spire, I would blast it to dust!"

"Perhaps a good switching would serve us." Fiany nodded in agreement with her companion's assessment of the unseen twin magicians. "Often it is the best way to deal with unruly children."

"We should've cut a switch from one of their rose bushes," Cor'Mid added.

Bertam lifted his head when he turned back to the tower of rock. "Stay your spells! You tempt the wrath of three who would meet with you in the name of Prince Felrad, who would follow his father Bedrich the Fair to the Velvet Throne."

Cor'Mid coughed to gain Bertam's attention. "Think you that this will change their insolence to hospitality?"

Bertam stood for a moment as a wave lapped up along the beach to wash around his ankles. The mage's gaze traveled across the strand to the base of the rocky spire and upward to its summit. Twin beacons shone there, one reflecting brilliant sunlight and the other radiating an ebon intensity as though the mage stared into the depths of a moonless night. Bertam knew the twin mages studied him, and found him lacking.

"A tidal wave!" cried Cor'Mid. "They conjure a wall of water to swallow us!"

"Use your magicks to dissolve it," Bertam ordered curtly.

Bertam never shifted his gaze from the dual points of light and dark atop the unscalable peak. To display weakness now meant he would have to find two others to join his quincunx.

Only through a pentad could the rent be repaired and Yannis' damnable source of Faceless Ones closed. Even if Prince Felrad regained the Sword of Kwerin Bloodhawk, this was a chore that must be done. The demons could not be allowed to pour forth endlessly to bedevil Raemllyn's lands.

Cor'Mid and Fiany began working to halt the tidal wave. Bertam was aware they did it subtly, with gentle magical nudges rather than overt power. The tidal wave slid along a magic knife's edge and crashed onto the beach far behind them. Relief suffused Bertam; no second wave followed the first.

"Why do you seek us?" boomed the question from high above the beach.

Bertam spoke in a soft voice, aware the mages could hear even a whisper so close to their keep. "We seek to enlist your aid in a project worthy of your immense talents."

Tacllyn-lin-Bertam carefully detailed the plan to weld shut the tear in the space-time fabric and concluded with, "So it is obvious that your talents are required. Only Wok-Lamol and Wok-Manol exhibit the power we need for such an undertaking."

"He recognizes our ability, dear brother." A black-dressed man winked into existence to Bertam's right.

Bertam contained his surprise. The mage had simply appeared with no hint of spell preceding him. Alert for such magicks and failing to detect them, Bertam admitted to himself the two were full masters of the conjuring arts. Their abilities equaled their reputations.

"Why shouldn't he, dear brother?" came the reply to Bertam's left. A mage cloaked in eye-searing white linen, so pure that Bertam knew it must be kept spotless through constant magical vigilance, nodded solemnly.

Looking past their robes, Bertam saw they were, indeed, twins. Long, hooked noses and high-domed foreheads were their most prominent features – and they were mirror images of one another. More than this, they moved in mirrored unison. If one lifted a right hand, the twin duplicated the movement with his left.

"Such unity of purpose lends vigor to your spells," Bertam said with an inkling of the pair's strength. "You represent both sides of magical power. Together you comprise a whole."

"But of course," said the white-dressed mage. He bowed deeply. "I am Wok-Lamol."

"And I," chimed in the black-dressed twin, "am Wok-Manol. Your mission is of some slight interest to us. Therefore, we will entertain your plans, at least for a few seconds."

"It is of vital interest to the people of Raemllyn," Bertam cut in.

"Why should we . . ." started Wok-Manol.

". . . indulge in aiding you?" finished Wok-Lamol. "It is none of our concern. We live here in peace, meditating and . . ."

". . . performing our experiments." Wok-Manol stood with his arms crossed defiantly.

Bertam didn't have to see his twin to know the white-dressed mage adopted a similar insolent pose.

"Perhaps we have chosen poorly," spoke up Cor'Mid.

"Yes, I must agree. They will not do," added Fiany.

Bertam kept from smiling. They understood the egos involved and worked to maneuver the twins into agreement.

"Why not?" the twins cried in unison. "We are the finest mages in all Raemllyn. None stands against us!"

"We fight magicks not of Raemllyn," Bertam pointed out. "Fiany and Cor'Mid are correct. We apologize for disturbing your meditation and will seek mages better suited to . . ."

"Stop!" commanded Wok-Manol. He stalked around and planted himself firmly before Bertam. His brother joined him, adopting the same pose. "You saw our descent into Peyneeha. Who else among all the mages in this pitiful world dare tweak Black Qar's nose as we did?"

"Who would be so foolish?" muttered Fiany.

They ignored the small woman and moved closer to Bertam until they rudely bumped against him.

"Try us. Let us show you our power."

"We must work as a team, in a quincunx of power, if we are to project the most potent spell possible. We repair, not destroy," warned Bertam.

"Do it, do it," the twins said. "We want to prove you cannot find better mages, more powerful ones. We have spent our lives in practice."

"Let us put an end to the rent. Your spells must protect as well as mend," said Bertam, speaking more to Cor'Mid and Fiany than to the twin mages.

He motioned the twins to opposite ends of a diagonal, the other vertices occupied by Fiany and Cor'Mid. Tacllyn-lin-Bertam placed himself in the center where the lines of power would cross with searing intensity. His role was not to provide magical power, but to guide as the swordsman's strong wrist and sharp eye caused the sword tip to nick its target.

Bertam staggered when the spell began. An overwhelming power flowed from their five-fold combination. The sand crunched beneath his feet as he widened his stance to keep from collapsing beneath the force focused on him from four sides. While his body stayed on the eastern coastline, his mind soared northward faster than any airborne denizen.

"It reeks," complained Fiany.

"No, it blinds me," said Cor'Mid.

The twins made no comment about the rift in space. They arrowed directly for the hole, allowing Bertam to accept thousands of sensations and reject them all. This was a magical tear, not a smell or a sight, and it held more danger than any force to threaten Raemllyn in the memory of humankind.

"Such a small hole," he marveled, but Bertam knew its deadly potential. Beyond the rent he saw things writhing.

Bertam swallowed hard and began careful spell-casting, for what he saw were not things. They were *things, things* unclean and lethal to any mortal. Using his honed skills, he guided the power generated by the five straight at the hole – and through.

He screamed at the same time as Cor'Mid and Fiany. Wok-Manol and Wok-Lamol joined that silent shriek echoing across all eternity a heartbeat later.

"What is it? Such a break – two tails – nothing I have ever seen rivals it!" The woman ducked, throwing up hands instead of magicks to ward off the *keedehn*, a dragon creature from the dimension of Gohwohn.

More ferocious creatures crowded behind the dragon, each waiting for an opportunity to rush from their respective worlds into Raemllyn. Bertam's resolve faltered; their mission was ill-conceived. They could not close this gaping hole. Their meddling only further ripped the fabric of time and space!

"Away," he cried. "Get away. Back before the creatures find us!"

The *keedehn* snapped and clawed and flew at them though their bodies were secure on a beach near Orji. Bertam did what he could to focus deadly magicks on the other-worldly beast. The *keedehn* wobbled and shimmered, turned translucent – and then, it simply vanished.

"Away," Bertam repeated, breaking the bonds that held the five together as a single mind. He took a step, stumbled and fell to the beach. Salt air stung his nostrils and he knew they had returned. He looked about him and saw a shaken Cor'Mid and a trembling Fiany. When he saw the twin mages, though, his heart turned to stone and coldness seized him. They had been boastful of their incomparable magical ability. Now they stood as daunted as their companions.

Tacllyn-lin-Bertam hated to admit it, but they had failed. Simply examining the tear had drawn the fearsome creatures – monsters of mystical substance as much as physical form. If he and his companions were to prevail, they had to be stronger and more clever than they had been during this foray. If they failed, nothing could stop Yannis from summoning legions of Faceless Ones.

Not even the Sword of Kwerin Bloodhawk!

13

"Fight? You call this a fight?" Disgust brimmed in Goran One-Eye's voice while he swung his deadly axe high and brought it down on the arm of a swordsman foolishly rushing forward. "This is more like hacking weeds with a scythe."

The Ianyan yowled in pain when Goran yanked the axe from his opponent's forearm. The man fell silent when another quick lash of the Challing's blade caught him beneath the chin. Two more guards ran down the stairs and were met by the Challing's axe, and died.

"Friend Davin, there's no need of you here." Goran twisted to face three new guards who pushed through a doorway into the hall. "Find Berenicis and my Kulonna. I could sleepwalk and hold this position all night."

Davin Anane parried a feeble lunge by the swordsman he faced and deftly drove his own sword tip between the man's ribs, thrusting to the heart. Goran did not brag; the Ianyans with their stone-headed spears and soft iron swords posed no real threat. Whether in bravery or stupidity, they raced into the fray and died like animals led to the slaughter.

"As you will, my friend," Davin answered, stepping over the bloody bodies of four guardsmen. "The time for Berenicis and me to stand before each other is long overdue."

Davin darted through an open doorway to his left while Goran readily dispatched the first of the guards to reach him with an upward swing of the axe that disemboweled the man. The Ianyans' vulnerability stemmed from more than a lack of weaponry, Davin thought, as he moved down another hall lined with doors. The Ianyans were ill-trained for what weapons they bore – and more, they were weaklings. It was as though the long centuries of banishment to this land of eternal cold robbed their muscles of the strength given to the men of Upper and Lower Raemllyn. The Jyotian recalled the Urro mentioning rampant famine. Perhaps such was as common as ice and snow here, and the Ianyans' weakness was born in their lack of nourishment?

The thief had little time to ponder the possibility. He threw open the third door, expecting to find the room beyond as empty as the first two, and found himself leaping aside to avoid a spear thrust meant for his stomach. When the Ianyan who sought to ambush him stepped into the hallway and jerked his weapon back for another thrust, Davin's wrist flicked his sword to the right. The blade parried wooden shaft and sliced inward. The guardsman died with his throat slit from ear to ear.

The remaining nine rooms that opened from the narrow corridor proved as empty as the first two. Davin halted before a door at the end of the hallway. Unlike the others, iron bands reinforced heavy wood and an iron lock latched the doorway. As massive as the lock appeared, it provided little resistance to the bite of tempered steel. Three times the Jyotian's blade rose and fell before the lock thudded to the wooden floor, the hasp cut through. Davin shoved back an iron bar and pushed the door inward.

Fetid air washed over his face, warm and carrying the heavy coppery tang of spilled blood. Dim light from guttering torches offered a shifting, shadowy glow that spilled onto hewn rock steps leading downward into the bowels of the palace.

Berenicis would never have selected such gloom as a bedchamber if given the choice, Davin thought while he picked his way down the stairs, carefully avoiding slick patches of red-tinted ice. Then, the Blackheart might not have been given the welcome Valora found in this gods-forsaken realm. A wise ruler would have deemed a dungeon cell an appropriate accommodation for the likes of Berenicis.

The spiraling stairway ended in a lofty chamber hewn from the same bedrock as the stairs. The walls about the Jyotian sported manacles bolted into the stone, but the room lacked the torture devices usually contained within a dungeon. A large fire blazed in cheerful counterpoint to the dingy walls and their dangling black iron chains. A pot of pitch boiled above the flames, hinting at a less innocent purpose for the flames.

Davin crossed to a heavily barred wooden door. He shoved back the locking bar and cautiously opened the door. The stench of death and dying staggered him. The interior corridor was cast in darkness too intense for his keen gray eyes to penetrate.

The Jyotian backed away and found a wood shaft and dipped its end in pitch. He thrust the makeshift torch into the fire pot until it ignited and sputtered with hissing sparks that popped through the air like miniature comets. Holding the torch at arm's length, he returned to the cheerless corridor.

Bars on either side of the passageway caged Urro. Davin had seen suffering in his travels across Raemllyn, and more since Zarek Yannis had stolen the throne. The atrocities imprisoned within the cells rivaled those devised by the usurper.

On both sides of the narrow corridor, he saw hideously starved Urro, dismembered and tortured. Male, female, and child, the torturer who labored here made no discrimination of either sex or age. Parts of Urros' bodies had been frozen and others burned to blackened stumps. One seemed to have been fed his own arm – raw. Davin barely contained the violent churning of his stomach while he opened cell after cell.

"Out," he called. "Everyone is free. Return to your homes!"

The freedom offered and the ability to take it were two separate things. Most of the Urro could not walk, their powerful legs twisted and broken. He waved three ambulant Urro to him and ordered: "Search other corridors. Do what you can to get out of the dungeons, but do not fear if you cannot. I'll fetch your companions to aid you."

Davin made his way up the stairs, all the more aware of the blood on the stony steps. Those Urro who had died on their way to the dungeons were the lucky ones.

At the top of the stairs, Davin rushed down the lit hallway to where Goran One-Eye still fought with gusto. Davin sidled toward the open palace door and called to his companion, "What? Still fighting? Why so gentle on them?"

Goran snorted and renewed his efforts to hack to pieces each of the soldiers rushing him. The piles of dead around him were testament to the Challing's success.

"Berenicis? Kulonna? Did you find them?"

"I found only the dungeons and scores of tortured Urro," Davin answered as he ran outside, assured his friend faced no imminent danger from the weakling soldiers.

Following the path that had led him to the palace, the Jyotian retraced his steps to the ice wall and the hole melted through it. Davin shook his head. Not only were the citizens of this viper-pit they called a city cruel, they were stupid. No attempt had been made to seal the breach in their city's sole defense.

"Bonn, Yeeha, attack now!" Davin called outside.

For a moment, he thought the Urro had deserted their position. Slowly, shadows took substance and moved forward. Bonn led a small group of Urro, all swinging spiked bludgeons and brandishing knives. Behind him came Yeeha and a larger party.

"Hurry, those in the dungeons are freed, but they can't escape on their own. They need you," he urged.

The Urro came hesitantly, as if Davin Anane led them to new bloody slaughter. The thief's head spun when he felt the magicks cast by the Urro rise like a wall about the hairy creatures. Not Urro but shades stepped into Draymo-Vor and drifted toward the palace.

Unwilling to wait for their slow procession, Davin turned and ran back to the palace. Goran still fought without any sign of tiring, his barrel chest not even heaving from exertion. The Challing shot him a sour look, then bellowed, "Take these worthless scum and kill them for me, will you, Davin?"

"Are they too much for you?" Davin adroitly parried and gauged his response. His thrust sank home beneath a guardsman's gorget. The Jyotian freebooter whipped around, his blade a silvered blur. He cut two more of Goran's attackers, then joined his friend.

"I grow weary of them and their ineptitude," grunted Goran. "The time has come to end this playing. I've come here for Kulonna and Berenicis' head!"

Davin saw how the Challing's good eye burned brighter, a sure sign of magicks walking the streets of Draymo-Vor. The Urro cast new spells while they advanced.

The focus of those spells became apparent. The guardsmen facing the two thieves grew increasingly slow and clumsy in their fighting. Davin wondered if the Urro had constantly barraged the city and its inhabitants with this spell over the years in an attempt to weaken human resolve and sword arm. Magicks rather than lack of food drained the strength from those who inhabited the city.

"Yo, friend Bonn, down there!" Goran kicked a dying soldier in the direction of the dungeon. "Rescue your countrymen." In a lower voice meant for Davin's ears, he added, "If that is the proper term for such malformed savages."

Davin glanced over a shoulder to see the Urro reform and move down the corridor toward the dungeons below.

"I want my Kulonna and Berenicis," Goran growled out.

"And I want the one who calls himself Draymo-Vor. It is time he paid for all he has done." Davin felt a rush of guilt for his earlier doubt – doubt that the ruler of this realm tortured the Urro.

"We'll not find them here. The guards seem endless," Goran said.

As though understanding the pair's predicament, ten Urro stepped forward and faced three new soldiers who came running down the hallway. Movements impaired to sluggish imitation of thrusts and parries by the Urro magic, the swordsmen died beneath an onslaught of spiked clubs.

Davin nodded to the Challing. "They free us for our search."

"That way," Goran said with a tilt of his head toward the stairs Lijena had taken earlier.

"No." Davin hesitated. Had Draymo-Vor been on the second floor when attack began he would have answered the clash of arms. Instead, the thief guessed the ruler hid on the lower floor and directed his men against those who invaded his keep.

"You search this level while I go above!" Goran did not wait for an answer. With a swing of his battle-axe, he cut down a guard harried by four Urro, shoved aside the man's dying body and ran up the stairs.

Following his friend's lead, Davin stuck out his foot and tripped one guardsman rushing to the fray. When five Urro swarmed over the fallen man with their deadly bludgeons, Davin pushed down the hallway. Two swordsmen stood outside a door adorned with a round seal of handworked gold. Their swords rose menacingly when the thief approached.

"So this is where the coward you call a king hides." Davin's sword tip lifted. "Timidity will serve him little this morn."

Davin attempted to sidestep a lunge from the nearest guard and found his feet mired in molasses. His arm, however, was not. His sword leaped up, clanged against the soldier's blade in an easy parry. The thief replied with his own lunge that drove straight and true into the guard's throat.

Yanking his sword free, Davin forced sluggish legs to move, turned, and deftly battered away the second guard's attack. With equal ease, Davin thrust his sword into the man's chest.

The Urros' spell, he realized as he moved past the fallen men and cautiously opened the door they had guarded. The magicks the Urro wove apparently affected all humans, be they Ianyan or Jyotian. Davin told himself if all were equal, he retained his advantage over those of Draymo-Vor. That he found it increasingly difficult to make his legs take simple steps did nothing to bolster his confidence.

Beyond the door stood a spacious room with walls draped in tapestries. The scenes woven by the thread were of green forests and fields, neither of which were known by Ianya. Taken from ships wrecked on these frozen coasts, Davin realized, as he stepped toward a raised throne at the end of the chamber.

Although the thief saw no one, he felt a presence. His eyes darted from side to side. Nothing – no secret panels that opened to admit a fresh flood of guards.

"Hiding will buy you nothing this day," Davin called out. "If you live, it will be by your own mettle."

No answer came, but a slight shift in a curtain hanging beside the throne drew the thief's attention. Davin hastened forward as quickly as his spell-hampered legs would carry him.

He was greeted by a half-dozen well-dressed soldiers who pushed into the room from behind curtain and throne.

The Urros' sluggish spell, combined with his own abrupt halt, almost toppled the last son of the House of Anane facedown on the floor. These were no common foot soldiers like those the thief had faced in the hallways of the palace. Each of the six he now faced wore breastplates and helmets crafted of hardened leather. Although the capes that trailed from their shoulders were cut from fur rather than silk, there were no tattered edges or coarse stitches binding the furs.

Draymo-Vor's personal guard, I'd wager, Davin appraised the six when he noticed all drew double-edged swords of tempered steel rather than soft iron. *The king cannot be far away.*

The Jyotian took the offensive rather than wait for the swordsmen to surround him. Willing his legs to move through treacle-thick air, Davin lunged at the man nearest him.

As he suspected earlier, the Urros' magicks slowed his opponents in an equal proportion to his own lethargy. The soldier's sword lifted no more than a finger's length when Davin's blade sank into the man's exposed throat.

The thief did not wait to observe the effects of his lunge. Instead, he yanked his sword free of its gory berth and shoved the dying soldier into his two companions behind him. While the two jostled to free themselves of the unexpected dead weight, Davin turned his attention to the remaining three who attempted to circle for a rear attack.

With practiced ease, the Jyotian parried a lunge meant for his chest, then slipped his own blade inward. He saw a brief instant of relief on his opponent's face when the sword thrust into empty air between arm and torso. Horror replaced relief when Davin's blade leaped up and pulled out. The keen-edged sword sliced deep into the soldier's underarm to sever vein and artery. The guard fell away trying to staunch the gush of crimson down his side.

In a slow-motion pivot, Davin ducked beneath a sideways slash designed to separate his head from his shoulders. His own blade answered in an upward arc that opened a second mouth on the throat of the man who sought his head. That flashing flight of silver ended with a quick twist and thrust to the throat that ended the life of the third would-be rear attacker.

Davin turned to face the remaining two of the original six. Both men blanched when the Jyotian's sword lifted to them. Instead of attacking, they fled the room. Their death cries echoed from the hall outside as the Urro completed what Davin had started.

The thief's attention returned to the throne and the open doorway he discovered behind the curtain. Davin crossed the threshold and entered a small, sparsely furnished room with but a single chair and small table. Backed into a corner five strides away stood a lone man dressed in a purple cape.

"Draymo-Vor?" the thief questioned.

Davin's answer was a battle-axe hefted high and hurled directly at his head.

Rather than hindering, the Urros' spell aided Davin. He saw the axe's trajectory as a lazy turning in the air. Shifting sword from right to left hand, he reached up, caught the axe's haft and snatched the weapon from the air. Without pause, Davin sent the axe spinning back at its owner.

The Urros' magic was not as kind to the Ianyan. There was only time for the man's eyes to widen in terror before the heavy blade slammed into his forehead and lodged in the brain. Then, there was only time for dying. The man slid down the wall to the floor and jerked spasmodically as life fled his body.

With sword leveled before him, Davin cautiously approached the dead man. If dress were any indication, the corpse at his feet belonged to King Draymo-Vor.

"I see you found Draymo-Vor." Lijena confirmed the thief's suspicion.

Davin looked up to see the frosty-haired blonde step into the room with the Sword of Kwerin Bloodhawk in her hand. Behind her strode Goran One-Eye and three Urro.

"Lijena had luck, too. As you can see," Goran said with a tilt of his massive head to indicate the ensorcelled blade. "She found the witch Valora in a bedchamber on the second floor. Dispatched her quite ably, too."

"What of Berenicis and Kulonna?" Davin asked while his companions moved to his side.

"They did not sail with Valora," Goran replied. "It is as I feared when I heard the Urro mention only a woman joining forces with Draymo-Vor. But the Blackheart will not escape me. I will find the whoreson if it takes the rest of my days on this ball of mud."

"We'll both find him," Davin assured his friend.

"Like we've found A'bre and returned me to my own world of Gohwohn?"

There was no disguising the bitterness in Goran's voice, nor the twinge of guilt that twisted within the Jyotian. Time and again Davin's promise to help the Challing find the gate back to Gohwohn had been broken – not shattered – in their quest for the Bloodhawk's sword.

"I've given my word," Davin said firmly. "When Felrad is served, I'll fulfil my promise."

"What's this?"

Whether Goran heard him, Davin was not uncertain. The Challing squatted beside the dead king and reached out as though intent on throttling the corpse.

"He's dead, Goran. Let him be," Davin said. "Though he deserved to die a hundred times more, there's no way to exact that payment."

"Here it is. Look, Davin, look," Goran said in a low voice.

The Challing slipped a necklace from the Ianyan's neck. He wiped away the blood with a thumb to reveal a curious pendant dangling from the golden chain.

"A broken leaf," Davin whispered when he saw what had caught his friend's eye. "Like the one around your neck."

Goran fumbled inside his tunic and drew forth the portion of a golden leaf he had discovered on the ghost ship*. The pieces fastened together to fashion half of a completed leaf.

"What does it mean?" asked Davin.

"I cannot say," replied Goran, staring intently at the intricately wrought golden half-leaf, "but I am sure it is part of the key needed for me to return home." A tear welled in the corner of Goran's good eye as he added in a low, choked voice, "Home to Gohwohn."

The Challing straightened and tucked the partial-leaf medallion back under his tunic, patting the bulge as if to reassure himself of its safety.

"There was reason for you to come to Ianya, then," Davin said.

"Thank you, Father Yehseen," said Goran, lifting his battle-axe in salute to the Father of the Gods. "I am one step closer to returning home."

"And Prince Felrad is closer to conquering Zarek Yannis," came Lijena Farleigh's voice.

Davin watched the woman sheath the legendary blade. Surprisingly, the sword hung well from her hip. *She carries it as though born to bear it.* The thought was equally surprising to the thief as was the uneasiness that suffused his breast when his gaze caught the defiant gleam in Lijena's eyes.

"Now all we need find is a vessel to take us from this iceberg,"

* See *Beasts of the Mist*

Goran said. "I feel the need of warmer climes. Such was it after my first visit to Ianya. It was here that I lost my left eye, you know. I was shipwrecked on these frozen shores and beset by an ice worm. Not just an ice worm, but the *grandfather* of all ice worms. I was near the point of freezing to death when . . ."

Lijena and Davin groaned as they turned and walked from the small chamber, leaving the one-eyed Challing to entertain the Urro with his outrageous yarn.

14

Once Lord of Jyotis and now Duke Berenicis of the Isle of Prillae, the Blackheart stifled a yawn while his chamberlain rattled on in a monotone voice about problems abounding in the castle. Some details required opinion, but most were trivial. Berenicis wished he could ignore them. If he did, however, what control he garnered would trickle through his fingers as quickly as water.

A dead Berenicis would be as missed as the unlamented Duke Tun, he pondered on his precarious new role. Eliora remained obtuse and secretive whenever questioned about her original plot to depose Tun. Even as the new duke, Berenicis had been unable to uncover the lady general's fellow conspirators. Too many considered their new duke an interloper rather than someone in whom they could confide, no matter the reward or torture. With Eliora and the other conspirators free, he walked a path as narrow as the blade of a knife. Stumble and well-honed death awaited on either side of him.

"Very well, do as you see fit on these matters." Berenicis waved the chamberlain away. The new duke was more concerned about the staff the chamberlain installed than if the cook's assistant stole food for his starving family.

"You are most wise, Duke Berenicis." The chamberlain bowed low so his bald pate gleamed like a polished mirror in Berenicis' eyes.

When the man retreated, Berenicis reached over and pushed Kulonna upright in her chair. He glanced around for the drugged woman's maids; they were nowhere to be seen. Impatiently, Berenicis gestured to General Eliora. The woman's expression told him he would get no help from her. She busied herself with a report on some secret mission and had no desire to be bothered with Kulonna.

"Duchess Kulonna is ill again," Berenicis said in a loud voice that froze the chamberlain in his tracks. "See to her."

When no one responded, Berenicis was forced to stand and use both hands to keep his wife of three weeks erect in her seat.

"Goran?" Kulonna muttered. "Things are so blurred. Cannot see."

Berenicis silently cursed, starting with the Sitala and working through the entire pantheon of gods and goddesses. Always the red-haired giant! Whenever Kulonna edged toward lucidity, the name *Goran* sprang from her tongue. Berenicis should have killed his bastard brother's companion and his worthless thief of a brother, Davin Anane, for that matter, when he had the chance.

"See to her, Qar take your soul!" Berenicis shouted.

A half-dozen servants rushed forward. Berenicis took note of those who answered and those who held back. The latter would eventually find their hesitancy rewarded with a visit to the torturer's station in his dungeons.

My dungeons! *Duke Berenicis of the Isle of Prillae.* In spite of the shark-infested waters surrounding him, he had to keep the ultimate goal clear in his mind. Jyotis had been a start, though a small one. The Isle of Prillae was a larger stride toward that goal. While servants took Kulonna to her chambers still mumbling about Goran One-Eye, Berenicis studied the dingy audience chamber, visualizing something more.

Kavindra – the Velvet Throne!

Berenicis never had allowed himself to dream of that exalted seat. Now, however, if he maneuvered quickly and positioned himself correctly, he would be waiting when Felrad and Zarek Yannis managed to kill each other – or be there to deliver the fatal blow to the survivor of the conflict that scarred its way across Raemllyn. After all, the blood of Bedrich the Fair flowed in his veins and he intended to support his claim to the Velvet Throne with might.

"Duke Berenicis." A gravelly voice shattered the reflections of the splendid future the Blackheart attempted to mold.

Berenicis swung around, glancing over his shoulder. Captain Pendross approached the dais with his rolling sailor's gait. "The messenger's here for you."

"Messenger?" Eliora strode forward, hand on a dagger's hilt. Today she wore a uniform, a severely cut gray outfit lacking in ornamentation save for the dual purple gem-studded pips bouncing on her left breast denoting her rank as Commander of the

Realm. "You have me send a courier out *and* this barnacle-brained old salt as well? Why do you not trust me?"

"In my chambers," Berenicis ordered.

The Blackheart silently damned Pendross for not holding his tongue until they were alone. There were no benefits to be gained by arousing Eliora's suspicion and ire. Until he discovered the foundation of her power and removed it, she was too big an unknown to be handled safely. As a commoner, Eliora could never assume the throne herself. But before his arrival, she had plotted to replace Tun, Duke of Litoyna and Melisa while she remained the iron-gloved force behind the throne.

With whom? That was the question that gnawed at Berenicis the Blackheart. Who would she have placed in Tun's stead had he not appeared with Kulonna? Until he held the answer, Eliora was not to be trusted.

In a smaller room off the audience chamber, Berenicis dropped into a chair and faced the two who followed him. He trusted neither of them, but felt more kinship with Pendross. The old sailor's ambitions were limited, and Pendross viewed Berenicis as a leader, not an impediment to power. Eliora's ambitions ran wild; she longed to cast off the foreign demon who sat on the throne – and to execute Kulonna.

The latter Berenicis considered as a bargaining counter. It would be a pity if his wife happened to die, but such would be the case if Kulonna's death could buy a few more weeks of Eliora's compliance.

"You sent out two couriers? To whom? Zarek Yannis?" Eliora tossed back her hair and leaned forward with fists resting on the table in front of Berenicis.

"Your messenger did not reach the usurper." Berenicis delighted in the shock that froze the woman's face for an instant. Eliora thought she hamstrung him. The knowledge that he had developed his own intelligence network would give her pause in the future.

For an instant, Berenicis considered killing Eliora here and now and being done with her intrigues. He discarded the idea as foolhardy. His foothold was slippery at best and he was not ready to face his enemies in the open. Instead he'd keep Kulonna alive for the moment. Tun's daughter provided a thorn in Eliora's side and distracted her from an all-out assault on his power.

Captain Pendross' expression was unreadable as his gaze shifted between Eliora and Berenicis. He coughed and hawked a thick black gob of *mylo* weed onto the floor near the general's feet. Eliora went for her dagger.

"Yes, Captain," Berenicis said in a voice that demanded both their attentions, "you should report. Your duties elsewhere are pressing."

"Right, Duke," Pendross said with a nod. "We been sailin' up and down the coast and regulatin' trade, as you ordered. My crew's unloadin' more 'n five hundredweights of gold into your vaults as we speak."

Berenicis kept a pleased smile from his lips. Piracy, when backed by the Duchy of Prillae's navy, exceeded his expectations. But simply extorting cargo ships along Raemllyn's western coast was not enough, would never be enough. Wealth bought power, and that was what he sought.

"What news of our naval operations?" Berenicis asked, pointedly ignoring how Eliora fumed. "Are the new warships harmonizing with existing units?"

"We impressed six ships into service." Pendross spat again. This time he directed the gob away from Eliora's feet.

Eliora's hand tightened on her dagger, obviously prepared to teach the old sailor a lesson in courtly manners with the point of her blade.

Berenicis moved to deflect her anger. "Marines, General Eliora, we need six new companies of marines. Can you recruit them?"

"Yes," she hissed.

"Accommodate them, Pendross." Berenicis stalled with trivial matters, trying to reach a conclusion about the captain's report from Yannis. Eliora would discover the contents of the communiqué eventually, but did he want her to hear it directly? He reached a quick decision. Eliora was still valuable to him and angering her further would serve no purpose. "Now, Captain Pendross, tell how the High King of Raemllyn responded to our overtures."

"What overtures?" asked Eliora. "I was told only that we desired to remain neutral."

"Neutrality is a fool's game in this war. It will bring down the armies of both Felrad and Yannis on the one who plays it." Berenicis stared at Eliora, enjoying the discomfort she displayed. "I ordered a ship to be sent to Kressia. From there, a courier took my greetings and good wishes to Zarek Yannis and offered naval support against the realm's enemies."

"This is why you seek more marines," she accused rather than questioned.

"In part. Much depends on Yannis' answer." Berenicis turned to his captain, eyebrows rising in query. From the way Pendross grinned like a fool, he knew the answer already. Power begot power, and Berenicis the Blackheart, Lord of Jyotis and Duke of Prillae, bargained from a position of authority.

"The usurper needs you, Duke," Pendross said. "He desires a meeting to discuss future alliances."

"Current ones are more to my liking," Berenicis replied. Let Felrad and Yannis cripple their armies. He would raise a force to defeat whoever was left standing.

"A few more weeks of battlin' Felrad will leave the usurper bled white, it will," Pendross added as though reading the Blackheart's thoughts. "With a good force and enough naval power to back it up, you could seize Kavindra and the throne."

"Ridiculous!" Eliora snorted. "More than a few companies of marines will be required."

"Yannis offers Duke Berenicis all the land from Kressia to Faldin as his personal fiefdom," cut in Pendross. "What ruler gives away such vast tracts of land if he truly rules?" Pendross reached into his pocket and drew forth a new packet of *mylo* weed and bit off a large piece. He chewed contentedly as the narcotic plant exerted its subtle, unknown influence on the seaman.

"A ruler with a plan. He seeks to bleed you, Berenicis," Eliora said. "You defend 'your' fiefdom against Felrad and his navy, then when you have defeated the prince and weakened yourself, Yannis attacks and recoups what he has so generously bestowed."

"An interesting insight into Yannis' thoughts," Berenicis said sarcastically. "It will never work that way. I will not permit it. *We* will not permit it, will we?"

His gray eyes bored into Eliora's brown ones. Neither duke nor general flinched. Pendross broke the silent power struggle.

"We're layin' keel on a half-dozen new warships, Duke. I got my good eye on a frigate 'bout ready to launch. Can I name it *Far Traveler*? The old scow's ready to sink from all its fightin'. A new *Far Traveler* shows resolve."

"A splendid idea, Pendross," agreed Berenicis. "If Yannis wants to meet face to face, we shall require a new ship to fetch him here."

"Sorry, Duke, he spoke on that and wasn't too keen about leavin' the mainland. Not got his sea legs," Pendross opined.

"He's the High King, not you," said Eliora. "No matter how grandiose your fantasies of power, he still rules Raemllyn."

"A neutral point might be necessary for our meeting," said Berenicis, considering the matter from different vantages. He had entertained a notion he might assassinate Yannis, but until Felrad was crushed totally such a move would accomplish little.

Five hundredweights of gold provided a start to empire. A small step but one which would draw Zarek Yannis' attention. First, he needed to consolidate power within his own ranks.

"Captain Pendross, see to commissioning the new *Far Traveler*."

The sailor grinned crookedly, his ambitions fulfilled. "Seein' to it right now, Duke."

Pendross turned and walked away, his rolling gait carrying him from the room with surprising speed.

"Now, General, we've other matters to discuss."

Berenicis stood and moved around the table. He reached out and placed his hand on Eliora's shoulder. The muscles beneath his fingertips tensed, but before the woman could slip away, Berenicis pulled the tall brunette closer, his eyes trying to plumb the depths of her soul – and her treachery. Berenicis the Blackheart drew her even closer and covered her mouth with his own. Slowly, oh, how slowly, Eliora melted to his advances. Berenicis had no illusions why the woman allowed him to make love to her.

"Kressia lies yonder, Duke." Captain Pendross lowered his spyglass. "We'll reach its harbor within the hour."

"Any sight of Felrad's corvettes?" asked General Eliora. "We cannot outrace them in this wallowing barge." She clutched the rail of the newly christened *Far Traveler* and stared longingly toward the beaches.

Berenicis read her desire to land with marines and seize the harbor, the city, the entire peninsula connecting Upper and Lower Raemllyn. This stretch of land had been the site of countless battles over the generations.

An invasion here would not be the beginning of High King Berenicis' rule, at least, not this day, the Blackheart thought. Prince Felrad's navy had badgered them all along the coast as they made their way southward to meet with Yannis. Intelligence reports placed the prince's armies spread out across all of Upper Raemllyn and sweeping downward to drive Yannis' forces back to Kavindra.

"A naval assault across the Isthmus of Brykheedah cuts off Yannis' retreat and keeps him in Kavindra," said Eliora. "He must deal with us or Felrad will have him trapped between land and sea."

"More marines on the way, Duke?" Pendross hiked an eyebrow in question. "You'll need a full legion of 'em to hold back a real sea-launched attack if Felrad tries it."

"Will Yannis demand transport on duchy ships should Kavindra fall?" Eliora posed possibilities. "That might prove dangerous for us. Felrad victorious, Zarek Yannis retreating. Such an outcome will turn the new High King against us."

"Yannis has nowhere to retreat." Berenicis had spent the week-long trip down Raemllyn's western shore considering how to approach Yannis. With Felrad's army driving the usurper ever southward, Yannis had to make his stand in Kavindra or admit total defeat. Yannis needed the navy of Prillae to protect Kavindra from naval assault – and to furnish an avenue of escape should Felrad seize the Velvet Throne.

He needed what Berenicis the Blackheart offered, and he could not quibble over the price.

Half a continent to rule is better than none for Yannis. Berenicis considered the outcome of an alliance with the usurper. To lose half of Upper Raemllyn would insure the eventual collapse of Yannis' power – and Berenicis' inevitable rise.

"How do we guarantee that they hammer each other into the grave, Duke?" Pendross spat overboard.

One of the few benefits of being aboard the *Far Traveler*, the Blackheart thought. He abhorred stepping over the sizzling patches of narcotic weed the captain constantly spat, but said nothing to his most trusted ally for fear of alienating him.

"Ship approaching!" came the cry from the crow's nest.

Berenicis craned his neck around and saw the sailor pointing landward. He took the spyglass from Pendross' hands and peered through it. The rise and fall of the *Far Traveler* prevented him from getting a good view, but the flash of Zarek Yannis' colors fluttering at the distant ship's stern told him all he needed to know.

He had won; Berenicis' pulse pounded with excitement. Yannis sailed out to meet him personally!

"Prepare for boarders," Pendross cried an order to his crew.

"They come to parley," Eliora warned as she squinted into the sun to get a better view of the approaching vessel. "They show the flag of truce."

Pendross grunted and shouted at three sailors who were slow to obey his command. No one, not even Lady Commander of the Realm, countered Captain Pendross aboard his own ship.

"They're a treasonous lot, General," Pendross explained. "A little prevention now keeps from swallowin' a whale of a load of bad medicine later."

Pendross strode off across the heaving deck to double-check the *Far Traveler* and her crew. Berenicis leaned against the rail near Eliora. He reached over and placed his hand on her callused one. She started to pull away and hesitated.

"Kulonna?" asked Eliora.

Berenicis smiled; Kulonna was no longer a concern. "She's below in a drugged stupor. She sees nothing of this." He nodded to the mainland. "The poor fool does not comprehend how close her husband is to being crowned High King!"

"*He* stands in your way." Eliora's gaze fixed on the approaching ship bearing Zarek Yannis' colors. "He is no fool and will not be deceived easily."

"All men can be deceived," Berenicis said, "by any woman as lovely as you."

She pulled away. Berenicis grunted. How transparent her behavior! Did she think he was unaware of her plot to overthrow him? How provincial they were on the Isle of Prillae. Duke Tun had been too forgiving a ruler and had allowed his nobles and officers to become soft while he frittered away his time in the ducal gardens. They lacked the hard edge of intrigue and treachery Berenicis Blackheart so admired in those inhabiting the court of Kavindra.

"What do you want of me? To sleep with him, then drive a dagger into his foul heart?" Eliora stared at him with disdain.

"He would never sleep with you," Berenicis said, distracted. "His tastes are – different."

"Ahoy, *Far Traveler*!" came the cry from the bow. "Prepare for His Majesty, High King Zarek!"

"We should put a shot across his bow," grumbled Pendross, returning to Berenicis' side. "Or," he amended, "burn it to the waterline."

Berenicis had pondered such a move and discarded it. Better to let Yannis face Felrad's force than fight that battle himself. Let them bleed one another dry, *then* launch his attack. The marines aboard this and the other ships in his growing navy would quickly take Kavindra with little resistance from Felrad's battle-weary men.

"Let them board," Berenicis told the captain. "We mean to parley and form alliance, not to make war."

Eliora spoke, but the Blackheart only caught her tone and not her words. He chuckled softly at her reaction to Yannis' arrival. Eliora would never do as consort at Kavindra's court. Perhaps Kulonna might remain as his queen, for a while. She afforded a buffer against many different assaults, not all of which would be might of arms. None dared deny she was of royal blood. Her father was a distant cousin of Bedrich the Fair, strengthening any legitimate claim Berenicis might have to the throne.

"Welcome, King Zarek," greeted Berenicis, making a deep bow as the haggard ruler of Raemllyn scrambled between the ships along a heaving plank and lines.

Berenicis stiffened when he saw the king's attendant. Every footstep on the gyrating plank was firm and solid and left a smoldering footprint. The robe barely stirred in the brisk breeze whipping off the Sea of Bua, but the glowing eyes beneath the hood were unmistakable. Berenicis wondered how this Faceless demon had eluded Felrad's magical sword.

"Get the demon off my ship," cried Pendross, undaunted by

the sight of royalty aboard the *Far Traveler*. "It's bad luck, a curse, an affront to Nalren!"

"The God of the Sea cares little if my servant sails over his dominion," Zarek Yannis answered coldly. "Might your god appreciate your heart being given to him in sacrifice?"

"Please, King Zarek, no affront was intended. My captain is overly protective of a powerful new ship," Berenicis said smoothly while he swept an arm about the ship. "I might add that such a ship, laden with well-trained marines, as it is, might find exemplary duty under your leadership."

Watery blue eyes skipped past Berenicis to the ship's deck, examining every detail. Yannis nodded slowly. "A trim vessel, even if its master should have his tongue cut out and fed to seagulls."

From the corner of his eye Berenicis saw Eliora restrain Pendross. He appreciated her sudden diplomatic tendencies. He wondered what words she whispered in the old salt's ear to calm him so quickly.

"Would Your Majesty care for some fine Litoynan wine? The grapes are made all the headier by rains swept over the sea and . . ."

Yannis spun about to face him; the usurper's composure was that of a wild wolf. Berenicis barely caught himself before he leaped back in surprise, in fear. The light of intelligence that had burned in Yannis' eyes faded, replaced by stark madness. Berenicis drew a slow breath to steady himself.

"I come to seal our agreement, not drink filthy wine with you," snarled Yannis. His broken, yellowed teeth clacked together and froth speckled his cracked lips. "I give you the richest portion of Raemllyn in return for your support. That swine comes after me and I cannot stop him without aid."

"Felrad?" asked Berenicis, trying to remain calm in the face of madness. "How strong is his army? After your defeat at Rakell, I thought he lacked sufficient strength to . . ."

"I was not defeated at Rakell," shrieked Yannis. "I only retreated to lure him into a trap. The trap closes on his neck even as we speak!"

Berenicis held his tongue. Yannis would never deal with an upstart duke if victory over Felrad was assured. Eliora's warning that Yannis only toyed with him until Felrad was defeated haunted the Blackheart. His strategy was simple – keep his own forces away from the fighting until either Yannis or Felrad proved the victor, then attack whomever claimed the Velvet Throne.

"King Zarek, I seek only to serve. How may my forces support your noble cause?"

Berenicis stepped away when the Faceless One lifted a skeletal hand and pointed. Yannis jerked around and stared across the waves.

"Qar take him! Felrad's navy sails on us, thinking to trap me at sea. I must return to Kavindra immediately."

Zarek Yannis whirled about and hastened back to his ship. The demon remained a moment, eyes like burning coals, then it, too, retraced the bucking path to the ship.

Within minutes, Yannis sailed a course that would bring landfall north of the Isthmus of Brykheedah.

"What do we do, Berenicis?" Pendross spat into the sea. "Support the crazy barstid or keep our distance? He runs from shadows on the water. There's nothin' to be seen."

Berenicis surveyed the ocean, trying to recall where the Faceless One had pointed. A tiny speck grew on the horizon. Seconds later, the watch in the crow's nest called, "Heavy frigate to the north bearing down on us!"

"What do we do, Pendross? Why, we prepare for battle!"

15

"How are they likely to attack?" Duke Berenicis asked his captain.

Pendross spat out a gob of *mylo* and rubbed his stubbled chin. His milky eye turned in the direction of Felrad's approaching frigate. For a moment, Berenicis stiffened. He saw more than translucent film in Pendross' cataract-fogged eye.

He saw a disturbing image flashing across the whiteness, the silhouette of a man he remembered from the ship that had brought Davin Anane to Felrad's aid. Berenicis struggled to put a name to that face. The *Twisted Cross* was the ship's name, and the man was the first mate.

"Bertam," muttered the Duke of Prillae.

"What? What's that?" Captain Pendross spun about, his jaw tense and his hands clenched into fists.

"I . . . nothing," Berenicis said. The image vanished from the captain's eye. He might have imagined it in the heat of the moment. "How do we prepare to defeat those fools?"

"I'm a'runnin' colors to tell 'em who they face," Pendross said.

The captain tossed a string of brightly colored pennants to his mate. The first officer hesitated, then rushed off to raise the flags when Pendross glared at him. "We wait for 'em to come near, then we ram. The *Far Traveler*'s got a steel prow just under the figurehead. No frigate run by a cross-eyed landlubber can withstand that."

"Landlubber? You know Felrad's captain?" asked Berenicis.

"All those not born on Prillae are landlubbers," Eliora said sourly. "Pendross is a capable captain. Let him do his job."

"Strike those colors, Qar take you!" Pendross ran to the upper deck and grabbed the lines from the first mate. "Not in that order. Make a mistake like that again and I'll feed you to Nalren, one piece at a time!"

"But, Captain, you wanted . . ."

Pendross struck the officer across the face, knocking him to the rail. The captain's booted foot drove into the man's side and sent him rolling toward the edge of the deck.

"We need every hand for battle, Captain," Berenicis called in a cold voice that halted Pendross before he kicked the man overboard. "We have an agreement with Yannis to land marines on the Isthmus of Brykheedah to support his troops."

"Might be all that saves the barstid," grumbled Pendross. He glared at his mate, then spun about and hastened to the wheel to prepare for battle.

"They're breaking off, heading for shore," came a cry from the crow's nest. "They're flying off to keep us from putting them on the bottom!"

"So it seems." Eliora lowered the eyeglass Pendross had abandoned and nodded at the Blackheart. "They have no taste for battling the *Far Traveler*."

"Then we wait for the remainder of the fleet," Berenicis announced, ignoring a rootless uncertainty that shivered through him. "There is nothing to be gained by chasing after yon vessel. We wait for the remainder of our fleet and the marines to arrive, then we sail to support Yannis."

"The battle is raging even as we speak." Eliora turned to the mainland. "I read it in Yannis' panic. If we wait too long, we might find ourselves bowing to Prince Felrad."

"We wait," Berenicis repeated firmly to hide the apprehension that gnawed at him anew. "Not long, but we wait."

Berenicis leaned against the rail, his eyes fixed on the shore. Yannis fought for his life. In hours he would be back in Kavindra facing Felrad's army. Delay the promised support, and Felrad and Yannis would bleed one another, making the pickings that much easier for a duke with a strong fleet and a force of fresh, well-trained marines.

Victory. Soon, Duke Berenicis told himself. Victory soon.

"No question about the pennants," said the captain of the frigate *Nalren's Beard*. He turned to the mage huddled on the deck. "That match your information?"

Tacllyn-lin-Bertam shook like a wet dog when he pushed to his feet. Too many leagues had passed under his boots these past weeks and left him physically exhausted. Worse was his mental state, the wizard realized. He had never regained his confidence after the failure of the quincunx to seal the rent between dimensions. Wok-Lamol and Wok-Manol recovered their power the fastest of the five mages; Fiany and Cor'Mid barely kept to their feet. The latter two should have been placed in a physician's care, but there was no time.

Bertam motioned to the captain who came to his side and helped him stagger to the highly polished *chiin* wood rail. Bertam appreciated the decorative nature of *chiin*, but more important was its strength. The wood would withstand the ravages of war far better than boards cut from lesser trees. Felrad had constructed a durable vessel for his western seas flagship.

"We've sailed beyond the range of my power," Bertam said, rubbing his eyes. "But I concur. We must reach Felrad quickly with the information given us."

The colorful pennants fluttering above the *Far Traveler* had conveyed a few tidbits of important data, but Bertam had gained much more through his magicks. It surprised him that Berenicis had not brought along at least one mage to cast ward spells to guard against magical scrying.

"We can reach Amayita by sundown," said the captain. "Will that give you enough time to travel overland to meet Felrad's forces before the battle is joined?"

Bertam nodded absently. It was good to be at sea again. He had forgotten the freedom granted by the brisk wind, the delight of the sharp tang of sea air in his nostrils. No direction held any encumbrance, and he felt like simply pointing at random and sailing that heading. But such luxury was denied him. Duty bound him to Felrad with invisible chains.

To sail away, the mage realized, reflected only the desire to flee from his failure to seal the rent in space. Even if Felrad defeated Yannis in the forthcoming battle, a danger far greater than the usurper and his Faceless Ones would remain. With each passing second, the rent grew. In less time than Bertam wanted to think about, the rent would rip Raemllyn apart at its seams.

* * *

"At last." Berenicis made no attempt to hide the relief in his voice.

Four days at sea had crept by like four years. Now the remainder of his fleet from the Isle of Prillae sailed into sight.

Berenicis stared toward the Isthmus of Brykheedah as Eliora stepped to the deck from below. During the wait for the fleet, she had not once countered him or questioned a command. Her display of loyalty tripled Berenicis' suspicion of her motives. When the chance to eliminate her duke presented itself, she would seize it with both hands.

Knowing how she would act did not reveal the moment of that treachery. Berenicis felt like a man walking over thin ice. The ice would break beneath his feet, but when? At that first crack, he had to be prepared to kill Eliora swiftly and in the next instant resolutely sweep up the fallen mantle of her authority. If only he had unearthed her conspirators!

She had mentioned the old surgeon, Summeant, in slighting terms. Berenicis had arranged for Duke Tun's chirurgeon to be put to death an hour after the *Far Traveler* sailed, believing her anger toward the physician to be but a ruse to hide a pact between Summeant and Eliora.

Berenicis had also ordered the executions of many holding high rank under Eliora. Word of these assassinations would reach her ears when the marines landed, and he needed to be on guard doubly then. His hand drifted to the dagger at his waist when he remembered how the ambidextrous lady commander routinely carried three more.

"No warships in sight, Duke," came Pendross' voice. The captain grinned from ear to ear, pleased with the fleet's arrival and the total lack of opposition to the invasion. "Should we land the marines and post our fleet a few leagues away to protect against surprise?"

"No need." Berenicis shook his head. He had weighed odds and risks for four days. Victory would not belong to the timid. "Felrad's main navy sails the Gulf of Qatera, not the Sea of Bua. The frigate we sighted days past was the only hint of Felrad we've seen and it was not the flagship of a fleet."

"How can you be so certain? If you don't mind my askin'?" Pendross turned his milky eye toward the landing site Eliora had chosen.

Berenicis studied that clouded orb but saw no hint of the *Twisted Cross*'s first mate. The vision he had seen when Prince Felrad's frigate approached still gnawed at him. He had no explanation for that brief glimpse of Tacllyn-lin-Bertam reflected in the captain's eye.

"Better to attack us while we were alone than to wait for our fleet to arrive. No, that was nothing more than a spy ship. We will sail the western coast unopposed for some time, Pendross. Mark this, my friend. We will sail a navy unrivaled in Raemllyn's history – and you will be its admiral."

"Don't seek any such thing, Duke. All I want is to have enough strength left to spit in Qar's eye when he comes gropin' for me." Pendross turned and yelled at the topsailmen struggling to furl the sails.

"Eliora," Berenicis called to his general.

"My Duke?" He saw a flash of irritation cross her face when she turned to him. She held her true feelings in rein carefully. "I must coordinate the landing to insure we do not walk into a trap. Felrad's forces . . ."

". . . are occupied with breaching Kavindra's gates," Berenicis finished for her. "We need do nothing more than protect Yannis' rear – and establish a chain of posts across the Isthmus of Brykheedah. That is our path to the Oceans of Kumar and complete encirclement of Upper Raemllyn!"

"You aim high," Eliora said, her eyes narrowing. "Let's fight this battle before going on to the next."

Berenicis laughed aloud. The thrill of the coming battle coursed through his veins. Even the finest wines of northern Prillae did not give such a heady feeling.

"Launch the boats. Land the marines and let the greatest fight since the Time of the Called begin," Berenicis ordered haughtily. "I will drink victory with my dinner!"

Eliora glared at him but issued the order to launch her detachment of marines for the distant shore.

By nightfall, messengers brought reports that the Isthmus of Brykheedah was taken with a minimum of resistance encountered. By dawn of the next day, the entire contingent of Prillae troops had landed. Berenicis gave the order to move toward Kavindra and the battle there raging so fiercely.

* * *

"He goes too far!" Felrad pushed to his elbows from where he lay on the narrow bed. His body shook from the effort. "Yet it is to be expected. I hoped Yannis had rid us of Berenicis at Rakell. The Sitala play games with all mortals, both Berenicis and me. But the Blackheart goes too far murdering Duke Tun and then marrying his daughter!"

"He keeps Kulonna drugged. I saw this, Majesty." Bertam sat in a chair beside the bed.

Felrad's health was unimproved, but he appeared none the worse than when the mage had left his side. That the prince still lived and found strength to fight was a balm to Bertam's frayed nerves. Like his liege, he would have to find a way to continue.

"Berenicis the Blackheart is hereby declared a traitor to Raemllyn, stripped of his rank as Lord of Jyotis and for ever banned from the Isle of Prillae for his murder of the rightful ruler, Duke Tun." Felrad gestured at a scribe detailing the edict. "Put something in there about Kulonna also. From all Bertam has reported, she is an unwilling participant and deserves full consideration. Duchess Kulonna of Prillae is granted a freehold."

"Majesty, is there any reason to go that far?" asked Bertam.

"It sends the proper message to her people. If she dies before accepting it, the freehold reverts to the crown. If she lives, Kulonna will be bound to us for our generosity." Felrad dropped back to his bed while the scribe rushed off to put the official document into proper form. Felrad lay as still as death, but Bertam saw his chest moving in shallow breathing.

"Majesty, how long do we permit Berenicis to remain in power?"

"No longer. Send the message to those willing to mutiny in the fleet. There are enough officers who will betray their new duke?"

"More than enough," Bertam agreed. "Further, General Eliora will support us, though she had no love for Kulonna."

"Duchess Kulonna," corrected Felrad. "Is this Eliora an able commander?"

"She is more adept at field command than palace intrigue," Bertam said after a long pause while he considered the tall brunette soldier's abilities and failings.

"Offer her command of our western forces," Felrad decided. "We have few enough competent generals and far too many willing to engage in politics."

"Are you ordering the mutiny in Berenicis' fleet *and* marine forces?" asked Bertam. He had to be sure of Felrad's intentions. Such a dual thrust would deny Zarek Yannis a retreat route into Lower Raemllyn across the Isthmus of Brykheedah.

"Do it. And see to turning your magicks against Kavindra. Our military forces are having a poor time of it. The city is so strong, so very strong." Felrad's voice slipped away as the man who would be king drifted into a shallow, troubled sleep.

Tacllyn-lin-Bertam uttered a small sleep spell to aid his liege, hoping healing would come with the brief respite from consciousness, then left to issue the commands. For all the distance they had come, there was still such a long way to go.

"Pendross, Pendross!" Eliora shook the *Far Traveler*'s captain hard enough to rattle his teeth. The old sailor stood and stared vacantly, as if unaware of her presence, but Eliora pressed anxiously for his answer. "What is it? Has the time come for action?"

"Yes," the captain said softly, answering a distant ally. "See to Kulonna now. We – I – do not know how to counter the drug, but see if you can bring her out of her stupor."

Pendross sagged and the image dancing in his fogged eye vanished. He felt limp, exhausted, too gloomy to lift his head. "Damn you, Bertam, damn you! Why do you send me your problems when I have plenty of my own?"

Pendross stood taller and looked around for Berenicis. The Blackheart walked on the starboard side, watching a patrol of marines on the beach. Pendross' fingers dropped to his cutlass, but he hesitated to draw the blade. Bertam's spellbound message had been explicit. First, they must see to Kulonna. Then, they dealt with the Jyotian interloper. Pendross went to the hatch and dropped to the bottom of the cargo bay where the marines had huddled for long weeks.

"I have her," came Eliora's soft voice.

With unerring knowledge of his new ship, Pendross made his

way to a small hatch leading into the officers' quarters. The pale yellow rectangle of light spilling forth guided him to where Kulonna lay on a small bunk. Eliora sat beside her, a bottle of pungent spirits under her nose. Kulonna shook her head, blonde hair flying as she tried to avoid the harsh odors released.

"Kulonna, arise. We – you – I must take charge quickly. Many of the crew favor Berenicis," Eliora said without an attempt to stem her distaste for the woman she aided.

Pendross laid his hand on the general's shoulder to reassure her. "You have reason to hate her, dear niece, but she is our rightful duchess. Felrad has made it official."

"She does not deserve the title," spat Eliora.

"There is more. You have drawn Felrad's attention. He will elevate you to western commander of all his forces."

"What of you, Uncle?" Eliora asked. "Do you get some worthless title? Admiral of the Seas?"

Pendross laughed harshly. "Berenicis has already offered that to me. I seek nothin' save for my younger sister's child to prosper."

Bending over Kulonna, Pendross used his thumbs to lift the newly named duchess's eyelids. Bright sapphire eyes came into focus.

"Hurry, my Duchess, hasten to the deck above. We will do what is necessary after that. You need only show yourself to the crew." Eliora spoke the words as though each seared her tongue.

"Eliora, what? I remember so little. My father!" Kulonna sat upright and struck the overhead. She recoiled, but the sudden pain apparently drove away a greater portion of the drugs' effects. "Who are you?"

Kulonna stared at Pendross. Her eyes widened as she took in the sailor. She edged away from the unkempt man.

"He is my uncle, Duchess Kulonna," said Eliora. "We have orders from Prince Felrad to depose Berenicis."

"You support Felrad? Berenicis?" A distant expression washed over Kulonna's face as though she half remembered all that had occurred since leaving Rakell. Tears welled in her eyes, but she brushed them away when she swung off the bed and stood. She

took several unsteady steps, then a slow smile crossed her lips.
"We are at sea. It is good to feel a heaving deck beneath my feet
again. Tell me more."

"There is no time," Pendross urged. "Berenicis becomes
suspicious of Eliora. If he ever doubts my loyalty, all might be
lost. He has done much to solidify his ascendancy over your
father's best officers."

"You are Eliora's uncle?" Kulonna shook her head then
nodded in acquiescence. "Very well, I will do what is necessary.
I'll need a weapon – a dagger will do."

She locked eyes with Eliora, then held out her hand.

Eliora reluctantly passed over a dagger, finished with the inner
battle she fought, and gave the duchess a second knife, this one
with a wickedly serrated edge.

"For Prillae," Kulonna said. "For my father!"

As fast as her unsteady legs would carry her, Kulonna moved to
the door and went up the narrow gangway. With Pendross and
Eliora crowding behind her, she burst onto the deck.

"Back." Pendross used his cutlass to wave off the crewmen who
moved forward to greet their duchess. His head jerked from side
to side, unable to locate Berenicis.

"Where is he?" demanded Eliora, not caring if she warned the
usurping Jyotian. She still carried two daggers and her sword.
Dressed in armor and ready for battle, she had no fear of any
man.

"There, there he is!" cried Kulonna.

The duchess attempted to sprint across the deck to where a
startled Blackheart stood with back against the rail. Pendross and
Eliora were far quicker than Kulonna's shaky legs. Eliora's arm
snapped back then jerked forward. A sliver of silver cartwheeled
through the air to embed itself in Berenicis' thigh.

"Damn!" the Blackheart cursed through pain-gritted teeth.
"Qar take you, bitch!"

Wrenching the slim dagger from his leg, Berenicis half-
heartedly tossed it at Eliora with his left hand while he struggled
to draw his sword with his right.

"Pendross!" he called out. "Get her, Pendross. Stop her!"

Berenicis recognized his error as he ducked beneath a cutlass
swung hard enough to sever head from shoulders. Instead of

flesh, the blade bit through ropes on a davit, dumping a longboat intended to carry Berenicis to the shore. The boat fell prow first into the ocean to dangle there by a single line attached to its stern.

Before the Blackheart could slide farther along the rail away from Pendross, Eliora was there, her sword tip nicking his left cheek. "Lay down your weapons and surrender. Kulonna now leads us."

"Kulonna? Would you place a woman you hate on the throne? I can give you the land, the sea, the moons above!" Berenicis' arm shot up barely to parry Eliora's expert thrust.

"She is Prillae-born and bred – rightful heir to the throne." Pendross brought his heavy cutlass down on the flat of Berenicis' sword.

The slimmer double-edged blade shattered. Neither Pendross' nor Eliora's steel struck next. Instead, another dirk, this one from Kulonna's hand, sailed across the deck and sank hilt-deep in the Blackheart's right shoulder. Berenicis staggered back into the railing. Balance lost, he fell, tumbling from the ship. Wood cracked and splintered when he crashed into the swinging long-boat, breaking the last rope holding it to the *Far Traveler*. The boat turned over and floated away, capsized.

Kulonna, Eliora and Pendross huddled against the railing and peered at the waves below. Minutes passed and still Berenicis did not break the surface of the water.

"He's dead," Kulonna finally pronounced.

"Let Nalren gnaw his bones, and may his soul be tortured for ever in Peyneeha by Qar's most creative demons." Pendross spat into the water, then faced his duchess. "Time has come to make your presence known. Prince Felrad has need of your fighting men this day."

Kulonna swallowed hard, drew a deep breath, then nodded before turning to the ship's crew behind her. "I am Kulonna, daughter of Tun and Duchess of Prillae. Berenicis is dead, and I claim all rights and powers bestowed upon him. Are there any among you who disputes my claim to my father's throne?"

The crew's glances shifted between Eliora, Pendross and Kulonna. When both their lady commander and captain knelt and pledged fealty, a sigh passed through the men. Five of the sailors stepped forward to join captain and general. Seconds later the entire crew of the *Far Traveler* dropped to a knee to pledge their loyalty to the restored Duchy of Prillae and its duchess.

"Another spell. By Ychsccn's rusty rod, send a different spell against their gate!" raged Felrad's field commander.

Bertam tried to remember the man's name and failed. What seemed more important was keeping young Cor'Mid and the twin mages from frying the impudent rascal with their spells. Fiany's weakness kept her bedridden within her tent, robbing her fellow mages of their cohesion. The result was the remaining four had toiled without rest to break the magical barriers guarding Kavindra.

They had fought and they had failed for almost a week.

"Make a frontal attack that carries your forces into the city," Bertam said, keeping the anger from his voice. "You have failed repeatedly to breach the gates."

"The Faceless Ones! The demons fight like a thousand soldiers," protested the officer. He turned to his prince who sat in light armor listening to the raging argument. "Majesty, use the Sword of Kwerin and lead us into Kavindra."

Before Felrad could speak, Bertam interrupted with, "We await reinforcements, General. It is not your decision when to use the magic blade – or our magicks. Zarek Yannis has only a single mage in his service, but potent ward spells placed long ago on Kavindra's battlements thwart us."

Bertam did not add that the loss of Fiany's much needed assistance hampered their spells, and he definitely did not want to reveal that the Sword of Kwerin Bloodhawk had been stolen. Should Felrad lead an attack with his false blade, the results would be disastrous. One meeting with a Faceless One would rob Raemllyn of its rightful ruler.

"We make some progress," Felrad said in a strong voice that belied his true condition. "Duchess Kulonna has pledged her support. We now control the western seas and have blocked any retreat Yannis might attempt across the Isthmus of Brykheedah."

"He is trapped inside Kavindra's walls, true," said Bertam, "but we cannot reach him. How long can he laugh at our siege?"

"We argue for the same end, wizard," snarled the general. "Free your most awful spells. Turn them against Kavindra's walls and let me lead my troops with Prince Felrad and the Sword of Kwerin Bloodhawk at the forefront!"

"The time is not yet right," Felrad said. "It comes."

"Soon?" asked the general, hand gripping his sword hilt.

Bertam saw Felrad straighten. The prince nodded slightly, then said in a forceful voice, "We attack – soon!"

16

"It's bewitched," Goran One-Eye said uneasily.

The red-maned giant stared at Lijena Farleigh with his single good eye in a silent plea for her to dissuade Davin from his insane notion of taking Valora's beached ship. Eyebrows arched high above Lijena's aquamarine eyes and she shrugged. It did not require a mage to know the fishing boat had been propelled northward by evil magicks. Cold flame still crackled and sparked on the masts and the canvas sails hung rumpled, never fully unfurled for true running.

"We have little choice," Lijena finally said. "Our own boat was completely wrecked by the storm."

Davin Anane picked his way carefully down the icy slope to the beach's snow-covered rocks. Hunks of ice as large as his fist dotted the way, but footsteps coming from the marooned vessel had been burned into the beach to show where Valora had disembarked, her body radiating the power of her spells.

Davin shuddered, remembering similar tracks left by the Faceless Ones' horses. The hairs on the Jyotian's neck stood at attention. Magicks, whether caused by demon or human mage, were not to be taken lightly. The Sword of Kwerin Bloodhawk had given Valora immense power for the brief time she held it. How she employed the blade lay beyond the thief's ken or that of any living human. Only Dark Qar might draw those secrets from Valora now.

The last son of the House of Anane squinted against the glare of Ianyan's snow to evaluate the ship's seaworthiness. On the prow, near the granite boulders at the water's edge, gleamed a patch of shiny new wood. Davin moved closer and bent to examine the repair. His eyes narrowed and he chewed his lower lip.

This was no ordinary patch. The boat had obviously crashed into the boulder when Valora arrived at Ianya. But no human hand had repaired the rent. The new wood appeared to grow from old to seal the hole. Residual magicks left by the witch-woman's spells had allowed the vessel to heal itself.

"She's right, Goran." Davin stood and turned to his companions. "There is no other way to return to Upper Raemllyn. I have no love of magicks, but we must risk them to return Kwerin's Sword to Prince Felrad."

"Truth be told," Goran said, still edgy, "I desire only one thing more than to be off this frozen lump of an island that is . . ."

The Challing's voice faltered when he looked at Lijena. "The sword! It comes alive!"

Lijena glanced at the sheathed blade slung at her hip when she stepped toward the fishing boat. A pale blue glow enveloped sword and scabbard. The fingers of her right hand cautiously touched the hilt. "I can feel its power like when I fought the Faceless. But this is different. It's as though the sword is drawing me to the boat."

Her right hand enclosed the hilt of the Sword of Kwerin. Pale green fires danced higher along the ship's upper masts – cold green fire without heat.

Goran's single eye now blazed with witchfire. "I feel no evil, Lijena?"

"No, none." She shook her head. "I sense no evil – just power flowing from the sword. It is as though the blade attempts to speak to me – to direct my steps."

Davin tried to suppress a shudder that ran through his body and failed. He had little use for magicks and even less knowledge of how spells were woven. In truth, he would have preferred to sail an iceberg south rather than set foot on Valora's abandoned boat, but he was pledged to return the ensorcelled sword to his prince.

Sucking down a breath, Davin steeled himself for what he recognized as inevitable. All he could do was follow Lijena and try to protect her and the sword from danger, be it human or demonic in origin. He motioned Goran to the beach when Lijena went to the side of the boat.

For a moment, she eyed the vessel, stranded and tilted heavily on its port side. She lifted her hand, laid it on the wooden vessel and shoved gently.

Before Davin could laugh and explain that more than a mere push was needed to free the craft, his jaw sagged wide. The fishing boat eased gently away from the boulder-strewn beach.

"The skinny ones often hide amazing strength," Goran said with a chuckle. "Our frosty-haired companion reminds me of a wench I once arm-wrestled in . . ."

Davin paid no heed to the Challing. Lijena now drew the Sword of Kwerin Bloodhawk from its unadorned sheath. She held out the glow-bathed length of steel and touched it to the hull. As if running away from unutterable pain, the large ship creaked, moaned and protested, timbers straining. The craft edged through the ice floes clogging the narrow bay until it was totally free of the beach. Only a trailing gangplank ran from shore to ship.

"We must board now," Lijena said in a distant voice. "The tide is going out and we must ride with it."

"She and the sword speak as one." Goran waved Davin onto the gangplank after Lijena. "I fear this will not be the finest of journeys, my friend."

Davin silently agreed with the Challing.

Sheathing the Sword of Kwerin Bloodhawk, Lijena strode to the prow and hauled the anchor onto the deck. Immediately, the fishing boat slid into the bay, turning on a southward heading of its own volition.

"I like this not." Goran selected a biscuit of hardtack from a tin and bit into the rocklike excuse for bread.

"Neither do I." Davin shook his head when he scanned the endless ocean surrounding the fishing boat. "We traveled from Rakell to Ianya in the space of two days. Today marks our seventh since leaving Ianya and still we've yet to sight land."

"I didn't mean that." Goran popped the remaining portion of hardtack into his mouth and crunched down loudly. "I meant this tin. It's the last of the food stores below. If we don't make landfall soon, we might starve to death."

Davin waved off the tin when Goran offered him a piece of the hardtack. He looked at Lijena. "Any idea why it takes so long to reach Rakell?"

"Time," Lijena answered with an uncertain shrug, "perhaps it's as Goran suggested. The storm that drove us to Ianya was a rent in time and space. Without the rent propelling us, we must live every moment."

"Perhaps," Davin replied, hesitant to admit at least a month had been lost to them in what felt like no more than three days.

A month? He shook his head. The truth was, if the constellations that filled the night skies were to be believed, a full two months had passed since leaving Rakell.

"At least we didn't face the storm again," Davin said. "I don't believe this vessel would have withstood that gale a second time."

"Gale? You call the puny breezes that blew us to Ianya a gale?" Amazement filled Goran's expression. "Why, friend Davin, it was nothing compared to the time I lost my eye. A seacoast town, somewhere in Lower Raemllyn, and a harsh place it was. The blistering desert inland burned the incautious traveler and vicious storms perpetually racked the coast."

"Your eye?" Davin turned to stare at his Challing friend. "Not too long ago you said a big oyster ate your eye. Or squirted ink at it. I misremember what you said."

"The pearl-bearing fiend *almost* blinded me and allowed the lady pearlers to steal it as it popped from its socket. No, Davin, you must listen more carefully. This is the *true* story of how I lost my eye. Struck by lightning, I was."

Goran rambled on, telling his outlandish yarn while Davin's thoughts drifted away. The horizon offered no promise of landfall. Nor did the fishing vessel require a crew; the ship sailed itself. To where was the question he could not answer. That the sun rose on the port and set on the starboard said the course was southward.

His gray eyes studied the mast. The green fire still gamboled on the upper masts while sailcloth hung limp. The naked wood creaked like a thing alive, as if invisible winds blew to send the craft on its way.

Wherever that way might be.

"Valora still touches us, even from the grave. Her magicks live after her," Davin said, more to himself than Goran One-Eye.

The Challing rambled on with the improbable anecdote of losing his eye to lightning spirits who had then used the eyeball for a prize in some bizarre spot encompassing storm winds and the private parts of a desert beast.

"The sword does not react poorly to the magicks she wove." Lijena touched the blade on her hip. "I feel no evil."

"I'd prefer you to *feel* land," Davin replied. He came from Jyotis, a district renowned for its seafarers, yet he had always preferred both of his boots securely on the land. How was he expected to make a quick retreat when he had to swim to unknown shores? "It would also be nice if you might *feel* exactly where we are and where this boat takes us."

He saw Lijena wince at the bite held in his words and added. "I meant no offense. Magicks never have set well with me. I prefer to hold my life in my own hands."

Again Lijena touched the blade of the Bloodhawk; her hand then moved to her stomach and rested there. "For over a year, I've had no control over the forces enveloping my life. Now the sword commands me. One does not grow accustomed to such forces. The best anyone can do is accept."

It was Davin's turn to wince with guilt. He had put into motion the forces that had dominated Lijena's life when he had been tricked into kidnapping her from her uncle in Harn. He studied the blonde-tressed daughter of Bistonia and found the surprising desire to take her in his arms and hold her close. More surprising was the lack of lust in that desire. There was a vulnerability about the young woman that he had never seen before, something that called for comfort.

And be skewered on Kwerin's Sword for the effort, he thought, remembering Lijena's pledge to kill him one day.

Lijena's head lifted, and her aquamarine eyes turned to him. As though she read his thoughts, she said, "There is no need to fear that, Davin. The time of revenge is past. We are both called to a higher purpose now."

Before he could answer, her neck craned back and she studied the high gray overcast that had settled over the sky shortly after sunrise. "Might we have slipped through the rent in space without knowing it?" she asked, more to herself than to him.

Davin's gut twisted, and a cold shiver ran along his spine. The notion that they had somehow left Raemllyn had entered his mind more than once, but he had refused to contemplate the possibility. To be adrift on an endless sea for eternity was not the end to his life he had always envisioned.

"I think the magicks that hold this boat make one's mind run wild at times," Davin said without a trace of condescension in his tone. "The ceaseless waves stir the imagination."

"There aren't any birds," Lijena replied. "And fish? Have you sighted any?"

"I can slip overboard and explore," offered Goran. "This human form is becoming tedious. A nice fish shape might . . ."

"No!" Davin Anane's aversion to Goran's shape-changing brought his quick response. "The ship moves too quickly. It might leave you behind."

"Then I shall shift into a bird and soar. There is no way this ship can travel faster than a denizen of the air can fly!" Goran peered at Davin, his good eye ablaze with witchfire.

Magicks abounded and Davin had no power to control any of it. But he saw that his friend only argued out of boredom.

"Do so, if it pleases you." Davin shrugged. "Perhaps we might harness you with one of yon ropes and let you pull the ship all the faster."

"I . . ." Goran snapped his mouth shut, then pointed behind Davin.

For a moment, Davin wasn't sure what the Challing saw. Then he made out white clouds and soaring mountains. Land!

"Where are we?" Davin shook his head, unable to recall the features of the coastline. "I do not remember any land along the northern shore of Raemllyn that looks that way. And it seems – warm."

"The Isthmus of Brykheedah," Lijena spoke up. "It has been years since I traveled there with my father, but I recognize the twin peaks."

"The Winged Rams!" exclaimed Davin. "Yes, I recognize them now. The rams stolen by Kaga. But how can this be? We have come halfway around Upper Raemllyn in only seven days."

"You spoke the truth, friend Davin," said Goran. "Ensorcelled, this ship. I, for one, am glad finally to see a way off this miserable, leaky vessel."

"We've come almost to Kavindra," Davin said carefully, his mind racing. "What of Felrad?"

Lijena drew the Sword of Kwerin and held it high. She staggered as though some unseen hand tried to prise the blade free of her grip. The blade's blue glow intensified, turning it incandescent. Davin held his hand up to shield his eyes from the radiance. The sword turned slowly in Lijena's grip until it pointed north of the distant peaks.

"Felrad is there," she said. "The blade desires a return to his hand."

"No," Davin said slowly, "I think not. Felrad cannot be in that direction. Kavindra lies that way," he said, pointing to the ship's prow. "The blade points to something else."

"*Keedehn*!" Goran spat like an angry cat and scrambled back while he tugged the battle-axe from his belt.

Above the ship drifted one of the fierce denizens of Goran's home world of Gohwohn. Merciless green eyes spied them while twin tails raked the air with short, confident beats. The serpentine head turned slowly to home in on the Challing in man form. The dragon's great serrated beak opened, and the creature's hideous hunting scream filled the air.

"It recognizes a Challing no matter what shape I occupy!" Goran hefted his axe high ready to meet attack.

Davin recalled vividly their first encounter with a *keedehn*. He also remembered the dragon had a decided preference for Challing flesh.

Another scream tore the air. The *keedehn* tucked its batlike wings to its scaled side and dived.

Davin was fast. Goran was faster. Fastest of the trio was Lijena Farleigh!

She swung the Sword of Kwerin Bloodhawk in a lofting trajectory blurred by the speed of her attack. The *keedehn's* head exploded from its body the instant the magical blade touched leathery neck. A shower of iridescent scales showered onto the deck. The dragon's headless body twisted and wrenched violently in the air, then plummeted into the ocean to sink beneath the water.

"The rip in space!" Davin stared at the foam that marked where the creature had disappeared. "It is like Agda's Wood. It allowed a *keedehn* to enter this world."

Goran scanned the sky. "If there is one, be assured others follow."

"I fear you are right," Lijena said. "This sword pointed not to Felrad, but to the real danger facing our world. The hole must be closed."

"Does the blade hold such power? Or only the ability to slay the monstrosities freed on this world?" Goran slowly lowered his axe, but his eye remained on the sky.

"I don't know." Lijena sheathed the sword, her hand remaining on the hilt. "Sometimes I understand the forces that flow from the blade – at others, I merely react to them."

"What if the Sword of Kwerin draws the monsters, rather than merely detecting their presence?" Davin suggested.

Neither Lijena nor Goran had time to answer.

The enchanted boat swung about without warning.

Man, woman and Challing clung to the railing to keep their feet under them while the craft completed a tight turn and headed directly for land. All three watched the rapidly nearing Winged Rams thrust through white clouds in a suddenly blue sky. The boat seemed to fly toward the coast. Distances that should have taken hours to cover were crossed in minutes. The craft did not slow its headlong race toward a now visible sandy beach.

"Overboard," Goran called to his companions. "Throw yourselves overboard before we . . ."

There was no time to act. The vessel lifted from the water and glided over dry land before settling gently atop the sand.

"It appears we've arrived," Davin cautiously released his hold on the railing.

"And I for one am quite pleased to see dry land." Goran vaulted over the railing and dropped twenty feet to the ground, landing nimbly.

Davin and Lijena took a less precarious route. Tossing the anchor over the side, they climbed down the knotted rope. The instant Davin's feet touched Raemllyn's soil, the ghostly ship slid backward, returning to the sea. A bank of thick fog appeared and tendrils of mist opened, engulfing the boat.

Then the fog dissipated, leaving only gentle ocean – and emptiness. Valora's vessel had vanished totally.

"Kavindra lies yonder." Davin pointed inland, unwilling to ponder the ways of magicks. "We've at least two days' walk ahead of us."

"That's if we can avoid Zarek Yannis' troops. This is the heart of his territory, you know?" The Challing swung battle-axe to his shoulder and started in the direction Davin had pointed.

Davin followed with Lijena at his side. On her hip the Sword of Kwerin Bloodhawk glowed and pulsated with light as though a mystical heart beat within the steel.

"The soldiers are not Felrad's." The realization brought Davin little comfort. "They appear to be a marine force."

"Of what city-state?" Lijena clutched the Sword of Kwerin more tightly as she peered from the bushes that hid them from the patrols marching past. "They oppose Yannis, that much is certain. It was Yannis' troops we saw them fighting."

Davin cautioned, "Enemy of our enemy might not be our friend."

"You are growing too cautious in your old age, friend Davin," complained Goran.

The Challing started to stand and summon the marine officer passing some fifty paces from them, but both Lijena and Davin restrained him until the marines were well past their position.

"We know Felrad's army is near," Lijena said. "I saw banners on yon hill bearing his colors. Rather than upset the balance of power, we should explore more."

"The fewer who know of the sword's return, the better it will be," agreed Davin. "Felrad might have hidden its theft. We should not stir unwanted rumors that would undermine his authority."

"All the authority Prince Felrad needs is clutched in her hands," Goran said, preferring a direct approach. He glared at Lijena in accusation of turning his friend into a doddering imbecile fearing even the hint of adventure. "Since you insist on such circumspect behavior, we should march in that direction."

"Why?" asked Davin, looking north where Goran pointed.

"The blade shines brightest when facing that way. Either Felrad camps there or we find the hole leaking *keedehn* into the world. Either way, we accomplish more than sitting here arguing endlessly." Goran shoved from the tangled bushes, heavy axe resting on his shoulder.

"He is right." Lijena's hand left the sheathed blade and her fingertips brushed her belly for an instant before returning to the hilt. "We must move on."

Davin studied her features while he used an arm to open a way through the bushes for her. The pace thus far had been an easy one, yet she appeared pale and drawn. Her breath became increasingly deep and labored. Did some guardian spell left aboard the fishing boat now hold her in its grip?

Davin placed little weight on the possibility. Other than being constantly tired, he detected no trace of magicks at work. Lijena's behavior appeared normal and her desire to return the sword to Prince Felrad steadfast.

"Ah, now there is a fine sight," grumbled Goran. A meaty hand rose and a stubby finger pointed in the direction of an immense, walled city-state. "Kavindra lies under siege. But where is Felrad, and where is Yannis?"

"A question easily answered." Davin tilted his head to Felrad's colors fluttering on a tall flagstaff a league north of Kavindra's gates.

While they watched, a horde of Felrad's warriors stormed the city's main gates and were repelled as quickly as they charged. The ancient fortifications were too secure for such haphazard assault.

"He needs the sword," Lijena said softly. "The battle cannot be joined until Felrad again swings the Sword of Kwerin Blood-hawk."

Without another word, Lijena started toward Felrad's camp. This time Goran and Davin were hard pressed to keep up. Resolve gave her strength and speed.

"He is weaker than before," Tacllyn-lin-Bertam said softly. The mage rested his hand on Felrad's brow.

The prince stirred feverishly and tried to move the hand away. He lacked the strength even for such a simple task.

"Heal him with your spells," Lijena demanded. "Surely, there must be some magic to aid him."

"We have tried. The five of us assembled for . . ." The mage hesitated, afraid to reveal the purpose of their task and their abject failure.

"Ah, you tried to seal the rent in space," Goran said boldly, enjoying the surprise on Bertam's face. "Why else would Felrad have five mages so obviously unversed in healing arts?"

"To the point, to the point," urged Davin. "How can Prince

Felrad wield the Sword of Kwerin in his present condition?"

"Without him, the rebellion fails," Bertam answered, obviously troubled by this simple truth. "Another of royal blood might be found, but Felrad has the loyalty and confidence of the army."

"Tie him onto his horse and lead him to the battlefield," Goran suggested. "He can be a figurehead and let another carry the sword."

"No!" Lijena Farleigh's emphatic denial froze those gathered around Felrad's bed. "I can give the sword to no one else!"

"Goran is strong. He could wield the sword," Davin suggested. "Or give me . . ."

"No! You hear but you do not listen." Lijena stared at the Jyotian. "The blade is changed, is changing. Its time has arrived. Only one it has . . ."

"You would deny us the magicks locked within the steel?" Bertam's face twisted with anxiety. "There is much you do not know about the coming battle."

"Such as the way Zarek Yannis summons more Faceless Ones to do his bidding?" asked Lijena. "Or do you mean the otherworldly beasts that invade Raemllyn?"

Bertam's body sagged with defeat. "We five, Wok-Lamol, Wok-Manol, Fiany, Cor'Mid and I, attempted to repair the rift Yannis has somehow opened. We failed. Fiany remains bedridden from the undertaking. We must try again, but Yannis pressures us constantly."

"How is that possible? Is he a mage of such surpassing power?" asked Davin.

Again Bertam sagged; his shoulders slumped in abject failure. "I do not know how he derives his power. I fear Felrad's condition is partly due to Yannis' magicks. Perhaps intentionally, perhaps only as a side effect of the usurper's meddling with forces beyond his control."

Bertam turned to Lijena. "Only one thing is certain – without the Sword of Kwerin Bloodhawk we have no hope of ever defeating Yannis. You must give the blade over."

Lijena shook her head. "Don't you understand? I want to. More than anything, I want to do just that. But I can't. The sword is more than some enchanted length of steel. Edan placed more than magic in the blade. He gave it a life of its own. It chooses who will bear it, not I!"

Outside Felrad's tent rose a panicked cry. The clank of sword and shield echoed in a rattling chorus. The twang of taut bowstrings and the hiss of arrows taking flight sounded above all.

Lijena spun. The Sword of Kwerin Bloodhawk burned a brilliant blue as she wrenched it from its sheath.

"A demon!" came the cry from outside. "A demon rides through the camp!"

Goran reached for the sword. He yowled in pain and jerked his hand back. Angry red blisters mottled his fingertips.

"Now you understand." Lijena stared at the Challing, her eyes filled with pain. "With Felrad ill, the blade has chosen another to carry it into battle. No other may touch this hilt until its task is complete."

Lijena did not wait for an answer. She ran through the tent flaps and stared at the dark death charging through the camp.

Hooves flaming, the massive midnight-colored courser carried a Faceless One on its back. Every time the steed reared, its hooves set tents ablaze wherever they touched. The demon horse kicked out and caught one of Felrad's soldiers in the face. The man screamed, fell to the ground and then exploded.

Nor did the charger's rider sit motionless. The Faceless One wielded its sword of crystalline flame like a scythe. The blade rose and fell. With each deadly slash three of the prince's warriors died in screaming agony.

Lijena strode forward, her jaw set, her eyes narrowed with determination.

"No!" Davin burst from the tent, his own sword in hand. "It's certain death!"

When the Jyotian started for Lijena, Goran's heavy hand locked on his shoulder, holding him in place.

"Man-forged steel cannot aid the sword-bearer." The Challing held tight no matter how Davin twisted and turned. "You can do no more than watch, my friend. She is beyond your help or love."

Lijena abruptly halted and planted her feet in a wide stance.

The Faceless One wheeled about and charged with fiery blade raised for the kill.

In a movement too swift for the eye to follow, Lijena dropped under the demon's crystal sword and drove the sword of Kwerin straight up into robed body.

A skeletal hand clawed at the magical sword but failed to free it. Lijena did that, yanking back hard with both arms. A hideous scream lacking any semblance of a human voice filled the air and died as the demon vanished in a cloud of noxious black smoke.

Lijena stepped back, judged her distance, then lunged. The enchanted blade skewered the demon charger's side. Like its rider, the massive animal screamed then was gone in a billowing black cloud.

"See?" Goran released his hold on Davin's shoulder. "Nothing you can do will aid the sword-bearer. The blade has chosen her."

"There are more coming," Davin cried. "A dozen of them! Yannis has unleashed an army of Faceless Ones!"

"The battle is upon us." Battle-axe clenched in his fists, Goran One-Eye went to meet the tide of death charging out of Kavindra's open gates.

17

"Back! Guard Felrad!" Lijena cried out when she saw Davin and Goran One-Eye rush to her side. "The Faceless are not meant for you. Protect the prince!"

"There are too many of them!" Davin Anane calmed himself and answered with the hiss of steel freed from sheath. How could there ever be too many demons to defeat the best thieves in all Raemllyn?

"We stand together." Goran One-Eye took a wide-legged stance to the swordswoman's left. He held the twin-bladed axe at the ready.

As they positioned themselves to each side, Lijena realized the two adventurers thought they provided her protection. They did not understand that no human swordsman armed with mere steel could survive long against the Faceless Ones – not now.

"You don't understand!" A wild blue light filled Lijena's eyes when she turned to Davin. "This isn't Rakell. All is changed. The forces loosed here are stronger. The Faceless are in full power. A mere brush of their swords will steal your life. Get back! Both of you, get back! Damn you, get back before you're killed!"

When neither man nor Challing retreated, the daughter of Bistonia took the only avenue open to her. Sword of Kwerin Bloodhawk grasped in both hands, she ran forward to meet the demon riders and their flame-hooved chargers. The courage her companions displayed deserved a greater reward than certain death.

"No!" Davin cried out in horror. In the blink of an eye, Lijena separated herself from the two thieves by a hundred strides and there was nothing he could do to stop her.

Goran stared after the woman with wide-eyed disbelief on his face. His massive head turned to the Jyotian. "She seeks to protect us. Something is amiss here, my friend. Something beyond our understanding."

Unimaginable terror filled Davin as he stared at a full dozen

Faceless Ones riding straight for Lijena. The tenderness, the warmth, the caring – all the feelings Awendala had first awakened in him now swelled in Davin's breast and flowed outward to Lijena. The tidal wave of passions that broke over him tripled the terror. The Sitala once again cast a cruel fate – to discover his love for Lijena Farleigh only to lose her in battle the same way he had lost Awendala!

"Not again!" Rage and frustration roared from his chest! His head jerked from side to side in a desperate search for something, anything, with which to aid the swordswoman. Nothing! There was nothing. No human-wrought weapon was a match for the blade of flaming crystal the Faceless wielded.

The opening flaps of Prince Felrad's tent caught the Jyotian's eye. Tacllyn-lin-Bertam stepped out.

"A spell!" Davin screamed at the wizard. "Protect her with your spells!"

For an instant, Davin's gaze held Bertam, then the mage pivoted sharply amid swirling robes and retreated down a line of tents.

"Damn him and all his breed!" Goran roared. "If he'll provide no magicks, then we'll use the steel given us to conjure our own!"

The Jyotian spun back in time to see the first of the Faceless reach Lijena. Rather than meet the assault upright, she abruptly dropped to one knee.

Lijena Farleigh first had faced the Faceless Ones in the forest of Agda. Three of the demons had died that day. Her own prowess with sword and sheer luck had brought her safely through that battle. Today, she was allied with a man dead for ten thousand generations.

More than mere magicks bound the honed steel she wielded. She had told those with Felrad that the sword had a life of its own. Only now did she recognize that life. Edan, mage to Kwerin Bloodhawk, dwelled within the steel. The power, the skill required for such a transformation, was beyond her comprehension. But the reason was all too clear now – Chal had taught her well. Love! So great was Edan's love for humankind that he sacrificed himself, forged his own life into the sword he created for his king. He died so that Raemllyn would live!

Not dead – Lijena drew the Sword of Kwerin Bloodhawk back

above a shoulder when she dropped to one knee before the charging Faceless Ones – *but alive this day in the steel!*

A glow of brilliant blue-white enveloped the sword when she struck, not at the rider, but at the midnight-black mount carrying the foremost demon. If the blade met flesh or bone, she felt the harsh jar of neither; the sword sliced through the charger's shins as though they were mist. The animal's nostrils flared, but before a death scream was born in its throat the beast vanished in a cloud of greasy black smoke.

As did its rider when Lijena arched the sword upward to hack into a black robe-covered thigh.

No voices echoed in her head; no unseen entity commanded her body. Yet Edan stood with her. She saw with the eyes of two. Her own vision tunneled in focus when she swung her blade upward to block a thrust by the second rider.

At the same time, she saw with eyes that surveyed all that surrounded her. While she sent the second of the Faceless Ones to oblivion with a flick of her wrist that nicked a skeletal wrist with the blade's tip, Edan's eyes prepared her for the two demons that attacked as one.

It was Edan's spell flowing from steel into her body that provided the burst of speed needed to carry her safely beneath the descending swords of crystal fire when she dived forward. Lijena hit the ground in a roll and sprang to her feet. In a wide figure of eight, she lashed out left then right with the mage-bound sword. The blade sliced through the rumps of the fire-breathing steeds on both sides of the swordswoman. Two more clouds of black erupted to dissipate in the wind.

The gift of Edan's second vision allowed her to thrust upward in answer to the fifth of the Faceless Ones who charged before pivoting and eliminating the two horseless demons with one wide sweep of the Bloodhawk's Sword.

While the sixth demon rider reined his charger straight down on her, the seventh jerked the head of his steed to the left. Rather than Lijena, his target lay beyond the swordswoman.

"For one so skinny, she has an understanding of tactics!" This from Goran One-Eye. "Yannis sends a demon for Prince Felrad!"

Imitating Lijena's earlier tactic, Davin dropped to a knee and swung his sword back over his right shoulder. With every ounce of strength in his body, he struck. Steel bit deep in the demon horse's right shin and lodged there. In the next instant, the Jyotian was thrown backwards as the sword's hilt was wrenched from his hands.

Rather than exploding into a cloud of black, the charger stumbled, then collapsed. The Faceless One astride the muscular mount kicked free of stirrups and leaped from the saddle. Without so much as a break in its forward motion, the demon landed on the ground with its own sword leveled at Goran One-Eye.

"Steel against demon blade!" Goran's eye blazed with green witchfire; he grinned broadly.

With deft grace, the Challing whipped out a battle-axe now aglow with the same green witchfire that fired his eye. The heavy blade slammed into the Faceless One's forearm to sever a bony hand at the wrist.

"Perhaps a might more than mere steel!" Goran chortled while he swung anew, driving the axe straight into the demon's burning eyes. "I see you care little for Challing magicks!"

The Faceless One toppled; greasy smoke smoldered through its black robe.

"Its sword!" Davin scrambled to his feet and leaped for the blade of crystalline fire that tumbled from the dying demon's hand.

The instant his fingertips touched the sword's hilt, the weapon shattered like a length of breaking glass. A heartbeat later, the crystal shards exploded in a thousand crackling sparks of fire.

"What?" The Jyotian jerked back, eyes saucer-wide. "How can it be? In Rakell we used the Faceless Ones' own swords against them."

"This is not Rakell," Goran repeated Lijena's earlier words. "All is changed. The Faceless Ones are in full power."

Davin blinked at his companion while Goran used his witchfire-glowing axe to end the life of the crippled demon horse that hobbled on one foreleg behind him. The Jyotian retrieved his sword when the cloud of smoke thinned. "What does that mean?"

"It means the sword-bearer wins or loses this battle," Goran answered. "Men and their weapons cannot hope to stand against the Faceless Ones this day. Pray to your gods, friend Davin, that your skinny blonde has the mettle to stand before all Zarek Yannis will throw at her!''

Davin's gaze darted back to Lijena. All but three of the dozen riders were dead. Two reined their chargers toward the swordswoman. The third rode straight down on the pair of thieves with fiery sword raised high for the kill.

The Jyotian reacted rather than thought. He jerked his sword high to block the descending blade of crystalline fire meant to cleave him in twain. Parry the blow he did, but the impact sent him reeling to the ground once more.

"Stand clear! Let me handle this!" Goran roared as he drove his axe into the chest of the charger that bolted between them. "Even a scratch from the demon's blade will drink away a man's life!"

If Davin had ever forgotten his companion was not a man, the difference became all too apparent in the time it took the Jyotian to lift himself from the dirt.

As with Davin's blade, the Challing's axe lodged solidly in the demon horse's body. The mount reared, jerking the handle from the one-eyed giant's grip. The Faceless One astride the black steed leaned down and stretched out a skeletal hand for Goran's throat.

Goran's shape shifted like molten rock. No longer did a savage red-haired giant stand before the demon, but the Faceless One found itself confronted with its twin. Davin had never seen one of the Faceless display any hint of emotion. This one did! The demon reeled back as it found itself fighting a comrade from the lowest depths of Peyneeha.

"Goran, no!" shouted Davin when he realized the Challing's intent.

The warning came too late!

Goran, in demon guise, leaped high, his own bony claws locking about the Faceless One's neck. Together, two black-robed demons spilled to the ground.

Davin hefted his sword, ready to aid his friend. He took two strides and skidded to a halt. He could no longer discern Goran from Yannis' soulless killer. Each was a mirror image of the other.

Except—

A brief glimpse beneath the dark cowls when the two struggled to their feet provided the answer the thief needed. A single eye of brilliant emerald burned beneath the hood of the nearest demon.

Davin reacted swiftly, his sword sweeping about in a fierce cut that caught the true demon behind its knees – or where its knees ought to be. Off balance, the serpentine spirit crashed to the ground. Challing in hellspawn form pounced. Skeletal claws aglow with the flames of witchfire tore and rent like a savage beast.

And the Faceless One died.

Davin stepped back when the triumphant demon rose from the smoldering corpse and shape-shifted back into the more familiar form of Goran One-Eye.

"A fine fight, eh? Not like you puny humans. They give me a true challenge!" Goran turned to the still-rearing demon horse and yanked his axe from its flesh. Without batting his eye, he brought the twin-edged blade down on the animal's head the way another might use a hammer to slaughter an ox. The charger followed its rider to Hell.

"Ah, a truly great fight, one that bards will sing of for centuries to come." The Challing laughed and slapped Davin on the shoulder. "How did you know which of us was the true immigrant from Gohwohn?"

"The eye. One eye. You had only one," Davin Anane gasped out.

"Indeed, how odd. When I shape-change, I usually show the proper number of orbs. Only in this body am I magically constrained to just one eye."

Davin's eyes widened in terror. The Challing was right. He must have been mistaken. "I could have killed you," Davin said in alarm.

"You, you a mere human? Kill a demon? Never! Now let me see if the Faceless One's sword will fit my hand." Goran reached for the Faceless One's fallen sword of crystalline flame but recoiled when it shattered and burst into hissing sparks at his touch. "By Yehseen's great quivering shaft, it seems weapons from Qar's lowest hell are not for the living this day."

"Rally, warriors of the realm! Rally to her who wields the

Sword of Kwerin Bloodhawk!" Prince Felrad's voice thundered behind the pair of thieves. "Zarek Yannis sends demons against us. Meet them with cold steel!"

Outside his tent, Felrad stood in full armor with sword raised high. The rightful ruler of Raemllyn betrayed no hint of weakness in tone or posture. "To the Sword! Warriors of Raemllyn, rally to the Sword of Kwerin Bloodhawk. Drive the demons back through the gates of Kavindra!"

Soldiers who had fled when the Faceless Ones approached now turned and charged the hell creatures with sword and spear raised. Single battle cries rose from individual throats to join in a thunderous roar.

Davin recognized the source of the prince's sudden strength. Tacllyn-lin-Bertam and his four assistants stood behind Felrad. Even the ailing Fiany chanted and wove patterns in the air with her hands.

With certainty in his gait, Prince Felrad approached the two adventurers. "She fights like a legion. Even with the Bloodhawk's Sword in my hand, the blade was never wielded with such skill and deadly accuracy."

"The blade has chosen her," Goran answered. "She and it were forged for this day."

Davin watched as Lijena finished the last of the twelve demon riders with a tireless thrust to the chest. As death scream and black smoke rose to the sky, Lijena lowered the Sword of Kwerin Bloodhawk and glanced over her shoulder.

"My liege, return to your quarters. You and Bertam need to counsel," she called out, then added for Davin and Goran, "Guard him well. Yannis' fingers slip. Soon Hell will reign over this battlefield. Felrad will have need of you."

"She speaks the truth, my Prince." Bertam approached Felrad. "Your appearance has rallied your troops. They will follow the sword-bearer now. You must return to your tent while our spells hold. We've other matters to attend to, else her valor will be for naught."

"Other matters! Damn you, Bertam!" Felrad winced in pain; color fled his face. "I should stand at her side. It's my crown she fights to regain!"

"He is right, my brother." Davin edged closer to the prince

when he noticed him sway. "Your men have heeded your battle call."

Shaking, Felrad acquiesced. Placing a hand on Davin's shoulder for support, he returned to the tent and the five mages who waited outside.

"The city gates open wide!" rose the cry from the soldiers. "Faceless Ones! Yannis unleashes a whole army of demons!"

Below the rise on which they stood, Davin watched while human troops flooded from Kavindra's open gates. At their center rode a hundred Faceless demons.

"To the Sword of Kwerin Bloodhawk!" Lijena's voice rang out clear and true. "Warriors of Raemllyn, rally to the Sword!"

Her cry was more effective than the orders of a score of generals. Foot soldiers and cavalry fell into rank and file to form a solid wall to meet Yannis' attack.

"Can she hope to stand against so many of the monsters?" Helplessness filled Felrad's voice.

"They are only the beginning," Bertam answered. "You heard her warning. Yannis' control slips away. We must act now before it is too late."

Felrad turned from the armies that surged toward each other to determine who would sit atop the Velvet Throne. Davin glanced back toward Kavindra. No longer did Yannis' human forces stream through the city gates. All he could see were the Faceless Ones – not hundreds, but thousands!

"Place him on the bed," Bertam ordered the two thieves. "Guard him well. Where we must travel will place us far beyond his needs."

While Goran and Davin seated Felrad on the edge of his bed, the five mages lowered themselves cross-legged to the ground. They formed a simple square with Tacllyn-lin-Bertam at the center intersecting invisible diagonals running between the mages.

"Yannis has opened a rent in space to such a degree that he can never close it. The Faceless Ones pour through in an endless stream he can never stem," Bertam said, arranging his robes around him.

"How does he accomplish this?" asked Goran. "We saw the Beasts of the Mist. They had to squeeze through, one or two at a time."

"We know not what spells he used, what powers he controls," Cor'Mid answered. "I think he only sought to bring a few more Faceless Ones to his aid after the prince slew so many at the Battle of Rakell."

"Something went wrong," Bertam picked up. "The tear grew, widened, lengthened. Zarek Yannis has lost his control, if he truly was ever in control. That is what the sword-bearer warned our Prince."

"The Faceless Ones attack without a commander?" Davin's pulse quickened. The demons were deadly enough when guided by a human hand. Unbridled, they could destroy all of Raemllyn in a matter of days.

"What is the difference?" Goran asked with a sharp edge to his words. "They do of their own volition what Zarek Yannis would order them to do anyway. How will you stop them?"

An ice floe crept along Davin's spine when he saw the apprehension on the Challing's face. Nothing in Raemllyn fazed Goran. For him to show fear—

"I scouted for a force to oppose Yannis when we sailed the northern seas together. You faced that force," Bertam answered the Challing.

Davin failed to grasp the mage's meaning, then it dawned on him. "The Beasts . . ."

Goran was far ahead of the Jyotian thief. "You would open a gateway of your own and bring the Beasts of the Mist to do battle with the Faceless Ones? Are you all fools?"

"That well may prove the case," Fiany spoke up.

Bertam added, "Yannis opened the gateway when he first summoned the Faceless Ones – it was an unexpected and unwanted side effect to the spell he wove. Left alone, the two rents will eventually spread across all Raemllyn, tearing apart our world at its seams."

"We will summon the rent you faced in the north," Cor'Mid explained. "When the two forces meet, they will destroy each other and seal the tears between the planes of existence."

"Or so you hope," Goran replied with doubt brimming in his tone. "It is the plan of madmen."

"Does it matter?" Felrad's pale face lifted to the Challing. "If my army fails, we die and the Faceless Ones overrun the world.

Better to stop them – or try – than simply to die."

Davin's mind raced in rhythm with his pounding heart. Lijena and the others who fought outside were but a delaying tactic. Within this tent the fate of Raemllyn would be decided. A world would live or a world would die.

"You waste time," Felrad said to Bertam. "Do what must be done, and may the gods walk with you."

Simultaneously, the five mages closed their eyes. Although each of their lips moved, the chant they sang lifted as if in a single voice.

Davin Anane gasped aloud. Forces moved into the tent, around him, *through* him.

"If we have seen our last sunrise, friend Davin, know that we have drunk of life to its fullest!" Goran's head turned toward the Jyotian, but his features blurred. His face shifted through every form the Challing had ever worn – all in a single moment!

The Challing's words were meaningless, and at the same time contained the deepest of philosophies. Davin felt supremely uplifted and transfixed, more than merely human. As surely as power flowed into him, so did it flow out. His knees buckled, abruptly transformed to rubber, and he collapsed to the ground. Above him, he saw Goran stagger under the onslaught of power the mages unleashed. The Challing collapsed to the bed where Felrad sat stoically, his expression one of utter pain, an agony of the soul as much as of the body.

Lijena! He needed to warn her of the beasts – of what Bertam called forth.

Davin crawled weakly to the tent flap and pushed it aside. Through blurred eyes he saw Lijena Farleigh in the distance. With untiring strength she wielded the Sword of Kwerin Bloodhawk. Endlessly, the horde of Faceless Ones charged, only to die in clouds of black smoke.

How long could she persist before one of those crystalline blades found a way through her guard?

The chant behind the Jyotian rose. Louder and louder it grew – a shout, a clamor, a roar that shook the very foundations of the world. Davin clasped hands to ears, but nothing dampened it. The roar only mounted.

Below on the plains, human and demon foe no longer fought.

All heads turned to the sky. Davin's own gaze lifted.

"Goran, above us!" he cried out, uncertain if his words were heard above the deafening roar. "The sky opens."

Even as he spoke, the heavens split apart and beasts defying description teemed forth in a horrifying torrent. He tried to put names to those creatures and failed. Serpents and griffins and sea dragons and *kloyt* beetles and *keedehn* and malformed oddities with no specific shape at all crashed from above – and all sought the Faceless Ones.

The demons' crystalline blades of searing flame worked no better against the magical menagerie summoned through this tear in the fabric separating the planes of space and time than the humans' steel cut demonic hide.

"More, give them more!" Goran stumbled from the tent, nearly stepping on the Jyotian.

The Challing's body shimmered as if seen through drifting fog. His shape altered subtly, then he began to glow like a rainbow, shifting from one color to another so fast it seared Davin's eyes.

"Goran?" Davin fought to stand. He reached to touch his friend and recoiled when searing fire raced through his hand. "Goran? What is happening?"

"The hole pulls me back to Gohwohn, yet I am compelled by Roan-Jafar's geas to remain here," the Challing answered in a quavering voice. "I am pulled and pushed in all directions!"

Goran One-Eye raised his arms – now writhing tentacles – to the sky. Maniacal laughter tore from the Challing's throat as he staggered forward to vanish in the chaos below.

Amid that mindless turmoil stood Lijena Farleigh. No longer did she wield the ensorcelled sword. She held it with both hands directly above her head. Blinding blue-white light, as bright as the sun itself, flared from the length of steel.

No! The Jyotian's mind screamed. Not Tacllyn-lin-Bertam and his fellow wizards, but Lijena and the Sword of Kwerin Blood-hawk stood at the vortex of the colliding rents! The blade focused the opposing powers! The sword drew the tears in space together!

The power! Lijena's mind reeled. In the same instant, she was nothing and she was all. She was the nexus – all magicks gathered in her. She was the conduit through which cosmic forces sizzled and rushed into the Sword of Kwerin Bloodhawk.

Madness lay around her, ready to suck her soul into the churning chaos. To focus her thoughts on any single event that raged lay the path to insanity. Time and space were torn, shredded into myriad fragments, then reassembled to be folded atop each other. To allow her mind to grab hold of even a single second of the maelstrom, to attempt to find solidity where none existed, would have wrenched her away into a shattered oblivion from which there was no return.

She closed her mind to thought and drifted with the flow, accepting that she was nothing and that she was all. A gentle melody wove; a soothing calm surrounded her and mingled with every cell of her body.

Chal!

Tears welled from her eyes and rolled down her cheeks. The tender song was Elysian, one Chal often used to soothe her pain and confusion. She sensed rather than heard its affectionate refrain. It resonated from the heart of the sword and was chorused by a lilting voice within her own belly. The melody was life; the melody was a shield protecting her from raging forces that ripped at the fabric of time and space. She would survive within the song.

Above Lijena's head bolts of actinic light shafted into the sky. Clouds awoke, swirling in an ever-increasing vortex. Beneath Lijena's feet the earth trembled.

Earthquake! Davin threw his legs wide in a futile attempt to ride the ground's undulation. Like a child who had not yet gained control of its own muscles, he fell facedown on the ground. The solid earth under him rolled and tossed as if it had been transformed to ocean waves. His head lifted and his jaw sagged open when he again saw the sky.

In pulsating rhythm shafts of blinding white light shot from the Sword of Kwerin Bloodhawk and lanced into the sky. Like a tornado abirthing, the clouds churned. Faster, faster, faster, ever faster they whirled with cyclonic fury. The swirling column darted, twisted and dipped until it danced on the very tip of the Bloodhawk's Sword.

Thunder rolled with the voice of ten thousand thunderstorms, an explosive crack that ripped through the air and rent gaping chasms in the earth. The wind screamed in tortured agony while it rushed toward the raging maelstrom dominating the sky.

And with the wind rose Faceless Ones and demon chargers. Drawn upward, too, were the Beasts of the Mist. One by one, the other-worldly creatures that had spilled onto Raemllyn through their separate rents in space were yanked from the earth and wrenched aloft where the maelstrom waited to swallow them.

When the last of the monstrosities flew upward and disappeared into the spinning clouds and wind, the maelstrom lifted to the sky. Its churning column retreated ever higher until it was a mind-numbing disc flying across the heavens.

"Bertam!" Lijena's voice, calm and steady, cut through the ear-shattering roar. "The rents are joined into one. Seal them! Seal *it*!"

Davin twisted around. From Felrad's tent deliberately filed the five mages. Their eyes were lifted to the sky. Simultaneously, their gazes shifted to the sword-bearer. In a single voice, they answered Lijena's call.

"We are the needle. We are the thread. You are the hand by which all will mend."

Light, bright and yellow like the rising sun, sprang from the tip of the Sword of Kwerin Bloodhawk. It lanced through the air in an ever expanding globe that swept down and encompassed the line of wizards. And then it burst open!

Five beams of light bounded from earth to sky. The roar died. The winds stilled. The earth quieted. The maelstrom winked into nothingness, leaving a peaceful sky of cloudless blue.

Davin Anane blinked. He surveyed the world that remained around him. Clean, he felt. The air, the world, had been swept clean.

A mountain in the form of a man trudged up the hill toward the Jyotian. "Closed! The gateways are gone! How can I ever return to Gohwohn now that the doorway has been slammed in my face?"

"There is still a way." Lijena reached out and pulled the half-completed golden leaf pendant from under Goran's tunic. She tapped it with a forefinger, then added, "But for now, there is work that must be finished."

With that she darted past the Challing and by Davin to disappear inside Prince Felrad's tent. Before Davin and Goran reached the entrance, the flaps parted and the prince stepped out with Lijena at his side. Although his pallor remained ashen, a new strength sustained him.

"Much has been sacrificed this day. It must not be in vain." His gray eyes shifted to the city below. "My army remains and Kavindra's gates are wide. It is time we entered the royal city!"

18

Lijena knelt before Prince Felrad and with both hands lifted the sheathed blade. "My Lord, the Sword of Kwerin Bloodhawk."

"This moment is one that should be surrounded with pageantry. But circumstances press close and call us to arms." Felrad accepted the sword and strapped it to his waist with no further ceremony. He motioned for Lijena to rise. "If we live through this day, I hope to show the depth of my gratitude for what you and your companions have done for me and for all Raemllyn."

Felrad mounted a charger a guard held for him. "The final assault will be two spearheads, one from the north and one from the south."

Lijena stood, a portion of the weight she carried lifted from her shoulders. The ensorcelled sword now sat with its rightful owner. She said a silent prayer that he would never learn the truth of the blade. Edan's secret would remain her burden; to reveal Edan's power would be insanity.

The ancient wizard's wisdom could not be questioned. Edan realized the blade's chance of survival through the ages was greater if shrouded in myth and mystery. Were the truth known, there would be those who sought to destroy the soul that dwelled in the sword rather than attempt to divine the blade's power.

The hint of a wry smile lifted the corners of Lijena's mouth. Nor did she believe those rallied here to win back their world were prepared for a greater truth. They believed they acted of their own free will, when in fact it was the sword, Edan's subtle influences, that had brought them to this point.

Nor was her own part any different. Her kidnapping from Harn had been no random event but a plan to join her with Davin and Goran. Nor was the demon who possessed her soul and drove her across Raemllyn to Agda's Wood mere happenstance. The wild flight had brought her to the sword and its missing sheath – and eventually Chal.

Chal, my love, not even you knew your part in Edan's grand scheme. Chal taught her the ways of the Elysian, prepared her mind for the greatest of all the Elysians – Edan himself.

Perhaps at the end Tacllyn-lin-Bertam and the four who gave their lives to seal the rents understood, she thought. But Valora had never suspected Edan guided her northward so that the sword's magicks might prepare the way for Tacllyn-lin-Bertam and his spells.

So intricate, so finely woven was Edan's work that Lijena's mind spun when she attempted to comprehend all the lives he had touched, changed, molded to bring them together at this moment.

More mind-numbing was the realization that the Elysian mage had recognized humankind's need for this moment ten thousand generations before. He had seen that magicks were not the way of humans, that spells hindered rather than aided their growth. Since Kwerin Bloodhawk first wielded the blade, magicks had diminished across Raemllyn. Edan knew that the forces brought to life by those magicks would one day surge forth in an attempt to claim this world. Thus he locked himself in the steel for eternity to await that rebellion.

Not magical, Lijena thought as she gazed at the sword hung on Felrad's hip, *but the antagonist of magic!* Now once again, magicks would continue their slow death in Raemllyn until the day, generations hence, humankind would be free of mystic crutches and adequately prepared to delve the true greatness of its birthright.

That is, if this day is stolen from Zarek Yannis. Her gaze rose to Prince Felrad's face. Color returned to his cheeks as the sword's spells gradually destroyed the tapestry of magicks the usurper had subtly cast about the prince to assure his wounds would never heal.

"Majesty," called an aide, "the Prillae forces are ready for the attack. Their commander moves her troops into place and awaits your command."

"Her forces?" An eyebrow arched high above Goran's single good eye. "My beloved Kulonna was of the Isle of Prillae."

"Lady Commander Eliora leads the forces from Prillae." Lijena let slip a portion of all she had learned from the sword.

"Ah," said Goran in obvious disappointment. "It was too much to hope that Kulonna was here. Why should she be? After

Berenicis the Blackheart kidnapped her . . ."

"Berenicis!" a nearby officer exclaimed. "Why, he was deposed in a coup. Duke Berenicis . . ."

"*Duke* Berenicis?" roared Goran. "By Yehseen's gold gonads, he is no duke. What are you saying?" Goran reached out and wrenched the poor man into the air and shook him like a terrier with a captive rat.

"H-he died. They stabbed him and filled him with arrows and threw him overboard," the aide stammered in obvious terror for his life. "That was what we heard. Berenicis became duke upon Tun's unfortunate demise."

"Goran, enough." Davin grasped his friend's arm. "We face Yannis. There will be time enough to find the Blackheart and deal with him."

"He's dead. Someone has robbed me of his blood! I'll kill the whoreson who robbed me of my revenge!" Goran tossed the officer aside. "No one robs a Challing of revenge!"

Before Davin could answer, Prince Felrad drew the Sword of Kwerin Bloodhawk and thrust it to the sky. His voice thundered: "Look above! See? See the pentagram of stars? Those are new stars, brilliantly shining stars cast into the heavens by Brykhee-dah, God of Warriors, to honor Tacllyn-lin-Bertam and the brave mages who gave their lives this day. By their pure white light we fight for Raemllyn and victory!"

Goran craned his neck and stared above. "What new stars? The sun still lights the sky."

Davin cast a disgusted glance at the Challing, then surged forward when Felrad gave the order: "To Kavindra!"

The city's gates lay wide open as Felrad led the charge. And the wide avenues within stood barren – until a quarter of the attackers passed through the gates!

Then Yannis' men attacked. Although deprived of the Faceless Ones, they came streaming from the buildings like hordes from hell. With sword, spear and arrow they threw themselves at Felrad's warriors.

With a deft sidestep, Davin met the attack of a spear-bearer, then ended the man's life with a hacking slash to his neck. Immediately, he ducked beneath another spear and drove the point of his blade into the gut of the man who thrust it at his chest.

"They charge us like berserkers!" Davin cried to Goran.

The Challing's axe separated a swordsman's head from his neck. "Look at their eyes! Yannis still has magicks at his command! He's transformed his soldiers into mindless killers!"

Davin saw it now as he blocked an overhead blow from a swordsman who stepped forward to replace the warrior who toppled when Davin wrenched his own blade free. The battle for Kavindra was far from won. Before it was decided, Goran might glimpse the five stars Felrad had mentioned.

Davin hissed a curse against the night while he and Goran crept down the unlit alley. Ahead and to the right, he heard the din of fighting but saw no one in the soft glow of torchlight issuing from the street at the end of the alley. "Half the night is gone, and still Yannis' men wait to ambush us."

"Isn't that the way it ought to be?" the Challing asked. "Ah, you humans! You fail to experience your richly emotional lives. In Gohwohn there is nothing like this. Fear, yes. *Keedehn* abound and cause us woe, but there is no love, no passion, no pathos, nothing to relieve the tedium of eternity."

"I would appreciate endless boredom now," Davin answered, sword leveled before him. "Never did I expect the fighting to be like this. Yannis' men attack, then flee, forcing us to hunt them down and draw them out like rats hidden in walls."

"The usurper's general understands and uses what strengths are at his command," Goran replied. "Worse than his fighters are the damnable traps he has set everywhere. They've claimed more lives than sword or arrow."

"Would that we could find some of our own fighters." Davin paused at the end of the alley and peered right and left. Except for the orange glow of buildings burning in the distance, he saw nothing. "The stars have moved the length of a hand since we lost ourselves chasing those bowmen."

"You might be lost, but I know where I am – in the City of Kavindra!" Goran replied enthusiastically.

"Such wisdom blinds my eyes with its brilliance." Davin grunted and stepped toward the street.

A vicelike hand clamped on his shoulder and jerked him back.

"Take another look at the cobblestones that line the street, friend Davin," Goran whispered in the Jyotian's ear.

Davin did; a shocked hiss escaped his lips. The cobblestones moved, slithered! "*Pletha* snakes!"

"Never have I seen so many hide belts and wrist straps wriggling," said Goran. "And each with enough venom to kill ten men."

Davin now saw the trap that lay before them. A section of the street had been dug out and filled with hundreds of the poisonous vipers. Yet another of the traps meant to ensnare Felrad's forces.

"Back, we'll find another route."

Retracing their way down the alley, they hastened to the west and discovered direwolves penned and waiting for the unsuspecting. From the way the fanged beasts snapped when the two passed, it was apparent the huge, shaggy gray beasts had been starved for days to prepare them for the attack. Two streets deeper into the city, the pair of thieves wove a path between pits lined with poison-tipped wooden stakes. Three more streets brought them to another snake pit.

"Yannis' general thinks more of defense than offense." Davin maneuvered toward the light of burning buildings. "He thinks more like a sapper than a commander."

"A real possibility. We meet little armed resistance. His stratagems are designed to slow us." Goran stopped and cocked his head to one side as if thinking hard. "Perhaps Zarek Yannis has no remaining army. These pitfalls might only serve as delays for the usurper to find a way from the city."

"He might have perished when the Faceless Ones tore wide the rent in time and space." Davin picked his way carefully along a street pockmarked with a series of potholes, each filled with needles meant for unwary feet. Although the light was too dim to confirm, the Jyotian imagined each of those needles tipped in poison.

"No, not Yannis," replied Goran. "Others, yes, others by the hundreds, but not Zarek Yannis."

Davin had to agree. Furthermore, the evidence lay in support of this conclusion. What general fought with such diabolical traps and ambushes when his liege had already perished? Davin was certain any soldier in Yannis' command would think of nothing but escape if the usurper no longer sat on the Velvet Throne.

"Ahead! It appears we've found Felrad's main force." Goran boldly strode forward.

Davin Anane heard a click and the creak of groaning wood. The Jyotian dived head first, straight at the Challing. With arms wide, he crashed into the back of Goran's knees.

A cry of surprise roaring from his throat, Goran toppled backward as a spring-loaded board sprang from the ground. Silver flashed as a length of wood sliced the air the width of a finger's joint from the end of the Challing's nose. Knives embedded in the board had hacked away a handful of Goran's thick red beard.

"Two good eyes often serve better than one." Goran sat up and stared at the still vibrating board. His toe tapped a loose cobblestone that had triggered the trap. "Wars can be fought in ways other than sword-to-sword."

"I prefer more open combat." Davin dusted himself off before proceeding toward the soldiers Goran had sighted.

"He is inside. The captured soldiers all agree on that," the Jyotian heard Prince Felrad's voice.

"Prince, a moment," Lijena called out. "This one was caught while laying traps for your soldiers."

Davin saw the swordswoman bring out a captive at the point of her blade. The man wore a uniform, but the insignia had been ripped away.

"Your name?"

"Lonch Porry, sublieutenant of sappers," came the immediate reply. "I am in High King Zarek's personal guard entrusted with setting snares."

The man's face was pale, but there was a firmness to his chin and voice. Neither hid the fact from the Jyotian that Lonch Porry lied.

Nor was Felrad deceived. "Since Rakell, the name of Lonch Porry has been known as the architect of the usurper's defense."

"Put him to death and be done with the whoreson," Goran suggested. "I know of a pit of furred *pletha* that will provide him a warm grave!"

"I am Yannis' field commander," Porry admitted, "but I had no choice. How could a mere mortal stand against one who summoned the Faceless Ones to do his bidding? All I ever desired was to return to my home. I am from a poor family of farmers living outside Yaryne. I seek no one's death."

"Yet you caused many," Felrad said, using the Sword of Kwerin Bloodhawk to point at Lonch Porry's handiwork. "You serve a cruel master without protest. There can be no mercy."

Felrad lifted the magical sword to dispatch the man, but Lijena interceded, placing herself between sword and intended victim.

"Stay your blow, my Prince," she pleaded. "There is a ring of truth to Porry's words. If he pledges fealty to you and returns to Yaryne, would that be enough to satisfy you?"

Felrad faltered. Puzzlement clouded his face and he stared at the sword in his hand.

Knowing the blade spoke within the prince's mind, Lijena pressed. "The time has come to put an end to the killing. This man can no longer harm you or your men. He is no threat to Raemllyn."

Felrad's gaze returned to the captive. "Do you swear loyalty to the High King of Raemllyn?"

"I will pledge loyalty to *you*," Porry answered quickly, "though you are not yet on the throne. Long live Felrad, High King of Raemllyn!"

Those soldiers nearby had not heard what passed between prince and enemy general, but they took up the cheer.

"Leave Kavindra immediately. Take no weapon with you and never again set foot outside a ten-league radius of Yaryne. These are my conditions."

"King Felrad, I accept them," Lonch Porry said, kneeling in obeisance to his new king. "As my parting gift, let me warn you of this keep. Yannis has traps in every corner."

"It shall be destroyed, taken apart stone by stone after he is put to death," promised Felrad.

Lonch Porry bowed again and backed away, then turned and hastened down the street. He tore away his uniform as he went until he wore only tattered trousers.

"As with my father before me, mercy, not fear, will be the watchword of my reign," Felrad called out to the warriors around him. He turned to the doorway to the keep. "The time has come for that reign to begin."

"Brother, wait!" Davin rushed forward when he realized the prince's intent. "Heed Porry's words. Let me enter first. My life has prepared me to avoid the traps that await inside."

Felrad's gray eyes turned to his half-brother. His chest heaved and he shook his head slowly. "The usurper's reign of terror must end by my hand. Anything less will spawn a dozen plots to unseat me. He killed my father. For that his life belongs to me alone."

Davin started to mention that Bedrich the Fair also was his sire, but Lijena pressed to his side and whispered, "The sword protects him. Let him go, Davin."

Reluctantly, Davin Anane nodded acceptance. "But allow my sword to guard your back, my King."

"Such a guard will be an honor." Felrad pivoted and walked into the keep.

Davin pressed close to Felrad to guard his back and to position himself for a hasty dash forward should the need arise. To his surprise, the keep stretched empty and forbidding. Shadows crept along the walls and only small, frightened rodents raced the corridors.

"He has slain everyone in the keep," Davin guessed.

"Or everyone has fled," the would-be king of Raemllyn answered softly.

"Not everyone, Felrad!" A voice echoed through the empty keep. "I await you."

"There!" Davin pointed to double doors opening on a central courtyard. "Zarek Yannis is there!"

Seated on an ornate, gem-encrusted throne completely surrounded by stacks of firewood was Zarek Yannis. Only the light of flickering torches set around the courtyard burned in his eyes as he gazed at the prince. Nor was there a trace of panic in his tone when he spoke: "Ah, Felrad, you have come with the Sword of Kwerin Bloodhawk. Would that I could summon Qar to take you and devour your entrails! Such was my power – but that is gone now."

Yannis' quiet composure sent icy tingles racing up Davin's spine. His eyes darted from side to side, searching for a trap.

"Qar will next dine on your soul. The true tragedy is that I cannot feed you to him time and time again for all the suffering you loosed on Raemllyn's realms." Felrad moved forward steady and unflinching.

"I'm afraid you will be cheated of the pleasure of sending my soul to Qar even once." Resignation hung in the usurper's voice. "Your hand is not fated to take my life. Divinations long ago told of my death, and it was not by steel. It was by fire – and my own hand!"

Zarek Yannis' hands lifted from the arms of the throne. Witchfire danced along his fingers, then sparked out as rushing gouts of flame that poured onto the wood surrounding him. The dry kindling wood exploded; a sheet of fire blasted high, engulfing both throne and occupant.

Zarek Yannis' death screams rent the night, echoing and rebounding off the walls of the courtyard. Then there was only the crackling and hiss of flames as the inferno hungrily devoured the tyrant who had ruled Raemllyn for far too long.

"Gone," Felrad whispered, as though unwilling to believe the fiery scene that raged before him.

"Gone," Davin repeated, sheathing his sword.

19

"Can there be any of Yannis' supporters left in Kavindra?" Lijena Farleigh stared from a window on the left side of the audience chamber's anteroom.

For the three days following the usurper's suicide, King Felrad's troops scoured the city in a building-by-building search for the remainder of Yannis' troops. Nor had the new High King overlooked those who openly or covertly aided Yannis. The bodies piled in the streets below served as a grim reminder that a new ruler sat upon the Velvet Throne.

"Weeks will pass before all are ferreted out, and longer to discover all the traps left by Porry and his men." Davin Anane moved beside her. The stench of rotting corpses wafted in the breeze.

"Felrad proclaimed his reign would be one of mercy." A distant quality echoed in Lijena's voice.

"Give him time," Goran said. "Had he let those be, he would not have lived long enough to enjoy a reign. He does only what must be done. He is even-handed in his judgments. Those who profited by the blood Yannis spilled now give their blood to assure peace will come to the land."

"Mages." An aide rushed out of the audience chamber running a hand through his hair. "The king seeks mages to advise him. Is there one wizard remaining in this kingdom?"

"He'll have a difficult time filling that request." Davin shook his head. "Zarek Yannis was particularly hard on those versed in the arcane arts. In one of the palace's upper chambers the freshly slaughtered bodies of thirty-five men and women were discovered yesterday. All were mages of varying power, none too adept yet all with some skill. It makes no sense. I would have thought Yannis would have used their powers rather than kill them."

Lijena held her tongue. Amid the knowledge gleaned from the Sword of Kwerin Bloodhawk was the secret to Yannis' summoning of the Faceless Ones. The blood and souls of those trained in magicks were the keys to unlocking the rent between dimensions.

"Mages! Traitors! By Yehseen's potent staff, I care little for such prattle." Goran scowled, his gaze shooting about the ante-room like a man seeking something to rip apart with his hands. "It's Kulonna I care about. I've sailed from Ianya to Kavindra in search of the wench. Rumor places her in Kavindra, but I've yet to find her. One hour she is supposedly with the marines in the south, the next she's aboard a Prillae flagship, and an hour after that she meets with Felrad's commanders. I've sought her from one end of this city to the other a hundred times, yet she eludes me."

"These times are hectic . . ." Davin began.

He was cut off by a page who questioned, "Kulonna? Kulonna, Duchess of Prillae? Do you seek her?"

The Challing glared at the page. "My Kulonna was of Prillae, daughter of Duke Tun. Do you know of her?"

The page swallowed hard. The fear in his eyes said he recog-nized the barrel-chested giant was more than capable of dislocat-ing an arm or two if he answered wrong. "Duchess Kulonna and her retinue now enter the palace. The High King is scheduled to speak with her before he sees you three."

"Kulonna, my Kulonna is here?" A joy Davin had never seen before on the Challing's face lit Goran's features like a beacon. "She needs me. She must know I did not fail her, searched from one end of . . ."

The outer doors to the anteroom opened and a tall brunette wearing the uniform and medals of a Prillae general entered. "Did I hear my duchess summoned?"

"Kulonna!" Goran One-Eye called. "Kulonna, I am here!"

The woman eased two dirks from sheaths at her waist and held them ready to skewer the Challing when he hastened toward the door. "What? You called my duchess's name? What possible need could the Duchess Kulonna have with a ragged street beggar like you?"

"He's her lover," Davin answered with an amused smile.

"And your death, if you don't stand aside and let me see my Kulonna!" Goran reared to his full height. Angry sparks of witchfire crackled in his good eye.

"Think twice, you overgrown oaf." This came from a one-eyed

man with cutlass drawn who stood behind the general. "Even think of layin' a hand on my niece and you'll be greetin' Black Qar!"

"General Eliora, Captain Pendross," a feminine voice called from outside the doorway, "there is no need for rudeness. I know this one."

Davin blinked, then his eyes went as wide as saucers. The woman who stepped to the threshold transcended mere beauty; she was a goddess come to earth. The admiral's uniform she wore or the twin swords adangle from her waist could not hide the voluptuous proportions of her body. Long tresses like spun white gold cascaded about her shoulders.

Goran's reaction echoed the Jyotian's. The Challing stood with mouth agape and disbelief plastered on his face. "Kulonna? Is that you? Is that really you?"

When Kulonna stepped toward the Challing it was the regal dignity and an air of absolute command. Her whole bearing bespoke a woman whose simplest utterance was to be obeyed.

This was Kulonna, but not the Kulonna Davin remembered. Kulonna, daughter of Duke Tun, had never been timid, but neither had she been so self-assured. Davin could well imagine this woman ordering the executions of any crewman in her fleet who balked at her commands. From the dark stains splattered down the left side of her uniform, it appeared she had done so recently.

"Ah, friend Goran, it has been a long time since last we met." Kulonna smiled at the Challing, then glanced at the two with daggers and cutlass drawn. "Eliora, Pendross sheath your weapons. Goran is harmless. I would talk with him a moment – alone."

Taking the Challing by the arm, she led Goran into the hall outside the anteroom.

Davin pursed his lips. There was something in the way Kulonna pronounced the words "friend Goran" that sent a chill along his spine. This was not the lusty wench who had whiled away the days in Goran's embrace. Nor was Kulonna the helpless beauty the Challing had rescued from a wizard gone mad with power. No, this was Kulonna, Duchess of the Isle of Prillae.

"She struggles to keep control of her island," Captain Pendross said when he crossed to Davin and Lijena. "The Blackheart

Berenicis kept her drugged for months. She's had a rough go of it, but there's real metal in her. Killed Berenicis herself, she did.''

"She killed him?" Davin stared at Kulonna while she whispered to Goran. "Kulonna killed Berenicis?"

"With her own dagger," Pendross assured him. For a moment the old captain studied Davin with his fogged eye. "You have the look of the Blackheart about you. Jyotian?"

Davin Anane swallowed hard. "Aye, I hail from Jyotis. The Blackheart was well known to me. Would that he had died by these hands rather than her dagger. He owed me a heavy debt."

The thief made no mention that he and Berenicis both claimed Bedrich the Fair as their father. There was no pride to be found in such a brother.

"Hmmm—" Pendross chewed thoughtfully on a wad of *mylo* weed. "Were you here for the battle? Eliora and I were with Duchess Kulonna's marines. Without us blockin' the south, Yannis would have escaped the High King."

Davin listened with half an ear while Pendross and Eliora told of their mutiny and Kulonna's rise to power. His attention focused on Goran and Kulonna. The joy he had seen on the Challing's face earlier faded to a grim mask.

"Kulonna, daughter of Duke Tun, Duchess of the Isle of Prillae, High King Felrad the Merciful herewith summons you to audience," a page called when the doors to the audience chamber opened.

Rather than a kiss, Kulonna lightly touched Goran's shoulder, then waved Eliora and Pendross to her side. The three disappeared into the audience chamber as the doors closed behind them.

"How went your reunion?" Davin asked tentatively, unable to read the Challing's expression when he walked back to the window.

"She has changed," Goran said softly. "She has assumed her father's mantle. And the Blackheart, he did – did *things* to her – things no woman should have endured . . ."

Goran's voice trailed off. He stared outside, but Davin was uncertain what his single eye saw.

"She is changed," Goran repeated, his voice as distant as his stare. "She has found another lover – a kingdom that is more demanding than any man or a Challing ever could be."

"There are others, my friend," Davin began, but Lijena silenced him with a touch to his arm. She tilted her head to indicate he was to follow her across the anteroom. "What is it?"

"Goran needs to be alone," she whispered. "He feels pain for the first time."

"Pain? Goran?" Davin's head snapped back in surprise. "Are you saying Kulonna broke his heart? Goran isn't human. He's a Challing."

Lijena's gaze fixed on him. "He's more human than you realize. Each day in human form makes him more so. Kulonna taught him what it means to love. Now she has taught him what it means to hurt, really hurt as only a human heart can when it has lost love."

"You make too much of Kulonna." But Davin's brow furrowed with doubt. That doubt deepened when he glanced at the Challing. A single tear trickled from his good eye and traced its way down his cheek.

"Sadder yet is that Kulonna loves him as deeply as he loves her," Lijena said. "But with the matters of Prillae pressing, she cannot see that or how Goran might find a place in her new life. Had they met a year from this day, things might have been different. Kulonna needs time to grow into the role the Sitala cast for her."

"Kulonna loves Goran, yet she denies him?" Davin turned back to Lijena. "How could you know that? Does she speak to you with her mind like the Urro?"

"In a way." Lijena's right hand rose to rest lightly on her belly as the Jyotian had seen it do a hundred times since they set sail from Rakell. "Davin, I am with child – a miraculous child."

Again the Jyotian's head snapped back. He was not sure that he heard her correctly.

"When I returned from Agda to my home in Bistonia, I was not alone. There was one who traveled with me, a man named Chal," she said. "No, he was more than a mere man. He was Elysian, a blind poet who saw more than any man gifted with sight."

"Elysian? They are myth!" Every word she spoke increased the Jyotian's doubt.

"Not myth, but real." She explained the Elysian ability to read and touch the emotions of humans. "It was as though Chal and I spoke with our minds to each other. There was no need for words."

The chill returned to Davin's spine when he saw the warm light in Lijena's eyes when she spoke of the blind bard. Her expression said more than her words. The love she shared during her days with Chal was greater than she would ever find with a mere man such as Davin Anane. His stomach knotted and then knotted itself again. All the things he wanted to say to her, the feelings he wanted to share now meant nothing in the face of the love she had found with the Elysian.

"My child has his father's gift. Even within my womb, he can sense the thoughts of those around us. He shares those thoughts and feelings with me. It is how I spoke with the Urro, and how I know Kulonna's true feelings," she revealed, careful not to mention that it was the son who grew within her belly that had first touched Edan's presence in the Sword of Kwerin Bloodhawk and allowed the ancient mage to touch her.

"Why do you tell me this?" Lost in his own confusion, Davin could think of nothing else to say. "Can you see into my mind?"

"Had I not, you would have died by my blade," Lijena answered. "I know now why you did what you did. You were unwittingly drawn into your actions as surely as I was. For that there is forgiveness. But I can't erase the memories or all that happened to me. Not even time will wash away the memories."

Davin understood why she had drawn him aside. Gently, she told him that the love he felt was not returned, nor would it ever be. "I . . ."

The doors to the audience chamber opened. Kulonna, Eliora and Pendross stepped out. Goran turned, his lips parted, but whatever he intended to say went unspoken when Kulonna passed through the anteroom without a glance in his direction.

"The High King Felrad will now see you," the page called.

"We should not keep the High King waiting," Lijena said as she looked at Davin, a gentle smile on her lips.

Davin nodded and called to Goran. The giant pushed from the window and walked by his companions' side as they entered the audience chamber.

Felrad, the sheathed Sword of Kwerin Bloodhawk resting

across his knees, sat upon the Velvet Throne. He smiled and motioned the three forward. "I had no wish to keep you waiting, but the affairs of state are pressing. The battles are won, but I have a kingdom to reunite. Were that all my allies of the ilk of Duchess Kulonna. The woman is open and a loyal subject. She will make an able leader for her people."

Davin felt Goran wince at the pronouncement. Where moments ago he had doubted the Challing's pain, the Jyotian found he now shared a loss with his friend.

"You look well, my liege," Lijena spoke up. "The crown of Raemllyn sits well with you."

Felrad smiled and tenderly touched the sheathed blade. "I think you know from where my good health stems."

She nodded, wondering how much of the sword's real power had been revealed to the new king. Without the interpreter she carried within her belly, she might not have known. Lijena doubted that Edan had revealed himself to Felrad in any way approaching what she had experienced because of Chal's unborn son.

"I've summoned you this morning in an attempt to show I recognize the full weight of all you have done to help me regain my father's throne." Felrad leaned forward and stared at the Challing. "Goran, called One-Eye, you above all present a puzzle to me. I am uncertain what is an appropriate boon to express my gratitude. Would you be a lord? If so, there are several city-states that find themselves in need of a ruler. The choice is yours."

"Nay." Goran shook his head when he stepped before the High King. "My arse is not meant to sit on a ruler's throne. I would weary quickly of the petty problems that plague those who wear the mantle of power. Better would be a fine saddle and a horse to go under it. Aye, and a new sword and battle-axe. A pouch with a handful of golden bits to hang from my belt to balance the weight of the new sword also would be welcomed."

Felrad laughed and nodded. "So you ask and so you shall have. My chamberlain will attend your needs."

When Goran stepped back, Felrad motioned Davin forward. "For you, my brother, there can be no greater reward than what has been denied you for so long. From this day hence you shall bear the title Davin of the House Anane, Lord of Jyotis. I have ordered a ship to be prepared to carry you back to your homeland whenever it suits you to sail."

"My liege, you do me great honor." Davin's thought spun in a dizzy procession. Years had passed since he had last stood on Jyotian soil. To return now and right all that Berenicis the Blackheart had . . .

His mind stumbled. As much as his heart yearned to return to Jyotis, another task lay ahead of him. "But I request you appoint a regent to serve in my stead, Your Majesty. Before I can return to my homeland, I have a promise to a friend that I must keep."

Davin glanced at Goran and smiled. The Challing grinned from ear to ear.

"Then I will see that you have what you need to fulfil that promise," Felrad said.

"A horse and saddle as Goran requested," Davin replied.

"So be it." Felrad nodded to the chamberlain, then turned to the last of the three. "We, Felrad, High King of Raemllyn, do hereby confer upon our most loyal subject, Lijena Farleigh of Bistonia, the title and responsibility of Bearer of the Sword of Kwerin Bloodhawk."

Felrad lifted the magical blade from his knees and held it out for the woman who knelt before him. Lijena's eyes lifted to her king, to the blade she had wielded against the Faceless Ones and accepted it with whispered words only Felrad could hear.

"Rise, Lady Sword-Bearer." Felrad held his arms out, encompassing all within the room. "Know all of you these words we speak this day. No one has fought as bravely and well as Lijena Farleigh, and none shall ever sway the confidence we have in her. In her able hands rides the defense of Raemllyn and its salvation!"

Lijena drew the Sword of Kwerin Bloodhawk from its sheath and raised it high. A faint blue radiating from the steel bespoke magicks still alive in the blade.

"Know all of you, Lijena Farleigh is now Bearer of the Sword of Kwerin Bloodhawk and captain of my personal guard!" Felrad's words echoed through the keep to be drowned by a cheer that rose from all gathered within the audience chamber.

"It's time we made our exit." Goran nudged Davin's side. "She no longer has need of us."

Davin Anane nodded and backed away at the Challing's side. Beyond the double doors, they hastened through the anteroom. Behind them the king's audience chamber reverberated with another cheer for the new captain of the Royal Guard. Davin silently prayed that the Goddess Jajhanna would shower only good fortune on Lijena and the son that grew within her.

20

"*Fish!* What kind of city serves fish when a man orders red meat!" Goran One-Eye's words came as a throaty growl when he stared at the platters of broiled fish the serving wench placed before Davin and him.

"A city where every oxen and sheep have been appropriated for use of our army." The well-endowed redhead slammed two tankards of ale to the table with no mind that the foam spilled from the mugs. "Be happy there's bread on the plate. Zarek Yannis' army appropriated all our wheat three days after they entered Kavindra."

"Fish!" Goran's shaggy head shook from side to side while he glared at his plate. "This is no fit meal for a hungry man."

Davin smiled across the table at his friend. After all the wine the Challing had consumed throughout the day, the Jyotian was amazed there was room for food even in Goran's capacious belly.

"Excuse me, sir, but I've others calling me to their tables." The serving girl stared at the Challing with eyebrow raised and hand extended.

"At least you could have asked Felrad for your own pouch of gold, friend Davin," Goran grumbled while he dug a meaty hand into a leather bag hung at his waist. He dropped a silver coin into the girl's palm. "A horse and a saddle – did you think he'd give more than was asked? Kings are as tight with their purses as money-lenders!"

"Two hundred bists should more than suffice." Davin tasted the fish; it was far more savory than it appeared. "If not, there are always gem merchants with coffers awaiting two skilled thieves."

"And there are gaming tables." A delighted gleam, the first Davin had seen since the Challing's meeting with Kulonna that morning, flashed in Goran's good eye. He hiked his tankard, held it out in a mock toast, then drank deeply. "Bah! They call this ale! Mountain spring water has more flavor!"

"I've heard they drink *lantha* piss up north," came a husky voice from the table beside the pair. "If you'll allow, I'll stand you to real ale, ale that's sailed the western coast of Raemllyn all the way from Litonya."

"Litonya!" Goran's hands clenched into hammers of flesh. "Nothing from Litonya is worth my while."

"Not even the duchess?"

Goran shoved from the table ready to demonstrate the full extent of the damage he was capable of inflicting with those fists. He took one stride toward the stranger and halted. A bushy eyebrow arched high. "Eliora? General Eliora? What are you doing here, swilling down foul Kavindran liquor?"

"Where else might I be this night?" The tall brunette stood, never flinching from Goran's one-eyed, defiant stare. "I am a soldier, not a diplomat or politician. There's no need of me in court for the High King's tedious ceremonies."

Goran's head cocked to one side for a moment as though pondering some deep thought, then he laughed. "Aye, you're right! The royal court is no fit place for man or beast. It's best left to politicians who are neither!" Goran turned and hailed a serving wench. "A round of fine ale from Litonya for the three of us!"

"No!" Eliora countered. "I am buying for him and his friend."

"Bring us *two* rounds," Goran amended and waved the general to a seat beside him.

The Lady Commander of Prillae settled to a stool; her expression was as dour as the one that had shadowed the Challing's throughout the day.

"For one who should be celebrating victory," Davin said, "you appear to walk under a cloud of gloom."

"Aye." Eliora hefted one of the tankards the wench brought to the table, drained it in a single draught, then wiped her lips. "Good."

Goran followed her example, then upended a second flagon. While Eliora lifted her second tankard, the Challing called for three more rounds. "The night is still young and the damnable heat here in Kavindra leaves one's throat so dry."

Eliora chuckled when she reached for a full tankard in front of Davin. "You are not such a bad sort, it seems. Your professed love for Kulonna blinded me to your finer qualities this morning. Myself, I hold little affection for my new duchess, or she for me.

It's been that way since we were children. In truth, she would as soon slip a knife between my ribs as look at me."

"And you, her?" Davin asked.

Eliora drained her third ale and nodded. "Now I serve her. The world has changed much in the space of a few days. I am a trained warrior, skilled in the ways of battle. But with peace upon us, I will be little more than an administrator over patrols that come and go to assure all is quiet on the Isle of Prillae. By Yehseen, the tedious task would be best served by a sheriff, not a general!"

"Aye, we are fighters, adventurers, *thieves*!" Goran's good eye flared with witchfire that died when he lifted another tankard of the heady, dark ale.

"Mayhap we should seek other places. Kavindra settles quickly into a monotonous routine," Davin suggested, but neither of his companions listened. He lifted his own flagon and downed it, hoping the ale would keep Lijena from his thoughts.

It did not. His mind kept slipping back to the morning and the secret she had revealed. Nor could he keep from exploring might-have-beens. The child she carried might have been his. Lady Lijena Anane of Jyotis might have been her title had she . . .

Davin drained the rest of the ale and reached for another. The path to madness lay in might-have-beens. Lijena's words had been clear and concise. She held no love for him, nor could he ever hope such love might spark in her heart. In time, he told himself, he would learn to accept that.

"With Felrad on the throne, thieves will not be lightly treated," Eliora said to Goran. "My orders call for all thieves to be summarily executed when caught. The High King hopes quickly to rebuild order from the chaos Zarek Yannis created throughout the realm. Catching thieves and cutpurses – bah! – is not a task fit for one trained for battle!"

"No thieves – a travesty." Goran shook his head sadly. "We risk our lives a thousand times over to find the lost sword and he repays us thus. Humans have no concept of justice."

"No adventure left," Eliora continued. "Kulonna appoints herself High Admiral and sails the western seas. She leaves me in Litonya, no more than a common sheriff. I've no desire to govern the Isle of Prillae in her stead. Is she as big a fool as old Tun, her father? Doesn't she see her absence will stir those who would plot against her as we – uh – *they* did against Tun?"

Davin's ear perked. The free-flowing ale loosened Eliora's tongue. The woman was talking treason against the duchy of Prillae! Did the lady commander seek to replace Kulonna?

"I love that woman, truly I do. But you named her right. She is a fool. She casts off all things that should be of real importance to her." Goran's tone edged toward the maudlin. "But for you, my lovely general, it seems the best of all possible worlds. An absent duchess is no duchess at all. Rule for her. Take what you can! Let her sail north and south along the coast doing Felrad's bidding, if that's her wish."

"Perhaps, but such a course is far from the path for which I was trained. What of you? There seems no place for such as you in Felrad's new world." Eliora's gaze lifted to Goran's face and remained. "And that is a pity. Men such as you are a rarity."

The Lady Commander of Prillae leaned closer to the Challing. Her hand lifted and rested on Goran's shoulder. What might have been taken as a comradely gesture proved to be a less than subtle invitation to something far more intimate. Her fingertips played their way to the Challing's neck and twirled curls in Goran's thick red beard.

"It is too bad that your heart still aches for my duchess," Eliora said in a low, husky voice. "Were it not so, my one-eyed thief, you and I might . . . uh, what is this?"

Eliora's fingers eased away, tangled in the leather thong about Goran's neck. The golden pendant forming half a leaf glimmered in the tavern's faint light.

"Never have I seen its like," Eliora said, turning the delicate pieces of the leaf in her hand. "The radiance from it intrigues me, as though it calls from some distant realm."

"The lost City of A'bre – my return to Gohwohn," Goran mumbled, apparently unaware of Eliora's advances. "When the rent in space was sealed, so was my fate. I am trapped in this miserable place for all eternity!"

"Remember the map on the ghost ship where we found the first quarter of the leaf?" Davin leaned toward his friend. The time had come to put as much distance as possible between a Jyotian thief and the new captain of Felrad's personal guard. "The map pointed the way to ancient A'bre. And if that is not enough, by all the gods, I sense your divided leaf will reveal the rest! Gohwohn still awaits you."

"Gohwohn awaits me?" Goran blinked at his friend. "Can I truly hope?"

"No, but we can seek and find," Davin urged, ready to place Kavindra leagues behind him. "The time is upon us, Goran. A'bre calls."

"A'bre! My precious leaf, my key to Gohwohn!" A wide grin spread across Goran One-Eye's face. "Yes, Davin, I can sense it, too! It is time we sought the lost city."

"You have found a destiny awaiting you." Eliora sighed forlornly. "I have nothing but tedium before me."

"Join us," Goran invited. "We can always use a strong sword arm!"

Daggers flashed in the smoky light and bit deeply into the table top. Eliora's hands clutched both; light blazed in her eyes. "I accept! I will join you!"

The trio shot to their feet, lifted their flagons high.

"South to A'bre!" Davin Anane cried.

"South!" Eliora echoed.

"To A'bre and Gohwohn!" finished Goran One-Eye.

The three upped their tankards and drained them. Goran tossed a golden bist to the table and they strode from the tavern to where Goran's and Davin's mounts waited.

"Horses? I had not considered horses." Eliora swayed in a drunken stance while she stared at her companions' mounts.

"The finest horseflesh in all of Raemllyn," Goran said proudly. "Hand-picked from High King Felrad's own stable."

"But I have no horse." Eliora blinked at the massive giant.

"You are part of a company of thieves now, General," Davin answered while he swung into the saddle.

Eliora blinked again, then grinned. "Right!"

Without concern for who watched, she untied the reins of a sorrel filly standing next to Goran's black charger and managed to climb into the saddle. "We waste time. A'bre calls to us!"

The three spurred their mounts toward Kavindra's gates. Their laughter hung in the night as they reined southward along the Isthmus of Brykheedah toward Lower Raemllyn. Only when the pinks and golds of predawn lit the summer sky did Eliora raise a hand to halt their headlong ride.

"My Prillae marines stand guard ahead," cautioned Eliora. "Their orders are to stop all who travel south. Initha, on the other side of the isthmus, is a notorious city filled with criminals and traitors. Felrad fears Yannis' supporters will gather there and attempt to rise against him."

"A city of criminals," Goran repeated. "My kind of metropolis."

"Can we get through the guards?" The night's ale no longer blurring his mind, Davin realized they faced the first obstacle between them and A'bre.

"I am Eliora, Lady Commander of the Isle of Prillae, and these are my troops. They will not question their general. I trained them too well for that." Sadness crept into Eliora's voice. "Brave men and women they are. All fought well these past few days. I shall miss them. There is no company of warriors better anywhere in Raemllyn."

Davin and Goran exchanged glances. With a nod of their heads, they silently agreed.

"There's no need for the Lady Commander of Prillae to lie for two thieves. Goran and I will find a way around. Your marines are good – we are better!" Davin winked at Eliora.

Doubt shadowed Eliora's face and then she grinned. "Are you telling me that my short life as a thief has come to an end?"

"Friend Davin is saying he understands a sense of duty and how it calls to one of honor," Goran replied. "Keep the sorrel as a memento to your brief partnership with the greatest thieves in all of Raemllyn."

"I can give you safe passage . . ." Eliora started.

Goran waved away the offer. "Davin and I will find a way, no matter how many marines patrol. Besides, as you'll discover from that fine filly, things that are stolen are sweeter."

Eliora leaned to the side in her saddle and wrapped an arm around the Challing's neck and pulled him to her. Her lips planted themselves on Goran's mouth in a loud kiss. "Kulonna is a fool for ever letting you get away, you walking mountain. I hope I don't prove to be the bigger fool for not riding with you!"

"I fear it will be I who regrets this moment." Goran returned her kiss with unbridled relish. When they parted he added, "If life on the Isle of Prillae grows too hard under the rule of its new duchess, give Kulonna my love before you drive your dagger into her heart!"

With that, Goran turned to Davin. "To A'bre!"

"To A'bre," Davin chorused, spurring his mount southward.

THE TOMBS OF A'BRE

1

Davin Anane licked dry lips and swallowed hard. The latter action merely served to remind him of how parched his throat was. A goblet or twelve of wine would go far in washing away the taste of the muddy river water circumstance had forced him to drink during the past week. The journey south from Uhjayib, a city renowned for its fierce gorillas – not all of the bestial variety – had been difficult. It had proved far more arduous than normally since it had been made on foot rather than on horseback.

"The people of Pahl are most generous with their bounty." Goran One-Eye swept wide an arm as thick as a tree limb toward the tables laden with earthenware jugs. His nostrils flared when he inhaled deeply. "Savor the aroma of all the wine brimming in those containers. And the intoxicating perfumes worn by Pahlese women! Breathe it in, friend Davin! It's enough to make your head spin."

Davin, last son of the House of Anane and recently proclaimed Lord of Jyotis by High King Felrad, gazed in wonder at the snaking line of Pahlese men and women dancing down the cobblestoned street lined on both sides with countless tables bearing a thousand times that number of bowls and jugs of wine. In Lower Raemllyn's city-state of Pahl the time of midwinter festival had arrived, and the residents of this western coast metropolis celebrated with wild abandon.

In and out through the long wooden tables twirled and pranced men and women in multihued costumes that flowed like bright liquid about the dancers. Laughing gaily, the revelers flung small presents wrapped in refulgent red and yellow ribbons to cheering onlookers who scrambled to snatch the prizes from the air.

As comely as were the women with their celebration-flushed cheeks and wide smiles and as anxious as Davin was to add the weight of coins to his empty purse, he could not pull his attention from the wine.

The Jyotian and his Challing companion, Goran One-Eye, had

spent the past month traversing the western coast of Lower Raemllyn, leaving Felrad and his victorious fighters to reclaim the Velvet Throne of the High King far behind. The road had been dry, dusty and hotter than any winter ever sent by Jalya, Goddess of the Seasons. At least hotter than any winter he recalled, Davin thought as he wiped his hands on the thighs of his breeches and edged closer to the tables and their tempting goods.

"Wine, Goran! Fine drink to tempt, then please the palate. I never thought to see wine again after you lost our horses." Davin maneuvered closer to a table on his left. If his money pouch lacked weight to purchase a jug to quench the fires in his throat, he had other talents that would provide. Davin Anane was not known as a master thief without reason.

"Lost our mounts? Me? You wound me deeply, friend Davin. 'Twas bloodthirsty brigands who cut our horses out from under us as though they were pincushions for their arrows. Where lies my fault?" Goran's single good eye followed the progress of a red-haired maid whose ample breasts appeared they would escape her bodice with each bouncing step she danced. The walking mountain in man form clamped a meaty paw to the Jyotian's shoulder. "Now there is a sight that awakens life in my weary eye! The women of Upper Raemllyn pale beside the beauty found here in Pahl."

"Brigands? Those were angry townsfolk of Elkid seeking your hide for tanning in return for the way you cheated them at the gaming tables!" Davin tried to shake off Goran's hand, but the Challing's grip remained firm.

Davin cast an irritated glance at his hulking companion. Besides the wine, the Jyotian caught sight of a table spilling over with smoked meats, sausages, loaves of bread and wedges of cheese. More important, the merchant who peddled his wares stared fully engrossed in the weaving line of dancers. What was wrong with Goran? Usually the sight of such tempting morsels set his stomach to growling. It would be easy to move while the dancers provided a diversion.

"Townsfolk – brigands? Details of little concern," Goran replied with a shrug of massive shoulders. "We eluded the whoresons! That's all that matters."

"The dust caking my throat and the protests of my belly matter more," Davin answered, trying to shake free of the Challing's grip. "If you'd unhand me, I'll tend to both in the blink or two of an eye."

"Wine, food, who cares?" Goran shrugged again. "I spy something far more interesting."

"The red-tressed wench?" Davin Anane jerked away from the Challing to watch the maid with pillowy breasts prance down the street. "You're thinking with your gonads again!"

In all the time they had traveled together, Davin had yet fully to understand his friend. The only things predictable about Goran One-Eye were his unpredictability and his unerring penchant for finding trouble where none existed but an instant before.

No man born of woman was the barrel-chested giant. Goran was a Challing, a shape-changing entity nine parts mystic and one physical. Yanked from another plane of existence by a sorcerer who bound Goran to human flesh and soon found his throat slit by Goran's hand for the effort, the Challing journeyed across Raemllyn seeking the means to return to his home world of Gohwohn.

Although *why* the Challing sought this homecoming lay beyond Davin's reckoning. To be certain, Goran described Gohwohn as a realm of perfection – a world of eternal peace and serenity, except for the occasional *keedehn*, a dragonlike creature that relished the taste of Challing flesh. For the Jyotian it sounded like the most boring place in all the universe.

Gohwohn lacked emotion, the wide variety of sense-stimulating experiences found in human realms – the very things that most appealed to Goran while trapped in solid flesh. And by all the gods, the Challing did his able best to sample every human vice, depravity and corruption available to him.

"Ah, Davin, my dear friend," Goran chided, "must you always be so single-minded? Wenches? There are wenches aplenty throughout Raemllyn. I speak of other things in this fine world – bigger things to occupy our attention."

The one-eyed, flaming-haired giant abruptly stepped forward, turned his imposing bulk and blocked two men who strode toward the wine-laden table that so mesmerized the Jyotian. With a quick sweep of hand and arm Goran artfully lifted a wineskin and passed it to Davin.

The Jyotian thief did not question but sidled into the crowd as he tugged cork from mouth, lifted the skin and let a stream of deep red liquid gush forth over his lips. While Pahl's grapes could not compare with the vineyards of Jyotis, Davin's throat offered no protest to the sweetness that rolled down it. Nor did his flagging body complain when renewed energy spread through his limbs in a warm glow.

"Ahh," a pleased sigh pushed from deep in his chest when he lowered the skin after the third long sampling. "I almost feel like a new . . ."

Davin swallowed the remainder of his words as his eyes lifted and his gaze alighted on the object Goran had spied earlier.

"Magnificent, isn't it?" Goran took the wineskin from Davin and drained half its contents in a single swallow. "An unexpected treasure, wouldn't you say?"

Davin moved forward, oblivious of dancers and merchants hawking foodstuffs that had captured his full attention only seconds ago. "How many do you count? At least fifty diamonds the size of a child's fist, I say. And the rubies – twenty rubies as big as *kelii* bird eggs, if there is one!"

"And gold!" Goran added with gusto. "Why, the platter is so immense even I would strain to lift it."

"I can barely make out the lettering on it." Davin squinted into the brightness of the noonday sun. "Something about the royal city of Pahl. Perhaps it's a gift to the citizens of Pahl from Bedrich the Fair during his fight with Zarek Yannis. It was rumored he sojourned in Lower Raemllyn seeking sanctuary for a short while. Could he have left *that* as a symbol of his appreciation?"

"No High King shows such gratitude." Goran shook his head. "Especially one fighting to keep his throne in Kavindra."[*]

"Where it came from matters not. That it offers riches beyond our dreams does."

For another, the gem-encrusted disk held aloft above the city's square by thick ropes would have been a marvel of beauty to behold. Not so for the Jyotian. When he had been falsely accused of murder and driven from his homeland, Davin discovered a quick wit and even quicker hands provided the means for the

* See *Blade of the Conqueror*

necessities of life as well as more than a few of its luxuries. The gold alone contained in the disk was enough to see to the needs of a man into his sunset years. The diamonds and rubies would assure he spent those years in a palace fit for a king – or a newly named Lord of Jyotis.

To steal the disk – Davin could not deny the race of his heart or the rush of adrenaline that coursed through his body – would be the stuff from which bards wove their songs over the generations. To be sure, it would be no easy task. Perhaps even impossible.

"No," Davin said aloud. "Nothing is impossible. It just requires thought and careful planning."

Without thinking, the Jyotian shoved aside a cleric who rudely stepped into his path. The robed priest pivoted and a growl rumbled from his throat. Remembering himself, Davin bowed and added a hasty apology. It never paid to draw attention before a theft, especially one of such magnitude.

The priest tugged his cowl lower, then straightened and looked directly at Goran One-Eye.

"Good day to you, Father," Goran greeted the priest cheerfully. "My friend has sampled too much of Pahl's fine wine this morn. You must excuse his oafishness. What temple do you serve, if I may ask? We are strangers in your fair city."

"I humbly serve Ediena, Goddess of Love and Pleasure." The priest's gaze remained locked on the Challing. The man's arm lifted and he reached out to touch the gold chain around Goran's thick neck. Dangling at the end of the chain rode half a golden leaf.

Goran eased the amulet away from the priest's fingers and tucked it inside his tunic. Davin caught a green flash of witchfire in his companion's good eye and caught his breath. The divided leaf of gold somehow held the key to the Challing's return to Gohwohn. Just what that key was had brought them all the way from Upper Raemllyn's northern reaches to Pahl in Lower Raemllyn. A show of anger from the Challing would ill serve them now.

The Jyotian breathed a silent sigh of relief when Goran contained his temper and answered, "A fine lady to serve, Ediena. I shall worship at your temple ere the day is out. Ediena has always smiled upon me, and I have always favored her with ample donations of gold."

"Your generosity will be received with gratitude," the priest replied, adjusting his cowl so his face remained hidden in shadow.

Davin cocked an eyebrow when the priest bowed again, then turned and hastened away to disappear in the crowd of revelers. Did light and shadow play tricks on his eyes or did the cleric wear a sly smile on his face when he left?

"How best do we filch such a massive gewgaw?" Goran's voice drew Davin back to the disk hung high above the town square. The winter sun set gold and jewels afire.

"Daring, my friend." Davin's mind raced in time with his pounding temples. There had to be a way to get to the disk.

"Daring, hmmph! Daring could also cause our heads to be separated from our shoulders by an executioner's blade, if that daring isn't tempered by caution." The Challing took another swig from the wineskin before passing it back to Davin. "However, it would be a pity to allow such a bauble to remain in Pahl. Look at these debauched people. Why, I spoke to a priest of Ediena. They worship only pleasure in this city!"

Goran's mock disapproval broke Davin's concentration for a moment.

"What priest? Never mind," he said while he crossed the square to a wall atop which the ropes supporting the golden disk were tied.

The Jyotian freebooter drank deeply from the skin, then leaned heavily against the wall as though drunk as most of Pahl's population. His gaze returned to the massive suspended disk. Only two ropes held it.

"Where are the guardsmen?" Davin looked at the Challing. "Were someone to reach the top of the wall, how long before they reacted? Seconds? Minutes?"

Goran's reply was a guffaw. "They won't reach us 'til they sober up. Never have I seen such gluttony and excess, save when I happened to lose my eye. But I have told you the story of how my eye came to be lost in a tun of summer wine produced by the stamping feet of a dozen Litonyan maidens."

"Later, Goran," Davin said, refusing to be distracted from the task at hand by yet another of the Challing's improbable tales of how he lost his eye. "Are you game?"

"I think we should consider another game. Mayhap cutting a few purses. 'Twould be easy enough in these crowds." Goran tilted his shaggy head to an avenue running off the square to the right. "Pahl's citizens appear to worship the platter if those paintings are any indication."

"Paintings?" Davin's head snapped to the right.

Along one side of the broad street Goran indicated, artists displayed canvases. Like religious icons, at least half the proffered works of art were of the gold and jeweled disk.

"From here they almost look real," Goran added.

"Especially that *big* one." Davin's racing heart doubled its pace as the seed of an idea began to sprout in the Jyotian's mind. "You were right about cutting a few purses. We'll need coins if we intend to be patrons of the arts today."

"Patrons of the arts?" Goran stared at Davin as though the Jyotian had suddenly lost his wits.

"Patrons of the art of thievery!" Davin laughed aloud when he lifted the skin and downed another swallow of wine made sweeter by thoughts of the gold and jewels that would soon be theirs.

2

Davin Anane cast an anxious glance over a shoulder. He saw nothing except garbage strewn along the alley. He shook his head, silently admonishing himself for what he could only describe as a case of the jitters.

Since joining the fight to overthrow the usurper Zarek Yannis and return Prince Felrad to the throne, there had been little opportunity to ply his chosen profession. He felt as nervous as the first time he had purloined fire opals from a gem merchant's heavily guarded shop.

At least a half-dozen times during the afternoon he had felt the sensation of eyes following him. Yet, whenever he had felt the hairs prickling on the back of his neck, a cautious survey of the streets had revealed only Pahl's ceaseless revelers. The Jyotian shook his head again and looked at Goran One-Eye who licked the last traces of a honey cake from his fingers.

"Are you sure you can do it?" Davin asked, unable to rid himself of the uneasiness.

Goran smacked his lips with obvious relish and grinned. "You just see to hanging that masterpiece and I'll do my part."

Davin shifted the weight of a long roll of canvas he carried from one arm to the other. An unwitting Pahlese artisan had prepared the "masterpiece" in the space of half an afternoon, his able hands steadied by a plump purse bulging with brass and silver coins. The generous payment, as well as a few golden bists bouncing gently in Davin's pouch, were supplied by the citizens of Pahl, or at least supplied by their slit purses.

"I am Challing," Goran continued. "Of course I can do it. The cart is prepared."

Davin wrinkled his nose but offered no comment on his friend's chosen method of smuggling the golden disk from Pahl. Less than six months ago they had used the same method to slip a king's ransom in gold beneath the nose of Zarek Yannis' army. He had no doubt it would fool a few provincial guards.

If there were a kink in the cat's tail, it lay in his part in the theft. Should something go awry, at least a thousand pairs of eyes would be able to identify him. There would be no denying what he did should he be caught.

"They gather for the speeches." Goran cocked his head to one side, listening to the din of buzzing voices that rose from the other side of the wall they stopped beside.

Davin hastily tied a rope to each end of the rolled canvas, then slipped it over head and shoulder to carry it as an archer might wear a quiver of arrows. Next he drew his dagger and tested its edges with the flat of his thumb. The tinker found earlier near the town square had honed both edges to razor's sharpness with his grinding wheel. Davin shoved the knife securely into its scabbard, let his gaze trace to the top of the wall, fully the height of five men standing on each other's shoulders, and finally looked at the Challing and gave a determined nod. "Shall we give the fine people of Pahl something more to talk about than local politics?"

"May Jajhana be with you," Goran invoked the name of the Goddess of Chance and Fortune.

"May she smile on both of us," Davin replied. "If she veils our risks, we'll have the fortune of a lifetime – two lifetimes!"

"Aye, that we will!" Grinning from ear to ear, Goran pivoted and with quick strides moved toward the opposite side of the wall where he would position himself beneath the jewel-encrusted disk of gold.

Davin turned to his own task, the wall itself. He found a fingerhold half an arm's length above his head. The width of a hand higher some mortar had worked loose between the blocks of rock in the wall. That was enough for his left hand. He pulled upward until his boots found purchase in a slight crack between the massive blocks. Thus he worked upward by hand and toehold until an arm stretched over the wall's edge let him scramble to the top.

Flat on his belly, Davin inched along the wall until he reached the two steel rods that jutted out from the stone above the town square below. From the ends of each rod, both at least the length of two strides, was tied a rope. At the end of each rope dangled the massive disk of gold embedded with diamonds and rubies. Below the disk on the ground stood Goran One-Eye waiting to catch the prize when it fell. Within the square at least a thousand of Pahl's citizens crowded close to a raised wooden platform where the local leaders took turns in praising the city-state, the festival, the revelers, and exhorting the blessings of Raemllyn's pantheon of gods.

Wiggling the rope over head and shoulder, Davin unknotted it from the ends of the rolled canvas and sliced it in twain with his dirk. He then unrolled the canvas half a turn to reveal two holes cut in opposite sides of one end. Through these he threaded the pieces of rope and tied them in two loops.

Once more he risked a glance over the edge of the wall. Goran looked up and signaled he was ready. Davin returned the nod before drawing a steadying breath and pulling back.

He aligned the canvas roll's width with the two steel rods, sucked down another breath and shoved the roll forward with both hands. The canvas unrolled over the rods, reaching their ends and unfurling downward to display a painting of a golden disk sprinkled with diamonds and rubies hung by two ropes against the background of a stone wall.

Belly down and with one leg wrapped around each of the steel rods, Davin left the wall and scooted out along the supports. He easily hooked the rope loops over the ends of the rods so that both the canvas and disk hung from them.

With a whispered prayer to Jajhana that the painting would disguise the truth long enough for him to sever the ropes holding the disk and make good an escape, Davin once more tugged dagger from sheath. Precariously balanced atop the rods, he pressed the knife's honed edge to rope and started sawing.

The first of the ropes parted with a twang that seemed to echo around the square. Heart lodged somewhere in the middle of his throat, the Jyotian thief glanced up. A nervous sigh of relief escaped his lips. Those gathered below never so much as turned a head, their attention held by a city official who promised increased profits for all in Pahl from taxes on merchant ships with the coming of spring.

The second rope proved as difficult as trying to slice through a hawser. Thin strands of metal were interwoven with hemp, an obvious ploy to hinder those who might attempt exactly what Davin attempted. The metallic threads left the Jyotian undaunted. Grasping one rod with his left arm for greater support, he increased the pressure behind the blade. Ever so slowly the rope frayed wide.

The final portion of the rope, no thicker than a woman's little finger, parted with another violent twang. The disk, rather than dropping straight down, swung inward, grated against the stone wall and bounced outward.

The final twang and the grinding of gold against stone was loud enough to turn half the heads below. Whether it was the light of a setting sun or the quality of the workmanship of the Pahlese artist who painted the canvas, or a combination of both, he did not know, but none in the square looked toward the disk. The simple rush held.

As he shinnied back along the rods to the wall, Davin saw Goran struggling with the immense platter. Cords of muscle stood out on the Challing's neck and arms as he caught the falling disk and held it firmly. He cleverly tossed a large cape about his body and clasped it tightly about his chest. Bent as he was by the sheer weight of purloined treasure, he gave the look of an improbably large, flat-spined hunchback who shuffled across the square toward the city's interior.

With solid wall beneath him again, Davin scrambled forward on all fours like an overgrown spider missing two pairs of legs. A chorused gasp followed by a cry of dismay brought a chill to the Jyotian's spine. He lifted his head and peered below, expecting the worst.

Davin found it!

And evening breeze stirred, and with it the canvas that flapped from the rods like a flag aflutter in a gale. Those gathered for the speeches thrust accusing fingers at the breeze-stirred painting. Politicians brimming with promise of prosperity a breath ago shouted for the city guards and demanded the heads of those who violated the Great Seal of the City-State of Pahl. The guardsmen responded, running here and there across the square, doing more than a little pointing and shouting of their own.

A hasty glance to Davin's left revealed Goran was far from safety. The Challing's escape was hampered by the seal's ponderous weight. He needed a minute or two more to reach the relative security of a nearby alley. Without a distraction to divert the now alert eyes of the guards, Goran would never make it.

Telling himself that he had prepared for such a situation, Davin sprang to his feet and began to sing at the top of his lungs the most ribald ballad he could recall from visits to thousands of taverns across Raemllyn. He staggered unsteadily from side to side and slurred his words to provide his best impression of a drunk who had been swilling Pahlese wine throughout the day.

If the bawdy song and his sudden appearance was not enough to draw all the eyes below, the bright scarlet blouse the Jyotian wore was, that gaudy blouse slipped from a merchant's table earlier while Goran held the man's attention discussing the purchase of three dozen hand-tailored eye patches. In the rays of the setting sun, the red fabric appeared to blaze with fire.

As Goran disappeared into an alley, the guardsmen below Davin began to display signs of organization. Three pairs of men rushed toward the wall with long ladders. Whether the ladders' span was enough to reach the top of the wall Davin could not judge. Nor did he have the inclination to wait around and find out. He swirled, took one quick stride and leaped into the air.

"He's escaping!"

"Stop the bastard! Or it'll be your heads that roll!"

Davin heard the guards call while he dropped to the street behind the wall. His legs gave way when he hit the cobblestones below. He fell forward, tumbled in a roll and came back to his feet in a full run. Down an alley to his right he darted as though the very demons of Peyneeha nipped at his heels. Within the alley, he ripped the scarlet blouse away and tossed it to the ground without missing a stride.

"City guards by the gate." Goran nodded toward the torches ahead while he drove the cart down Pahl's streets. "Act as stupid as you look, and we'll have no problem getting past them."

"If stupidity is the key to escape, then we'll find no snags this night," Davin answered, disgust heavy in his tone.

He eyed his manure- and urine-stained rags with disdain. These were not the togs of one recently named Lord of Jyotis, or even a man known as a master thief. Yet, if they were to pass by the guards and slip from Pahl, it was their smelly garb and the equally malodorous mountain of dung filling the cart that would disguise them. Not thieves in the night were they but simple ostlers going about their lowly task of mucking stables and disposing of the resulting manure – or that's what Jyotian and Challing wagered their lives on.

"You, there!" a voice called out. "What have you got in your cart?"

"Horse apples," Davin replied in a cracked voice that was half coarse giggle. "Fresh picked from our orchard they are. You and your men are welcome to sample to your hearts content, Cap'n. Me and Utur here always are willing to give Pahl's protectors whatever they wish."

Goran joined the charade with a deep-throated chuckle of obvious amusement at his companion's vulgar wit. "Aye, take all the apples you want. Anything for the brave men of the core!"

When Goran eased back on the reins to halt the swaybacked mare pulling the cart, an officer strode forward with a torch held high in his left hand and a drawn sword in his right. From the way his protruding gut bobbed with each step, Davin realized either Goran or he could best the man without raising a sweat if it came to a fight. The Jyotian was not as certain of the ten soldiers behind the officer. With weapons, in hand, Davin judged it would be an even match. However, his sword, as well as Goran's sword and battle-axe, were buried at the bottom of the cartload of dung beside the Great Seal of Pahl.

The guard captain stumbled and bashed a knee into the side of the dung cart when he jerked his torch higher to peer at the two grimy ostlers and their cargo. Cursing the lesser gods for the games they played with him this night, the captain glared at the cart's occupants. "If I didn't have enough on my hands tonight, I'd see you two spent a few days in chains for suggesting those in Pahl's guard ate such as this."

"'Twas the simple joke of a simple man," Davin offered softly as though attempting an apology.

"Simple mind is more like it!" The captain shook his head and waved the men behind him back to the gate. "Get this filthy wagon out of my way! It's the Great Seal of Pahl and it's thieves I want this night. And remember my leniency with you."

"Eh, how's that? The steel grate?" demanded Goran in a loud

voice. He canted his head to one side and cupped a hand behind an ear.

"Never mind." The officer shook his head again as he turned to his men. "Let them pass."

"They're of no mind to sample the fruits of our labors," Davin almost shouted in Goran's direction to bolster the Challing's deaf act. "The good cap'n says we can go, and that we should remember his kindness."

"Good, good." Goran grinned and nodded in the officer's direction. "I *will* remember him." He added under his breath as he clucked the mare forward, "and I doubt he'd forget us after this night."

The gates to the City of Pahl swung inward and freedom lay but two dozen strides away when a gravelly voice Davin half recalled hearing before called, "Be not so hasty, good Captain. Your search has come to an end. The men you seek are seated atop the dung cart.'

"What?" The captain turned and peered at a robed man who stepped out of the night from behind the cart. "Who goes there?"

Goran clucked impatiently at the mare to quicken her pace. Before the swayback could respond, two guards grabbed the horse's bridle.

"I am Juusapt, of the Temple of Ediena," the cowled man replied.

"The priest you ran into this afternoon!" Goran whispered to Davin.

"These are the men who stole the Great Seal." The priest pointed at Davin and Goran. "Look beneath the dung. You'll find the seal beside their weapons."

"I think we should abandon this tenuous position and try for the gate," Davin said softly.

"Aye," Goran answered. "Better to leave with . . ."

The two spears that pricked at his throat left the Challing's sentiment unspoken. Another pair of spears impolitely nudged Davin's side.

"I fear we've been found out." The Jyotian shrugged at his companion.

"Aye." A syllable that bespoke a heart of woe rolled from Goran's lips.

* * *

"It's not as dark as it seems." Goran's voice came from the shadows across the cell from Davin.

Peer as he might, the Jyotian's eyes could not part the darkness to reveal his hulking companion's massive form. "I know what you mean. There is a beam or two of moonlight coming between the bars of our window. See how they glint off the skull by the cell's door? Looks as if the last man to use these quarters was left where he fell and the rats stripped him clean."

"Davin, my friend! What are a few chains? Or the stone walls of a cell?" The Jyotian imagined the Challing shaking his shaggy head in mock disappointment. "I've endured far worse and lived to enjoy a long line of fine days and nights. This is nothing compared to the time I was held prisoner in the sewers of Bistonia by that city's emperor of thieves. We have merely encountered a temporary obstacle."

Davin started to point out that it was he who had rescued Goran from Bistonia's sewers and, at the moment, not one, but both of them were manacled within the Pahlese prison. "Perhaps the light you see is the coming dawn. You remember the morning? That's when the captain promised we'd be marched before a judge and sentenced to place our heads on the block. Or do you view the executioner's axe a temporary obstacle also?"

"There *is* a bright spot in all this, friend Davin," the Challing insisted above a sudden rattle of chains as though Goran tested their strength. "We were the first to steal their Qar-damned golden seal!"

"Goran," Davin said softly after a moment of lost hope that the Challing's strength had been enough to snap his manacles, "change form. Perhaps you can save yourself."

For all the charitable ring to it, Davin knew if Goran One-Eye could use his Challing shape-changing abilities now there was a chance he could save both their hides.

"I've tried, and cannot," Goran moaned. "The power has fled me."

Davin pursed his lips and sucked at them with disgust. Goran's ability to alter his form was a fickle magic at best. His power came and went without rhyme or reason. If Jajhana smiled, the

Challing might regain his power before they faced the executioner in the morning.

"Would that I could become Glylina," Goran said wistfully. "She would set our guards' eyes to bulging and find us a way out of here before sunrise."

Although Davin would have preferred the shape of some monstrous beast with the strength to batter down their prison door and make short work of the guards outside, he would have settled for Goran's female persona of Glylina. Glylina's slender wrists would easily slip from the wide manacles holding Goran.

"I think the wizard cheated me when he sold me his potions," Goran said. "He promised a return of my Challing powers. Instead, they are here one moment and gone the next. As wizards go, he was lacking."

Again Davin made no attempt to correct his friend. The sorcerer in question had promised but a partial return of Goran's shape-changing power. As long as the Challing remained in Raemllyn, he was prisoner in his human form with the occasional ability to shift that shape.

"Davin, have you thought about the priest? The one that calls himself Juusapt?" Goran abruptly asked.

"Only about getting my hands around his putrid throat," the Jyotian replied.

"A noble purpose," the Challing replied, "but not what I had in mind. For the past hours, the man keeps nagging at me. I can't get him out of my head. There is something familiar about the priest, but I can't lay a finger on it. Can you recall seeing him before?"

"Except for our accidental meeting in the afternoon, I never saw him before," Davin replied, uncertain what Goran was getting at.

"I would swear the same," Goran said. "Yet, I can't shake the feeling that I've seen the man before."

Davin remembered the sensation of being followed throughout the day. That Goran and he stood manacled to a prison wall said he should have heeded those feelings. Had he a single copper to his name, he would have wagered that Juusapt had spied on them during the day. But why? How could the man have guessed they planned the theft of the Great Seal of Pahl?

"No," Davin answered after probing his mind to recall encountering Juusapt before, "I've never met the priest before."

"Does Harn stir your memory?" a gravel-filled voice asked from outside the cell's door. There was the metallic clink of a key being inserted into the lock. The door creaked on rusty hinges and edged inward. "Almost two years ago, it was – during the Spring Festival."

"Harn's Spring Festival?" Chains rattled when Goran twisted toward the opening door. "What about the festival?"

Davin remembered the festival well. Like stealing Pahl's great seal, purloining the festival's prize money had been done brazenly in the daylight while half the city's revelers stared on in disbelief. The difference between Harn and Pahl was that Goran and he had escaped then, the prize money tied to their mounts' saddles.

"I was there." The Priest Juusapt walked into the cell with a lantern in one hand. He pushed back his cowl to reveal a pleased grin on his lips as he stared at Goran. He nodded toward the Jyotian. "I wasn't certain about you, but there was no way to mistake the big one. I only met Goran One-Eye once, but once was enough for me to remember him the rest of my life. You can never imagine the times I've dreamed of having you right where you are, Goran with the one eye."

"Me? I have never harmed a priest in the service of Ediena! There are none among Raemllyn's gods I admire more – or the pleasures she offers," Goran answered. "Why would you wish me ill?"

"I did not wear Ediena's robes in Harn," Juusapt answered. "I wore the crest of commander of the city guard then."

"Commander of Harn's city guard," Davin repeated, unable to accept the twists of fate the Sitala cast with their dice.

Goran and he had made good their escape when Goran had leaped to the judge's stand, lifted the commander of the guard high above his head and tossed him into the crowd. In the chaos that reigned afterward, the two thieves easily slipped from the city with the prize money.

"Commander of Harn's guards, hmmmm," Goran finally said. "I can see how our introduction might have made an impression on you. Not that such a dramatic touch is usually needed to etch me into a mind."

"I was driven from Harn in shame after you two escaped my men." Juusapt turned to Davin and stood studying him. "I would have become a worthless wanderer had not my own brother brought me to the worship of Ediena. I welcome the opportunity to come to Pahl and open a temple to my goddess. Pahl is far from Harn and the humiliation you two heaped on my shoulders."

"Now you've come to gloat as the wheel comes full turn," Davin said. "Will you ask to wear the executioner's hood on the morrow?"

"It is a possibility that has passed through my mind more than once since your arrest," Juusapt answered while his smile broadened. "But I fear it would not do to have a priest of Ediena seen with an executioner's axe in his hand. Rather, I bring you the opportunity to escape the fate that awaits you with the coming of the new sun."

"Escape?" Again Goran's chains rattled when he straightened with interest.

Davin's suspicion flared. Why would one who obviously relished the prospect of their deaths offer freedom – especially after he had personally seen to their capture? "Why? There's no sense in bringing the city guards down on our backs, then aiding in our escape from this prison."

Juusapt hiked his eyebrows, smiled and rubbed at his chin. "Let's say that as certain of Goran's identity as I was when I saw him this afternoon, I wanted to make doubly sure. I knew that if you two were indeed those I remembered from Harn, you'd be up to no good. All I had to do was wait and you would show your hand. After you stole the Great Seal, I couldn't allow you to slip from Pahl – not until we had this little talk. Besides, the seal is nothing . . ."

"Nothing?" Goran's eye widened in disbelief. "It is worth a king's ransom!"

". . . nothing compared to what I would suggest for a pair with your obvious talents. What I propose is worth a *High* King's ransom – or his entire kingdom!" Juusapt concluded.

Davin began to glimpse what the priest had in mind. He didn't like it, but then he had no desire to be introduced to the executioner's axe. "You want us to steal for you?"

"No, not for me. For Ediena! Your freedom in return for a

prize to adorn the Temple of Ediena!" Juusapt stared into the air as though his eyes peered somewhere in the distance beyond the cell's walls.

"Our lives for pilfering some religious icon – it sounds like a fair enough exchange to me. Release us from these chains and we'll be on our way to complete your mission." Goran did his best to hold out his manacled hands.

"And the instant you stepped on the streets outside, I would never see either of you again." Juusapt blinked several times as his attention returned to the Challing. "No, I am not fool enough to accept the promises of thieves. Remember, I once commanded the Harnish Guard."

The priest dipped a hand beneath the neck of his robes and brought forth a golden chain with a small medallion dangling from it. "Instead, I offer you this in return for the object I desire. Do you recognize it, one-eyed one?" He swung the medallion before Goran's good eye.

"Your friend has half of this medallion around his neck." Flashing in the darkness, shining with an inner magical light of its own, was a quarter of the medallion Goran sought to complete.

"The leaf! It's a quarter of the leaf!" The Challing's undivided attention hung on the swaying bauble of gold. "How did you know that we seek A'bre and . . ."

"Goran!" warned Davin. "Your tongue is waving . . ."

"He has a portion of the golden leaf." Goran's expression was a plea for help when he looked at the Jyotian. "He holds part of the key needed to return me to Gohwohn."

"Gohwohn?" Juusapt rolled the name around on his tongue. He shrugged, apparently unable to dredge up any memory of the name in his mind. "What the broken leaf means to you is of no import to me."

He reached out and pulled the two pieces of the leaf Goran wore from beneath the Challing's tunic and demonstrated that the section he wore would snap in place with the others. "This and the fourth quarter are the reward I offer as payment for your services – and, of course, your lives. As a show of good faith, this portion of the leaf is yours now. The final quarter needed to complete the design will be placed in your hands when you deliver my – bauble."

"We accept!" Goran answered without hesitation or the slightest thought to maneuvering for a bargaining position.

Not that men destined to meet with the executioner at dawn ever had much of a bargaining position to begin with, Davin thought. Still, Goran's overeagerness to commit them to an unknown task surprised the Jyotian. The lure of returning to his home world was too much for the Challing to contain.

"What is it you want us to steal?" Davin finally asked.

"Davin? Does it matter? Let the good priest free us so we can be about the task. He dangles the key to my return in front of me!"

Juusapt chuckled when his gaze shifted back to Davin. The sound came dry and broken from his throat, devoid of any humor. Goose flesh crawled up Davin's back until the hairs on the back of his neck stood on end.

"The Belt of the Virgin Goddess – that is all I require of you," the priest answered. "Bring me the Belt of the Virgin Goddess."

The chill running along Davin's spine faded as his eyes grew saucer-wide. "The belt – it is real – not legend?"

"Aye, it is real," Juusapt replied, his gaze locked on the Jyotian's eyes. "And I would have it adorn the Temple of Ediena."

In spite of himself, the last son of the House of Anane shivered with anticipation. How could any self-respecting thief turn down the opportunity to purloin one of the greatest treasures in all of Upper and Lower Raemllyn? Especially, Davin mentally amended, when it would aid a friend! And he was pledged to help Goran return to Gohwohn. Stealing the Belt of the Virgin Goddess would be an added pleasure!

3

"You entered the prison with ease. How did you manage it? We passed a small army of guards when they dragged us to the cell." Davin rubbed circulation back into his wrists, glad to be free of the manacles.

"Those from the Temple of Ediena are trusted within Pahl's walls," Juusapt answered as he unlocked Goran's chains. "Here, as I promised, a quarter of the golden leaf."

While the Challing fumbled to remove his prize from the priest's gold chain, the Jyotian eased to the open cell door. The glow cast by Juusapt's lantern dimly illuminated the corridor outside. Two Pahlese guards lay crumpled on the floor. "Trust, eh? It appears these two required additional persuasion."

Davin stepped beside the fallen men and placed a finger to their necks. He felt no pulse. Neither trust nor the Goddess Ediena had trod this corridor, but Black Qar, Raemllyn's God of Death, accompanied Juusapt into the prison.

"I'm afraid you're right. Not all in Pahl have yet to come to the way of glorious Ediena. To assure my success, I brought several jugs of wine to the guards as a show of appreciation for their service to the city," the priest answered from within the cell. "I added a few spices to the wine to induce sleep, to be certain the wine provided the desired results."

Davin frowned and pressed his fingertips to the nearest guard's neck again. He had not misread the man's condition. The chill of the guard's flesh spelled out death even if the Jyotian had somehow overlooked a pulse the first time.

A cold shiver worked its way up and down Davin's spine when his gaze moved to the guards' faces. Neither corpse possessed the blank, expressionless mask of death. Instead, their features were those of bliss as though death claimed both while lost in the deepest of pleasures.

The Jyotian's eyes widened then narrowed when his attention shifted to the unmistakable bulges straining the dead men's breeches. Something was terribly amiss here. Death released a man's bowels and bladder; it did not leave his . . .

"No need to worry yourself with them. They will awake by morning to find their heads aching with a hangover and two of their prisoners mysteriously missing." Juusapt bumped into Davin's back when the priest stepped from the cell.

Unable to contain his surprise at the unexpected contact, the Jyotian thief bolted upright and sprang away from the priest, nearly throwing himself against the cold stone wall across the corridor.

"You are needlessly nervous. We have an – agreement," Juusapt said in an unctuous voice that tripled Davin's suspicions.

"I was going to take their dirks and swords," Davin managed to reply. "If you remember, we left our own buried beneath a mountain of horse manure."

"They are there no longer. I rescued them also. They await you outside, with the mounts I have secured for you," Juusapt assured the thief.

"The third piece of the leaf is genuine!" Goran ducked from the cell and held up the three-quarters-formed amulet for his friend to see.

The soft green glow radiating from Goran's prize bespoke the authenticity of the priest's quarter. Once again witchfire sparked in the Challing's single good eye.

"Would I offer counterfeit merchandise to thieves of such renown?" Juusapt asked. "And the last portion of the leaf is yours as soon as you bring the Belt of the Virgin Goddess to me. A task you should be about. The dawn grows near, and it would not be wise for you to be found within Pahl's wall come daylight. There are few among the city guards who don't know the faces of the two who attempted to steal the Great Seal."

"*Stole* the Great Seal of Pahl," Goran corrected. "There was no fault in the thieves. It was our escape that was lacking."

"But I have remedied that." Juusapt's grin returned to his lips as he waved for the pair of thieves to follow him from the prison.

At Goran's heels, Davin moved down the corridor into the prison's receiving chamber. There a door opened onto the darkness-cloaked streets outside. From cell to street, Davin counted an additional eight guards sprawled on the floor. Like the first two, none of the eight showed the slightest sign of life.

Whatever Juusapt had slipped into the wine had not been a sleeping potion but a powerful poison. Those who trafficked in secret murders were never to be trusted, Davin thought. They lacked even the honesty to stand before man and face him with bared steel – or a knife for his back.

"The horses I have waiting are near the city's south gate," the priest said, leading the two into an alley beside the prison. "There is a small pouch of coins tied to one of the saddles. Not much – the Temple of Ediena is not rich – but enough to see that your bellies do not go empty while you seek the belt."

The weight of Davin's distrust for the priest did not tilt the scales of reason against the audacious theft Juusapt set for them. For a lifetime the Jyotian had heard rumors and tales of the magical, bejeweled belt. For a woman to wear the Belt of the Virgin Goddess meant that she was transformed into the most beautiful in all Raemllyn. Her mere smile demanded and received any wish she desired from the male who fell beneath the shadow of that smile.

It was said that Galitena, queen to the ancient High King Fuskil, once donned the belt and within the space of an afternoon set ten kingdoms at each others' throats in a war that lasted for two generations.

Should a man gird the belt about his waist, any woman he desired became his. Tytallilon was rumored to have worn the Virgin's Belt when he wooed and won Queen Mytulia's heart – and the Velvet Throne for himself.

The value of the jewels said to adorn the belt were rumored to be worth half of all of Raemllyn, but in the belt's power lay its true value. Davin could think of few, be it man or woman, who would not be tempted to slip on the belt for an hour, for a day, to obtain their innermost desires.

What would a priest, a priest of Ediena, want with the fabled belt? One who served in the Temple of Ediena had little problem finding those willing to sate his carnal lusts, be his taste for woman or man, or both. Perhaps it was not the power of the belt itself he sought, but the power the belt would give him over others Juusapt desired.

There was a fortune to be made if a man could guarantee that the most forbidden of desires might be obtained without undue risks. Ruler of city-state or the lowest of peasants would willingly pay whatever price Juusapt demanded to have their carnal dreams fulfilled. Morcover, to wield such power meant the ability to influence, if not control, those who ruled.

Davin could only speculate as to Juusapt's motivations. But the bodies of ten dead men were silent testimony to the lengths the priest was willing to go to possess the Belt of the Virgin Goddess.

"Take this." Juusapt handed Davin a folded piece of parchment when he stopped outside a darkened inn. Two saddled horses stood tied in front of the caravanserai. The promised weapons hung from the saddles. "It is a map of Faltren. The house where you'll find the Belt of the Virgin Goddess is plainly marked."

"Faltren?" Goran asked, as he admired the newest addition to the medallion around his neck.

Ediena's priest glanced at the Challing. "It is a town a day's ride south of the River Kouloun, between Pahl and Rattreh. In Faltren you'll find the home of Smeem, a merchant hired to deliver the belt to me but who has betrayed my trust and kept it for his own perverted desires."

Juusapt turned back to Davin. "Two days' ride to Faltren and back, to that add a night to retrieve the Belt of the Virgin Goddess – I will expect you here two nights hence. Follow this street south to the city gate. The guards there will pose you no problem."

Before either Goran or Davin could answer, the priest turned and hastened away, turning down an alleyway and disappearing from sight.

"How do you judge this man who allowed us to steal the Great Seal as a test of our prowess?" Davin tied sword and dagger about his waist, then unknotted the reins of a bay gelding and slipped them over the horse's head.

"Better than I would have judged him had he let us face the executioner's axe." Goran mounted a black steed with one white fore ankle. "And he did give me the third part of the leaf."

"Slip that beneath your tunic," Davin ordered when he swung to the saddle. "It still casts a green hue and will draw attention to us."

"Whose attention?" The Challing glanced about and saw no one but complied with his companion's request nonetheless. "Pahl sleeps. The only ones who might notice us are other thieves out on this pleasant night."

"There is more to what the priest wants of us than a simple theft." Davin reined toward Pahl's south gate. "Juusapt was less than generous with details of what awaits us in Faltren."

"Not that generous with his money either." Goran found a small purse tied to his saddle and opened it. "Brass and copper pieces, every one. Not one silver or gold. Enough for a few meals and nothing more. But then, that's all Juusapt promised."

"Did you notice the guards in the prison?" Davin asked, uncertain whether Goran listened or if he talked to himself.

"A fine job the priest did of drugging them," the Challing answered. "I would have preferred to have fought my way to freedom, but then I realize you often follow a more sedate way."

"They weren't drugged," Davin said. "They were poisoned. They weren't sleeping; they were cold and dead."

"Dead?" Doubt welled in Goran's voice. "Why would Juusapt kill when a sleeping potion would have sufficed?"

"Perhaps for the same reason he killed those two guards." Davin nodded toward the prostrate forms of a pair of soldiers one on either side of the open south gate ahead.

It was Goran who dismounted and confirmed what Davin already knew. "They felt Qar's embrace at least an hour ago." Goran nudged one body over with a boot, then did the same with the other. "Look at this, Davin. Have you ever seen a dead man with his member standing at attention?"

"Aye," Davin replied. "'Twas the same with those in the prison. And their expressions – are they ones of ecstasy?"

Goran bent close to one of the dead guards' faces. "As though he found in death the greatest of all pleasures. 'Tis the same with this one. Most strange, I'd say."

"Twelve men dead to assure our escape," Davin posed while Goran remounted. "I can find no reason or rhyme in it. And your gold leaf – it takes no wizard to see it is bound with magicks. Why would Juusapt give his portions away so freely?"

"Why would any except a Challing desire a key to Gohwohn?

For him the leaf holds no importance," Goran One-Eye suggested.

The possibility had occurred to the Jyotian. It did not ring true. A priest relished magicks almost as much as a sorcerer. To give away a relic that held power, even undefined power, did more than suggest Juusapt's feet trod a course known only to the priest. Nor did Davin believe Juusapt had need of companions on that treacherous path.

Davin shook his head as he nudged the bay through Pahl's south gate. "I fear Juusapt's scheme is at least twofold. He uses us to steal the Belt of the Virgin Goddess, yet he somehow devises a method to repay us, by our own actions, for the shame he suffered in Harn."

Goran glanced over one shoulder and then the other when they reached a wooden bridge spanning the River Kouloun. "We cannot abandon the theft. I *must* have the remaining quarter of the leaf if we are to find the lost city of A'bre."

"I know." Davin had no intention of forsaking the reason they had traveled to Lower Raemllyn. He was pledged to help the Challing return to Gohwohn. It was a matter of honor, even if only among thieves.

"Perhaps we should rein about, relieve Juusapt of the last piece of the leaf and leave Pahl far behind," Goran proposed.

Davin's head turned to the east and the faint hue of purple that heralded predawn. "Had we a full night, we would do just that. But Pahl is no place for us in the light of day. Not with twelve dead guardsmen behind us."

"So we ride to Faltren, steal the Belt of the Virgin Goddess, then back to Pahl and filch the final piece of my medallion from Juusapt – and mayhap reclaim the Great Seal while we're at it," Goran said in a tone that announced he considered the subject closed. "What could be easier?"

Davin tried to smile at his companion's display of bravado but could not. Instead, he tapped the bay's flanks with his heels and urged the animal into a long-strided gallop. The sooner he entered Faltren and put that city behind him, the easier he would feel.

For the fourth time in a two-hour span Davin Anane and Goran

One-Eye strolled by the home of Smeem the merchant. And as with the first three visits what they saw brought a string of mumbled curses from their lips.

"Little wonder Juusapt needed *us* for his theft. The merchant's dwelling is a fortress!" Davin paused beside the trunk of an evergreen in a small park across from the house.

"Fortress? Smeem's house is a veritable vault disguised as a human dwelling. No man would willingly live in such a place." Goran's single eye darted around, repeatedly returning to the merchant's home. "Who would expect to find such as this in a lovely town like Faltren?"

Davin almost expected the Challing to wring his hands in desperation. In their years together, in all the times they had stood face to face with Dark Qar, the Jyotian had never seen his friend so agitated. Since arriving in Faltren, Goran had fretted and worried like a young maid about to embark on her first liaison.

"I think we've overstepped ourselves, friend Davin," the Challing said with a massive shake of his head. "Smeem's dwelling appears impenetrable. Mayhap we should ride back to Pahl and rid Juusapt of the burden of the final piece of my leaf. There's no need to risk our necks going after this Virgin's Belt."

Davin did not disagree with Goran's assessment of the merchant's stronghold. High walls enclosed a wide yard. Glinting off the top of the walls came the undisputable reflection of sunlight cast by sharp shards of broken glass. Mounting those walls would quickly slice a man's hands, and probably his knees and shins, to bloody ribbons. Nor did the Jyotian spy a nearby tree with weeping limb that might provide a route above the wall and allow them to drop into the yard.

Not that the yard presented an easier course than the wall. It was worse. Packs of hounds, large, muscular boarhounds trained for the hunt, roved freely in the grounds. Twenty dogs in all, Davin counted, each with the look of a mongrel only too willing to separate a thief from an arm or a leg if that thief managed to find a way over the stone walls with their embedded glass.

"Guard patrols." Davin nodded to two pairs of armed guards who made a circuit of the grounds along a narrow dirt path just inside the walls.

Goran glanced back to the walled fortress and frowned. "Does my eye deceive me, or do the hounds remain on the grass while the guards never step a foot from their path?"

"It seems to be so." Davin watched for several moments before offering an explanation of the seemingly invisible barrier that separated men and dogs. "Mayhap there are spells keeping them apart. If so, what purpose do the guards serve save to examine anyone passing through the gates?"

"Gates?" Goran's head lifted high, and he strained to locate some overlooked detail. "I see only the front gate. The wall stretches unbroken around the estate."

"If we get past the guards, how do we reach the house unseen?" Davin continued, thinking aloud. "Smeem's strength lies in the openness of his home. There's not a tree or a shrub anywhere – nothing that might hide a man between the gate and the manor's front door."

"Assuming one can clamber over the walls and sneak past guards and dogs," Goran replied, the hint of desperation returning to his tone.

Perhaps his friend's agitation stemmed from the nearness of the last part of the golden leaf, the Jyotian thought. There was nothing else to explain Goran's uncharacteristic behavior. Nothing ever vexed the flaming-haired giant, except perhaps the unfavorable tumble of dice at the gaming tables.

"No one can get beyond those walls," Goran said.

"Wrong!" A smile uplifted the corners of Davin's mouth as the glimmering of a plan ignited in his mind. "The guards will give us a key to that gate. There must be someplace that draws them when they aren't on duty. A place where they might lift a tankard or two of ale and share complaints about their superiors."

"There was a tavern we passed down the road," Goran answered. "Shall we find a guard within and ask him to hand over the keys to the gate?"

Davin glanced at the sun that drifted toward the western horizon. "Perhaps we should consider sugar to draw the flies we want – barflies."

"I'd rather down a tankard or two myself," Goran answered starting after the Jyotian as he hastened back toward the tavern. "If my mind is blurred enough by ale, I might hope to understand you."

Entering the low door of the tavern a quarter of a league from Smeem's estate, Davin squinted until his eyes adjusted to the interior dimness. He restrained the pleased smile that sought to climb to his lips. Huddled at a corner table were two armed men sporting the same uniforms the Jyotian had seen minutes ago worn by the sentries patrolling beyond the merchant's high walls. From the look of the muscles that strained those uniforms, both men had spent more than a few years of their lives working the shipyards for which Faltren was known.

"What do you think of their livery?" Davin whispered to the Challing. "Either uniform is big enough to cover you."

"Huh?" Goran blinked with puzzlement as his gaze danced between Davin and the two guards. "Ah! Your ruse begins to take shape!"

"Now all we have to do is . . ."

Goran did not give his companion the opportunity to complete his sentence. In a resounding voice, the red-haired giant bellowed, "Ale. We require two tankards of ale to wash the dust from our throats."

Goran swaggered to a table near the guards and sank down, making a great show of brushing off his clothing. "'Tis a thirsty journey all the way from distant Kavindra and the new High King's court."

Davin settled on a three-legged stool across the table from the Challing. From the corner of an eye, the Jyotian studied the guards' reactions. Both cocked their heads slightly as though pointing an ear in Goran's direction in hope of gleaning news of any recent battles faced by Felrad and his armies.

Davin patiently waited for a barmaid to bring the ale before openly sprinkling his sugar bait. He lifted an arm and waved the men to the table. "You two, yes, you. Would you join us? We appreciate the work of the local guard. Your forces fought bravely for High King Felrad, and we would honor you."

"Us?" The larger of the two muscle-bound guards frowned in confusion. "We weren't in any battle."

"But the Faltrenians fought gallantly," Goran shooed away the man's doubts. "What does it matter if you were not there in person? Your fellows were, and your support for them helped win the day. Such succor won the day for good King Felrad. Join us."

Goran turned and signaled the barmaid. "Two more rounds for our gallant allies!"

The offer of free ale proved too great a temptation for either man to resist. For an hour they sat and listened with rapt attention to Goran's retelling of the Battle of Rakell and the fight to win Kavindra. Both seemed oblivious to the fact Davin and Goran only sipped at their own ale, ordering tankard after tankard for them. The effects, however, soon revealed themselves; one guardsman slid from table and stool to lie on the floor, snoring loudly.

"Boro, wake up, wake up." The remaining guard swayed unsteadily when he peered down at his companion. "We're on duty in less than an hour."

Davin inquired innocently, "When do you stand watch?"

The guard, eyelids heavy and neck rubbery, turned to the Jyotian, opened his mouth and stared as though he had forgotten the simple question or lost the ability to reply.

Loud enough for the tavern owner and barmaid to hear, Davin continued, "Let us help you to the estate."

Shoving from his own stool, Davin hefted the inebriated guard from his seat by an arm and escorted him to the door. Goran lifted the fallen man to a shoulder like a sack of potatoes and followed the Jyotian outside where Davin tilted his head toward the rear of the tavern. There the handle of a dagger applied to the back of the ambulant guard's head left him on the ground snoring beside his companion.

In seconds the two thieves wore the guards' uniforms over their own garments. They did not stop stripping the two unconscious men until they were as naked as newborn babes. Jyotian and Challing then dragged the men behind a clump of bushes and deposited them there to sleep off the ale.

"They will hesitate before running to Smeem in their present state should they awake unplanned," Goran said, tossing the man's undergarments to a trash heap.

"That is the general idea," Davin replied hoping Goran and he would be halfway to Pahl when the two recovered their wits. "Shall we see how effective our new garb really is?"

"The fit is tight, but who is likely to notice in the night?" Goran flexed his arms, muscles straining the seams of the stolen uniform.

Here and there, he tucked and poked away the parts of his clothing that stuck out beneath the livery.

Goran exaggerated the lateness of the hour or yearned for darkness to disguise the ill-fit of the uniform. Sunset lay at least an hour away. It was the Jyotian's hope the fading light would help conceal their purpose. What captain of the guard would expect his master's home to be pilfered during daylight hours?

Davin glanced at his own uniform and realized it half swallowed him. Even with his own clothing underneath, the uniform jacket flapped loosely on his muscular frame. He busily tucked and folded in an attempt to appear less slovenly.

"Without the aid of two or five tailors, we'll do no better. It's time to steal Juusapt's trinket," Goran said. "I am eager to get the last piece of my little puzzle." His meaty hand touched the spot where the almost-completed medallion rode on a gold chain around his neck.

"Do your best to appear disciplined. We've no desire to attract the captain's eye," Davin cautioned as they hastened toward Smeem's estate. "And stay clear of the other guards, if possible. We've no wish to be recognized as interlopers."

"The gate is open." Goran inclined his head toward the merchant's home. "No need to fret about being recognized. We simply march in and walk through the front door."

The Challing settled his heavy sword at his side, inflated his chest, and threw back his shoulders.

It would take a man with more courage than himself to challenge the image of a walking mountain in uniform Goran presented, Davin thought. Yet, he could not argue with the Challing's course of action. Boldness would allow them to seize the day – and the Belt of the Virgin Goddess.

And it was a course that would have taken them straight through Smeem's front door had not the sharp command to "Halt!" stopped them in their tracks, just a pace outside the gate.

"Why are you two late for duty?" The epaulets on the shoulders of the guard who stood in the doorway of a guardhouse built next to the wall marked him as the very captain Davin had hoped to avoid.

"Sorry," Davin muttered with head downhung before Goran attempted to bull his way through an apology. "We overstayed our evening meal at the tavern . . ."

The Jyotian let his words trail off to allow the officer to reach his own conclusion.

"Over a dozen cups of wine or tankards of ale?" The conclusion was not the one Davin had hoped for. "I won't tolerate either of you being drunk on duty again. I warned you last time that it would be the last."

"Why we . . ." Goran bristled beside Davin. The Challing possessed no tolerance of any man who would give him orders.

"No, no!" the Jyotian interjected, drowning Goran's voice with his own. "We're sober. Only a tankard each with our dinner. No more, no more than that, good sir."

The officer grumbled when he stepped from the guardhouse and approached them. He eyed the pair critically, then pronounced, "A loss of five brass pieces from your pay for tardiness. Another five for sloppy dress. Your uniforms are an eyesore. You know how Master Smeem feels about that."

Davin nodded and nudged Goran to do likewise. The Challing's shaggy head bobbed up and down, but the set to his chin showed mounting anger at this delay. He ground his teeth and his fists clenched into fleshy hammers capable of felling the officer with one blow.

"May we get about our patrol?" asked Davin, silently praying Goran could contain his rage. "We've learned our lesson – we have, we have."

"Sure you have," grumbled the officer as he walked back to the guardhouse to reach inside the door and retrieve a tightly rolled scroll. The man opened the parchment and began reading to himself.

For what he searched, Davin was not certain. However, he was sure it did not bode well for them. He had to distract the captain's attention and lead the man's thoughts down another path. "How can we work off the demerits? Ten pieces of brass is a heavy price. You know how little we are . . ."

"Password," the officer demanded. "Give the password immediately."

"Why make us even later for our patrol?" Goran could no longer hold himself. "You pleasure yourself with your petty power the way a boy finds pleasure with his own hand! Can . . ."

"Guards to me! Seize them! They are impostors!" the captain cried out. "To me, now!"

Davin's right hand dropped to the hilt of his sword, but before he freed steel from leather, Goran lunged. The Challing caught the man's left arm and flung him into the wall. The officer's head thudded against the stone wall, his eyes rolled back in his head and he slid unconscious to the ground.

"The front door!" Davin turned to the palatial home. "We can make it and . . ."

"No, Davin, I don't think so," Goran One-Eye answered.

Davin looked back at his companion and saw the reason for the Challing's denial. Ten uniformed men shot from the guardhouse each bearing a crossbow leveled at the two thieves. Davin froze. A single misstep now meant their lives.

4

How cruel are the Sitala! Juusapt sighed with deep regret when he saw Smeem's personal guard surround Davin Anane and Goran One-Eye. *They play with men's lives the way children trifle with their toys.*

He had hoped for better from the pair who had shamed him so grievously in Harn. During the Spring Festival there and again in their attempt to steal the Great Seal of Pahl, the two thieves had displayed such daring. Perhaps it was merely that Jajhana occasionally smiled on them rather than any modicum of skill on their part. His suspicions should have been alerted when he followed them through Pahl's festival without being noticed by either thief.

And last night, they never once noticed I rode behind them! The priest of Ediena thoughtfully rubbed his ample waist, noting how it had grown since losing command of the guard in Harn. The Belt of the Virgin Goddess would rest well under his robes during the day, and it would be a magically shining symbol of the Goddess of Love and Pleasure throughout the night as he inducted acolytes into the mysteries of his chosen temple.

Turning from Smeem's estate, further evidence of the pair's incompetence presented itself. Two naked guards ran up the road, wobbling in their drunkenness and shouting a warning to those within the compound. Had Davin and the one-eyed giant managed to gain entrance to the mansion, their discovery would have come but moments later.

The thieves were not only inept but unable to kill when necessary. Such softness always led to disaster.

Juusapt looked over a shoulder and saw the captain of the guard motioning his men to move Davin and Goran deeper behind the walls. Surrounded as they were by crossbowmen, their fate soon would be sealed. Juusapt traced an arcane sign in the air, wishing them a slow and painful death and realizing it was a wasted benediction. Captain Rorseg was efficient in his duties. He believed in sweeping trash out the instant the wind blew it in.

Knowing the captain's habits as he did, Juusapt felt not so much as a twinge of uncertainty. Neither thief would live long enough to whisper the name of the man who had hired them nor to reveal what treasure they sought within the merchant's home.

"Other days, other ways," Juusapt accepted the failure.

He pulled the cowl over his face and strode briskly toward Faltren's harbor district and the Temple of Ediena he had opened on the waterfront a year ago. The only thing that continued to eat at him was how the two clumsy oafs had managed to succeed so spectacularly in Harn. Had they been this inept during the Spring Festival he would still wear the epaulets of city commander!

A wry smile touched the corners of Juusapt's mouth. Mayhap he owed the two thieves a debt of gratitude he had never considered before. Had they not escaped with the festival's prize money that day in Harn, he would never have donned Ediena's robes. The priesthood offered far more opportunity for rapid advancement than did the life of a soldier – advancement that would gain the speed of a meteor once he obtained the Belt of the Virgin Goddess.

Juusapt mounted the temple's wooden steps, lost in thought. The last fading light of sunset brought a chill to air that quickened thoughts. Davin and Goran long pushed from his mind, the priest's brain churned with new schemes to relieve Smeem of the Belt of the Virgin Goddess.

There was a way, Juusapt was certain of that. Just as certain as he had been of opening a temple to Ediena in Faltren a year ago. Those in Kavindra who sat at the heart of the inner circle labeled him a madman and would have cast him from the order had it not been for his brother's influence. Ediena's worship did not prosper in small communities, they argued. It needed the desires and lusts of the city to survive.

Ediena's elders were short-sighted. They held no intimate knowledge of Faltren. Neither village nor city, Faltren was a prosperous town that thrived on the ships that continually came and went from her harbor and the dry docks along her wharves. Faltren was a town populated by the finest shipwrights in Lower Raemllyn. A town that saw a constant flow of sailors through her streets had need of Ediena and the pleasures offered in her temple.

Juusapt smiled with self-satisfaction. The first night he had opened the temple's doors a full two dozen visited Ediena. Worshippers numbering a hundred or more now visited the Goddess of Love nightly – and all brought gold, often more than collected in city temples. The elders of the Inner Circle now praised his efforts and spoke of elevating him within the priesthood.

It was here in Faltren that Smeem had first entered Ediena's worship, and here Juusapt first had learned of the belt Smeem possessed. With the Belt of the Virgin Goddess, Juusapt would assure that he ruled the Inner Circle in a not too distant future.

Comfort and pleasure were paramount in the pursuit of Ediena's ultimate grace. He knew Smeem's vices and considered the possibility of turning them against him.

Juusapt laughed aloud at his own mental stumblings. Of course, Smeem's foibles could be exploited. Juusapt saw evidence of this every day in the temple. Men and women came to him with the most improbable requests. Ediena never turned away those with gold coin desiring a quiet place to worship by following their individual paths to erotic bliss.

Smeem's carnal hungers were as great as any. The priest realized how foolish it had been to consider using thieves to steal the belt – and how fortuitous it had been for him to follow the pair of rogues here to Faltren. With Ediena's blessing, he might win the Belt of the Virgin Goddess this very night.

The temple Juusapt entered was unadorned wood on the outside. Its interior rivaled the opulence of the homes of Faltren's town leaders, all the more opulent since a goddess, not mere men, dwelled within these walls.

Crushed velvet hangings deadened sounds of footfalls that otherwise would have echoed off the beaten gold-leaf flooring. Stained-glass skylights admitted the dying light from outside, giving a softness to the corridor that belied the fabulous amounts of gold and gems visible everywhere. All this and more had been purchased in a mere year through the generosity of those who worshipped here nightly.

Juusapt ignored the glittering trappings. They did not address the inner spirit, the true essence of Ediena.

Four life-sized marble statues crafted by justly famed Inithan sculptors lined the temple's hallway, each glowing with magical inner light. Juusapt halted by his favorite – a slender, unclothed woman with delicate hands clasped behind her head, arching her back and with an expression of incomparable ecstasy cunningly graven on her upturned face. The priest reached out and placed his hand on the cool curves of the woman's artistically captured posterior.

Juusapt's eyes drifted closed as he stroked tenderly. Delicious tingles passed into his fingers and spread up his arms as he caressed the stone. The warmth grew when he pressed his palms to the statue's breasts.

For Juusapt there was more than imagined heat within the marble. The statue's substance flowed beneath his touch and responded to his intimate caresses. Moving closer, Ediena's priest placed his cheek against the statue's gently rounded thighs.

A distant bell rang three times.

Startled, Juusapt jumped back from the statue. A misty veil blurred his vision as though he saw through the mysterious inner glow of the statue depicting his ideal woman.

The melodious tolling sounded again, louder, more insistently. The priest's vision cleared to reveal the cold marble surge of an adroitly crafted sculpture. A wan smile replaced the ecstatic expression that had been in Juusapt's face but a heartbeat before. The concerns of his calling demanded his attention.

"Later," Juusapt whispered as his index finger lovingly traced the region between the statue's slender legs.

He stepped away and settled his robes before hurrying off to the evening's calling. Work – he had work to complete and acolytes to select. And there was Smeem. It was time to unburden the merchant of the Belt of the Virgin Goddess, this night if possible.

The priest paused at an open doorway beneath an intricately carved lintel depicting men and women entwined in the thousand and one positions of Ediena's Divine Love. The glow of twilight still hung in the sky, but at least three dozen worshippers already gathered in the temple's central chamber.

Juusapt smiled and shook his head, wondering how he could ever finish the calling in time for evening assembly. The calling in Faltren normally rested with Atarit, Juusapt's hand-picked priest for this fledgling temple. This evening he would oversee the duty himself. Selections had to be made for those who would pay for assembly.

A smile crept across the priest's thin lips. The eve's calling required a special acolyte, one selected to fire Smeem's loins and willingly fulfil Ediena's desire. And if not willingly, there were other means to assure the chosen did his bidding.

"Greetings, Ediena's children of love." Atarit entered the chamber from behind a flowing drapery of the purest silk.

At the sound of Atarit's voice a tremor rippled through those gathered. The anticipation of the night's duties awoke guilt. Why, Juusapt was never certain. But it was ever so, even in Pahl. The masses sought Ediena's blessing, yet felt uneasy in the revelations of their hidden passions. With time, he would change that. It was his duty.

While Atarit passed among the gathered, Juusapt entered the chamber. His sharp eyes appraised those who sought entry to the temple as acolytes. Like Atarit he dismissed most for age – too old, but never too young – physical deformities or general lack of aesthetic appeal. The majority of those who paid for the assembly held little appreciation of malformed and ugly bodies. On the other hand, it was wise for a priest to be aware of those with such tastes and provide such a menu when required.

Juusapt halted when his gaze alighted on a young woman, hardly more than a girl, who wove her way through those gathered on a path parallel to Atarit's. Dirt smeared the young, dark-haired waif's face, concealing, at first glance, her beauty.

Juusapt's eyes narrowed. The smudges on the woman's face lacked a randomness about them. Rather, they seemed to be applied with intent and purpose the way another woman might apply red powder to blush her cheeks or allow the juice of cherries to deepen the color of her lips.

If such was the case, she succeeded in blending with the other derelicts seeking only a meal and a warm bed for the night. Beyond physical beauty, the girl displayed a talent that caught Juusapt's eye. Her quick fingers worked with the blur of hummingbird wings as she lifted the light purses of those she bumped against.

This is the one, Juusapt thought as he turned to Atarit and signaled his fellow priest with a tilt of his head toward the girl. The soiled garments she wore could not hide the comely curves of a lithe body from Juusapt's trained eye. Smeem would be unable to resist the choice, and the girl would serve Juusapt – and the Goddess Ediena – well.

When Atarit motioned apprentices toward the girl, Juusapt hastened from the chamber to private quarters farther along the hallway. Atarit could attend the others selected in the calling; he would personally see to the young cutpurse himself.

Entering the sparsely decorated room, Juusapt seated himself in a chair and poured a cup of wine from a pitcher on a table beside him. He drank deeply to quiet a thirst that had nagged at him throughout his day of spying on Davin Anane's and Goran One-Eye's movements. As much hope as he had placed on the two thieves, he doubled that with the girl. He knew Smeem's tastes and desires. The merchant would be unable to resist the pleasures Juusapt would dangle under his nose.

Footfalls came from the corridor outside. Closer they grew until two apprentices, one on each side of the young woman, appeared in the open door to the room. Apprehension widened the woman's eyes although she did her best to appear calm.

"Be at ease, my daughter. Enjoy the bounty of Ediena this night and then choose your most pleasurable route through our world of woe and travail." The words came from Juusapt's lips without conscious thought, having uttered them countless times before.

The priest smiled to congratulate himself on his choice more than to soothe the girl. Standing so close, there was no way for her tattered garments to hide the fine flare of hips or delightful bulges of breasts. Her cheekbones were slightly too high for Juusapt's tastes, but her clear, green eyes held the light of emeralds in them. That was good. Smeem had a definite affinity for emeralds.

That the young woman did not desire calling this night, Juusapt realized. She sought only a few coins to get her through another day. *Still*, be reflected as he studied every alluring curve of her body, *she will be called.*

"Come closer, my daughter." Juusapt gauged the way she moved. She held herself like a young gazelle, prepared to bolt if she could not brazen her way out of this situation. *Good, very good!* She had spirit and courage. Both would be needed if she were to fulfil the mission he intended for her.

"I made a mistake," she said. "I did not realize whose temple I entered. I merely followed the others, wondering what called them."

Juusapt nodded his approval at her protest. Her voice came like soft music to his ears. Grating words spoken by a voice trained in the gutter diminished the pleasure of the flesh while softly enticing words augmented them.

"How much did you take from those in the calling?" Juusapt's dark eyes bored into hers. She did not flinch. Courage flowed in her veins. Another point in her favor.

"Not enough," came the reply. She brushed back in a very feminine gesture a heavy fall of ebony hair to keep it from her eyes.

The woman was taller than Juusapt originally estimated. When she stood straight, shoulders back, the aspect of a very young girl vanished and maturity presented itself. That was not good but a small obstacle that could be overcome with the correct attire. By the time Smeem even noticed the deception, if he did, his lusts would control him – and then it would be too late.

"Do you have a name, child?" Juusapt leaned back in the chair.

"Iesella, and I repeat, I do not care to join your temple. You run nothing but a high-priced brothel. That does not match my belief in Ebil."

Juusapt was not certain whether to laugh or explode in anger. He rose, hands on the arms of the chair. "You are not ebilsis. You do not worship the Goddess of the Frenzy. You think to irritate me in the hope I will find you displeasing and order the apprentices to cast you into the streets."

"Believe what you will," Iesella said haughtily. In a lower tone she added, "and I am sure a pervert like you will."

Her right hand darted beneath her tattered cloak and came out with a glinting dagger. Cautiously, Iesella began to back to the doorway.

"Do not go. I've need of you for a special worshipper this night."

Juusapt lifted his left hand and gestured to the apprentices.

The signal was not lost on Iesella. She spun, her dagger slashing out wildly. Juusapt had trained his acolytes in many ways of pleasure; inflicting pain was only one of those methods. Artfully the two men ducked beneath the knife and grabbed the woman's arms. The dagger fell from her grasp as fingers found the soft flesh of her wrist and gouged deeply. In the next instant Iesella lay writhing on the floor, prisoner to followers experienced in Ediena's more brutal canons.

"Prepare her," Juusapt ordered. "Use the Flame of Desire on her, but only a small sampling."

The apprentices stared up at the priest. Their expressions said either would have killed Iesella to obtain such a reward. Instead the cleric they followed carelessly gave the drug to a woman from Faltren's gutters.

"Do it," Juusapt said coldly. Softening his tone, he added, "You will share in the bounty this night. The assembly will reward you with your hearts' desires. It is Ediena's will."

Juusapt sank back to the chair and watched the acolytes drag Iesella away. He would attend her later, after the Flame of Desire boiled in her veins. Its passing would make the woman tractable – she would beg for more once she had tasted the libidinous heights to which the drug could carry her.

But first, he had to send a message to Smeem. The merchant would be Ediena's guest this night. Her *loving* guest.

Iesella moaned and thrashed. Her eyes darted about unfocused.

Juusapt stood at the foot of the bed, drinking in the woman's luminous beauty. He had been correct in his earlier assessment of the dirt on her face – a simple attempt to place a mask over the blazing radiance of her beauty.

Cleaned and groomed, the young woman equaled any courtesan Juusapt had ever admitted to the temple. Draped in gauzy veils that hid little and suggested much, Iesella awaked sensations within his core he had thought under his control long since the tempestuous days of puberty in Harn.

"Are you certain?" Juusapt asked Iesella's attendants. "It seems incredible, too incredible."

"It is so, Master," a middle-aged woman said. "She is a virgin."

"How is that possible?" Juusapt shook his head. Perhaps the young thief was indeed a devotee of Ebil. Titters passed through the gathered attendants. Juusapt silenced them with a reprimanding glance. "I would have the Flame of Desire administered again. No more than before."

"It will leave her in a few minutes," warned the woman.

"Do as you are ordered," snapped Juusapt, his patience waning.

Did they take him for a fool? How their attitude would change when he fastened the Belt of the Virgin Goddess around his waist! Even the carnally potent addictive Flame of Desire would be refused for a single minute with him!

Juusapt watched a diluted drop of the Flame roll across Iesella's lips. The woman's lush body stiffened, then she began writhing in uncontrollable rapture as though entwined in the embrace of an invisible lover. She arched her back off the bed, reached between her thighs, and then rolled over, clutching a long silk pillow while every inch of her body shuddered.

As quickly as the drug seized her, it left. Iesella sagged and rolled to her back. Her eyelids fluttered open and she peered up to Juusapt who hovered above like some bird of prey.

"More," she gasped out. "I must have more! I need it. Please!"

"You shall have more, my dear Iesella," the priest said, settling to the edge of the bed.

He repressed the desire to reach out and touch her, surprised by the attraction he felt for this woman who had wandered into the temple from Faltren's streets. This was not the Goddess Ediena come to earth in human form but a common cutpurse. The very thought of such a wench firing his blood disgusted him. Yet, Iesella's beauty tugged at him as surely as a lodestone draws iron. He could not deny the desire she fanned within him or how he ached to sample the pleasures of her body – a gift that she would offer with abandon were he to administer another drop of Ediena's Flame to her lips.

"Listen carefully, dear Iesella. You will do as I ask, and if you do, every night will be filled with unspeakable ardor. You will have as much of the Flame of Desire as you want." Juusapt reached into his long sleeves and drew out a tiny vial filled with pale blue fluid. He sloshed the liquid inside and hastily thrust the vial back into hiding when Iesella sat up and snatched for it.

"No," Juusapt said with a shake of his head as though he spoke to a child.

Undiluted Flame would kill with ecstasy. He needed Iesella. Her beauty and her abilities as a thief were perfectly matched for Smeem.

More than this, Juusapt needed her. After she stole the belt, Iesella's nights would be filled with more than the Flame. She would also have the most irresistible man in all Raemllyn sharing her bed!

Smeem strutted into the bedchamber, his eyes widening with pleasant surprise when his gaze dipped to the bed. His multiple chins quivered as he soaked in the beauty of the woman stretched languorously amid the silken pillows.

"Child, your loveliness takes away my breath." The merchant barely kept from slobbering on himself when he spoke. "Why have Juusapt and Atarit hidden you from me for so long?"

"I am only recently come to Faltren," Iesella answered, hating herself with each utterance that passed her lips.

She was weak. She felt hollow inside, an empty cavity resonating with self-loathing. Yet, loathing and hate were nothing. The drug, Ediena's Flame, was all that mattered. To obtain it she would even give her body to this loathsome toad. Never in her life had she known a man, and now she offered herself willingly to one who churned her stomach just to taste the priest's damnable drug one more time.

"I am pleased." Smeem reached into the folds of his robes to withdraw a heavy sack of gold coin. He tossed the pouch onto a low stool. "I am sure you will be well pleased, also."

Iesella almost blurted out she would rather mate with a sea squid when her eyes dropped to the merchant's middle. He threw off his cloak and opened his tunic. His chest was pasty white and looked more like dough than flesh. Smeem's gut bulged grossly like a bloated alewife, but Iesella could not slow the race of her heart or the pounding in her temples. Her breath came fast and shallow – the same sensations ignited within her by the Flame of Desire.

"Never have I thought a man could awaken this in me," she

whispered as she reached out to strip away what remained of the merchant's clothing.

The merchant danced back, batting away her groping hands. "Do not touch the belt," he cautioned. Smeem locked his fingers under a canvas money belt cinched about his waist. He thumbed it back. Beneath it rested a gaudy, heavily ornamented belt. "It is to remain about my waist at all times. *Both* are to stay fastened."

"Anything . . . anything you desire."

She made her meaning abundantly clear by stretching on the bed and opening her arms to the rotund man.

More than desire for the Flame possessed her. The source of her fiery need radiated from the merchant Smeem. As disgusting as he was to the eye, she wanted him to possess her virginal body, needed him to take her. She would not be denied.

Every cell in her body cried out in glorious agony when the merchant's hands found her body, roughly caressing the silken texture of her flesh. She groaned beneath his intimate probing, begged for him to consume the passions he set raging within her.

Only then, with her pleading for release, did the bulky merchant slip atop her and begin his obscene movement.

Although a prisoner of the desire this swine of a man awakened in her, Iesella somehow managed to recall the priest. For the belt the merchant wore, Juusapt would provide her with an endless supply of the Flame. Her body moving in rhythm with Smeem, she let her fingers run down the man's back and prise loose the golden pin holding the belt around the merchant's midsection. In the next instant the world exploded around her while her body sought and found a glorious culmination to all its carnal hungers.

Smeem spent himself quickly. As rudely as he had come to her, he now pushed away and rose to stare down at her. His expression lay somewhere between contempt and ecstasy. He shivered and rubbed his hands over his sweat-dripping arms. "The room is suddenly cold."

Through the lingering veil of pleasure, Iesella remembered the task Juusapt repeatedly had drilled into her mind earlier – a task that must be completed if she were to receive the ecstasy of the Flame. With a playful squirm, she sat up in bed, an action that caused the veils and bedclothes to tumble tauntingly from her shoulders and gather about her waist. As Ediena's priest predicted, the bloated merchant's gaze shot to the uplifted cones of her breasts.

"Allow me to provide you warmth," she offered in a soft voice of seduction while she reached for Smeem.

The merchant's multiple chins quivered again and a leer slipped across his pudgy features in answer to the undeniable temptation she presented.

The belt – the belt – the belt, Iesella repeated over and over to focus her mind on the task at hand when she once again felt the effects of the ensorcelled girdle encircling Smeem's waist. Anger, loathing and revulsion once more railed within the cutpurse. Not her own unbridled passions but the belt was responsible for the unspeakable act Smeem had performed to her virginal body – the same belt Juusapt required of her in return for the Flame.

Instead of cool fingers teasingly caressing his naked flesh, Smeem found his head abruptly covered by a silk coverlet Iesella whipped from the bed.

"Oh! I'm sorry!" Iesella exclaimed in a mock apology when she pushed to her knees and added another layer of bedding to the merchant's head. "I meant to cloak your shoulders from the cold with the silken sheet."

While her left hand tugged and pushed at the bedclothes as though attempting to free Smeem's head, her right hand found the counterfeit belt Juusapt had tucked beneath the mattress. As deftly as she snatched money pouches from unwary citizens on Faltren's streets, her expert fingers eased the true Belt of the Virgin Goddess from Smeem's waist. It took little more effort to replace it with the fake by the time she at last yanked the covers from the merchant's head.

"Will there be anything more you desire?" came Juusapt's loud question from outside the chamber.

Smeem wobbled unsteadily when his head snapped up, and he tried to push from the side of the bed. Iesella aided his disorientation by whirling another silken coverlet about him. "Please come back to bed. The night air is chilly."

Iesella yanked the sheet and sent the merchant tumbling to the wooden floor amid startled cries and groans. Had Juusapt not been so close, she would have wrapped the belt about Smeem's throat and repaid him for what he had done to her. Instead she stuffed the purloined belt under the mattress.

When the merchant gained his feet, Smeem wanted nothing more than to draw his own clothing up in front of his pudgy, soft body and hide the fat layers of his nakedness. However, when his eyes shifted toward the door to find Juusapt there, anger turned his face beet red. "How dare you interrupt! This is an outrage! I'm a paying custo – worshipper. My generous offering to Ediena is there on the stool!"

"You have sampled the delights offered by the Goddess. Would you seek more?" Juusapt answered in a tone that bordered on patronizing. A smile that reflected the same attitude twisted his lips.

Huffing indignantly and with his clothing gathered in a crumpled bundle to hide himself, Smeem stomped past the priest and stormed into the brazier-illuminated hall outside.

Juusapt closed and bolted the door behind the merchant, as Smeem should have done if he had desired privacy. Not that it would have availed him, the priest thought. In the Temples of Ediena there are no doors worshippers can totally secure. After all, there are those whose pleasure is derived by watching others lost in the heat of passion – and Ediena provided for all carnal hungers.

"You have it?" Juusapt's worried expression became a gloating grin when Iesella nodded. "Give it to me."

"The Flame," sobbed Iesella. "Give it to me!"

Juusapt pushed past the unclothed woman and yanked the Belt of the Virgin Goddess from under the mattress. He flipped it around his waist and fastened the cinch. Anticipation on his face, the priest stood leering at Iesella.

The beautiful thief merely stared back at him.

"This is not the belt!" Juusapt's shock of realization erupted into rage. "You fool! You stupid bitch! You took the wrong belt!"

"It was all he wore." Iesella blinked, trying to remember what had occurred during those fiery moments when the power of the belt controlled her mind and body.

"No, no! He wore more than this. I saw how you responded to him. Smeem wore the true belt," Juusapt insisted. "You did not steal it!"

"I . . ." Iesella's words faltered when half-memories edged into her mind.

Smeem had worn two belts. The first was only a money belt; the one beneath, the one she filched looked like the replica Juusapt had placed beneath the mattress. She moaned with sudden understanding. The money belt had not contained gold coins but had concealed the Belt of the Virgin Goddess.

"You failed me, you miserable little guttersnipe! You failed glorious Ediena!" Juusapt glared at the naked woman in utter contempt. Revulsion churned his stomach when he remembered the desire this common thief had stirred in his loins less than an hour ago. How could he have considered sharing the pleasures of the flesh with one who mated with a pig like Smeem?

"Don't blame me for your mistake," Iesella countered. "The belt sashed around your waist is the same in appearance as the fake you gave me. The fault is yours, not mine. I did as I was ordered."

Juusapt wrenched the belt from his middle and lashed out with the bejeweled strap. The end caught Iesella on the arm and left a burning blood welt. Twice more the priest struck before Iesella fought past the pain and confusion to leap from the bed and snatch the belt from Juusapt's grip. She had returned one biting lash for the three received when Juusapt cried out for his apprentices.

There came the clink and grate of metal as the door's lock slid back. Two robed men burst into the room. As they had eluded her dagger earlier, the apprentices dodged the lash of jewel-studded leather Iesella swung. Writhe and kick as she did, she could not break the hold on her arms once they seized her.

"By all rights, I should slit your throat for this." Juusapt gingerly touched the bleeding welt that rose on his left cheek. His eyes narrowed and his body trembled when he saw the wet crimson on his fingertips. "For this you deserve the agonies of Peyneeha's lowest depths. But that would be too merciful."

Juusapt pulled a silken sheet from the bed. He glimpsed darkening splotches already in the sheet, testimony to Iesella's lost virginity. The face she had given such a prize to that swine Smeem only stoked the flames of his anger. Pressing the sheet to his bleeding cheek, he turned back to the woman he had whored to obtain the Belt of the Virgin Goddess.

"Yes, Peyneeha will be a welcome residence when I have finished with you," he said. "You will return with me to Pahl. There in the lowest levels of the temple, you will serve the Goddess Ediena. There will be no Flame to fire your loins. Instead, you will service those who can offer but a few paltry coppers to Ediena – the crippled, the diseased, the beggars and any other riffraff."

Juusapt waved the apprentices away. "Take her to a secure room and see that she is bound and gagged until I am ready to return to Pahl."

The priest turned his back on the woman and the obscenities she screamed. The apprentices would soon silence her foul mouth, he thought, as he settled on the side of the bed.

Twice in a single day he had been cheated of the Belt of the Virgin Goddess. The Sitala were far crueler than he had ever imagined. He reached out and lifted the pouch of gold with which Smeem had purchased Iesella's maidenhead. It was little recompense for the loss of the real prize he had hoped to possess this evening.

"Damn them," he muttered aloud. "Qar take them all!"

They cheated him – first Davin Anane and Goran One-Eye and now Iesella. It was as though they all conspired to cheat him.

Worse, Ediena had been cheated!

5

"We simply sought food – handouts that might silence the rumble of bellies that have not known a meal in three days." Davin let his tongue follow the first course that popped into his mind.

His sharp gray eyes scanned the guardsmen who encircled him and Goran as he tried to locate the proverbial weak link that might provide an avenue for escape. He found not so much as a glimmer of sympathy in eyes that stared coldly at him. If anything, the crossbowmen's fingers tightened on the triggers of their weapons with each word he uttered.

He saw no sympathy. Only death.

The Jyotian thief swallowed hard and closed his mouth. His brain raced, searching for anything that might distract the guards for one brief instant. Given the opportunity to draw their own weapons, they would have a fighting chance of freedom.

"Inside the walls. Over there." The captain pushed to his feet and stood on shaky legs while he rubbed the back of his head. "Get them inside *now*. We've no need of gawking passersby when we dispose of these two."

Even Goran gave no more than a throaty growl of protest before submitting when two of the guards jabbed his side with arrows. Davin's hopes sank as he approached a rough-hewn post driven in the ground beside the wall, less than twenty-five feet from the gate. Though he recognized the post's purpose, the rusty red stains on the stone wall gave silent testimony to how many times this spot had been used to dispose of those attempting to enter Smeem's estate uninvited. Those who gave unholy sacrifice to omnipresent Black Qar might have worshipped here – for the past ten years or more.

"Captain, Captain!" rose a cry from the road. "Intruders. You got intruders!"

The officer turned to see two naked men dart through the gate. The guardsmen with their crossbows never diverted their gaze from their prisoners. They were too well trained. Davin cursed

Smeem's care in selection of these guards.

"Idiots!" The captain coolly inspected the two when they stumbled to a halt. "Boro, Clinn, do you think me as big an idiot as you two? You don't see my privates waving in the wind, do you?"

"We don't think you an idiot at all," Clinn began. "We ran here to warn you of . . ."

Boro nudged his companion's side with an elbow and pointed a shaking finger toward the two captives surrounded by their fellow guardsmen.

Clinn swallowed hard but kept talking. "Them's the ones. They drugged us at the tavern, they did. They stole our uniforms and . . ."

"Enough! Clinn, you and Boro tie them to the execution post," the captain ordered. "We will discuss how many tankards of ale it took to *drug* you after we dispose of them."

"Sir, our uniforms," protested Clinn. "Let us . . ."

"Now, do as you are ordered *now*," barked the officer.

Neither naked man noticed the captain's eyes narrow to slits, but Davin did. The officer's next command turned his already chilled blood to ice.

"Taat, Willit, Croman, Jate, kill the slackers," the captain said as though he did no more than call for a cup of wine in a caravanserai.

"Captain, we didn't . . ."

Boro's words died as did he when two crossbow bolts slammed into the center of his chest. The double impact threw the naked man to the ground where he lay twitching while the last vestiges of life fled his body.

The arrows that shafted into Clinn were not as kind. One caught a shoulder and the other buried itself in the man's stomach. Clutching the second shaft with both hands, Clinn sank to his knees. His eyes lifted, and he blinked at the officer who had condemned him to death. "Why, Captain? We didn't do nothing, 'cept try to warn you."

"Let it be known," the captain said in a clarion voice. "Captain Rorseg of the House of Smeem does not tolerate fools in his command. As you died, Clinn, so shall any other who fails in his duty."

With that Rorseg freed the sword hung at his side and hoisted it high above his head with both hands. Clinn mutely stared up at the weapon as he watched it fall. He died with only his spine holding his head to his shoulders.

"Let none say Rorseg is without mercy," the captain proclaimed while he wiped his blade clean. "Clinn was gut shot. He might have lived an hour or more in pain before Qar claimed his paltry soul. I eased his misery. I take care of my men – in all ways!"

Davin was so stunned by the officer's cold-blooded murder of two in his command that he forgot the guards and the crossbows aimed at Goran and himself. When he sucked in a breath to regain his senses, he saw that not one of the remaining six men had taken their eyes off their prisoners.

It was this single-minded purpose that saved Challing and Jyotian from sharing Clinn and Boro's fate.

A chorus of sheer terror tore from the guards' throats. Crossbows held rock steady a beat of a heart before tumbled from hand to ground. The ten soldiers abandoned their posts as quickly as their legs could pump. In all directions they ran as though the demons from Peyneeha were nipping on their heels. Even Rorseg turned pale and ran from the estate to disappear down the road.

Uncertain what panicked the guards, but not wishing to stand around and find out, Davin turned to Goran. "Come, Jajhana smiles on . . ."

The mountainous red-haired giant was gone. In his stead stood a creature that would rival any of Peyneeha's demons in monstrous appearance. Where a face should have been bobbed two eyes awash in a sea of melting green flesh. Rather than hair, the creature sprouted writhing silver snakes, each with darting head and snapping fangs.

For a body there was a cylindrical trunk covered in shining silver fish scales. The creature's legs were flippers better suited to an ocean seal. Worst of all were the thing's arms – reed-thin limbs that appeared more like the wings of a plucked chicken than anything else that came to Davin's mind. Both limbs thrashed about as though the creature possessed no control over them.

"Goran!" Davin blinked away a momentary start as seal flippers transformed to the hairy legs of a tricorn, the wild bull of

Raemllyn's forests. Whatever caused the return of the Challing's shape-changing ability, the Jyotian did not know, nor did he care. All he wanted was to take full advantage of their unexpected reprieve. "Goran, we have to leave! Now! Goran, can you understand me? We must escape before the guards regain their wits!"

His answer was an increased hissing from the writhing serpents growing from his friend's head. Davin took a cautious step forward and reached out, immediately jerking his fingers away before three of the vipers could sink their fangs into his flesh.

The Jyotian's chest heaved when he sucked in a steadying breath. Another might abandon the Challing to fend for himself, but not Davin. Far too many times Goran, in human and bestial form, had wrenched him from Black Qar's embrace. The time to repay one of those debts was upon him, no matter what fear he experienced. Davin launched himself shoulder first into the Challing's scaly midriff.

With a liquid gurgle from the melting green face, the shape-changing Challing staggered a step before he toppled to the ground. Davin offered no apology for his rude approach. He snatched the three-quarter golden leaf medallion from Goran's neck and rolled away from the grotesque monstrosity.

"If you want this back, you'll have to catch me!" Davin dangled the partial leaf in front of the creature's eyes, then spun around and dashed for the open gate when the Challing scrambled to legs that now resembled those of an Uhjayib gorilla.

Reaching the road beyond the wall, Davin risked a glance over a shoulder to make certain the guardsmen had not recovered their wits. However, the grotesque *thing* that Goran had become apparently had. With snakes hissing and a bubbling growl gurgling behind the melting face, the creature ran but three strides behind the Jyotian. The Challing's featherless chicken wings beat the air furiously.

"That's it, you cross-eyed excuse for a demon. If you want your precious broken leaf, you'll have to take it from me!" Davin shouted to urge on the Challing.

Instead of turning left or right on the road, Davin's long strides took him directly into the park across from Smeem's estate.

Beyond a glade of manicured grass, past a wind-rippled pond and into a dense thicket of trees and bushes he ran.

"Davin," a grating but recognizable voice called behind him. "Return the medallion. Its magicks hold my body within acceptable bounds. I – cannot keep from changing without it."

Davin skidded to a halt. Turning to the creature that lumbered to a stop on splotched legs that might have belonged to a cow, he tossed the leaf to his friend. Goran batted awkwardly at it with denuded wings, but that was enough. The mere touch of the bauble evoked an immediate metamorphosis. A pale wing transformed into a muscular arm and ham-sized hand. The clawed feet of a predatory bird shifted shape until leather boots again stood solidly on the ground.

Davin released a sigh of relief when Goran's familiar features, complete with gaudy orange eye patch covering his left eye, replaced the flowing green blob. "Can you get rid of that?" The Jyotian pointed to a single viper that poked sinuously from the Challing's forehead. "It will make it difficult finding a hatter willing to fit you."

"Never could abide hats." Goran avoided the snapping fangs as he slipped the medallion around his neck again.

As though preparing for meditation, he sank to the ground and crossed his legs. Gradually the snake receded and changed into a wayward lock of bright red hair. Goran's good eye lifted to his companion.

Seldom had Davin seen the witchfire burn so brightly in that orb.

"What went on back there? I remember the two naked guards being slaughtered like lambs, but . . ." Goran shook his head.

Davin arched an eyebrow. "You don't remember?"

Goran shrugged. "I don't even recall thinking about altering my form. For weeks the power has eluded me."

"You lost control of your shape," Davin said half in question and half in explanation. Since Goran had regained a portion of the ability to shape-shift, he had always remained fully cognizant of those changes. "The transformation was not complete – or rather it was too complete but with too many different creatures. Snakes and birds and who knows what else, all seizing your body at the same time. The way they shifted was a sight to behold."

Davin tried to repress a shudder and failed. Goran had been too frightening.

"When you plucked the medallion from my neck, I remembered how to return to this body." Goran stared down at the partial leaf. "It is curious, is it not, friend Davin? Only when I lost the medallion did I recall Goran One-Eye. Yet, without these three small pieces of gold I could not will my shape to change. There are powers within this metal I cannot fathom. What will be revealed to me when it is whole?"

A new shiver worked its way along Davin's spine. He never relished the working of magicks and did not like to consider what transformations might occur within the Challing when they acquired the last part of the leaf. "Unless we discover a way into the merchant's house, you will never see the final piece of your leaf puzzle."

"True." Goran began to strip away the confining uniform he wore. "'Twas a good plan, but not good enough. Perhaps if we had waited until twilight passed, we might have had better luck with the ruse."

Davin was not interested in "ifs" or "might have beens". Nor was he willing to abandon the task they had begun, although common sense and caution told him the priest Juusapt wanted their lives as well as the Belt of the Virgin Goddess.

"Brains," Davin said decisively. "We need to use our heads for something more than hats – or snake pits."

"We tried to move too quickly," Goran said. "We need more time to study the merchant's estate."

"Or the merchant and his family," Davin added. "Perhaps if there is no way for us to get within those walls, there is a way to make someone within bring us what we need. Does Smeem have a family? Does he value a wife or daughter? An only son to inherit and carry on the name and fortune?"

"Kidnap a member of Smeem's family?" Goran's single eye widened. "We are thieves! Could you lower yourself to such an act?"

In truth Davin felt the same but said, "Stealing a belt or another human – is there any difference? I stole Lijena Farleigh to free you from Bistonia's sewers. Why not a member of the merchant's family in exchange for the belt? It might be the only way to get the last piece of your leaf."

Goran fell silent but nodded his head in acceptance.

"If need be, we'll watch the mansion this night and the morrow. That will give us tomorrow night to get the belt, the next day for the return to Pahl where we'll meet with Juusapt as planned," Davin said, slipping out of the uniform he wore. "We can hide in one of the trees closer to the house."

The rough bark of a *chiin* tree had begun to turn their backsides to ground meat before either man or Challing saw a hint of movement near the house. A carriage drawn by two horses rolled from behind the mansion and halted before the front door.

"A fat old poltroon, I would say," Goran said while he stood on the limb that had held him for the past hour. "He has no fewer than five guards with him inside the carriage, riding outside and dangling from those flimsy handles at the rear. It must be the merchant himself."

"Then we follow. Better to take the merchant than some innocent." Davin swung from limb to ground. "Five guards to protect a merchant seems far too many, unless Smeem has countless enemies in Faltren. More likely, he wears the Belt of the Virgin Goddess and wants to make sure he doesn't run into thieves."

"Like ourselves?" Goran dropped to the ground beside the Jyotian.

"Exactly!" Davin moved through the shadows after the carriage as it rolled from the estate and moved toward the central portion of the town.

Goran turned to his companion in puzzlement when the carriage finally rolled to a halt. "The bazaar? The man goes in search of turnips at night? Most food stalls have closed. Only a few shops have lights in their windows."

"A task more suited for servants," Davin agreed, watching Smeem disappear into a shop with a sign outside proclaiming the freshness of the fruits and sweets it carried. "Unless Smeem prepares his own meals?"

"Might be how he achieved his immense proportions," Goran answered. "The man *does* have a girth about him that would serve two men well."

Davin eased closer to the carriage, careful that he remained deep within the shadows. One face-to-face confrontation with the merchant's guards was enough for this day.

"This makes less sense by the moment," Goran whispered at the Jyotian's side. "Now Smeem enters a butcher's shop. Does he buy a lamb chop to go with his turnip?"

"And the five guards stay right at his side," Davin replied. "What need does a man have of bodyguards when he's purchasing parsnips and mutton?"

"Mayhap he's here for other reasons." Goran tapped his companion's shoulder and pointed down the cobblestone street. "He has the look of a priest about him – a priest of Ediena by the hue and the fine weave of his robes."

With that Davin agreed. Those in the service of Raemllyn's other gods usually wore coarsely spun fabric. For the priests of Ediena, who profited in one of humankind's oldest enterprises thinly veiled as religion, linen and sometimes silk robed their dissipated bodies.

"The priest pauses outside the butcher's shop," Davin noted aloud. "Perhaps Smeem seeks more than meat and vegetables tonight."

As the two thieves watched from the darkness of an alley, Smeem and his guards exited the butcher's shop. Nor did the merchant appear surprised to discover the priest waiting in the night. After several minutes of unheard words and arm gesturing, Smeem, the priest and five bodyguards got into the carriage. The driver flicked a whip over the horses' backs and the carriage trundled down the street.

When the two thieves stepped from the alley intent on following merchant and priest, a cart drawn by a single ox rolled in front of the butcher's shop. Two men began to load sides of beef into the cart.

"Ho, Knilen." The door to the fruit vendor's shop opened. "Is there room enough in your cart for my goods tonight?"

One of the men carrying the dressed beef turned and answered. "More than enough room, Paloten." The butcher Knilen paused to scratch his bald head. "I'm not complainin', mind you, but have you noticed Smeem buys enough to feed an army?"

The other shopkeeper laughed. "He *is* feeding an army. Haven't you noticed all the guards he employs? It's the late hours he keeps that I mind – although not *that* much. He's worth ten of my other patrons. And he sometimes even pays promptly!"

"I think we both know why Smeem keeps such hours," the butcher chuckled. "The priest from the Temple of Ediena was waiting for him again. I overheard them mention Juusapt's name and something about a virgin waiting this night."

It was Paloten's turn to laugh as he turned back to his shop. "A virgin in the Temple of Ediena? The day that happens Father Yehseen will walk among us again."

Goran chuckled in Davin's ear. "Did you hear that? It seems Juusapt has followed us to Faltren. Do you suppose he lacks trust in us?"

"Would you trust someone who sent you flying into the crowds at Harn's Spring Festival?" Davin answered. "More likely, our erstwhile employer is trying to filch the Belt of the Virgin Goddess without our aid."

"Bah, an amateur meddling where he shouldn't." Goran spat onto the street. "He'll end up a pincushion for crossbow bolts ere he succeeds."

"Not that such a fate would ever happen to two such as we," Davin replied sardonically, although he agreed with the Challing. Had Juusapt thought himself capable of purloining the Belt of the Virgin Goddess, he would never have gone to such great lengths to secure their aid.

Still, Juusapt's presence in Faltren bothered the Jyotian. What did the priest plan that went beyond simple theft – although snatching the Belt of the Virgin Goddess had been anything but simple to this point? Davin could not forget the malice in Juusapt's voice when the priest recalled the day they first had met in Harn. Whatever payment Juusapt had in mind for their services, Davin was certain, did not include delivering the final piece of Goran's golden leaf. More likely it entailed a slow and painful death for one born of Jyotis and a Challing plucked from the realm of Gohwohn.

"Were there a way to assure that Juusapt doesn't snatch the belt while Smeem is in the temple," Davin thought aloud. "But there is nothing I can think of to stop him."

"Except Ediena," Goran answered with a wink.

"What?" Davin frowned, uncertain what the Challing was trying to say.

"There is none among those who follow Ediena who can do the deed, my friend," Goran continued. "Not that one with my ability to attract women has ever had need to purchase a roll in the hay in one of Ediena's temples, you understand, but it is well known that priests who follow Ediena can't thieve or rob. I first learned that fact from a comely young thing just entered as an acolyte to that most gracious of Raemllyn's goddesses. It was how I lost my left eye, you know. It was in Ahvayuh, which sits across the width of Lower Raemllyn from Pahl that I . . ."

"Goran!" Davin did not have time for another of the Challing's far-fetched yarns detailing how he lost his eye in some lusty adventure. "What do you mean the priests of Ediena can't thieve or rob?"

"It's against their beliefs." Goran shrugged. "All pleasures of the flesh are permitted them, but they are not allowed to obtain material goods, except those given by the church. To steal or rob a mere mundane item is their greatest sin, punishable by death should any in their order learn of their act. Why else would Juusapt hire us?"

"Why else indeed!" Davin grinned. With five alert guards at Smeem's side, the Jyotian doubted Juusapt would be stupid enough to attempt a theft within Ediena's own temple. "If he hired us, he could hire others."

"He probably has." Again Goran shrugged as they started down the street to find Faltren's Temple of Ediena. "Someone's blood had to stain the wall within Smeem's estate. That's why he chose us. We do have a reputation that often precedes us."

Davin rubbed a hand over his chin. Religious conviction or not, he did not put it past Juusapt to try something in the temple tonight. Why else would the priest have journeyed to Faltren? A man who poisoned twelve men in Pahl was definitely not to be trusted.

"There." Goran pointed to a brightly lit building near the town's wharf district. "You can smell the perfumes and incense from here. A copper will get you a golden bist if that's not Ediena's temple."

Goran failed to mention that Smeem's carriage and guards stood outside the wooden building.

"If there's a back entrance, we could sneak in and snatch the belt from under Juusapt's nose." Goran grinned from ear to ear. "Master Smeem will be too busy to notice until it's too late!"

Davin shook his head. "I think it's already too late."

While the two watched, a naked man, rolls of fat aquiver and clothes clutched over his privates, ran from the temple's open door. In the space of three blinks of the eye, Smeem and guards were in the carriage which did a sharp turn and raced down the street right past the thieves.

"I fear Juusapt tried something untoward, as you suspected, friend Davin." Goran turned and watched the carriage disappear around a distant corner. "From appearances, the priest accomplished no more than angering the merchant."

"And cost us the possibility of getting at Smeem while he was outside those damnable walls of his!" Davin felt frustration well within him. He was certain the priest had attempted to steal the belt, and in doing so destroyed any chance of getting to Smeem this night.

"What we need is a fancy carriage like the merchant's," Goran said wistfully. "Then we could just ride through his gates and roll up to the front door."

"Carriage!" Davin's head snapped around, and he grinned at his companion. "But there is a carriage waiting for us. One heading right to Smeem's house!"

"Carriage?" A grin to match Davin's spread across Goran's face when he grasped the Jyotian's meaning. "The butcher's cart!"

"We've hidden beneath worse than slabs of meat and fruit to get where we've wanted to be before." Davin started running along the cobblestone street with Goran at his side.

They found the cart and its driver still outside the butcher's shop. Darting down a side street, the two thieves ran ahead, then moved through an alley that opened along the route to Smeem's mansion.

"A good spot," Goran said with a nod of approval. "There is little light here, and I see glows in only a couple of windows, which means most people sleep instead of watching the street."

"Those potholes will serve us too," Davin added, pointing to a series of rough spots in the street. "If we time it right, the driver will never notice us. He'll think the jostling of the cart as we climb aboard to be no more than the bumpy road."

The pair of adventurers had to wait but a handful of moments before they heard the abrasive grate of steel-rimmed wooden wheels on uneven cobblestones. Another handful passed before Davin darted from the shadows and leaped to the back of the cart. While he wriggled beneath two sacks of dried apricots and figs, the Challing timed his own gamboling jump to coincide with the drop of a wheel into the largest of the potholes. Neither ox nor driver noticed the massive giant squirm beneath several cloth-covered wheels of cheese.

"My stomach reminds me we haven't eaten since our arrival in Faltren," Goran whispered while he freed his dagger to open one of the cheese cloths. "Ah, and here's some smoked fish and candied dates. Not a meal to be found on Felrad's table, but my belly has no complaints."

For the first time in hours Davin noticed the protests of his own stomach. Plying Clinn and Boro with ale and then barely eluding the crossbows of Smeem's guards had left little time to consider food. He wriggled around, finding neither cheese nor fish near his hiding spot. Never caring for the gritty taste of figs, he quieted his stomach by downing a handful of chewy, tart, dried apricots all the while cursing the occasional muffled smacking of lips he heard coming from the Challing's hiding place.

However, the Jyotian's ears were more attuned to the harsh sound of the cart's wheels on the cobblestone street. When he noticed a slowing of the rhythm of rim against road, he wormed upward to poke his head from between the sacks. He twisted around and strained to peer over the front of the cart.

"We approach the gate. Two guards stand ready on either side." He described what he saw for Goran in a whisper of a whisper. "But I see no sign of Rorseg."

"The captain knows not how Jajhana beams on him," the

Challing said between two smacks. "As fit as I feel now, I would rip him limb from limb with my bare hands if I were to lay eyes upon him."

Braggart though he was, Davin often found it difficult to know when Goran merely prattled or spoke with deadly intent. Besides having discovered a hearty appetite for the pleasures of human flesh, the Challing also had a decided relish for a fight, whether it be with the double-headed battle-axe he usually carried over a shoulder or face to face using only bare hands.

"We're pulling up to the gate," Davin continued to report the cart's progress.

"Get down!" Goran warned from under the wheels of cheese.

Beneath the piles of foodstuffs, a massive hand closed around Davin's left ankle and yanked. Balance rudely jerked from under him, the Jyotian disappeared beneath the apricots and figs once more.

"Get down!"

For a moment, Davin thought the Challing repeated himself. Instead the command came from outside. One of the guards ordered the driver to step from the cart. The Jyotian's right hand felt its way through the tight confines of pressing sacks to his waist and rested on the dagger at his belt. If the guardsmen found them for the second time this day, it would not be without a weapon in hand.

The wagon clattered on a few more feet, then halted. A scuffling of boot on board came from above when the driver scrambled from box to ground to comply with the guard's order. "Just the usual provisions Master Smeem ordered."

"We'll see about that."

Davin's fingers tightened around the dirk's handle ready to meet the man who lifted the sack of figs covering him.

An ant nipped at the back of his hand. Before his mind could comprehend what had happened, an army of angry ants covered every inch of his body. And each of those ants opened their jaws wide and ripped into his flesh.

"A ward spell!" Davin identified the source of the hot needles pricking his body. "The toad of a merchant has cast a ward spell to protect his home."

The Jyotian twisted to escape the unrelenting assault. There was no relief. The needles no longer pricked at his flesh but slid inward to worry at his innards.

"I feel nothing," Goran's voice came. A soft glow of green flooded the bottom of the cart. Magicks! Potent magicks!

The needles that gouged deep into Davin's body transformed into white-hot brands of steel. A ward spell rather than true steel it might be, but magicks could kill a man as surely as a blade. Fight as he did, Davin could not hold back the scream of agony that raced upward from his chest, prised open his clamped teeth and tore into the night.

6

Ward spell?

A half-eaten chunk of cheese dropped from Goran's hand. More than once during his years of confinement in human flesh he had felt the burning tongue of a ward spell licking at his flesh and knew the torturous pain of the protective spell.

Now he felt nothing, except the warm satisfaction of a filled belly gone too long without so much as a crust of bread.

However, he could see. And what the Challing saw opened his single good eye as wide as a saucer. He *saw* the ward spell! Not felt it but *saw* it!

Like shafts of light transformed to blazing bolts of flame, he watched the magicks slice through cart and sack alike seeking a target. He lifted a hand and stared in amazement when the arrowlike shafts of magicks passed through his flesh without the slightest resistance or twinge of pain.

How? His fingers found the three-quarters leaf about his neck and lifted it. Glowing green witchfire danced from the medallion. Goran blinked. It was as though the gold drank the power of the ward spell and nurtured his body with the captured magicks. His Challing powers tingled, alive within him.

A scream twisted with agony rent the night!

"Davin!" Goran shifted beneath the wheels of cheese. The Jyotian was no Challing nor was he protected by the leaf's power. Working on a mere human, the ward spell would turn Davin's brain and every nerve in his body to cinders in seconds.

"Qar-damned fool!" Goran realized his friend had attempted to endure the spell's effects rather than reveal their hiding place. "Get out of here before your brain bursts into flame!"

Goran's boots found Davin's shoulders. With all the strength he could manage within the cramped confines of the cart, the Challing shoved with both legs.

Davin Anane's scream died to an aching groan of relief as he and three sacks of figs shot out the open rear of the cart as though hurled from a catapult. The Jyotian hit the ground on his back, air forced from his lungs by the impact. He didn't care. The fiery brands were gone. Not even needles or fire ants remained. The cool night bathed his sweat-drenched body.

"Only Master Smeem's provisions, huh?" a guard said somewhere behind the Jyotian. "Looks like you were carrying a rat with you, too!"

"Captain Rorseg!" the second guard called. "We got us another one trying to slip in!"

Davin did not wait to see if Rorseg answered the warning. The Jyotian scrambled to his feet and ran toward the park across from Smeem's home as fast as his legs could carry him. He risked one glance over his shoulder and saw Goran One-Eye's shaggy head poke out from between two cloth-wrapped wheels of cheese. The Challing wore a broad grin and green witchfire sparked in his one good eye.

"He's getting away!" Captain Rorseg darted past the cart with every man in his command at his heels. "Qirt, you and three men head to the left! Cleatin, you and another three to the right! The rest of you with me. We'll run down Jaitus' rat!"

Rat? The thought no more than formed in Goran's mind than the muscular giant shifted shape into a black-and-white speckled rodent a foot in length with a tail twice as long. If a rat were capable of grinning, the one that scurried through the maze of foodstuffs to the rear of the cart and leaped to the ground would have worn such an expression stretched between pointed ears.

Pausing but a moment to watch Davin disappear in the darkness far ahead of Rorseg and his men, Goran spun about and darted belly to the ground beneath the cart on a beeline toward Smeem's front door. No guardsmen could catch the Jyotian, of that Goran was certain. Unless his friend was clumsy enough to step in a gopher hole and break a leg, Davin would lead the guards on a merry chase until dawn awoke a new day.

In the meantime, there was no reason for a Challing cloaked in rodent form to waste a golden opportunity. The Belt of the Virgin Goddess lay somewhere within the house ahead, and he intended to get it before daylight pushed away the night. Without guards or magic to stop him, no obstacles stood between him and success.

One of the hounds that patroled Smeem's closely cropped lawn viewed the situation from a different perspective. The long-fanged monster, standing taller than a small child at the shoulders, bounded across the grass, barking like a hunting dog on the fresh scent of a fox.

Goran's beeline became a twisting zigzag as the Challing in rat shape darted and dodged slavering jaws that snapped at his furry rump with the deadly intent of ending a rodent's life.

In a surprising move, Goran abruptly spun around and ran straight at the hound. The dog gave a startled yap and stared as the rat ran directly between its legs.

Chittering a series of high-pitched squeaks that served to voice the curses streaming through the Challing's diminutive skull in reprimand for forgetting about Smeem's canine guards, Goran pivoted to scurry beneath the hound again while the dog struggled to resume the chase.

Goran realized he played a fool's game as he prepared to repeat the maneuver a third time. It was only a matter of time before the hound's size and speed won out. The Challing wished he had fully considered the situation before assuming the form of a rat. A dog at least a hand taller than the hound doing its able best to turn him into an evening snack would have been a more appropriate body.

Goran's metamorphosis was instantaneous. When the hound resumed its chase of a black and white speckled rat, it found standing in the rodent's stead one of its own ferocious breed looming with fangs bared, hackles raised, and feral growl rumbling from its throat. Smeem's canine guard made no attempt to challenge the larger hound. The rat was, after all, no more than sport to break the monotony of the night.

With tail tucked between hind legs, the dog turned and made a hasty retreat.

This is more like it! Goran's canine chest expanded with pride. Whether his shape-changing ability stemmed from the medallion dangling from his fur-covered neck or was simply an unexpected return of his powers, he was not certain. Nor did he wish to let them pass without putting them to good purpose.

He turned and ran straight to the mansion's front door. A paw lifted to the door's handle, but it was human hand that opened it. A hand that shifted back to a paw when a hound nuzzled the door open, entered, then used a leg to close the door behind it.

Far more cautious as a dog than a rodent, Goran studied the hallway with a careful eye before willing himself to human shape again. He had no intention of underestimating the merchant again. It had taken a return of his Challing abilities to gain entrance to the house. Now that he was here, he was determined to take full advantage of the situation. When he left, be it in canine or human form, it would be with the Belt of the Virgin Goddess – and with that he would barter for the final portion of the leaf.

Moving down a hallway paneled in richly stained and polished *chiin* wood, the Challing opened door after door and peered within the revealed chambers. More than the Belt of the Virgin Goddess Smeem protected with his guards and spells. The house proved to hold a veritable treasure trove in each room! It took every ounce of restraint the Challing could muster to edge aside instincts sharpened by years of thievery. Rulers of Raemllyn's lesser kingdoms could have fed all within their realms for a year with a quarter of the wealth in any of the rooms.

Only a finely crafted figurine of pure gold proved too great a temptation for the Challing. He stepped into a room that appeared to be a library lined with shelves of scrolls and tomes, crossed to a wood stand, and caressed the figure of a young woman with robes loosely flowing around her. From the small statue's heft Goran estimated in gold weight alone it was worth thousands of bists. He considered tucking it beneath his belt but feared the weight might slow him should fighting prove necessary.

"What use is it to sit down to a banquet and do nothing but sniff the bounty offered?" he wondered aloud.

The banquet set before him was a feast of vases, tapestries, paintings and statues, all of which would bring fabulous amounts if delivered into the right hands. Goran picked up the hand-sized figurine again. What did a little extra weight mean to one who could transform himself into a winged dragon if the need warranted?

Goran shoved the golden figurine under his belt. He faded into shadows cast by heavy cloth wall hangings at the approach of footsteps in the hallway outside the library. The owner of those footsteps called out, his words muffled by the walls separating him from the Challing.

A door on the opposite side of the library opened and a man in servant's livery entered. Goran was none too certain if the summoned servant was indeed human. He appeared to be the offspring resulting from a grudge mating of an Uhjayib gorilla and the ugliest human in all Raemllyn. The man easily equaled Goran in height and bulk, although his hair was black, all of it growing on his chest and arms, since his head was as bald as a *kelii*'s egg.

Muscles rippled on the servant's arms when he crossed them over a barrel chest. Squint and twist his head from side to side though he did, Goran found it impossible to discern the man's neck. Cordlike muscles stood out in thick bundles that began at the earlobes and ended at the shoulders.

If size and physique gave an indication, the servant would be a doughty opponent should Goran be discovered. However, muscular strength was not the sole threat the man presented.

The two wide-bladed knives, each as long as a man's foot, shoved under the servant's broad leather belt provided more than a hint to the man's real duties. No simple manservant was this one, Goran realized, but a trained bodyguard willing and able to cut the heart out of any unwanted intruder who approached his master.

The Challing's fingertips dipped to the purloined figurine and tenderly caressed the gold. Jajhana protect him this night, and the goddess would receive a generous tithing when he managed to slip from the merchant's house with the Belt of the Virgin Goddess in hand.

"Haco!" the voice in the hall demanded. "Haco, by Peyneeha's depths, where are you? I desire a bath. My visit to Juusapt's whorehouse has left me feeling defiled and dirty."

"At once, Master Smeem," the servant called, hastening his strides. "I have hot water ready and waiting for you. Allow me a few moments to add the oils and perfumes."

"Good, good," Smeem replied when Haco stepped into the hall. "I'll disrobe in my bedchamber. Fetch me when the bath is prepared."

"Yes, Master Smeem," Haco answered, his remaining words lost as the pair moved deeper into the mansion.

A smile upturned the corners of Goran's mouth. Pliaton, Raemllyn's God of Thieves, walked at his side tonight. So shortly returned from the Temple of Ediena was Smeem, the Challing was certain the merchant still wore the enchanted belt. All he had to do was follow the man, then make off with the belt when Smeem soaked in his bath oils and perfumes.

Goran frowned when he poked his head into the hall. Neither Smeem nor Haco was in sight. Had they moved that quickly or stepped into one of the rooms that opened onto the hallway?

With a step as light as an autumn leaf floating to the ground and an agility that belied his bulk, Goran edged into the hall. From door to door he slipped to press an ear against ornately carved wood. At the seventh, he heard the muted sounds of movement. Pressing splayed fingers against the wood, the Challing inched the sliding door back enough to allow his single good eye to peer inside.

He blinked and blinked again letting his vision adjust to the interior darkness. He pursed his lips with surprise when at last he was able to make out yet another room lined with shelves crowded with scrolls and tomes.

A scholar? Goran shook his head when he slid the door back and entered the carpeted room. A merchant with a taste for literature and histories was an oddity. Or were these volumes a collection of Raemllyn's pornographic rarities? That would tally with Smeem's visit to the Temple of Ediena and his possession of the Belt of the Virgin Goddess. It also explained two libraries within the mansion – one to impress visitors, another to feed the merchant's secret lusts.

The Challing caught himself when he started toward the nearest shelves to examine one of the tomes. Whether Smeem delighted in drawings and paintings of men and women coupling was not his concern; stealing the belt was. He glanced about. He no longer heard the muffled sounds that had drawn him into the library, nor did the room's dimness reveal any indication Smeem or his muscle-bound servant Haco had passed this way.

Dropping to a knee, Goran ran a hand over the thick weave of the carpet. What eyes could not see, the tactile sense discerned. The rotund merchant's weight gave him away. Depressions in the carpet's rich pile marked each footstep he had taken.

In a waddle-walk, Goran followed the trail across the library to two doors standing side by side. Light glowed from beneath the one on the left. On hands and knees the Challing bent low to peek beneath the door. The carpet's thickness which had aided him a moment ago now thwarted his efforts. With a silent curse on his lips, Goran eased the door back. The smile returned to his lips.

Smeem's sleeping chamber lay on the other side. More important, so did the merchant. Unaware of the peering eye that watched his every move, Smeem mumbled and cursed to himself as he tugged off the layers of his clothing and tossed them in disarray to the floor.

Goran's smile widened. More than once the merchant derided Juusapt's canine mother, declared the illegal state of the priest's birth and speculated about the destination of Juusapt's eternal soul which would not be snuggled safely to Ediena's bosom.

As amused as he was by Smeem's scathingly inventive tirade, the Challing's attention hung on the common canvas money belt that remained about the merchant's bloated belly. The belt lacked the telltale circular impressions of gold bists hidden within, but there was no denying the belt's thickness. Something was hidden within.

A belt within a belt?

Goran's forehead furrowed with doubt, but the more he considered it, the more the possibility appealed to him. He had no idea what the Belt of the Virgin Goddess looked like. He supposed it was studded with the finest of gems. *But to what purpose?* The belt's power, not its appearance, was its worth. A plain, leather strap within a canvas belt would appear to be no more than added support for an unusually weighty burden of gold the wearer carried.

Goran nodded to himself. Yes, that had to be it. The Belt of the Virgin Goddess was concealed within a common money belt. Why else did Smeem keep the belt girded about his middle?

A belt within a belt!

"I don't know how you managed to get in here," a low voice growled behind Goran as a meaty hand grasped the back of his neck, "but you'll live to regret it!"

His speculations about the belt and the carpet's deep pile conspired against the Challing. While he spied on Smeem, someone had crept up behind him. Goran rolled to the side when the hand on his neck attempted to lift him from the floor. His own hand darted to his belt but found a gold figurine rather than the hilt of his dirk.

Hand on Goran's throat rather than thc nape of the neck now, Haco leered above his captive. "You're a big one for a thief. But I like 'em big. Makes for an equal match. Get tired of the others always saying I can only best those that are smaller than me."

Goran cared little about the equality of their size or what others might say about Haco's ability to murder his fellow man. He was concerned about the fingers squeezing his throat. This was not Gohwohn, and the human form he wore required that he breathe if he were to continue living.

Rat! The Challing thought, willing his form to shift shape. He had never met a man who did not cringe when he encountered a rat. In that instant of revulsion, Goran could escape the vicelike grip that slowly clamped his windpipe closed.

Rather than rodent, Goran remained a hulking mountain of a man. *Dog!* he thought, more than satisfied to trade human form for that of a canine with teeth big and sharp enough to shred Haco's wrist and arm.

Again his shape remained unaltered. There was no time to ponder the abrupt loss of his form-shifting ability. Goran kicked out with his right leg and drove his boot heel into Haco's left kneecap.

Not only was the force of impact enough to free the Challing from the choke hold, it also sent the muscular cutthroat turned bodyguard hurling across the room into a floor-to-ceiling bookcase. Haco grunted and dodged a small shower of scrolls that fell from the shelves above his head.

However, he did not go down. There was no escaping the rage in his glaring eyes, even in the library's dimness, when his hands dropped to the hilts of the two broad-bladed knives stuck under his belt.

"Is my bath ready, Haco?" Smeem questioned from the bedchamber when Goran pushed to his feet.

The manservant's hands closed around the knives' handles.

Like some large predatory cat, Goran launched himself in answer to Haco's challenge before it was fully spoken. The man's hands abandoned the blades and clamped around the Challing's wrists when Goran's fingers closed around his throat, thumbs pressing into heavily muscled windpipe.

Yanking, twisting and jerking from side to side, Haco's eyes widened in shock at encountering one whose strength was equal, if not greater, than his own. Goran exerted enough strength to keep Haco's warning cry bottled in his throat.

"Almost ready, Master," Goran grated out in reply to Smeem's inquiry.

Haco's eyes narrowed to slits at such effrontery. The servant drove a knee directly into Goran's groin.

Had the Challing possessed his own misty form, the attack would have passed through him like a cool evening breeze. Goran, however, was trapped in the flesh of a man and was burdened with all that body's weaknesses and vulnerabilities. Thus, Challing reacted like a man. He released the servant's throat and clutched at himself with both hands as he stumbled back.

That Goran doubled over saved him from a sledgehammer-sized fist meant for his face, which whistled a hairsbreadth above his head. A wobbly duck to the left evaded another would-be punishing blow and an awkward bob to the right was enough to dodge Haco's third punch. It also proved time for the waves of excruciating pain to diminish and Goran's head to clear. When Haco charged with both hands clamped together and raised high to slam down into the back of the Challing's neck, Goran threw himself shoulder first into the man's muscle-rippled stomach.

The impact sent man and Challing through the door beside the entrance to Smeem's sleeping chamber. Rather than cushioning carpet they careened across cool ceramic tiles. Goran came to an abrupt halt when the top of his head banged into the side of an immense sunken bathtub.

"Now you die!"

Goran blinked his eye and stared up at Haco who had somehow managed to regain his feet and free both wickedly long knives.

"I'll gut you the way I used to gut *bloaterfish* when I was a kid workin' the wharves!"

Haco did not wait for an answer and threw himself toward the Challing. Both of Goran's legs jerked up to catch the servant in his midriff and send him sailing across the bathroom. It was a good counter except that Haco's twin blades met and drove solidly into Goran's own midriff when the Challing's legs sent the man hurtling through the air.

Goran grunted, his palms shooting to his stomach to stem the flood of blood. Not blood but cold hard gold met the Challing's fingertips. Goran glanced at his belly to find both of the knives embedded in the soft, pure gold of the figurine he had lifted from Smeem's outer library.

Jajhana protected those who promised her tithes, he thought, when he pushed to his feet and spun about to meet Haco's renewed attack. There was no continued challenge. The servant lay face down on the tiled floor, his neck twisted grotesquely to one side and the side of his face flat against a shoulder.

Goran released a soft sigh of relief. As muscular as Haco's neck had been, it proved too little to protect him when his head struck the bathroom wall. The servant's spine had snapped like a dry twig. No longer would Haco gut *bloaterfish* or men.

"Haco!" came Smeem's shrill summons. "I want my bath *now*!"

"Another moment, Master," Goran answered, hoping the merchant was still too upset with Juusapt to distinguish the sudden difference in his servant's voice.

As Goran crossed to Haco, intent on dragging the servant's body from the room, Smeem's voice came again, this time directly behind him. "Haco, what happened to this door? It's shattered! And the bath! Look at all that steam. You know I like warm baths, not scalding! Have you lost your mind, man?"

"Not his mind," Goran said coldly when he turned to face the fat merchant. "Haco lost his life."

"You're . . . you're *not* Haco!" Smeem stared in disbelief at the giant wearing an eye patch. "How did you get into my house?"

"If I told you I transformed myself into a dog, you'd never believe me."

As Goran's right hand tugged one of the blades free from the gold figurine, his left snaked out and grasped the belt around Smeem's middle to yank the merchant toward the steaming bath water. When Smeem staggered past on his way to the waiting water, Goran slipped the knife blade beneath the money belt and tugged. The simple iron clasp gave way. The belt fell from the merchant's waist into Goran's hand as Smeem tumbled into the water.

"Yes!" A triumphant shout rebounded off the bathroom wall as Goran tossed aside the knife and tore away the canvas with his bare hands to reveal the treasure hidden by the coarse cloth. Not simple leather as the Challing had speculated, but there were no jewels studding the girdle either. The Belt of the Virgin Goddess was fashioned exquisitely from fine strands of gold woven into a flexible band half the width of Goran's hand.

The fat man in the bathtub moaned when the Challing dangled the prize in front of his eyes. "A good night to you, Merchant Smeem. There is no further business we need to transact this eve."

"On that you are mistaken!" Water splashed high about the merchant's waist when he took two strides to cross the length of the tub and slapped his hand onto an ornamental rose blown from colored glass. Smeem twisted the rose to one side and glared at the Challing. "Whoever you are, you will die horribly!"

A rusty creak came from overhead. Goran's gaze darted to the ceiling to see one white tile drop on hinges. The tiny hidden doorway posed no threat to the Challing's life. The *gauline*, a winged serpent of jungles stretching across the middle of Lower Raemllyn that fell through the opening, did.

Winged though it might be, the membranous appendages fluttering against the air behind the snake's triangular head had lost the power of flight ages past. The poisonous viper flopped to the floor a mere stride from where the Challing stood. Goran backstepped to place added distance between him and the serpent.

Those useless wings beat with increased agitation when the snake lifted its head and peered at the Challing with eyes as black as obsidian. A forked tongue darted in and out of its mouth, tasting the air for the scent of man. Silently, the *gauline* drew its length together, then writhed forward.

Goran took another backstep and was stopped by the room's wall. His gaze darted toward the shattered doorway. To reach it meant leaping over the snake. A bird might accomplish the task, but even that was doubtful. Birds formed the mainstay of a *gauline*'s diet. The serpent was capable of striking a distance three times its body length.

Closer the viper writhed, drawing its body of glinting blue scales into coils.

Had Goran not known what to expect, he could have guessed that the *gauline* prepared to strike. The Challing readied himself to meet that attack. His arms crossed his body, one hand grasping the hilt of his dirk and the other finding the handle of Haco's knife still protruding from the golden figurine. When the snake's head arched back, Goran pulled at both of them.

Rather than wait for the *gauline* to strike, the Challing shoved the figurine straight at the snake's head. The serpent responded with membranous wings beating the air. Rather than flesh, the *gauline*'s jaws snapped closed around soft, pure gold, embedding its poisonous fangs in the metal.

Simultaneously, Goran drew his dirk's tip down along the snake's cream-colored belly, opening it from stomach to spine. Before the ocherous blood could splatter on him, the Challing tossed serpent and figurine into the bath.

The steaming water turned from crystal clear to the sickening yellow of the *gauline*'s blood. And in the next instant, the bath began to bubble and sizzle as if transformed to acid. Goran peered into the churning water and frowned. Snake and gold figurine dissolved as he watched.

"My apologies, Jajhana," the Challing said aloud realizing that he had faced more than a poisonous snake, that it had been a serpent driven by diabolical magicks. "There will be no tithing from that bauble – unless you care to dip your own delicate, divine hand down there and retrieve your treasure."

Goran held up the Belt of the Virgin Goddess and grinned. "It seems this little trinket will have to suffice for the night, doesn't it, Merchant Smeem?" Goran frowned when no one answered. "Smeem?"

The Challing's head twisted from side to side. Smeem was gone – vanished as though into the air itself.

"Likely some hidden passage," Goran speculated aloud.

There was no time to hunt for a concealed corridor. Goran had what he had come for. The Challing whirled around and dashed from the bathroom. Rather than retracing his path through the house, Goran darted into the merchant's bedchamber. A stained-glass skylight over Smeem's bed offered an unexpected exit from the mansion. If Smeem somehow had managed to summon aid, there was no need to walk outside into their waiting crossbow bolts.

Goran leaped onto the bed and jumped toward the multihued window. His left hand caught and held a heavy cornice that edged a slight chimney in the ceiling into which the skylight was set. Ducking his head, he sent his right fist through the glass, shattering it into a thousand shards. With the Belt of the Virgin Goddess tucked under his own belt, the Challing pulled himself upward onto the roof and into the velvet soft night.

A commotion at the front of the house drew his attention. Slunk low, the Challing deftly maneuvered across the roofing tiles and peered below. He smiled. He had chosen his escape route well. Smeem *had* managed to summon help. Below, the merchant berated a now-mounted Captain Rorseg who ordered two guardsmen and their crossbows into the house.

Goran crept closer to the edge of the roof. It would take only a few moments for the guards to discover his escape route, and the roof offered no place to hide. There would be no better time than the present to take what small advantage surprise offered.

The Challing sprang outward, leaping into the night. He saw Smeem look up, but it was too late. The Challing landed solidly on the rump of Rorseg's mount. Before the guard captain understood what was happening, Goran shoved him to the ground and used both hands to vault into the saddle. While Rorseg tried to find his legs, the Challing's own legs swung out and drove down to slam heels into flanks. The horse bolted straight for the open gate.

"Bowmen! Bowmen!" Rorseg screamed.

The cry came too late. The instant the horse shot through the gate, Goran wrenched its head toward the road that led from Faltren. Somewhere behind him, Davin had found a hiding place safe from Smeem's army of guards. Tomorrow, when the sun was up, Goran would return to the town and find the Jyotian.

For now, he needed his own refuge. Two days had passed since last he slept. A few hours of rest were needed to clear his mind before he sought Juusapt and exchanged the belt for the final portion of the leaf.

When the Challing reached the crest of a small hill, he drew the horse to a halt and twisted in the saddle to glance behind. He cursed Father Yehseen, Black Qar the Destroyer, the entire Sitala and four other gods of Raemllyn's crowded pantheon who popped into mind.

Smeem refused to admit defeat and relinquish possession of the Belt of the Virgin Goddess. A small troop of mounted guardsmen poured from the gate of the merchant's estate and reined down the road after the thief who had so artfully eluded them.

"Son of Lukiahn," Goran evoked the name of the stallion from which all of Raemllyn's horses traced their bloodline. "It appears your work is not done this night."

Goran's heels brought no more than a grunt from the animal. Nor did coaxing bring response from the horse. In the silvery light of Raemllyn's two moons, the Challing saw the reason. A crossbow bolt protruded from the animal's neck. Goran swung to the ground and yanked the arrow free. Its sharp iron head was buried only the depth of a finger joint, not enough to kill but more than enough to send the horse into shivering shock.

Affectionately patting the animal on its muscular chest for the brief ride to freedom it had provided, Goran pivoted and fled toward a thick wood that lay just beyond the plowed field of a farmer. If he were to evade Rorseg and his guards, it would have to be there. The open road offered no cover whatsoever.

7

"Keep to that course and Rorseg and his guards will turn you into a porcupine with their arrows!" called a voice behind Goran One-Eye. "The stand of trees is narrow with a sandy beach and the Oceans of Kumar on the other side."

The Challing skidded to an uneven halt, twisted about to find the voice's owner, and grinned widely. "Davin! Your appearance is more than well-timed! I had hoped to find you in Faltren after I lost the captain and his men."

Davin nudged the bay gelding he rode with his heels and led the black whose reins he held to the Challing. "Get your sizable backside in the saddle or we'll both be dodging crossbow bolts." Davin jerked his head to one side. "There's a stream less than a quarter of a league that way. It will hide our tracks, and if we move with haste, we can be there ere Rorseg reaches the top of this hill."

"I thought you'd be slinking in the shadows of some alley until morning." Goran swung onto the black's back and slammed heels into the animal's flanks to follow the Jyotian eastward across another plowed field, over a rock fence and into a sparse wood.

Half a league down the promised stream, Davin drew his mount to a halt and looked back. "I can't see anyone behind us. I think we've lost them. Rorseg might be quick to execute those who offend him, but the man and those he commands know little of the chase. After you so rudely kicked me out of the cart, I eluded them simply by climbing a tree and watching them run beneath."

"It's well you did, friend Davin," Goran replied while he studied the night behind them and found no trace of pursuers. "It was a tight spot back there. Reminded me of a time in Cahri when I was caught within the home of that city's high judge with a particularly valuable golden figurine in my possession. Not that possessing a statue of gold or being in the judge's home are in themselves a crime – unless one is uninvited and the statue in question belongs to that judge. It was there I lost my left eye, you know. The judge had one hundred guardsmen, each armed with short bow or spear. You can imagine . . ."

"You transforming into a gutter rat and scurrying away," Davin cut short the Challing's attempt to launch into another long-winded yarn about the loss of his eye.

"Rat?" Goran squinted at his companion as their mounts continued along the stream in a leisurely walk. "Why do you mention rat?"

"Because I happened to see one jump from the butcher's cart and go running to Smeem's mansion – one with the green of witchfire in its eyes," Davin answered. "I realized you had regained your shape-changing ability and had chosen an appropriate camouflage."

Goran nodded enthusiastically, missing his friend's verbal jab. "A most excellent choice, I admit. It would have taken me right to Smeem's door had it not been for the most vicious rabid hound in all Raemllyn and its decided taste for rodent flesh."

Davin patiently listened as the Challing recounted his escape from the hound and eventual entrance into the merchant's house. In truth, the Jyotian was uncertain what portions of the adventure to believe. He was sure a kernel of truth grew in Goran's tale, but separating chaff from grain was a mental task far beyond his sleep-deprived mind. When Goran paused to take a breath, Davin suggested:

"I think we should find a place safe for the night. We'll need our wits about us when we return to the merchant's home in the morning."

"Return to Smeem's estate?" Goran's head snapped around. "Why would you want to do such a thing?"

"The Belt of the Virgin Goddess – or have you forgotten why we're here?" Disgust filled the Jyotian's voice. "Without it, we cannot claim the fourth portion of that precious leaf you wear."

"But I have the belt!" Goran yanked the golden girdle from beneath his own belt and held it high. "Did you think I failed to get what I sought?"

Davin stared at the band of woven gold that caught the light of the two moons overhead and used them to spark inner fires.

Although his mouth opened, the Jyotian found himself unable to speak.

"Rather plain, isn't it? One would have thought it would be studded with a few diamonds or maybe emeralds – green does go well with simple gold," Goran prattled on. "Smeem had hidden it within a canvas money belt, as though such a simple deception would fool the greatest thief in all Raemllyn."

Non-human thief, Davin started to correct but pushed the thought aside. There was no reason to diminish the Challing's accomplishment – the proof of his daring dangled in a golden stream around his hand. "Then we'll get no sleep this night. We can make half the journey back to Pahl before the sun rises."

"Pahl?" Goran stared at his friend as though the Jyotian had lost his mind. "Juusapt is in Faltren. Why not deliver the belt to him this night?"

"The priest followed us here," Davin explained. "It's obvious Juusapt is prepared to deal with us here. He doesn't want us back in Pahl. Why else would he have left twelve dead men behind us, except to assure we would never attempt to enter the city again?"

Goran nodded. "A good enough reason not to return to Pahl, I agree. The city guards will kill us as we approach the gates."

"And Juusapt and Smeem are as likely to kill us in Faltren should they lay an eye on us," Davin replied. "I prefer the maneuvering room of a city. Faltren is too small and offers few places to hide a man and a Challing should the need arise."

"But Juusapt doesn't know we have the Belt of the Virgin Goddess," Goran countered.

"By morning, he will. Faltren is too small to keep your theft a secret," Davin replied. "He is unaware we know that he followed us. The moment he hears that someone managed to enter and escape from the merchant's house, he'll know what happened and will return to Pahl as fast as a horse can carry him."

Goran sat silently for a long moment, then acquiesced with a heavy nod of his shaggy head. "You are right. For whatever reason Juusapt followed us to Faltren, you can be certain it was for no good. I fear the man still carries ill-will in his heart for our unfortunate meeting in Harn."

Davin chuckled. "I would say that. I would also say it was time we returned to Pahl."

The two thieves reined their mounts northward, riding toward the distant city beneath Raemllyn's two moons.

"Davin! Davin, wake up!"

Rough hands shook the Jyotian's shoulder. He forced leaden eyelids open and stared past the sleep cotton that blurred his vision to the imposing figure of Goran One-Eye.

"It's Juusapt," Goran said. "He comes up the road. We should surprise him here in the open."

Half-asleep, Davin pushed from the ground on legs turned to rubber. "To what advantage? I doubt he carries the last portion of the leaf on him but keeps it in the temple. There is no way past the guards at the gate if we approach him now."

"We could demand he bring his piece of my leaf here to us," Goran answered as they wove through dense underbrush toward the road running between Faltren and Pahl. "He would have to return for the belt."

"No doubt," Davin said sarcastically, "and bring every guard in Pahl with him, each one of them ready and willing to avenge the twelve who died in our escape. No, we'll let the priest pass, then find a way into the city. Tonight, when Juusapt's guard is down, we'll have our meeting."

Squatted behind a clump of *jhain* bushes the two peered beyond the plants' prickly leaves to watch the robed priest ride past.

"He brings an acolyte from Faltren to Pahl." Goran stood when Juusapt rode far beyond their hiding place. "Quite a comely wrench she was, too, although a mite too skinny for my tastes. She would appeal to you, though, Davin, my friend."

Davin shook his head, not in denial of the young woman's beauty, but to refute the Challing's assumption about her religious ardor. "No acolyte, that one. She had no more desire to be here than we do. Her hands were tied at the wrists, and Juusapt kept a firm grip on her mount's bridle."

"Little matter to us," Goran said, shrugging his massive shoulders. "It's time we concerned ourselves with getting past the guards at Pahl's gates."

"The sooner the better," the Jyotian agreed.

* * *

A rope slipped from a passing farmer's cart, a gnarled limb from a *morda* tree cut into a makeshift hook and the cover of late evening were all Davin Anane and Goran One-Eye required to scale the high walls that surrounded the city-state of Pahl. They were well on their way to the Temple of Ediena before the sentry who walked the wall passed the spot they had ascended from one side and descended on the other.

The throng of Pahl's less fortunate who gathered outside the temple when the chimes signaled the evening calling gave a ready-made cover for them to enter the House of Ediena. While Juusapt stood on a dais to oversee which of those answering the calling would be selected to provide for the lusts of Pahl's more fortunate who would visit the temple later that night with pouches of gold in offering to the Goddess of Love, Davin and Goran slipped behind a heavy velvet drapery and moved from the calling chamber into the heart of the temple.

Statues, immense tapestries, massive arrays of flowers, flowing draperies on every wall, all were enough to conceal fifty thieves, let alone hide two. Davin and Goran waited and watched when Juusapt finished his daily task and retired to his own chambers. Neither Challing nor Jyotian made their move. Instead they waited until Juusapt abruptly left the temple, then let themselves into his rooms.

Awaiting the priest's return from their prearranged meeting near Pahl's south gate, the two thieves searched every closet and drawer in Juusapt's chambers.

"Nothing," Goran announced after the exploration was completed. "He doesn't keep the last part of the leaf here."

Davin held his tongue. He did not like the nagging doubt that wriggled nastily at the back of his mind.

Goran slumped down in a chair and stared glumly about the outer room of the three comprising Juusapt's chambers. "For a temple overflowing with riches, one would expect the priest's quarters to be furnished with finer appointments. These rooms are as bare as those of a monk in the service of Ansisian and seem to be of little use but for clerical work and sleep."

Davin dragged an unadorned wooden chair from another room and seated himself beside the door to Juusapt's chambers. "Mayhap Ediena's followers grow jaded to the treasures their religion

amasses and require the drab to remind them of the beauty that
fills their temples.''

"That we could grow so jaded," Goran said with a snort of
disgust.

Davin's gaze traveled over the monotony of the whitewashed
rooms, trying to push aside the niggling apprehension that kept
edging to the forefront of his mind. Had the priest played them
for fools from the moment they accidentally bumped into each
other on Pahl's streets? His eyes shifted to the three-quarters
complete golden leaf about Goran's neck. Juusapt gave no hint of
placing any value on the portion of the amulet he had given
Goran. If he saw the leaf as worthless, then why wasn't the last
piece here in his chambers? Why would he go to the trouble of
hiding it?

The answer repeating in the Jyotian's mind brought no surcease
from worry.

Nor did his restlessness quiet as a stick of incense stuck in a
burner near the priest's bed slowly smoldered to ash. Another
incense stick burned full length before he sat straight in the chair.
Footfalls came outside the door. He pressed finger to lips to signal
the Challing to silence. The clank of brass on brass came when the
door bolt slid back.

Juusapt stepped a full stride into the chambers before his head
jerked up and he came to an abrupt halt. "You! You're here?"

Davin closed the door behind the priest, then positioned
himself between Juusapt and the exit, lest the cleric should feel
the sudden urge to bolt. "You didn't believe us fools enough to
await you and the city guards at the tavern did you?"

"Guards? What do you mean?"

In spite of the indignity Juusapt forced into his words and the
shocked expression on his face, he could not conceal he had
just returned from the tavern – in the company of Pahl's city
guards.

"In all likelihood he told the guard commander that we had
filched a certain belt from his temple," Goran suggested, "to
make certain he got away with the Belt of the Virgin Goddess
when the guards dragged us off to visit the executioner."

"The *belt*! You have it?" Juusapt quivered with excitement.
"Show it to me."

Davin chuckled. "You knew we had the belt when you left Faltren this morn . . ."

"Faltren? What are you talking about?" Juusapt's cowl-shadowed features furrowed in confusion.

"Apparently *truth* is not one of the virtues Ediena demands of her worshippers," Davin said with a shake of his head. He then glanced at the Challing. "Show the most reverent priest his precious belt."

Goran tucked a hand behind his back and yanked forth the Belt of the Virgin Goddess which he dangled before Juusapt like a carrot tempting a stubborn ox. "Took it from Smeem's fat belly as he stepped into his night's bath, I did."

"The Belt of the Virgin Goddess!" The words came in a soft whisper of awe from the priest's lips as he pushed back the cowl and reached for the golden girdle.

Davin shuddered. Never since their chance meeting during Pahl's festival had he seen the cleric's visage in full light but always cloaked by the shadows of his cowl or a prison cell. Now he wished he had not been so graced. Seldom had the Jyotian beheld a man less favored by Ajeuni, Goddess of Beauty. Tiny blue veins stood out on Juusapt's bald pate. The ring of thin hair above Juusapt's ears was speckled with white, although the priest was hardly more than thirty summers in age.

Strangest of all were the cobwebs of scars on his cheeks, turning his face into a crudely drawn map of some desolate wasteland. How the priest had earned those scars lay beyond Davin's guessing. Had they been his reward for allowing a pair of thieves to escape Harn with the prize money from the Spring Festival?

"Be not so greedy!" Goran snatched the belt away when the priest attempted to grab it with both hands. "There is an item you promised in return for this."

"What?" Juusapt blinked in surprise. "Item? Why do you prattle on?"

Davin's doubts returned in full assault.

Goran lifted the incomplete leaf with two fingers. "You promised the last portion of my leaf. Where is it?"

"Oh, yes, yes." Juusapt answered quickly his eyes darting about the whitewashed room. "I had no desire to cheat you of your reward. It's the belt, you don't know how long I have . . ."

Davin cut the man short. "The last piece of leaf. Where is it?"

"In there." Juusapt tilted his head toward the second room. "I keep it in the top drawer to that chest. Give me a moment and I'll get it and you can be on your way."

Davin clamped a hand on the priest's shoulder, halting him when he stepped toward the other room. "That wouldn't be the same drawer that contains two daggers, would it?"

Juusapt cringed with the obvious realization the pair of thieves had searched his apartment while they waited for him to return. His eyes darted about and his tongue licked at his lips. "I'm no fool, either. I had to consider the possibility of you breaking into the temple rather than riding to Faltren. There's a key in the drawer. I need it to unlock the vault below the temple where Ediena's special treasures are kept."

Davin motioned to his Challing friend. "Get the key, and be careful of the knives. Their tips appeared dipped in poison."

Tucking the Belt of the Virgin Goddess beneath his own belt once more, Goran entered the room, opened the drawer and brought forth a key he held up for the Jyotian to see.

"Now," Davin demanded of the priest, "summon one of your assistants and have him retrieve the piece of leaf while we three wait here."

Juusapt shook his head. "I can't do that. Only a temple's high priest may enter the vault. It's a death sentence for any other of our order to gaze inside."

While Davin's mind raced seeking an avenue out of a possible trap, Goran answered. "I think this vault may very well need our personal inspection. Who knows what other trinkets it might hold as recompense for all the trouble and lies friend Juusapt has heaped upon our shoulders?"

Davin pursed his lips, then gave his head a tilt. "We'll accompany you to this vault. And remember, the swords we wear are not ornamental."

Juusapt swallowed hard and nodded, his eyes dipping to the blade sheathed at Davin's hip. "The way to the vault is short. At the end of the hallway is a flight of stairs that leads to it."

"Then take us to it," Goran said impatiently. "The sooner I have my leaf, the sooner you get the belt."

Outside the priest's chambers, Juusapt moved steadily down

the hall. Davin eyed the cleric closely, alert for any signal that might pass between Juusapt and the other priests they passed. The man apparently took Davin at his word about the thieves' ability with blades. Juusapt merely nodded and smiled at those they passed.

"Down here." Juusapt stopped at the head of a twisting flight of stairs that led downward beneath the temple. "The vault is below, near the foot of the stairs."

Hand on shoulder, Davin halted the priest as he started below. "It's too dark. We need a light."

Juusapt took a candle from a nearby table. "There is a brazier on the lower level. We can light it with this."

Goran motioned the man to proceed, and Juusapt started down the narrow stairs that spiraled in a series of right angles toward the dungeonlike chamber below.

"Just a few more turns," Juusapt said, turning back to the pair of adventurers and holding his candle high. "The vault is . . ."

The priest left the sentence unfinished. With a flick of his wrist, he tossed the candle aside. Blackness fell on the stairs like a curtain. The clack of hard-soled sandals on stone steps echoed through the darkness.

"He's getting away!" Goran's words came in a throaty growl. "After the whoremonger!"

The Challing shoved by Davin to chase after the vanished cleric. Hesitating, uncertain whether to proceed or retreat to the illuminated temple above, Davin chose and moved to join Goran.

"Qar-damn the son of a *pletha*! He grabbed the belt!" Goran roared a moment before Davin reached the foot of the stairs and stumbled into his companion. "He was waiting and took the belt as I passed in the dark!"

Davin blinked his eyes against the featureless pitch that engulfed him. Nothing! He could see nothing. Even Goran's imposing bulk was lost in the black that swallowed them.

"Quiet!" Davin ordered. "He can't be far. Listen!"

Challing and Jyotian fell silent. Except the pounding of their own temples, they heard nothing.

"The belly crawler is near," Goran whispered. "I smell him. I *feel* him. When I get my hands on his scrawny neck, I will finish the job I started in Harn two . . ."

A scurry of sandals on stone came from the right. Davin and Goran moved together and collided once again. Amid grunts and disgusted curses, they managed to move together, first bumping into a wall, then feeling their way into a narrow passage.

"It twists like a maze," Goran said. "First to the right and then to the left."

"Stay with Juusapt's footsteps. As long as we can hear him, we can find him."

Abruptly the footfalls were gone. The narrow passage opened into what felt like a chamber.

"Where's he gone?" Goran whispered. "He couldn't have been more than twenty strides ahead of us."

Twenty strides was as good as twenty leagues in the darkness, Davin thought. Juusapt might be standing right at his side and he would never know it. "Best we retreat to the stairs. Sooner or later, Juusapt will have to come out, and we'll be waiting for him."

"Why wait at the stairs when Juusapt is right before your noses?" The priest's voice taunted in the darkness. "The time has come to settle unfinished business between us."

"Finish it I will!" Goran returned. "You'll wish your mother had been barren when I get my hands on you!"

"Goran, no!" Davin reached out in the darkness, his hand clamping onto the Challing's shoulder. "He baits you! He . . ."

The warning came too late. Goran yelped in surprise and fell forward. Had the Jyotian's hand not been locked to his companion's shoulder, Davin might have escaped. As it was he, too, was carried into the yawning nothingness that opened beneath their feet and sent them tumbling downward.

Davin could not judge the distance they fell but thanked the gods that he landed squarely atop Goran's stomach, breaking his fall rather than his neck.

"Soft living has caused you to gain unwanted weight." The Challing groaned when he shoved the Jyotian from him. "Were it not that I always keep myself in perfect physical condition, I would surely be dead at this very moment. That is a lesson you humans should learn from Challings."

Davin reached out with both hands. Rather than stone, earth was beneath them. He pushed to his knees and crawled through the darkness until his head collided with a wall – this of stone rather than dirt. Hands exploring, Davin found that the obstruction curved.

"We're in a pit!" the Jyotian cursed aloud. "Juusapt led us into a pit!"

"In truth, it's an old cistern," the priest's voice came from above. "It was discovered when these underground chambers were dug a generation ago. Most suspect it is a remnant of an ancient city on which Pahl is built."

Light flared overhead. Juusapt stood twenty-five feet above them, holding a torch high and peering down as a king might view an insect.

Davin instinctively slid dagger from sheath. The cleric was within range, although the angle was all but impossible.

"Save your weapon, thief," Juusapt called down. "You will need it soon. You might consider using it on your own throat! Others in your position have taken that route."

"My leaf!" Goran demanded. "You never had the last piece, did you, you whoreson!"

"Actually, no, though I know where the trinket is. I was afraid you might have discovered it in Smeem's home. He keeps it with a small chest of baubles in his bedroom." A dry chuckle pushed from the priest's throat. "Had you found it, however, I suspect I would never have seen this."

While Juusapt held up the Belt of the Virgin Goddess in triumph, Davin's gaze darted about the pit. A full ten strides it measured in diameter. The stone walls were dry and held a bounty of hand- and footholds. No master mountaineer's skill would be needed to scale it. What puzzled the Jyotian was the rusted iron grate directly across from him. Was it also a remnant of a civilization that dwelled in this land long before Pahl was built – a shaft that connected with an underground water source?

"I thank you for your service. Ediena will be well served by the belt. And you two will be well served to my friends who will soon arrive." Again the priest chuckled as though he had uttered a joke that only he understood. "Here, take this. I want you to see what I have arranged for you."

With that, Juusapt tossed the torch into the pit, turned and vanished beyond the cistern rim.

"My dirk will provide a new mouth for him to smile with," Goran said as he moved to the wall. "A mouth that opens his throat from ear to ear. Come, friend Davin, we can be out of here before Juusapt burns another stick of his incense."

Davin's nose crinkled. Not the heavy sweetness of incense gushed forth from the grate but the overpowering effluvium of sewage. The pit connected with sewers – sewers still used by the Pahlese by the strength of the odor.

"Qar-damn!" Goran dropped from the wall and plopped to his backside. "The rock is sandstone! It is old and brittle and breaks away under my weight. Perhaps if you climbed onto my shoulders, you might find . . ."

Goran's head twisted around sharply, his words forgotten. A series of squeaks came from behind the grating. Two rats slipped through the wide openings formed by the grate's flat crisscrossed bands and ran directly for Davin.

The Jyotian pulled sword from sheath. With one stroke he sliced both furry creatures in twain as they reached his boots.

"Davin, there's no time to stop and play with pets," Goran chided. "We've other matters to attend. A couple of sewer rats are no problem."

"Rats!" Davin repeated.

Goran's eyes followed the Jyotian's gaze across the pit. Rats, hundreds of them, poured through the grating!

8

With alacrity that belied his muscular bulk, Goran pushed from his backside, leaped halfway across the pit and snatched up the burning torch. Flaming brand clutched in both fists, the Challing swung out in a wide swath.

A full dozen snapping muzzles came away with mouthfuls of oily flame rather than living flesh. The squealing cries of alarm from their injured leaders were enough to give the rest of the invading rats pause. They halted, hundreds of pairs of tiny glinting eyes turned upward to stare at the one-eyed giant challenging their attack.

"They've been down here so long, they aren't sure what light is!" Goran kept the torch swinging back and forth, holding the rodents at bay. "It won't take them long to figure out I can only burn a few of them before they take me. The wall, Davin! Climb the wall and find a way to get me out of here!"

Davin didn't need urging. He was already a full ten feet up the wall when the Challing spoke – and would have scaled another five feet before Goran finished had not the ancient sandstone crumbled beneath his right hand and left boot at the same instant. Instead of scrambling over the top of the pit, the Jyotian fell, unceremoniously sprawling on his back in the dirt.

Sensing an easy meal in the fallen man, the rats surged forward.

The red-eyed creatures received faces full of flame when Goran leaped to defend the Jyotian from the snapping maws that could strip a man of every ounce of flesh on his bones in a matter of minutes and when done start on the marrow within those bones.

"The wall's too old to support my weight." Davin rose and applied sword blade to a phalanx of rats attempting to maneuver behind the two thieves. The ten twitching rodent corpses left in the wake of flashing steel immediately became dinner for the remaining rats in the broken line. "Try shape-shifting! A bird could fly to the top of the pit."

"Would that I could," Goran said with another swipe of the

torch as the horde of sewer rats pressed forward, growing bolder by the moment. "Since my brilliant entry through Smeem's front door, my abilities seem to have abandoned me."

Before Davin commented on the uselessness of a partner in crime whose magical powers were as fickle as the favors of a courtesan in the high king's palace, a woman's voice called from above, "Use this! Hurry!"

Two bed sheets knotted together floated over the edge of the pit and dangled above the Jyotian's head. The young, dark-haired woman Goran and Davin had seen with Juusapt on the road that morning peered down at the thieves. No longer were her hands bound but now held tightly to the opposite end of the sheet rope.

"Hurry!" she repeated. "I can hold the smaller one of you."

Goran glanced at his companion and nodded.

Without comment, Davin once more attacked the wall. His right hand firmly clasped the end of the dangling sheet when the wall dissolved to sand beneath his left fingers. Instead of falling, he threw his left arm high and caught hold of the sheet and began pulling upward. He heard the woman above groan under the sudden burden of his weight, but she maintained her grip as he worked his way up the sheets and over the top of the pit.

"Goran, we can both support you! Up the wall!" Davin called down as he grasped the sheets and solidly braced boots on the stone floor.

Below, the Challing made a running attack at the rats with torch brandished before him. A chorus of squeaks and squeals announced the rodents' retreat, and in the next instant Goran tossed the torch into the furry horde, swirled, took three quick strides and half ran up the wall to grab the end of the sheet. In the space of ten heartbeats he sat on the edge of the pit, grinning up at Davin and the young woman.

"Fair lady, I know not your name, but you have my most heartfelt gratitude for saving my friend here from certain death," the Challing said. "By myself, I could have escaped easily, but I could not leave my friend to become dinner for that ocean of teeth and fur."

"It's not gratitude I want from you, Goran One-Eye," the woman said, her gaze holding on the Challing then shifting to the Jyotian, "or you Davin Anane, but . . ."

"Our fame spreads wide for her to know our names," Goran said with a shake of his head. "Ere long we will have to find a new profession. What good is it to be a thief if all Raemllyn knows of you?"

". . . your help in escaping this temple and that damnable Juusapt, and passage away from these cursed shores," the woman said. "Other than that the rats could have feasted on your carcasses."

"A fair enough exchange," Davin agreed. "But how did you learn our names?"

"The whole ride from Faltren to Pahl this morning – all Juusapt did was curse you," the woman replied. "From his colorful descriptions of both your parents, it was easy enough to recognize you."

"And you, fair lady?" Goran rose, took her hand and kissed it in his most courtly manner. "Whom do we thank for saving our backsides?"

"My parents named me Iesella," she answered. "Nor am I of the blue blood or a lady. Like you, I was born a thief. I sailed from Gatinah toward the Isle of Prillae. There is a new ruler there, I hear, a woman. Seemed to me Prillae was an island ripe for one of my talents. When my ship put in at Faltren, I thought to add weight to my pockets by visiting the Temple of Ediena."

Iesella quickly recounted all that had befallen her while the pair of rogues had sought the Belt of the Virgin Goddess within the walls of Smeem's estate. Nor did she shy from sharing the plans Juusapt had for her beneath this temple devoted to Ediena. "A chair firmly applied to the back of the head of the guard outside my room served me well when I heard you two chasing Juusapt through the darkness."

"One would think you would want Juusapt's head for what he has done to you," Davin said when she finished.

"That will be mine – eventually." A nasty glint fired Iesella's eyes. "We of the Sisterhood of Ebil have our ways of dealing with those who defile a true believer."

Davin could not contain the shiver that ran along his spine. Ebil was Goddess of the Frenzy. Her followers were all women – and virgins. A man who forcibly took an ebilsis signed his death warrant. When the frenzy was upon the ebilsis, a man's head was not safe, nor were his other body parts.

"The Isle of Prillae is a fine place," Goran said with a grin when she finished. "I have a friend there who will most certainly find one such as you interesting. Yes, Davin and I will help see you on your way to Prillae."

The friend the Challing spoke of was Kulonna, recently named Duchess of Prillae, Davin realized. Before High King Felrad had given her that title, Kulonna and Goran had been passionate lovers. Sending Iesella to the northern island kingdom would be Goran's way of giving Kulonna a personal message reminding the duchess he had not forgotten her.

"Of course, we'll need coin for Iesella's journey." Goran looked at Davin. "Then a way out of this Qar-damned dungeon."

"I can get you to the stairs." Iesella tilted her head to a candle burning on the stone floor. "There are two more back in my cell if they are needed."

Davin rubbed his chin. "Juusapt mentioned a vault here. That should provide more than enough for Iesella's passage to Prillae."

"And a little for our efforts," Goran amended. "Then there is a certain belt we need to retrieve before leaving."

"First we locate the vault, then find a way to the streets above," Davin reminded the Challing of their immediate situation.

"The vault and then the streets!" Goran repeated as Iesella led them through the darkness with her burning candle.

The vault proved easy to locate; it was the only room below with a door and a lock. The other small chambers stood wide open and contained simple straw mattresses and tables.

Davin grimaced, recognizing that it was to these dark cribs those who served Ediena with their bodies were eventually relegated when they grew too old or no longer interested patrons willing to offer gold and silver to partake of the pleasures of their flesh. Here they served Ediena on their backs for pennies taken from the poorest of Pahl's poor. Ediena was the Goddess of Love and Pleasure, but the men who worshipped in her name had perverted the temple into nothing more than the lowest of brothels.

"This lock wouldn't keep a child out." Goran gave a solid tug on the vault's brass handle, tearing it and lock from the wood. A gasp escaped the Challing's throat when the door swung inward and the candlelight fell over the casks and chests within.

Davin stepped inside, his own awe of the wealth collected by Ediena's whoremongers escaping his lips as a soft whistle. "Copper, brass, silver and gold, all neatly separated and arranged in their own places."

He opened a small box similar in size to one used for jewelry. It brimmed with gold bists. "This should be ample coin for your journey to Prillae and enough to assure that you are well established on the isle after you arrive." He passed the box to Iesella, then lifted a leather pouch of bists. "A hundred coins by the feel of it. Enough to aid us in our search for A'bre." He tossed the bag to Goran.

The Challing stared at his friend with doubt written across his face. "This is all? Davin, there's enough here to buy all of Lower Raemllyn! We could be kings in our own kingdoms!"

"We could be dead if we don't get out of here before we are discovered." Davin edged the red-haired giant from the vault. "There is a time for greed and a time for flight. The latter time is upon us."

Iesella's candle led them to the stairway which they mounted two steps at a time, then halted when they reached the upper hallway only to duck back inside the veiling darkness.

"Patrons arrive for the night. The temple is swarming with priests and acolytes," Davin whispered. "There's no way to the street without drawing attention to ourselves. One cry to the city guard and we might as well throw ourselves on our own swords."

"What we need is a diversion." Goran took the candle from Iesella's hand, elbowed past Davin and darted into the hall. He returned a few moments later wearing a wide grin and sniffing the air.

"What happened?" Davin questioned.

"You'll smell it soon." Goran continued sniffing like a hound trying to find a lost bitch. "There!"

Davin caught a whiff of the smoke. "A fire? You set a fire?"

"A small one," Goran replied with a sheepish shrug. "No more than a couple of silk curtains – and maybe a tapestry or three. A few buckets of water will suffice to put out the flames. In the meantime, it will provide our needed diversion." To make certain, the Challing cupped hand to mouth and yelled in his booming voice. "Fire! Fire! The temple burns!"

Two heartbeats later chaos reigned. Priests, acolytes, patrons and apprentices swarmed from every nook and cranny within the temple. Nor did one give more than a fleeting glimpse at the other. When faced with the possibility of meeting the Black Destroyer amid a torrent of flames, it was a simple matter of every man – and woman – for themselves.

Goran waved an arm toward the panic in the hallway, beaming with obvious pride in his accomplishment. "That way to Pahl's streets."

Seconds later three thieves separated themselves from the crowd that grew in the street outside the Temple of Ediena. The sudden appearance of two members of the Pahlese city guard was more than enough to warrant slipping into the shadows of a nearby alleyway.

Sired by a thief and with a dame of the same ilk Iesella might have been, but as she walked up the gangplank to board a three-masted vessel called *Minima's Kiss*, she appeared every inch the lady, dressed in rich apparel and with three sailors at her heels bearing her luggage. A morning devoted to spending a portion of the gold taken from the Temple of Ediena prepared her well for her journey northward.

She paused at the ship's rail to glance back and throw the two waiting below a kiss.

"I could almost feel her lips on my cheek," Goran sighed when he turned from the wharf, Davin at his side.

"That's as close as any man will get to those lips without incurring the wrath of the Sisterhood of Ebil." Davin smiled up at his friend.

"'Tis a pity – Iesella is a rare woman. Had my powers been with me, I would have considered allowing Glylina out to play." Goran's voice held a distant quality about it as though he walked in an unshared daydream.

"Do I detect sudden affection in your voice?"

Goran shook his shaggy head and shrugged. "I fear I've worn human flesh far too long. I begin to accept human emotions as my own. In truth, I grew quite fond of Iesella in the few hours we shared with her. Had circumstances been different, who knows what might have developed?"

"Between Iesella and Goran, or Iesella and Glylina?" Davin posed.

"I'm a Challing, man or woman makes no difference to me."

Davin smiled. "First Kulonna and now I find you pining for a love that might have been. Mayhap you are right – you have been in human form too long."

"Kulonna!" Goran threw back his head and laughed. "I do believe I have placed a thorn in my love's side. Iesella has a head on her shoulders. A single bist against a thousand says that before Iesella is done with Prillae, Kulonna will find herself face to face with a lovely young thief capable of stealing control of the isle out from under her."

"Iesella will definitely make her presence known in Prillae," Davin agreed. "But at the moment, I think we should concern ourselves more with making our own presence less obvious. A room in a tavern and a few hours sleep until nightfall would be welcomed."

"Then over the wall and a return to Faltren?" Goran asked.

"By morn, we shall again greet the merchant Smeem," Davin answered, "this time as conspirators rather than thieves."

9

Captain Rorseg's mouth dropped open in surprise. His eyes darted back and forth taking in the two faces that grinned at him through the gate's steel bars.

"I know what is passing through your mind," Davin said before the captain could utter a sound. "You think to call your archers with their fine crossbows and transform the pair of us into porcupines in the space of a heartbeat. If that be your desire, do so. Neither one of us will run."

The captain's eyes narrowed to suspicious slits, but he did not signal an alarm.

So far so good, Davin thought. He had Rorseg's ear, more than he had truly hoped for. The plan to reenter Smeem's house seemed flawless when they rode from Pahl last eve. But in the light of day, and standing before Rorseg, it had the feel of madness about it.

Davin nodded a thank you for the captain's silence. "Were I standing in your boots, I would be tempted to summon the archers. It would be the easy way to erase a black mark on your good name, but Captain, we are not common thieves who bested you and your men. Nor did we do it alone. Magicks forced us to criminal ways and defeated you and your command."

"Spells?" Rorseg's eyes widened. "I told Master Smeem it was so. No mortal men could get past my men."

"Do you think mortal men can shift shapes as I did when you caught us attempting to enter this estate?" Goran asked.

"But it is as mortal men we come here today," Davin hastily added. "We are men of honor who seek to have our own good names wiped clean of the shame smeared on them – and help the good merchant recover the item stolen from him."

"Magicks," Rorseg repeated as he eyed Goran. "I should have known that no demon walks Raemllyn in the form of a man. Even such a horrible creature would have the good sense to select a more eye-pleasing physique. You two wait." The soldier waved three guards with crossbows to him. "See that these two remain where they stand while I speak with Master Smeem."

Mere minutes passed before Rorseg returned and opened the gate. "Smeem will hear you out – but be forewarned – if he suspects a single lie, he'll have your hides flayed from your bodies before he orders your heads separated from your necks."

Smeem awaited the pair in the house's outer library. With fingers steepled on his chest, he sprawled in a chair carved to accommodate the spreading fat of his body. The merchant's slightly bulging eyes speared Goran. "I never saw that one, but this is the man who assaulted me in my own bath."

"I didn't assault . . ."

Davin stepped forward, cutting Goran short with an elbow in the ribs before the Challing cost them their lives with his temper. "Master Smeem, my name is Davin Anane. I hail from far Jyotis . . ."

"Davin of the House of Anane?" Rorseg asked. "Half-brother to High King Felrad?"

Smeem's head twisted to his captain. "You know this man?"

"Of him, Master Smeem," the captain replied. "All who served in Kavindra under Felrad's command know of Davin Anane." Rorseg looked at the Challing. "And you, big one, must be Goran One-Eye." The soldier glanced back at his employer. "These two served Lijena Farleigh who now captains the high king's personal guard and carries the title of Swordbearer."

"Lijena, Goran and I returned the Sword of Kwerin Blood-hawk to High King Felrad," Davin corrected.

Rorseg's knowledge of the two did not lessen Smeem's suspicion as he shifted his bulk in the chair. "Thievery is not what one would expect of one born of royal blood – at least, not breaking into the home of an honest man. One would expect a brother to the High King to be in a more prosperous position."

"Half-brother to Felrad," Davin explained. "Enough of Bedrich the Fair's blood flows in my veins that I cannot be denied. Alas, not enough to demand that I share the luxuries of Kavindra."

Smeem nodded but said nothing.

Davin drew a breath and began the tale he had rehearsed during the night's ride from Pahl. "After Felrad regained the

Velvet Throne, my friend Goran and I traveled to Pahl seeking to make our own fortune. My plan is simple – like my homeland in the north, Pahl is known for its wines. Goran is a close friend of Kulonna, Duchess of Prillae. Our thought was to begin a shipping line to supply all Raemllyn with the finest wines and rich Prillae ale. It's easy to see there were fortunes to be made in such an enterprise."

The glint in Smeem's eyes said the merchant did see the profits to be gained in such a venture. However, all he uttered was, "Continue."

Davin had mentally pared down his yarn as he rode toward Faltren, eliminating twists and details that might ring flat. Straightforwardly, he spun a simple lie of visiting the Temple of Ediena in Pahl for an innocent diversion while Goran and he awaited their families' arrival in Pahl.

"When our wives and daughters' ship docked, the priests of Ediena greeted them while we were kept drugged in cells beneath the temple," Davin wove his tale. "The choice the high priest gave us was simple. We did as he asked or we would die and our wives and daughters would spend their lives as whores in the temple."

"Juusapt!" The name hissed from Smeem's lips like a curse.

"You know the high priest?" Davin forced surprise in his voice.

"I have dealt with him in the past," Smeem answered, impatiently waving for Davin to continue.

Davin did, explaining he and Goran were wrapped in magicks to assure they would not retreat from the task Juusapt demanded of them. "As though the lives of our families were not enough to move us to whatever Juusapt desired."

"Magicks explain why they repeatedly tried to enter the estate," Rorseg interrupted. "No man, except one under a spell would attempt to breach these walls after seeing all the security here."

"It also explains this one's transformation into a demon," Smeem said, staring at Goran. "But what of the belt stolen from me?"

"When we took it to the temple as Juusapt had ordered, our families were not delivered to us as promised," Davin said. "Instead we were given into the hands of Pahl's city guards.

Juusapt poisoned twelve members of the guard and left several of our personal items by their bodies."

"There *is* a demon at play here," Smeem said, "and his name is Juusapt. He covers his evil by laying blame for his insidious acts on the backs of others."

It was Rorseg who now grew suspicious. "How came you here? Pahlese guards are able men."

Goran grinned and shrugged. "There were but four guards. Able they were, but we are veterans of Kavindra. The guardsmen are used to policing a city, not dealing with battle-trained men."

Rorseg nodded, accepting this as truth. However, it was Smeem who spoke, "Why come here? Why not free your wives and daughters?"

"There are but two of us," Davin answered. "Juusapt has too many priests and apprentices, as well as his magicks."

He paused and held out a hand in which Goran placed the pouch taken from the vault beneath the temple. "There is more. This comes from a treasure trove hidden under Juusapt's temple. There are chests upon chests hidden there, each filled with those."

Smeem opened the leather pouch and poured a hundred gold bists into his lap. The Belt of the Virgin Goddess was a road to pleasure, but coin was a merchant's lifeblood. He understood the power of a golden coin above all else.

"Enough in those vaults to allow four men to live like kings for the rest of their lives." Davin's eyes shifted between Smeem and Rorseg. "And enough for a small army of guards to live like lords."

Smeem scooped the bists from his lap and returned them to the pouch. For several minutes he sat there, feeling the weight of the bists in his palm. "I feel you have a plan for retrieving this treasure – as well as freeing your family."

"Master Smeem," Davin answered with a smile, "of course I have a plan."

"Smeem wears the final piece of the leaf," Goran said as they hauled Rorseg up the side of the wall enclosing the city of Pahl. "Did you notice?"

"I saw," Davin answered. "It would pay us to stay close to the merchant and make our move at the first opportunity. The sooner we leave Pahl behind, the better I will like it."

"Agrccd," Goran answered, "but I don't understand why you had to give Smeem all our gold. Surely, a fcw bists would have sufficed."

"To catch a whale a man must bait his hook with more than a minnow." Davin fell to silence when the captain's hand grasped the top of the wall and the man scrambled up beside the two adventurers.

"How far to this temple?" Rorseg asked.

"We'll be there in time to meet Smeem as planned," Davin assured the soldier whom the merchant had ordered to stay with the pair to assist them. "By the morn, you'll have gold enough that you'll never have to serve another man for the rest of your life."

"Mayhap." Rorseg's attempt to interject a dour note to his voice could not contain the symphony of greed in his tone.

"Worry about Smeem after we're below on the street," Goran cautioned. "The sentinel will pass this way soon, and it would not do to have him find us here."

Neither Davin nor Rorseg questioned the Challing's wisdom. Holding dagger and sword to keep them from rattling in the night, they leaped below. Freeing makeshift grapnel hook and rope, Goran followed.

Outside the Temple of Ediena the three wove through the crowd waiting for the nightly calling. More than the city's poor gathered. Davin spied both men and women in fine attire who would sell their bodies for the Goddess of Love this night. The lusts and desires of human flesh, the Jyotian understood well. Disguising those passions as worship lay beyond his comprehension.

"Smeem," Rorseg whispered and tilted his head to the left.

The fat merchant was easy to discern even in the flickering light of torches held high. Smeem's guardsmen were not. Like the crowd, they dressed in the garb of the street; unlike the others, they concealed weapons beneath the folds of their clothing.

"The chimes of the calling," Smeem said when the three reached his side. "It's time we paid the demon Juusapt a visit."

With the others on the street, they entered the wide temple

gates and crowded into the main chamber like human cattle. Unlike cattle in a slaughterhouse, there were those mingled among the human herd ready and willing to strike before the sledgehammer fell and robbed them of life.

The instant Juusapt seated himself in a hand-carved throne of ivory to preside over the ritual selection, Rorseg's guards struck. As planned, twenty-five men, battle cries tearing from their throats, cast away the capes and robes hiding their swords and charged priest and apprentice alike.

"Juusapt!" Smeem called. "Get Juusapt before he escapes!"

Davin responded by lunging into the fat merchant. When they toppled to the floor, the Jyotian's deft fingertips found the clasp that held the last piece of the gold leaf and its chain about Smeem's neck. Both were tucked securely in Davin's blouse when he shoved to his feet.

"Time to leave, Goran," the Jyotian said.

And found Rorseg standing before him with sword drawn. "I thought as much. Trick Master Smeem, mayhap, but not me . . . uggggh!"

The soldier collapsed as a meaty fist the size of a ham came out of nowhere and connected solidly with his jaw.

Goran stepped before Davin, grinning. "He was watching you, so I watched him. Now, as you said, it's time for a hasty retreat."

Shoving aside man and woman alike as the crowd gathered for the calling panicked and rushed for the temple doors, the two thieves made it to the streets. There was no need for them to cry out in alarm as had been their plan. Those around and behind them screamed at the top of their lungs, warning all within earshot that the city of Pahl lay under siege by an army of bloodthirsty murderers.

"I fear Iesella and her sisters will be cheated this night," Davin said while he followed Goran into the darkness of a nearby alley. "Smeem's guardsmen are likely to rob them of Juusapt's life."

"And the Pahlese guard likewise will rob them." Goran paused and looked back over a shoulder to see the first of the city guardsmen arrive at the temple. A heavy sigh of regret passed over his lips. "All that gold in the vault will end up in the pockets of city officials, more likely than not. Such a waste."

"Aye," Davin said as they proceeded at a more leisurely pace toward the wall they had scaled but moments before. "All the gold except these hundred bists!"

He tossed the pouch he had retrieved from Smeem's belt to the Challing and received a broad grin in reply when Goran hitched the bag to his own belt.

"We could ride back to Faltren," Goran suggested. "There is always Smeem's house and all the riches within."

"Nay," Davin said as he tucked a hand into his blouse and withdrew the final piece of leaf and passed it to his companion. "First we climb the wall, then we retrieve our horses and put a few leagues between us and Pahl. We must see what type of key to A'bre we've found."

"Why wait?" Goran tugged the three-quarters leaf from under his shirt.

Before the Challing could attach the final piece, Davin snatched it from his hand. "Later, I'll give this to you later. I've seen the magicks the other pieces awakened in you, and I've no wish to try to smuggle a snapping purple kraken over the city's wall."

Goran looked at his friend sheepishly and gave his head a tilt in acquiescence. "You're right. Each piece has brought a renewed vigor to my unique Challing ability."

"Good," Davin answered, relieved Goran offered no protest. "There lies the wall and our horses are on the other side. It is time we found long lost A'bre!"

10

"A hundred bists weigh heavily in my pouch, and we sit here in the middle of nowhere roasting rabbits for supper. If one can call these scrawny things rabbits!" Goran turned the spit where two dressed hares hung over a small campfire. "Do we have bread to eat with this pathetic excuse for a meal? No! Where are our cups of wine or tankards of foaming ale?"

Davin chuckled. "We have fresh meat and clear water. *And* we still live. For the moment that seems enough for me. Tomorrow may be another story, but for now it is enough."

With hands behind his head and legs crossed at the ankles, the Jyotian stretched on the ground with his back propped against a *morda* tree. After a hard night's ride north from Pahl, they had reined from the road into a heavy wood. A small glen beside a clear running stream provided the quiet sanctuary needed for a long overdue sleep.

Long, wonderful, undisturbed, hours of sleep, Davin thought with the full satisfaction of a man who had slept deeply throughout most of the day. Except for the persistent nagging of an empty stomach, he felt better than he had since arriving in Pahl. Nor could he complain about the wealth that hung heavy from Goran's belt. Although not the Great Seal of Pahl or the Belt of the Virgin Goddess, he was content with their treasure. The majority of those dwelling in Raemllyn lived out their lives without ever seeing a hundred bists in a single pile.

The Jyotian's nostrils flared wide as he savored the rich aroma of roasting rabbit.

"I wonder what will become of the Belt of the Virgin Goddess?" Goran gave the spit another turn.

"In truth, I can only guess," Davin answered, scanning the blue skies above the treetops. "I suspect that it, as well as all the wealth beneath the Temple of Ediena, has been confiscated by Pahl's dignitaries. To them it will be nothing but another item of gold to be melted down and molded to coin."

"Bah, it seems like such a waste . . ."

Davin admitted a twinge of disappointment as well for the fate he was certain awaited the Belt of the Virgin Goddess. The temptation to strap the belt around his waist and sample its power was one few men or women could resist. Imagining what delights he might have tasted had he worn the belt but for a single night provided the stuff for a tantalizing daydream.

". . . yet, it may be for the best. The Jewel of Tih was endowed with similar magical powers, and I feel the world is a safer place without that bauble," Goran said.

"The Jewel of Tih?" Davin asked absent-mindedly. "I have never heard of such a jewel, and it *is* my business to keep track of Raemllyn's rare gems."

"Little wonder you haven't heard of it. I was responsible for destroying the Jewel of Tih. It was how I lost my left eye, you know," Goran answered and received a moan from his companion in reply.

The Jyotian tried to let his mind drift back to his fantasy of wearing the Belt of the Virgin Goddess, but the Challing's voice kept intruding to force Davin's thoughts back to Goran's improbable yarn. "Cloud Dwellers? There is no such race in either Lower or Upper Raemllyn."

"Aye, if not the case, it soon will be." Goran passed one of the rabbits to his friend. "The Cloud Dwellers, with their magicks, fashioned the Jewel of Tih from the very sunlight. You see, they are, or were, a dying race and needed the powers of such a potent gem to seduce humans, both men and women, to add new blood to their lines. Because of my obvious attributes, they selected me first, not realizing that I was a Challing."

Davin tore into the rabbit. It tasted every bit as good as it smelled. That surprised him. Goran and he had lived on rabbit throughout most of Upper Raemllyn's winter, and the Jyotian had sworn he would never dine on hare again. A man's empty stomach often makes a liar of his tongue.

"After satisfying a full dozen of the most beautiful women of that winged race, I fell into a deep sleep. I'm uncertain whether it was physical exhaustion or the thin air of their cloud-bound city that caused such a sleep, but I did not awake until one of those fair, recently-had-been-maidens popped my eye from its socket with the tip of a dagger. Unlike the others, the poor thing was not satisfied with a lock of my hair as a souvenir of that night of ecstasy," Goran continued while he downed sizzling bites of his own rabbit.

"You're lucky she didn't pick another one of your parts for a keepsake," Davin commented with a wicked chuckle. "After all, you had provided her with such ecstasy."

Goran ignored him. "When my eye came free, every one of those beauties went wild, each desiring my orb to treasure as a souvenir. A fight – a no-holds-barred brawl – broke out. All the time, my eye was flying through the air. I called out for them to cease and return that precious orb. Imagine my astonishment when my eye flew directly toward me and landed in my open mouth."

"Not surprising," Davin said. "Your mouth is all too often yapping when it should be closed."

"So startled was I that I swallowed my own eye," Goran went on. "That's when all twelve of those delightful beauties turned on me with daggers drawn and ready. They fully intended to cut my eye from my belly."

"Goran! Enough! This is the most ridiculous of all the lies you have ever uttered about your missing eye," Davin chided. "Can't you admit the truth? Did the sorcerer that brought you into this world somehow lack the power to give you a fully formed body? In your fight to kill him, did he poke out your eye?"

Goran sadly wagged his head from side to side as he tossed away the last rabbit bone and licked his fingers clean of grease. "Lie? You wound me deeply, friend Davin. Not once have I ever told a single falsehood when recounting the loss of my eye. It is a lacking of your human brain that you cannot comprehend the truth spoken in each of my tales. The fault is not mine."

Davin studied his companion. Something in Goran's tone and demeanor rang true. But how could that be? In all their years together, Davin surely had heard at least a thousand versions of how the Challing had lost his eye. How could they all be true? Yet, something told the Jyotian that they were – at least to Goran. That possibility bothered him even more than Goran's continuous outpouring of outrageous yarns.

Davin pointed to the leaf hung about the Challing's neck.

"You've yet to join the last portion of the amulet."

Goran slipped a hand into his tunic and brought it out with the final piece of the leaf nestled in his palm. "I hesitate." His tone held uncertainty. "For a year I've believed this to be my key back to Gohwohn. What if I've been led astray by some sorcerer who draws us to him the way we were pulled to the Blood Fountain*? What if your damnable Sitala merely play a jest on me?"

The Jyotian's brow creased. Did he sense fear in the Challing? It was hard to believe, to accept that even a mote of fear might exist within Goran's mountainous frame. Yet, Davin now saw fear reflected in his friend's single eye.

"There is only one way to find out the truth," Davin said. "If the leaf is but the beginning of a new adventure, so be it. Neither of us is a stranger to adventure."

Goran frowned, obviously unimpressed by the Jyotian's bravado. "I suppose you're right." The Challing's gaze shifted about the glen. "And I suppose this tranquil spot is good for my purpose. Should magicks overwhelm me, there will be none to see – save you."

Slipping the small piece of veined gold between his meaty fingers, Goran lifted the last piece of the medallion to its siblings hung from his neck. A soft metallic click sounded when he snapped the final portion of the leaf into place. "There it is. Do . . ."

The hairs on the back of Davin's neck stood at attention. The Jyotian's eyes narrowed while his heart doubled its pounding beat.

The medallion glowed. Not the soft green Davin had seen when each piece had been found but colors that shifted through the spectrum, colors vivid, vibrant, *alive* in their radiance. Like a kaleidoscope, the hues shattered and reformed in patterns that held the Jyotian mesmerized.

"Time and space are singular," Goran spoke as though from the depth of a trance. His single eye stared into distant nothingness. "The soul shifts from one place to another immutable in its form. Only memory flees when the soul darts from existence to existence. Few truly glimpse this infinity, recognize the endless

* See *Blood Fountain*

procession that dwells in the heart of Life . . ."

Davin barely heard the Challing's words. Instead, his attention was transfixed by the dark shadow the leaf projected across the ground. The form was not that of a leaf, but a—

The Jyotian's head twisted from side to side attempting to recognize the familiar shape. In truth it appeared to be the continents of Upper and Lower Raemllyn, yet the land masses were changed. Here a well-known bay was missing and there a mysterious peninsula jutted into the Sea of Bua. The isthmus connecting the two continents was swollen and wide.

Patterns appeared within the shade like the dappled shadows cast by sunlight shafting through a canopy of wind-tossed leaves.

"A map!" Davin stared in awe as the shadows within the shadow formed miniature mountains and twisting rivers. "I am sure of it, Goran. It's the same as appeared on the ghost ship!*"

If the Challing heard, he gave no indication, not so much as a blink of an eye. ". . . not life, but lives. Finite souls afloat among infinite planes of existence within infinitely extended universes. All caught in a single instant we name time . . ."

Davin tried and failed to repress a cold shiver that began on his neck and worked down his spine. The shadow transformed to map continued to mutate like a living thing. The Jyotian stared as the land masses of Upper and Lower Raemllyn swelled and shrank as if they marched through the slow procession of the eons in mere instants.

For a brief instant, the map was exactly the one he had known since childhood. In the beat of a heart, the Isthmus of Brykhee-dah stretched thread-thin and snapped. The two continents floated apart, then abruptly swung back on each other, colliding with such violence a vast wall of mountains rose along the point of impact.

"There is our destination." Goran walked across the map. He knelt on one knee and jabbed a finger at a pinpoint of brilliant silver that burned like a small sun near the inland sea men called Lake Woe. "A'bre."

Recalling the map within the ghost ship, Davin committed the position to memory, fearing the shadow map would vanish as

* See *Beasts of the Mist*

surely as had the ensorcelled vessel.

"We must sail up the coast, past Fayinah toward Uhjayib. The road to A'bre will be revealed." Goran stared directly at Davin, but that distant, trancelike glaze remained in his eye. "Finite souls, infinite lives – we have trod this path a thousand times and will tread thousands more in both past and future."

Davin had no understanding of metaphysical babble. He could reckon distances from a map. "It is shorter if we travel overland to Lake Woe."

"Death has claimed us on that path – claims us at this very instant – though the realm is called by a different name. Only a sail and the wind will guide us to A'bre. Any other path is held by Qar."

Dark writhings that were neither jungle nor mountain crawled to life on the map to stretch tendrils from the coast to the silver glow that was the lost city of A'bre. The Jyotian swallowed hard in an attempt to relieve the sudden dryness in his throat. If the Death God were to take life in cartographer's ink, those serpentine tentacles crawling on the map would surely have been Qar's.

Davin's gaze traced up the coast. "We can approach Lake Woe by the Tesska River."

"A sailing vessel leaves Tamiler Point on the morning tide," Goran announced as though his single eye gazed into the future. "It will carry us toward A'bre."

The Challing gave his companion little chance to reply. Standing, Goran strode toward the horses tied beneath a *morda* tree. At his first step, the map vanished, leaving only dry winter grass that gave no hint of A'bre or amulet-cast shadow.

"I only hoped to gain a few extra bists. I didn't even charge you full fair." Captain Stoweg clung to the *Stalwart*'s rail when a wall of water disguised as a wave broke against the side of the ship, nearly capsizing it. "I never should have taken on passengers at the last moment – especially two who appear from nowhere with gold dripping between their fingers. It weren't no more natural than is this storm."

"You blame us for the weather?" Davin Anane stared at the young captain in disbelief. "Are we mages who command the forces of nature? Did we speak directly to the Goddess Minima and ask for these hurricane winds?"

Davin tried to spit to emphasize his contempt, but the howling wind forced the spittle back into his mouth. In disgust he turned and clung to a stanchion, barely able to maintain his footing in the rush of water washing across the *Stalwart*'s deck.

"Why else? Winter seas are always peaceful. Nalren promises it to those of us who worship him faithfully."

Stoweg staggered beneath the onslaught of another wave and would have been crushed against the ship's wheel had not Goran grabbed him by the collar and saved him the ignominy.

The captain offered no word of gratitude. A disgusted growl rolled from deep in his throat while he fought to hang onto the wheel which he had long since lashed himself to. "Do ye think me deaf? I've heard ye whispering – 'soul's marching from one plane to another – infinite realms – time but a single blink of the eye.' Is that the talk of normal, working men? I say no. It's the conversation of wizards. Evil ones, to boot!"

Davin wiped the stinging seawater from his eyes and peered into the towering walls of heaving green water. He damned his luck aloud. The scream of the wind drowned his curse. Stoweg had overheard him explaining all that had happened after Goran had pieced together the golden amulet. The Challing remembered nothing except pointing to the glowing spot of silver he labeled A'bre. Any attempt to explain the truth would only make Goran and him appear sorcerers more than they already did.

"I've no use for mages nor the bad luck that sits on their shoulders." The captain spun the wheel, turning his ship into a swell that would have swamped the vessel had it broken over the boat. "I want double your passage or I'll throw you over the side. You'll pay for your trickery or you'll not stand long on this deck."

"Try and you will find yourself combing Nalren's seaweed beard the rest of your days," Goran bellowed. The captain cringed but did not appear to rethink his demand.

"This is no normal storm. Magicks stir it. I smell them on the gale. You brought this on the *Stalwart*. There is no other explanation. Rumors back in Tamiler Point were abuzz about two mages who destroyed the Temple of Ediena in Pahl, killed the high priest and a prosperous merchant from Faltren. To cover their escape, these two materialized chests of gold and set the citizens of the city at each others' throats in a scramble to possess those riches. I think you are those mages and have brought Ediena's wrath down upon my ship."

"Your imagination runs away with itself. If your leaking scow were half as fast, we would be in a safe harbor by now," Goran declared with a shake of his head.

"Mayhap, but my crew will believe me," Stoweg replied with a sly smile twisting his lips. "Then see how fast your arms can carry you to a safe harbor!"

Davin recognized the captain's tirade for what it was – no more than a wily game to milk a few more bists from his passengers. The price was almost worth it to have learned all that had transpired in Pahl after their hasty retreat from the Temple of Ediena. He made a mental note to avoid Pahl at all costs during any future journeys to Lower Raemllyn's southwestern coast.

"Utter one word to your crew, and I'll skewer your scrawny body like I would a gutter rat." Goran rested his hand on the pommel of his sword to make certain the greedy seaman understood his meaning.

Davin turned toward the captain intent on bolstering the Challing's threat. The Jyotian's words deflated to a startled gasp.

A monstrous head with the height and breadth of a full-grown man ripped through an undulating swell amid a storm of flying foam.

Hand dropping to belt, Davin wrenched dagger from sheath as he stumbled away from the rail. The leviathan that broke from the ocean's depths defied all memory or description of sea serpents found in the Oceans of Kumar.

The broad head that shifted toward him appeared born of both land and sea. Aglitter with green scales like a *surrin* fish, it sported a flat snout more appropriate on a wild boar from the forests of Upper Raemllyn. The eyes belonged to neither fish nor boar but were reptilian, each moving independently of the other.

The cavernous maw that opened to split the head in twain had been spawned in the bowels of Peyneeha. The foot-long recurved tusks that filled that mouth snapped closed and with a toss of the monstrous head tore away the section of railing Davin had clung to but a heartbeat before.

The gaping nostrils flared and snorted in disgust at the taste of splintered wood rather than warm human flesh. Another toss of that grotesque head set the portion of railing sailing through the air. Wide-spaced eyes flecked with yellow and gold rotated forward to focus on the Jyotian when the head arched back to prepare for another lunge.

Attention held by eyes and yawning mouth, Davin did not see a rubbery tentacle that lashed from the sea and swept across the deck toward his legs.

Goran One-Eye did!

In spite of the rolling deck and the seawater rushing in sheets across the wood, the Challing bolted from the wheel and launched himself straight at his companion. Arms wide, Goran caught Davin about the waist. The Challing's momentum and weight lifted him from the deck and carried him beyond the coiling green tentacle.

Together, they hit the deck with arms and legs flailing out for support, careening into the legs of five crewmen huddled near the main mast.

"You were an eye's blink away from ending your life as fish bait!" Goran grinned when he managed to sit up and twist around to his friend.

"Close," Davin agreed with a nod. "Closer than I want . . ."

"Overboard with them!" Stoweg's cry carried over the roar of the wind. "The creature comes for them. Feed them to it! Do it now before the monster claims all of us!"

Before he was certain what happened, anxious hands grabbed for Davin. They held his arms and legs, lifting him from the deck. He kicked and twisted to no avail.

"Heave them over the side! Give them to Nalren, God of the Seas, so that he will calm the waters!" Stoweg continued. "Make haste, men! The creature has gone between the waves. Throw them overboard before it rises again!"

"Unhand me, you slimy sons of a . . ."

Goran's curse abruptly ended in a heavy splash. The next moment, Davin went hurling through the air, a flight that ended when he landed in the roiling sea. He kicked upward, fighting the current that dragged him downward. Arms and legs thrashing against the salt water, he broke the surface. He sucked in air when an ocean swell lifted him high.

"Goran!" he called out.

The Challing did not answer nor was he to be seen!

Higher the swell pushed toward the slate gray sky. The *Stalwart* now rode in a deep trench between two swells a full twenty feet below Davin. He searched in all directions. Goran was nowhere to be seen.

The head of the monstrous sea creature, however, was very visible as it thrust through the wall of the swell opposite the one he rode atop. Not one but two of the ship's crew were snatched from the deck when the tusked maw opened wide and shot forward.

In the next instant, Davin's world transformed into a tumbling chaos of spray and foam. The swell peaked and broke into a roaring wave with the Jyotian caught on the tip of the curl. The force of the breaking water sent him tumbling head over heels. The Jyotian threw arms and legs straight out in the hope of being thrown forward like an arrow rather than tossed to the depths like a spinning rock.

The wave did neither. Davin found himself caught at the crest of the wave's curl like a piece of driftwood. Belly down he rode the wave like some watery steed, allowing the ocean's unbridled power to carry him toward a distant shoreline.

Halfway to the sandy beach the wave died and left the Jyotian treading water. When the next swell rose beneath him, he was ready. With arms stroking long and hard and legs kicking with all their strength, Davin swam with the swell. When it broke he was there, once more riding the churning foam toward the shore.

11

Davin's boots touched sandy bottom. With arms wide for support and balance, he managed a springing step and then another and then another. Soon he pushed through waist-deep water and trudged onto a beach littered with tangled seaweed.

"I wondered when you would see fit to come ashore. I have been waiting for you half the day."

Davin's head jerked up. Ten strides away Goran One-Eye sat in the sand, grinning from ear to ear. "How? I thought you'd drowned!"

"I found a porpoise's shape suited me well in this brisk sea." The Challing laughed. "I would have offered you a ride, but you appeared to be enjoying yourself surfing."

"*Surfing?*" Davin stared at his friend. The term was unknown to him. "What is this *surfing*?"

"Surfing," Goran rolled the syllables on his tongue. "Surfing – I'm not certain where I heard the word before – but be assured that is what you were doing. Perhaps it was on one of the other infinite planes you said we exist on."

"I said no such thing." Davin collapsed to the beach beside the Challing. "I merely repeated all you uttered while entranced by the leaf about your neck."

"I remember no such utterances." Goran shook his head. "Though such a philosophy lies at the heart of Challing knowledge."

Once, Davin would have argued against the existence of other planes and dimensions except the rock solid reality of Raemllyn. Meeting Goran and living with his shape-shifting abilities had undermined those beliefs. The rent in time and space the now dead Zarek Yannis had opened to admit the demon Faceless Ones defeated in the battle to regain the Velvet Throne for Prince Felrad had shattered Davin's concept of a singular world in a singular universe.

"However, your metaphysical beliefs explain the feeling I have that you will be at my side when I lose my eye," Goran continued.

Davin's head snapped around. "When you *lose* your eye? Unless I'm mistaken, there's no eye under the patch you wear."

Goran tentatively touched the fur eye patch. "Aye, you're correct, no orb dwells beneath this spot of fox fur. That does not change the fact I've yet to lose my eye . . ."

"No, Qar-damn you, no!" Davin refused to hear another word. In all their years together, he had listened to endless wild tales of how the Challing had lost his eye. Now Goran claimed he had yet to lose that eye! "You do this because you enjoy irritating me. You see it as some kind of Challing jest!"

"I speak from what I see as the future and what has been the past," Goran said, voice level and a trifle distant. "I readily admit finding your race of humans more than a little humorous."

Davin's mouth twisted in disgust. "Suddenly I find myself befriended by a seer! Where stems this new-found ability? Has your leaf amulet bestowed upon you the power to divine the future?"

Goran laughed, apparently enjoying Davin's irritation and confusion. "I make no such claims, but the leaf has restored my memories – in full, I believe – memories robbed from my head when I was wrenched from Gohwohn to this ball of mud. Those memories of the future say I have yet to lose my eye."

"Ahhgah!" Davin shook with mounting frustration. Each word the Challing let slip from his tongue made less and less sense. "And how *will* you lose your eye?"

"Davin, my friend, calm yourself. Your anger is not with me but at yourself for nearly getting us killed."

"Me? I nearly got us killed?" Davin's eyes went wide, then narrowed to slits. "How did *I* nearly cost us our lives?"

"You spouted your metaphysical philosophies within earshot of Captain Stoweg, not I. Your words made him brand us wizards and decide to sacrifice us to Nalren," Goran replied with a smile that said his twisted logic made perfect sense in the mind of a Challing.

"Had I not pledged my word to help you find ancient A'bre," Davin said as he spat to the sand, "I would leave you here to rot in your tangled memories!"

"Not that offering us to the God of the Depths has aided him or his ship." Goran pointed to the sea. "It appears yon sea monster was summoned for the *Stalwart* and her crew rather than for you and me."

Davin's gaze scanned the watery horizon. In the distance, he made out the silhouette of a finned serpentine body rising from the waves and falling across the *Stalwart*. He could almost hear the crack of timbers and shattering of the decks beneath the creature's ponderous weight.

Goran pushed to his feet. "The ship is breaking up."

Davin could barely see the shape of the vessel's bow as it lifted toward the stormy sky, then slowly sank below the waves.

"The serpent will have a full belly when it returns to the depths," Goran said without a trace of emotion in his voice.

Davin, however, shuddered with each rise and fall of the monster's head. The distance spared him from actually seeing the creature's mouth close around helpless sailors, but his mind was not so kind. He had seen that tusk-filled maw and knew what it could do to a man.

"All in all, Captain Stoweg and his ship served their purpose," Goran said when he turned his back on the ocean.

"But we are without a vessel," Davin said. He then reminded the Challing, "You said we had to travel to A'bre on the deck of a ship."

"No," Goran corrected. "I said a ship would show us the path to A'bre. And there is a path. See?"

Davin didn't like what he saw. The forests and woods that had surrounded Pahl transformed into jungle this far northward? The path Goran pointed to led directly into the jungle's tangled vegetation.

"Our path is obvious." Goran started toward the jungle. "All that remains is for us to follow it."

"Goran! You don't know where that leads!" Davin called to his friend.

The Challing's strides remained strong and determined as he disappeared into the green wall of vegetation. Davin cursed aloud. There was nothing else he could do but run and catch up with his stubborn friend.

Goran cupped his hands in the stream and threw both handfuls of water onto his face. He used a shirtsleeve to wipe the water from his eye when he sat back in the tall grass. "There is a sweet whisper of breeze today. It offers a small respite from this hellish heat."

Davin knelt by the stream, drank from a cupped hand, then thrust his head beneath the water. The respite Goran mentioned was small indeed, barely noticeable. "And this is the jungle's winter. Jajhana graced us by not placing us here in the middle of summer."

Goran sniffed at the air, his nose wrinkling and his lips pursing. "A curious scent hangs on the breeze." He pulled the intact amulet from beneath his tunic and inspected it carefully. "I sense no magicks, nor does my leaf."

Davin saw no hint of witchfire on the golden leaf nor in his companion's single eye.

"The odor is there, though – heavy – musky." Goran slipped the medallion beneath his shirt again. "Do you smell it?"

"All I smell is my own reeking sweat." Davin washed his face again. "It's been a full week since the *Stalwart*'s crew provided us with our last bath. If you don't begrudge me a few moments' delay, I shall partake fully of this stream."

"A bath can wait," Goran said, halting the Jyotian when he began to strip off his shirt. "A'bre lies near. I can feel it."

"Goran, Lake Woe lies weeks ahead of us in the north," Davin answered. "That is, if you can tell one direction from the others in this jungle. Surely we have time for a bath and the chance to wash our clothes?"

"There will be time for a bath when we reach A'bre." Goran shoved to his feet and drew his longsword. With a wide swipe, he cleared the leafy undergrowth to reveal once more the path they had trod for a week.

"Is this a guess, or is my bath held in your *future* memories?" Davin asked as he jumped across the narrow stream and moved after his friend.

Less than a hundred strides from the stream, Goran paused, threw his head back and sniffed the air again.

"What's wrong?" The Jyotian stared up into the Challing's sweaty face and saw something more than weariness. A shadow of doubt flickered across his companion's features. "Goran, what do you see?"

"Nothing. I see nothing." Goran shifted uneasily from foot to foot. "Nor do I hear anything. It is what I smell, and what I *feel*. Something stalks us. Can't you feel it?"

Davin slowly drew a deep breath. He then made a complete turn, scanning the tangled vegetation surrounding them. "There's nothing, Goran. You are as weary as I. I think it best to return to the stream. A bath and a long sleep would do us both good. We've been pushing ourselves . . ."

"No." Finality clung like a barnacle to that single syllable. Goran's eye shifted from left to right to search the dense vegetation. "They are close – moving in closer."

"They? They? What *they*?" Davin drew another breath to continue and fell silent.

A musky scent lay hidden beneath the ever present sweetness of rot permeating the jungle. Another breath and the odor had vanished. A third and the Jyotian smelled it again. This time there was a familiarity to the scent, raw and bestial.

"You sense it now?" Goran asked while he continued to study their surroundings. "It grows stronger – and they move closer."

The odor came and went with each breath Davin drew, but he no longer doubted the Challing. Making another slow turn, his gaze probed the tangle of trees and vines that towered around them. High above, more than the slight breeze stirred a branch. He nudged Goran and pointed toward the suspicious movement.

"Some *thing* stirred the leaves, but I cannot make out more than shadows." Goran sniffed hard. "The smell is stronger there. Come, it's time we found a place to defend ourselves."

"In the middle of a jungle? Better to put a tree trunk to our backs." Davin continued to scrutinize the trees while he followed the Challing as he sliced through fanlike fronds to clear the path.

Nothing. The Jyotian saw no more movement but could not escape the prickling sensation at the back of his neck. Someone or something watched them. And whatever it was held the advantage. It remained hidden while Davin sensed Goran and he might as well have walked across a flat, open plain. They – it – saw every move the Challing and he made.

"Here," Goran announced abruptly half a league from the now half-forgotten stream. "What we seek is here."

"Here?" Davin glanced around the small clearing where the Challing halted. "Goran, this clearing is barely twenty strides across."

Goran moved to the lightning-shattered trunk of what had once been a giant of the jungle at the center of the clearing. With back pressed to the rotting remains of the bole, he eyed the green wall of tree and vine that encircled them. "Here, it's here somewhere. I feel it."

"It? Or they?" Davin took a stance beside his friend and slipped sword from sheath.

"They come, Davin," Goran replied, never taking his gaze from the jungle. "But I feel *it*. A'bre lies close – closer than they are."

With a sideways glance, the Jyotian noted the Challing's eye. No glint of witchfire sparked there. Davin was not certain whether to be relieved or not. The lack of witchfire indicated whatever stalked them did so without magicks. It also said the Challing's own shape-shifting powers ebbed.

"Above!" Goran's elbow jabbed Davin's side. "They come at us from above!"

The Jyotian heard it now. Something heavy moved through the branches. It sounded as if it dropped, moving from limb to limb on a path straight for the—

Ground! It – a massive Uhjayib gorilla – dropped directly across the clearing from the two adventurers. The black-furred ape stood motionless, arms planted firmly on the ground, human-imitating eyes locked on Challing and man.

"It," Davin said in near relief as he studied the muscular master of Lower Raemllyn's western jungles; "there is only one."

He spoke too soon. Again branch and leaf stirred. Two more of the flat-headed monsters swung from the trees and positioned themselves beside the first gorilla.

"Three," Davin said aloud. "Our blades more than make up for the third."

"What about the fourth and fifth?" Goran tilted his head when two more of the yellow-fanged creatures descended from the heights. "Or those?"

The five became ten as more furry bodies dropped from the branches to the ground. Like the first, all ten stood and stared at the humans who dared intrude into their domain.

"It is said their bite is poisonous," Davin whispered.

"It could definitely cause death," Goran answered, "but I doubt poison would be the reason. Rather, those fangs might rip out a man's throat."

Davin did not argue. Fangs or arms, the gorillas were equipped to rend a man's body into pieces – small pieces. "They don't move. Why don't they attack?"

Goran shook his head while he kept sword level and ready. "Mayhap men are unknown to them? We are an oddity rather than a threat? Surely, humans cannot be common this deep in the jungle."

The possibility brought Davin little comfort, nor did it ring true. Men had once come and gone freely through this portion of the jungle. The path they followed marked that passage. Although, Davin thought, that it was overgrown also said years had passed since it had been used.

"They don't attack," Goran went on. "They just stand and stare at us."

As though in answer to the Challing's words, the gorillas moved. Not in attack, not in a random shifting, but one step forward in perfect unison. Then they halted again and continued to stare with unblinking eyes at the two humans.

"What?" Davin's head jerked back, not knowing whether to believe his own eyes. "It isn't possible."

"It happened," Goran said.

And it happened again. All the gorillas advanced one step simultaneously, then stopped.

Davin's gaze darted to the Challing. Still no hint of witchfire burned in his eye. If magicks were at play, Goran did not sense them.

The black apes took another step.

"They move like a precision-drill unit in King Felrad's own guard," Davin said, still uncertain whether to believe what he saw. "It makes no sense. Why don't they charge?"

"They are not here to kill us, friend Davin." The trancelike quality the Jyotian had heard in Goran's voice each time he found a piece of the leaf amulet returned to the Challing's voice. "They have been sent to see that we remain on the path to A'bre."

The distant gaze which usually accompanied Goran's trance was missing. The Challing's good eye darted left and right, searching. "It's here, Davin. It's here, I can *feel* it. But I can't see it."

The gorillas took two steps forward, still in perfect unison.

Goran tugged the leaf from beneath his tunic. He cursed under his breath. No glow radiated from the gold. "It's here, I tell you. I can feel it."

Ignoring the ten gorillas when they took two more steps forward, Goran edged around to the other side of the trunk. "I knew it! Davin, I've found the way to A'bre."

Facing ten Uhjayib gorillas alone, in spite of the fact they moved like marionettes on invisible strings, did not sit well with the Jyotian. He edged closer to the Challing.

"There. See the spot of light," Goran said softly. "See how the speck brightens? That is A'bre and our goal. I feel it pulling me strongly now."

"I see the spot." Davin also glanced over a shoulder to see the gorillas advance once more. "It's no more than sunlight filtering through the trees."

"No, it is the gateway to A'bre. The sea monster and now the gorillas were sent to guide us," Goran insisted.

To Davin the circle of light no wider than the length of a man's foot still appeared to be sunlight on the ground. "Lake Woe lies hundreds of leagues to the north. I suggest we cover a few dozen of those leagues while the gorillas are practicing their close-order drills."

Goran turned to his companion and shook his head. "Step into the light, friend Davin. That is all we need do."

"I think we'd be better served by stepping straight through . . ."

A blood-chilling roar split the jungle's silence. Behind the two thieves, the Uhjayib gorillas suddenly came to life. Ten monsters charged, each capable of tearing a man to shreds in a matter of seconds! Nor were their movements in unison now although they did move with singular purpose – the lust for blood!

"The light! Into the light!" Goran urged.

He did not wait for Davin to respond. The Challing's arm snaked out, hand clamping to the Jyotian's shoulder.

In the next instant, Davin went hurling into the light – a light that shattered into a spinning spectrum of colors never meant to be viewed by the human eye. Solid ground dropped away beneath the Jyotian's feet and he fell into nothingness.

12

Davin heard a cry – his own. It screamed up from the depths of the pit, raced past him, echoed in the distance, then rolled back over his head, and all the while he tumbled headlong through the swirling light of ever-changing color.

In the blink of an eye or the winking out of a lifetime, he knew not which, the ground abruptly returned. He hit, shoulder first, grunting in pain as he rolled in an attempt to regain his feet, only to flop gracelessly on his backside.

Beside him a disembodied leg appeared in the air. That familiar leg was soon followed by the equally familiar body of Goran One-Eye who stepped out of nothingness as though passing through an unseen doorway.

"We have arrived, friend Davin." Goran reached down and slapped his companion on a shoulder. "We made it! We have found lost A'bre!"

Rubbing his throbbing shoulder, Davin climbed to his feet with another grunt. His gaze moved over their surroundings. All he could do was shake his head and mutter, *"This* is A'bre?"

He was not certain whether to laugh or cry at the sight that met his eyes.

A perplexed expression clouded Goran's face. "It isn't much to look at, is it?"

"An understatement, my friend." Davin continued to stare in disbelief. "Are you certain you shoved me through the correct portal?"

They stood in the middle of a village – no, Davin decided, describing this pitiful collection of hovels as a village was an insult to every *real* hamlet in both Upper and Lower Raemllyn. The squat mud huts with dry straw roofs were simply a dozen shoddy structures assembled in a rough circle.

The Lost City of A'bre – throughout his life the very mention of the ancient metropolis had evoked images of elegant buildings with soaring spires crafted out of marble and silver and gold. The artistry and splendor of those edifices reflected the nature of the city's inhabitants who spent their days in pursuit of philosophy, literature, art and music.

This – this was a heap of dust that would blow away in a strong wind!

"I am no mage. I cannot direct the magicks in the leaf." Goran winced like a wounded child. "But surely *this* can't be legendary A'bre. It's more a pigsty than a palace. Yet, it has to be our destination. The leaf brought us here. There can be no other answer."

"I can think of a few." Davin watched two gaunt men wearing no more than loincloths exit a nearby hut. Their dark bodies, baked by years under the harsh sun, seemed to absorb the day's light as they moved toward the blue water of the lake on whose shore the huts were built. Neither gave the two strangers in their midst so much as a curious glance. "To begin with, the Sitala have played a cosmic joke on you, and taken me along as spice for the jest. Then there is the very real possibility that this isn't A'bre, that A'bre never existed and we were never meant to find it. These mud hovels could never be mistaken for a magnificent city even by the wildest dreamer."

Goran turned to Davin and frowned. "Mud hovels? I see no hovels. This is a town no more or no less than one would expect to find in any of Raemllyn's realms. Smaller than most, I would reckon, but large enough to attract those three ships tied to the wharf."

Davin followed the Challing's gaze to the water's edge. All he saw were the two half-naked men squatted barefoot in the mud with fishing poles and lines in hand. "Goran, there are no ships, no town, no wharf – only miserable mud huts and two skinny men fishing in the lake."

"No, friend Davin, the town stretches for at least . . ." Goran stopped abruptly and peered down at the leaf about his neck. No glow came from the gold. "No magicks are at play. How is it our eyes see different sights?"

"Do the dwellers in your hamlet notice us, Goran?" Davin saw a child dart from another hut and run toward the men by the lake. The boy appeared oblivious to their presence.

"Of course they do. See those two lovelies there? Let me hail

them and let them direct us to the nearest tavern." Goran lifted
an arm and called toward a withered *morda* tree.

"Ask them about a bath while you're at it," Davin suggested
while he watched his friend's features twist in disbelief.

"They acted as though they were deaf," Goran said. "They
didn't so much as glance my way."

"I don't believe they will," Davin answered, trying to ignore
the prickle of the hairs on his neck. "I think we've stepped into a
land of ghosts."

"Nay, those you see are not ghosts," a broken voice came from
behind the two thieves, "though there be ghosts aplenty to be
found if you're of a mind to go looking for them. For me it's hard
enough keeping up with the living."

Davin and Goran turned. To the Jyotian's eyes an old crone
bent low shuffled out of one of the hovels. The Challing perceived
a hag who pushed a flower cart over a street of cobblestones.

"It took you long enough to get here. I sent the ship northward
for you over a year ago. Why didn't you just stay aboard? It
would have brought you straight here, it would." The ancient
woman walked right up to Goran and lifted the gold leaf with two
grubby fingers. "You found all four parts? One of them was
enough. Didn't you see the map on the ship? You can read, can't
you? It's hard to remember your exact mettle. Too many memories for a single mind to juggle around at once."

The woman's brazen approach widened the Jyotian's eyes. In
appearance she might have been one of a thousand beggars who
inhabited the streets of Raemllyn's cities. Her clothing was a
mismatch of colors and fabrics, no more than rags held together
by coarsely stitched patches. Her hair was a wide tangle of matted
silver that looked as though it might have recently served as a
bird's nest. Dirt and grime equaling her abundant years smeared
both hands and face.

The hag's eyes, however, shone a clear blue. Light caught in
them and fractured in a blaze as bright as any sapphire or
diamond. And the right corner of her mouth lay slightly upturned
as though eternally twisted in humorous irony.

"One part?" Goran stared at the woman. "I needed but one
part?"

"Should have been more than enough." The crone noticed a

louse that crawled on her shoulder. Capturing it between thumb and forefinger, she sliced it in twain with dirty fingernails. "All the parts contained the same message. It's often a problem with men of action. They rarely use what's in their heads. Oh well, it matters not how you arrived, just that you *did* arrive. Although not a moment too soon. My time grows short." She turned, lifted an arm and signaled them to follow. "Hurry. The sooner we get to the cave, the sooner I can be on my way."

"Old woman!" Davin hastened to her side. "Hold. Neither of us has the intention of going to any cave until we know what is happening to us."

"Aye!" Goran stepped beside Davin. "I came in search of a way to return to my home world of Gohwohn – to find A'bre. Instead my friend and I find a town that is, or isn't, depending on whose eyes view it. Davin sees a cluster of hovels, I see a prosperous town. Which is true?"

The crone halted, turned slowly and eyed the pair while she scratched at her side. "Two A'bres – is that all you see? A thousand times a thousand A'bres dance before these eyes."

"All time, but a single instant." Davin's mouth twisted in disgust. The hag babbled nonsense as ridiculous as Goran when lost in the trance of the amulet. "Infinite planes – finite souls."

The crone arched her right eyebrow high and studied the Jyotian. "Perhaps I misjudged you. You appear to be aware of the erudite . . ."

"He repeats something he heard me say," Goran interjected, his chest puffing out.

"Then you should understand that A'bre is a nexus, a vertex, where the universes intersect, connect, overlap." The woman glanced nervously over a bony shoulder toward a nearby hill. "There isn't time to discuss the obvious. I must sleep, and you should be on your way. We have to get to the cave."

"No cave," Goran said firmly. "I came to return to Gohwohn."

"And he wants to return to his home world." The crone pointed at Davin.

"But this is Raemllyn," Davin corrected.

The woman shook her head, and her shoulders slumped as though bent by an unseen burden. "This is A'bre. I thought you understood that. In A'bre you are nowhere and everywhere at the same moment. We must go to the cave. We haven't time to waste. Of that you can be certain."

"Then explain." Goran's expression said he was as confused as Davin.

The woman sighed heavily in acquiescence. "Walk with me toward the cave and I will explain what I understand." She smiled wistfully up at Goran. "You were less stubborn when we first met in the city of the Cloud Dwellers. You were after the Jewel of Tih."

"I *stole* the Jewel of Tih," Goran corrected when they started toward the hill.

"But not before I stole your eye." The woman cackled with obvious delight. "I wore it strung about my neck until my death. It was a constant reminder of the pleasures we shared that night."

"Death?" Davin's head jerked back. "But you live and breathe this very moment!"

"Infinite planes – finite souls," she said with a wink in the Jyotian's direction. "A single life is but a step in the endless procession. My curse, or treasure, are the memories. I recall all my lives past and future. They grow confused, you know. There are so many, so many sad ones, so few pleasant ones."

She looked back at Goran. "You remember, too. At least in part. Do you remember the Cloud Dwellers of Marrces?"

"Could I ever forget?" Tenderness flowed in Goran's voice. "Moreover, could a man ever forget Mettatine? What man wouldn't readily sacrifice an arm – or an eye – to share the passions and pleasures that were ours!"

A tear welled in the crone's right eye and trickled down her cheek, turning to mud along the way. "Or forget how I took your eye." She sighed again. "But that is another time, another life. Perhaps it lies ahead of us. That would be something to look forward to, would it not?"

"Aye, it would, my Mettatine." Goran's arm encircled the hag's waist and drew her close in a tight squeeze. "Now I seek to return to Gohwohn."

Madness! Davin had often doubted that his companion was in full control of his mental facilities. Now he was certain the Challing carried more than the seed of insanity within his brain.

Goran and the hag were both raving lunatics! Nothing either said made sense.

"Yes, yes," Mettatine said with a nod. "Let me see – Gohwohn – Roan-Jafar – yes, yes that is it."

Goran stiffened. "What of the mage Roan-Jafar?"

"Roan-Jafar and Etol-Sammo," she said as though lost in memory. "Roan-Jafar played with powers he could never control. You were a victim brought from another world." She looked up at the Challing. "Not an innocent victim, you are one who has never been innocent, but an unknowing victim. You were to serve as pawn. Through you the universe would shatter, but you were not tainted with the ambitions of those mages. You were simply you. That was a force they were not prepared to reckon with."

"You speak in riddles, woman." Davin could make neither head nor tail out of her babble. "Goran has told me of Roan-Jafar who drew him from Gohwohn to Raemllyn and then bound him to human form. But who is Etol-Sammo?"

"Aye," Goran added. "His name is unknown to me."

"A mage of great power and greater ambition, more grasping than even Roan-Jafar," Mettatine answered. "Together they came to A'bre to steal its greatest possession – the Grimoire of the Ages."

Davin shook himself. Goran had slain Roan-Jafar, and this Etol-Sammo was of little concern. "My friend seeks only the doorway back to Gohwohn. Can you help him resolve his plight?"

"His plight?" The old woman cackled. "His predicament is nothing compared to the black destiny facing the universes!"

The old crone offered nothing to ease Davin's skepticism. More than once he had worked crowds, large and small in the cities, taking on the role of a mind reader. The technique employed was simple: dribble forth tidbits of knowledge in piecemeal fashion and use the mark's reaction to point the way as to how to proceed. Eagerness in the voice, anticipation in the eye or a ready smile hanging on the corners of the mouth all provided clues for the observant.

The Jyotian sensed Mettatine employed similar methods to read Goran and feed him what he wanted to hear. Yet he could not deny that it was she who first spoke the name of the mage who had brought Goran One-Eye to Raemllyn.

"Did you know Roan-Jafar is dead?" The woman's question was disjointed and unconnected as seemed to be all her sentences.

"Of course he is dead," Davin answered with no attempt to hide his growing disgust. "Goran killed the mage with his own knife."

"Yes," she went on, as if she had not heard the Jyotian, "Roan-Jafar is dead but Etol-Sammo lives! And the battle rages. You do not see it here. The battleground is elsewhere. Elsewhen. Etol-Sammo is winning."

Goran fingered the leaf that dangled from his neck. "You used this amulet to summon me to your aid?"

"Me? No, my wild one, not I but the mages of A'bre. You must stand beside them against Etol-Sammo's incredible power. Should he triumph and gain the Grimoire of the Ages, the power would be his to sever the nexus. Universes would be lost and all the souls they contain within them."

"The mages of A'bre?" Davin scoffed. Had Goran truly lost his mind? The Challing hung on the hag's every word. "Where? In *that* A'bre? There are no mages in those mud huts, only half-naked fishermen."

"There are – were – will be," the old woman muttered. "The battle rages wide and far, far beyond what we see. You must help us or all will be lost. I feared I had chosen the wrong time to find you or perhaps you would not recognize this leaf that once adorned the Jewel of Tih."

Without so much as glancing about, Goran entered the cave at Mettatine's side. Hand on his sword, Davin paused at the entrance and cautiously surveyed the interior. It appeared to be a single room dug out of the hillside. The furnishings were no more than he expected, a solitary bed made of straw. The old woman and Goran squatted beside a low fire that burned within a ring of stones at the center of the cave.

"Watch and you will see glimpses of that of which I speak." She reached out again and touched the medallion at Goran's neck.

The brush of her fingertips awoke the gold. A soft white glow radiated from the amulet.

"Look! See!" Mettatine pointed to the cave's unadorned wall.

Davin blinked and blinked again. Images there came to life as though he stared out of a wide window. In spite of himself, Davin gazed at the progression of armies and magicks, of towering triumph and unutterable loss. And flashing across the picture was a tall, slender man of handsome disposition. He appeared benevolent, smiling gently as he dispensed – death.

"Etol-Sammo now kills the mages of A'bre. This is how it is unless you travel to this A'bre and stop him," Mettatine said. "That is your task. You must change this history. You must return to that A'bre and prevent Etol-Sammo's victory."

"Change history? Impossible!" Goran shook his head as though he were a man casting off the veils of sleep. "I seek only a return to my Gohwohn."

"There is no path open to Gohwohn or any other plane as long as Etol-Sammo reigns. The mages of that bygone A'bre can give you what you seek, but you must earn it by defeating Etol-Sammo. His evil is transcendent now."

"We are not mages." Goran shook his head again. "We are only simple . . ."

"You are what you have always been and will be a – a thief – but not a simple one. It is the same for your friend, Davin Anane." Her head lifted to the Jyotian. "Although for the last son of the House of Anane, another path will eventually call you home. That is, if you defeat Etol-Sammo and pass through the door to Raemllyn."

Davin said nothing from where he stood at the mouth of the cave. The old woman's images continued to flare, popping up brightly and fading as death seized the people in the passing images. The ebb and flow of a history – Davin could almost believe that, rather than what it was, a conjured mirage.

He saw beautiful women and men of clean chin and strong lines destroyed in unspeakable ways. Some fought, some argued, some pled for mercy.

All died.

"That is A'bre as it was?"

"Yes," the old woman said softly.

"When? When are we watching?"

"Eons ago – this very instant," Mettatine answered. "All time is one and the same. If your mind cannot grasp that truth, then think of it as the past or consider it the future. That it is, is all that matters – that, and the fact Goran and you can change it."

"It can't be." Doubt upon doubt piled high in the Jyotian's mind.

How could a man accept what she proposed? How could life, a hard struggle to survive from one moment to the next, all exist in a single instant? Moreover, how could a single soul live an infinity of lifetimes in that same moment? To contemplate such for more than a few moments invited insanity.

Davin drew a heavy breath and slowly released it. "If what you say is true, this Etol-Sammo must have sought A'bre throughout all his lives and found it again and again."

"Some of those you are watching die believed it so." Mettatine nodded. "Others believe he has simply lived and died for eternity upon eternity dreaming or seeking A'bre. That was until forces were unleashed upon your own world of Raemllyn – two great tears in the fabric of time and space. The whole structure of the planes and universes weakened. Etol-Sammo found a door to A'bre and stepped through.

"From A'bre, all times and all histories were his. The mage drew not only from the power of his own world but the powers of countless worlds. Time and again, he has attacked A'bre first on one plane and then the next. And time and again, he has been turned back – until now. He views himself as a god. But his power is only that to destroy. He can and will destroy A'bre, and when it fails so will the other vertices that intersect the planes of existence."

"What matter is that?" Davin could not grasp her point. The more she spoke, the more it all seemed like nonsense to him. "Why does it matter that the planes are connected? The individual worlds will live on. The universes will continue. Only A'bre and these other vertices will cease to exist."

"Infinite planes – finite souls," Mettatine repeated the phrase as though it were a litany. "A'bre and those other vertices are the paths for the progression of souls. Close them and a soul will have no route to its next life. In the space of a generation, all worlds will be barren and dead for all the eternities."

Davin frowned and turned to stare back to Lake Woe. If he believed what she suggested, there was no death. Death as he had been taught was merely a transition from one plane of existence to another. Personally, the possibility appealed to him, but the thought that one born of evil such as Zarek Yannis might now live again on another world, or worlds, was abhorrent to all that was decent.

"This mage will become the embodiment of Qar himself," Goran said. "Death, true death, will reign throughout the universes."

"Here is the way to Etol-Sammo's A'bre. Take it and this geas and both of you will be returned to your separate worlds – if you triumph," the old woman said. "Now it is time for me to sleep. I have waited long for this rest."

Davin glanced over a shoulder. Where the images had played on the wall now stretched a gaping hole that led only to darkness.

"She's dead, Davin!" Goran sat on the floor of the cave holding the hag in his arms. "She gestured with an arm, opened the wall then leaned her head to my shoulder as though to sleep – and died."

Davin moved beside his friend and placed a fingertip to the old woman's lips. No breath moved from or into her body.

"My eyes see the snow in her hair and the wrinkles of her face." Goran gently stroked Mettatine's cheek. "But my mind remembers her as she was among the Cloud Dwellers. Rarely has any world known such beauty or depth of passion."

"We should bur – but what is this?" Davin found a delicate gold chain around Mettatine's neck. He tugged it lightly.

"Davin, we do not steal from the dead. We will bury her with her . . . What? It's my eye! She still wears my eye!" Goran reached down and cupped a hand tenderly beneath the orb that dangled from the chain. "She said she wore it to her grave."

Davin stared with mouth ajar. There was indeed an eye attached to the chain, although he could discern no physical device binding eye to gold. It simply lay snuggled against the chain.

Rather than snatching up the orb, Goran tucked it back beneath the neckline of Mettatine's tattered dress of rags.

"Aren't you going to take it back?" Davin stared at his friend.

Goran slowly shook his head as he stretched Mettatine out on the floor of the cave and crossed her arms on her chest. "Nay, that eye belongs to another time and another plane. Mayhap it will help her find the next life that awaits her."

Davin's head spun like the swirling of a maelstrom. The tales Goran told of his lost eye were true – all of them – if he believed what Mettatine had revealed.

The Challing lightly kissed Mettatine's forehead and rose to face the dark mouth of the cave across from him. "There is nothing more we can do here. There is another A'bre awaiting us, and our own worlds to regain, my friend."

"Goran, wait. Don't!" Davin reached out to stop his friend, but the Challing brushed his hand away as though it were no more than an irritating fly.

The instant Goran's foot entered the dark mouth, the Challing vanished. One instant he was there, the next he was gone.

"Goran! Come back! Qar damn you, come back!" Davin crossed to the yawning darkness. "Goran, Goran, can you hear me?"

When no answer came, the Jyotian tentatively stuck a hand out to test the blackness. It was a mistake. The world crumbled beneath him, and he plummeted downward into eternity.

13

"Goran!" Davin called as he fell. The Challing's name was ripped from his lips and lost in the blackness before any sound touched his ears. "Goran!"

If the Jyotian expected an answer, none came. In truth there was no sound, not even the rush of wind.

Davin threw his arms wide, fingers seeking solidity. There was nothing, not even the sensation of wind surging over his palms.

He jerked his head from side to side, eyes opened wide for any glimmer of light. There was none, nor did he feel the coolness of wind in his eyes.

Yet, there was air; he breathed, although each breath he drew into his lungs twisted his gut into convulsing knots that threatened to double him over in agony.

And he fell. Of that he was certain. There was no mistaking the sensation that he plummeted downward as though he had leaped from Raemllyn's highest mountain and hurtled into his world's deepest canyon.

But this is not Raemllyn!

In the maddening fall through blackness, his mind attempted to grasp and comprehend all that Mettatine had revealed. He could not. His world was one where the sun rose with each day and twin moons illuminated each night. Time could not be one single moment common to all planes and universes. A'bre was an ancient city lost in Raemllyn's long-forgotten past, not some point through which souls passed from one lifetime to the next.

It can't be!

Yet, in the same moment, the Jyotian doubted the reality of a lifetime spent beneath sun and moons. There were other planes, other dimensions. He had seen the rents ripped into time and space by Zarek Yannis. His closest friend was not of Raemllyn but from a mystical world called Gohwohn.

Time? Is it time I fall through?

That made no sense. If Mettatine had spoken truly, all time was but a singular moment. Nor could he hurtle through space if each dimension existed in one point. Madness, only madness lay in contemplating the crone's revelations.

"Uggh!"

Davin slammed nose first into Goran One-Eye's back. The massive Challing turned and stared while the Jyotian gingerly tested that nose to make certain it was not broken.

"You followed?" Goran smiled. "I was not certain you would."

Assured his nose remained in one piece, Davin replied. "I gave my word that I would help you find A'bre and the way back to Gohwohn, did I not?"

Goran rubbed his right temple as though beset by a headache. He tilted his head to one side. "I'm afraid all we've found is the inside of a cave."

Davin's gaze darted from side to side. They remained in the crone's cave! Nothing had changed. It was all the same!

"Your old paramour cast a spell over us before she died." Davin now rubbed at his own temples to ease the throbbing ache that crept into his head. "I thought I saw you vanish into nothingness, then imagined I followed. It seemed as though I fell down some deep shaft – for ever. But we've gone nowhere. It was an illusion, a trick and nothing more sinister."

"I fear that you are . . ." Goran fell silent when he made a new appraisal of the cave. "No, Davin, it is not the same."

Unsure what the Challing meant, Davin took a quick inventory. The straw bed lay against the cave's earth wall. The ring of stone stood where he last saw it – but no flames flickered. Only a pile of ash marked where a fire had once burned. And—

"Mettatine's body is gone!" The Jyotian stepped to the spot where Goran had carefully arranged the old woman on the cave floor. "I see no mark in the dirt to show she was here."

Goran knelt beside the ring of stones, testing the ash with his fingers. "They're as cold as it's suddenly grown in here." He rose, rubbing hands over arms. "And my stomach growls as loudly as those Uhjayib gorillas we escaped. I am famished. I feel as though a week has passed since I last ate."

Davin's own stomach rumbled in protest, and his throat felt as dry as a desert dune. "We're not likely to find a fit meal in those dung huts outside."

"But I saw a tavern only a few feet from where we first met Mettatine." Goran paused and grimaced. "I forgot. A'bre was a different vision for each of us." He scratched his head and shrugged. "So be it. Find what you can in your hovels. I'm off for the tavern I saw."

When the Challing turned to the mouth of the cave, he halted in mid-step. "Friend Davin, was it not day when we entered this cave?"

Davin's eyes followed Goran's gaze. The light that shafted into the cave came not from sun or moons. "The whole village must be ablaze to create that much light."

"Where has the daylight gone?" Goran cautiously approached the mouth of the cave with hand resting on the hilt of his sword. A single word cloaked in unmistakable awe slipped from his lips, "A'bre."

Davin Anane stared open-mouthed when he reached the Challing's side. Two syllables pushed over his own lips, "A'bre."

"Do we see the same city?" Goran asked softly as though the sound of his voice might shatter the metropolis that lay spread below the hill.

Davin's head slowly shifted to one side in a noncommittal gesture. "Near the lake – central to the city – an edifice with two towering marble spires . . ."

"And a banner flying from each," Goran finished in the same soft voice. "I can see no walls, although the city encompasses . . ."

". . . half the lake," Davin completed. "It's three times larger than Kavindra."

"And three times as beautiful," Goran said while he stepped into the night. "Surely, more than the hands of men constructed such edifices."

Davin offered no argument. The architecture was unlike any he had ever seen in any city of Raemllyn. Even Kavindra, royal city of the High King, was but a shabby shadow compared to the wonder below. A'bre – the city could only be A'bre – and it surpassed even his wildest imaginings. What wealth it must have taken to raise this city!

"Nothing like it," Goran uttered. "Even on Gohwohn, there is nothing like it."

The light that radiated from the city came not from fires or torches but the buildings themselves. The flaming stone glowed with an inner light. Raemllyn's northern province of Norgg was renowned for its opalescent rock, but it was no more than common marble beside this stone and the light it cast. Nor was the stone's use restricted to buildings. The roads, too, appeared paved with the same glowing rock.

"Why do we linger here?" Davin finally asked. "What we seek lies yonder within A'bre."

"True, friend Davin," Goran answered, "but I think it would be pleasant to wander A'bre's streets and marvel at its wonders a bit before seeking the way to Gohwohn. Surely, treasures abound within A'bre ripe for the picking, especially for men with talents such as ours."

"What of Etol-Sammo?" Davin hiked an eyebrow high when he looked at his companion.

"What concern is another mage to me? My travels across Raemllyn are marked by the wizards who have fallen before me," Goran answered with his usual braggadocio. "Did I not slit the throat of Roan-Jafar with the mage's own knife? If this Etol-Sammo was in league with Roan-Jafar, how much of a problem could he pose? No, first we'll enter yon city of majestic wonders, perhaps find a joint of beef and a few tankards of ale, then take care of this Etol-Sammo. What could be . . . ahhgghh!"

Goran danced back a step, reached down, and yanked the gold amulet from beneath his tunic. "It burned me!"

"What?"

"It burned me!" He dangled the leaf as far away from his body as the gold chain would permit.

Davin saw no glow surrounding the metal, but he detected a soft humming emanating from the leaf. He lifted a hand to touch the medallion and immediately jerked his fingers away. "It does burn!"

"Magicks – from the city." Goran's gaze shot toward A'bre. "No, Davin, there above the city."

The Jyotian saw nothing except low hanging clouds illuminated by the light from the city. Then he sucked in a hard breath. "There's something in the clouds!"

No, he was wrong. Nothing was *in* the clouds. The clouds themselves came alive. As though stirred by the Beasts of the Mists they churned restlessly, but no grotesque creatures from other planes of existence poured forth from the sky to rain upon the city.

As he watched, the clouds solidified into a monstrous coil of dark scales. Gradually, these shifted and took on sharper definition until a writhing serpent hung above A'bre. Two malignant emerald green eyes glared down at the glowing buildings with their needle-like spires.

Without so much as a blink of those haunting eyes, the gargantuan struck. Its thick triangular head darted below. Fangs, a full fathom in length, sank into a street as though the stone was no more than soft flesh.

Then those fangs ripped. Jagged furrows rent the ground and from the deep wounds billowed clouds of yellow mist.

"Poison!" Goran pointed to the dark shapes in the distance that crumpled and fell whenever touched by the yellow fumes.

More than vaporous poison the cloud serpent delivered to towering A'bre. Again and again, its head arched to the skies, then fell. Spires snapped within its jaws. Buildings shook and collapsed when its blunt snout slammed into them like some gigantic battering ram. A full twenty times that horrible head rose and fell. With every blow it delivered death and utter destruction.

"City guards! They fight back!" Goran pointed to a small horde of men, no bigger than ants in the distance, who swarmed onto the streets. "But what arrow or spear can reach that high?"

There was no need for either arrow or spear. In the space of a single breath, the serpent dissolved into the clouds and was gone.

Below, the ragged gouges left by the monster's fangs slowly filled as if smoothed by some invisible hand. Likewise, the toxic vapors dissipated on the cool night breeze.

"Cold," Goran said, tucking the leaf beneath his tunic. "The magicks have passed."

"Not so." Davin stared on in wide-eyed amazement.

Crumbled buildings rose from the streets and again challenged the skies. Shattered glass flew through the air in a rain of shards to reform into windows that slipped back into their frames. Only the bodies of those struck down by fumes or falling debris did not rise. Qar, or whatever dark god ruled these people's realm of death, had exacted a heavy toll tonight.

"If this be Raemllyn, the memory of such powerful magicks has long ago faded from the minds of men," Goran said when he started toward the city. "It's as though each of these edifices was born of magic or sustained by the spells of ten mages."

"A city of mages," Davin said. "A'bre has often been called that in lore. Until now, I always thought it only a child's tale."

"This is not Raemllyn, my friend." Goran continued to stare at the city as it righted itself after the attack. "This is A'bre. It is as Mettatine said – this place spans the planes, intersects the dimensions of the universes."

Davin's mind refused what the Challing proposed. It was easier to accept that they had somehow been flung into Raemllyn's forgotten past or hurtled into a distant future.

The Jyotian mentally stumbled. Wasn't that what Mettatine had told him to do? If he could not accept the reality of A'bre, then believe in the span of time – past and future.

His mind revolted against the possibility Goran and he had somehow been transported to either Raemllyn's past or future. To be certain, he accepted a past. Man's histories were a record of that past. But how could one live in a time before he had been born?

And the future? It was a dream of things yet to be. It did not exist save in the guileful minds of the gods.

His logic brought him full circle. If they had not entered either past or future, then the path they trod, the ground beneath their feet, did not belong to Raemllyn but to some other place, a hitherto unknown plane of existence or unheard-of dimension.

"Can a man die before he is born?" the Jyotian spoke aloud his thoughts when his mental weaving returned to the possibility of having somehow been cast across the years. "How can one die before he is even conceived in his mother's womb?"

"Accept the known and let the rest pass you by," Goran said as they entered the city. "This is A'bre. Where or when it exists will not change the fact that it *is*. As to where we are, we are *here*. And the time is as it always is – *now*. Beyond that, there is no need for either of us to know."

"What of the magicks that gave birth to the sky serpent?" Davin posed.

"I fear I misjudged this mage Etol-Sammo," Goran admitted without his usual twisting of the facts. "We must find A'bre's defenders and offer our services as Mettatine directed."

Davin glanced overhead. Thinning clouds rather than the gargantuan snake seen from the hill ruled the skies. If Etol-Sammo controlled forces powerful enough to summon such a monster, Goran had more than misjudged the sorcerer's strength; he had walked blindly into waters far above his head – and dragged a Jyotian with him.

"What difference does it make *when* we are? Gaze about you, friend Davin. A man – or a Challing – might make a fine life here! At least until he has the urge to move on to other things and other places." Goran's head turned this way and that while his single eye soaked in the magnificence of A'bre.

Davin did not deny the beauty that rose around him. However, he found little pleasure in the intricate architecture of the sky-challenging edifices or the marvelous statues that lined the avenue they walked. His eyes kept returning to the sky that had given birth to the viperous gargantuan.

Through holes in the clouds he saw twinkling stars. The bright pinpoints of light brought him little comfort. The patterns they took were strange and unfamiliar, doubling the sensation that he did not belong in A'bre, that he was both out of place and out of time, that he had somehow intruded into a world not meant for the eyes of a mortal man.

Have I been transformed into an old woman? Afraid of my own shadow? In a lifetime that had yet to see the passing of twenty-five cycles, he had faced the dangers of any ten men. He had stood at High King Felrad's side the night Zarek Yannis was destroyed and his nightmarish reign over Raemllyn ended. He had seen the Narain and their malevolence[*]. And he had survived

* See *Blood Fountain*

the underground empire of the self-proclaimed Emperor Jun*. Then there were the Beasts of the Mists and the countless monsters it had unleashed.

So much faced and conquered. Yet, here and now, all that had gone before during his lifetime lost its meaning. The Jyotian felt insignificant, his triumphs and conquests no more than flitting flies batted aside by forces beyond his comprehension.

Nor had he ever felt so menaced. No trace of the monstrous serpent remained in the sky, but he sensed it moving above him, hovering over A'bre, ready to appear suddenly and strike without warning.

Out of the corner of an eye, Davin caught Goran studying him, a worried expression on the Challing's face. "You feel it too, don't you? The presence of something malevolent surrounding us and this city of wonders?"

Goran pursed his lips and glanced around for several moments before giving his head a heavy nod. "The serpent remains. It had merely slipped between planes and now attacks an A'bre of an elsewhere. You feel its eternal evil like a knife wound in the belly."

It was Davin's turn to drop into a long silence as the weight of truth pressed onto his shoulders. "Mettatine had not lost her mind, had she? All she said was true, wasn't it?"

Goran released an overly held breath and nodded once again. "There are those souls blessed, or cursed, with minds that span the dimensions and the lifetimes of the progression of souls."

Goran touched the leaf amulet. "Since obtaining the final piece of this trinket, I have glimpsed a portion of what Mettatine and others within A'bre can see. Whatever god or gods who molded the universes use those individuals to protect the balance of the dimensions, to keep the vertices open."

"And you and me?" Davin asked, probing his mind but finding no memories of past or future lives.

The red-haired giant shrugged with uncertainty. "We are what we have and always will be – souls drawn to adventure. Maybe there is more. Perhaps we are merely pawns used by the gods for their amusement, but I can't see it or feel it."

* See *To Demons Bound*

"And we have been friends in other lives?"

"Countless lives," Goran replied. "In others we have hated one another as surely as you hated Berenicis the Blackheart. Infinite planes – finite souls – and combinations of lives as infinite as the universes themselves."

Davin openly shivered as a chill that was not carried on the night air crept along his spine. "I sense we are in a time far removed from our own. And that invisible creature hovering over us is something more evil than even the Faceless Ones."

"I, too, feel we are in a place ancient to our time in Raemllyn – before Nnamdi and the Time of the Called," Goran said. "Imagine, no Faceless demons and no Sword of Kwerin Bloodhawk, none of what you or I call history has yet to pass."

"Or will ever come to pass." Davin's gaze returned to a now-clear sky with its unknown constellations. "Mettatine described Etol-Sammo as though he were Qar himself."

"Qar is but death, Raemllyn's harvester of souls," Goran answered, rubbing his own arms against the cold. "Etol-Sammo stands as Death. Should he destroy A'bre, the progression of souls is shattered. Only ghosts will inhabit the worlds of the universes – even Qar will die. Etol-Sammo is the end to all life, everywhere, in all times."

As surely as Davin recognized his boots no longer trod Raemllyn's familiar soil, he knew the Challing spoke unerringly. The horrors, the dangers the Jyotian had faced and triumphed over *were* meaningless; they still lay far in the future. Nor would they ever come to pass, if Etol-Sammo were not stopped here in this elsewhere.

"Where or when we are does not diminish the growling of my belly," Goran abruptly said. "Nor will our sword arms serve any purpose if we don't find food to give them strength."

The hollow rumblings of Davin's stomach, forgotten when the sky serpent appeared, returned with renewed insistence. "Agreed. It is time to break our fast."

Decision and conclusion are not the same. Stars shifted their positions in the heavens as the two thieves wandered aimlessly through the unlittered streets of A'bre. Streets without pothole or rut they saw. Statues crafted by skilled artisans they passed. Structures built of stone and glass they moved beneath. Open

354 Robert E. Vardeman & Geo. W. Proctor

parks with manicured lawns and neatly trimmed trees they strolled through. What neither saw nor smelled was anything that appeared to be a caravanserai or a tavern.

"Don't the people of A'bre eat?" Goran spat on the ground in disgust.

"Are there people within the city?" Davin realized other than those they had seen die from the hill, they had not encountered another soul in A'bre. "Every street we've walked has been empty."

"Mayhap they cloister within these buildings and focus their powers to ward off Etol-Sammo." Goran glanced at the sky. "The night fades. Perhaps the daylight will bring them out."

Davin drew a long breath. His nostrils twitched. He sucked in another breath and smiled. No matter what the time or place, the tantalizing aroma wafting in the air was unmistakable. "Bread! I smell bread baking."

Goran sniffed the air and a grin replaced the scowl on his face. "Right you are. And it comes from that direction."

The Jyotian did not question his companion's olfactory sense. When it came to ferreting out food or drink, Goran One-Eye was without equal. Davin doubled his pace to keep up with the muscular giant when he hastened down the street. Reaching an intersection, Goran turned to the left and skidded to an abrupt halt.

"Dinner, Davin, and breakfast!" The Challing's chest expanded broadly while his eye drank in the sight before them. "A veritable banquet stretched before us! All for the taking!"

Although "banquet" was not the term Davin would have used to describe the immense square that opened before them, he did not quibble. All the ingredients of a banquet were laid out before them. And for able-bodied thieves, selecting which of the items required to silence protesting stomachs offered little challenge.

"A market district." Davin scanned the carts and wagons that stretched across the square from warehouse to warehouse collecting foodstuffs. "Fruits, cheeses, smoked meats – and there's a wagon loaded with casks of wine."

"Dinner and breakfast rolled into one!"

Before Davin could restrain him, Goran double-timed it toward the open doors of a bakery and a table piled with fresh loaves of bread. The Challing had torn one of those loaves in half and busily stuffed bread into his mouth by the time Davin reached the table.

"It tastes better than it smells." Goran handed his companion half the loaf. "Now we need some of that . . ."

"Halt!"

Feminine though the voice was, Davin recognized the tone carried in that single syllable. It spelled out but one thing – city guard! His hand dropped to the hilt of his sword.

"Keep your hands away from your blades and turn around so I can see you."

Jyotian and Challing complied, to find themselves facing a young woman cloaked in a flowing white robe. Dark hair was piled high atop her head and studded with tiny, shimmering pearls.

More radiant than those precious jewels was the woman's face. Davin did not deny the beauty of those features, but there was an inner force in her bearing and composure that demanded his attention. What perplexed him the most was the woman's ebon-dark eyes. He had never seen her before this moment far before his own birth, yet he felt as if he knew her well.

"Your clothing marks you as strangers to A'bre," she said.

"We are just arrived," Goran answered with a tilt of his head to the bread in his hand. "We've traveled far and have gone long without eating. The aroma of this fresh baked bread was irresistible. We have coin to pay for what we've taken."

"How did you get into the city?" Her eyes narrowed to slits while she studied them.

"We walked in," Davin answered, judging that she was in no mood to tolerate an artfully woven tale. "We've done no wrong. It's as my friend said, we can pay for this loaf of bread."

"You felt nothing at the edge of the city?" The woman apparently had no interest in the pilfered loaf.

"No," Davin replied with a shake of his head. "We felt nothing, nor were there guards to question our entry. We simply walked into the city and followed the smell of baking bread here. Is there a crime . . ."

"Silence!" The woman's hand rose. The small jeweled rod held in those graceful fingers pointed directly at the Jyotian's chest.

"No one just enters A'bre in these dark times – none save agents of Etol-Sammo. Every peace warden in the city has standing orders to banish anyone even suspected of serving Etol-Sammo."

"Etol-Sammo? We were sent here to . . ."

Shafts of blue and white light erupted from the rod. They struck the Jyotian squarely in the middle of his chest like the blow of a massive hammer. The force of the impact lifted Davin from his feet and threw him into the bakery's opened door. Like a limp rag, he slid to the ground, still conscious but unable to move a muscle, even to blink his eyelids in confusion.

The peace warden turned the rod toward Goran.

14

Bolts of blue and white burst from the jeweled rod and shafted straight toward Goran One-Eye's barrel chest.

The Challing glanced down, watching the light fizzle into a puffy white cloud that rose into the air like a mounting thunderhead only to dissipate. Goran took another bite from his portion of the loaf.

"There's no need," he said as he chewed, "for extreme magicks. We *can* pay for the bread. Do we look like thieves?"

A gasp escaped the woman's gaping mouth. Her hand tightened around the rod to send another barrage of bolts blasting into the Challing's chest. The results were the same. Whatever power froze Davin motionless on the ground had no effect on the Challing. He swallowed and tore off another bite of bread.

"Spies! Only an agent of Etol-Sammo could withstand the power of the wand!" She sent a third series of bolts into Goran's chest only to create more clouds of white mist. "Saboteurs! Etol-Sammo sent you to destroy our food supply."

"No." Goran shook his head while he leaned against the bread-laden table. "We were sent here to aid in the fight against Etol-Sammo and Roan-Jafar."

The bitterness with which Goran spoke the name of the mage responsible for his tribulations surprised Davin and caused the peace warden to step back, eyes widening.

"You fight against both Roan-Jafar and Etol-Sammo?" she asked cautiously.

"I have killed Roan-Jafar once, when he drew me from my own world of Gohwohn," Goran answered. "I used his own knife to open his throat from ear to ear. If the whoreson lives *here* and *now*, I will be only too happy to perform the task again. He died too quickly the first time to give me any real satisfaction."

"But you entered the city without triggering the alarms!" The peace warden kept the jeweled rod in her hand. "Only Etol-Sammo's spies have slipped by those ward spells in our long years of warring."

"Were we spies or saboteurs, would we be stupid enough to risk discovery by stealing a loaf of bread?" Goran tore another large piece of bread from the loaf and popped it in his mouth. "Not that we intended to steal this bread, you understand."

"Then you are mages with magicks to counteract the A'brean spells that encircle the city?" The woman's tone still held doubt, but her body relaxed its guarded stance.

"Mages? Nay." Goran hooked a finger beneath the gold chain about his neck and pulled the leaf from his tunic. "This little bauble sometimes diverts ward spells. Recently in Faltren, it allowed me to pass through a ward spell that almost killed my friend." Goran motioned in Davin's direction.

The expression on the warden's face transformed from caution to shocked surprise. "Who are you? How did you come by the Four Keys of A'bre?"

"Keys? This leaf? All it has brought me is grief." Goran let the amulet fall to his broad chest. "With each portion, the promise of return to my home has been dangled before me and then snatched away."

"You come from a plane called Gohwohn? Is that where you discovered the Keys?" The woman stepped closer to Goran, her midnight eyes fixed on the magical medallion.

"Yes and no," Goran answered. "I am Challing wrenched from my own world to a ball of mud the inhabitants there call Raemllyn. It was Roan-Jafar's magicks that drew me forth, for which I slit his throat. Or I will slit his throat – I am uncertain of the time we have entered. I've come to A'bre because one called Mettatine directed me here. She said the mages of A'bre could return me to Gohwohn and send my friend Davin back to Raemllyn."

"Yet you said that you oppose Etol-Sammo?"

Davin's throat constricted, then relaxed. A groan escaped his lips.

The peace warden turned and once more pointed her wand at him. Orange light burst from the rod to bathe the Jyotian. When the brightness faded, life slowly returned to Davin's frozen muscles.

"Mettatine told us of the Grimoire of the Ages and Etol-Sammo," Davin said, his vocal cords working again. "She promised that in return for our aid, those in A'bre would show us the paths to our separate home worlds."

The woman's gaze moved back and forth between the two thieves she had caught pilfering a loaf of bread. Furrows formed on her brow and deepened as though she were lost in thought. Eventually, her ebon eyes focused on the golden leaf she had called the Keys of A'bre. She nibbled at her lower lip, then drew a heavy breath before she said:

"By all rights, I should summon other wardens and set your souls on new paths – but you carry not one but all four of the Keys. Never has one returned with all the Keys. I cannot decide alone. The others must share the burden of the decision. Come with me."

Set your souls on a new path, the phrase repeated in Davin's mind. If A'bre was truly the nexus through which souls passed on their journey from one dimension to another, then the warden had just pronounced the local euphemism for a summary execution, if these "others" found fault with Goran's and his tale.

Goran stared at the woman in white robes as he rubbed the gold leaf between his fingers. Then he shook his head. "We come to your city with our hands extended in friendship, offering to aid in your fight against Etol-Sammo, and you would place us on trial like common criminals?"

Her eyes dipped to the half-eaten loaf of bread still in his left hand. "There is evidence that you are no more than that. And there are powers in A'bre more potent than my Rod of Discipline that could force you to comply. It would be best if you accompanied me of your own accord."

The Jyotian expected the Challing's usual reaction to the less than subtle threats of authority – a string of curses and the promise to dismember the one voicing those threats with his bare hands. Instead, an amused smile touched Goran's lips.

"We came to aid, not to hinder," Goran finally said. "Yet common courtesy rather than that *stick* you carry, would serve you better." He paused and stuck out a paw disguised as a hand. "I am called Goran, although there are those who add the appellation One-Eye for obvious reasons."

The woman tentatively shook the Challing's proffered hand. "I am Jennona, acting Warden of Peace in A'bre."

"And I am Davin Anane, Lord of Jyotis."

If Davin expected Jennona to be impressed by the title recently bestowed on him by High King Felrad, he was sorely mistaken. The woman merely tilted her head in his direction while her eyes remained on Goran. "Come. If you can aid A'bre, then it must be determined how best to use your powers."

"And if we cannot," Davin added, unable to shake the sensation he knew Jennona, "set our souls on a new path."

"There is no need to repeat the obvious," she replied with no attempt to disguise the disdain in her voice. Looking back at Goran, she said, "Where we go is close-by, near those twin spires that mark the Academy of the Moment. The others await us . . ."

Thunder cracked overhead and shook the ground beneath Davin's feet. White light like the brightness of a thousand lightning bolts covered the city in a blinding sheet.

"Etol-Sammo!" The name hissed through Jennona's teeth like a foul curse as she leveled her Rod of Discipline and slowly turned. "He attacks again – so soon!"

Davin blinked to part the red glare that hung over his eyes. The glow grew as a column of flames erupted from the street a hundred strides ahead of him. Thunder faded from his ears, replaced by the roar of a furnace fanned by howling north winds.

"It's alive!" This from Goran who freed the sword at his side. "It takes shape!"

Davin's own blade hissed from its sheath when the Jyotian saw the tongues of flame churn and twist into the form of a man made of living fire. An arm muscled by crackling fire reached out. A ball of molten flame burst to life in his fiery palm.

The fire creature drew back his arm and hurled the ball at the nearest building. A river of flame shot up the side of the edifice, flowing from ground to pinnacle. The blazing man turned and launched a second fireball at a building on the opposite side of the street. An instant later, the second structure raged as fire covered it in a liquid sheet.

"Goran," Davin called. "Together!"

The Challing nodded. "If the creature has a heart, our blades will find it!"

Before either man or Challing could begin their charge, Jennona shouted, "Stand aside! Steel cannot bite a heart of fire!"

A'bre's Warden of Peace pointed her wand at the man of living flames. Dark clouds appeared at the end of the jeweled rod. Like a miniature thunderstorm they roiled. From those black clouds shot a single bolt of jagged lightning that burned blue-white.

The furnace roar doubled and the creature of flame spun about. Both arms of fire jerked back, balls of flame again bursting to life in fiery palms. The creature's arms snapped forward, sending the twin globes straight toward Jennona.

"No!" Goran roared and threw himself directly into the path of the balls.

"No!" Fear tore the word from Davin's throat as he watched the conflagrant globes explode and engulf the Challing.

Instead of a smoldering mass of black-jellied flesh, a second man of flame stood in the wake of the fiery explosion. The flames of the second creature burned bright green.

"Die, you misbegotten spawn of Peyneeha!" Goran's voice roared as he hurled two globes of green fire at the burning man.

"Witchfire! How?" The words escaped Jennona's mouth in confused gasps.

"The power is upon him," Davin's answer was almost a sigh of relief. "He is no man, but a shape-changer, and the power is upon him again!"

Etol-Sammo's fire demon staggered when Goran's assault broke over him, but he did not fall. Instead, with a resounding roar, Etol-Sammo's minion launched another pair of globes in reply.

These sputtered and fizzled to nothingness when they struck not a being of living witchfire but a man of ice!

Davin's jaw sagged. Faster than his eye could perceive, the Challing shifted shapes. No longer did Goran stand his ground but charged straight for the fire creature with a battle cry that imitated the splitting of ancient glaciers.

"It cannot be!" Jennona uttered, her head moving from side to side as though she refused to believe the scene that unfolded.

Fire and ice collided in a billowing cloud of sizzling steam. If Goran's form had diminished his strength, Davin could not discern it. With hands that were no more than animated icicles, the Challing tore the fire demon's left arm from its body and tossed it aside. The limb of flame fizzled out in a cloud of greasy black smoke.

As did the right arm when Goran ripped it away. Last came the burning man's head. Along with a headless body, the head vanished in billowing smoke.

Rivulets of water streamed down Goran's melting body when the Challing stood and peered about as though uncertain what had happened. Stumbling, he turned back toward Jennona and Davin. Swaying unsteadily, his mouth opened to emit the sound of cracking ice. His arms reached out.

Then he collapsed.

"He's hurt!" Davin ran toward the Challing, his heart pounding as he watched the pool of water spread about the inanimate heap of ice. "He's dying!"

"Back," a voice barely discernible as Goran's whispered when the Jyotian reached the Challing's side. "Back, Davin, back."

"Do as he says." Jennona placed a hand on Davin's shoulder. "Come away."

"But he's hurt. We have to help him." Davin looked at the woman, then at the cracking ice that was Goran One-Eye.

"Back," the Challing whispered again.

Torn between the desire to aid his injured friend and knowing it was beyond his ability to help, Davin did as the Challing requested.

"He dies! By Yehseen, he dies. Can't you use your magicks to heal him?" Davin dropped to his knees, wanting to reach out and holding himself back only through great force of will.

Jennona's head moved from side to side. "He must do what must be done. His powers are unknown to me."

In mute horror, Davin stared helplessly as the ice that had been Goran One-Eye melted into a small lake of crystal clear water. A thick lump filled the Jyotian's throat. "He's dead – he's dead."

Jennona said nothing, nor would her words have eased the pain that filled Davin. From every corner of his mind marched a thousand memories of all he had shared with the Challing, of the dangers they had faced and overcome. How many swords had sought to claim Goran's life? How many wizards' spells had failed to deliver his soul to Qar's frigid embrace? Death was a simple fact they both accepted, but for one who had stood against the Faceless Ones to have died thus, no more than rainwater trickling away in a gutter, was a cruelty beyond even the fickle Sitala's conjuring.

"His soul walks another path," Jennona said softly. "All we can hope is that his new path is . . . No, look!"

Davin stared in disbelief. A mist formed above the puddle. As it rose to the air, the water slowly sank in size, nor was there a trace of moisture left on the street. Colors, soft, gentle pastels, blushed through the lolling cloud. Here and there tiny pinpoints of light flashed within the mist like miniature stars flaming to life, only to wink out in an instant.

"Look!" Jennona pointed above her head.

Threadlike strands of mist formed in the air and drifted down to join with the larger cloud. The colors shifting through the mist grew in intensity.

"Goran," Davin whispered in awe.

The Jyotian knew not how he realized he gazed upon the Challing in his natural form. This ethereal, misty form that folded in upon itself was the real Goran One-Eye as he would be in his home world of Gohwohn. No wonder the Challing cared little whether he bore the body of Goran One-Eye or his female persona Glylina. This light-speckled cloud appeared to be without sex, or if so endowed, the condition was only discernible by another Challing.

"What is it?" Jennona moved closer to Davin and whispered. "Is this a soul?"

"I don't believe so," the Jyotian replied. "I think my friend has assumed another shape."

Even as he spoke the mist shifted, elongating so that it stretched from the street to an inch above Jennona's head. Then the cloud widened to assume a vaguely human form.

In the wink of an eye, Glylina popped into existence. A grin spread across the flaming-haired seductress's full lips. Goran's eye patch hung loosely about her neck beside the gold leaf.

"And this?" Jennona asked, obviously disturbed by the sudden presence of such a voluptuous woman.

"May I introduce Glylina?" The Jyotian discovered he didn't

care whether his friend wore male or female body – only that the Challing still lived. "This, too, is one of Goran's shapes."

"I preferred any of the others to *this*," Jennona answered, making no attempt to hide her instant dislike for the Challing's new body. "Can't you change back to the handsome, muscular one with the one eye?"

Glylina shrugged in familiar Challing fashion. "Not at the moment, I'm afraid. As soon as I am able, I shall do so to accommodate your desires."

Whether Jennona understood Glylina's less than veiled meaning, Davin did and found the possibility of the Challing sharing a dalliance with the A'bre Warden of Peace disturbing. That Jennona answered Glylina with a pleased smile only increased the Jyotian's rootless annoyance.

"Have your powers left you again?" Davin asked, annoyed at himself for feeling irritated.

Glylina shook her head which stirred the long red hair that cascaded over her shoulders. "Weak. I lost a portion of myself, up in steam, so to speak. It took more strength than I realized to gather myself together. I'm sorry if I frightened you, dear Davin, but it took all my concentration to regain those missing parts from the air."

"But you still have the ability to shift shapes?" Davin asked, surprised by what Glylina implied.

She nodded again. "Whether it's this amulet or that I am free of Raemllyn I know not, but my Challing powers feel fully returned to me."

"Then," Jennona interrupted, "I suggest we meet with the others. They will determine how best your unique abilities can be used."

"Yes," Glylina agreed.

She took one step and faltered. Davin reached out and caught her in his arms before she collapsed to the street.

"Weaker than I thought." She smiled sheepishly at the Jyotian, then passed out in Davin's arms.

"The Keys of A'bre obviously increase the magicks that define you as an entity, Challing." The one called Parthlin lifted the amulet from Glylina's ample breast and let a thumb slide across its surface. "You might have died today without it around your neck when you fought Etol-Sammo's fire warrior."

"Before we arrived in A'bre, I felt that the leaf drew strength from other magicks and transferred those magicks to me," Glylina replied.

Parthlin let the leaf fall and turned to the others. "More important, this woman, this shape-changer, is the first ever to return with all four Keys. Never have any of the other heroes appeared with more than one."

Davin didn't care for the sound of that. It gave little comfort to realize others had come to A'bre to stand against Etol-Sammo – and had failed.

"Nor can we overlook that Glylina and the Keys seem to resonate as one. Why else would the Keys have demanded she find all four?" This from a middle-aged woman named Toiyah. Dressed in white robes similar to Jennona's, she paced restlessly back and forth across the room of glowing white stone. "But how can that be? The Keys were endowed with no spell except those of summoning."

Davin kept a close watch on Glylina out of the corner of an eye. After the full day in a coma-like sleep within a private apartment inside the Academy of the Moment, she had awakened with the evening, declaring she was starving and ready to meet with Jennona's "others".

Although a bloom had returned to her cheeks, Davin was unsure of her true condition. Glylina, like Goran, often refused openly to admit any vulnerability. Moreover, this was not the Goran-Glylina the Jyotian had called friend for years. Gone was the wildness, the damn-the-gods-and-all-who-stand-in-my-way attitude that had been Goran-Glylina. In its stead was a sobriety, a somber mood totally alien to the Goran-Glylina Davin knew so well.

Vulnerable?

The Jyotian did a mental double-take. Thinking of either Goran or Glylina as vulnerable was inconsistent with the Challing Davin had known during their travels across Raemllyn. Yet, after this morning, he fully recognized how defenseless his friend was. Whether Glylina admitted it or not, she had teetered on the very edge of the grave. That she still lived was nothing short of a miracle.

"The Keys have been cast into the universes countless times since they were first crafted and spellbound," Jennona spoke up. "Who can say what changes have occurred within them, what powers and forces have touched them?"

"Nor can we discount that all four Keys found their way to this world of Raemllyn," Toiyah added. "The very world that gave birth to Etol-Sammo and the now dead Roan-Jafar."

"But what of him – Davin Anane?"

A slender man also dressed in white pushed from the chair he had sat in since Glylina and Davin had entered the Council Chamber within the Academy of the Moment. Davin recalled his name as being Harri'Alin.

"Never have we had two sojourners answer the Keys together. And this one doesn't even carry a Key." Harri'Alin stabbed a finger at the Jyotian.

"It's obvious, isn't it?" This came from Meerium, the last of Jennona's "others".

As to Meerium's sex, Davin could only guess as he did with the mage's features. One moment Meerium appeared male and in the next female. It was as though the A'brean shifted between the planes of existence that intersected in this city, and with each transition changed countenance.

"There are bonds forged between souls. This we have known for generations," Meerium continued. "Such bonds exist between Glylina and Davin." The mage paused and bowed his-her head a moment. "Davin is here because he is needed. Perhaps his presence stems from Etol-Sammo and the now dead Roan-Jafar both hailing from the realm called Raemllyn."

"Or that Glylina's and Davin's abilities complement each other," Toiyah proposed. "What matters more is how best to employ their abilities in our struggle."

Davin glanced around the white chamber with its white tables and chairs. The monotony of the room equaled the monotony of the five mages' ceaseless speculations and endless hypothesizing. In the two hours they had sat in the chamber, first retelling their journey to A'bre and then listening to the "Chosen" spout theory after theory or why the two adventurers had been drawn to A'bre, Davin had learned little of Etol-Sammo or why he attacked the city.

The best Davin could discern was that Etol-Sammo and Roan-Jafar worked together. Their combined spells created a nexus of their own, one that allowed Roan-Jafar to draw the Challing to Raemllyn from Gohwohn. Etol-Sammo, however, had not been satisfied with summoning creatures from other planes; he had entered the nexus himself. Now he could shift from dimension to dimension, drawing on the magicks of all the universes.

"Enough prattle!" Glylina abruptly burst out in a very Challing-like reaction. "Etol-Sammo gains power over A'bre with each passing moment. What will you do – talk yourselves to death?"

The Council fell silent. The five mages stared at the Challing as though uncertain how to answer.

"Gor – Glylina is right," Davin spoke up. "From all I've heard, you fight a defensive battle against the mage. No battle is won by defense. You must attack! You must strike at Etol-Sammo – put him on the defensive! Anything else and this city will crumble beneath his power. Brick by brick it will fall."

Still the five remained silent, their heads turning to each other, faces shadowed by befuddlement.

Jennona eventually spoke. "You are right. Etol-Sammo is an abomination – something that should not have been – cannot be by all we know or knew. Not once did he appear in the Grimoire of the Ages. Yet, in a single instant, he has been written on every page."

"We are lost," Parthlin added. "In its own way, A'bre is as solid and unmoving as your own worlds. While we know of the infinite planes, we are confined to this place. Not so Etol-Sammo. He shifts through the dimensions as readily as Glylina shifts forms."

Davin saw Glylina wince at the mage's final statement. Did the reaction come from Etol-Sammo's power or some limit to the Challing's own ability? Either way, Davin did not like it.

"This Grimoire of the Ages," Glylina asked, "what is it and why does Etol-Sammo seek it?"

"Immortality," Jennona answered solemnly.

"True immortality," Harri'Alin amended. "Not the immortality of the progression of souls but the single life of a soul throughout all time."

Meerium spoke up. "Until now, none in A'bre has ever considered evoking the grimoire's power. Now . . ."

"Now?" Davin hiked an eyebrow in question.

"We are the Chosen," Jennona replied. "We have been selected as sentinels – guardians of the moment. Should we find a way of defeating Etol-Sammo, ours will be the burden of immortality."

"Ours will be the task forever to safeguard A'bre, to defend the vertex should another such as Etol-Sammo suddenly appear and threaten the universes." This came from Parthlin.

Davin's head spun. "Burden? Immortality a burden?"

"Boring, Davin." Glylina glanced at her companion and shook her head. "Think of it, my friend. To be forever locked in one body, one life. Can you think of anything more boring when there are infinite worlds and universes meant for each soul, unending lives to experience!"

Jennona turned to the Jyotian. "Glylina sees the truth. But for Etol-Sammo to escape the small deaths that claim all lives, for him immortality means an ascension to godhood."

"In that lies the reasoning of a fool." Meerium turned her-his gaze on the two thieves. "Etol-Sammo's power is death – the total annihilation of all life. A god must also have the power to give life – that will never be his."

Davin could not deny the seduction of immortality. All men had considered it, yearned for its lasting taste. Yet, something deep within the Jyotian was repelled by the notion of living for ever. Perhaps it was simply that life as he had known it was meant to end in death. He saw it as a natural order. Or maybe it was the attraction of the progression of souls. Infinite lives and infinite worlds were the very heart of adventure.

"Where is this grimoire?" Glylina asked. "Where do you hide it?"

"Hide it?" Harri'Alin made a subtle pass with his right hand. "It is where it has always been."

From nowhere a white pedestal appeared in the middle of the chamber. Atop the stone sat a tome bound in immaculate white leather.

"What spells could Etol-Sammo find within that?" Davin stared at the slender volume. "It has no pages, only binding."

"Open it," Jennona said. "You will see."

Davin and Glylina rose and walked to the pedestal. Without hesitation, the Jyotian threw open the pageless book.

Images assailed Davin. The rush of lives, of worlds, of universes was relentless. They tore at his brain, etching themselves into his memory but refusing to allow him to grasp a single solid vision.

"Enough!"

Harri'Alin stood before the pedestal. His hand rested on the closed Grimoire of the Ages. "Madness lies in reading more of the tome in one viewing. Those who study it are trained from childhood to withstand its power."

Jennona stepped forward. "You saw him, didn't you?"

Davin closed his eyes and held onto the pedestal for support while he calmed his trembling body. Vestiges of that onslaught of images slid before his mind's eye. The tableaux formed a parade of nightmares – torture, destruction – with Etol-Sammo's grinning face looming above all.

The Jyotian cringed. Lorennion, Valora, even Zarek Yannis, were but kindly grandfathers and grandmothers when cast in the bloody shadow of Etol-Sammo. He maimed for the sheer pleasure it gave him. The more his victims suffered, the greater Etol-Sammo exulted.

And this spurred him to greater depths of depravity. He sought out individual victims, learning all he could of their history, their lives, their desires. Then the mage used his victims' innermost fears against them, sometimes ending their lives in a single flare of misery and at other times drawing out the torture over long years.

Sons watched their fathers die slowly. Mothers were forced to kill their own children. Lovers turned on one another in vicious, hideous ways, loving even as they slew. No length of time was too long for Etol-Sammo to wait if he could learn the precise way of inflicting the most agony.

Nor was the horror limited to those of human blood. Nameless creatures, unimaginable races, all fell beneath Etol-Sammo's rule. And when the wizard recognized even eternity would not provide the time needed to destroy infinitely, he annihilated A'bre – severed the nexus of the planes to bring an end to all life.

"I saw our deaths," Glylina whispered beside the Jyotian. "The bastard has the power to kill us – for ever."

The fear Davin felt within his own soul resonated with the Challing's pronouncement. "I saw the same."

Jennona moved closer and reached out to touch lightly the two thieves. "It was not always so within the grimoire's pages. What you saw is mutable. It can be changed."

Glylina's eyes rose to shift over those in the Council Chamber. Her voice came cold and devoid of any trace of emotion. "Etol-Sammo will die. If any means exists to kill this butcher, I will find it. As surely as I opened the throat of Roan-Jafar, I will draw my blade across Etol-Sammo's gullet and spill his blood to the earth."

"Aye," Davin said. "We both pledge that to you – or we will die in the attempt."

The Jyotian closed his eyes again, trying to vanquish the images of his own death revealed by the Grimoire of the Ages. "It can be changed. It can be changed."

15

Parthlin made a pass with his left hand and the Grimoire of the Ages vanished. Davin tentatively reached out. His fingertips felt the tome and pedestal, but his eyes did not discern the slightest hint of either.

"A simple spell," Jennona explained. "Not only does it conceal the physical but also the metaphysical. No trace of the grimoire's power escapes to allow Etol-Sammo to trace its location."

Harri'Alin cleared his throat to draw the attention of all within the chamber. "If we accept that these two represent a counterpoint to Etol-Sammo's intrusion, then what power do they hold? How do we employ it?"

Davin felt the eyes of the Chosen turn to them, seeking an answer from the two thieves. The Jyotian held no answer. His mind still reeled with the vision the grimoire left burning in his brain: on the morrow he would die, impaled on the spears of an army of creatures called forth from time and space at Etol-Sammo's command.

Davin's gaze moved to the Challing. Glylina, too, would die, ripped asunder by a ball of sizzling energy cast by a sorcerer who would be a god. After that A'bre would fall, and Etol-Sammo would take the first steps to the destruction of all life.

It can be changed, Davin repeated over and over in his mind, although how it would be accomplished evaded him.

"We must study the matter at length," Toiyah answered. "The grimoire has always revealed the correct course to us."

"Study?" Glylina's eyes went wide and her nostrils flared. "More talk? More endless debate? Tomorrow every one of us in this room will die, and you want to haggle over possibilities? There's no time for talk. We must act!"

"How? Where? When?" Meerium asked. "How can we move against Etol-Sammo when we can't find him? Don't you understand? He slips through the planes at will. One moment he is here, then elsewhere."

"The grimoire will serve us as it has served countless generations of A'breans." This from Parthlin. "It will show us . . ."

A trumpet blared in the distance. Closer, another echoed the strident wail. A third returned the urgent call, then a fourth and a fifth and a sixth and a seventh until Davin's ears could not discern the number of horns raising that single note.

"An attack?" Parthlin's head jerked to the left and then the right. "It cannot be!"

"The grimoire revealed no attack this night!" Panic filled Toiyah's voice. "How can it be?"

"The signal can't be ignored. Etol-Sammo renews his attack on the city." Meerium slowly turned in a complete circle as she-he spoke. "This was not shown to us."

Of the five mages, only Jennona seemed to retain her wits. "To your positions! Hurry! Get to the roofs!"

When Jennona pivoted and ran for a door at the front of the chamber, the remaining four magic weavers darted to two doors at the back of the room.

"What about us?" Davin called out. "What do you . . ."

"Forget them! We will do as we always have." Glylina's voice deepened into familiar tones. "We shall fend for ourselves!"

Davin glanced to his side to see the one-eyed Goran standing with sword drawn.

"A better body for what now must be done," the Challing said. "Come. There is no need for us here or atop the spires with those four. Our blades will be of more aid to Jennona and her peace wardens on the streets."

Freeing his own sword, the Jyotian joined Goran as he ran for the open door at the front of the chamber. Down a long white hall, featureless except for doors and other hallways leading off it, they ran until reaching a massive portal that opened onto the streets.

Not the darkness of night eased aside by the glow of A'bre's buildings and streets but a blazing hell burned at their eyes. Gouts of light exploded over the city. Like a thin mist, the light fell to blanket the city of wonder – light that was acid at its core, blistering the skin where it touched.

The strident wall of the alarm blared by a thousand trumpets died in a high-pitched whine that sliced into the ear and drove to the center of the brain. Davin threw hand to eye and then to ear, unable to block either whine or glare.

"What kind of magicks are these?" he shouted at Goran.

"The kind that can summon *that*!" The Challing thrust an arm to the sky.

The monstrous serpent once more writhed over A'bre. Again and again, its blunt triangular head struck downward, ripping into the city's towering buildings.

"And that!" Goran's arm swung to the west.

Davin gasped. Towering above all the buildings of A'bre lumbered a creature that dwarfed the giants of Raemllyn's myths. With each step both A'breans and structures fell. Human in shape, the gargantuan's features, however, were a mockery of all that was human. Four black eyes with white pupils stood in a line across its forehead. Two crimson slashes served as nostrils for that purple head. Not one but two mouths, one above the other, opened and snapped at the air.

Long, whip-thin arms dangled at the giant's side. Their scrawny appearance was put to the lie when taloned fingers at the end of those arms closed on a statue in one of A'bre's neatly kept parks. As a man might pluck a wild flower, the creature pulled off the stony head and cast it aside. Then in two bites, one for each mouth, it devoured the remaining marble. When the monster belched, fire billowed from its pair of mouths and flames ignited the building before it.

Davin watched helplessly as beams of blue light ripped across the night and tore into the chest of the stone-devouring behemoth. The monster roared and the earth trembled beneath the Jyotian's feet.

"The roofs!" Davin pointed to the twin spires of the Academy of the Moment. "That's where the others went! They work their magic from above!"

Two more blue beams blasted from the spires. When they struck, the four-eyed giant no longer roared but vanished in a sizzling ball of red flame. The sapphire rays then shot upward, turning their power onto the sky serpent.

"Davin!" Goran cried out. "Hurry! Jennona's surrounded!"

Davin twisted. The Challing no longer stood at his side but ran down the steps leading from the academy and raced into the street. The Jyotian's gaze leaped ahead of his friend. A'bre's Warden of Peace stood at the center of a grassy plaza across the street. Twelve warriors in gleaming, blood-red armor and horned helms encircled her with sword and spear leveled for the kill!

Davin did not hesitate. Down the stairs he raced, taking them three at a time. As quickly as he ran, he skidded to a halt with equal alacrity when his boots touched the street.

A pard winked into existence directly before him. Twice the size of the direwolves that roam Upper Raemllyn's wilderness it stood. Nor was it the color of any feline Davin had ever seen. From its nose to the tip of its lashing tail, the leopard was covered in sleek emerald green fur.

The pard, growl rolling from its muscular chest, crouched. Eyes of jet focused on the Jyotian an instant before it launched itself with taloned paws outstretched to ensnare its chosen victim.

Davin reacted rather than thought. Sword held before him in a two-handed grip, he attacked instead of retreating. Imagined or not, he thought he saw a glimmer of sentient light in those black eyes just before he shot between outreached claws and drove steel into the giant cat's broad chest.

In the next instant, man and pard collided. Together they tumbled to the street. Only one rose – a Jyotian with back and sides aching from the massive weight that had threatened to shatter ribs and spine like so much dry wood. He wrenched his blade from the cat's chest and turned.

Goran stood face to face with a stone knight armed with a gleaming marble sword and shield. Davin's brain reeled. This was no hellish demon of flesh and blood but one of A'bre's own statues animated by Etol-Sammo's devilish spells.

"Davin, get your arse over here and do your part," growled Goran as his blade clanged against unyielding stone. The Challing then ducked beneath a broad swipe of a marble blade that would easily have crushed his skull.

Again the Jyotian chose the direct approach and charged. Rather than hacking at stone with steel, Davin launched himself at the living statue feet first, kicking out with both legs. A cry of pain tore from his lips as boot soles slammed into marble and the force of the impact jarred through shin and thigh.

By luck or purpose, Goran was not certain, the Jyotian's attack caught the marble knight in mid-stride. For an instant the statue tottered on one sandalled foot, then toppled. It struck the street and shattered, head and arms sliding across the smooth pavement.

"Close," was the only thank you the Challing uttered when he reached down and yanked his friend to his feet. "My blade had no effect on it. What took you so long?"

"A leopard." Davin gritted his teeth to fight through the onslaught of aches that now beset his whole body. "A green pard attacked me by the stairs."

"Pard?" Goran glanced toward the academy. "I see no leopard – only a butchered alley cat."

Davin looked back and saw the sword-mangled cat. "But it was a panther – as green as an emerald!"

Goran examined the shattered statue at his feet before his eyes lifted to the street around them. As empty as A'bre had been when they entered in the predawn, the streets now swarmed with the city's citizens. Man, woman and child all fought myriad creatures and monsters. Goran blinked, then blinked again.

"Qar damn his soul to the depths of Peyneeha!" Goran roared. "The treacherous bastard! He mingles demons with illusions! Blink your eyes and see the truth!"

Davin did, and he saw. The blink of an eye revealed the truth: a stare allowed the illusion to fill the brain. Here and there A'breans battled common house pets transformed to demons in their minds, while others struggled against true horrors called forth from other dimensions.

"Help!" Jennona's scream rose above the battle's din. "Anyone who can hear, help me!"

Challing and Jyotian spun around. A'bre's Warden of Peace remained surrounded by the warriors in red armor and helms. She danced from one side to the other to elude the points of spears and swords that jabbed at her. All the while, bolts of miniature lightning shot from her Rod of Discipline to strike the chests of her opponents – to no avail.

Goran blinked. "Illusion! She is beset by a mirage."

"For one with only one eye, you see much, especially for a Challing."

A young man materialized beside Jennona. A gentle smile rode on his lips when he reached out and touched her shoulder. A'bre's Warden of Peace froze like a statue of hewn ice. A wave of the blue-robed man's left hand evaporated the red warriors in wisps of smoke.

"Etol-Sammo!" The name hissed between Goran's clenched teeth.

A pleasant smile remained on the sorcerer's lips as he bowed slightly. "Roan-Jafar was supposed to deal with you, but now it no longer matters. Tomorrow, you and all in this city will die. It is too late, Challing. There is nothing you can do. I have what I came for. When I come on the morrow, I will know where to find the Grimoire of the Ages."

The mage's fingers danced and Jennona vanished. "I would prefer that you direct me to the tome, but the wench will tell me what I need – eventually."

Davin's right hand eased to the dagger slung from his belt. He eased the dirk from its sheath.

"Will you point the way, Challing?" The wizard's voice was as gentle as his smile, without trace of threat, which made it all the colder. "You will save Jennona untold pain and suffering. And I will spare your own world."

"Gohwohn?" Goran's sword tip lifted to point directly at the sorcerer. "What know you of Gohwohn?"

"I know it will be a dead realm ere I come here tomorrow if you don't reveal where these fools have hidden the grimoire," Etol-Sammo answered without inflection in his tone. "Not that the passing of such a monotonous world would be mourned. Still, I suppose there are those, such as yourself, who might feel a loss."

Davin's arm shot out. His hand opened and the dagger hurtled forward.

"No!" Goran's own arm snaked out to slam into the Jyotian's forearm, blocking the attack.

Too late! One and a half times the blade turned in the air to end its flight by sinking hilt-deep in the mage's left shoulder.

Crying aloud, Etol-Sammo jerked back. His right hand jumped to the knife and wrenched it from his flesh. A confused expression washed over a handsome face suddenly gone ashen as he stared at the blood-covered steel. "How?"

The mage's eyes rose, and he glared at Davin. "You? You aren't of A'bre!"

Wide and round in terror, Etol-Sammo's eyes went. His right arm jerked up and his fingertips wove symbols in the air. As he appeared, he vanished, leaving the two thieves standing amid the grassy plaza as A'bre warred around them.

"Damn you, Davin Anane!" Goran spun around to face his friend. "How could you be so stupid? If you were going to kill him, why not attack with your sword? By all the gods! You used a dirk! All you did was alert him!"

Davin took a startled backward step. He was familiar with the Challing's rage but had never seen it directed at him. "Alert him? I meant to drive my dagger into his throat and kill him!"

"Humans!" Disgust brimmed in Goran's voice and his mighty body sagged as though an unseen weight settled on his shoulders. He shook his head when he turned from his companion. "I shouldn't blame you. It's not your fault. You were born a blind creature. As blind as all those who inhabit A'bre!"

"Blind?"

"You have stared into the Grimoire of the Ages and you still cannot see." Goran's head slowly turned to survey the fray. "Blind like everyone around me and as big a fool!"

Davin stared at his friend. "What in Peyneeha are you talking about?"

Goran's features softened, shifted. Rock-hard musculature melted into voluptuous curves. One eye became two. Glylina once more stood beside the Jyotian.

"I'm talking about the inability of human beings to see truth when it stares them in the face," Glylina answered. "Etol-Sammo expected me to be here, Davin. He knew I was a Challing. But he didn't know about you. He didn't even notice you until you bungled your dagger throw."

"Of course he knew of you through Roan-Jafar," Davin answered as the Challing's words penetrated his mind. "You're right. He didn't notice me until I threw my dirk. Until then he thought I was of A'bre."

"I saw that, why didn't you?" Glylina started toward the Academy of the Moment. "Come. Fighting Etol-Sammo's power here is futile. He is too strong."

"We can't abandon these people. And what about Jennona?" Davin protested. "And why should I have noticed Etol-Sammo didn't see me?"

On the steps to the academy, Glylina stopped and turned back to Davin. "These people are dead, as is Jennona. You've seen it with your own eyes. The same as we will be if we remain here. As to your seeing or lack of seeing, you are supposedly a trained thief who observes the minuscule."

"Abandon A'bre and Jennona?" was all Davin could mumble. Had the Challing gone mad?

"Davin, you are not supposed to be here. Didn't you listen to anything said in the Council Chamber?" Glylina lifted the leaf that nestled about her neck. "This brought me here. I couldn't escape its power. But you – it has no hold over you. You are here because . . ."

Glylina stopped abruptly, stared at the Jyotian, then laughed aloud. "You are here because you are blind, dearest Davin. You're as blind as Etol-Sammo and every human in the city." Glylina reached out, cradled his cheeks in both her hands and pulled him to her for a loud, smacking kiss. "That's it! Etol-Sammo is as blind as you. That is his weakness!"

Davin still wasn't certain what she meant, but he wiped the kiss away with a sleeve and stayed by her side as she entered the open doors of the academy.

"Time is not one moment, Davin dear. It flows! There is a past and there is a future. Perhaps it is a circle – past connecting with future – who knows? The A'breans proclaim loudly that all time exists in a singular moment. They even erected glorious monuments to that concept." Her arms swept out to the building they walked through. "But the Grimoire of the Ages speaks to the opposite."

She paused again and looked at her companion. "Can't you see it yet? Time is not granite. It is mutable. The future is but infinite possibilities – unlimited paths our feet may choose. The grimoire is not a window to the future but a glimpse at what might be should we continue down the present path."

Glylina started toward the Council Chamber again. "That is what blinds those in A'bre. They see *a* future and believe it to be *the* future. That belief locks them to that future. Though they see how Etol-Sammo's sudden appearance changed what can be, they cannot accept how mutable the future is. It is a blindness shared by all seers, all who divine the future. What they see blinds them to truth."

"So we run from the battle?" Davin could not disguise the disgust that welled within his chest. "Have you turned into a coward?"

"No, but I refuse to die with these fools. They have seen their deaths, and though they say the future is changeable, they don't believe it. Their deaths are shown in the Grimoire of the Ages, so they are prepared to die." Glylina strode into the Council Chamber and walked to the center of the room with arms outstretched. She winced when she bumped into the invisible pedestal. "If we are to save these fools, and manage to protect our own necks, it won't be here or now."

Davin stopped as the Challing's meaning sank in. "Elsewhere? Elsewhen?"

"Think, Davin! Recall Etol-Sammo's words. He said Roan-Jafar was supposed to *deal* with me. Since my arrival on Raemllyn, I believed Roan-Jafar sought to bind me as a slave. I was wrong. It was the wizard's task to slay me. Roan-Jafar and Etol-Sammo had slipped between the planes, had glimpsed the future. They saw me in this moment, recognized me as a danger. Roan-Jafar yanked me from Gohwohn to eliminate that danger."

The Jyotian's mind reeled while he tried to piece together the shifts in times and places. Just as he mentally grasped what Glylina said, it slipped away from him.

"This past has become your future as surely as it has become Etol-Sammo's." Glylina tried to prod him toward the conclusion she wanted him to see.

"True," he realized what she said. "But if you were the danger Etol-Sammo and Roan-Jafar saw, why didn't the mage show fear when he found you today?"

"He has had time to weave the spells needed to protect him from me and from this." Glylina held up the leaf. "He wasn't prepared for you."

A smile of comprehension crossed Davin's face. "That is why I was able to wound him! Why, you tried to stop me!"

"You start to see!" Glylina exclaimed. "I believe Etol-Sammo has bound himself in spells like a knight binds himself in armor. There is but one chink in that armor – he has not protected himself from those born of his home world."

"Raemllyn!" Davin now began to see a glimmering of where Glylina led him. "Why should he protect himself from any who come from Raemllyn? None on Raemllyn even suspect the power that resides in this place."

"Exactly!" Glylina said. "Tomorrow, when Etol-Sammo leads his horde of death into A'bre, he will be prepared. Not even one Raemllyn-born will be able to stop him. He will fulfil the prophecy of the Grimoire of the Ages."

Davin now understood Goran's earlier rage. But how was he to have known the sorcerer's weakness? He could only see the here and now. Nor did he have memories of past and future lives such as Goran had claimed to possess.

"If we are to stop his madness," Glylina said, "we must move to another time and place."

"How?"

"With the help of this, I hope." She clasped the leaf tightly in one hand. "And what I can see in the Grimoire of the Ages."

Releasing the leaf, she blindly felt over the invisible pedestal. "It is here. I have it in my hands. Now to open the cover and see if the grimoire reveals the past as well as the future."

Davin watched as Glylina's fingers felt along the invisible tome. Her hands moved as though she opened the covers, then—

She disappeared!

16

"Glylina!" Davin took two strides toward the invisible pedestal, then skidded to a halt. "Glylina!"

Alarm furrowed the Jyotian's brow. The Challing did not answer. Did the spell cast by A'bre's Chosen now envelop Glylina, hiding her as it concealed the Grimoire of the Ages? Cautiously, he edged toward the center of the chamber. His right hand stretched out, fingers feeling only empty air. He crept closer, boots shuffling across the white floor. Still his hand met nothing but thin air. Twice more he inched forward before his fingertips brushed against Glylina's shoulder.

She remains here. Relief flowed with the thought. He had no desire to stand alone in this mind-twisting everywhere men named A'bre.

Lightly, his fingers slipped down the Challing's arm to find her hands pressed against the open binding of the grimoire. What visions filled her mind? To what times did she travel? Did wonders or horrors parade before her mind's eye?

"Glylina," he whispered.

The Challing did not answer.

"Glylina, have you found Etol-Sammo?"

Glylina still did not reply.

Nor did she move. Davin nudged her hand with his fingers. There was no response. He pinched the soft flesh between her forefinger and thumb. Instead of a startled yelp, there was only silence.

Something was wrong!

From the back of the Jyotian's mind came the memory of Jennona's earlier warning – to stare into the Grimoire of the Ages for too long could bring madness. How long had Glylina and he viewed the tome with the five Chosen? No more than seconds? Glylina had disappeared over a minute ago.

"The last thing I need now is a raving Challing." He remembered how Parthlin had snapped the book shut to end the visions.

Removing Glylina's fingers from the binding, he did likewise.

Nothing.

Davin's pulse raced. He had never given the Challing credit for possessing a large brain, but no matter how small his friend's mental capacity, he did not want what was there driven to lunacy. Grasping Glylina's wrists with both hands, the Jyotian yanked her toward him.

One moment there was empty air, the next the Challing winked back into sight. Her eyes were wide and stared straight ahead as though still locked in the visions of the Grimoire of the Ages.

"Glylina," Davin called while he lightly patted her cheeks. "Glylina, come out of it. Speak to me."

A soft moan, little more than a whisper, pushed past her parted lips.

Then her eyes closed and she collapsed into his arms. Gently Davin lowered her to the floor. The rise and fall of her breast said that she still lived. But what of her mind?

"She is lucky to be alive," the voice of a child came from behind Davin. "Not even the Chosen stare into its pages without someone at their side to draw them away."

Davin's head jerked around. A girl still years shy of the first signs of blossoming womanhood stood at the door to the chamber. Her blue eyes were big and round and black hair fell about her shoulders. She moved to the Jyotian's side in a brisk walk.

"You should take her to her room and let her rest." The girl knelt and pressed three fingers to Glylina's forehead. "She will be all right. She merely saw too much at one time. Those who have lost their minds to the Grimoire of the Ages have come away foaming at the mouth and screaming at the gods."

"You've seen others?" Davin frowned, certain he had seen the child before.

"Two – and my grandmother Mettatine has told me of others. The madness the grimoire brings is always the same."

"Your grandmother is Mettatine?" Davin's mind darted back to the old crone who had brought them to the cave by the side of Lake Woe.

"I am named after her," the child answered with a nod. "It is what I will name my own daughter and what she will name hers. Mettatine is a name that has followed the women of my bloodline for untold generations. It is a good name, and I hope it will continue through the future generations."

An amused smile uplifted the corners of Davin's mouth. Somewhere in the future another Mettatine would live and meet the Challing now stretched out on the floor. That Mettatine would steal Goran's eye and wear it about her neck like a charm.

"She is very beautiful, don't you think?" Young Mettatine scrutinized Glylina with the curiosity of a child.

"Very," Davin agreed, relieved Glylina was unable to hear that single word. The Challing's recent transformation to Glylina was one of the few times she had not attempted to seduce him.

"My mother is beautiful, too." Mettatine looked at the Jyotian. "Do you know her? Her name is Jennona."

Davin's heart sank. This was Jennona's daughter. How could he tell her of her mother's danger? "Yes, I've met her, and she is beautiful."

"I hope I am as beautiful as she is when I grow up." Mettatine smiled wistfully.

"You will steal the hearts of men like a thief in the night."

Davin's and the child's heads swung to Glylina who smiled up at them.

"You're all right?" Davin asked.

"My head swims like I have drained a keg of Litonyan ale, but I still live." Glylina rose to her elbows. "Why are you here, child? A battle rages outside. Shouldn't you be somewhere safe?"

Mettatine looked up. "I am bound to the Grimoire of the Ages when Etol-Sammo attacks. I can feel it when someone disturbs its pages. My task is to warn the Chosen if someone attempts to steal it."

Glylina sat up and massaged her temples with her fingers. "I merely wanted to look, not steal."

"I know," Mettatine answered. "I can feel that, too." The young girl stood and smiled at Jyotian and Challing. "However, I wouldn't let the Chosen find you here. With Etol-Sammo so near they might think that you are thieves."

Davin nodded while he pushed to his feet. "A good idea." He held a hand out to Glylina. "Can you stand – walk?"

She grasped his hand and allowed him to pull her to her feet.

"I'll be fine, but young Mettatine is right. It is time for us to be going. I saw what I needed."

When the two turned to the chamber's door, the girl said: "If you see the one-eyed giant outside, tell him that he was brave when he tried to save my mother."

Davin and Glylina turned back. Davin asked, "You know?"

A sad shadow moved across the girl's face. "I watched from my room above."

"We go to try to save Jennona." This from Glylina. "If there is a way, we will bring her back to you."

The smile returned to Mettatine's lips, but the sadness remained in her blue eyes. "My mother is prepared to die if that is what is needed to save A'bre. Don't let her life be a waste."

"Child, your mother's life is not wasted," Glylina assured the girl, then turned to Davin. "Come, we must make our way back to the cave. It is the heart of the nexus." She reached up and touched the golden leaf about her neck. "With this, we can travel to elsewhen."

Outside the Academy of the Moment, three fur-clad barbarians armed with spiked bludgeons charged Jyotian and Challing with weapons raised high. A blink of the eye proved them to be more of Etol-Sammo's illusions.

However, a demon with the body of a naked woman and the head of a tigress brandishing a trident and net did not vanish in a blink.

Davin met the thrust of her three-tined spear with a swipe of his sword. At the same time, Glylina's own blade leaped forward and drove into the demon's heart. The roar of a tiger tore from the creature's fanged mouth as it dropped to the street and keeled over face first to die.

Glylina glanced from the dead demon to her Jyotian friend and winked. "We make quite a team, don't you think, Davin m'dear?"

"We always have, *Goran*." Davin placed double emphasis on the Challing's male name to make certain Glylina clearly understood his position remained unchanged since her last appearance.

Glylina shrugged. "If you find me 'very' beautiful, why do you fight nature?"

"You heard?" Davin felt embarrassed heat rush to his cheeks.

"I heard." Glylina gave him another wink. "Nor will I forget what I heard."

"Then I suggest you change back into Goran before we take another step toward the cave."

The Challing shrugged. "Sorry, that's not possible."

"But you said that your powers are fully . . ."

"They have returned fully," Glylina confirmed. "But Etol-Sammo knows Goran One-Eye. He has never seen me. If I am to get close enough to him to divert his attention while you slay him, I must keep this body."

"Then you have found a way of returning in time! You weren't just dazed in the chamber?"

"The leaf comprises the Four Keys of A'bre – each key opens a portal for the wearer. The Grimoire of the Ages revealed that," she said. "The three dimensions as we know them are unlocked by the first portion. The second molds time and the third shifts one through the planes of existence. The fourth controls the other three, bringing them into harmony with each other."

"Then we travel back to when Etol-Sammo first discovered A'bre." Davin waved an arm toward the distant cave.

"That was my original thought," Glylina said, "but the grimoire did not reveal all that I needed. We will travel back to this very night, before Etol-Sammo's attack."

Four knights mounted astride black bulls charged down the street straight at the pair. Davin blinked his eyes and watched them disappear. "Tonight? We failed to kill Etol-Sammo tonight!"

Glylina started toward the cave. "We weren't prepared. But when this night comes again, we will be waiting for Etol-Sammo's arrival in the park."

Davin's frown of uncertainty faded as he began to understand Glylina's plan. "Etol-Sammo was unaware of me this night. He wore no spell to protect him from my attack."

The confirming grin that slid across Glylina's lips was as bloodthirsty as any expression the Jyotian had ever seen on Goran's face. "While I draw his attention, you will slip up behind him and slit his throat."

Davin felt an uneasy shiver quake through his body. He had faced and killed more than one man with his sword and knife. But this was not the same. What Glylina described was assassination – cold-blooded murder. The Jyotian slowly drew in a deep breath to quell the restlessness. Such a deed would change the course of history – histories.

The thought brought him no comfort. Did not all assassins strike for the same reason – to eliminate a man or woman whom they saw as a great destroyer?

"There is one more thing, Davin." Glylina reached out, took the Jyotian's shoulder to stop him, then turned him to face her. "Roan-Jafar still lives. My blade will finish what it failed to do when the wizard first snatched me from Gohwohn!"

17

"Roan-Jafar? Alive?" Davin stumbled forward when Glylina started toward the cave again. "How can that be? You killed him when he dragged you from Gohwohn! And why have the A'breans not seen this?"

"They haven't seen because they haven't looked. They are trapped by the seduction of the future, never peering into the past." Glylina bit at her lower lip and shook her head. "I searched past and future, I killed but one of the mage's apprentices who posed as Roan-Jafar."

Davin's gaze constantly surveyed the street for new attacks while Glylina revealed what she had seen in the pages of the Grimoire of the Ages. The din of battle died behind them as they neared the edge of the city.

"Roan-Jafar discovered the path to A'bre in his youth. He spent his life exploring the worlds A'bre opened to him," Glylina explained. "Although the mage understood the progression of souls, he could not resign himself to its simple truth," the Challing continued. "Death and the loss of all the knowledge he had gathered in a lifetime was more than he could accept. He had lived a full sixty world cycles when he discovered that time also joined in a nexus. He used this discovery to move through the ages to a time when the Grimoire of the Ages was uncovered by the A'breans. There he first read the pages and set upon his path to immortality."

"But Etol-Sammo?" Davin questioned.

"Like the apprentice I killed, Etol-Sammo is no more than a pawn Roan-Jafar manipulated – still manipulates like a marionette on rubber strings." Glylina paused and turned back to A'bre when the paved street gave way to a dirt path. She shivered. "The sky serpent is gone. We must hurry before he finds that we are missing and attempts to stop us. And as soon as Mettatine reveals that I read the Grimoire of the Ages he will know that I know."

"Know?" The more Glylina revealed, the more confused Davin grew.

"Roan-Jafar," she answered. "He will know that I have discovered he still lives."

Davin shook his head. "Dammit! It's Etol-Sammo who wages war on A'bre."

"But it's Roan-Jafar who controls his every move," Glylina countered. "When that black-souled mage learned that the Grimoire of the Ages held the power of immortality, he found the A'breans standing between him and eternal life. None in A'bre would consider evoking such an unnatural power. Roan-Jafar had to push them to that point. War – the destruction of A'bre – was the only threat that could possibly force them to use the grimoire for his horrible purpose. To achieve his goal, he needed men to wage that war," Glylina explained. "Thus he chose two apprentices, Etol-Sammo and Telun Roct. Each in turn, he escorted through the portal and let them view the infinite worlds.

"Think of it, Davin. You glanced at the Grimoire of the Ages for mere seconds and your mind reeled under the onslaught." Glylina's fingers once more crept to her temples and rubbed. "Roan-Jafar held his apprentices suspended between the planes watching the endless progression of worlds for days. When he brought them back to Raemllyn, they had no minds. Both had traveled beyond madness. Their thoughts, desires, personalities were gone, totally erased. Both men were no better than turnips in human form."

Glylina quickened her steps as the distant hill that first admitted them to A'bre loomed like a dark shadow on the horizon. "Roan-Jafar was beyond what men of Raemllyn call a master mage. His knowledge was drawn from a thousand worlds. With Telun Roct he molded a new Roan-Jafar to replace himself. Etol-Sammo he simply molded. Each movement the two made was controlled by spells implanted into their blank brains. He imparted his knowledge to two men who were in essence nothing more than mirror images of himself. Then he sent them into time to wage war against A'bre.

"Throughout the ages, Roan-Jafar and Etol-Sammo appeared and drew minions from the dimensions to battle the A'breans. With each appearance their might grew and A'bre gradually weakened. While his two puppets pushed the A'breans closer and closer to evoking the power of immortality held within the Grimoire of the Ages, the true Roan-Jafar assumed a new identity. He married an A'brean woman and left her with a child before he slipped forward in time. Like a farmer breeds stock, he watched his line progress through the eons, weaving a spell here and there to assure his ultimate goal."

"To place one of his descendants among the five of the Chosen!" Davin suddenly saw the twisted path the Grimoire of the Ages had revealed. "When the grimoire is used, he will be there to gain eternal life!"

"Exactly!" Glylina paused at the foot of the hill and hugged her arms against the growing chill that hung in the night. "While Etol-Sammo and his armies invade A'bre on the morrow, Roan-Jafar will slay his own descendant and take his place among the Council of the Chosen. He will then oppose Etol-Sammo and slay him. In that moment he will become A'bre's greatest hero. No one will ever believe he is more than he appears to be – A'bre's savior."

"There is something amiss. We saw the future in the grimoire," Davin said. "It was Etol-Sammo's face written on every page, not Roan-Jafar's."

"That, too, is his working," the Challing said when she began to climb toward the cave mouth. "Roan-Jafar is not here. He uses the Chosen's weakness: their addiction to the future. He hides himself in the past, waiting until Etol-Sammo's final attack to leap across the eons and claim his victory. Unlike those in A'bre, he recognizes that what is to come can be changed and uses that fact."

"Which of the Chosen is his descendant?" Davin asked the question that nagged at him.

"All five," Glylina said simply. "He has had all of time to weave his plot, and he has been thorough. He has seen a possible future where we kill him. Why do you think he used Telun Roct to draw me from Gohwohn and attempt to kill me? He failed in that, and is only too aware he might fail again."

"But what of Jennona and Toiyah? They are women. Surely we can eliminate them from possible plotting?"

"Davin, think." Glylina halted at the mouth of the cave.

"Roan-Jafar controls the magicks of endless worlds. Do you think the changing of shapes is beyond him? That is the danger I pose. I can recognize a form that has been shifted."

"By Yehseen's staff!" More than the night's chill sent ice coursing through the Jyotian's veins. "He intends to use Jennona."

Glylina's eyes lifted to Davin, and she slowly nodded. "Your thoughts run with mine. On the morrow, Etol-Sammo will appear with his armies. At his side will be a battered Jennona who will stave off death long enough to kill miraculously Etol-Sammo and allow A'bre's healers to reach her side. What better disguise to hide behind than a hero recovering from near-fatal wounds?"

The tableau painted was a possible future, Davin reminded himself. But it had an undeniable ring of truth to it that could not be ignored. Though he saw myriad possibilities that would allow them to thwart the sorcerer, he also admitted that they were about to step into a realm Roan-Jafar had manipulated through eons upon eons.

They were but neophytes pitted against a past master.

Glylina tilted her head to the cave's darkness. "It's time we step back in time and force Roan-Jafar to come forth and meet his future."

18

Twice Davin had stepped into A'bre's damnable portal. The third venture did not increase his liking of slipping between the rapidly passing moments of time. The blackness, the sensation of falling through an endless void and the knotting pain in his gut all returned, as did the throbbing headache when the darkness parted and he again stood within the small cave with its straw bed and circle of stones.

"Davin!" Glylina's voice came to him, weak and trembling with fear. "Davin, help me, please!"

A glowing veil of witchfire surrounded the Challing in a pulsing sphere as she stumbled toward the cave mouth.

"Please, Davin. Help me!" She turned. Her face twisted in pain as she clutched her stomach with both hands and doubled over. "Please, help me. Something tears me in twain."

Davin took a step toward the quaking Challing and almost collapsed facedown in the dirt. The strength in his legs fled; his arms fared no better. The power required to stand seemed more than he possessed in his whole body.

"Please," Glylina pled, her voice echoing the agony that knotted her facial muscles. "I'm being ripped apart. Please help me!"

Ignoring the hammer that slammed into an anvil buried at the center of his brain, the Jyotian forced legs more rubber than flesh and bone to stagger forward. He stretched a hand toward Glylina. His fingertips brushed her shoulder when her whole body convulsed. She dropped to the floor and trembled like a woman caught in the throes of the falling sickness.

The leaf!

Davin blinked against the actinic glare that burst from the amulet when Glylina tossed to her back and writhed uncontrollably. Never had the medallion burned with such intensity, even in the presence of threatening magicks. Something was wrong, terribly wrong.

The Jyotian tried to throw himself forward and discovered the best he could manage was a fall that brought him stomach down on the cave floor beside the flaming-haired beauty. His right hand reached out and closed on the chain around Glylina's neck. He yanked. The chain held. Five times he tugged with all the strength he could muster before the soft links of gold separated. Chain and magical leaf came free of the Challing's neck.

Immediately, Glylina's shuddering body quieted. Her eyes opened and shifted to the Jyotian. A weak whisper slipped from her lips. "The portal – throw it into the portal."

Rolling to his side, Davin found enough strength to lob chain and leaf into the black mouth in the cave's wall. The amulet vanished into nothingness.

"Ohhh," came a moan of relief from the Challing.

Strength creeping back into his body, Davin rolled to his other side to see Glylina swallow twice then slowly draw in a deep breath. Her eyes fluttered closed and her chest heaved three more times before she said, "Better. Weak but better. I'll live."

"What was that?" Davin pushed up and sat cross-legged on the floor. His head still throbbed but no longer did a hammer pound at the anvil inside his skull.

"The amulet," Glylina said, sitting up and facing her companion. "It could not exist in a time where it already existed. It was trying to escape into another time and tearing me apart to get there."

For a moment Davin was not certain what the Challing meant, then it occurred to him that they had stepped back in time to a moment they had already lived. They sat on the floor to the cave – they were also in A'bre.

At this instant two Glylinas and two Davin Ananes existed.

"I don't think we are supposed to be here either." Glylina stood and swayed. "My strength has not totally returned, and I feel – strange."

Davin recognized the full force of that "strange" when he rose. "You feel sick. Not bad but as if you had stood outside in a winter rain and taken a chill."

Glylina nodded. "I do feel chilled, but my face also feels hot and flushed. It is unusual. I have never felt this way before."

"Fever," Davin said. "It is a fever."

The Challing looked at him. "How do you know how I feel?"

"Because I feel the same way." Davin closed his eyes and shook his head to cast off the sensation. All he did was succeed in making his head spin. "Mayhap neither Challing nor man is supposed to exist in a time they have already lived. I feel worse by the moment."

"Mayhap," Glylina agreed, "but we have no other course. We *must* get to the city."

"Even if it kills us?" Davin moved to the cave entrance where the sun sank toward the western horizon.

"It will kill us if we don't!" Glylina elbowed her way past him and started down the path toward A'bre.

"Right," he answered as he started after her. "I, for one, feel too bad to die this night."

They huddled together beside a building opposite the Academy of the Moment. Both shivered and hugged their arms to their chests for warmth that refused to come. Man and Challing stared across the grassy plaza separating them from the entrance to the academy.

"I fear this is what it feels like to die," Glylina said, teeth chattering hard. "I sense my strength slipping away with each beat of my heart."

"If we're to join the progression of souls tonight, so be it." Davin's eyes lifted to the sky. There was no sign of the sky serpent. "But I'll not start that journey until we've completed our task."

Glylina's eyes rose to him. He saw no glimmer of hope in them, only the vulnerability he had recently come to know in his friend.

"Would it warm you if I held you?" he suggested.

The Challing shook her head. "It is not the way I have wanted you to hold me. And I am not one to be pitied. When we get out of this Qar-cursed city, ask me again. I *might* be more receptive – then again, I might *not*."

Glylina's head turned back toward the academy. Davin studied her and found himself surprised that he thought of the Challing as "her" rather than Goran One-Eye, the red-haired giant warrior. Before Glylina had always been merely Goran in female form. He now saw all the differences he had denied over the past year.

Goran and Glylina were truly two separate entities.

He smiled at his foolishness. Such thoughts now made no sense. Yet, since seeing the Challing in its natural form, he had come to realize how little he knew about this being from another dimension he called friend.

What if he had met Glylina rather than Goran first? Would he find the blatant advances she made such an affront?

An elbow nudged his side. Glylina tilted her head to the sky. The night took the form of glinting scales.

"The sky serpent," Davin said softly.

"The time is here." The strident blare of a trumpet sounded in the distance punctuated her words. A warning that was soon chorused by a thousand horns across the city.

"Your dirk," Davin said urgently. "Give me your dirk. I don't think I can lift my sword."

Glylina's right hand freed the knife and passed it to him. "Strike true this time. You'll have but one chance."

The Jyotian shivered as the cold sank deeper into his body. "Just draw Etol-Sammo's attention, and I'll do my part."

Glylina rose on tiptoe and lightly kissed his cheek. "May your gods protect us, Davin Anane, because I feel they may be the only ones standing with us."

With that she turned and walked toward the grassy plaza to position herself for Etol-Sammo's arrival. Across the green, Jennona burst from the Academy of the Moment. Two yellow-skinned man-things armed with spears appeared at the front of the steps and died as white bolts shafted from the Warden of Peace's wand.

From every building surrounding the plaza came the citizens of A'bre, each beset by creatures drawn from other worlds or monstrous illusions meant to befuddle their minds. The chaos of war reigned in the streets of the city within minutes.

Davin ignored all, forcing his quivering legs to carry him across the manicured grass. A beetle, serrated jaws stretched wide for the kill, appeared before him. He blinked. The sorcerer-conjured illusion vanished. A sign of relief escaped the Jyotian's lips when he walked unscathed through the mirage. Had the giant insect been real, he would have died a terrible, painful death. The strength to fight had forsaken his body.

Two dozen strides from Glylina, he halted. If their pooled memories served them correctly, Etol-Sammo would materialize directly between them.

Davin's right hand tightened about the dirk's handle. Closer, the time grew closer. Jennona moved across the street, bolts from her wand slicing into three fish-headed warriors brandishing long, curved silver swords.

"Davin!" Glylina's voice snapped his mind back to the task at hand. "Get ready!"

Three warriors in red armor, each wearing horned helms, winked into existence. With war cries tearing from their throats, they charged Jennona. The crackling bolts from her wand passed through the three illusions and brought three more to life who joined the other mirages to drive Jennona toward the center of the plaza. Another blast from the wand and ten faced A'bre's Warden of Peace – then twelve. The red-clad warriors spread out, meaning to encircle her.

Blink! Davin willed the A'brean to see that only illusion surrounded her. He wasted precious strength on the impossible.

"Help!" Jennona cried in desperation as she danced from side to side, dodging spear and sword. "Anyone, help me!"

Goran One-Eye ran down the steps of the academy to answer the cry. Halfway across the street the living statue of a knight in full armor blocked his way.

Davin did not bother to blink when he saw himself charge an alley cat and drive his sword through the unwitting creature. The Jyotian watched himself butchering a cat transformed to green pard, then in the blink of an eye he stared at Etol-Sammo's back and the loose folds of a blue robe that hung there.

"You finally decided to show yourself, eh?" Glylina forced herself to face the wizard with back stiff and straight. "I wasn't certain such a craven would crawl out from beneath his rock."

"What?" Etol-Sammo swung about to face Glylina squarely. "Have they sent a madwoman to greet me?"

"Nay," Glylina answered with a shake of her head. "They sent no woman at all."

"You!" Davin could not see the mage's face, but he had no need. He had viewed that cool expression before. "It is you, Challing. Roan-Jafar was supposed . . ."

The Jyotian struck. Gripping the dagger with both hands, he wrenched it high above his head, then drove it down straight between the wizard's shoulder blades. Hilt-deep the long sliver of steel sank as Davin's wrists twisted to guide the tip between ribs.

A howl of rage and shock ripped from Etol-Sammo's throat. He spun around, a flailing arm striking Davin in the chest and sending him to the grass.

"Who?" Etol-Sammo's eyes went round when they alighted on the fallen Jyotian. "You're no A'brean. How did you get here?"

Davin tried to answer, to spit a curse in the dying man's face. He couldn't. That one stroke had drained his reserve of strength. All he could do was stare up and watch Etol-Sammo sink to his knees while his arms stretched over his shoulders in an attempt to free the solidly lodged dagger.

"Damn you! I was not meant to die this way!" Realizing the futility of his clawing hands, Etol-Sammo's arms stretched toward the Jyotian. "Die I might, but your soul shall precede me to Peyneeha's depths!"

"No!" Glylina screamed defiantly. Somehow she had managed to free her sword and stagger toward the mage. "Die, damn you! Die!"

Downward the blade swung, striking Etol-Sammo's neck as miniature bolts of red lightning danced between his splayed fingers – lightning that blasted from the wizard's hand when he toppled to the grass, his head half-severed from his torso.

Not Glylina but Jennona reeled back when Etol-Sammo's final spell found a target. The jagged bolts of red lightning struck her full in the chest and exploded in a ball of flame.

"Noooooo!"

Davin barely recognized Glylina's wail of agony as the ice that flowed in his veins tugged him downward into a blackness where only Qar could dwell.

"Davin!" A voice echoed in the featureless darkness. "Damn you Davin. Wake up!"

The voice refused to let him be. It was as persistent as the hands on his shoulders that shook him.

"Davin, this is no time for a nap! We aren't finished!"

Glylina – he recognized the voice. It belonged to Glylina.

"Let me die in peace," he groaned, his own hands rising and batting at those on his shoulders. "I'm ready to join the progression of souls. I've had enough of this world."

"Not quite enough, it seems! This is going to hurt you more than it does me."

"Damn you, woman!" Davin's eyes flew open when an open palm slapped his right cheek. "I was willing to die on my own! You don't have to kill me!"

He shoved up on one elbow while rubbing the sting from his cheek with his right hand. "If you weren't . . ."

"There's no time for threats," Glylina cut him short. "I don't know how, but you live – we both live."

Davin pushed from the ground. The cold was gone from his arms and legs – gone from his whole body. Other than a mild throbbing in his head, he felt – *alive*!

"And this is back." Glylina lifted the golden leaf around her neck.

The Jyotian glanced around. The battle still raged on A'bre's streets, but Etol-Sammo's body lay still and dead a few feet away. They had succeeded in eliminating Roan-Jafar's brainless creature. However, Davin saw no sign of Jennona. "Where is she? Where is Jennona?"

"Joined the progression of souls," Glylina said softly. "She was dead when I reached her, then I passed out. I awoke only moments ago. I think it was the return of the leaf that brought me around."

"If the leaf is back, that can only mean . . ."

"I'm not certain what it means, nor do we have time to discuss it." Glylina's head turned toward the Academy of the Moment. "The demon who caused this blood bath still lives. We've achieved nothing while he remains alive."

"Immortality lies in but one direction." Davin tilted his head toward the academy. "When he appears, it will be there."

"And we will be waiting for him." Glylina bent and scooped her sword from the ground. She started to retrieve the dagger protruding from Etol-Sammo's back, then halted. "Better to leave it there. A dirk comes cheap enough."

Steel on leather hissed when Davin pulled his own sword from its sheath. "Shall we go and introduce ourselves to Roan-Jafar?"

"I go to sing his death song." Glylina pivoted sharply and strode directly to the academy, up its stairs and through its open door. "The Council Chamber is open."

That Roan-Jafar might have already found his way to the Grimoire of the Ages struck them at the same moment. Together they ran down the long white hall and burst into the chamber.

Four mages in white robes stood around a table on which was stretched Jennona's bloody body. All four swung around to stare at the two adventurers.

"Glylina? Davin? How?" Parthlin spoke. "We received reports you were devoured by a cyclopean dragon outside on the steps!"

"Perhaps another Davin and Glylina," the Challing said. "As you can see we're very much alive."

"A one-eyed dragon," Davin whispered. "Seems like an appropriate end for a certain Challing I know."

Glylina's lips twisted in disgust. "To me it seems time found a way of eliminating the problem of having two Davin Ananes running around."

And two Glylina/Gorans, Davin thought, remembering what the Challing had said about time offering unlimited possibilities. How he could both live and die the same night was beyond him. That he somehow managed to live was all that mattered at *this* moment.

Toiyah stepped away from the table. "We promised to return both of you to your worlds if you aided us in Etol-Sammo's defeat. And so we shall, but now we mourn the passing of one of the Chosen."

"And prepare to greet our new member." This from Meerium.

"Yes," Parthlin added. "After we have opened the Grimoire of the Ages together, we shall fulfil our promise."

"You intend to go through with your lunacy?" Glylina edged toward the center of the chamber. "You intend to succumb to Roan-Jafar?"

"Roan-Jafar?" Harri'Alin questioned. "You killed Roan-Jafar."

"*A* Roan-Jafar – a man he bound with spells to stand in his stead," the Challing said as she reached the spot where the invisible pedestal stood. "The same as he bound Etol-Sammo to do his bidding. It was Roan-Jafar who has always threatened

A'bre – still threatens the city. I saw him in your book."

The four mages' gazes shifted among each other as Glylina's meaning slowly sank into their minds.

"What you propose is impossible," Meerium said. "I know these three, have known them since childhood."

Parthlin, Toiyah and Harri'Alin nodded in agreement.

"Be that as it may," Glylina reached out and tapped the invisible grimoire. "This is what Roan-Jafar wants. And until he shows himself, no one will open this tome."

None of the four spoke but all roused as a single entity. Their arms lifted, their mouths moved in a joined chant. Glaring light, white-hot and sizzling, burst from their fingers and cracked across the room straight at Glylina.

An inch in front of the Challing, a shimmering green mirror abruptly formed in the air. The mages' blast struck the barrier rather than the Challing.

In the next instant, Davin felt an invisible hammer slam into his chest as white heat exploded through the chamber. The force lifted him from his feet and threw him against the wall. Like a child's cloth doll, he slid to the floor beside the opened door.

He shook his head and peered up at a grinning Glylina, then glanced at the four mages sprawled flat on their backs on the white floor.

"The keys," Glylina said before he could ask the obvious. "They belong to A'bre. Not even the city's protectors may destroy them."

Davin staggered to his feet and leaned heavily against the wall to gather his strength. The world refused to slow its wild spinning. "What about them? Which one is Roan-Jafar?"

"None," Glylina answered simply, then turned back to the four who groaned on the floor. "Who have you chosen to replace Jennona?"

"Mettatine," Parthlin answered.

"A child?" Glylina stared in disbelief. "You chose Jennona's daughter?"

"No," a cool voice came from the door and a stately silver-haired woman stepped into the chamber. "They chose me, Jennona's mother."

Glylina's head snapped around. The Challing's eyes filled with horror. "Davin, it's him! It's Roan-Jafar!"

The Jyotian's sword tip leaped up. Davin's arm jerked back, prepared to drive steel straight to the woman's heart.

"Not her!" Glylina cried. "The child! Roan-Jafar is the child!"

Davin's gaze dropped to see a blue-eyed, dark-tressed girl step back from her grandmother's side. This was the small Mettatine who had knelt at his side when he revived Glylina, the same gentle child who so wistfully wished for beauty when she blossomed to a woman.

"It's Roan-Jafar, Davin! Kill him!" Glylina insisted.

The child's image was but an illusion that hid a mad wizard seeking to become a god. Glylina's eyes could see beyond the veil of magicks blinding him, Davin told himself. It was not a child who would—

"Too late, Jyotian!" Mettatine's lips moved, but the voice that came from that mouth cracked with the weight of years rather than flowing with sweet innocence.

An invisible hand closed around Davin's neck like a vice and threw him against the wall. Sword falling from his fingers, he reached up and grasped – empty air!

"I summoned a dragon. I saw it devour you. How you still live I know not," came Roan-Jafar's voice from Mettatine's mouth. "But I promise you this second death will be final."

The unseen fingers tightened about Davin's throat, closing off his windpipe.

Mettatine's small hand turned palm up and lifted.

Davin's feet left the floor. Inch by inch, the force that clutched his throat raised him three feet into the air. Still his hands found nothing to fight against. His fingers merely clawed at the air. He gasped but no air found its way to his burning lungs.

"A second and final death!" Glylina's voice rang out. "Exactly what I promised to deliver you!"

Through tear-blurred eyes, the Jyotian saw the Challing charge with sword clasped in two hands and drawn back over her right shoulder.

Mettatine's head twisted around. Her right hand rose.

Too late!

Glylina swung. Cold steel whistled through the air. The honed blade bit into the child's neck, severing head from body.

Instantly, the invisible hand opened. Cool air rushed into Davin's lungs. He dropped to the floor, the withered head of a white-haired wizard thudding against his boots. Neither fear nor shock was written on the lifeless face that stared up at the Jyotian. The mask Roan-Jafar now donned was the same slack, emotionless expression worn by all dead men.

"This time you will stay dead!" Glylina used a well-placed kick to the midriff to topple the mage's still standing body.

The headless corpse fell amid a spray of crimson that splattered across the immaculate white floor.

The Challing turned to Davin. "Are you all right?"

The Jyotian nodded and swallowed hard. The glint in Glylina's eyes was the familiar light of blood lust he had seen in Goran's single eye hundreds of times.

"Good, because Roan-Jafar has loosed an army of demons on this city, and I'm of no mind to face them alone." Glylina snatched Davin's fallen blade from the floor and tossed it to him. "Are you with me?"

Davin raised his sword in silent salute to the woman, then followed her from the Academy of the Moment.

19

"More wine?"

Davin glanced away from the dancers who reveled around the plaza outside the Academy of the Moment. A lovely blonde with a pitcher in her hands smiled at him. He nodded and watched her refill his cup to the brim. With another smile, she moved on to three women who held up their empty chalices.

"You think she's pretty, don't you?"

Davin smiled at the child who sat beside him on the grass. "Aye, but not as beautiful as you, Mettatine. Of all the beauties in A'bre, you are the one who has won my heart."

The girl's bright blue eyes sparkled when she blushed and giggled with obvious delight. "Even with this blackened eye?"

"Even with your wounds of war." Davin let his fingertips brush her left cheek, then raised his cup to her and drank deeply.

The child had been lucky. In Roan-Jafar's panic to ensure that he stood with the Chosen when they opened the Grimoire of the Ages, the sorcerer had merely employed a fist to drive Mettatine into unconsciousness rather than a blade to end her life. The ugly, swollen purple and green bruise around her left eye would fade, leaving but a memory and a tale she would one day tell her grandchildren.

"If I have won your heart, why won't you stay here in A'bre?" Mettatine asked.

Davin took another sip of the sweet wine. "Because Glylina and I have finished what we were called here to do. And A'bre is not our world. You wouldn't like to be taken from your home, never to return, would you?"

"No, I guess not," the child admitted reluctantly.

The Jyotian's gaze drifted toward the Academy of the Moment. Glylina was nowhere to be found. He pursed his lips. A'bre had brought changes in the Challing. In the seven days of celebration that followed the obliteration of Roan-Jafar's minions, he had seen Glylina only in passing. Instead of losing herself in wild revelry, she chose to be locked away within the academy debating with the Chosen.

For an hour on the first day of the celebration, Davin had sat beside her, then left in disgust. He had no mind for the metaphysical nor ceaseless debates over the numbers of souls who passed through A'bre each moment as they moved onto a life in another plane of existence. As much as he prided himself on being a man of the world and educated to the finer things of life, he admitted to himself he preferred the feel of reality to dreaming of "might be".

"Still, I will miss you," Mettatine said, her eyes lifting to the Jyotian. "You will not return to A'bre, will you?"

Davin glanced down. "Who knows what fate the Sitala cast for a man? I never expected to travel this way, yet I am here."

Mettatine looked at her feet. "I think you'll not be back – not in this lifetime."

Davin reached out and rested a comforting hand on her shoulder. "Then we have other lifetimes to look forward to."

Again he turned toward the Academy. Glylina pushed through the edifice's broad double doors and came down the stairs three at a time. Without more than glances at the revelers, she walked directly to Davin, took the cup of wine from his hand and downed it in hasty gulps.

"We have overstayed our visit to A'bre, Davin dear." Her gaze moved over the city of wonders. "It's time we returned to our own lives."

"The Chosen are prepared to send us home?" Davin asked.

"We never needed them." There was a trace of bitterness in the Challing's tone. "The cave is the nexus. All we have to do is return to the moment we entered and the way home will be open to both of us."

"The cave?" Davin's head jerked back toward the academy, unable to escape the feeling that A'bre's Chosen had artfully manipulated and used them.

"You go now?" Mettatine asked, her eyes turning to Glylina.

The Challing squatted to look the child in the face. "Aye, we have lives of our own that need tending." Glylina reached into her blouse and withdrew the gold chain that had once held the Keys of A'bre. She placed it around the child's neck. "Here's something to remember us by." She then lightly kissed Mettatine on each cheek and rose.

"I won't forget you," Mettatine said when the pair of thieves started toward the city's edge.

Glylina glanced back. "I know that, child. Nor will I forget you!"

Davin smiled and chuckled while they walked from the grassy plaza and down A'bre's streets. "Your gestures grow more human each day."

Glylina winked at him. "I did that for Goran."

"Goran?"

"The Keys of A'bre are woven with powerful magicks," the Challing answered. "Some are now instilled in that gold chain. Nothing dangerous, you understand, but enough to hold a stolen eye to its links without need of clasp."

Davin laughed, remembering the chain and eye the crone Mettatine had worn. "I notice you no longer wear the gold leaf. Did the Chosen take it back?"

Glylina nodded. "They felt there was no further need of the Keys."

The Challing dipped a hand into a pocket and brought it out with the four-sectioned leaf in her palm. "On the other hand, I thought it too powerful a tool to leave with them. Besides, it's been over a week since I practiced my arts. None of them noticed when I slipped it from Parthlin's robes."

Again Davin detected a hint of bitterness in his companion's voice. "Did all go well in your talks with the Chosen?"

Glylina shrugged. "Who knows with you humans? I tried to convince them of the dangers of using the Grimoire of the Ages – that seeing a possible future locks one to that vision rather than exploring the possibilities. I urged them to destroy the tome, yet it remained when I left the Council Chamber. I'm afraid the desire to divine the unknown is too great for them to overcome."

When they moved from pavement to dirt path, Davin broached the matter he knew bothered the Challing. "And immortality – did you sway them from that path?"

For several minutes Glylina remained silent, lost in thought. Finally, she shrugged again. "I believe so. I hope so. History is the only guardian from the past that the future requires. If sentient minds cannot heed the lessons to be gleaned from what has gone before, then they deny their only salvation." Glylina quickened her pace. "Come, we've been too long in a place we were never meant to be in."

Nor did the Challing glance back over her shoulder once along the path to the cave or look back at the magnificence that was A'bre when Davin paused at the cave's entrance to gaze a last time at the legendary city.

"I've passed that way once. Why would I want to see where I've been?" she said, urging him to enter. "We have been too long in the past, Davin dearest. The future is long overdue."

"And Gohwohn?"

"Aye, and for you that mud ball Raemllyn." She walked into the blackness of the portal and vanished.

Davin followed at her heels. This time he fell not downward but up. The change in direction did nothing to ease the cramping in his gut or lessen the throbbing of his head when he abruptly found himself in the cave once more.

"It's changed!" The Jyotian's head jerked from side to side.

No longer was the cave simply a hole dug in the hillside. The interior had been plastered over. The smooth surface formed a perfect canvas for the murals painted there.

"Here, Davin, look." Glylina laughed when she pointed at images that could only be a certain Challing and Jyotian as they slew Etol-Sammo and led a charge against the sorcerer's minions. "It seems at least one history will remember us as heroes!"

Davin's gaze traveled over the murals, seeing the whole history of Roan-Jafar's eons-long battle unfold in vivid brush strokes. He smiled when he found a small child holding a golden chain in the final celebratory scene of the mural. Though he found no signature, he sensed Mettatine's hand had directed the brushes that decorated the walls. Her own image was a message to assure two adventurers she had never forgotten them.

"Davin, the Grimoire of the Ages!" Glylina moved across the tiled floor of the cave to a stone pedestal where a white volume rested. With trembling hands, she opened the cover. "They listened to me! My words weren't in vain. See, there is nothing inside. No images! The grimoire has been destroyed!"

The joy on Glylina's face faded when she turned to the Jyotian and found him staring into the doorway of a second chamber. "No. The fools!"

"All five are here." Davin stepped into the room and walked among the five crystal cases. "Jennona's mother Mettatine, Parthlin, Toiyah, Harri'Alin, and Meerium – all the Chosen."

Davin peered closely through the transparent crystal, still unable to determine Meerium's sex or features.

"Would they were what they appeared," Glylina said as she moved to each of the cases. "But these are not coffins, and they are not dead. They merely sleep and wait. Such is the curse of immortality. Five souls wasted. Fools. Fools!"

Glylina turned to the Jyotian, tears welling in her eyes. "I tried to sway them from this folly – I tried."

She cries. Never before had he seen the Challing display grief. He found himself at a loss as to how to react. Had Glylina been human, he would have taken her in his arms and held her close in comfort.

"Davin, I must leave this place," Glylina said. "So much wasted – this is the legacy A'bre has left the future – five tombs that enclose the living. It is madness."

The Jyotian followed her back into the mural chamber where she withdrew the Keys to A'bre and snapped the leaf into its four quarters. One at a time she tossed the separate portions into the portal that was the nexus of the planes. Each vanished when it struck the blackness.

"Why?" Davin stared at his friend.

A sad smile hung at the corners of Glylina's mouth. "The temptation is too great, even for one with the strength of a Challing. The progression of souls is enough for anyone. There is no need to rush into what will eventually be. Here, I'll have no need of this." She took the money pouch filled with a hundred gold bists from her belt and handed it to him. For a long, heavy moment, Glylina's eyes hung to his. "I have no liking of good-byes, my friend. But if you wish – I can become Goran One-Eye a last time."

"No." Davin slowly shook his head, trying to ignore the sudden hollowness opening within him like an abyss. "But if you should see him, tell the ugly ape that he will be sorely missed, that he was a brother, more than those with whom I share the same blood."

Glylina smiled. "Goran has felt the same for years. As for me, I have something I would like to give you as a parting gift."

Before Davin could question, Glylina stepped forward, threw both her arms around his neck and kissed him with unrestrained passion. When at last their lips parted, it was for the Challing to step to the waiting portal.

Glylina glanced back. "That's what you missed, Davin Anane!"

With a toss of her head and a laugh, she stepped into the blackness.

And was gone.

"Fare thee well, my friend," Davin said softly, then turned to the open mouth of the cave to escape the urge to follow the Challing. Gohwohn was no more his world than was A'bre.

Stepping into the hot sun outside, he stared toward Lake Woe. Gone was the magnificence of glowing buildings with towering spires. Once again hovels of mud and straw sat on the lake's shore.

He turned once more to gaze upon the murals for reassurance that all that had occurred was real, that he had not been caught in some mad god's dream. A wry smile slit his lips. The simple cave with earthen walls, straw bed and ring of firestones met his eyes.

With a shake of his head, he turned away and walked down the dirt path toward the lake. If he had been held within the dream of a god, that deity had a sense of humor. He had fought and triumphed over a sorcerer who would have destroyed the universes – and no trace of that adventure remained – not even an entity from another world he had come to know as a friend. The Sitala did relish twisting the fates they cast for men.

A crackling chuckle greeted the Jyotian when he reached the ten huts. A wizened old man with three front teeth missing sat cross-legged in the dirt, a small hammer in his hand. He grinned at Davin and chuckled again.

"Another come to seek the great treasures of A'bre! Must be at least a hundred I've seen since I was a boy." The old man bent and hammered at an object set before him on a flat stone while he laughed to himself. "Been up to the old cave, have you? That's where I go when my wife kicks me out of her bed after I drink too much *paloa* beer. You can see a lot of wonders up there, you know."

"You can?" Davin's temples pounded. "Then you have seen ancient A'bre!"

"Of course, I've seen it many times. Seen flying horses and purple pigs, too." He laughed with obvious glee. "It depends on the amount of *paloa* beer you drink."

Davin joined in his laughter. "I think I could use a cup of your *paloa* beer right now."

"And I'd share a cup with you, but it's mid-winter and there won't be any *paloa* berries until spring." The bald man tilted his head toward a white-haired woman who hung cleaned fish over a smoking fire. "Best I can offer is a couple of those fish. Ain't much, but smoking makes 'em mighty tasty."

Davin waved off the offer. His eyes narrowed when he glanced at the object the man worked with the small hammer. "Is that gold?"

"Aye, I make these from the few gold bists I get when I take my smoked fish across the lake to sell twice a year. Can make four from one bist. People seem to like them. What they bring is enough to buy my Mettatine there a few pretties." He looked back at the woman curing the fish. "She ain't much to look at now, but there was a day when she was a real beauty."

Mettatine? Davin studied the woman for a moment. If he squinted and twisted his head, he could imagine a resemblance to the blue-eyed child he had bid farewell to eons ago.

"You interested in one of these?" The old man drew Davin's attention again. "You might have a lady whose neck this would grace."

The man held up a small golden leaf that had been divided into four equal parts. "See, the pieces snap together like a little puzzle. And this loop lets you hang it on a chain."

Davin accepted the leaf and turned it over in his palm. "The Keys to A'bre."

"Keys?" The old man shook his head. "I think you've already had a portion of *paloa* beer. That ain't nothing but a leaf. Not even a real leaf, just something I made up in my head."

"But interesting." Davin's hand closed around the ornament. "How much?"

"Two bists," the man answered. "I know it seems a mite high, but that's what I get for 'em across the lake."

The Jyotian dug two fingers into his money pouch and passed four gold coins to the old man.

"Too much," the man said with a shake of his head. "I only ask two."

"Keep the bists," Davin answered. "It reminds me of a place I once knew, and a friend."

A thousand memories of a Challing with a single eye crowded into Davin's mind, while his fingers rose to his mouth where the taste of a kiss he would never forget lingered on his lips.

"Then I'll offer you to sup with me and Mettatine," the old man said. "It's the least I can do to repay your generosity."

"Better would be to point me toward a nearby town. The sun is high and I can travel far before it sets."

The old man lifted an arm and pointed. "Tale'Qaw ain't much of a town, but you'll come upon it, if you stay to the eastern shore."

Davin nodded his thank you and started toward the lake.

"When you reach Tale'Qaw," the old man called after him, "where will you go?"

"Raemllyn!" Davin answered as he glanced at the leaf in his hand once again. "I've got all of Raemllyn ahead of me!"

THE JEWELS OF LIFE

1

Davin Anane pulled a threadbare brown cloak about his broad shoulders and hunched over in an attempt to appear insignificant while he adjusted the thick padding beneath the faded cloth. In a sluggish shuffle, the soles of his boots scraping noisily over the cobblestones, the Jyotian thief edged through the main bazaar in Gatinah. His keen gray eyes darted about even though his head hung down and bobbed erratically from side to side like an unfortunate beset with palsy. Occasionally, he lifted fist to mouth and coughed loudly or cleared his throat as if preparing to hawk a gob of phlegm to the ground.

Across the market two of Lord Hormachi's elite guard, resplendently arrogant in their crimson and azure uniforms and dangling swords sheathed in golden scabbards, strolled among merchants hawking breads still steaming from the oven and sausages sizzling atop charcoal-fired grills. Should any of the savory aromas tantalize the soldiers' nostrils, they openly sampled the feast spread about them without leaving so much as a single brass coin before striding toward a brewmaster's table to wash down the tasty tidbits with an equally free draft from that merchant's wares.

Davin Anane concealed an amused smile behind fist and cough. Lord Hormachi's guards were as reliable as the rising and setting of Raemllyn's sun. No matter the time of day, the soldiers never failed to route their patrols of the bazaar through the tables laden with foodstuffs. A wise thief confined his activities to the remaining areas of the vast, open market.

With equal wisdom, the son of Jyotis did not underestimate the predictable guards. During his four months in Gatinah such caution had kept him beyond the grasp of the overbearing authorities and their decided tendency to throw freelance thieves into the lower levels of the dungeons, seldom releasing their prisoners, and if they did, always minus vital body parts. Nor were the guards particular about which parts they sliced from a man. The Brotherhood of Pliaton paid well for, and demanded, such harsh treatment of those who transgressed the rules of their society.

Davin spat to the ground, bile rising within him at the mere thought of the Brotherhood. Organized unions of thieves were not unheard of in Raemllyn's cities, nor was the practice of liberally bribing local officials to assure that the wheels of illicit commerce were greased and rolled onward with no more than an occasional squeak. The Brotherhood of Pliaton spread tentacles far more insidious than a mere guild of thieves.

Pliaton, God of Thieves, normally gathered prayers and tribute from those who whispered his name under their breaths. In Gatinah, Pliaton was worshipped openly by those who trod on each side of the law. Not thieves but priests ruled the Brotherhood, presiding over the rituals they performed within their great marble-columned temple. The merchant who gave generously to the temple's coffers found that thieves shied clear of his business ventures. Those who did not quickly discovered that thievery fell on them like a plague.

To assure the generosity of Gatinah merchants when the offering plate was passed, the priests kept thieves not aligned with the Brotherhood outside the city walls. The perfect henchmen to deliver the Brotherhood's bloody form of justice were city guardsmen whose palms were spread with silver and gold. Simplicity from axle to gear, the priests had constructed a machine equal in strength to those that rolled across the fields of battle. Merchants either tithed regularly or were beset by a series of insoluble thefts; freelance thieves either embraced the way of the Brotherhood or never saw light again, lost for ever in Gatinah's deep dungeons.

Davin admitted that he had rarely encountered thieves so strongly organized, even in the Upper Raemllyn city of Bistonia where thieves ruled a kingdom constructed in the sewers beneath the city's streets. At the same time, the Jyotian also admitted the challenge Gatinah presented had kept him within the coastal city for four long months. Gatinah afforded the perfect arena to hone the fine art of thievery.

Or, as it was for the Jyotis-born Davin Anane, to relearn the intricacies of his chosen profession. After a year spent in the fight to return his half-brother Felrad to his rightful place on the throne of Raemllyn's High King, Davin knew the edge to his skills had dulled, becoming nicked and pitted from disuse.

With the clarity of hindsight, he now saw how those once finely whetted abilities had slipped away. With their minds focused on returning Felrad to the throne, he and his former companion, Goran One-Eye, a changeling from another realm of existence, had bungled theft after theft, nearly costing themselves their lives time and time again. Luck more than ability had seen them through one misadventure after another. A year and a half ago Davin openly called himself the master thief of all Raemllyn. This had not been a mere braggart's claim. Now he carefully trained himself to reclaim that title.

Nor was there a better instructor, Davin thought as he shambled toward a merchant sporting a rounded belly heralding his prosperity, than the presence of constant danger. Nothing honed a man's senses more nor sharpened his skills, than the possibility of forfeiting one's life should the slightest mistake be made. And nothing was sweeter than snatching a sparkling treasure from beneath the very nose of Black Qar, the God of Death.

So it was, to practice the quick fingers of a pickpocket and the sleight of wrist of a cutpurse, Davin Anane came to Gatinah's bazaar, selected a target and bumped into the gaudily dressed merchant, sending the man reeling.

"Swine. Get away from me, you piece of filth!" The merchant recovered his balance and spat his anger at the brown-clad beggar.

Davin bowed and backed away muttering apologies. "Sorry, Master, sorry, so sorry. I am an awkward pig unworthy of your spittle."

To the untrained eye, so busy was the Jyotian in making obeisance that he clumsily backed into another merchant, knocking an armload of goods to the cobblestones. In truth, Davin's movement was a perfectly timed ballet of thievery.

"Sorry, so sorry. I did not see!" Davin bent double as the second merchant used a small quirt to smite him repeatedly on his shoulders. He winced but felt nothing as the heavy padding beneath the worn, brown cloak absorbed each blow. With just the right touch of awkwardness, Davin bent to help the man retrieve the bolts of gold thread-chased cloth spilled onto the ground. The toes of his boots sent three skittering over the dirty cobblestones.

"Leave me, leave me be, oaf!" the merchant shouted, ire rising. He raised the short leather whip and lashed at Davin's face.

The Jyotian thief dodged artfully, taking the blow on an upraised arm. Real pain brought a wince to his face this time. The quirt's bite would leave a nasty welt on his forearm. Biting back his own anger, Davin silently thanked whichever of Raemllyn's gods had given him the foresight to leave his weapons behind today. Had he worn sword or dirk, he would have opened the merchant's throat from ear to ear. Thief though he was, Davin Anane was also royal born, albeit a bastard son of the now dead High King Bedrich, and it sorely tried his patience to endure the merchant's blow.

"Leave or I summon the guard! You fool!" The merchant turned red in the face from his ranting, then bent to pick up the merchandise knocked from his arms.

Davin cast a hasty glance across the marketplace and saw the guardsman paid no attention to the little drama he authored. Again hiding a smile with fist and cough, he scuttled away, maintaining his bent posture every step of the way. Only when he found a narrow alley far removed from the crush of Gatinahese citizens did he straighten to his full height. Shrugging precipitated a minor torrent of coins to shower from under his voluminous cloak.

Rubbing his left forearm, he knelt to examine the rewards of a day's hard labor. A pleased smile lifted the corners of his mouth. The treasures scattered about his feet lessened his arm's stinging and dulled the edge of the insult of being spat at.

"Nice, very nice!" he evaluated the two long golden chains of a single necklace he lifted from the ground.

Taken from the round-bellied merchant, the chains were an unexpected prize. The gleaming gold provided value enough for the risks he had taken, but the small Norggstones mounted in the intricate braiding offered the real prize among those metallic strands.

Davin's smile grew when he touched one milky white, opalescent stone mined in the frigid northern province of Norgg.

Although valued throughout the realms of Raemllyn, Norggstone with its warm inner light was particularly revered here along the southernmost coast of Lower Raemllyn where even the smallest samples of the gem were difficult to obtain.

A rootless sigh escaped the Jyotian's lips when he traced a fingertip down the chains. The stones' interior light evoked a peculiar mingling of exaltation and melancholy within his breast. It was as though he triumphed in the greatest undertaking of his life and, at the precise moment of victory, found himself struck by the cruel realization his endeavor was hollow, devoid of meaning.

Davin shook off the curious sensations and shoved the necklace into a leather pouch hung from his belt. The necklace was beautiful and the emotions generated by the stones proved interesting, but not as valuable or interesting as the gold coins to be gained when he sold the delicate strands.

His nimble fingers snared coin after golden coin he had taken from unsuspecting shoppers in the marketplace. Two small coins he threw away; they were counterfeit.

"There is no respect for law any more," he said aloud with a sad shake of his head. "Too many think to make a quick fortune illegally."

Davin feared the recent flood of counterfeit coins appearing in the city was a weather vane to stormy political times within the Gatinah city-state. Whether external or internal, he sensed an unseen force building to undermine and topple Gatinah's economy – and with it Lord Hormachi's rule. He made a mental note to convert the cache of local coins he had safely hidden away to golden bists or other equally stable tender. He then amended the thought by adding the very real possibility of leaving Gatinah soon. A city afire with revolution was no place for a thief trying to earn a living.

"Now, for what the last merchant offered so generously." Davin stood and performed a little hopping dance from foot to foot that shook free two bolts of the luxurious cloth from beneath his cloak.

He leaned both against a wall and ran his hand over the dense weave, nodding in appreciation. The risk in pilfering such bulky items had been great, but when opportunity knocked, only a fool left the door bolted.

The Jyotian smiled at the wit of his mental pun, then grinned with satisfaction. Once again he proved himself equal to the challenge. Stealing under the watchful eyes of Lord Hormachi's guard and two angry merchants, strengthened his bid to regain the title as best thief in either Upper or Lower Raemllyn.

The overwhelming sensations of triumph and melancholy flooded back into Davin's breast with such a heavy weight that he sank to the ground and leaned against the cold brick wall. Another sigh slipped from his lips.

The best thief in all Raemllyn echoed in his mind, taunting him. Six months earlier, he had been half of the best pair of thieves in Raemllyn.

What had appeared moments ago now revealed itself to be a tangle of memories wedged into every nook and cranny of the thief's brain. They all pointed to one simple fact – he missed Goran One-Eye. As often as the young son of the House of Anane had avoided admitting that fact to himself, he missed the Challing he had come to think of as a brother over the years spent adventuring across Raemllyn. Now, here in a cold, dank Gatinah alley, it seemed as if the Challing had been gone for years rather than only months.

Silently, Davin wished his friend the riches of a good life and the hope that Goran's return to his homeworld of Gohwohn had been all he had yearned for during his years of imprisonment in human form within the realms of mankind.

Over the past months Davin had proven that he had not come to rely on the abilities of the red-bearded giant with his single good eye lit with green witchfire to carry a lion's share of their adventuring. Alone, the Jyotian had proven there was a fortune to be made with quick fingers and quicker mind. *His* fingers and mind. In truth, he admitted, he had sidestepped danger and eluded death with a greater ease than when the changeling traveled at his side.

Yet, the bond of brotherhood forged between man and Challing was missing. The brilliance of a daring theft lost its gleam when there was no one with whom to share the thrill of adventure. And how could he revel in triumph when the slip of a phrase to the wrong ear could result in the loss of his head?

Glylina . . .

Davin felt an uneasy squirming within himself when Goran's feminine persona edged into his thoughts. The feelings the beautiful redhead stirred within him were far from comforting. Seeing Goran-Glylina in a Challing's natural body in A'bre had driven home that a Challing was not merely a human with shape-shifting ability but a being from another world.

Nor could he forget the passionate kiss Glylina had left him with before she stepped through the dimensional gate to return to Gohwohn. That kiss had awakened the desires of a man for woman. In that lay Davin's uneasiness. He found it impossible to resolve the fires Glylina had sparked with the bond of brotherhood he felt for Goran.

Nor is there need for resolution, Davin thought as he pushed to his feet. *Goran – Glylina is gone*. He tried to edge aside the sadness that came with the realization he would never see the Challing again in this lifetime, whether it be in the form of Goran One-Eye or Glylina.

Davin hefted the heavy rolls of cloth and tucked them beneath the brown cloak again. There was nothing to be gained in reminiscence when he had treasures to convert to gold. Besides, when night finally arrived even greater prizes awaited!

2

Davin Anane rapped the heavy door three times with his bare knuckles, waited a heartbeat, then knocked four more times.

From inside came muffled sounds as if a giant rat scurried from its lair, frightened by the unexpected noise. The scratching of claw on wooden floor transformed to the distinctive shuffle of nearing boot soles. A bolt disguised as a massive brass screw in the top of the door's three immense hinges vanished inward. A bloodshot eye blinked on the other side of the revealed hole.

Davin threw back the hood of his cloak and let Fole, the owner of that peering eye, study him. The bolt head grated back into place, followed seconds later by the metallic clank of the locking bar retracting. The door opened on surprisingly quiet, well-oiled hinges. Davin slipped into a cool darkness that wrapped around him like a spring night.

"What excrement do you bring to defile my home this time?" a high-pitched voice with the edge of a razor in it demanded.

A hand more skeletal than human reached out to touch the cloth Jyotian proffered in reply. Davin's gaze followed the angular bend of a bony arm to a body that appeared to be no more than a skeleton with dry, pale skin stretched tautly over it. Fole's eyes blinked from deep within their sunken sockets and the man gave his gourd-shaped head a disdainful shake.

"This? Do I look like a tailor? Can I burn it to stay warm?"

"The winter comes early, even for this southern clime," Davin admitted with a nod, "but consider how royal you would feel wrapped in such fine cloth. Gold thread works its way through the fabric at every point."

"It is always winter in Gatinah. This is land's end! A man freezes whether he's wrapped in gold or not. Cold, always cold." Fole gave another dubious shake of his head, but his fingertips remained on the bolt Davin held out.

"Fifty bists," Davin flatly announced his price. Such fine cloth would fetch ten times that, even sold back to the merchant from whom it was filched, but the Jyotian had no time to haggle and sensed Fole was in no mood to argue over the price.

"Forty."

"Fifty." Davin stood firm, irritated that Fole would even consider trying to chisel away at the price. There was no time to waste on pettiness. Tonight he would reclaim the title of Raemllyn's master thief. All the exploits of his lifetime would stand in the shadow of the coming night. When he finally bade farewell to Gatinah, he would leave its citizens with a tale of daring to retell for generations.

"Done." Fole lifted the bolts from Davin's hands, set them aside on a table. "Anything else?"

Davin dangled the twin-strand, braided gold necklace under Fole's thin nose.

A jaded dealer in stolen goods Fole might have been, but he could not hide his reaction. His nostrils flared, and he caught his breath. "Norggstones – no other jewel glows with such fine light and delicate warmth."

A palsied, thin hand reached out to brush lightly over the luminescent gems. Davin allowed only a fleeting touch, then yanked the necklace away. From the jerk of Fole's hand as he tried to prolong contact with the stones and the ineffable sensations they evoked, Davin Anane knew he could name any price – and get it.

Norggstones did not cause the addiction of narcotics such as *mylo* weed or *chalokin*, nor did they affect all who came in contact with them. But when one attuned to the gem encountered a Norggstone, its seduction proved more insidious than simply captivating the body. After experiencing the admixture of emotions once, a person desired another touch. Just for a moment, they might say, but another caress of the stones from the cold northern province was all that sated their need. And then another, less surreptitious touch. And another and another until life became unbearable without constant contact.

"How much?"

Fole's question shocked Davin. Never had he heard the conduit for most of the stolen goods in Gatinah ask a thief to name a price. Fole's reputation was one of hard dealing and utter adherence to the principles of paying little for the products of a thief's métier.

As if realizing how he had momentarily shocked Davin, Fole reluctantly eased his hand back and grumbled, "I have a market for such a bauble. Price is no object."

Davin's thoughts leaped ahead, considering the possibilities. He knew the market lay no farther than this room; Fole desired the Norggstones for himself. That was the Jyotian's lever, one best employed later.

"A gift for you, friend Fole," Davin announced casually.

"What? You mock me?" At the unexpected pronouncement, Fole's hand dropped to a knife hidden in the folds of his overly large tunic.

"You are a valued friend, a colleague with whom I wish to conduct still more business."

Davin watched Fole's bloodshot eyes narrow. The dealer in purloined merchandise did not believe the thief for an instant. In Gatinah, or anywhere, there was no honor among thieves – and no friendship.

"What do you want in return?" Fole demanded.

"Top money for fine gems I will bring you before the sun breaks on a new day," Davin replied. "No quibbling, only fair valuation – and all in gold coin immediately."

"Bists," grumbled Fole. "You want the stash in Bistonia's currency, not Gatinahese octens."

"Such a fine example of Norgg craftsmanship," Davin went on, dangling the necklace in front of Fole. "My requirements are extensive. Be prepared to pay out as much as I can stagger away carrying."

"What? Nothing in Gatinah is worth that much!"

"A fair appraisal," Davin said, swinging the glowing stones in a slow, hypnotic arc. To add to the enticement, he lied, "And perhaps another of these baubles."

"Another!" Fole's arm shot out with the speed of a striking snake.

Davin permitted the man to snare the necklace, then stepped away while Fole examined the stones. The merchant of other merchants' wares looked up to acquiesce with a sharp nod.

"I shall return before dawn," Davin repeated, "with enough trinkets to make us both fabulously wealthy."

"Just don't get caught," Fole said uncharacteristically. He

coughed, spat a gob of phlegm onto the rotting wooden floor, and added, "I want another of these. Remember that. You promised!" Fole clutched the necklace to his breast as if it were a small child. He even cooed softly as he cradled and rocked it.

With a shake of his head, Davin turned and stepped to the door. As in all the times he had dealt with Fole, a small box lay beside the portal. Davin had never heard or seen Fole's assistant, but the master fence's wishes were always carried out to the letter at the conclusion of any negotiation. Davin flipped open the box and smiled at the fifty bists shining inside. He scooped them out and shoved the coins into his pouch before stepping outside.

The hairs on the back of the Jyotian's neck prickled as they did whenever he entered or exited Fole's door. Hand resting lightly on the pommel of the sword beneath his cloak, Davin mounted the short flight of steps and climbed to the alley. Lord Hormachi's guardsmen, whom he always expected to find at each end of the alley, were absent. An overly held breath escaped the thief's lips in a soft sigh of relief. Fole's reputation for arranging a quick, bloody end for those who opposed him might hold the guardsmen at bay, but more likely, Davin reflected, heavy bribes kept guard patrols to a minimum in this section of Gatinah.

In a casual stride, Davin moved to the alley's south exit, paused and surveyed the street ahead of him. Finding no guardsmen waiting to snatch up the unwary, he turned toward the center of town and the hub of Gatinah's commerce. He rearranged his cloak to appear as presentable as possible while he bypassed the shops of silversmiths, rug merchants, perfume importers, goldsmiths, potters, glass blowers and countless other merchants who catered to the city's wealthy.

Each and every shop was like a ripe fruit ready for the plucking for a thief with the daring needed to breach lock and door. Yet, the last son of the House of Anane strode down the street without so much as a glance toward the tempting feast on each side of him. His destination was the shop of Aotesja, master jeweler of Gatinah. There was no greater prize within the city. For one ready to reclaim the title of master thief of Upper and Lower Raemllyn, there could be no better proving ground.

He had first spied Aotesja's establishment on his second day in Gatinah. Nor had it taken more than a few visits to the less than respectable inns and taverns in the city to learn of the shipment of gems and jewels that entered Aotesja's establishment every three months. The largest of those shipments came today as the jeweler prepared to create a line of exquisite baubles he would peddle to Gatinah's elite before and during the city's renowned Summer Festival. For four months Davin had schemed and dreamed of the shipment's arrival – for four long months, he had waited for this day.

Had the Jyotian any doubt when the cache of jewels would arrive, they were dispelled when he approached the gem merchant's shop. Two squads of uniformed private guards, six men in each, stood sentry on either side of the store. Another six men, dressed less conspicuously, mingled with the thick crowd outside the door, although the heavy swords worn beneath their capes were obvious even to the untrained eye. Two uniformed guards, bulging with muscle enough for three men, confronted every client entering Aotesja's emporium whether the prospective buyer be man or woman.

The increased activity told Davin this was the day he had awaited. All knew Aotesja's ability to find and purchase only the finest of gems. Few of Gatinah's nobles escaped buying from the portly merchant as Aotesja often crafted intricate pieces of jewelry exclusively for special occasions.

With Summer Festival and its tradition of lavish gift-giving mere weeks away, the city-state's aristocrats flocked to the extravagantly appointed emporium, each willing to lay forth a small fortune to purchase an intricate piece of jewelry crafted for the occasion by the portly master jeweler. It was unheard of for Aotesja to turn away any with gold enough to acquire one of his designs. To fill the heavy demand, Aotesja kept a large staff working the year round, and hired a greater number as Summer Festival approached.

That fact, rather than lockpick, was Davin's key to entering the jeweler's shop.

A steel vice masquerading as a paw-sized human hand crushed down on the Jyotian's left shoulder as he moved toward the shop's open door. Davin turned his head toward the hand's owner and stared up at a giant of a man. For a fleeting moment, Davin thought he gazed at Goran One-Eye. But this red-bearded giant carried too much loose bulk on his frame, and he sported two good eyes – both fixed squarely on Davin.

"Where do you think you're going?" the giant challenged in a voice that rumbled from deep in his chest.

"Into Master Aotesja's store." Davin pointed at the entrance only a stride away.

"Ain't one of Aotesja's customers dresses in rags like these." The muscular guard made no attempt to hide his scorn for Davin's attire.

"But—"

"Let him pass," one of Aotesja's liveried servants called from inside before Davin could explain. "He works as a gemsman. Aotesja himself hired him two weeks past."

The giant grunted with obvious reluctance and gradually loosened the clamping fingers that dug into Davin's flesh. Mumbling something about Aotesja hiring riffraff, the guard pivoted to fade into the crowd.

"Thank you." Davin bowed slightly to the uniformed assistant when he entered the shop, then tilted his head toward the street. "Why are there so many new watchmen? Has someone threatened Master Aotesja?"

"The guards are no concern of yours. Rather, you should worry yourself with getting to the back rooms before Aotesja notices that you're at least half a stick late from your noon break." In the next instant, the man totally ignored Davin and turned his attention to a fur-cloaked matron who entered the shop with three rouged servants trailing at her heels.

Davin heeded the advice. On this of all days, he had no wish to draw attention to himself. He hurried to a suite of rooms at the rear of the building and took his place at a wooden table. As he shifted his weight on a three-legged stool, Aotesja entered the room and approached the table beside Davin's. Without so much as a nod, the rotund jeweler's sharp tongue began to flail a woman named Irisli whose only job was to sort the gems brought into the shop.

The Jyotian bit his lip and contained himself while Aotesja berated Irisli's parentage, her limited skills and what the jeweler saw as a total absence of a brain within her head. This was no time gallantly to come to the aid of a simpleminded young woman,

Davin reminded himself over and over. The new sentries pacing outside the shop and the additional security inside were clear signs that the gem shipment was due this very day.

Davin occupied himself as he had for two weeks. He screwed a jeweler's loupe over his right eye and began to work his way through a bin of low-grade stones, removing those of minimally acceptable quality. Those he found unacceptable, Aotesja sold to lesser jewelers in Gatinah and other Lower Raemllyn cities. Only the finest were kept for Aotesja's intricately wrought creations.

Expertise garnered from years as a thief afforded the ability to evaluate a precious stone with a quick glance. Davin discerned an internal fracture in the first emerald he lifted, a flaw that made the gem worthless except to be cut into small accent stones. Instead of immediately sorting the gem into its correct box, he studied it for several seconds, slowing himself to match the pace of Aotesja's other workers.

"Out!" Aotesja's bellow was punctuated by the sharp slap of the jeweler's open palm on Irisli's cheek. "Out! I'll not tolerate your incompetence any longer!"

"Master, please," the simple woman pled with tears in her blue eyes. "Please, Master, I promise to do better. I need the wages you so generously . . ."

Double chins aquiver, Aotesja cut her short with a snap of his fingers. Two guards immediately rushed into the room, grasped Irisli's arms and dragged her to the shop's rear door where they rudely heaved her into the alley.

Silk robes hissed like a snake when Aotesja turned and glared at Davin in challenge. The Jyotian drew a slow, steady breath to hold his anger in check and returned his attention to the bin of emeralds that needed grading. No matter what Irisli's imagined transgression, the gem merchant had no cause to abuse the woman. Irisli's work sorting stones by color had been more than adequate while Aotesja's pay was less than adequate compensation.

Ignoring the jeweler's glare, Davin turned back to his work, lifted another emerald from the bin and studied it through the loupe. With a gruff grunt, Aotesja muttered something about eliminating all the slackers in his shop when the festival had passed, then stalked from the room.

Even on a good day Aotesja was not an easy man to work for. To Davin, his unexpected outburst was yet another signal that today marked the date of the quarterly shipment of uncut gems.

A dozen emeralds came from the bin and were sorted into their appropriate grade boxes before Davin glanced to the shop's showroom. Aotesja and his assistants were fully occupied with patrons demanding to see every ring, bracelet and necklace before deciding which item to purchase. The Jyotian's gaze shifted to the right and a doorway hung with a curtain of beads, separating him from the gem cutters' room. The four men beyond the sparkling strands bent over their worktables, oblivious to all but their work.

Davin's right hand slipped beneath his own table, fingers finding the small glass vial secreted there four days earlier. With vial in hand he slipped to the back door through which Irisli had been cast moments ago. The massive, solid iron portal hung on heavy hinges embedded in seasoned wooden posts, a design meant to withstand the assault of a battering ram. Nor did the intricate lock offer a thief a better avenue of entry. Although not invulnerable to pick and skilled fingers, mastering the lock by such basic means would take far too long and leave one exposed to passing patrols of city guards.

The slow-working, odorless acid Davin poured from the vial so that it trickled over the hinge pins would transform the metal to the consistency of soft cheese by late night. Then would come the test to determine if the Jyotian could once more claim the mantle of master thief in all Raemllyn. Not only did he have to elude the patrolling bands of Aotesja's private guards and Lord Hormachi's vigilant elite guardsmen wandering Gatinah's streets to enter the shop, but he had to repeat the deed to make good his escape.

If caught, at least they'll find no evidence on me. Even Hormachi's guards cannot hold a man as a jewel thief when there are no stolen jewels anywhere on his person. Davin allowed himself a small smile when he returned to the table and bin of emeralds. If there was a stroke of brilliance in his scheme, it was the method he would use to empty Aotesja's shop of gems without slipping a single damning stone into his own pockets.

* * *

"Make way, make way!" the demanding cry rose from the shop's showroom.

Removing the loupe from his eye, Davin looked up to see Aotesja hasten toward the open door. Behind him four men carried on their shoulders two poles from which hung an iron-banded chest sporting triple locks. Veins stood out on the bearers' necks, and the men's faces were red from the weight of their burden.

Davin's brow furrowed. If the strain of the men's expressions was any indication, he had underestimated the weight of the gems in the shipment. When night came, he might have to alter his plan. Rather than completely cleaning Aotesja out, he would have to satisfy himself with only the choicest of gems.

"Out!" Aotesja entered the room with arms and hands waving as though shooing away flies. "All of you. I'm closing early today. Go home. Hurry. All of you, out!"

"But, Master Aotesja, I have yet to finish my work!" protested Davin as though unwilling to leave his labors unfinished.

"Out!" Aotesja repeated. "Consider this an unexpected holiday. But be here promptly tomorrow morn as usual."

Forcing a grateful grin, Davin nodded in appreciation, pulled cloak about his shoulders and hastened past the ranks of guards at the shop's entrance into the cool afternoon that had settled peacefully on Gatinah. Two streets north of Diamond Avenue in which lay Aotesja's emporium, the Jyotian entered an open door beneath a sign bearing the name Inn of the One-Eyed Harlequin. There he found an empty table and waited, more to kill time than in patience, until a busty serving wench with raven black tresses eventually brought a flagon of mulled wine. The spiced wine had grown as cold as a freshly drawn ale before he downed the last swallow, left two brass coins on the table, once more stepped into the streets and returned to Diamond Avenue.

The front windows of Aotesja's shop boasted metal shutters now. In the time Davin had worked for the gem merchant, he had never seen them closed before. The Jyotian also noted two men positioned on the roof with crossbows and four sword-carrying private sentries circling the block. Davin lingered at the nearby stall of a brass merchant, haggled over the price of a lamp for which he had no need and diligently counted the seconds required for those sentinels to make a single circuit. Rather than making another patrol around the block, the four swordsmen split into pairs, one working clockwise around the shop while the other moved counterclockwise.

Davin wandered through the bazaar, idly poking at fruits and hefting a few items to peer myopically at them in the setting sunlight. As he held aloft an ancient leather-bound tome, he saw Aotesja's watchmen complete their complicated circuit, rejoin, and move about the block again. The thief smiled. The patrol pattern was just that – a pattern and every pattern was riddled with holes through which a clever, bold thief could slip.

"A fine volume, sire," a book dealer said when he approached Davin. "Written by a poet of Bedrich the Fair's court and . . ."

"And of inferior quality." Davin placed the book back on the peddler's cart. "I seek only the finest works."

"But, sire, it is!"

"Do you have any books retelling the travels of Goran One-Eye?" Davin worked around the display to watch the four guardsmen once again split into pairs. For a moment, his gaze lifted to Aotesja's shop. He could almost hear the weight of gems inside causing the foundations to creak and settle.

"I have never heard of this hero," the bookseller admitted with a shake of his head.

"Humph! An unread man should never attempt to peddle what he believes to be literature!"

Davin turned and walked away, leaving the bewildered book huckster blinking in confusion. The last son of the House of Anane had seen all he needed. Escaping with the jewels offered the greatest challenge of the night ahead, but he had anticipated that.

Stopping at a meat vendor, Davin bought a double-weight parcel of scraps meant for a stew pot. He then made his way through the maze of alleys off the marketplace and entered a small wooden house he rented for an exorbitant amount. For the first week in Gatinah, he had been hard pressed to steal enough to pay the daily hire, but the expense now seemed minimal when a king's ransom awaited for the taking on Diamond Avenue.

A chorus of gleeful yaps rose from the darkened interior of the house when Davin found an oil lamp on a table near the door and lit it. Six sleek hounds with coats as black as a moonless midnight bounded toward the Jyotian with tails wagging.

"Quiet, my pups. Speak softly lest you draw the attention of our neighbors." Davin tore open the package he carried and carefully apportioned bits of meat among the six large hounds, their yips giving way to the chomp of jaw and smack of lips. "Tonight, you earn your keep."

The last of the scraps wolfed down, six heads turned upward with the hope of a second serving. Davin grinned and reached down to scratch behind each of their ears. It would be difficult to leave such fine animals behind, but when he slipped from Gatinah tonight the fortune in bists Fole would pay for Aotesja's gems would be more than enough burden for a lone man.

"Now back to your beds and rest," Davin shooed the dogs toward the back of the house. "When I return there'll be work to do."

With that he left the house. He still needed to visit the stable where two horses had to be prepared for his escape this night. After that, he and the hounds would pay a visit to Aotesja's shop.

In a day that seemed so lost in the past as to belong to another age, before Berenicis the Blackheart toppled the House of Anane and drove Davin from Jyotis with a price on his head, the Ananes kept in their employment a hound master. Few men ever had such a hand with dogs as Tomfar-Ris, training them to perform feats that would amaze even the Huata, Raemllyn's wandering bands of fortune-tellers, tricksters and thieves, with their dogs that jumped through loops of fire. For the House of Anane, Tomfar-Ris trained the most intelligent of his canine students as messengers to carry communiqués the length and breadth of Jyotis.

It was from Tomfar-Ris a young Davin Anane learned the use of a whistle attuned to the ear of a dog, yet unheard by human beings, to signal commands to canine companions. He also had learned a gentle, loving hand, rather than a whip, quickly brought loyalty and unquestioning obedience from even the most slap-happy dog.

Thus it was Davin trained his six canine cohorts for five months, until each responded to the piping of a silver whistle pitched beyond the hearing of any man. And thus it was six black hounds followed silently at the heels of a thief determined to reclaim the title of master thief of Upper and Lower Raemllyn as he wound through the night-cloaked alleys of Gatinah.

A single note from that whistle and the six hounds silently dropped to their haunches and sat with ears alert while Davin peered from the shadows toward the alley that opened behind Aotesja's establishment.

Three times the patrolling guards made a circuit of the block before the crossbowmen on the shop roof turned their backs and shifted positions. Sucking down a breath to quiet the race of his heart, the Jyotian raced from the shadows and darted into the alley. Mentally, he counted off the seconds before the patrol would once more pass the alley's mouth as he darted to the shop's rear door.

Mouthing a whispered prayer to Jajhana, Goddess of Chance and Fortune, that she had assured the acid had weakened the hinges, he reached out, placed both palms flat against the door and shoved inward.

The acid had done its job.

Davin gasped as the door fell inward. He caught it by both sides, straining to prevent it from crashing to the floor inside the shop while he managed to wobble the dead weight to one side and lean it against the wooden frame. A hasty inspection assured him that the only way anyone would notice anything was amiss would be to stand directly in front of the door.

Wasting no time, Davin moved like a ghost across the floor to the huge cask Aotesja's four bearers had brought into the shop that afternoon. A few twists of a pick in each of the three locks opened them wide. In less than a minute, the thief ran his hands through the minor sea of jewels contained within.

The darkness drove away thoughts of selecting only the finest stones. Not that it mattered now. Even poor quality gemstones in such quantity would provide the beginning of a life of luxury in a city far from Gatinah.

Davin lifted the whistle hung around his neck to his lips and blew hard twice. He heard nothing. No human did. But across the street from the shop a canine-shaped shadow separated itself from the darkness, padded into the alley, and entered the opened door.

One by one he signaled the hounds until the dogs crowded into the store. Davin scooped the jewels out of the chest in double handfuls and shoveled them into deep leather pouches strapped to the dogs' backs like miniature packs meant for horses. More than a few of the gemstones fell to the floor. Davin ignored them. What were a few droplets of water lost to the breeze when a fountain sprayed into the air?

As each dog's pouches filled with their weighty loads, Davin piped new commands on the whistle. Without a sound, the animals vanished back into the night, powerful legs carrying them to the distant house. Davin idly wondered how Tomfar-Ris, if he still lived, would react to the knowledge he had given a young boy being used thus.

He shoved the image of a grinning Tomfar-Ris from his mind. There wasn't time for such a luxury. As soon as he loaded the last hound with its precious cargo, he had to make his own way to the stable for the horses and then to the house to transfer the treasure to his pack animal. Then it was on to Fole's burrow to exchange jewels for bists. Time would be tight, but he would ride from Gatinah with a fortune in gold before the dawn broke.

"There, go swiftly!" Davin patted the last hound's head before blowing the signal for him to depart.

Resisting the urge to fill his pockets with the few jewels remaining scattered about the bottom of the cask, Davin stood and settled his cloak again to be sure he did not betray himself with a stray glint of light off metal when he exited. The last thing he wanted now was to be stopped by city guards as he hurried toward the stable.

Light – the glare of exploding witchfire – filled the air when the thief stepped into the alley!

Davin threw up his arm to protect his eyes from the dazzling flood of white light as he spun and reached for the dirk beneath his cloak. In the doorway leading to the front of Aotesja's shop stood a tall, well-built man dressed in silver-chased purple velvet.

Davin gasped in recognition. "Lord Hormachi!"

Pivoting around, Davin did not consider how or why Gatinah's ruler-mage stood within the shop of a jeweler in the dead of night. Instead, he shot out the open door into the alley.

He skidded to an uneven halt a stride beyond the threshold.

Four leveled swords agleam in the witchfire blocked his escape. Whirling about to avoid the sharp sword tips, the Jyotian leaped back into the shop and grasped the unhinged iron door to send it toppling toward the crimson-and-azure-uniformed Gatinahese soldiers.

Not waiting to see the damage wrought by the falling door, Davin tossed the dirk to his left hand and wrenched sword from sheath with right. With both blades free and ready, he turned to face Lord Hormachi.

An amused smile danced on the ruler-mage's thin lips. Hormachi lifted a long-fingered hand and made a pass in the air, leaving the smoky remnants of a magical rune trailing lazily.

Davin's legs locked at the knees an instant before his arms transformed to stone. The last thing he saw as he fell facedown onto the floor, completely paralyzed by the mage's spell, was Cal'Dreth, High Priest of Pliaton, step from behind the Gatinahese ruler with a grin that split his face from ear to ear.

3

"We have done well, Cal'Dreth. It has been a good night."

Soft-spoken though it was, Lord Hormachi's deep voice resonated through the room, and strain as he did to locate the
Gatinahese ruler-mage, Davin could not. Every muscle in his
body had forsaken him except for those commanding eyes. If he
concentrated and focused his will to a fine point, the thief could
force his gaze to slide slowly from side to side. When he did, all he
saw were polished military boots treading perilously close to the
tip of his nose.

"How long will the spell bind the Jyotian, my liege?" the higher
pitched voice belonging to Cal'Dreth questioned. "This is the one
I spoke of earlier, the one who has been overheard making claim
to being the Lord of Jyotis."

"Aye, the one who has eluded both your men and mine for at
least three months, Cal'Dreth."

Four months! Davin mentally corrected, cursing the Sitala,
Raemllyn's Gods of Fate, whose unlucky toss of the dice left him
in such an untenable position.

"It is the absurdity of absurdities to consider this common thief
to be the bastard brother of High King Felrad," Hormachi
continued with a chuckle weaving beneath his voice. "At most he
shares a common name, Davin Anane, with the Jyotian lord.
After all, Cal'Dreth, why would one with blue blood in his veins
choose to live in the gutter?"

Davin had to agree with the logic. If he had used the sense he
had been born with, he would have journeyed to his home the
moment Goran had stepped into the portal that sent him across
the dimensions to Gohwohn. However, the staid life of a ruler of
a city-state that awaited him in Jyotis lacked the seductive call of
adventure he had grown to relish since he had fled his homeland
after being branded falsely as a murderer. One day, he fully
intended to return to Jyotis and cloak himself in the mantle of
respectability and responsibility, but until that day came, he had

been content to allow the regent Felrad appointed to rule in his stead.

Now, breathing the dirt of the floor in through his nostrils, Davin was not that certain of his decision. More important, he was even less certain about another decision – what Hormachi intended to do with him. He could well imagine such a resolution with his neck being rudely introduced to the executioner's blade.

Somewhere behind him, the last son of the House of Anane heard the heavy thud of something weighty striking flesh.

"You, there!" Lord Hormachi called out. "If I'd wanted this one kicked, I would have given the command. I don't recall issuing such an order. Do you?"

"No, milord," an unseen man answered with a quaver of fear in his voice.

Davin realized for the first time that not only was he paralyzed, but every inch of his body lay totally numb. Whatever spell Hormachi wove, it was powerful. Later, Davin was certain he would feel the full brunt of the guard's boot, but for now he was as grateful as his humiliating position would allow to be spared the pain.

"Bind him," Hormachi ordered.

Davin felt nothing as hands shifted and tossed him from one side to another like a sack of flour. Nor could he determine how he was bound, since he felt no strand of rope or chain about wrist or ankle. Hormachi was no mere caster of spells. Davin recognized the mage-ruler had more than a glimmering of the mind he dealt with and considered it as dangerous as the unfettered body.

"The last in our pride of lions," Lord Hormachi said. "This one proved to be the most inventive of the lot. He doesn't appear damaged by the blow. Good. He's of no use to me crippled."

"More like a pack of alley cats, my liege," Cal'Dreth corrected. "You are wise to rid the city of such."

Hormachi laughed. "And you, Cal'Dreth, do you think me blind? Do you believe I can't see that your Brotherhood of Pliaton stands to profit by eliminating the most successful thieves in Gatinah?"

"Let us agree that my scheme is mutually beneficial, milord." Cal'Dreth's voice came as slippery as oil floating across water.

Qar-damn the man! Whatever Davin had stepped into, it had

not been by accident but part of a well thought-out plan by the Brotherhood of Pliaton to exterminate the independent thieves they viewed as pesky vermin.

The world around Davin transformed into a blur of light and dark as unseen and unfelt hands lifted him to his feet. When his gaze focused, he found he stared directly into Hormachi's cold dark eyes. Had his muscles not been already paralyzed he was certain the cast of those emotionless eyes would have frozen him in mid-stride. The Jyotian's mind went aswirl, then sank into a bottomless pit, spiraling downward. Hormachi chained the thief's body. Now the ruler-mage's gaze accomplished the same with Davin's mind. Thoughts refused to flow. Even hope of escape, to which the son of Anane clung so fiercely, fluttered from his brain.

"Away with him. To the others. We have a full slate for the next competition."

In the distance, Davin heard a whining like the sound of a whipped dog; somehow, he recognized the noise as Aotesja's voice.

"Lord Hormachi, the jewels," the jeweler moaned. "What of them? Those mongrels carried off a fortune. My whole livelihood is strapped to the backs of those dogs!"

"That is your worry, Aotesja," came the Gatinahese ruler's icy reply. "Might I suggest you put out food and hope they return? Or use this."

Davin heard rather than felt the leather cord around his neck snap. He saw Hormachi hand the silver whistle to the gem merchant. "He used this to command the hounds. Perhaps you may learn to play the necessary tune on it."

The world melted into another dizzying blur as Davin was lifted and borne along by at least two men. With no regard for his safety, they smashed him into walls and door jambs while they wrestled his inert body from Aotesja's store. Davin felt nothing. He found himself unable to fear or rejoice or experience any emotion. Thoughts and body frozen, Hormachi's spell held him totally in thrall.

Outside, they might have carried him along the Gatinahese streets for a minute or a year. He neither knew nor cared. When a distant buzzing reached his ears, he fought to draw it closer. It provided the only stimulation he had received other than the crunching of boot soles against gravel.

Davin cried out when the buzzing invaded his body and expanded like a pool of spilled liquid, completely inundating his mind. Pain! The buzz was the crackle of every nerve ending in limbs and torso sparking alive. With the same alacrity with which Hormachi had stolen the Jyotian's volition, the ruler-mage returned it.

Davin blinked up from where he sat on a stone floor to stare at Hormachi. The thief then glanced to his side to find the soiled outline of a boot sole on his blouse matching the ache beneath. The well-placed kick throbbed, but this didn't hurt nigh as much as the sharp pain at the back of his neck. It took several seconds for him to remember that Hormachi had ripped away the leather thong that had held the dog whistle.

"You are a decent-looking sort, once the shabby cape is pulled away." Hormachi slowly circled the Jyotian as though he were studying some animal he considered purchasing. "You played the role of the slow and dim-witted fool quite well. I might add, you are the only one actually to get away with stealing Aotesja's jewels."

"Better had I cut them off," grumbled Davin. "And Cal'Dreth's, too!"

"Fire, yes, of course, and wisdom. You display an ardor beyond that of a normal citizen. Yet, you have the sense not to threaten the one that holds you captive. That makes you different from the common horde droning on endlessly about their worthless, miserable lives." Hormachi gave an overly dramatic sigh and shook his head. "Do you truly call yourself Davin Anane?"

"'Twas the name my parents gave me," Davin answered, his eyes meeting the gaze of the mage-ruler. "It is also what my brother Felrad calls me."

Hormachi laughed. "Do not cling to such an absurd tale. It only lowers my estimation of you."

Davin shrugged as though saying, "It was worth a try." In truth he did not expect Hormachi to believe he was the Lord of Jyotis, yet it *had* been worth the small effort.

Davin shifted slightly to give himself a clearer view of the room in which he found himself. Shadow bathed the rear of the chamber and drawn draperies hid what might be a large bed. To either side stretched rows of wooden chairs, unusual for a boudoir. The Jyotian thief frowned. Perhaps Hormachi preferred an audience as he slept – or made love.

The chamber's furnishings were lavish but far from ostentatious. The gold Fole would have given for Aotesja's jewels could have provided a flamboyant splendor far exceeding this. And Davin would have surrounded himself with such, he told himself. What good was earning a mountain of gold if he never enjoyed it?

Little chance remained of making off with either gems or gold now. Behind Hormachi's highly polished boots Davin heard the shuffle of leather on stone. He coughed and bowed his head enough to glance in the direction of the sounds.

Six soldiers, all cloaked in the unmistakable crimson and azure uniforms of Hormachi's guard, stood behind the ruler-mage. No mere guardsmen were these. Tight rows of bejeweled medals and multi-hued ribbons adorning their chests marked them as officers in Hormachi's army. High-ranking officers, if Davin had to make a guess.

Davin straightened while his mind rushed through the possibilities open to him. Escape would be difficult, yet not impossible. He felt the weight of dirk and sword sheathed on his hips. For some unfathomable reason, Hormachi had not ordered his weapons removed. That might prove a bigger mistake than the Gatinahese ruler had foreseen. With dirk pressed to Hormachi's throat, the Jyotian would have a royal shield to protect him as he made his way from Gatinah.

"Yes, you begin to get a glimmering of your interesting situation." Hormachi smiled as he strode back and forth before Davin. "I have no reason to rob you of your weapons. In fact, I permitted you to keep that ample purse stuffed with gold coins. Since you apparently lack skill or desire to earn such a sum legally, I can only assume you have introduced yourself to a certain unsavory but enterprising creature called Fole. There is no one else willing to pay bists for stolen goods in the city."

David cringed inwardly. *Master thief of all Raemllyn!* How bitter the title tasted rolling silently on his tongue. Not only were Hormachi and that damnable priest Cal'Dreth aware of his activities in Gatinah, but they apparently had been for months – aware enough to know his name and the fence he used to dispose of the items taken in his thefts!

A dark, ugly thought wriggled free from the back of the Jyotian's mind. "Were Aotesja's gems real?"

"Quite real, varied and of the first water." Hormachi chuckled and rubbed a slender hand over a beard that neatly fringed the jawline and chin of a face most would deem handsome. "When Aotesja petitioned me for a company of guards to protect his shipment, Cal'Dreth first suggested the possibility of employing the jewels as others use a sliver of cheese to trap unwanted vermin."

"Such traps usually kill, but I live. To what purpose? Torture? Public execution?"

The mage-ruler appeared talkative, which Davin milked for all that it was worth. He bought time with simple questions, time needed to find an avenue to freedom.

He doubted he could draw either sword or dagger before the Gatinahese ruler could evoke a new spell to halt a direct attack. A bit of misdirection might buy him precious seconds, though, and allow him a better chance. The lump of his cloak tucked to one side might provide the needed diversion, if he could send it sailing out in a blinding arc.

"Torture? Never! Such has never been of pleasure to me. Death is a tool to be used with a quick, clean cut to eliminate those who oppose." Hormachi's amused laugh carried a vicious edge to it. "Nor do you still live so that your head might roll to entertain Gatinah's pathetic, bloodthirsty populace."

Hormachi halted and pointed a slender finger at Davin's sides. "And as to those weapons you undoubtedly consider using – you retain sword and dirk because you will need them. As will the others."

"Others?" A half-memory of hearing Hormachi mention something about "a pride of lions" returned to the Jyotian.

Hormachi gestured to an unnoticed officer who stood behind Davin. The Jyotian thief turned to see four men and a woman herded into the room, their hands bound tightly behind them.

"Irisli!" Davin exclaimed, startled to see the simple-minded stone sorter from Aotesja's shop included among a band who obviously employed means outside the law to provide a livelihood.

"Ah, you know her," mused Hormachi, rubbing his bearded chin. "But of course you do. She worked alongside you for two weeks. Were you in league? I think not. Her scheme to steal the jewels proved less adventuresome than yours."

Hormachi paused and looked from Irisli to Davin. He laughed harshly. "No, you were not in league. And I do believe, thief who runs with dogs, you did not realize she sought the same treasure. She tried to waylay the caravan bringing the jewels to Aotesja's ship, as did the other four at different points along the route. All she required of her employment with the gem merchant was the time of delivery. You, however, used your position to full advantage. Clever, very clever. I greatly anticipate seeing how you will fare, dog thief."

Davin ignored Hormachi's tirade, studying Irisli more closely and realizing what a thespian she had been. Not once had he assumed she was more than the dim-witted soul she pretended. The woman's hair swept back now in wild disarray suited her better than the matted style she affected in the shop. Her once dull cow eyes now burned with hatred – and intelligence. Davin saw schemes ebb and flow behind those eyes, clever plans, ones he had never suspected to exist.

"Had I made off with the treasure, Hormachi, I would have spent every octen it brought to see you deposed!" She spat in the Lord of Gatinah's direction, her aim spoiled by the officer's backhand that brutally smacked the side of her face.

"I am disappointed in you, dear Irisli," Hormachi said. "Your ambition extends no farther than seeing my soul fed to Black Qar?" Hormachi studied the others but made no further comment.

Two Davin remembered from the bazaar, as often caught by their intended victim as not. That they still had all their hands and feet told him they were more fleet of foot than they were quick of fingers. The other two were unknown to him.

"I'll cut her throat, Lord," offered one of the two unknown faces.

"If I allow you to go free?" Hormachi's bantering tone held an echo of amusement.

Only Davin and Irisli, from her unworried expression, noticed the ruler's intent. The other four obviously scented blood and a method to earn their freedom.

"Yes!" the thief assured Hormachi with decided relish. "I'll flay the skin from the traitorous bitch before I open her gullet, if that's what suits you!"

"Ah, a clever offer!" Hormachi's voice barely concealed the ruler-mage's disdain. "So clever, in fact, I give each and every one of you the opportunity to win your freedom."

A sense of dread trickled like a cold stream along Davin's spine as he pushed from the floor and stood to face the Gatinahese ruler. Hormachi's dark gaze shifted among the six thieves he had trapped this night as though expecting all to question the offer of freedom he dangled like a carrot before them. A wry hint of a smile played at the corners of Davin's mouth. He sensed that the others glimpsed danger at the heart of the ruler's words.

The shadow of a frown darkened Hormachi's face when none of the six posed a question. His eyes shifted toward the curtain at the rear of the room. "By the right of law each of you should forfeit anything from a hand to your head for your acts this night. Instead, I magnanimously extend a chance of freedom. All you have to do is take a simple stroll through – the maze!"

4

"Freedom!" Hormachi repeated, delight firing his dark eyes. "All you need do is survive the maze. All six of you enter. The first one to leave wins the honor of serving me as a trusted lieutenant. Nor is that all. He – or she – shall have great wealth heaped upon him.'

"Aotesja's jewels?" Davin's right hand rose to his side and massaged the ache left by the guardsman's boot. It would not do to be distracted by minor injuries when facing death, and Hormachi had said survive. To the Jyotian if one did not survive, one did not live.

"The thought had not occurred to me, dog thief. But it seems appropriate." Hormachi smiled broadly with no evidence of mirth in his expression. "Yes, yes! I shall give you all Aotesja's jewels. It is only fitting, since those gems brought you here. Why not? Make a note of it."

Davin noticed none of the officers hastened to summon a scribe to commit their ruler's words to paper.

"What of this maze?" Irisli spoke.

If any of the others fully comprehended what Hormachi planned, Davin decided it was this young woman who had fooled him so easily. He could almost hear the thoughts turning busily in her brain.

"There." Hormachi's right arm swept dramatically toward the far end of the room.

The draperies drew back with a soft hiss. Davin now understood the chairs in the room. The chamber was not a bedroom, but a box that overlooked a huge coliseum lit by a thousand torches burning along its circumference. The arena's floor was covered with a complex series of sliding walls that formed a maze. From here Hormachi and his officers would watch their six prisoners' progress through the labyrinth.

"You need only be the first to reach the far side and exit – and life and riches will be yours." Hormachi looked back at the six thieves.

"What of the others?" asked the man to Irisli's right.

"What others?" Hormachi arched an eyebrow. "There are no rules in my maze. If none of you succeeds this night, then more of your ilk will be recruited until I find my champion."

With a snap of his fingers, the ruler-mage brought his officers to attention. "Take them below."

Two men grabbed Davin and shoved him forward. He stumbled and regained his balance just before two pairs of arms shoved again to send him tumbling over a low balustrade. With the grace of a cat, the Jyotian thief turned in the air and got his feet under him. The instant his boots touched the packed dirt floor, his right hand wrenched sword from scabbard.

As though anticipating the thought that flashed in Davin's mind, the maze's walls came alive. In the blink of an eye, four walls slid to form a box about him. Nor did the walls stop their movement, but shifted away from Lord Hormachi's balcony. The possibility of leaping back to the ruler's box was forgotten as Davin scrambled back to keep from being crushed by the moving panels.

The Jyotian heard rather than saw the others enter the maze. Grunts and groans accompanied the heavy thuds of bodies hitting the ground. A defiant curse that maligned Hormachi's parentage marked Irisli's ignominious introduction to the maze. Again the walls shifted, opening so that all six thieves stood together boxed like penned animals.

"Your goal lies on the opposite side." Hormachi stood high above them with arms crossed. "Remember this. The first to reach that goal will survive. The others will be left in the maze – to die!"

A wall shifted and the maze opened to the six.

Two men darted forward with sword and dagger drawn.

Davin hung back, letting the others enter ahead of him. Hormachi would not simply put them into a labyrinth to fight among themselves. There had to be more – of that he was certain. A heartbeat later he saw that there was. A wall ahead began to slide. Davin dashed forward before the passage closed completely. Hormachi's maze would trap any who moved too slowly to suit the mage-ruler.

A roar rent the air, followed by an all too human scream. Then the latter died away, leaving only bestial grunts and growls and the sounds of joints being popped and flesh ripped hungrily from bone.

The last son of the House of Anane could not identify the creature by its roar, but it waited ahead, big and hungry. Worse, the bestial foe sounded close. Davin ran a hand along one panel. Vibrations trembled through the wall. He glanced down to see blood oozing under the panel. Whatever it was feasted on its grisly meal on the opposite side of the wall. Leaping the pooling flood of crimson, Davin quickened his pace. With the way the maze's panels shifted without warning, this was no place to linger.

Around three angular twists in the maze he worked, and walked head-on into a dead end. Pivoting to retrace his steps, a wall slid across the corridor to barricade his way. Before he could weigh his predicament, another wall moved to open on a square at least twenty-five strides on a side. Across the chamber stood one of the thieves Davin had seen in the bazaar.

The man grinned in shaky relief and held out a hand in obvious greeting. "The walls closed around me seconds after I entered. I've been trapped here ever since."

Davin's right hand tightened about his sword's hilt as he cautiously approached the man. Hormachi decreed there could be but one winner of this insane race through the maze. This was no place for an open hand of friendship.

"Fool!" the man cried out. "It's time for you to die!"

The hand he held at his side leaped up and opened. A dagger tossed in an underhanded pitch flashed in the light of a thousand torches.

Prepared for attack, the Jyotian spun and whirled his cape in a dark cloud before him. The threadbare fabric was too thin to stop the razor-honed weapon. However, the cloth proved enough to deflect the needle-pointed knife and send it sailing to the left.

Davin completed his pivot with sword raised and leveled for renewed attack. It came as the other thief rushed across the pit, arms wide to ensnare the Jyotian in a powerful hold meant to snap his spine.

There was no need for the drawn blade. When the charging man reached the center of the open square, the arena's floor gave way beneath his feet. A startled cry tore from his lips as he tumbled into a chasmlike pit.

"Help me, help me! By all the gods, don't let me die this way!" the man shrieked in fear and agony that could never be feigned.

Stepping to the edge of the pit, Davin looked at his adversary. A single glance was all it took to see the man was far beyond mortal help. Furred *pletha* snakes swarmed over his body, sinking fangs dripping with venom into already dead flesh.

An uneasy breath escaped Davin's lips when he turned away, scooped the man's dagger from the ground, and slipped it beneath his belt. Had he met the man's attack with a charge, the pit might have taken him rather than his foe.

Two of the thieves stretched out dead in the damnable maze. Two other men and Irisli still lived. *And myself*, Davin amended. How long that would remain true, he feared, lay in the hands of the Sitala rather than his own. He could only guess at the traps Hormachi had placed within his insidious tangle of sliding walls.

He glanced around. A misstep might trigger another of the ruler-mage's deadly devices. Placing his fate in the hands of dice-tossing gods and goddesses he had cursed most of his life sat ill with him. Davin had not survived this long by trusting to such caprice. Skill, quick reflexes and an even quicker mind had been the tools used to keep his body in one piece.

The harsh grate of wall across dirt pulled his gaze to a panel that slid back to his left. The Jyotian pursed his lips and his gray eyes narrowed. Even the mightiest of traps contained a weak point. Lord Hormachi's maze was no different. The shifting walls were the weakness; designed to slip and slide, they needed solid ground beneath them to work. Hormachi would not place traps near the walls – the panel movement might spring them.

Unless the walls themselves contained death, Davin considered spring-loaded spikes and poison-tipped darts that could easily be concealed in the panels as he stepped to the nearest wall and edged through the opening. Remedying those possibilities, he walked with sword held before him like a blind man's cane in the hope that steel rather than flesh and blood would spring such traps.

The wisdom in his method made itself apparent less than a

hundred strides deeper into the maze. The tip of the sword struck a trip wire no thicker than a man's hair. Not spikes nor poisoned darts exploded from the wall ahead of the thief; a stream of acid belched forth in a fountain that splattered against the opposite wall.

Davin danced away to avoid the burning droplets and drew his cloak over his face to protect nose, mouth and eyes from the searing vapors until they dissipated. When at last he lowered the thin brown cape, he blinked at the man-sized hole the acid had eaten through the wall. Beyond, Irisli struggled to escape one of their fellow contestants who caught her by the arm and flung her to the ground.

Davin reacted rather than thought. Hugging his cloak tightly around his body to protect him from the acid that still dripped from wall to ground, the Jyotian shot through the breach with sword ready.

The thief who now sat atop the young woman with knees pinning her shoulders to the ground jerked around. Davin judged his distance and lunged, missing an outright kill by the span of two fingers. His blade sank deeply into the other thief's chest and red blossomed.

Beneath the thief, Irisli heaved and threw off her assailant. She rolled to her side with the speed of an attacking jungle cat and drove a dagger directly into the man's gut – and cursed like a Gatinahese longshoreman when her blade struck a large metal belt buckle that turned away the tip.

"Back!" Davin shouted while he shifted from side to side to find a clear opening.

Irisli reacted too slowly. Her assailant struck out, his fist landing solidly on her chin. The brunette jerked back, eyes rolling up in her head as she fell directly in front of Davin, preventing him from delivering a final stroke.

Clutching the red stream that ran from his chest, the wounded thief kicked away, scrambled to his feet and staggered into the maze. As Davin started after the man, the walls slid shut, blocking his way.

"Where's the way out of this room?" Davin swung in a circle, searching for an opening. There was none.

"The doors come and go." Irisli sat up, the fingers of her right hand inching toward her fallen dagger. "There! There is one now!"

As she spoke, she grabbed for the dagger. Davin never turned, prepared for the trick. He held his sword *en garde*, waiting for the woman to attack.

Irisli shuddered, her body going limp. "I have no reason to kill you. You were good to me when I worked for Aotesja."

"Perhaps I only pitied a simple-minded girl," Davin suggested.

"No, not that. Not that alone." Irisli shook her head. "You have a kind heart. You cannot hide that."

"Don't say that too loudly," Davin answered, his gaze scanning the walls that surrounded them. "It'll ruin my reputation for ruthlessness."

Irisli's head lifted, and she smiled weakly at him. Though she retained the dirk, Davin saw no menace in her grip.

"Will you kill me now? Hormachi said there can be but one survivor."

Davin drew a heavy breath, pursed his lips and stared down at the woman. "I have no idea what Hormachi has in mind for the one who finds a way from this maze. However, if two exited side by side, he might be convinced those two could offer him twice the possibilities."

Irisli sat silent for a few seconds, then nodded in acceptance. "At least together we might find a way out of here. Alone, I fear there is no hope of getting through."

"Haven't we come this far?"

Again a bestial roar echoed through the maze.

This time the sound sent an ice floe up the Jyotian's spine. He recognized the cry. That familiarity did nothing to lessen his unrest. As Goran One-Eye and he had crossed the continent in search of the lost city of A'bre, he had first heard the roar of an Uhjayib ape. There was no mistaking the hunting cry of that fierce creature.

"Hormachi has every conceivable menace planted in this Qar-damned maze," Irisli said, spitting when she mentioned Hormachi's name. "If no one watches your back, you are doomed."

"If those apes find us, it won't matter who's watching whose back." Davin cringed inwardly as the hunting call of a bull

Uhjayib sounded closer. He stepped to a wall and reached toward the top with a hand.

"Don't!" Irisli warned. "Every edge sports a razor along it. Grab hold and lose a finger or two!"

Davin jumped just enough to confirm the young woman's words. He nodded a thank you when he looked back at her. Another roar sounded closer. "The pack of apes will be on us in a few minutes. Is there any place we can put our backs to a wall – and have the wall remain there?"

"The edge of the coliseum," Irisli suggested when she pushed from the ground. "This used to be the sports arena. Hormachi closed it a year ago when the spectators rioted after a favorite *reto* team was defeated. I had no idea that he had turned it into his own personal execution chamber. Another reason to see him thrown into the lowest depths of Peyneeha!"

"Curse him to Qar's home later," Davin said, growing nervous. He no longer heard the Uhjayib apes, but his nose picked up their distinctive musky scent. They fell silent just before attack.

"There, Irisli, get over there!" Davin drew his dagger and swung about to face a blank wall.

The odor grew overpowering, and it came from the direction of the wall.

"What? Why?" Irisli questioned, but she stepped back with a pair of daggers drawn toward the spot the Jyotian indicated.

The partition slid to the side to reveal four Uhjayib gorillas with high-crested heads that marked them as males. On all fours, the apes rushed into the chamber, the small dark beads of their eyes darting from side to side. The foremost's gaze centered on Davin first. The creature rose to its full height and roared in a defiant challenge that exposed yellow fangs that looked more like tusks than teeth.

While the dark furred monster pounded its chest with balled fists, Davin did the one thing the immense ape did not anticipate. He charged!

His thrust drove forward smooth, long and clean. It also missed its mark! Rather than slicing straight to the ape's heart, the tip of the blade entered the creature's gaping mouth when the beast suddenly dropped to all fours again. The Jyotian's wrist twisted to the left in an attempt to use the sword's edge the instant he felt the point meet the back of the animal's throat.

Davin was certain the blade found and, at least partially severed the spine, but the muscular beast refused to die. It fought forward, working its way down the steel skewer that now protruded from the back of its neck, dripping a steady stream of crimson. The royal-born thief's wrist never stopped its sawing motion, yet the monster still came. Dirk rather than sword ended the ape's life. In an upward arc, Davin lashed out with the knife to open the creature from groin to shoulder.

"Back! Damn you, back!" Irisli's cry rose above bestial growls.

Davin stepped away from the two gorillas that waddled forward to dip their hands curiously into their companion's spilled entrails and then sniff their fingertips. Assured the monsters' attention was held for a few heartbeats, the Jyotian whirled toward the young woman.

Irisli's pair of daggers barely held at bay the creature menacing her. The bloody trails along her arms gave silent, painful testimony to how close she had come to dying by the ape's talonlike claws.

While Irisli held the beast's attention, Davin danced behind the monster. His sword leapt high, then descended in a two-handed swing that hacked deep into the gorilla's neck. Flesh, bone and spinal cord opened. The ape dropped to the hard ground, body twitching in the last spasms of death.

"Retreat." Davin pointed to the hole the acid had eaten through the wall. "The other two already lose interest in their dead brother."

Irisli did not hesitate but dashed across the chamber and ducked through the opening. No more than a stride behind her, Davin followed. He paused on the other side of the hole long enough to send his dagger hurling toward the breast of the gorilla charging after them.

"Davin, hurry! The walls open!" Irisli urged.

The Jyotian did not wait to see if his blade flew true. Pivoting on his toes, he saw his fellow thief dart through an opening that now began to slide closed. Whether the chamber Irisli entered held a new threat mattered not. The roaring danger behind Davin was all too real. He bolted forward. A quick sideways twist allowed him to slip through the opening before the partition snapped shut. He lost his cape, but that was a small price to pay to escape the fearsome apes.

"Above you, above!" shouted Irisli in warning.

Davin dropped to one knee and placed the hilt of his sword on the floor, bracing himself for the impact of a heavy ape. Instead, he endured a shower of ape fingers and blood. Angered by the loss of its prey, one of the apes had tried to climb the dividing wall and discovered the razored blade meant to prevent such a shortcut. Deafening screams shook the panel separating man from beast.

Davin closed his eyes and let a sigh of relief gust from deep in his lungs – and in doing so, almost died.

The soft crush of dirt beneath boot sole saved the Jyotian's life. His eyes went wide and his head jerked up. The last two of their fellow thieves crept into the maze's chamber through a panel that inched open. The first moved behind Irisli and caught her in a stranglehold. The remaining thief lunged straight at Davin's side with a rapier extended before him.

Davin rolled to a side, feeling the blade meant to deliver death pierce the fabric of his tunic and slice over the surface of his ribs. Time did not permit accuracy, only a wild lashing blow to answer the attack.

The thief yelped then fell to his knees when the flat of the Jyotian's sword slammed into his shins. Again Davin's sword struck. This time the silver steel traced a line across the side of the man's neck. When the would-be assassin collapsed facedown in the dirt, it was with both hands trying to stem the life-draining spray of blood that fountained from his severed jugular vein.

Davin clamped a hand to side and felt a trickle of flowing warmth. The rapier's gash was shallow, although his own sweat set it on fire as though salt had been sprinkled into the open wound. He winced when he pushed to his feet and turned to Irisli.

Irisli remained firmly in the man's hold but had forced his arm away from her throat. Struggle though she did, she was out-matched. It was only a matter of time before the man overpowered her.

Two quick steps brought Davin to their side. Freeing the spare dagger tucked under his belt, he struck. His hand moved as if guided by Brykheedah, God of Warriors. The knife's sharp point slid between ribs and upward through the man's lung and heart. The thief stiffened with the thrust, then died before he sagged to the floor.

Irisli tumbled away, gasping for breath. On her knees, she stared up at Davin. Her wide brown eyes were filled with astonishment. "You saved my life."

"It was as we agreed," Davin answered simply.

The grating of panels on dirt announced the walls moved again.

Davin's and Irisli's heads snapped up to see what new perils the maze unleashed on them. At the far end of the long, narrow corridor the moving walls shifted to reveal an open door outlined in white paint. Lord Hormachi stood at the threshold with a pleased grin on his face.

"Two have reached the goal. Which one of you will cross first?" his question rang out a challenge. "Quickly now, before the walls shift anew and all is lost!"

"We cross togeth—"

Davin's answer was cut short by the point of a dirk that jabbed into his left thigh. He jerked away from the lancing pain, spun and drove his sword deep into Irisli's breast.

The treacherous woman recoiled, face deathly pale and twisted in agony. Irisli swallowed hard and let the dagger stained with his blood drop from her hand. Her head moved slowly from side to side as she collapsed to her back.

"I meant not to kill," her voice came in an unsteady rasp. "I only meant to wound, to give me time to get to Hormachi first. I would have killed him, Davin. I would have slit his throat. I meant you no . . ."

Irisli's body sagged and her unseeing eyes rolled upward as life fled her body.

The Jyotian held back the cry of injustice that burned in his throat when he turned and staggered toward the waiting ruler of Gatinah. Before he said his final farewells to this city, both the priest Cal'Dreth and Hormachi would pay dearly for the blood shed within this damnable arena tonight. The high priest would die for the lives of cutpurse and thief alike he sacrificed in the name of the very god supposed to protect them. Lord Hormachi would die for Irisli – this Davin Anane silently promised himself.

5

"My dog thief! You truly astonish me with your skill and ingenuity." Lord Hormachi held out his hand in greeting to Davin. "No one has ever survived the maze before, and you simply walked through with hardly a scratch. Yet even those will be soon healed as part of your promised reward."

Davin winced at the pain racing along his ribs and the deep throb where Irisli had driven her dirk into his thigh. The Jyotian realized neither wound was life-threatening, nor was either a mere scratch.

He considered employing his still drawn sword to draw a *scratch* across Hormachi's throat but held his hand. Irisli had been willing to sacrifice her own life to rid Gatinah of its ruler; Davin was not. As easy as it would be to slay Hormachi at this moment, the Jyotian saw little chance of his own escape. Not only did he tread dangerously close to exhaustion, but he had no idea where he was other than in a coliseum somewhere within the city. Hormachi would live – for this night.

"My Lord," Davin called, sheathing his blade. "You do me great honor." He made no attempt to stem the sarcasm that seeped into his words.

"You have no idea of the honor before you." Hormachi's hands danced in the air.

Davin froze in mid-stride as a spell bound every inch of his body. The curse that rose in his throat lodged there, unable to escape tongue or lips.

"I read your face, dog thief. Not so much as an inkling of gratitude sparked in your eyes. Mayhap you thought to repay my generosity with a dagger slipped between my ribs?" Hormachi gloated when he stepped around the paralyzed thief. "You have proven yourself too valuable to allow an unthinking act of suicide."

Completing his leisurely circuit, the mage-ruler rubbed a hand over his beard-fringed chin. "Perhaps after you have served me, I will allow you to slit your own throat, but not before then. Understand that, Davin Anane, until you have completed the geas I place upon you, I shall own you body and soul!"

Again Hormachi's hands lifted and his fingers wove intricately patterned smoky runes in the air. A soft sing-song incantation whispered from his lips.

Had he still possessed his voice, Davin would have cried out as invisible bands of steel encircled his chest and squeezed inward. Gasping for a simple breath, the Jyotian felt life being crushed from him as surely as any constrictor snake might flatten its prey. He tried to inhale and failed. He exhaled and could not regain his breath. In a matter of seconds the last son of the House of Anane passed out.

Strange words filled Davin's ears. He tensed his muscles, inspecting the limits of his movement before daring to open his eyes and betray he had regained consciousness. Try as he might, he could not budge arm or leg.

The string of exotic words stopped for a moment and Lord Hormachi said, "No need to feign unconsciousness, dog thief. I know you are awake. I ordained it with my spells."

Davin's eyelids fluttered open and he immediately regretted it. Brilliant light shone in his eyes. He tried to turn from the glare and found it impossible. He was held spread-eagle in midair, and the movement of his struggles caused him to spin as if he had been fixed firmly to a rotating wheel. Wherever the Jyotian turned on his airy circle, the radiance followed him.

Squinting, Davin saw a tiny mote dancing inches from his face. Casting about, he began to spin faster and faster, and the speck of intense light tracked him easily. When he grew dizzy from his aerial turns, he relaxed and eventually came to a halt facing Lord Hormachi.

"There, just a bit more. Yes, yes!" Hormachi moved Davin so that he hung suspended at the Gatinahese lord's eyelevel. "I have worked diligently on this spell. If I do say so, it is the cleverest I have ever wrought. You will appreciate its effect, I am certain."

A cold breeze blew across Davin's sweaty chest, bringing the realization that he had been stripped to the waist. Craning his neck, Davin saw his arms held outstretched on either side of his shoulders. His hip joints creaked from the intense pressure put on them – and nowhere did he see physical bonds. Hormachi imprisoned him with the accursed magicks he wove.

"Irisli," Davin muttered, remembering.

"The wench in the maze?" Hormachi chuckled. "For a moment, I thought a streak of sentimentality ran through you, but when your life was threatened, you displayed nothing but the instincts of a cold-blooded killer. That is a quality I admire, one I appreciate greatly."

Davin grunted in disgust.

"Oh, it is true. Ask my chamberlain."

"Do I also ask for Aotesja's gems as my reward for surviving your labyrinth?"

"You did not outlive the others by being stupid, dog thief. A native, if simple, intelligence burns behind those gray eyes. You think to kill me, but under it all is nothing but stark greed. I could buy you off."

Not even Aotesja's trove would be enough! Rage flared, but Davin held his tongue.

"Your silence speaks louder than words. And what you think is nonsense. I am sure that I know your price to within a few brass coins." Hormachi hummed to himself as he opened a huge grimoire and balanced it on his outstretched left hand. His eyes, glazed over with concentration when he began the chant, stopped when Davin had come back from distant, dark dreams.

The Jyotian tensed, prepared for the worst, then relaxed when he felt nothing more than the intangible pinions on his wrists and ankles. He tugged gently, then harder in a vain attempt to free himself while Hormachi was lost in his spell-casting. No amount of twisting or wrenching could snap the invisible bonds.

When Hormachi moved closer, an artist's paintbrush in his right hand, Davin recoiled. The unseen shackles held him immobile as the mage drew a small circle around Davin's left nipple. Hormachi filled it in completely, wielding the brush with a flourish.

"Do you like the color?" Hormachi stepped back and studied his minor handiwork. A circle of purest white gleamed in the magical mote's bright light.

"I'd prefer something that didn't clash with my tunic," Davin said sarcastically.

"Ah, I know just the hue." Hormachi quickly drew a larger circle around the solid dot using his brush. The paint dripping from the bristles dried quickly, a violet tint that somehow frightened Davin.

"What are you doing to me?" demanded the pinioned thief.

"Patience, dog boy, patience. You will learn quickly enough to quiet even your feverish tumult." Hormachi continued to wield the brush, this time drawing a third circle around the other two. This he did in bright yellow. At no time did he dip the paintbrush into a pot or do anything to alter the color, yet it changed drastically according to the spell he uttered.

Davin stared down at the ring of yellow, then gasped when Hormachi began a new ring, a larger one concentric to the others. This splashed onto his flesh in bright crimson. And the merest touch caused him to scream in agony.

"Ah, you are even more sensitive to this spell than I thought. Good, good. Now for the final touch, the part that I worked so to achieve."

Davin's eyes widened as the dancing light mote shot away from him, hovered at the far side of the room, then rocketed straight for his breast. The speck of scintillation drove squarely into the center of the bull's-eye Hormachi had drawn on his chest, burrowing deep inside him, twisting and churning in his body, transforming every breath he took to stark torment.

"The final spell, the last one and it will be done," muttered Hormachi, more to himself than to Davin.

He passed his hand over the Jyotian's bare chest twice. The red ring exploded into virulent fire, charring flesh as it burned. The final pass of Lord Hormachi's hand extinguished the blazing ring. To Davin's surprise, only memory of pain remained. His flesh appeared unscathed by the fierce firestorm.

"Amazing spell, isn't it, dog thief?" Hormachi stepped back and stood, arms crossed on his chest.

"The pain vanished," Davin said, almost in awe. Dealing with mages frightened him, their power and arrogance surpassing any he might command personally.

"But you remember it. Oh, yes, you remember it, dog boy."

Hormachi tapped the yellow ring. "You will obey my every command. If you do not, in one week's time, this ring will blaze like the red one, only with a significant difference."

"What?" Davin wasn't sure he wanted to hear the answer, yet a curious, morbid fascination held him as he stared at the perfectly drawn yellow circlet on his chest.

"It will burn longer and hurt *ever* so much more."

"And the violet ring?"

"A week after the yellow flares, it will ignite itself."

"Hotter and more painful than the yellow?" Davin saw his answer in Hormachi's broad smile.

"You begin to understand. The final ring, the white dot holding the fire elemental I summoned, will consume you from the inside exactly one week after the violet ring has burned itself out. You will not survive that." Hormachi chewed on his thumb and looked thoughtful. "You might not survive the violet ring, though it is not designed to be fatal. The agony will be excruciating; only the strongest of the strong might live through its fire."

"What do you want from me?"

"Think, dog thief, think. What might I desire from you?"

"Obedience," Davin said, his mind raging when he recalled the mage-ruler's claim that he owned him body and soul.

"That goes without saying, though of course you had to speak it. Concentrate. Tell me more, more!"

Davin was in no pain, but he remembered the way the red circle had torn at his mind and body. The promise of worse to come in one-week delays told him he had a deadline. If he did not accomplish a task in that time, he would perish. And the only reason Hormachi had sent six thieves into his maze had to be . . .

"Yes, I see you understand now. Your mind works slowly but well, dog boy. I need the skills of a trained purloiner and that which I desire must be brought to me within the span allotted you by these magical rings. It might take less than one week to steal," Hormachi said, his finger lightly tracing the yellow ring.

"If so, no more pain. Or it might take more than two. Burning pain from first the yellow and then the purple circles will be your punishment for tardiness," he went on. "Let us hope that you accomplish your mission within three weeks." Lord Hormachi pressed down hard on the solid white dot.

"I grasp the situation perfectly," Davin said. "What is it you want stolen? Anything within the walls of Gatinah is yours for the asking – for the taking."

Hormachi smiled. "The trinket I wish you to obtain for me lies some distance from here. In truth, it is in Ohnuhn, a miserable flyspeck of a city."

"Ohnuhn?" Davin worried the name about in his mind finally to recall the city that lay half a continent to the west along Lower Raemllyn's southern coast. Even during his years as a sailor, he could not remember walking its streets. "What is in Ohnuhn that you go to such lengths to obtain?"

"A trinket. A bauble. Nothing of value. A mere soapstone statue less than a hand width in height." Hormachi's bantering tone hardened. "I want it taken from Vytellion. You have only three weeks. Travel fast, steal quickly, and return."

"Lord Hormachi!" Davin called as the Gatinahese ruler stormed from the room. "Wait! I need to know more. Who or what is this Vytellion? And the statue – what does it look like!"

Hormachi left without so much as another grunt. When Davin strained to look over his shoulder at the departing sovereign of Gatinah, his invisible shackles released and sent him tumbling to the floor. For long moments, Davin sat and stared down at the concentric circles ringing his left nipple. His fingertips traced over the smooth patches of color. Despite the memory of the fiery pain that had lanced into his chest, he felt no trace of the insidious paint on his flesh.

Cursing whatever gods had betrayed him into Hormachi's hands, he pushed from the stone floor to find a clean white linen tunic draped over a nearby chair. *At least Hormachi had the decency to provide a new shirt*, he thought while he dressed, remembering the rents and blood that had ruined the one he wore into the maze.

The mage-ruler had also healed the wounds the Jyotian had received in the arena. Both knife and sword cuts were completely gone, he realized as he found sheathed sword and dirk and strapped them around his waist. However, Hormachi provided no cloak to replace the brown one lost in the maze. He did leave Davin with the pouch of fifty gold bists Fole had paid yesterday – more than enough to buy a more suitable cape.

Thoughts of how he might retrieve close to five hundred bists he had pigeonholed around the city were forgotten when Davin turned and eyed Hormachi's grimoire on the table across the room. Agile of spell Hormachi might be, but he had overlooked a major flaw in his scheme to enslave the last son of the House of Anane. Given the original incantation, even an apprentice to the arcane arts could reverse a spell cast by another sorcerer.

A smile lifted the corners of the Jyotian's mouth. His small cache of hidden gold should be more than enough inducement for a mage of the inner circles to remove Hormachi's damnable rings. Then, Davin would see to removing Gatinah's ruler and his cohort, the High Priest Cal'Dreth.

Before he could take even a single step toward the tome, Davin heard the scuff of leather boot soles on the stone floor. Four Gatinahese officers stood in the door and hallway beyond, swords drawn.

"We are to escort you from the palace immediately," said a burly captain with a resemblance to the Uhjayib gorillas the thief had faced in the maze. "Lord Hormachi says you have been given your orders."

Davin cast a covetous look at the spell book, then with a helpless shrug went peacefully with the guardsmen. Each step of the route through Hormachi's palace etched itself into his mind as surely as the knowledge of returning pain burned in his chest.

Reaching a postern gate off the main palace courtyard, a guardsman opened it. The gorilla costumed as a soldier lifted Davin by the collar with one hand and tossed him through the portal. Any semblance of decorum was lost when the royal-born thief stumbled and fell heavily to one knee, tearing both pant leg and flesh beneath.

"Lord Hormachi told me to remind you – three weeks," the gorilla posing as a guard captain said gruffly.

"I need to speak with Hormachi." Davin climbed to his feet and stepped toward the soldier. "He hasn't given me enough information to . . ."

The guardsman's left hand shot out and like a battering ram slammed into the Jyotian's chest. Davin was knocked back three feet. A humorless chuckle rumbling in his throat, the captain yanked the gate closed.

As though resolved to the unwanted geas, Davin turned and started away. A journey halfway across Lower Raemllyn to Ohnuhn was the last thing in his mind. Instead, he listened until he heard echoes of retreating steps announce that the four soldiers had returned to their posts.

Once again the adventurer pivoted. Gazing up at the wall surrounding Hormachi's palace, Davin recognized the futility of even considering scaling its heights. His attention centered on the gate. Quick strides brought him back to the postern. He tested it with a single hand, then both. When that failed he added the weight of a shoulder. Nothing! The best he managed was a slight rattle when he gently pressed it with fingertips.

Undaunted, he slipped needles and picks from a pocket hidden within his belt. Ten minutes and a full measure of determination allowed him to coax the locking bar back far enough to use the tip of his dagger to slide it fully from its niche.

A pleased smile slipped across his lips when he eased the gate open, peered beyond the wall, then stepped back into the palace grounds. No common cutpurse or pickpocket was Davin Anane; he had faced and defeated the greatest sorcerers and magicians in all Raemllyn. No second-rate mage living here on the edge of the world would bind him as a slave with a death spell!

Replacing dirk in sheath, he moved on feet as silent as cat paws to retrace his steps through Hormachi's keep. Now, before the ruler alerted his elite guards that the last son of the House of Anane was again loosed upon the land, was the perfect time to strike! Not even Hormachi would expect such a brazen move!

Two steps at a time, Davin climbed a stairway to a second-floor landing and froze. A patrol approached straight toward his position. The thief pressed back flat against cold stone wall, sweat beading on his brow.

The troop continued toward him until a sergeant barked, "Punishment duty, to the rear, *march*!"

The men snapped about smartly and moved back down the hallway without pause. A shaky breath gushed from Davin's lips. How he managed to avoid detection was beyond him. He was certain at least half of the ten guards had stared right at him.

With a whispered prayer to the Goddess Jajhana for her fortuitous smile, Davin continued up the staircase until he reached the third floor. Here the maze of corridors might have befuddled a thief with a lesser memory, but the Jyotian moved unerringly to the door that led to the chamber where he had been held.

Pressing his hand against the door, Davin felt for vibration within. Nothing. Dropping to his belly, he tried to peer under the door. No shadows moved within the room. Although Hormachi might be seated and studying his tomes of magical lore, Davin sensed the ruler of Gatinah had no further use of the room beyond the door this day.

A soapstone statue? The object Hormachi desired wedged itself into the Jyotian's mind when he pushed to his feet. What value was a statue of common soapstone to the Gatinahese ruler? Perhaps it held no significance for Hormachi but might for Vytellion. Did an ancient rivalry rub raw the flesh of two old opponents?

"Or there might be precious stones set in this statue," Davin said aloud as his imagination blazed with visions of a statue with eyes of *drenn* jewels and fingernails of *mardak* stones. Such an object would command a fortune. The gems that filled Aotesja's emporium paled to bits of crystal beside such a treasure.

Perhaps it would be worth his time to journey to Ohnuhn after he finished his business here in Gatinah, Davin decided, as he eased back the door's lock. But first he had to purloin Hormachi's grimoire and find a sorcerer able to break the spell and remove the elemental that nestled in his breast.

He pushed the door inward and glanced inside. Empty. The mage-ruler was not inside.

Davin entered quickly. The grimoire lay on the table where Hormachi had left it. Davin suspected even he could reverse the spell lying dormant in his chest if he could but read the words marching in bright green runes across the parchment pages.

He took a step toward the book of spells and felt slightly dizzy.

A second step and the dizziness vanished, replaced with a nausea that boiled in his belly. A third step caused his eyes to blur. And at the fourth Davin fell into infinite space, tumbling head over heels.

From far away he heard Lord Hormachi's mocking voice:

"The statue, dog boy. Return with the statue or you will discover what it feels like to have all three rings ignite on your breast!"

6

Davin's hand shot to his sword hilt. Steel half drawn, he halted when he realized he faced a blank wall. He swung about and blinked in confusion. He stood in Gatinah's bazaar. Dawn warmed the far horizon, and yawning merchants shuffled toward shops and tables to prepare their goods for sale.

"Hormachi," Davin muttered, shoving the half-drawn sword back into its sheath. "Magicks!"

He spat on the cobblestones, disgusted that the ruler-mage had somehow spirited him from the center of the palace to the market in less than a heartbeat. Davin pulled open his tunic in the desperate hope that the memories of maze and burning rings were but remnants of some horribly vivid nightmare.

The nightmare lingered. The concentric rings, yellow, violet and immaculate white circled his left nipple. Licking a palm, Davin rubbed at the paint, hoping it would come off. It did not. Hormachi bound him with a spell and owned him body and soul as ruler-mage had boasted.

"Steal a statue, a small one," Davin mused aloud. "That's all I have to do. *All*?"

The sound of his unwanted task did not ring onerous to his ear. Yet Hormachi had gone to extremes to select the best thief in Gatinah to complete the chore. A man commanding the might of a city-state as prosperous as Gatinah could launch an army to take the statue if it proved so desirable. Or he could barter for it.

Vytellion, if this was indeed a man or woman, surely did not rival Hormachi in power or wealth. Davin delved his mind to find even a cobweb of memory about Ohnuhn. Nothing! He was certain he had heard of the city but failed to remember ever entering the Lower Raemllyn port.

What man but one of inconsequential power ruled over an unknown city? Davin attempted to rationalize the journey westward. In the next instant, bitter bile filled his gut. Davin Anane, son of High King Bedrich the Fair, was no man's slave! He did no one's bidding unless it was of his own free choice – not because of some wizard's arcane spell!

There would be no leaving Gatinah. Davin clenched his teeth in determination. No man who robbed him of a king's ransom in jewels, attempted to kill him time and again within a deathtrap maze and then embedded a fire elemental inside his chest would profit by Davin Anane's skills. The only thing such a man deserved was to feel the kiss of cold steel.

A glimpse of crimson and azure drew the thief's attention to a patrol of guardsmen who entered the bazaar for their early morning rounds. He doubted they sought him, but he had no time to waste answering inane questions should he awaken their suspicions. Davin slipped into a shadow-darkened doorway.

The guards passed by without so much as a glance in his direction.

The sight of their tailored uniforms and the flash of the golden weapons dangling at their sides tripled Davin's mounting anger. Hormachi used the taxes collected from his people for ostentation rather than defense. An image of Irisli dying on the arena floor, run through by his own sword, pushed into his mind. The young woman would willingly have given her life for a chance to slit the Gatinahese ruler's throat. Irisli's death was but another debt Hormachi had incurred that demanded full payment.

When he stepped from the doorway, the Jyotian's head turned northward. Even above the tops of Gatinah's stone and wooden buildings, he saw the spires of Hormachi's palace and mountainous walls surrounding the keep.

He cast away all thought of reentering the palace and attempting to steal the grimoire again. Hormachi had already proven he was more than prepared for such a move from his "dog thief".

Davin's hand lifted to the rings on his chest. Any spell that could be woven could also have the thread of that weave unraveled. All he had to do was find one with equal or greater ability than Gatinah's mage-ruler.

The Huata!

Davin's gaze moved toward the west. He and Raemllyn's nomads had aided each other on more than one occasion in the past. A week ago he had heard that a Huata band camped outside the city. He had intended to visit them, but preparations for his assault on Aotesja's gem emporium had kept him fully occupied.

Now was as good a time as any to make that overdue visit, he thought as he hastened toward the city's west gate. If there were any with the ability to remove Hormachi's spell, or the knowledge to direct him to one with that knowledge, it was the Huata.

A flood of memories filled Davin's head as he wove down street and alley. The Huata roamed both Upper and Lower Raemllyn freely, peddling remedies for mysterious diseases, giving a glimpse of the future for those willing to pay, even promising love and eternal life to the gullible. It was the Huata who first introduced the Jyotian to the ways of the cutpurse and pick-pocket.

More than most, the Jyotian enjoyed the Huata's company. They were an open and loving people to those who earned their trust. Once that trust was won, a Huata would willingly give his life to save a friend, and expected the same of a friend. If ever a code of honor existed between thieves, it could be found among the Huata.

The Huata also kept themselves linked closely to Raemllyn's magicks. Each band carried with it a wizard, mage or witch. It was that link so powerfully drawing the Jyotian to the nomads. Although, he admitted to himself, he knew nothing of the Huata who wandered Lower Raemllyn. He had heard Huata friends in the upper realms speak of a blood relative called Somora, a sorceress who had studied magicks among the mages in Kavindra, the city of Raemllyn's High King. Davin hoped knowing the woman's name would gain the Huata's ear, at least long enough to explain the fiery burden embedded in his breast.

Aotesja's shop came into view when the spellbound adventurer turned a corner. He noted how the companies of guardsmen so apparent yesterday were now absent. Whatever had happened to the gems strapped to the backs of his pack of trained hounds, Davin could only guess, but he was certain the six dogs and the treasure they carried had yet to be found. If Aotesja had recovered his shipment, the guards inside and outside the empo-rium would have been doubled – trebled!

The possibility that the hounds remained within the house they had been trained to return to sent the Jyotian's pulse racing. *No!* That was too much to ask, even of the fortune found in the

Goddess Jajhana's sweet smile. Davin had also trained the six to scatter should they be pursued – and Aotesja had definitely given chase.

In spite of himself, Davin felt his pace slow when he passed the shop on the opposite side of the street. Through now open windows he saw long tables draped with black velvet meant to display Aotesja's handicraft at its best. Ten seconds in that room and Davin would walk away rich. Not as rich as he would have been with the shipment of gemstones, but rich enough.

First, remove Hormachi's hex, Davin told himself, then he would pay Aotesja one last visit before he said farewell to Gatinah.

As he continued west, he found his hand had crept to his tunic. His fingertips lightly drew circles over the fabric as though to remind him of the danger inherent in allowing future visions to obscure the day at hand.

Hastening his strides, the Jyotian pushed through the city. Gatinah covered a huge tract of land, much of it open to the sea on the south. A long, curving wall swept eastward then meandered north and across to a western front protected by a swamp and roving beasts so fearsome most of the Gatinahese would not even boast about them. The city was well defended but rarely slept. Seldom did the gates close and traffic came and went in a steady stream bearing cargo from the port to the interior of Lower Raemllyn.

Davin relied on his feet in lieu of a good horse. By midday he reached a small stream forcing its way across rocky terrain to flow into the Ocean of Kumar. From all he knew of the Huata, their camp would not be far away. They required water for their draught animals, and more than one of their schemes to separate a man from his gold required elaborate mechanisms powered by falling water.

Davin had often marveled at the way a turning waterwheel could power an entire camp, bringing light and movement to the wilderness. With such displays, it was often easier to convince the Huatas' patrons of their insight and ability to conjure anything – for a price.

"The camp's not open for another six hours," a lilting voice intruded on the Jyotian's thoughts.

Davin turned to face a young girl, hardly fourteen summers, sitting on a large rock near the stream. "But then, not many coming here from Gatinah have your look about them. You're a handsome one, now aren't you?" She smiled prettily, flashing Davin a delectable view of her dimples.

'Work your wiles on another," Davin said, returning the smile. "I seek Somora, stepdaughter of Tymon of the Upper Raemllyn Huata."

"Tymon?" The girl frowned and shook her head. "I know nothing of any Tymon, but then I have lived my entire life in Lower Raemllyn."

"Somora?" Davin pressed. "You know her?"

"What do you seek from her?" The girl's caution bespoke a lifetime spent deftly redirecting the inquiries of local authorities who rarely welcomed the visits of Huata bands. "I remember hearing she was traveling across the country to – Initha."

Davin knew the girl lied from the way she struggled to recall a city distant enough to make it plausible that Somora could never be found. He went and stood by her, studying her features carefully.

"You remind me of another Huata," he said. "Are you related to Selene of Tymon's band?"

The answer came in the small widening of the girl's eyes, followed quickly by a narrowing as she appraised him.

"You know much of Huata genealogy," she said. "What is your business with our camp?"

"Somora," Davin repeated. "I require the services of one with her abilities."

"This is all you seek?" The girl turned somber.

"All? Certainly, this matter is of importance to me. Will you take me to your mother?"

"She's my aunt . . ." The girl broke off, then smiled and finally laughed. "Your words are skillfully set traps. Does your knowledge of my people come from first-hand contact?"

"I have traveled with Tymon now and then for varying lengths of time," Davin admitted, harkening back to the days when he and Goran One-Eye had tried to prise loose the demon bound to Lijena Farleigh.*

---

* See *To Demons Bound*, SWORDS OF RAEMLLYN: Book 1

"Come with me." The girl jumped from the rock and strolled off in a manner that bespoke complete awareness of her blossoming womanhood and the effect it had on men.

Davin remained aloof from her obvious, too obvious, attempts to draw his eye. A few years would bring subtlety, and then, Davin thought, this vixen would be a dangerous woman, as were all Huata women.

The encampment stirred when the girl passed through it on a direct route to a green-painted wagon parked beyond the loose ring formed by the Huatas' other wagons. Davin knew the woman-child paraded him along like a prize before the dark eyes that followed them suspiciously. The scrutinizing gazes that belonged to the dark-eyed Huata women, Davin answered with smiles. For the men, the Jyotian offered the traditional Huata greeting of morning, receiving only grunts in reply.

Friendlier bands existed, Davin thought, while admitting he knew little of Lower Raemllyn's Huata. Perhaps their ways were different from those in the north?

An older woman emerged from the wagon, long brown hair caught up in a colorful scarf. Heavy gold chains dangled from her neck and silver bracelets studded with precious stones decorated her wrists and ankles. Unlike most Huata, Somora wore no rings. Davin did not doubt for an instant this was the woman he sought. Power exuded from her like an aphrodisiac. A single glance into her dark eyes convinced him she was a sorceress of considerable power.

"Step away from him, child." The Huata woman held up a hand to signal Davin to halt. "He is ensorcelled. Have I not taught you to read the signs?"

"Somora, I . . ."

"You only had eyes for a handsome face!" The woman made no attempt to dull the bite of her tone. "Now do as I say. Step away."

The girl backed away. Her gaze nervously shifted between Somora and the Jyotian.

"Your niece was kind enough to bring me," Davin said, bowing deeply, as if he paid homage to a queen rather than a gypsy witch woman who spent her life wandering from town to town. "I am sorely in need of your powers, Somora."

The Jyotian took another step toward the Huata sorceress and Somora again raised a hand to stop him. When he started to speak she waved him to silence. Quietly, he stood while her fingers dipped and probed the air.

"You may come closer," she said eventually. "I detect no threat to myself or my people."

"I am an old friend to the Huata," Davin assured her. "I would never bring danger into your camp."

"Not on purpose," Somora answered, shooing her niece back to the camp with a wave of a hand. "But what you perceive as a threat to yourself might conceal a threat aimed at me or my traveling companions. Great magicks were unleashed at the Battle of Kavindra. The scales of balance are still out of kilter and there are those who would tilt them in their favor."

The Jyotian nodded in acceptance of her caution and glanced toward the departing girl. "She will break hearts one day."

"One day?" Somora scoffed with a raised eyebrow. "Already little Ceta causes fights. Only last week, Nabell lost a finger in a duel and Trofo walks with a limp that might never go away. I should send her to live with distant relatives until she learns self-control."

Davin nodded. He felt little desire to learn the ins and outs of this Huata band, but if such small talk put the woman at ease, then it was little enough price to pay. Still, he could not ignore the press of time. Half a day had gone by, leaving him less than a week to free himself before Hormachi's spell burned his flesh with its agony-ridden magicks.

"Tymon," the Huata said suddenly. "You mentioned his name. Do you truly know him or was that a ploy to see me, Davin Anane?"

"I know him," the adventurer answered when he reached the woman's side. She was younger than Davin expected, no more than two or three years older than himself. Although he could not call her beautiful, there was no way to deny that Somora was far more than merely attractive. Had circumstances been different, Davin realized that he would have been willing to explore more amorous avenues with Somora. "And Selene. I know Tymon's daughter Selene!"

"Everyone wearing pants in Upper Raemllyn knows my

stepsister," Somora replied with a snort that placed little weight on Davin's familiarity with Selene. "She and Ceta are cut from the same cloth, I am afraid."

Somora's fingertips wove a protective sign in the air, then she motioned for the Jyotian to follow her into a wagon crowded with shelves of glass vials, small pottery containers, tin boxes and dried herbs. Above the headboard of a small cot stretched two shelves crowded with tomes and scrolls; grimoires, Davin realized. Somora found a small three-legged stool on which she sat and pointed for the thief to take the side of the neatly made cot.

His backside halfway to quilt-covered mattress, the Jyotian suddenly stood straight and stared down at the woman. "You called me by name. How? I never spoke my name."

With a pleased smile, Somora signaled him to sit again. "You sought me because of my powers, friend Davin. Surely, you would consider the ability to read a simple crystal in my abilities. A week does not go by that I do not reach across the continents to speak with my father and see how his band fares. I first saw you, Davin Anane, when you joined Tymon as no more than a frightened boy fleeing the one you call the Blackheart."

Davin sank to the down-stuffed bed, uncertain what to say. He knew the Huata kept in close contact no matter what distances separated them, but he had never suspected they spoke through magicks. "How is Tymon this week?"

"He grows fat." Somora smiled. "He and his band now camp outside the walls of Bistonia. Selene, too, is well. But I hope you don't expect her to be pining for you?"

Davin grinned and shook his head. "I'm afraid Selene has yet to meet the man she will pine for."

"Now, let me examine the reason you came here." Somora nodded toward his chest. "Open your blouse and let me see this spell so tightly bound to your flesh."

Davin did not question how she knew so much about his predicament. Instead, he did as she asked, opening the tunic and pulling it wide. Somora leaned close, her dark eyes narrowing while furrows ran across her brow. She reached out to touch the colored circles with the tip of her little finger. She recoiled immediately.

"Can you lift the spell?" Davin pressed.

"Such power," she said, eyes fixed on the rings. "It will be a difficult hex to lift. The mage placing the spell was most adept and chose ancient methods in his weaving. Few bind elementals to flesh these days."

Somora's dark eyes lifted and locked on Davin's gray ones. "This will require great resources, materials I lack."

"What do you need?" If Somora's conjuring required less than a week to break Hormachi's spell, he would be well served. "I also have certain abilities."

"Huata trained skills," she smiled to say that she was aware of the Jyotian's abilities as a thief. "I need herbs, roots, ingredients I dare not put into words. Things you should not concern yourself with."

"What more do you need?" Davin knew what was next – Somora's price. A Huata's services never came free.

"In Gatinah, there is a gem shop. Aotesja is the proprietor . . ."

Davin laughed hard, interrupting her. When he noticed her frown, he waved for her to continue. "Please, go on. I know the shop well."

"Jewels, one hundred jewels," Somora went on. "No fewer than this number will provide recompense for such a dangerous, arduous spell-lifting."

"One hundred?" Davin shook his head firmly. To accept a Huata's price without haggling would be considered an insult. "I know the shop and this Aotesja. A hundred gems taken from his store would ruin the man. What purpose is there in killing a goose that lays fine eggs? Twenty-five stones will leave Aotesja ripe for the plucking on another day."

Somora's frown said she recognized the value in what the Jyotian said. A wise thief never totally cleaned out a merchant's stock but left enough for him to prosper and provide for future days. "Ninety jewels would suit me well, although truly not enough to pay for the dangers I will be exposed to."

"Thirty gems," Davin countered.

And so it went on for a full hour until the Huata woman proposed:

"Fifty gemstones and ten sword lengths of gold chain. Nothing less will purchase the magical materials needed for this effort."

"Agreed," Davin said, his mind already turning to breaching Aotesja's shop to steal the requisite baubles.

Davin drew a deep breath to settle his racing heart. The drop from the roof of the building across the street from Aotesja's shop might as well have been the Canyon of Affifs, reputed to be deeper than the ocean and wider than a hundred bowshots.

Davin could never hope to leap the chasm, but then he never considered doing so. He unlooped the rope coiled over his left arm and sent the grapnel with its three hooks soaring through the air. There was no way to muffle the metallic ring when the device landed on Aotesja's roof.

The Jyotian tensed, afraid the clatter might draw the attention of the single guard patrolling the block. For a full minute Davin waited to see if the unwonted noise alerted the sentry. No one came running, shouting out an alarm.

Tugging gently, Davin pulled the line taut and drew the grapnel along the distant roof until it caught on a gutter. He jerked as hard as he could in an attempt to dislodge it. The thief was not sure if he was glad when it did not pull free. The gutter was not the most secure spot to lodge a hook. He considered shaking the grapnel free and trying again.

Instead, Davin tied the loose end to a chimney and quickly dropped over the building's verge to dangle suspended by hands and heels on the line. Releasing his tight grip, Davin slid down the line toward Aotesja's roof. Inches away from his destination, he tightened his legs and hands to prevent crashing headfirst into the gutter. An agile twist brought him onto the roof, his catlike feet padding softly on the shingles. He saw evidence of where the guards had crouched a night earlier when the fabulous trove of gemstones was being delivered, but this night Davin walked alone on the roof. Going to the chimney, he stopped and surveyed the scene a final time to make sure he went unseen.

The bricks were hot to the touch from a fire that blazed below. Aotesja insisted on heating his shop to maintain a constant temperature for his gems. Davin had not noted any similar care for the master merchant's employees. Unwrapping a thick blanket from around his waist, Davin shoved it into the chimney. The time for hesitation was past. If he did not reach the bottom of the chimney quickly, smoke would billow back into the shop and alert either guard or firekeeper – or both.

Feet first, Davin jumped into the chimney, pushing the blanket downward as fast as possible. The heated bricks scared both shoulders and knees, but he ignored the pain. He crashed into the fire below and quickly rolled out of the large fireplace, pulling the blanket with him before it started to smolder. Hand on dagger, he listened for any hint that his intrusion had been noticed.

The only sounds reaching his ears were the solemn tick of a large pendulum-powered clock near the front door and softer, more distant, snoring from the back room. His unconventional entrance had not disturbed the firekeeper's stolen nap.

Davin opened a pouch to fill it with the trinkets Aotesja displayed so proudly on his tables. Soon the gem-studded sea of baubles disappeared, leaving nothing more than unwrinkled black velvet. Davin walked boldly to the front door and glanced out through a small barred window in the thick portal. He froze when he saw the guardsman standing outside.

Swallowing the curse that rose in his throat, his mind raced. The guard showed no sign of continuing his circuit of the block as he leaned against the door and began filling a pipe. Davin eased away from the door, realizing the sentry intended to smoke that pipe before returning to his duty. There was no time to wait. The firekeeper might awaken to notice the ashes strewn across the floor. Or the boy might see the missing jewelry. In either case, he would cry out in alarm.

Moving with the stealth of a feline, Davin crossed the shop and pushed into the back room where the firekeeper slept peacefully. The rear door Davin had burned from its hinges had been repaired, but leaving would prove no trouble. This door, like the one at the front, had been designed to keep people out. Davin had no trouble opening the repaired door from the inside.

He froze when the firekeeper stirred.

The boy rolled onto his side while he slept on the floor and tugged at his blanket which had fallen away. Sleepily, the youth's hand sought the covering. Davin crept to the boy's side and covered him with the blanket he had used in the chimney. It smelled of smoke and ash, but the dreaming boy never noticed.

"Night, my love," the boy said, never waking.

"Good night," Davin whispered as he slipped out the door and into the night-cloaked alley.

"You return so quickly," Ceta's voice greeted Davin as he reached the stream near the Huata camp.

"What Somora required was a simple task." Davin held up the pouch to display its bulging burden.

"Either you are a tremendous liar or the finest thief in all Raemllyn," Ceta grinned with obvious delight. "Somora will be pleased."

"Does it matter which?" Davin asked, laughing at the girl's enthusiastic reception.

"No, either is a fine accomplishment. Should I take you to my aunt's wagon?"

"I can find the way," Davin said. He noted the Huata were packing, preparing to move on. "Has there been no flow of coins from the Gatinahese purses to your own?"

"They are a tight-fisted lot," Ceta said sadly as she walked at his side. "Not even I could entice more than a few tin octens from then."

"Better luck next time," Davin said when he reached Somora's wagon.

Beyond the open door, the Jyotian saw the Huata woman bent over a table filled with magical apparatus, brewing a potion so pungent that green fumes poured from the wagon and caught on the breeze almost choking him. He had no idea how Somora kept from smothering amid the vapors she created.

He hesitated on the steps when she looked up. A slow smile crossed her face.

"Come in, friend of the Huata. Have you brought the required payment for this potion?" The sorceress held up a goblet fuming and boiling with the force of her magicks.

"All Aotesja had to offer," Davin said, dropping the bulging pouch onto a table at Somora's elbow. The woman made no move to examine the contents. Davin sat on the three-legged stool Somora motioned him toward.

"As to my promise, I have prepared the needed potion." She turned to fill a goblet with a thick, green brew. "This will break the spell and drive the elemental from your breast. But beware,

Davin Anane, it is not an easy thing. You will feel as though you struggle with a full score of men out to rip your head from your shoulders."

Davin swallowed back the cotton that grew in his mouth. "Better to feel like I face a score of men than to have Hormachi's spell burn away my life."

"Then drink, drink quickly!" Somora placed the goblet into his hands. "Every drop, to the very last, drink."

Davin hesitated but for the blink of an eye, then lifted the silver vessel with its runic inscriptions running about the lip and poured the concoction down his throat. It burned like the sun, then turned to ice in his gut.

"How long?" he choked out.

"Long enough," came Somora's answer.

Davin grew woozy, the world spinning in wild, crazy circles around him. He slumped forward, fighting against the dark curtain of unconsciousness that fell over his head rather than a score of assailants.

"He drank it without pause," Ceta's voice came as a distant whisper.

"I expected no less," Somora answered. "He is a desperate man. I almost feel pity to use him thus."

Ceta laughed. "Feel no pity for a fool. He actually believed you were Somora – that old dried up hag. I didn't think you would pull it off, Mairri."

Davin continued to sink, feeling his head hit the top of the table before him.

"Yes," the woman called Mairri replied. "We have our spies in Gatinah to thank for the information they supplied on this one."

"We earn the favor from the Brotherhood of Pliaton for this service, as well as a pouch packed with jewels."

The Brotherhood of—

Blackness engulfed Davin, drawing him downward.

The sun blazed down from the zenith when that dark curtain parted and he forced his eyes open. He groaned beneath the pounding assault within his skull as he sat up and stared about him. The wagons and the camp were gone – and the rings painted on his chest remained.

"Witch!" The single word came as a curse from Davin's lips

with the realization that the Huata had cheated him.

Worse still, he had wasted an entire day fulfilling Lord Hormachi's quest. He struggled to unsteady feet, vowing vengeance on the woman called Mairri who had posed as Somora should their paths ever cross again.

Turning back to Gatinah, he began walking. Stabled within the city, he still had a horse and pack animal. Riding would bring him to Ohnuhn's gate far faster than would his own feet. Like it or not, there was a soapstone statue in the west he had to steal.

After that, he would deal with both Hormachi and Cal'Dreth and his Brotherhood of Pliaton.

7

A low whistle escaped Davin's lips when the bay gelding topped a treeless rise covered by a dense carpet of coastal grasses. He blinked twice to make certain his eyes were not deceived by a mist-born mirage rising from a salt marsh.

The land gently sloped away from the Jyotian's position to fashion a verdant bowl of rich farmlands and open pastures. Cupped at the center of the luxurious, fertile greens rose Ohnuhn.

Again Davin whistled in amazement. How could one as well-traveled as he have missed visiting this magnificent place? Tapping his heels to his mount's flanks, he reined the bay toward the city. Nor were the multihued edifices of Ohnuhn an illusion, the adventurer realized when the horse moved onto a well-kept road that led directly toward towering walls of shining alabaster encircling the city. No soot-darkened bricks were here, but marble of soft pastel shades ranging from robin-egg blue to the gentle yellow of an *ofess* blossom.

Less pleasing to the eye were the patrols of alert soldiers dressed in flat gray uniforms that marched on either side of the road. Unlike the peacocks in Gatinah decked in crimson and azure with gold swords dangling at their sides, these soldiers carried weapons worn from training – or hard fighting. Not one of the guardsmen Davin spied had the look of a man grown soft from garrison duty.

Why so alert? Davin saw no sign of attacking hordes or armies come to ravage the city-state. The merchants traveling the roads appeared prosperous and happy and the peasants occasionally smiled. Again, the lone thief could not help wondering why he knew no more of Ohnuhn than its name.

Those he had met along the way from Gatinah could point the way to Ohnuhn, but none seemed to know anything about the city – or were reticent to speak of it.

Without knowledge of custom or law in this land of pastel

buildings, he would have to ease slowly into the vital currents flowing through Ohnuhn. Only when he blended with the populace would theft of Vytellion's small statue be possible.

The Jyotian's right hand crept to his breast. He felt no pain, but three days of hard riding had passed since leaving Gatinah. Davin felt the weight of time tightening like an invisible band about his chest. The first week Hormachi had given him would soon pass. He remembered only too well the searing pain of the mage-ruler's ensorcelled flame as it transformed his flesh to black cinders.

Davin urged his horse into a brisk walk toward Ohnuhn's distant gates, flung wide in open invitation to the countryside. Half a league from those gates, two men in gray uniform emerged from a guard station at his approach.

"Halt!" called the taller and thinner of the pair. "Your travel permits."

"Travel from Gatinah is proscribed?" Davin did not have to feign astonishment. Only in times of war were travel permits employed by Raemllyn's city-states, and then rarely. "I bring news to Lord Vytellion. No permit is required for such a task."

Neither man batted so much as an eyelash when the Jyotian mentioned Lord Vytellion. His guess that Vytellion was the city's ruler had been correct. However, the soldiers stiffened when he uttered the name of Gatinah.

"Gatinah? You come from Lord Hormachi?" The guard's eyes narrowed and suspicion filled his voice.

"No, you misunderstand," Davin said easily. "I have news *of* Hormachi. Lord Vytellion must hear it immediately."

"You have papers?" The guard did not relax his stance, nor did the man beside him.

Had he known of the travel permits, Davin would have waited until night and slipped over the city wall. Having committed himself to entry by the gate, there was no way he could turn and ride away without finding himself beset by guards. The only avenue open was to play out the charade he had begun.

"My papers are not meant for eyes of mere privates. Take me to your commander," Davin snapped with military crispness.

Both soldiers jerked rigid as though to attention – for an instant – then looked at each other. After a hasty exchange of buzzing whispers, the two turned back to nod simultaneously.

"Dismount and follow me," the first soldier said, motioning to the other guard to remain at the post.

Davin did just that. However, his mind raced with the increased pounding of his heart. If they reached the captain of the guard, he was certain to find himself taken prisoner owing to lack of travel permits. Any time spent dangling in shackles further reduced the meager time Hormachi allotted him.

The road took a turn through a small dell – and Davin acted. Slipping dirk from sheath, he slammed the knife's pommel behind the guardsman's right ear. The man grunted, half turned, then crumpled to the ground, unconscious.

Stripping away the soldier's uniform took longer than Davin liked, his eyes constantly darting up and down the road for the approach of a patrol. Nor did the uniform prove large enough in girth to fit Davin and was far too long in sleeve and pants' leg. Ripping open seams at the rear of both tunic and trousers allowed Davin to wriggle into the clothing. He would never pass muster, but he doubted he would need to. Handfuls of dirt smeared into several places on the uniform, then a few smudges to highlight the road dust on his face and the Jyotian deemed himself filthy enough to appear as though he had just fought a hard battle and barely escaped with his life. He turned and hastened down the road, slowing to a stagger when he came into view of the next guard station.

"The captain," cried Davin to the soldier who darted from the small structure when he approached. "I need to report! Brigands!"

"The Fellowship!" exclaimed the guard.

Davin had no idea what the soldier meant, not that it mattered. He willingly played on the guard's fear. "It had to be. A half-dozen or more!"

"The Qar-cursed swine! They grow too bold, venturing beyond the city walls." The guard rushed out and put his arm around Davin's shoulders, helping him toward the distant gates.

Davin alternately leaned heavily to convince the soldier of his injuries and walked on his own to reach the portal more quickly.

"The Fellowship!" called the guard. "This man's been in a fight with pillagers on the Gatinah road!"

A dozen more guards poured from the gate to answer the

alarm. Each had a barrage of questions which the Jyotian answered with dazed grunts and nods. Eventually the soldiers parted and allowed Davin and his assistant to enter. Still leaning heavily on the man, the rogue allowed the guard to guide him toward a barracks near a lavishly built structure that surely had to be the palace of Ohnuhn's ruler.

While being the center of attention served to get the Jyotian within Ohnuhn's walls, it was the last thing he wanted now. There was only one thing he could think of to remedy the situation. With a throaty groan, he went completely limp and collapsed to the ground.

When the guard crouched over him, Davin reached up and gripped the uniform collars. Thumbs pressed deftly into the man's throat. The guard's eyes rolled upward as he passed out. In the next instant Davin sprang to his feet and reversed their roles, hauling the guard to his feet and dragging the unconscious guard toward the barracks.

"Brigands!" he called out. "The Fellowship! There's been an attack. I've an injured man here!"

A full score of guards poured from the barracks and scrambled to get the unconscious soldier onto a cot inside, all the while cursing the Fellowship and how it preyed on Ohnuhn's honest citizens.

Forgotten in the guards' haste to comfort a wounded companion in arms, Davin drifted back, then slipped away. He stopped long enough in a nearby alley to tear away the tattered uniform and use it to wipe the dirt from his face.

Not a battered soldier but a mere citizen strolled from the alley onto the prosperous avenues of Ohnuhn. Again the question of how such a magnificent city had eluded his knowledge niggled at the adventurer's mind. Moreover, Davin could not recall ever hearing Ohnuhn mentioned by anyone in his lifetime. Other than being a point on a map, he recalled nothing about the city.

Time closed on him like red-hot pincers, forcing him to set aside Ohnuhn's wondrous architecture and focus on the task facing him. He had to locate Lord Vytellion and steal the soapstone statue Hormachi demanded.

The Fellowship, he considered. It had taken only a few of the soldiers' curses for him to realize that Ohnuhn's thieves were as organized as those in Gatinah, no matter what they called themselves. Although he usually had no use for such guilds, time might force him to consider an alliance, but only as a last resort.

Or was he letting pride stand as an obstacle to success? He knew nothing of Ohnuhn. Days, if not weeks, would be needed to garner the knowledge required to attempt entering a palace. No, he would work alone; how could one depend on hired thieves!

Davin sifted through various plans and discarded each as suicidal. No matter where his mental meandering traveled, they returned to this Fellowship. Time was of the essence. He had to take risks. Better to trust himself to fellow thieves than attempt to bribe his way into Vytellion's palace. Honest men bought with gold often were swayed by a sudden attack of conscience at a critical moment. Honest men simply were not to be trusted. At least with thieves a man knew where he stood as long as he kept in mind that greed guided their every movement.

Which meant he had to assure more than adequate booty for those of the Fellowship he convinced to aid him. He would limit his own plunder to the single statue Hormachi required. All else belonged to those assisting him. Surely, that would satisfy the Fellowship, even if the statue proved to be studded with the finest jewels he had seen this side of Aotesja's gemstone emporium.

While the Jyotian worked his way into the central market, Davin found it impossible to keep from noting the bulging purses of merchants and the level of prosperity shown by most of the businesses. He bumped into one man, spun and rocked into another.

"Excuse me, please, so sorry, didn't mean to, my fault," Davin muttered constantly.

He rebounded from three different men and came away with fat purses each time. After all, a man wishing to hire thieves needed coin to grease the wheels of criminality. Deciding not to push his luck further, Davin retreated from the crowded section of the bazaar to tally his easily obtained gains. Before he slipped even one of the stolen leather pouches from under his tunic, a cold voice spoke behind him:

"We've no need for such thieves in Ohnuhn."

"I? You mistake me for . . ."

Davin fell silent when he faced his accuser. The bulky man

stood with massive arms crossed over his chest. The set to the man's square jaw told of barely contained anger as did the fire in his eyes. The giant wore no uniform but carried three daggers thrust into his belt, two without benefit of sheath.

"You stole from men protected by the Fellowship. Hand over the money and everything else you carry."

"What!"

"No one but a sworn brother of the Fellowship may steal within Ohnuhn's walls." The man's voice rumbled like boulders grinding together. "You are not of the Fellowship. This being your first offense, you forfeit only your belongings. The next time, you die!"

"My belongings?" asked Davin, mind racing. "Even these pitiful rags?" He touched his clothing as if in shock.

"You go from this alley naked, but you will still possess your worthless life," the man said, a sly grin sliding across his face. "The Fellowship is generous."

"How can I join this fine organization?" asked Davin. He fumbled under his tunic to pull out the bags of coin he had filched.

"Forget it, friend. It takes a brother to sponsor you. I don't think that will happen. Your skills are obviously lacking. I saw what you were up to with a mere glance. The Fellowship admits only master thieves!"

Davin swallowed his ire. Who was this gorilla in human disguise to think, let alone give voice, to the possibility that the last son of the House of Anane was anything but a master thief! In a calm, steady voice, the Jyotian answered, "I think your leader would access my skills differently. I would speak with him."

"Him? You want to speak with *him*?" The giant member of Ohnuhn's Fellowship of thieves laughed heartily. "You are new to this fine city, I see. The gold!"

A huge, open hand shot toward Davin, waiting for the pouches of coin stolen in the bazaar.

"How would I go about finding others to help me in a small venture?" Davin asked, dropping the first of the three purses into the waiting palm. The heavy purse seemed small in the giant's paw of a hand. Davin added the second purse.

"No one will aid in any theft not approved by the Fellowship," the thief said. "The last purse. Then your weapons and clothing."

"Ah, well, so be it," Davin said, venting a huge sigh.

He dropped the third bag, missing the hand. Gold and silver spilled across the alley. As the colossus instinctively bent to catch the rolling coins, Davin launched a kick that landed solidly on the giant's knee. A sick snapping signaled breaking bone.

Davin recoiled, his foot hurting from the impact, but he had achieved his goal. The thief toppled like a felled tree.

"You fool!" the human gorilla roared, dropping the two bags of coins and grabbing his knee. "You will pay for this! By Pliaton, I swear you will pay!"

"No thieves able to think on their own in this fine town?" taunted Davin. "Only theft approved by the Brotherhood allowed?"

He danced around the fallen man, measuring the distance. The giant obviously did not consider the possibility that Davin would renew the attack – a mistake. The Jyotian moved with lightning speed, his boot slashing out a second time. The toe connected with the huge pilferer's chin, snapping his head back. It took only a few minutes for Davin to strip anything of value from the insensate hulk.

For a master thief, the gorilla carried little – only a small money pouch which Davin tied to his own belt beside the two he scooped from the ground. The fourth pouch was refilled with the spilled coins.

For a moment, the Jyotian considered stripping the man as he would have done to Davin. Instead, he pulled the man's cloak from his shoulders and tossed it around his own. It dragged on the ground behind him, but Davin's thoughts were far too occupied by his first encounter with the Fellowship as he hurried away to consider the sartorial insult.

If the Fellowship and their mysterious leader held Ohnuhn in an iron grip as his would-be assailant suggested, it might be difficult recruiting aid from the city's thieves. Yet Davin needed information about Vytellion and his palace, information he did not have time to gather on his own. Davin did not even know what the Ohnuhnian ruler looked like! What were Vytellion's faults, his strengths, did he ride freely and easily among his subjects or did he cower within the walls of his palace surrounded by a few select guards?

Davin tapped the pouches of coins dangling at his waist and knew he could buy information, even if the leader of the Fellowship sought to bottle and sell it at a premium price. Such knowledge was usually a double-edged blade, he admitted to himself. Those willing to sell were just as willing to sell the identity of those with whom they dealt.

Perhaps it was best to provoke Ohnuhn's Fellowship no more than he already had. A cold shiver worked along his spine when he remembered his fight with Velden, the self-styled Emperor of Thieves in the sewers of Bistonia.* The last thing he wanted was to face such a vicious and odoriferous conflict here.

Davin reentered the bazaar, this time purposefully staying clear of any of the tempting purses almost beguilingly offered to him through carelessness. He saw the informal patrols moving through the market now, both soldier and thief, protecting those merchants who had paid their tributes to the Fellowship. Rather than approach another of the Brotherhood, Davin sought a thief like himself trying to work the crowd. A freelance thief would surely have ample reason to defy the Fellowship and breach Vytellion's palace.

"You!" A heavy hand clamped on his shoulder.

Davin tensed. He had ignored his back while he studied those around him. He turned to find a squad of gray-uniformed soldiers arrayed behind him.

"Why, Captain, how good of you to check on my situation. Those thieves – I think they belong to the Fellowship. Will you . . ."

"Your accent says you are not of Ohnuhn. Give over your entry visa." The officer thrust out his hand.

Davin was beginning to believe Vytellion maintained order in his city by badgering everyone to frustration over infinite numbers of permits, visas and licenses. "The thieves . . ."

Davin was again cut off. The soldiers moved around him, hands resting on the hilts of their swords. The captain demanded, "Your papers!"

In other cities, a judicious bribe often was better met than naked steel. "Here, good sir, here they are."

Davin dropped one, then another of the stolen purses into the

* See *To Demons Bound*, SWORDS OF RAEMLLYN: Book 1

soldier's outstretched hand. The guard continued to glare at him.

"How clumsy of me. The papers are here somewhere," Davin said after assessing the situation. The remaining two purses dropped into the waiting palm with weighty clunks.

"Go on," the officer said brusquely.

Davin bowed and backed away while noting how the commander carefully divided the coins among his men. Davin also saw two men he pegged as being loyal members of the Fellowship making their own mental notes of a new player in the extortion racket. He stopped at the far side of the market to watch the two signal ten others who moved in to circle the soldiers.

"So many thieves, so little money," Davin said aloud in disgust.

He remained free but found himself in the same predicament as when he entered Ohnuhn. A thief without a copper in his pocket had little chance of inducing the most fumblesome pickpocket in the city into joining a raid on Vytellion's palace.

Deciding to leave fortune to Jajhana's whims for the moment, Davin wandered Ohnuhn's streets. He drew more than one questioning gaze as passers-by recognized him as a stranger, but neither member of the Fellowship nor Vytellion's guards approached him. Strolling along in a leisurely fashion, he circled the palace situated near Ohnuhn's north gate. Swirled minarets decorated soaring towers adorned in beaten gold leaf. If blocks of alabaster fronted the city walls, Vytellion had used pearl for the interior of his fortress. The prosperity so evident in the rest of Ohnuhn apparently was triply abundant for the city's ruler.

Although hints of such treasure were tempting, the Jyotian failed to locate an easy entrance to the palace. Those seeking audience with the city's lord patiently stood in line outside the palace's south gate. For several moments, Davin watched while teams of scribes wrote the required volumes of paperwork required to pass the guards at the gate. Beggars who approached were driven away, leaving only those able to pay the exorbitant entry fees access to Ohnuhn's ruler.

Even if Davin had carried the required sums, merely speaking with Vytellion would accomplish nothing. He needed to *steal* from him.

"Psst, you," came the *sotto voce* greeting from a doorway across from the palace. "A word, sir. You look to be a newcomer to Ohnuhn. Mayhap I can aid you?"

Davin recognized the introduction to a double-deal when he heard it. Yet, other than the clothes on his back, he had nothing to lose. Perhaps there was information to be gained by listening to the offer. He sidled over to the small, ratlike man. Davin swallowed hard. The shabby man reminded him of Velden, both in appearance and odor.

"Do you hide in the city sewers?" Davin asked, an idea forming. Ohnuhn seemed an advanced culture and might have a system of interlocking sewers running beneath the city – and the palace. It would be a noisome method of gaining entry, but a quick one not likely to be guarded heavily.

"Why ask?"

"Why did you call me over?"

"I'm sore in need of money, sir. For a fee, I can get you anything you need." The man's head bobbed up and down as if agreeing with every word he uttered. "And news. Whatever you want to know, Old Hooteg can tell you – or find out for you."

"For a price," Davin said. "Why are you making this offer? To what purpose do you solicit on the street?" Davin saw a flash of fear on the man's face.

"It's like this, sir. They don't let no one earn a living in Ohnuhn. No, they're cruel. Evil! And she's worst of all."

"She? What are you saying?" Davin crowded into the doorway.

"Her!" Hooteg exclaimed, eyes widening. "You know who I mean. She's vicious, cruel and cunning. Oh, yes, smart she is. And beautiful. It makes her all the more dangerous."

"The woman leading the Fellowship?" Davin chanced a guess.

"Who else, who else?" Rheumy eyes lifted to the Jyotian. "Give me gold so I can leave this terrible place, I beg you!"

Davin experienced a momentary pang of having to cheat this pathetic wight who sought nothing more than escape. Then he remembered the pain that would be his legacy if he did not return to Gatinah with the statue Hormachi sought.

"Ten gold pieces," Davin promised. "I need to know how best to get into the palace."

"You think to steal from Vytellion? But he is a powerful mage! He will fry you with his spells!"

Davin cursed, starting with the Sitala and moving through the entire pantheon of gods and goddesses presiding over the affairs of man in Raemllyn. He gripped Hooteg's shoulders firmly and shoved the small man against the door.

"You need not accompany me. I need only know where he keeps . . ."

Davin stiffened when he heard footsteps behind him. Hooteg shouted, then in the next moment the small man grunted as he doubled over, grasping the hilt of a knife embedded in his belly.

Davin spun from the confining doorway while freeing his sword. Three thieves he recognized from the marketplace confronted him.

"You're the one who got Benk," the nearest said. "Benk said you didn't look too smart. Guess he was right, what with you still wearing the cloak you stole off his back."

"Ain't no time for talkin'," another thief insisted. "The brothers of the Fellowship avenge their own!"

With that the three drove down on the Jyotian with their own blades bared. Davin swept aside the swords and stepped back, again cursing the gods of Raemllyn. He came to Ohnuhn to steal a simple soapstone statue and found himself fighting for his life against fellow thieves within view of Vytellion's palace and that lord's legion of soldiers.

8

Davin ducked beneath a wild dagger slash meant for this throat and drove his fist into what appeared to be a meaty gut. His knuckles reverberated as though they had struck solid rock. His own startled yelp drowned in a groan when a thief with a red bandanna knotted about his head staggered backwards. The Jyotian lord swung to the side, flicked his wrist and traced the tip of his blade behind the left ankle of a thief with one front tooth missing. The man yowled when steel sliced flesh, then dropped to a knee clutching his severed hamstring.

"Hooteg," Davin said, "can you run?"

"Yes," the ratlike man answered weakly. "It would serve you well to do the same. It's a death sentence to defy Fellowship enforcers. Their mistress won't rest until she has your head!"

The beggar's warning came a mite too late, Davin thought, as he parried a sword tip that drove toward his chest. Another twist of his wrist brought his own sword point arcing back to bury two inches of gleaming steel in his assailant's shoulder.

Retreating quickly, Davin paused, gauged distance, then launched a long, slow thrust. Granite Gut, who had recovered from the Jyotian's blow to the stomach, thought to evade the lunge with a simple parry of one of the two long knives he brandished. Again Davin's wrist flicked. His sword slipped under the shorter blade and skewered the man's heart. The would-be Fellowship enforcer collapsed facedown on the street when the Jyotian adventurer yanked his sword free.

A boot hooked behind the ankle of the thief with the bleeding shoulder sent the last man standing to the ground. A hasty glance around to make certain no more of the Fellowship's thugs threatened, Davin ran after Hooteg, afraid the injured beggar was not long for this world. With so much to learn, Davin refused to be cheated by Black Qar when Hooteg could reveal so much about Ohnuhn.

Hooteg had fallen to the ground, or so Davin thought, when he skidded to avoid tripping over the beggar. The Jyotian's eyes narrowed on second glance. Half of Hooteg's body had vanished! An instant later Davin realized no magicks were at play but that the beggar wormed his way into a manhole in the street.

The warning cries from the injured Fellowship thugs and the answering shouts of Vytellion's guards rushing from the palace were all it took for Davin to choose his own course. He climbed into the hole, pulling an iron grating after him to seal the mouth. Booted feet rushed past above as Davin moved down the rungs of a ladder inset in the rock wall of the hole, wondering what injury he had caused the Sitala, those dice-throwing goddesses who ruled Fate, that within less than the span of one afternoon they turned both Ohnuhn's Fellowship of thieves and the city's guards against him.

A thick trail of blood at the bottom of the manhole led the Jyotian through the sewer tunnel to where Hooteg lay atop a pile of rags. Curled into a tight ball, the man clutched his belly with both hands vainly trying to stem the flow of blood.

"Help me, sir, help." Hooteg's eyes rolled up to Davin. "I am not ready for Black Qar's embrace. There is so much to do . . ."

". . . and so many loose purses to rob," Davin finished as he dropped to a knee and eased the man's bloody hands away from the wound.

He grimaced. Belly wounds always bled profusely, but as Davin probed he found nothing but a shallow, long cut along Hooteg's abdomen. The entrails remained intact and nothing threatened to fall from the long gash.

"You might actually survive," Davin announced with more than a hint of amazement in his voice. "Jajhana, Goddess of Luck, favors you this day. I can bind the wound and make you easy, but alas, there is little else I can do."

"A chirurgeon," moaned Hooteg. "Get me a surgeon."

"That requires money – and most likely three scribes to write out the required permission forms."

The one truth Davin had learned about Ohnuhn during his brief time in the city was that Vytellion reigned with an iron grip. A complex bureaucracy demanding endless authorization for the smallest of deeds was the foundation of his rule. Vytellion had learned that piles of paper imprison a citizenry as readily as iron bars. Unlike iron bars, the constraints of bureaucracy were far more insidious, their purpose too often hidden behind benevolent claims of establishing order and law under which freedom might flourish.

What the Lord of Ohnuhn did not control, the mistress of the Fellowship apparently did. Her approach was far more direct and time-proven – cut down any who might oppose.

Hooteg nodded. "You're right. A physician would betray us." The beggar swallowed. "But there are others who can help – others like you and me – will you find them and bring them here?"

Others! A wild scheme planted itself, germinated and blossomed in the Jyotian's mind. Madness, he warned himself, but his mind refused to stop its frenzied flight. Worse, in spite of all the obvious peril the insane scheme held, he could not shake the sensation that it would work.

"Aye," Davin replied with a nod. "Where do I find these others?"

Hooteg closed his eyes and swallowed. "You will find them near, but you must listen closely. The sewer tunnels are countless. One wrong turn and you'll be lost. First you walk . . ."

"Say more and my knife will finish what was started above!" echoed a threatening whisper through the sewer.

Davin swung about. Four people, two men, a woman and a small child of indeterminate sex peered at him through frightened eyes from a dark hole in the wall that had gone unnoticed in the dimness. Both men had knives drawn and leveled at the Jyotian thief.

"Who are you?" Davin asked.

"Riffraff such as he." The woman stepped forward, pushing past Davin to kneel beside Hooteg. She eased the beggar's hands away from the wound and studied it a few seconds. "It ain't pretty, but I got powders back at the Nest that will help."

Standing, the woman motioned to the two men who hesitated long enough to glance at Davin, then slipped their blades beneath their belts and lifted Hooteg, carrying him into the darkness beyond the hole.

"Tell me, riffraff," Davin addressed the woman when she waved the child after the men, "do you truly hope to aid him?"

She shrugged. "Why do you care?"

"Hooteg promised to help me, and I he," Davin replied. "I need a few implements – and information about the sewers of Ohnuhn."

The woman laughed, then coughed harshly. "You've come to the right place. There is none in Ohnuhn who knows the sewers better. What speck of garbage do you require? And what will you pay?"

Davin watched the woman's eyes widen while he unraveled the plan that filled his head.

"By all rights, I should draw my own knife and slit your throat for sparking hope within my heart. All you've said is madness," she said with a slow shake of her head. "But I can't decide on my own. Come with me. The others will have to judge."

"Lead the way." Davin waved toward the open hole.

Under other circumstances, Davin would have felt little more than a tingle of excitement at the impending theft. Not this time. He chewed at his lower lip in constant nervous strain and his hands shook enough to give him a moment of worry. He needed full dexterity for the ambitious assault on Vytellion's palace. The slightest mistake and he would plunge to his death – if Lord Hormachi's spell didn't work on him first.

The last two days had been spent in frantic preparation. The small band of sewer rats allied with Hooteg knew little of the palace layout. Davin had to improvise once he gained entry, but from a full day of spying, he thought he had identified Vytellion's chambers. Unless the ruler of Ohnuhn kept his valuables in a vault hidden elsewhere, the statue would be somewhere in that suite.

"We filched it, Davin," spoke the young child the Jyotian had eventually identified as a boy. "The Fellowship's gettin' mighty upset, it is."

"Their mistress is a hard-hearted bitch," piped a man who had never revealed his name. "They're out to kill now, the enforcers are. Saw Pretty Prerry caught, I did. They chopped her hands off!"

Davin shook his head. Better to die than to suffer such a fate. He had been through enough towns and provinces where the petty lords ruling had similar laws. Never had he seen a place like Ohnuhn where the very thieves enforced the law so they could steal the more.

"Let me see it." Davin took the small box the boy held out and opened one side.

Within, rested a complex array of mirrors and lenses. He began fiddling with it, taking out two of the lenses and finally achieving the result he required.

"Very good work," he complimented. "This is exactly what I will need."

"You got the rest?" a woman's voice asked.

Terita sat beside Hooteg bathing the beggar's face with a rag she wet in a bowl of clean water. The woman's powders had not healed the man's wounds as she had hoped. In the relative cleanliness of the Nest, a hand-dug cave one entered through a crack in a sewer wall, she had carefully nursed him for two days. The only solace Davin found in the man's injury was that he hadn't died. In that lay a small ray of hope.

"The pole, the ropes and the hooks," Davin said, pointing to the pile of equipment he had accumulated.

He reached for the telescoping pole and winced. He touched his chest, then scratched. A flea dined on the succulent feast the Jyotian's body presented. Squeezing, Davin pulled the offending, blood-engorged insect off his flesh and cast it away.

The vermin's bite reminded him of the short time that remained until the yellow ring ignited on his chest. He hoped possession of the statue would be adequate to counter Hormachi's spell.

"It's nightfall," came an echo down a distant sewer pipe. "The palace has been flushed for the day."

"Then I go now," Davin stood and announced to his small band of burglars. "I will return with the information needed to steal all you can carry from the palace."

Davin hoped this was not a lie. He felt some respect for these dwellers in the underworld. Their ambitions were limited, none wanting more than to amass enough coin to leave Ohnuhn. If he could deliver them this small gift, he would.

If not, he wanted the statue in his possession as quickly as possible.

Davin carefully strung the rope about his waist, tucked the

collapsing pole into a back pack with the lens contraption, then bent double and made his way through the hidden ways below Ohnuhn's clean, swept streets. Knee-deep in sludge, the way quickly grew more odoriferous. Sewer gases rose to choke him. Davin tied a cloth over his nose and kept moving, following the path mapped out for him over the past two days. Now and then he had to avoid the sudden rush of waste, but never did the sewage rise above knee level.

Before midnight, floodgates would open and bring forth a roaring surge of water to flush the city sewers completely. For the moment, though, only the palace had been so cleansed. This afforded him his best chance of penetrating Vytellion's security and reaching the lord's quarters.

Davin twisted about and found a sloping tunnel leading upward. He thought he had come far enough for this to be the palace kitchens. Slipping and sliding along the grimy tube, he scooted upward until he found a locked hatch.

Working in almost complete darkness, fearing the striking of even a single spark because of the sewer gases, Davin labored to thwart the mechanism on the hatch. A single click announced he had succeeded. Sliding the hatch to one side, he stuck his filthy head into the kitchen, worrying that cooks and scullery workers might still be present. Distant clacking of huge pots came to his attentive ears, but he saw no one. He shoved through the hatch, pushed it back into position to hide his entry point. He glanced from side to side as he drew a steadying breath. He was in the palace, now all was a matter of cautious exploration.

Laughter echoed along the corridors and down into the kitchens. Davin smiled. Mayhap Vytellion entertained this night. If so, it made the thievery all the easier. The lord would be occupied with his guests rather than gloating over his possessions.

Slowly working through the lower levels, Davin eventually realized he could not hope to walk to Vytellion's chambers unnoticed. As in the city streets, the palace corridors were diligently patrolled. Nor did the guardsmen appear the least bit drowsy.

Davin had anticipated such a happenstance. Finding a doorway leading to an inner courtyard, Davin slipped into the cool night. Stars gave wan illumination as thin clouds blew across their faces.

Davin Anane pressed close to a stone wall and worked toward a tower across the yard. Earlier that day, from a vantage on the roof across the square, he had decided the tower provided the easiest access to Vytellion's quarters. Unlike other structures within the palace walls, the tower sported tiny outjuttings of stone ornamentation.

"Pliaton, God of Thieves, aid me this night," muttered Davin, testing the stone projections.

He found two outjuts thick enough to support his weight and pulled himself up. Like a fly on the wall, Davin climbed the rocky exterior until he reached the sharply slanted roof. He tumbled over a small lip, panting from the exertion.

Then he cursed. Pliaton had not smiled on him. Perhaps the Sitala, in their ever-willful ways, had cast the die against him. The angle from his distant spypoint had told him the distance between tower and Vytellion's quarters amounted to little more than a long jump. Now he realized even if he sprouted wings, he would have difficulty crossing the chasm.

The Jyotian frowned when he gauged the distance at more than ten full strides. Bracing his feet on the slippery tower roof, he began unwrapping the rope from his middle. He had used grappling hooks successfully in Gatinah; he could repeat the toss, though this was half again the distance.

Affixing the hooks, Davin began the slow unwinding of the rope as he whirled it above his head. He cast.

And missed!

The iron hooks clattered loudly against the stone tower wall beneath him. He quickly reeled it in, then peered over the edge to see if the palace guardsmen had noticed. Nothing stirred in the courtyard opening from the kitchens.

Davin tossed again. And again and again before the hooks founds purchase high on the roof of Vytellion's keep. It was then the thief realized there was nothing strong enough on the tower roof to serve as anchor for the end of the rope he held.

Desperation in the form of a yellow ring drawn on his chest kept him from turning back in defeat. Instead, he tightly grasped the end of the rope in both hands. There was but one way to reach Vytellion's chambers, and he had to take it.

"Yehseen take you all!" Davin hissed through clenched teeth

as he stood and stepped off the roof.

He did not care whom he cursed – Hormachi, Vytellion, the thieving Huata, the Fellowship and its mysterious leader – one and all could be damned. Doubly damned, he thought while he swung through the air to slam into Vytellion's tower keep. Boot first with legs extended to absorb the impact, he hit and almost lost hold on the rope.

Yet he did hold and began to climb upward. He ignored the burning muscles in shoulder and arm, fearing the far greater fire Hormachi embedded in his breast. With no chance of reaching a window from his present angle, he kept climbing until he pulled himself onto the roof of Vytellion's residence. Davin stretched out on his back and closed his eyes to let his heart slowly subside in its runaway pace.

The luxury of a few minutes rest did not leave him feeling refreshed, but it allowed him to find enough strength to stand and free the grapnel hook. Walking around the circular roof, he reached a spot above the room he had identified as Vytellion's chambers. The Jyotian pulled free the sectioned pole and lens box from his pack. A few more seconds passed and the pole was telescoped to full length with the box attached to its end.

Davin lowered the pole cautiously, twisting it now and again to keep the box's open faces turned inward and upward. He smiled when the box edged down past the stone lintel. The image reflected through lens and mirror reflected out of the box and to his eye. A complete view of the room was safely his.

Slowly turning the pole, he scanned the room and its contents. His heart sank when he saw this was nothing more than an antechamber. Drawing back the pole and its viewer, Davin worked his way around the tower to the next window. Dim light flickered within this chamber. A smile awoke on the thief's face.

On a table at the far side of the room stood a small gray-white soapstone statue. The figure was completely out of place in the opulently decorated sleeping chamber. Davin had no doubt this was the statue Hormachi desired. It had to be!

Davin drew back his pole and lens device, placing them on the slanting roof. He drove the grappling hook through the roof's shingles to find a supporting timber underneath. He tugged twice to be sure it was secured, then the thief tied the rope around his waist.

Grasping the edge of the roof, he dropped over the side to dangle fifty feet from the ground and above the window. He carefully lowered himself to the window ledge. Gentle taps with his toes kicked open the glass-paned window.

He lowered himself another few feet and balanced on the sill. All he could see in the deserted room was the statue. His heart sank a little when he got a better look at it. No precious gems studded its simple exterior nor was gold leaf in evidence. And artistry was lacking, the image being crudely hacked from the soft stone.

This was not the time to question why Hormachi desired a squat, ugly figure, Davin warned himself. His task was to steal it as quickly as possible, then make good his escape.

He dropped lower to sit on the window ledge and reached for the rope about his waist. Davin swayed, then almost fell.

His chest exploded in agony. The first wave drove into his chest like a heated knife. The second wave swirled inside him, twisting and grinding. He gritted his teeth to keep from crying out as Hormachi's damnable fire raged within his breast. Eyes blurring and heart threatening to explode, Davin tried to rip off his tunic and tear the yellow ring from his flesh.

Then paroxysms of real agony seized body and mind. Writhing amid the volcanic eruption of white-hot torment, Davin fell from the window and plummeted toward the ground below.

9

Somewhere beyond the lashing whips of pain that ignited in the core of Davin's soul, he sensed his body crashing into the stone tower.

Sensed, not felt!

There was nothing to feel beyond the most excruciating agony he had ever endured. Hormachi had given him a taste of the torment when he had ignited the magic-born red ring back in Gatinah. The yellow circle now tore at Davin's sanity, threatening to hurl him across the tenuous boundaries of reason into realms ruled by Yu-Vatruk, Black Qar's demon of nightmares.

"Father Yehseen," Davin moaned, unable to hold back the voice of desperation. "Stop the pain! By all that is holy, please, stop it!"

Whether the patriarch of Raemllyn's deities listened and granted a boon or Hormachi's spell merely ran its course, the Jyotian could not say. All he knew, amid heaving labored breaths, was that the pain subsided and his swirling vision gradually cleared. Nor was he certain how long he dangled limply in midair before the bite of the rope around his waist returned his mind to his precarious position.

Cautiously, he cast a glance below and above. Like a puppet with all but one string severed, he slowly swung from side to side. That he still lived and his rope held was more than he had the right to hope for.

Nor was it time to question fortune's grace. Feebly, he shifted to stretch out his legs and finally wedged his toes beneath a projecting stone. He used legs and toes to inch toward the wall until his fingers groped out and found purchase. Anchored by toes and fingers, he righted himself and allowed the rope to support his weight while strength crept back into his quivering muscles.

A vibration like the hint of a distant whisper running through the rope drew Davin's gaze upward. His eyes went wide. At the window, knife in hand, a guardsman sawed feverishly at the Jyotian's lifeline.

"Stop! Don't!" Davin hugged close to the tower, frantically seeking holds for hands and feet. "I'm repairing stonework!"

The preposterous lie brought a wide grin to the soldier's lips. He cut faster.

The last strand of slender hemp rope parted. Davin clutched desperately to stingy fingerholds the rock offered. No amount of cursing or gritting of teeth or sweat trickling from his brow could stop his fingers from slipping from the tiny crevasses.

Davin hurled backward from the tower and once more plummeted toward the ground.

As bone-jarring as the impact was, it did not walk hand in hand with death. Nor did jagged rock rip his flesh or hard-packed earth shatter his spine. Instead, the last son of the House of Anane found he had landed squarely atop large bales of cloth, silk from the rich feel of it. But Davin had neither the time nor inclination to confirm what his fingertips sensed.

Distant shouts echoed toward him!

Davin rolled to the left and dropped to the ground, landing hard, but on his feet. Dazed from Hormachi's fire and a fifty-foot fall, his mind focused on a single thought – refuge! He dared not confront Vytellion's guardsmen face to face. Arms and legs quaking from the ravaging torment that had gripped them seconds ago, a blind kitten would have a better chance in a fight than he would.

Davin took three steps before his legs melted to rubber and collapsed under him.

The cries of alarm grew closer.

The Jyotian thief did the only thing he could. He pushed to his knees and crawled toward the dark crack of an open door.

He was still on hands and knees when Vytellion's elite guardsmen poured into the small courtyard, swords drawn and bellowing contradictory orders in a chaotic scramble to find the palace intruder.

Tumbling headfirst down a dark flight of steps into the kitchen did little to renew the life Hormachi's hex had drained from Davin's body. At the foot of the staircase to the lower kitchen the thief sat and held his head in weak, shaking hands, grateful the

Sitala had seen fit not to break his neck in the unexpected fall.

When the sounds of the search above grew close, he slunk away, avoiding the wandering kitchen staff more by sheer luck than skill as he found his way to the grate leading to the sewers. Pushing the hatch aside, Davin hiked his feet up, then levered himself into the small tube leading downward. With the grate back in place, Davin hung in smelly darkness and listened to those who entered the kitchen.

"Where is he? A thief! He came through here!"

"I saw no one, Commander. No one's been through *my* kitchen this night who doesn't belong!" The smug voice turned churlish when it became obvious the soldier was not going to give up the hunt on a mere cook's word.

"Do you think I hide this nobody under my apron! Pah! Look where you like, look under tables, look up my arse, but do not disturb the bouillabaisse. It must simmer all night to be ready for tomorrow's supper."

Davin silently thanked the unknown chef for his intransigence. But the Jyotian froze when the metal hatch overhead rang loudly.

"Where's this lead?"

"Garbage. Do you wish to poke among the offal, Commander? Enjoy yourself, but be warned. The stench can overcome someone with your fine sensibilities."

Davin clung to the hatch's inner locking mechanism, praying to one god and goddess after another for deliverance. The voices in the kitchen softened, then died to be replaced by simple kitchen sounds.

Caring not which of Raemllyn's endless deities watched over him this night, Davin released his grip and slid noisily down the tube to land with a liquid *plop* amid sludge afloat with bits and pieces of discarded vegetables. Gagging, barely able to stand, he tried to recall being in a more humiliating situation and could not.

Two weeks! The thought repeated in his mind when he began to trudge toward the asylum of the Nest. Time ran out. Only two more weeks remained before Hormachi's vile magicks stole his life – his very soul!

Before then, in only one week, he must endure the torture meted out by the violet ring. He did not doubt that tonight's agony was only a taste of what the violet ring would bring.

* * *

"They seek you everywhere!" Hooteg whined as he pushed up
from his bed of rags to his elbows. "My friends tell me you have a
reward on your head."

"No one but you – and your friends – know who entered the
palace last night," Davin said with an arched eyebrow.

He winced when he started to turn. He had not broken any
bones in his tumble from Vytellion's tower, but every muscle in
his body felt as though it had been doubly knotted. Of greater
affront was the stench of the sewers that clung to him and his
clothing. Least offensive was the ineffable bouquet of rotting
garbage acquired in his escape from the kitchen. That overpowering odor threatened to choke him with each breath he drew.

"Fifty pieces of gold – that's what they offer." Hooteg's eyes
narrowed as though he evaluated the Jyotian like another man
might judge a side of beef hanging in a butcher's shop.

"I saved your life," Davin reminded the ratlike beggar-thief,
although Hooteg's unchanged expression said that the act carried
little weight. "Also, you can never leave Ohnuhn with a mere fifty
gold pieces. You need more, far more, and only I can deliver it to
you."

"You failed last night."

Hooteg sat upright on his mattress of greasy rags, propping
himself against a dirt wall. He still clutched his belly where the
knife had opened him like a rotted fruit.

While the rat-thief's injuries kept him bedridden, Davin viewed
the man as little threat. When Hooteg began to heal, he would
scurry to the nearest guardsman to point a finger at the man who
dared intrude on Vytellion's inner sanctum. Fifty gold pieces were
more than Hooteg could ever steal or beg on his own. As to the
others who called this cave their home, he trusted Hooteg would
keep them in line. After all, the rat man would not want to lose
the reward to another.

"So close," murmured Davin when his mind turned back to his
defeat.

He had been within a half-dozen paces of the statue and had
failed to take it! Worse, he now knew mere possession would not
relieve him of Hormachi's damnable spell. The lord of Gatinah
used magicks to flay the soul as others applied the whip to the

backs of their slaves. Davin could only guess at the agony that would consume his body when the violet ring ignited. He had to steal the statue within the next day or two to make the return journey to Gatinah before the remainder of the week allotted him passed.

"How will you filch this bauble?" Hooteg's eyes widened a bit, but remained locked to the Jyotian. "How will you steal it now that every patrol in the city has been alerted to watch for you?"

"I . . ."

"And how will you bring us the fabulous amounts of gold and gems you promised?" Hooteg continued, oblivious to Davin's attempt to speak. "That is as important to us as your pitiful example of art is to you."

"I understand," Davin interjected when the rat man finally paused to suck in a breath. "Concern yourself with your healing. Let me deal with Vytellion's guards."

"What of the Fellowship?" Hooteg shifted his weight, his face going white with strain when he moved. "They want your head on a pike. Are you going to accept their offer?"

"What has changed? The Fellowship has been after me since I bloodied their thugs." What troubled him more were the exact terms of the pact that obviously existed between Vytellion and Ohnuhn's society of thieves. There might be a way to turn one against . . .

His thoughts skidded to a stop as the beggar's words penetrated his mind. "What did you say about an offer from the Fellowship?"

"You haven't heard?" Hooteg blinked. "They want you to join. It's an apprenticeship they offer you."

Davin laughed in real amusement. His ribs hurt and his ears rang from the effort, but the notion of him working as an apprentice struck him as absurd. How many of the Fellowship ever ventured so close to the heart of Vytellion's wealth?

"What do they want with me, a foreigner come to steal the riches of their city?"

"Their queen bitch seeks to recruit only the finest in Ohnuhn and banish or kill the rest."

Davin discerned the bitterness in Hooteg's voice. The diminutive thief lacked the skill to be invited into the ranks of the city's elite pilferers.

"Tell me of this invitation," Davin urged. "It intrigues me strangely."

"Why strangely?" demanded Hooteg.

Davin abruptly came alert. If Vytellion offered fifty gold pieces for the Jyotian's arrest, what might the mistress of the Fellowship offer for Davin's death? "Have I made such an impression on this mystery woman who desires to control all Ohnuhn? I doubt it."

"Will you join the Fellowship?" Hooteg's sullen tone only heightened Davin's suspicion the beggar was involved somehow in a plot with the Fellowship to put an end to a certain Jyotian's life.

"They have shown me little hospitality," Davin replied with a shrug. "But I keep an open mind. Let us say I am willing to discuss the matter. Nothing more."

"Caution," Hooteg said, as if the notion had never occurred to him. "A useful trait for staying alive."

"It's served me well. Tell me of the Fellowship's offer." Davin's voice carried an edge to it that brought Hooteg up short.

"Sunset, at the rear of the mapmaker's store on the Way of the Dove."

"Is that a street?"

"The one running out of the marketplace toward the north gate. You are to bring tribute with you. Ten coins." Hooteg licked his lips as if lying came unnaturally to him.

From all Davin had seen, the weaving of falsehoods was part and parcel of the ratlike thief's existence. The only reason to do such a poor job of it lay in his injury and possibly the realization that the Fellowship was likely to turn on one who served them. Threats, too, might carry more weight than the promise of riches. Davin wondered which the Fellowship had used on Hooteg.

Bidding Hooteg farewell, Davin left the Nest to move through the maze of sewers to a manhole that led to the streets of Ohnuhn above. *Close, so very close.* The sour taste of failure filled his mouth as the image of the soapstone statue sitting on the table formed in his mind to taunt him again. In less than two weeks, the Sitala seemed to conspire against him at every turn. He had fallen from dreams of possessing a king's ransom in jewels to scurrying through subterranean Ohnuhn like a sewer rat. For a man who considered himself the master thief of all Raemllyn, the abrupt change in worldly status was humbling.

Humility was a cloak that sat ill on Davin Anane's shoulders.

Rather than the city's main avenues, the Jyotian slipped from alley to alley. He feared nothing from Vytellion's guardsmen since none had got close enough to see his face. However, the odor that surrounded him was certain to draw unwanted attention.

A bathhouse with its steaming waters and perfumed soaps offered a solution to that problem. When Davin stepped from the establishment, he rubbed a hand over cleanly shaved cheeks and chin and thoroughly savored the aromas of soap and oils that now clung to both himself and his laundered clothing. The clink of coins, generously provided by the careless patrons of the bathhouse who left their purses in plain sight while pampered by masseur, in a money pouch far too long empty, bolstered the Jyotian's flagging confidence.

A brief meal, a leisurely stroll past the palace, then a return to the market were enough to plant the seeds of a new method of gaining entry to the palace. But try as he did, Davin could not fathom the reason for the theft of the soapstone statue. Any of a dozen works of art on display in the bazaar were worth more. Either the crude carving contained an item of value hidden behind its ugly exterior or Hormachi and Vytellion waged a war of stark boredom, each seeking to win prestige through meaningless games.

The magicks Hormachi employed to achieve victory, however, pointed to more than meaningless games. Davin's right hand rose to his chest where the violet ring weighed him down as if it had turned into lead.

He shook his head. Time was too precious to squander in attempts to decipher Hormachi's motivation. Better would be another walk by Vytellion's palace to confirm the scheme germinating in his mind was planted in fertile soil. He glanced around and frowned. The sun dipped low on the horizon. The afternoon was gone. If he intended to hear the Fellowship out, it was time to find the Way of the Dove.

With a minimum of searching, Davin located the mapmaker's

shop and noted its three doors. The main entrance stood wide and inviting while the remaining two at the side and rear appeared locked. An army of cutthroats might lie in wait for him inside, and no matter how many times he walked around the shop, he would never see them.

Since subtlety proved fruitless, Davin took a direct approach and walked to the front door to peer inside. Rays of a setting sun angled across the mapmaker's cabinets, displaying his wares. The Jyotian slipped a spare lens left from his periscope box out of a pocket, held it between forefinger and thumb while he focused the sunlight on the corner of a parchment map spread atop a table just beyond the threshold. The instant the map began to smolder, Davin hastily walked across the street and waited.

"Fire! The shop is afire!" Cries of alarm came from the shop.

The side door flew wide and four thugs clanking with an assortment of weapons ran from the building. From the rear of the store came two more of the Fellowship's would-be assassins, one Davin recognized from the attack outside Vytellion's palace. The Jyotian pursed his lips and shook his head. The enigmatic mistress of the Fellowship proved less than inventive in her plan to ambush him.

"Fire!" rose a cry a block down the street.

Somehow, the sight of uniformed firefighters charging through the market did not surprise Davin. In Ohnuhn, Lord Vytellion ruled by controlling the smallest detail of daily life.

"Back, move back!" shouted a stout fireman bedecked with three lines of medals and ribbons on his chest. "To the side, to the side! Make way!"

Davin allowed himself to be pushed back with the gawking onlookers who crowded about for a glimpse of flame. Three strides back and the heel of his right boot landed squarely amid a puddle of black tar. He twisted in an attempt to free his boot; the sticky tar held fast. Cursing as the crowd pressed closer, he bent over to grasp his leg and yank it free.

He did not see the blanket that whirled through the air and dropped over him like a net. The loop of rope that followed the heavy blanket snapped tight to pin his arms to his side. Four more loops and the Jyotian was bound shoulder to ankle.

Davin cried out to no avail. The blanket, the orders of firemen and voices of onlookers drowned his shouts.

Strong arms scooped him up, blanket, rope and all, and dumped him down hard. Wood planking creaked under his weight, then groaned with a sudden jolt. If the uneven rocking and the sound of wooden wheels on cobblestones were not enough to tell the thief he now lay in the back of a cart, the braying of a mule was.

Damn! The thugs hidden in the mapmaker's shop had not been the trap, Davin realized as he struggled in vain to free the ropes around him. They had merely been the bait with which the Fellowship's mistress set her snare – a snare the Jyotian had walked into without so much as a blink of his eyes!

10

The thought of riding to his death trussed up like a pig ready for the slaughterhouse gnawed at Davin's brain while he struggled to free himself from blanket and rope. It took no more than a few minutes for the Jyotian to realize there was no quick escape from the coils looped about his body.

He could, however, reach the hilt of his dirk with his right hand, and with a couple of twists and squirms he managed to ease the blade free of its sheath. He caught himself before thrusting the knife through the blanket. There was too much risk that his abductors might notice the dagger before he freed himself.

Nor did he see any wisdom in waiting until the blanket was pulled from over his head and leaping on whomever waited. Whoever waited would surely outnumber a single Jyotian.

Instead, he flopped to his belly and continued to twist and turn as though trying to squirm free of his bonds. A single slash opened the blanket and allowed the dirk's tip to dig into the dry rot-riddled wood of the boards beneath him. The splintery wood parted readily as Davin whittled out a hole wide enough for hand and arm.

No man could slip through the narrow hole, but it opened access to axle and wheels beneath. Blindly, Davin thrust out with blade and fingers to locate the target he needed. His heart doubled its pace when he realized it lay within reach of a strong stab – and a single thrust was all he would get.

Pulling his arm back through the hole, the Jyotian maintained his charade of fighting his bonds while sawing through three-fourths of a rope loop. If his plan worked, escape hinged on his ability to toss aside blanket and ropes in the blink of an eye.

With a deep breath to quell the pounding in his temples, Davin stuck his arm through the hole again and once more located his target. He sucked in another breath, then thrust down with every iota of strength his confined position allowed. The blade drove between cart and spinning wheel spoke.

Immediately, the dagger was yanked from his grip. There was no time for a whispered prayer that he had struck true. A sound like a hammer against wood announced he had accomplished his goal. The dirk's hilt slammed hard against the bottom of the cart, forcing the blade deeper into the wheel.

The cart lurched to the left when the jammed wheel abruptly stopped turning. Cries of dismay rose around the Jyotian, followed by the sounds of chaotic scrabbling, and finally the solid thuds and groans of his captors spilling from cart to ground.

Although the Fellowship's ruffians were unprepared for the sudden halt, Davin was. He kicked hard against the partially severed loop, felt the rope snap. He shook free of the blanket, stood and vaulted over the side of the cart.

"He's gettin' away!" A scar-faced cutthroat with a wickedly bladed knife charged the Jyotian. "Our mistress will have our livers fried with onions for breakfast if we let him . . ."

The windy statement ended in a gusty rush as breath left the assassin's lungs for all time. Davin's sword thrust skewered the man's chest and drove straight through until the bloody tip protruded from his back.

A hasty backstep allowed the Jyotian adventurer to parry a tentative dagger thrust and kick out. His boot connected with his attacker's kneecap, dropping the man into the street to roll and yowl as he grasped his injured leg. A sliding shuffle to the left and Davin danced away from another of his abductors rushing him with a drawn knife. He slapped the flat of his blade onto the hand of the fourth man. The thug's knife fell to the cobblestones with a metallic clang.

The second gorilla staggered to his feet to test his knee. Davin kicked out again, this time planting his boot squarely between the man's legs. The thug's howls doubled when he again crumpled to the ground. On a single leg, the Jyotian swordsman spun and pressed the tip of his blade against the jugular vein of the thug who bent to recover his long knife from the street. The man blanched, dropped to one side and rolled clear.

The men who enforced the Fellowship's orders were far less clever than the mistress who gave those orders, Davin realized. While uncertain who ensnared him in blanket and rope, he wagered it had been one of Ohnuhn's firemen. He would also have given odds that the brain behind the Fellowship had set a series of traps meant to capture or kill him no matter how he approached the mapmaker's shop. His respect for the mysterious woman who pulled the strings of Ohnuhn's Fellowship of thieves mounted with each passing second.

"I have no wish to whittle down the Fellowship one man at a time," Davin said as he allowed the thug to recover the long knife. "I've skills to offer your mistress."

In a crouch, the thug glared at the Jyotian, then spat on the ground. "How is your skill at dying?"

When the man charged, Davin sidestepped and planted a foot on the thug's backside to shove him into the gorilla who once more attempted to rise. The two sprawled in a tangle of flailing arms and legs.

Hearing a chorus of angry shouts, the Jyotian twisted to the right. A small army of reinforcements turned a corner a block away and ran headlong toward him. Returning sword to sheath, Davin shrugged at the two men on the ground.

"Tell your mistress that we shall meet one day – on my terms."

With that the Jyotian spun around and darted down an alley. He found an open door and dashed through it. An iron locking bar fell securely into place behind him. Never slowing his pace, he made his way through a cobbler's shop and shot into the street in front of the store. There a brisk stride soon lost him in the flow of foot traffic moving along Ohnuhn's avenues.

It would be only a few seconds before the Fellowship realized its mistake. By then it would be too late. Whistling a jaunty tune, Davin cut back to the cart that had held him but minutes ago. He found his dagger and tugged it from the wheel, then continued along the street. His gaze shifted from side to side to survey the women who passed.

If the Fellowship's mistress had been present to watch the abduction, he could not locate her. From all Hooteg and the other men at the Nest said about her, the Fellowship's nameless leader was of unsurpassed beauty. While more than one of Ohnuhn's passing women caught and held Davin's eye, none possessed "unsurpassed beauty".

He frowned with the realization that he wasted time better spent elsewhere and in far less open surroundings. The Fellowship's mistress had proved clever. If she appeared in public, he suspected it would be with a full company of armed guards to protect her. No army of bodyguards enclosed woman or man.

Abandoning his futile search, Davin whirled and vanished into the back ways of Ohnuhn. The Fellowship's cutthroats knew their city better than he, but Davin had an innate sense of camouflage and used the gathering shadows well. There was no thief anywhere in Raemllyn who moved better or more clandestinely than the Jyotian freebooter. It took almost an hour, but he eventually slipped into a manhole and found his way to the Nest.

Hooteg's eyes went wide in surprise. Sweat popped out on his forehead.

"Davin? H-how? We heard the Fellowship had kidnapped you!"

"I had a brief encounter with a couple of would-be assassins. It amounted to little." The Jyotian pinned the beggar with his icy gaze. "I killed them."

The iron edge Davin put into his voice had the desired effect. Hooteg visibly cowered and his face paled two shades.

"A – and the palace?"

"I have another plan," Davin answered. "Assemble everyone in an hour. Then I will show you – and them – how to gain enough coin to leave Ohnuhn."

"Leave?" Hooteg's voice firmed, yet his eyes still stared at Davin with a mixture of fear and awe.

Davin doubted anyone who spat in the face of both Lord Vytellion and the Fellowship lived long. He had offended both grievously but had no intention of meeting Black Qar any time soon.

"Fetch them now." Davin sank to a pile of rags and kept from moaning while Hooteg signaled a man out of the Nest.

Davin closed his eyes and released a heavy breath. His body felt as if he had been beaten repeatedly by expert torturers. Between his fall from the tower and the ignition of Hormachi's magic fire ring, he was certain every muscle in his body was bruised or kinked.

"They come. They will listen – and obey," Hooteg's voice drew the Jyotian from a half-sleep.

The tone of the beggar's voice was filled with more than simple awe; it was reverent. Davin suppressed the smile that sought to climb to his lips. He had no liking for using fear as a goad, but Hooteg's treachery was obvious. If it took fear to command these sewer rats, then fear would be his whip.

"Listen carefully." Davin sat up, maintaining the charade that he had been lost in thought rather than treading near slumber. His gaze scanned the grime-smeared faces that stared at him in apprehension. "You will go to the marketplace in one hour when the shopkeepers begin to lock their doors for the night . . ."

Davin Anane carefully outlined a massive assault on a dozen profitable stores in unison and in force, and designed to produce the maximum response from Vytellion's guardsmen.

Hooteg and the others milled through the thinning crowds in the bazaar. Davin lounged to one side of the market, gazing at a sky veiled in the purples and deep blues of early evening. His attention returned to the changing of the guard at Vytellion's palace across the street from the shadow-darkened doorway where he stood.

A moment's diversion, he thought. All he needed was a moment to distract the guards and he would slip into the grounds. From that point Davin estimated he would have a quarter of an hour to reach Lord Vytellion's chamber and steal the statue. After that the guardsmen would grow wise to his ruse in the market.

Davin's head turned toward the bazaar as he pursed his lips. Why were things so quiet? It was time for—

"Thieves!" A lone man ran out toward the palace gate. "An army of thieves is attacking the bazaar! Call out the guard. Call out the guard!"

"Who demands the guard?" shouted a sentry at the gate when the man skidded to an uneven halt.

"Lieutenant of the Guard Sehik – the lieutenant told me to bring the order!"

The sentry turned and called out and, in turn, was answered by shouts from the garrison. Davin smiled in pleasure. Dozens of armed foot soldiers rushed from the palace, followed by a company of mounted lancers. And behind them came another, larger, detachment of guards.

The confusion inherent in such movement was perfect for a single man with a dark cloak drawn around his shoulders to slip into the palace. Davin crossed the street quickly and pressed against the wall near a guard post, his heart pounding while he waited for the right moment. It came. He stepped through the gate while the sentries watched their companions rush toward the bazaar. Without glancing behind him, the thief strode briskly to the palace's main entrance, opened a large wooden door and stepped inside.

Demeanor often provided the best cloak and was the one the Jyotian employed when he strode down the long hallway that stretched before him. He attempted to appear as though he belonged in the palace, that he had every right to walk through Vytellion's stronghold.

At least, that was his outward pose. However, the echo of his boot heels on the polished marble floor set his pulse racing. His hand lifted to rest on the hilt of his sword. Fear crept into his mind and swirled about. Each breath he drew was like a resounding wheeze. The beat of his heart came heavier than the pounding of a drum. Sweat prickled over his body and his mouth turned to cotton. His eyes darted from side to side searching the shadows for—

The Jyotian halted abruptly. He bit the inside of his cheek to keep from screaming out as a wave of abject terror washed over him. Try as he might, he could not continue. Taking even one more step would bring stark insanity!

No!

He filled his lungs and exhaled to force himself back from the precipice of madness. The horror, the fear, the terror were not his. They were spell-born! Vytellion employed a mage to work these magicks to guard his palace.

"Nothing will happen. Nothing will happen. The statue. I must reach it." Davin spoke aloud to force away the fear.

In spite of sweat pouring down his face in rivulets, he edged forward. Concentrating on a mental image of the statue helped but did not stop the breaking waves of terror that blurred the Jyotian's eyesight and set his legs quaking. The instant he passed beneath an arch at the end of the hall, the blanket of rootless fear lifted.

Before the grin of success was fully born on the adventurer's face, his gray eyes narrowed. A wet sound like the sloshing of some viscous liquid rolled down the shorter hallway he had entered. Davin swallowed hard when he saw small holes in the plain walls on both sides open.

Long, gray, glutinous tendrils flowed from the walls to ripple and snap like whips. Down the wall the slimy snakes writhed until they reached the floor where they pooled like gelatinous oil for a moment only. In the blink of an eye the pools metamorphosed into undulating lumps of featureless gray ooze.

What he faced was totally unknown to the last son of the House of Anane, but he sensed that each of the blobs pulsed with raw power that could easily maim, if not kill, a man.

As if possessing the sense of smell, the pulsating lumps slithered forward toward the Jyotian. No matter how he turned or tried to dodge the creeping masses of ooze, they unerringly followed his movements.

Davin's gaze darted about the corridor in a desperate search for table or chair. There was no furniture on which he might vault to escape. He jumped to one side, then the other. Rather than confusing the flowing blobs, the slime oozed together when they touched and formed a larger mass.

The Jyotian stepped back two strides, then halted. The pulsing globs stretched across the hall now as though they herded him toward the main entryway. At least that was the way it appeared until the ends of that line arched forward in an attempt to encircle the thief.

Davin drew his sword and poked at the nearest blob. Rather than injure it, the sword was simply subsumed. The tip disappeared into the heaving body and when Davin drew his weapon back was astounded to find the steel had been eaten away. The Jyotian leaped back as the gray blob surged up the length of polished metal toward his hand. He dropped the sword. A sucking noise marked the complete dissolution of his weapon a moment before the oozing monster once again advanced on him.

Davin retreated into the corridor of nameless fears that had tried to burrow into his soul but moments ago. This time he barely noticed the niggling doubts that wriggled into his mind – his legs moved too fast to spare a moment for baseless terrors. All too

real horrors slithered after him with inexorable speed, never
hastening their pace and never slowing for an instant.

Skidding to a halt outside the palace door, Davin sighted the
four sentries by the gate at the same time as they saw him. The
soldiers turned, weapons ready. His own sword dissolved, the
best defense the Jyotian could manage was a hard swallow.

One guard peered past Davin into the corridor and pointed.
"The hounds! The lord's hounds are loosed!"

All four guards backed away then spun about and ran headlong
for their garrison.

Davin did not question their reaction. He darted through the
open gate and into Ohnuhn's night-shadowed streets. Six full
furlongs he ran until he finally stumbled to a halt and leaned
against the wall of a bakery, gulping for air.

A horrified shriek caused him to jerk up his head.

A curse worked its way over his lips.

Two huge gray gelatinous blobs slowly rolled along the street
after him. Ahead of them, man, woman and beast scattered, all
crying out in fear.

Hounds! Davin now understood what the guard meant. The
smaller blobs in the palace had joined to form two creatures that
undulated to the height of a man's waist. Nor did the Jyotian
doubt that the two masses of ooze were on the trail of his scent.

As he had done outside Vytellion's stronghold, Davin ran! He
dodged into one alley and out another, climbed stairs to a tiled
roof and there leaped to an adjoining building, then to another
and another. Stairs on the side of the fifth led him back to the
street.

Still, he found the gray globs on his trail. They never increased
their speed beyond that of a fast walk, but they never slowed
either. They were implacable, and Davin realized that no matter
how he ran, they would follow now that they had his scent.

And should he rest too long in one spot, they would feast. Not
upon the cold steel of a sword this time but on his own flesh.

Turning away from the demons of ooze, Davin kept moving,
eyes and mind alert for anything that might serve to throw the
damnable creatures off his trail. Ten minutes passed before he
realized he was not the only one who hurried through Ohnuhn's
streets. A woman here, two men there, met at a corner then

hastened on toward others who gathered and moved toward the western portion of the city.

The Fellowship! Davin recognized two cutthroats he had faced earlier. A smile touched his lips when he slowed to catch his breath again. Apparently, Hooteg's sewer rats had done well this eve. And those thefts had not been sanctioned. That meant an emergency meeting of the Fellowship and plans for tightening an already iron-fisted hold on both merchant and freelance thief.

A glance over his shoulder to assure himself that Vytellion's hell-spawned hounds were not in sight, Davin sank into the shadows and crept quietly after the group of thieves ahead of him. Eventually, they turned down a street appropriately named Avenue of the Cracksmen. The Jyotian reached the corner, paused and peered after the small group as they greeted two men standing sentry outside the doorway of a two-story warehouse.

The unmistakable sucking sound of approaching slime was all the Jyotian freebooter needed to make up his mind. The time to introduce himself formally to the Fellowship's mastermind had arrived. He would also bring a pair of uninvited guests to the meeting.

He was three strides from the guards outside the warehouse when he recognized the taller – the would-be abductor he had hobbled with a well-placed kick to the knee. The man still favored the leg as he shifted his position.

"Has the meeting started?" Davin called when he reached the two, knowing it was too late to retreat, not that Vytellion's hounds left an avenue to retreat down.

"Half-hour back. You're late." The tall guard frowned. "Who . . ."

He never finished. Davin stepped forward and slammed a knee into an exposed groin. The man doubled over, retching violently. The second guard reached for his dagger and went down with hand on hilt as the Jyotian delivered an uppercut direct to the point of his chin.

Stooping, Davin snatched the unconscious man's sword from its scabbard. The blade was little more than that and the balance was poor. The Jyotian shrugged. The weapon was better than no sword at all. He entered the warehouse and stepped down a darkened passage to a room with its door propped open.

Within stood or sat fifty or more of the Fellowship. On a dais a smallish man ranted, often invoking the wrath of their mistress as reason for the meeting. He berated the gathering for lax security and for allowing so many thefts to occur simultaneously. When he swung into a jeremiad against one Davin Anane, the Jyotian decided the time had arrived to make his introductions.

"Excuse me," Davin called. "Excuse me, good sir. Am I the one you malign with your invective?"

A stunned silence fell over the room and every head turned back toward Davin who pushed through the cream of Ohnuhn's underworld and shoved aside the small thief on the dais. Davin held up his hands, using the confusion he caused to survey the exits on either side of the room.

"I would speak with your mistress. Where is she?" Though women were present, none was of overwhelming beauty – and none obviously held the strings of the marionette who picked himself off the floor to resume his ranting.

"No matter. I shall find her one day. I bear you no ill will," Davin said, aware that the shock of his entrance quickly dissipated. Those in the front rows already fingered their daggers. "In spite of the fifty gold coins offered for me . . ."

"One hundred!" a voice roared from the back of the room. "And I, Benk the Quick, claim the right to kill you!"

"A moment!" Davin saw the taller of the guards at the door limping toward him. "I seek nothing more than truce."

"And I seek nothing more than your blood!" The giant stumbled as he tried to reach Davin. Measuring his distances carefully, Davin kicked out and caught the man under the chin. Benk's head snapped back and he sagged to the rostrum, arms feebly thrashing.

Davin had bided his time and now saw what he had waited for. He used the momentary caution generated by the shock of his attack to dash across the stage. He bowled over the solitary guard at the door and spun through it as the gray guardians of Vytellion's palace entered the room. Screams of horror and pain rose when the two gelatinous hounds began attacking the Brotherhood.

On the far side of the heavy wooden door, Davin slid an iron locking bar into place. To make the room even more secure,

Davin leaned against two soft iron channels and bent them inward into the wooden door making removal all the more difficult. Let the scheming thieves struggle to escape along some other path, he thought, and let the spell-summoned monsters dine well.

Davin stepped into the street and heard the cacophony he had created inside the Brotherhood's headquarters. They deserved what they received.

He grinned as an outrageous idea took shape in his quick brain. Davin's feet turned back down the Avenue of the Cracksmen and into the marketplace. He had prevailed for the moment through quick wit and faster feet.

There was no reason to change that strategy.

11

Davin Anane abandoned caution and ran to Vytellion's palace as quickly as weary legs would carry him. In the light of torches hung from the palace walls, he saw uniformed guards patrolling in pairs, marching precise circuits about their ruler's stronghold. The security was more pronounced than before, but the Jyotian sensed the situation would change the moment word of his intrusion on the Fellowship reached the commander of the guard.

Davin barely restrained a gloating grin when the passing of a few moments proved how right he was about the nature of human forces in Ohnuhn. A mounted courier galloped down the street, reined to a halt, and swung from the back of his horse. A dozen heartbeats later the messenger and four officers stood nose to nose in heated discussion with arms flailing the air. The Jyotian could not hear their words, but it was easy to guess the focus of their conversation.

Proving him right again, one guardsman stabbed a finger toward the palace's front entrance where Davin had fled earlier. The soldier made wide, sweeping motions with both arms to indicate the gray blobs that had slithered out the door in pursuit of the would-be thief.

The arguing five snapped to attention when the unit's commander approached and gave the order for another push into the city. Columns of lancers rode forth quickly and two companies of soldiers marched out, their weapons drawn for the fray.

Davin watched and waited for his chance. He stopped in mid-stride at the gate. A figure, dressed entirely in black silk and appearing to be no more than a night shadow, moved across the far sentry post in a low crouch to vanish into the palace.

Davin frowned. Did another share his idea to strike while confusion was at its zenith? If so, Ohnuhn would take days to return to normal after all the chaos he set in motion this night.

As the guards at the gate huddled to discuss the affairs of the city, Davin slipped into the palace grounds. Rather than retrace his earlier route, the adventurer hugged the palace wall and followed it around the grounds. Although he knew the path was more likely to be patrolled by guardsmen, he preferred human foes to magic-spawned creatures Vytellion or his mage conjured.

Fifty strides beyond the gate, Davin stooped low to duck beneath an open window. Light from that window washed over the ground to reveal damp sand. The woman who had passed here had done so only moments ago.

Woman? Davin eased beneath the window and followed the tracks. Had the dark figure who slipped into the palace before him been a woman? His brief glimpse gave no clue. Whoever hid in black silk had been clever enough to draw the cloth across his or her face. Davin adopted this ploy by draping his cloak over his head and tucking the ends about his face to leave only his eyes uncovered. Now no stray beam of light could catch his face and reveal his position to guards.

The tracks ended at a small door. Davin pushed it open. Inside, a staircase spiraled upward into darkness. Taking a step back, Davin glanced overhead. The door entered a tower that connected with Vytellion's sleeping chambers four stories above the ground. The enclosed walkway provided ingress, protection from wind and arrow and gave privacy lacking by more traditional routes. He imagined Vytellion sneaking into the palace late at night using this door to reach his chambers, the castle workers none the wiser about his habits.

Davin moved up the tightly turning staircase. The presence of the woman somewhere ahead of him said that people other than Vytellion were familiar with the door. He imagined the silk-clad figure to be a lover come to her lord in the night.

As romantic an image as that was, it did not sit right. Vytellion was the city's ruler. He had no need of night-cloaked assignations. If he desired a woman, he simply commanded her to his bed. No, it was not a mere seductress who trod ahead. Whether assassin or thief, Davin did not know, but he was certain the woman's purpose was not dissimilar to his own.

Davin reached the walkway spanning the distance from the shorter tower to Vytellion's keep. He paused, studying the deep carpet and noticing how the nap slowly sprang back. The woman ahead of him had passed this way only minutes earlier. Raising an

alarm by startling her simply because he followed too close was
not what he wanted. He did not care why she was here. All he
wanted was one crudely carved soapstone statue.

Davin slowed his pace, gliding along the narrow passage and
stopping when he came to a window. From this aerie, he looked
down on the entire city. Parts were denied his view because of the
taller keep, but the view was impressive – and instructive. In the
courtyard, he saw another company of guardsmen forming rank
and preparing to march into the city.

Davin sucked in his breath and held it when he saw a tall, dark
man astride a white charger being led from the stables. Every line
of the man's body spoke of power, of command, of insistence on
instant obedience. *Vytellion!* The Jyotian recognized Ohnuhn's
ruler although he had never seen him before.

Or ruler-mage, Davin corrected himself. Vytellion might share
Hormachi's arcane abilities. Such might explain why Gatinah's
ruler placed such high value on a crude figurine.

Davin nodded to himself. A contest between sorcerers fitted
the facts he knew. Gatinah held prominence as a seaport and
Ohnuhn did not. Rivalry between mages was a vicious thing
before which the feuds of common men paled. Yet the theft of a
trivial statue might be no more than a game of one-upmanship
between two wizards.

"Father Yehseen," Davin whispered softly, "guide my feet and
fingers now. I need more than luck to aid me this night."

He shivered as he watched a stable hand release the bridle of
his lord's horse, allowing Vytellion to ride to the head of a column
of guardsmen who marched out of the gate. If Vytellion were
indeed a sorcerer, he would have to deal with the rampaging
blobs loosed from his palace and the conjuration might take long
hours.

Davin turned and advanced, carefully placing his feet in the
depressions left by the woman ahead of him. If any trap was to be
sprung, let it be on her head. Reaching the end of the walkway,
Davin pushed gently against the door. The door seemed stuck and
refused to budge with increased pressure. He cursed the Sitala
and several other gods for their capricious nature, then calmed
and stepped back to examine the portal.

The hinges on the far side were beyond his reach as was any

locking mechanism. Should he force the door? He hesitated, allowing his knowing fingertips to explore lightly the door's surface. His left hand brushed a cobweb at the top of the entrance.

He frowned.

How does a spider spin so rapidly if a woman has just entered? Closer examination showed a large portion of the web fastened to the door. The portal had not been opened recently. *A trap!*

But where was the true entrance to Vytellion's quarters? His gaze darted from side to side when he stepped back.

Ten minutes of examination brought Davin to the simple conclusion that anyone standing before the door had to either enter the trap or fly away. The woman in black silk had not gone through the door, so either she sprouted wings or vanished into thin air. As his eyes turned upward, he realized he had blundered onto the answer. Hidden in shadow above dangled a small chain.

All or nothing. Davin jumped, grabbed the chain and held onto it. Descending from the ceiling came a telescoping stairway. It silently unfolded and provided an easy way up. Hesitant at first, then with growing assurance in his instincts, Davin went up into the darkness. A short passageway led over the door below him. A narrow circular stair led down. Curiosity raging out of control, Davin went to examine this side of the door.

No fewer than three different traps guarded the door. If he had opened the door – he silently thanked the Sitala for allowing the door to have swollen over time thus saving him – a deadfall might have ended his life. And if the swinging weight studded with spikes had missed, the trapdoor might not have. He could only guess what deathtrap would be triggered by the tripwire stretched along the corridor.

The adventurer turned and made his way along the corridor, again finding evidence of someone with a small foot preceding him. A dangling curtain and a small niche drew him forward. Davin pushed through and came out in a small alcove just off the lord's sumptuous sleeping chamber.

He hesitated before entering the larger room. Ears straining, Davin edged aside a sheer drapery to scan the sleeping quarters for possible traps or the woman preceding him. Davin froze when he thought he detected movement in the bed. But the shifting coverlet proved to be illusion only – or perhaps the sleeping silks were stirred by drafts within the circular chamber.

The woman in black silk was nowhere to be seen. Save under the massive bed, there was no place one might hide. Wherever the unseen visitor to Vytellion's palace had gone, it was not into this room.

Davin pushed aside the drapery and stepped to the table where the statue stood. Time had not improved the beauty of the carving, it remained the image of a half-naked, bald, pot-bellied, squat-legged man with his arms stretched above his head, the smile of a drunkard well into his cups smeared across a fat-cheeked face. For whatever reason Hormachi desired the ugly piece of stone, it had nothing to do with aesthetics.

The Jyotian knelt and peered beneath the table for tripwires or pressure buttons. He saw nothing to indicate lifting the chubby statue would spring hidden death. Cautiously, he extended a hand and lightly touched the statue, thinking it might glow with some inner magic.

Cold, as cold as any other stone, Davin thought, shaking his head. If Hormachi and Vytellion were rival sorcerers as he suspected, then the soapstone might be some item of magic warmed by the power it held. He felt nothing but cold, unyielding stone.

With another mystified shake of his head, Davin closed his hand around the figurine and snatched it from the table. He had six days left before the violet circle on his breast ignited to sear his flesh. If he stole a horse this night, he could be in Gatinah within three days. In that time, he would carefully lay out a plan to ensure Hormachi fulfilled his promise to remove the spell. Any man who branded another with certain death could not be trusted to keep his word, of that the Jyotian was certain.

The thief froze when he turned to retrace his steps and make good a hasty escape. A woman in black stood at the entrance, the drapery pushed aside. This was the woman he had seen slip into the palace and whose footprints he had followed to the sleeping chamber, although her height almost equaled his own, which surprised him, as did her beauty. From the light that filtered into the room from outside, her blue eyes sparkled like gems from under arched brows plucked into perfect blonde bridges. A long, straight nose hinted at patrician lineage and ruby lips turned upward in a smile.

Or was it a self-satisfied smirk? Davin could not tell. However, he could not shake the feeling that he now stood face to face with the mistress of Ohnuhn's Fellowship of thieves. "Outstanding beauty" fell far short of accurately describing the vision of loveliness that stood before him. It was easy to understand how such a woman might win the hearts of the city's cutthroats and thieves then bend them to her will.

"You are careless," she said in a voice that mimicked a summer wind blowing through tall pine trees.

The soft melody of that voice enthralled the Jyotian. His mouth opened to reply, but the beauty lifted a graceful hand to her enticing bow-shaped lips to quiet his reply.

Davin cocked his head to one side, slightly pushing back the cloak masking his face to listen for the noise that had alerted the woman. He immediately regretted his shift in attention. She took two long strides across the room and swung a short club with painful accuracy.

The blow hammered into the side of Davin's head and sent him reeling to the left. He clutched the soapstone statue tightly, refusing to release the hard-won treasure. At the same time, Davin's cloak slipped and fell over his eyes to blind him. He ducked low to avoid another well-swung blow.

His movement was to no avail. The cudgel crashed down on the top of his head. Stars blossomed in dazzling patterns and Davin's fingers slipped on the statue. The woman grabbed at the figurine and the Jyotian answered with a wide sweeping kick. His intention was to drop the black-clad woman to the floor. Instead, his ankle became entangled in her legs and they both tumbled to the floor.

Both man and woman rolled and came to their feet. Davin ripped at the cloak blinding him but failed to free it from his face before the woman grabbed one end of the cape and tugged. Not only was the woman beautiful but her arms contained surprising strength and the Jyotian was sent spinning across the bedchamber.

The swirling failed to dislodge totally the tangled cloak although the cape fell away from one eye. The twisting also sent the Jyotian beyond the range of his opponent's club, a fact he gratefully accepted, having had a taste of the strength in her slender arms.

Feigning injury, Davin doubled over and groaned aloud. The woman came at him amid the whisper of silk. When she hefted the bludgeon for the kill, he launched himself to drive a shoulder into her midriff.

The pair stumbled back, Davin swinging the statue clumsily. The smooth stone figurine fell from his grasp but he found himself atop the woman. He stared down into her sapphire eyes for a moment, again startled by her beauty. More startling were the feminine arms that bodily lifted him into the air and tossed him aside as if he were a mere child.

Once more the Jyotian hit the floor in a roll. Davin came to his feet just in time to duck beneath the woman's arms closing to capture him in a bear hug. He threw out an arm to lock it around her long neck in a choke hold. This tactic would have worked to free him had her hands not closed around his arm and, by sheer strength, tugged the arm away.

Nor did the woman stop there. She spun around in a maneuver meant to wrench his arm behind his back. Only Davin's own quick twist managed to free his arm before she succeeded in tearing it from its socket.

How a willowy woman of comely face and such a perfect figure held such strength was beyond Davin's experience. Her skill matched his own, and her strength was superior, a fact that bruised the Jyotian's ego as surely as her bludgeon had left swelling knots on his head.

"You hail not from Ohnuhn," the woman said when they squared off and Davin tugged at the cloak to expose both his eyes. "You fight more like one from the north I once knew. By Yehseen's shriveled staff, if there were time, I would find pleasure in knowing you better, but . . ."

She rushed in, hitting low and bowling him over. Together they wrestled on the floor, vying for supremacy. The woman's strength was that of ten; her agility prevented Davin from gaining a decent hold; she knew and countered his every move.

"I surrender," Davin said suddenly when he managed to break away and stand. His chest heaved wearily. "I never thought it possible, but you, a woman, have bested me."

This declaration obviously startled the woman. She slowly pushed to her feet. In that moment, with her guard lowered, Davin struck. The Jyotian threw a short jab that ended on the woman's perfectly formed chin. Her head snapped back and she sprawled on the floor, her blonde hair spraying about her head in a wide fan.

Panting harshly, Davin rubbed his knuckles and stared down at her, marveling that one so beautiful could fight with the power of a great cat. If this was indeed the mastermind of the Fellowship, he found himself wishing their introduction had been under more pleasant circumstances. As it was, he had overstayed his welcome in the palace.

Waving an arm wide in a mock bow to the unconscious woman, he bent low to retrieve the statue from the floor. From the corner of his eye, he caught sight of a boot driving directly toward his head. There was no time to dodge the blow. All the Jyotian could do was groan as the toe of that boot slammed into the side of his head. He crashed facedown onto the floor, stunned.

12

Davin Anane shook his head, then moaned as the toe of a boot slammed into his side. Rolling to one side, he stared up into the face of Lord Vytellion. He blinked. Vytellion looked vaguely familiar, although Davin could not place where he had seen Ohnuhn's ruler before.

"Who are you, thief?" Vytellion, tall and dark-eyed, glared down at the Jyotian. "I ask your name."

To emphasize his words, Ohnuhn's ruler kicked out again. This blow glanced off Davin's shoulder and caught in the cloak still masking his face. Vytellion reached down and yanked hard, wrenching the Jyotian thief's head.

Rubbing his neck, Davin unfurled the cloak to expose his face and sat up in silence. A silver tongue would not stay Vytellion's hand should the ruler decide to put an end to the House of Anane then and there. Behind Vytellion stood four guardsmen with crossbows, their bolts centered on Davin's chest.

"Answer me! Who are you? Who sent you to steal this?" Vytellion demanded as he held aloft the crude statue.

"My name means nothing." Davin massaged ribs doubly tender from his recent tumble from the roof of this very keep and the toe of Vytellion's boot.

"Why do you seek this?" Vytellion shoved the soapstone figure toward the Jyotian's face. "There are means at my disposal to loosen a man's tongue should he decide that stubbornness might shield him."

The Ohnuhn's lord thrust out his hand. Red sparks arced from finger to finger while a nimbus crackling with miniature lightning bolts boiled from wrist to elbow. Vytellion's hand curled into a fist. His forefinger then slowly unfolded to point at the Jyotian.

Davin shrugged and nodded. The magicks Vytellion conjured would fry his flesh as surely as the circles Hormachi had painted on his chest. The only difference was that Vytellion's threat was far more immediate. "I was ordered to seek it. Were the choice my own, I would never have touched such a pathetic carving. It's crudely fashioned and wouldn't fetch a tin octen in the bazaar."

Davin's gaze shifted about. What had happened to his fellow thief – the Uhjayib gorilla disguised as a beautiful blonde? The hint of a smile touched his lips. A rumpled mound of black silk lay near the wall. Although he could not see her face, a disarray of blonde hair said his blow had left the woman still unconscious. It had been Vytellion's boot, not hers, that had caught him in the side of the head.

Vytellion's lips thinned to a razor slash. His finger stabbed out in Davin's direction.

Davin jerked straight up as a spider web of red light danced from the mage-ruler's fingertip to his chest. A tingling, burning sensation coursed through the thief, setting every inch of his body crawling. Worse, the violet ring began to sear his flesh. Whatever spell Vytellion wove shared much with the one Hormachi had used.

"Lord Hormachi." Davin saw no reason to withhold the name. With spells playing throughout his body and crossbow bolts ready to skewer his chest, it was not the time to remain silent. "Lord Hormachi sent me to fetch it."

"Hormachi!" shrieked Vytellion.

The ruler-mage's cold eyes abruptly blazed with unchecked fury. His lips pulled back in a feral snarl that reminded Davin more of a famished direwolf than a human. Saliva ran in a rivulet down Vytellion's chin and the man trembled as if his rage were a living creature that threatened to burst from his breast.

"You are Hormachi's minion," Vytellion accused in a suddenly calm voice that sent a chill down the Jyotian's spine.

The dark eyes snapped into focus from their berserk rage. The ruler-mage sighted along his index finger while the red pulsation grew in brilliance. Davin's throat tightened as he recognized the nearness of his own death.

A fiery bolt jumped from Vytellion's finger. Although the violet ring around the Jyotian's left nipple renewed its sympathetic burning, the sorcerer's brand ripped across the room rather than into his body. A table behind the thief exploded in a shower of burning splinters – then Davin saw the reason for Vytellion's poor aim.

As Vytellion focused on the Jyotian adventurer, the blonde had regained consciousness and grabbed the lord's left leg. If Davin had found her prodigious strength difficult to accept when they grappled, the present display of the power held in those slender, graceful arms left his brain spinning. The woman got to her feet, heaving Vytellion into the air. The beauty shot a quick glance at her fellow thief. Her exquisite features contained a mingling of sympathy, pity – and a hint of recognition.

As Davin struggled to throw off the weakness left by Vytellion's bolt and rise, the blonde woman moved with a speed that left a blur in the Jyotian's eyes. She tossed the lord directly into the legs of the guardsmen. The four crashed to the floor like so many skittle pins. In the next instant, she swarmed over them, her club finding more than one head to strike.

"Look out!" Davin cried out when a soldier lifted his crossbow and swung it toward the woman.

The warning was not needed. The woman ducked when the guard's finger squeezed the trigger. As the projectile sang through the air, the woman snared it in mid-flight with one hand.

The speed and strength required for such a feat amazed the guard as much as it did Davin. The soldier scrambled to his feet and ran over his companions in his haste to flee the bedchamber. Seconds later two more men scurried after their comrade. The fourth guardsman lay clubbed into unconsciousness with Vytellion sprawled across his legs in a similar state.

Davin reached for the statue on the carpet beside the Ohnuhnian lord, only to find a slender-fingered hand already there.

"So?" he asked. "We fight for it now?"

"Not this night, son of Anane. You carry it for now." Her fingers withdrew, slowly tracing over the back of his hand as they retreated. "We can discuss the statue's disposition after we are free of the palace."

Davin's eyes widened then narrowed, remembering his suspicions that this woman was the bloody leader of Ohnuhn's Fellowship of thieves. "You know me?"

"After we are free of the palace," she repeated, her sapphire eyes pleading with him. "*He* has laid traps everywhere, both magical and mechanical devices. He fears invasion and surrounds himself with precautions on top of precautions."

"It did him no good this night." Davin tucked the statue under his belt and smiled at the blonde. "We both got inside."

The woman laughed, the throaty chuckle captivating Davin. Her next words astounded him. "Why not both? Was not your father once the best thief in all Raemllyn? And did not my sword stand at his side?"

"You knew Bedrich . . ." Davin never finished the question.

The distant pounding of boots echoed toward the sleeping chamber. The three guards returned and brought a score of their companions with them.

"Vytellion!" urged the woman. "Use him as a shield! They will not kill their own master."

A dry, humorless laugh rolled from Davin's throat. Of all the rulers he knew, only a few commanded the respect of those they governed. The majority of citizens in most of Raemllyn's city-states would gladly sacrifice their lord and ruler if the opportunity presented itself.

The ravishing blonde seemed to read his mind. She nodded slowly. "I see the error of that. *I* would cut his throat."

"Then do it," Davin urged. He drew his sword, trying to accustom himself to the unusual balance of the pilfered blade. He wished that Vytellion's hounds had not possessed such an appetite for tempered steel. His own blade had served him well and delivered the precise control he required when the need for swordplay arose.

"Slit your own throat!" Vytellion came alive, springing to his feet with sword bared.

Davin lunged for the quick kill, refusing to allow the mage-ruler time to awaken new magicks.

Vytellion responded with a shift of his wrist that brought his blade up, deflecting at the last instant the sharp tip that shot towards his chest. The Jyotian's sword dug into the mortar behind the lord and produced a cascade of harmless sparks.

"The statue, damn you! Hand over the statue!" Vytellion's sword swung back, tip sliding toward Davin's throat. "Hormachi will not have my prize!"

The woman's club slammed into the lord's wrist. The sickening snap of bone resounded within the chamber as Vytellion's blade fell from his hand. The woman tried to finish off the mage-ruler with a backswing of the bludgeon. The man proved too agile for her. He moved his chin the barest fraction necessary for the blow to sail past harmlessly, then he charged.

Davin dropped his shoulder and drove forward, hitting Vytellion in the small of the back. The lord stumbled away, clutched at heavy draperies and twisted through the doorway into the corridor to escape further attack. His head hit the floor with a solid thud. He did not move when the blonde slammed the door closed and bolted it.

"We must leave now," the blonde said without so much as a quickened breath to mark the confrontation. "Keep the statue, young Anane. If we are separated, meet in the bazaar – at the mapmaker's shop."

She winked and smiled, then stepped to a window and struck open the shutters with a balled fist.

"What makes you think that I . . ."

"Because I knew your father, and you've just found the only friend you have in Ohnuhn. Or are you too dim-witted to know it?"

"What friend would invite me to walk into a deathtrap – not once, but twice?" Davin's nostrils filled with a waft of her perfume as they both leaned out the window. The fragrance was intoxicating, and the way the strands of her silky blonde hair played against his cheek was distracting.

"You've guessed that was me, eh? That was before I saw your face, young Anane." She shook her head when she pulled back into the room, "It's a long way down for those without wings."

"I survived before," Davin bragged, knowing he had been lucky to land on the bales of cloth, but unable to repress the desire to impress this beauty.

"Ah, so it *was* you with the periscope device. Very clever! A ploy that would have made your father proud. The window now, however, is suicidal." The blonde eased him back.

From outside came the cries of the guardsmen. One voice above all urged the others to use a bench as a battering ram.

"I see no other escape except the window." Davin's teeth grated when something big and heavy crashed into the door. "The guards will be in here within minutes."

"The bed!" The blonde grabbed his arm and dragged him

toward Vytellion's enormous bed.

"As much as a dalliance with you is tempting, I am afraid this is not the time."

"Like father, like son!" she said with a snort, releasing his arm to press her palms against the wall beside the bed. A metallic *click* sounded and a panel opposite the bed slid open to reveal a brass pole.

"A quick route of escape for a frightened lord," the mistress of the Fellowship said, grinning as she stepped toward the Jyotian.

Davin let out a cry of warning as the door's wood splintered. He leaped forward, snatched her up with an arm around her waist and dived for the pole. They slid downward as two guardsmen poked their heads through a hole shattered in the door.

"You and your father share more than one trait," she said when they landed below, dislodging his hand which had slipped upward to cup an ample breast during their ride down the pole.

She turned and slammed her shoulder into a door. It flew open, spilling her into the courtyard.

"How fast can you run, son of Anane? The main gate is distant and patrols lie between us and freedom."

"I have the statue," he answered without hesitation. "I can run with the fastest if it means escape."

He spoke to empty air. The blonde thief had already dashed off, her stride long and powerful, propelling her with a speed Davin found impossible to match. He shook his head. Never had he met such a woman. In a single night, she had tried to kill him – twice – and then saved his life.

Even the woman's astounding speed proved inadequate for a clean getaway. She crashed into two guardsmen rounding the building. Both went flying, but it slowed her and ruined any chance of reaching the gate before the hue and cry was raised.

Davin whipped out his sword and thrust into the throat of the first soldier trying to regain his feet. The woman again belied her delicate appearance by lashing out with a booted foot and breaking the other guard's neck with a single kick. She smiled, then pointed behind Davin.

"Our hosts. Too bad we dare not invite ourselves to partake of their hospitality." She stooped and drew each of the dead soldiers' blades.

With a dexterity Davin admired, the blonde rushed forward and engaged three more guardsmen. Swords swinging left and right she pushed back her opponents.

A war cry ripped from Davin's throat, and he rushed to join her as more guards poured forth. If this fierce fighter truly knew Bedrich the Fair, he could understand why the High King had selected her as a companion. It would not do to let such a woman be hacked into dog meat.

Davin wielded the awkward blade as best he could, hacking and cutting at arms and legs the guardsmen failed to protect. More than one scream rent the night when his sword found vulnerably exposed flesh. Had the soldiers from the tower been their only worry, the mastermind of the Fellowship of thieves and a lone Jyotian would have won their way to freedom with ease, for the blonde was a tireless fighter slashing with left or right hand with equal dexterity.

It was the guardsmen on the battlements that doubled the race of Davin's pounding heart. They reached the gates and threw themselves against the gigantic slabs of wood. The mere mass of those monstrous doors held them in place.

"We must get to the gate!" Davin swung a broad stroke that opened the throat of a man who carelessly attacked with a sword raised over his head.

"There's no way, unless . . ."

A startled yelp escaped the Jyotian's lips when the comely blonde beside him abruptly vanished in a quaking wall of shimmering flesh. In her stead stood a muscular giant with a mane of flaming red hair and beard to match.

And the eyes! The sapphire eyes transformed to two orbs dancing with green witchfire!

"Goran!" Davin gasped.

Two eyes or one – there was no way he could mistake the Challing!

A sudden rush by the guardsmen bowled Davin Anane over and strong arms pinned him to the ground.

13

The crush of bodies drove the wind from Davin's lungs. He gasped for air, but the weight on his chest was too great to breathe. He bucked, twisted and attempted to roll away from the soldiers. Nothing relieved the pressure that threatened to shatter his ribcage.

A startled scream rent the night somewhere above the mass of bodies piled atop the Jyotian. Another cry chorused the first, then another, and another. Air seeped into Davin's lungs as the weight pinning him to the ground gradually lessened. The next instant he saw the shaggy-haired giant Challing looming above him. In a beserk rage, Goran, now of two eyes, tore at the guardsmen trapping the Jyotian. Arm, leg, neck, it did not matter. The changeling's massive hands clamped tightly, wrenched and slung the soldiers aside.

Nor did Goran stop when he reached Davin. Grabbing the last son of the House of Anane by the front of his blouse, the Challing pulled him to his feet and tossed him halfway to the closing gate. "Run, young Anane! By Yehseen's great staff, *run!*"

Davin did, skidding to a halt just outside the palace wall. He turned back as Goran hammered a balled fist into an officer's face, then slid nimbly between the closing gates.

"This is no place to tarry." Goran's meaty paw hooked Davin's collar and shoved him forward. "They'll be on our trail like hounds after a fox in minutes."

Again, Davin did as told and ran. Down wide avenue and narrow alley, his legs stretched out in long strides trying to put as much distance between himself and Vytellion's palace as possible. He cast a glance to his left to see that the beautiful blonde again ran at his side, her graceful legs matching him stride for stride.

"Sanctuary!" the Challing called as she abruptly halted, using a vicelike hand that nearly yanked Davin from his feet. "We must find sanctuary. If we continue to run, Vytellion eventually will find us."

The Jyotian freebooter saw the problem the changeling had already noted. An entire company of Vytellion's guard herded the slithering blobs of all-devouring jelly toward the palace. The avenue ahead was blocked; Vytellion and his troops could not be far behind.

Worse, Davin felt an itching within the violet ring on his chest. "Ohnuhn's lord has cast scrying spells. I can feel them."

"Let Vytellion feed his own hounds this night." The Challing glanced at Davin with green witch-fire blazing in her eyes. "The Fellowship will protect us!"

With that she placed forefinger and thumb into the corners of her mouth and whistled.

The Jyotian thief glanced down the avenue. The approaching soldiers had not spotted them, but it was only a matter of moments before they did.

In answer to the changeling's signal a darkened second-story window to their right swung wide. A knotted rope tumbled out of the opening. The Challing waved Davin up first.

Leaping as high as he could, Davin caught the rope and scrambled upward. When his eyes came level with the window-sill, strong hands grabbed his clothing and tugged him inside and dumped him on the wooden floor. He rolled onto his back to see the Challing in feminine form surge through the window.

"Pull up the rope and scatter," she ordered those hidden within the dark. "When it is safe, I will put out the call."

The changeling reached down and hauled Davin to his feet. "The back window. We'll use the aerial avenues from here."

Davin discovered what she meant when he reached the window. Two wide planks stretched across an alley to the roof of the adjoining building. He quickly crossed. From roof to roof, over street and alley via rope, plank or ladder, Jyotian and Challing moved across Ohnuhn to the wharf district. There the blonde led Davin down a ladder to a dinghy tied among a line of fishing boats. Signaling him to remain quiet, she rowed to a two-masted vessel anchored in the middle of the harbor.

Once aboard, the Challing released a long sigh as she leaned heavily on the rail. "We're safe here. Not even the Fellowship knows of this vessel. Nor can Vytellion's hounds cross water. The beasts would go up in smoke if the smallest drop of seawater touched them."

"Goran-Glylina, this is yours?" Davin stared around. Even in the moonlight he could tell it was a rugged, well-crafted ship.

"I bought it two months back, but never before have I had reason to use it," she explained. "I have a cache of bists stored below – enough to see me through for several years. But now, I doubt they will be needed, since I have found you, young Anane. I know not what god or goddess led you to me, but they have my full admiration."

"And mine!" Davin laughed aloud. "All this time, I thought I faced some demonic bitch from the depths of Peyneeha, only to find my old friend Goran – or Glylina, as the case may be, has created an empire for herself."

He turned to face the blonde. "Tell me, what brought you back to Raemllyn from your beloved Gohwohn?"

"Gohwohn?" She stood straight. "Fifteen processions of the seasons have passed since I was drawn from Gohwohn, young Anane. Why would I wish to return to my boring birth world? Raemllyn is my home now, and will be until Qar opens his arms to embrace me. But as to why I am here – I followed Berenicis the Blackheart from A'bre to Ohnuhn after the treacherous whoreson murdered your father. Berenicis seeks to kill you and win the High King's throne for himself."

"What?" Davin frowned. The Challing's words made no sense.

"Berenicis is dead. And Berenicis did not kill Bedrich the Fair. Bedrich died at the hand of the usurper, Zarek Yannis."

"Aarrin Anane, was your head cracked by one of Vytellion's guards?" Glylina stepped toward him. "What nonsense is this? Your father was Davin Anane, Lord of Jyotis, and brother to High King Felrad."

"Glylina, it's you who suffered a blow to the head. Who is this Aarrin Anane? Don't you know me? It's me, Davin – Davin Anane!"

"Young Aarrin, this is no time for games. Don't you understand? Your father is dead. Davin died in my arms six months ago – killed by a poisoned arrow to the back from Berenicis' own bow."

Davin's head spun. Each succeeding word the Challing uttered made less sense than the one before. "Glylina, I am Davin Anane. I know of no Aarrin. When you returned to Gohwohn from A'bre, I eventually wandered to Gatinah and then here to Ohnuhn." Davin dug a hand into a pocket to produce a gold chain hung with a stylized golf leaf composed of four separate parts that snapped together. "Do you recognize this?"

Glylina took the chain from his hand. "The Keys of A'bre! No! This is but a reproduction. Yet, I sense the feel of A'bre about it. Where did you get this, Aarrin?"

"Davin, I'm Davin Anane," he repeated for the third time. "I bought the trinket from an old man outside a hut in what is called A'bre here and now. It is meant to remind me of you and Goran One-Eye."

"Goran? How could you know about Goran? Your father didn't like my masculine form, so I rarely transformed to Goran except when it was needed as it was tonight," she said. "And what is this 'One-Eye?' "

"I know Goran because I am Davin Anane," the Jyotian insisted. "Surely, you remember traveling from one end of Raemllyn to the other at my side? We were the greatest pair of thieves ever to walk this world!"

"Davin Anane was never a thief, except to serve Felrad! He was noble from the day of his birth to the day Berenicis . . ."

Without warning the Challing leaped forward, grasped the Jyotian by the collar, hauled him from the deck and carried him below where she tossed him into a chair. The sound of steel striking flint sounded in the darkness, followed by the soft glow of tinder burning. First, the Challing lit several candles and then three oil lamps making the cabin as bright as day. Glylina walked before his chair and stared down, studying him from one angle and then the other.

Suddenly, the blonde bent to cover his mouth with her own. Unexpected as the kiss was, Davin found himself lost in the warmth of her lips and the taunting play of her tongue. Once, just once, he had tasted Glylina's kiss. There was no doubt that this kiss was the same.

Apparently the Challing reached the same conclusion about him. When her mouth slowly eased from his, she hovered over him, sapphire eyes glistening with welling moisture.

"How? You died in my arms. Yet, it *is* you, Davin, my love. How?" She sank to her knees and threw her arms around him. Tears rolled down her cheeks as her head rested on his chest. "By the gods, I don't care how it is possible, my Davin. That you are here is all that matters. How I've longed for you! There were times I thought to end my life rather than live without you."

Davin's own arms cradled the woman tenderly. He lightly kissed the top of her head. The stirrings Glylina had sparked with her parting kiss before she stepped into the gate to return to Gohwohn awoke anew within the Jyotian. As difficult as it had been for him to reconcile the feelings Glylina created within him with her persona of Goran One-Eye before, it no longer mattered. For six months that parting kiss had lingered on his lips, igniting more than one fantasy of what might have been. Now to find Glylina suddenly returned—

A cold river of ice flowed along the Jyotian's spine when Glylina's face lifted and her full lips eased toward his.

"My love, what is wrong?" Her eyes widened then narrowed with doubt.

"Me," Davin said while pieces to a horrible puzzle tumbled into place within his mind. "I'm what's wrong – and you. The Sitala play with us as children do with toys."

A frown lined her bow. "Davin, I have known no other since . . ."

Her words faded and she slowly pulled back as her eyes traced over his face. Fingertips rose to brush over his left temple. "You are Davin. My eyes do not lie. Yet, the silver is gone from your hair."

He nodded, seeing the dawning of recognition on her face.

"You're not *my* Davin, are you?" She bit her lower lip, suddenly appearing small and vulnerable. "He died in my arms, didn't he?"

He watched her sink back to sit on her calves. There was a tension in the air. The fire-tressed temptress Davin had known as Glylina suddenly sat on the floor before him. The longing within him tripled. He had found Glylina and she had found him, only there weren't the ones they had known and loved.

"It was A'bre, wasn't it?" she asked softly.

"The intersection of planes of existence," Davin answered.

"A'bre was a nexus where infinite worlds touched – all the possibilities focused."

"And one of us has returned to a Raemllyn to which he does not belong," Glylina completed the thought in Davin's mind. She glanced up at him. "Which of us stepped onto the wrong plane of existence?"

Again Davin's mind reeled. He had never considered the possibility that the gate he stepped through had led to anything but his own world. Yet, he could not deny the existence of other universes lying beside one another like the layers of an onion's skin. In A'bre he had learned that on these other planes lived other Davin Ananes with lives similar but separate from his own.

The Jyotian shook his head. "I don't know. I never felt anything was out of kilter here until this night when I saw you transform into Goran One-Eye."

"Two eyes," she said softly. "When I am Goran, I have two eyes."

Another cold shiver ran along Davin's spine as he remembered the guardian of the gate revealing that his and Goran-Glylina's lives were entwined on all the planes of existence, that he was always there when Goran lost his eye. The Goran he knew had already lost his eye and delighted in cobbling together outrageous tales about the loss of that orb. All of which were true, the Challing claimed, since all had happened on one plane of existence or another.

Davin found Glylina studying him again. A sad, tiny smile hung at the corners of her mouth. She drew in a heavy breath and nodded. "Challings have glimpses of other worlds, other lives. I feel my Goran will one day lose his eye, but I know not when or where."

"But I will be there?"

Again she nodded. "Davin Anane is always there. Until now I didn't see how it would be possible."

Davin sank back into the chair and stared at the ceiling of the cabin. He did not relish the possibilities A'bre had revealed. To find himself living amid what a normal man would consider impossible only set his head to throbbing. "I need a drink – something to clear my mind or drive away the jumbled confusion. Either way, it does not matter. Were Ohnuhn's streets safe, I would find a tavern and drink it dry!"

Glylina rose, appearing more beautiful and graceful than Davin had ever recalled. She crossed the cabin and pointed to two small kegs. "Litonyian ale or Jyotian wine?"

"Your tastes are improved over the Goran-Glylina, I knew," he answered with a smile. "My Goran would swill whatever was available."

"And my Davin preferred only the finest." The sad smile still hung at the corners of her mouth.

"Can we begin with the ale?" Davin asked. "Wine from my homeland would taste like a cruel joke this night."

She nodded and opened a cask to fill two golden goblets. "There is no Aarrin Anane in your Raemllyn?"

"I have no sons," Davin answered as he downed a healthy gulp from the goblet she handed him. He amended, "Or daughters, that I know of."

"My Davin had a single child, born of a wife who died at childbirth – a Lijena Farleigh . . ."

Davin sat straight in his chair, eyes wide. On another plane Lijena and he had been husband and wife and brought a son into the world.

Glylina's gaze shot to him. "You know this woman?"

"Aye," Davin nodded, finding it surprisingly comfortable to talk with this strange Glylina. "But we are not husband or wife, or even lovers. Nor do I expect the Sitala will twist fate in a manner ever to make it so."

While he finished his first ale and refilled the goblet, he gave a hasty recounting of how he had kidnapped Lijena from her uncle as ransom to save Goran One-Eye. When Lijena was possessed by a demon, Davin and Goran had followed her across Upper Raemllyn to free her and reclaim the Sword of Kwerin Blood-hawk for Felrad.

Another round of ale and the Jyotian related how Goran, Lijena and he had battled with Felrad to defeat Zarek Yannis and reclaim the Velvet Throne for the rightful heir.

"Lijena is now Bearer of the Sword in Kavindra, captain of Felrad's own guard," Davin concluded. "After the Battle of Kavindra, Goran and I journeyed to A'bre where we defeated Roan-Jafar who sought to destroy all the realms of existence."

Glylina nodded. "After which Goran returned to Gohwohn and you to Raemllyn."

"Or what I thought was Raemllyn," Davin said, refilling her goblet.

"It is Raemllyn," she assured him. "A world that is strangely similar to your own." She paused to sip at the ale, then said, "I, too, was drawn from Gohwohn by the sorcerer Roan-Jafar. But rather than kill the mage, I managed to escape his keep in Kavindra. I was then as you see me now."

Glylina explained she had been found wandering the streets of Kavindra by Davin Anane. "Unlike your Goran, this world of carnal sensation frightened me, overwhelmed me with its power. Davin, in Kavindra to spy on Zarek Yannis, took me from the city and back to Jyotis. There he found his wife had died giving birth to their son, Aarrin."

The adventures Glylina unfolded followed those Davin and Goran had shared save that Lijena played no part in them. It was Felrad who took up the magical blade to defeat Zarek Yannis and his hordes of Faceless Ones.

"During that time Davin and I became lovers," Glylina said. "He grew upset whenever I transformed into Goran, saying he had never had the desire to bed another man. Since I shared no desire for another man other than Davin, it was easy enough to remain as you see me, except when Goran was needed."

"It was the opposite with me," Davin said. "I met Goran first and you – I mean Glylina – seemed unnatural to me. When I saw her, I saw Goran. I, too, have no desire to bed another man."

"Yet in A'bre, you saw her differently," Glylina reminded him of what he had just revealed.

Davin nodded. "Only after I saw her in her natural state as a Challing did I truly realize she was neither man nor woman but whatever she wished to be. What of you in A'bre?"

Glylina explained Davin's bastard brother Berenicis the Blackheart had not been slain but had joined forces with Roan-Jafar in the mad mage's attempt to rule the universes.

"For two years, Davin and I fought in A'bre before Roan-Jafar died his deserved death," she said. "But Berenicis escaped us. We thought he had returned to Raemllyn." She paused to wipe away a renewed flow of tears. "Instead, he hid in A'bre and waited until he could send a poisoned arrow into Davin's back."

"And you returned to Raemllyn to avenge my – your – Davin's death?"

"To save my love's son from Berenicis," Glylina said. "With Felrad slowly dying from never-healing wounds inflicted by the Faceless Ones, Aarrin is next in line for the Velvet Throne. Should he die, Berenicis has a clear claim to the crown."

Again the Challing's form shifted and the blonde once more sat across the cabin from the Jyotian. Glylina waved a hand to her body. "I took this shape to disguise myself from Berenicis whom I followed to Ohnuhn . . ."

"The Blackheart is here?" Davin jerked upright, his temples pounding.

"I believe he is still within the city, although in six months I have been unable to locate him," Glylina answered. "I suspect he now studies with a mage somewhere in Ohnuhn. While I have waited for him to emerge and make a move, I have done my best to gather as much wealth as possible. Davin taught me gold can often accomplish more than might or magic."

Davin drained his goblet and shook his head. The ale had not cleared his mind nor pushed away the confused bombardment of intersecting planes of existence. Glylina-Goran sat across the cabin from him, yet it was not Glylina-Goran. Or it was, but it was a totally different Challing, one who had been his lover for fifteen years.

And he had a son that he had never seen, not to mention that he had been killed by a poison arrow shot by a dead brother! The Sitala and their damnable dice were more than cruel. They now interwove the lives of those on two different planes of existence.

"I have heard no word of Felrad's wounds," Davin suddenly said. "Surely, you have returned to the wrong Raemllyn."

Glylina shook her head. "Would your brother be stupid enough to allow word of his illness to spread when his rule is so young? Raemllyn would be torn by war again."

Davin closed his eyes and sucked at his teeth. "Then traveling to Kavindra to see Felrad is the only way to judge whether you or I walk the wrong plane."

"Or to visit Jyotis and Aarrin," she added.

"Neither of which I can do," Davin said, his right hand creeping to his chest.

Glylina's sapphire eyes narrowed with suspicion. "It's your own son's life that hangs in the balance."

Davin wanted to tell the Challing that he felt no responsibility for a son sired by another man, but that would have been a lie. Though he had never known the Davin Anane who had shared a life with this Glylina, he could not help but think of him as an unknown brother, one who had given his life to save the universes. For that alone, he was willing to aid Glylina on her quest.

"This hinders me." Davin opened the front of his tunic and pulled it wide to reveal the sorcerous circles painted on his flesh. "I fear that I am spellbound to Hormachi of Gatinah. He sent me to steal Vytellion's soapstone statue."

Witch-fire sparked in Glylina's eyes when they alighted on Hormachi's handiwork. "A fire elemental hibernates within your flesh. When he awakes, he will devour you."

"If Hormachi's paint doesn't do it first," Davin said, explaining what had happened the first time he attempted to break into the palace. "Now that I have the statue, I must return to Gatinah and deal with Hormachi."

"And then to Kavindra?" Glylina arched an eyebrow in question.

"And on to Jyotis if need be," Davin added. Though he had only met this Glylina mere hours ago, he felt no inkling of suspicion as to her motives. It might be the reaction of a fool, he told himself, but he trusted her as surely as he had trusted Goran One-Eye. "Or through the gate to A'bre, if that's what it takes to save this son I've never seen."

The Challing hoisted her goblet high in a silent toast, then downed the remainder of her ale. "Davin Anane, I believe you are a man I could grow to like! Before we return you to Gatinah, I have unfinished business at Fellowship headquarters."

"Then we should be on our way." He tried to warn himself that wariness would be a better path to take than commitment, but he could not stop himself. This was Glylina, no matter what plane of existence they dwelled on.

"Before that, there is something you must do," Glylina said, her eyes shyly rolling downward and eyelashes fluttering demurely.

The Challing's almost embarrassed expression was something Davin had never seen on the face of the Glylina he knew. "What is that?"

"Bathe," she answered, her eyes lifting to him with hesitancy. "I've no desire to keep the company of a man smelling of offal!"

Davin laughed with the realization Glylina *was* embarrassed to mention the odor of the sewer he carried on clothes and person. There *were* differences in this Challing that he would have to get used to.

"A bath it shall be!"

14

Davin listened silently as Glylina gave orders to the three young men who took the dinghy and rowed toward the *Windsong*, the Challing's two-masted vessel. The Jyotian noticed the adoring gazes with which the three youths worshipped their captain. Glylina might be a being from another world but she understood the use of human feminine wiles better than most born to the flesh they wore.

"There's no need to worry about them," she assured Davin when she waved him down the pier toward Ohnuhn's streets. "Not one of them is of the Fellowship, and all are from seafaring families. I pay them well, which makes for a loyal crew."

Davin glanced back to the dinghy and then at the blonde beauty at his side. "They all look as if they are in love with you."

"Loyalty takes many forms." Glylina's smile said she had no qualms about using the young men's feelings for her benefit. "They have orders to prepare to sail the instant we return to the *Windsong*."

"It would be faster to travel to Gatinah by horseback," Davin said as they moved down a broad avenue.

"We will," Glylina replied, "but I've no intention of leaving behind the gold I've gathered in Ohnuhn. Who knows what we'll need when we face Berenicis?"

The Challing trusted her crew far more than Davin would ever consider trusting one man, let alone three. "You speak the name of the Blackheart as though it were a curse."

"In your Raemllyn, he robbed you of family and honor. In this world, he killed the Davin Anane I loved. The whoreson will pay for what he took from me if it takes all the bists in Raemllyn to see his head rotting atop a pike!"

A shiver shot up the Jyotian's back. Glylina shared another trait with the Glylina he knew. The Challing had a bloodthirsty streak that could not be denied. *Also loyalty*. Davin reminded himself that everything she had done in Ohnuhn had been to avenge his death or to protect a son he had never seen.

Davin shook his head, seeing the fallacy in his thoughts. With each moment that had passed since Glylina described all that had occurred in her world, he felt more and more as if those events were part of his own life rather than those of a Davin Anane who dwelled on another plane.

What of Glylina? he asked himself. She reminded him of the Glylina he had come to know while in A'bre. There the Challing had revealed a somber, reflective side he had never seen in the wild, Qar-be-damned Goran One-Eye. In truth, he admitted, he found that trait a strength missing in the Challing's male persona.

Nor could he dismiss the attraction he felt for Glylina. Although, he thought while studying the woman out of a corner of an eye, he preferred the red-haired beauty to the blonde.

"What of Berenicis?" Davin asked when they turned at an intersection. "Will we just leave him here in Ohnuhn?"

"I see no other course." Glylina's sapphire eyes darted about, alert for danger. "If we are to remove the bull's-eye Hormachi painted on your chest, we've got only four days to get you to Gatinah, Anane."

The use of his family name drove into Davin's breast like a dagger fashioned of winter ice. He had long accustomed his ear to Goran's "friend Davin" or Glylina's "dearest Davin." The appellation "Anane" rang distant and formal. It was as though the Challing purposely used it to separate him from the Davin Anane she had loved for fifteen years.

"I had hoped the statue dangling at your hip might be the key to locating Berenicis and exterminating the vermin here in Ohnuhn," she continued. "My plan was simple. I would return the figurine to Vytellion the day he delivered the Blackheart into my hands."

"Then you know why Hormachi and Vytellion prize this ugly chunk of soapstone so?" Davin patted the bulging leather pouch tied to his belt.

Glylina halted when they moved into an alley. "You don't know the significance of the statue either?"

The Challing's question took Davin completely off guard. "If you didn't know whether the figurine had value, why, by the gods, were you trying to steal it?"

"It had obvious value to Vytellion," she replied with a shrug. "I've spied on him from the window to his bedchamber on more than one occasion as a bird, bat or fly. I've seen Vytellion caress that piece of soapstone as though it were the most valuable item in this world. I was certain he would gladly scour the city for Berenicis to make certain it was returned to him."

"I think it's time we took a closer look at the figurine," Davin said, realizing he had yet to examine the statue closely. As he opened the pouch to extract the carved soapstone, he asked, "You used your changeling ability to spy on Vytellion. Do you have full control of your powers?"

"They wax and wane like Raemllyn's two moons," the blonde answered. "It has always been so. Here in Ohnuhn, however, my attempts to shift forms have rarely failed me. I've sensed subtle magicks weaving across this city and the presence of magicks has always increased my powers."

"Magicks?" Davin pulled the statue free and made a disgusted face when he looked at the crude, squat-bodied figure.

"I've never located its source, but it hangs in Ohnuhn's air like a thick smoke cloud." Glylina lifted the statue from Davin's palm and hiked an eyebrow high. "It *is* ugly, isn't it?"

"A child might shape a more eye-appealing figure from clay," Davin agreed.

"Hidden wealth?" Glylina turned the statue over in her hand. "That must be the answer."

Her fingers carefully probed every inch of the crude statue. A smile crossed her red lips when she pushed aside a layer of clay on the statue's potbelly.

"There is something hidden!" Davin's heart pounded.

"A diamond." Glylina lifted the statue toward the breaking dawn. "But it is hardly the largest I have ever seen."

Davin edged aside more of the clay with a thumb. "It is large, but a man of Vytellion's wealth and power could buy a dozen this size from the gem merchants in any of Raemllyn's cities. And if the stone means so much to Vytellion, why hide it under the clay?"

Davin held up the statue at arm's length. The more he studied it, the more perplexed he grew. Seldom had he seen such a surpassingly unsightly figure. Even the diamond gleaming where the navel should have been did not transform it into a work of art.

"Magicks," Glylina said slowly beside the Jyotian. "I feel something stirring within me."

The Challing shuddered and tried to speak, then started to fade and blur like a person dimly seen on a foggy night. Davin watched in fascination as Glylina became Goran, shifted halfway back to the familiar flame-tressed seductress he had come to know, then finally settled into the shape of the blonde mistress of the Fellowship.

Glylina shook her head and drew in a deep breath, her more than amply endowed chest straining the limits of the forest green linen blouse she now wore. No matter the plane, the Challing seemed to have a taste for the voluptuous when in female form. Not that the last son of Anane had any objections.

Davin caught himself. If he had truly been delivered into a Raemllyn other than his own, there was another son of Anane – one who faced death at the hands of the Jyotian's oldest enemy.

"Enough of this. The statue holds potent magicks. Or mayhap Vytellion uses his spells to locate us." Glylina motioned for Davin to return the statue to his pouch. "Come, Anane, let us not linger."

"My name is Davin," he said as he safely tucked the figurine away.

"I know," he answered softly. "You, however, are not *the* Davin. You look, sound and even *smell* like Davin, now that you've washed away the sewers, but . . ."

"But he was a great and noble lord of Jyotis and I am a mere *thief* from the gutter?" Davin watched the blonde give a hesitant nod. "Perhaps had Berenicis destroyed his family and driven him from his homeland branded as a murderer, the Davin you knew would have been the same as the one who now stands at your side."

Glylina glanced away, tears welling in her eyes. "There are more differences. After the Battle of Kavindra, you allowed Jyotis to be placed in the rule of a regent."

"Ah, but only to keep my promise to you – to Goran One-Eye – to return him to his beloved Gohwohn."

"And from A'bre, you traveled to Gatinah rather than Jyotis to take your place as the rightful lord." Glylina's gaze returned to him like an old accusation.

He nodded heavily, not wishing to give voice to the responsibility he shunned. "There are differences."

"Friend Anane, I had no intention of wounding you," she said, the words further emphasizing those differences. The Goran-Glylina Davin knew would have never noticed treading on another's feelings. "We both know each other intimately, yet there are subtle changes. We should give each other time to adjust to those changes. For me, you are the man whose love taught me the joy of living in human form, who made me more human than Challing. Yet you are not that man. It is hard to accept."

Again, the Jyotian nodded. She was right and it was a hard thing to accept and place properly in one's mind.

Abruptly Davin's head snapped up. An all too familiar wet sucking sound touched his ears. "Vytellion's hounds! I hear them! They're nearby!"

"Apparently you forgot to wash behind your ears. They still have your scent." Glylina playfully winked at him and pointed down the alley to a flight of wooden stairs that led to the roof of a building. "I've wanted to get rid of those *evipods* since Vytellion set them on three of the Fellowship. Come, I've prepared a little trap for just such an occasion."

"*Evipods*?" Davin ran after the Challing.

"They are magically enhanced slugs. Vicious and utterly dependable trackers. Never saw them fail, never." Reaching the roof, Glylina once again employed her aerial avenues to hasten along the tops of Ohnuhn's buildings.

"Wonderful news you bring me." Davin glanced below as he balanced his way across a narrow plank.

The gray blobs undulated down the street, mindlessly refusing to give up the hunt.

"There!" Glylina pointed to a row of barrels along a rooftop when she used a rope bridge to cross the deep chasm of an alley. "I prepared for any eventuality. Some contain oil to be set afire. Others have in them eye-burning acids. And there, that barrel. In it we shall find salvation from the *evipods*."

Davin went to the barrel she indicated and struggled to open the lid. Inside lay white grains. He dipped his finger into the contents, then lifted it to his lips to sample cautiously. "Salt. This is nothing but salt!"

"And we both know how slugs respond to a good dousing of salt. Why do you think I knew the *Windsong* would be a safe haven?" Grunting, the blonde heaved the barrel to a shoulder, staggered to the edge of the roof and emptied the contents in a white cascade to the street below.

An inhuman shrieking rose from the urban canyon.

Davin peered down at the street. The *evipods* were covered with a thin layer of salt. Where the grains touched, slug flesh sizzled. The keening increased until Davin clapped his hands over his ears to shut out the deafening death cry of the creatures. However, the *evipods* soon no longer posed a threat. Only bubbling pools of gray matter remained below.

"Interesting." Glylina dumped the barrel onto the small knot of soldiers who had followed the monsters. "The *evipods* had internal organs. That must be a heart still beating, and could those lumpy things be kidneys?"

"It'll be our heads floating in that ooze when the guardsmen find a way up here." Davin watched the guards start to regroup.

"This way." Glylina gracefully slipped to the far side of the roof and pushed aside a false chimney to reveal the mouth of a wide tube made of silk fabric.

"In. Jump in and slide!"

"Where?"

Davin was not given the chance to ask more. The Challing grabbed him by the back of the tunic and dumped him unceremoniously into the tube. Slide he did, downward through darkness until he popped out and skidded to a halt on his backside across a hardwood floor. Glylina exited the tube seconds later with a delighted grin wide on her face.

"I never tried this particular escape route before. It worked well!" She stood and offered a hand to pull her companion from the floor. "We are but minutes from the Fellowship's sanctuary."

"Wait! The guardsmen will follow down the chute."

"Let them." She drew a dirk from a sheath slung on her belt, bent, and severed a series of thin wires holding the mouth of silk open. "If they do, they'll end up somewhere on the street below

when the chute collapses under their weight. I doubt they'll be in
any condition to follow us if they survive the fall."

Two flights of stairs outside led to an alley into which Davin
followed Glylina and then through a maze of streets to the
Fellowship's headquarters. The Challing stopped and whistled
softly when she saw the gathering of thieves pressing into the
building.

"It seems Vytellion has stirred up the whole city to search for
us." Her eyes narrowed. "And Seonrho uses the occasion well."

"Seonrho?" Davin glanced at the crowd of cutpurses and
pickpockets.

"The big one with the black hair." Glylina nodded at a
mountain of muscle who spoke with a ring of listeners around
him. "He thought himself the finest thief in Ohnuhn until I
appeared and organized the Fellowship. That a woman accomplished what he couldn't rubbed him like a burr beneath a
horse's saddle. The sneak seeks to depose me. He has even met
secretly with Vytellion. The lord of Ohnuhn gladly supports
anyone he can control. I had intended to remove Seonrho
permanently, then you showed up and presented me with a new
set of problems."

"Had I known," Davin answered with a shrug.

"I had hoped to visit the headquarters without being noticed,"
Glylina continued, "but even if all the Fellowship is here, I won't
be denied. I have worked too long and hard to be thwarted now.
Come, we'll use a side entrance and hope that we don't draw
attention."

The plans of men and Challings are often twisted and set on a
new course by the dice-casting Sitala. So it was with Glylina's
scheme to slip inside by a side entrance. Both entrances were as
crowded as the one in front.

"Damn!" Glylina halted and stared around. "Anane, there are
magicks at work today. Stronger, they feel stronger than I've ever
felt them in Ohnuhn."

Davin had no time to question her. Several of the Fellowship's
thieves noticed her and called out. Glylina hastened forward and
pushed her way into the building, then through the sea of thieves
within to the raised podium at the far end of the room.

"This is not what I expected, Anane," she whispered to the

Jyotian as she held hands high to silence the drone of discontented voices. "Be prepared to follow me without question. We'll have but one chance to get out of here with our necks unbroken."

Turning her attention to the mass of thieves, Glylina called out, "The *evipods* that destroyed our meeting room are no more. I attended to them personally."

If the Challing expected applause or cheers, none came. Her only answer was a wave of grumbling that ran through the crowd. Davin suddenly realized she had not jested when she mentioned the possibility of having their throats slit.

Glylina motioned for Davin to stand to the right of the platform. His quick eyes saw no fewer than three possible exits. He could only guess which the Challing would choose.

"It's the outsider what's stirred up Vytellion and his guards!" a voice cried out. Another answered, "Cut the bastard's throat!"

Before the cry for blood could be taken up by the others, Glylina asked, "Is that what troubles you? We . . ."

"*You* trouble us, bitch!"

A hush fell over the room. Every head in the crowd turned to Seonrho who swaggered toward the podium from the back of the room.

"You have led us, or tried. And look where it has taken us! The man who stands at your side unleashed Vytellion's hounds upon us – and now Lord Vytellion's guardsmen hunt down every thief in the city as if we are animals!" Seonrho continued his slow deliberate strides toward the raised platform. "We have all seen that the one thing the Fellowship does not need is the gentle touch of a woman to guide it."

"What touch is needed?" Glylina's eyes blazed angrily, but Seonrho did not back down. "Perhaps you feel your touch is needed, Seonrho. Then again, I doubt the Fellowship would prosper under the hand of one in league with Vytellion himself!"

"Bitch!" Seonrho's right hand which had dangled at his side suddenly shot up. A spinning sliver of silver danced from his fingers and sailed through the air toward the Challing. "Taste *my* touch!"

Without batting an eye, Glylina snagged the spinning dagger

from the air, flicked her wrist and sent it sailing straight into Seonrho's throat.

In a single heartbeat chaos reigned within the thieves' sanctuary. Seonrho's supporters drew weapons and surged forward and were met by those still loyal to their blonde-tressed mistress. Glylina's own sword sprang free of its sheath as the Challing slashed the tip across the throat of a man with a cutlass who took one step too close to the podium.

While Davin's own sword disarmed a tangle-haired woman wielding a spiked bludgeon, Glylina's fingertips danced over the side of the rostrum to press at the bunch of grapes carved there. She called out, "This way, friend Anane!"

The blonde vanished into the black cavity that opened in the floor. In the blink of an eye, Davin did the same. The trap door overhead snicked closed and darkness enfolded him an instant before his feet hit solid ground.

"Hold tight to my hand and follow me closely." The Challing's hand found his and enclosed it. "There are hidden traps for the unwary."

"There are no torches?"

"What! Burn the building to the ground? Never!" Glylina laughed as she tugged the Jyotian through the darkness.

They covered a thousand paces before the Challing stopped to open what sounded like a latch. She pulled on Davin again and he heard a door close behind an instant before the thunder of crashing rocks shook the ground. A light flared and he blinked into Glylina's smiling face.

"The ceiling outside has collapsed to assure none follow to find this little treasure trove." She held a single candle high and nodded from left to right. "I had hoped to get it all aboard the *Windsong* before it became necessary to leave Ohnuhn. Now we'll take all that we can carry. If need be, we can return for the rest some day."

He released a low whistle of appreciation – and greed. For one who openly disdained thievery, Glylina had proved herself quite capable at the profession. Chests of jewels lined the walls. Bags, sacks! of gold coin underfoot made stepping difficult. Anything in Ohnuhn of any value that could be stolen resided in Glylina's treasure chamber.

Grabbing a canvas bag from the floor, she tossed it to Davin and pointed to a small mountain of neatly tied sacks. "Each of those contains a thousand bists. Take as many as you can carry."

Davin managed five bulging sacks while Glylina stuffed ten each into two bags. She then scooped up a handful of bists from an open chest and stuffed them into a pocket.

"First, we take this to the *Windsong* and then we'll see about finding horses for the ride to Gatinah." Glylina pushed a brick in the wall of the chamber and a door slid open. Once Davin and she had stepped into the sewer beyond, she pressed another brick and the door closed. "Not even the sewer rats you ran with, friend Anane, ever found this!"

With enough gold to buy a small army weighing them down, Challing and Jyotian sloshed into the sewers beneath Ohnuhn toward the sea.

15

"Yehseen's staff!" Davin yowled and clamped a hand to his right ear. Specks of red glistened on his fingers when the hand came away. "I'm bleeding! What did you do to me?"

Glylina, now form-shifted to the familiar redhead, smiled sweetly at the Jyotian and held up a long lock pick. "Just completing your own change, friend Anane. I pierced your right ear."

"Pierced my ear! With a lock tool!" Davin jerked up a mirror and stared at his skewered right ear lobe. "By all the gods, why?"

"To slip this in." While Davin watched in the mirror, the Challing inserted a large gold ring through the hole in the lobe. "There! Now tell me where I might find Davin Anane."

The Jyotian's head twisted from side to side to inspect carefully the reflected image. He pursed his lips and nodded. Glylina's scissors left his hair closely cropped to his head. Trimmings from her barbering were now neatly glued across his upper lip and chin to concoct a dark moustache and goatee.

"Certainly, he's not to be found in the mirror." Davin smiled, pleased with the transformation the Challing created in less than the passage of an hour. "But did you have to run me through with that needle?"

Glylina chuckled. "Quit whining, Anane. The wound is minor, has already stopped bleeding. When the ring is removed, it will heal in days. You'll never know you've been run through."

She turned, crossed the *Windsong*'s cabin, opened a small chest, and extracted a belt of *pletha* skin. Others might have used the nearby scissors, but the Challing employed strong hands to rend the furred snake skin. In seconds, she fashioned a crude eye patch from the orange fur and tossed it to her companion.

"Tie that around your head," she ordered.

Davin did so. A wicked smile slid across his lips when he looked
up at the redhead. He could not resist the urge that overwhelmed
him. "Did I ever tell you how I lost my eye?"

Glylina stared at him, brow furrowing with uncertainty. "Lost
your eye? What are you . . ."

"It was in the far-off realm of Humdrumaton." The Jyotian's
mischievous grin widened with obvious delight. "It was there
my extraordinary physique piqued the interest of the youngest
daughter of the aged King Getevon."

"Anane, have you lost your mind?" Glylina stared at him as
though she faced a madman.

"No, it was my eye that I lost," the Jyotian went on thoroughly
enjoying this sudden reversal of roles. He could not begin to
count the endless tales Goran had spun about the loss of his own
eye. "You see, I had been taken by a band of slavers and dragged
to Humdrumaton in chains. Stripped I was of all clothing except
the merest patch of ragged cloth which hid a certain region below
my navel."

"Anane, you have lost your mind!" the Challing exclaimed.

"It was as I told you," Davin answered with a shake of his
head. "It was my eye that I lost – aren't you paying attention? Or
is your Challing brain too small to grasp the intricacies of such a
noble tale?"

"Noble tale?" Glylina's frown deepened. "This sounds more
like a story born while staring upward at the bottom of a
flagon!"

"Aye, Getevon's daughter would have earned a king's ransom
in a single night in a brothel, so great was her hunger and
passion." Davin fought to keep from bursting out in laughter.
Glylina had no idea what he did, but that did nothing to sour the
sweetness of his verbal revenge. How many times had he yearned
to repay Goran for his ridiculous yarns? "You see, young Princess
Lustenbluem was so intrigued by the muscular proportions of my
body, she became obsessed to discover the secrets hidden beneath
that torn triangle of cloth."

"More likely she wondered if a brain existed within that head."

Davin would not be denied. "So it was that Lustenbluem crept
into the slave pen that night disguised as a simple peasant girl. It
would take a lifetime to detail fully the pleasures to which she

introduced me that night, but we should consider the journey before us. Suffice it to say, as dawn began to break and summoned a new day, she had totally drained me of strength and energy."

"And robbed you of a voice, I hope," the Challing mumbled.

"I was like a man in a coma, unaware of anything," the Jyotian continued. "It was then that Lustenbluem stole my eye. With the very long-nailed fingers she had used to rip bloody ribbons of passion into my back throughout the night, she prised open my eyelids and plucked out my left orb to keep as a memento of the carnal bliss we had shared. So it was I lost my eye."

Davin's grin spread from ear to ear as he gazed at his perplexed companion.

With her head tilted at an angle which sent her long flowing tresses cascading about her shoulders like a river of fire, Glylina studied him for a long silent moment. "Friend Anane, if you'll lift that *pletha* skin, you'll find that you have not one, but *two* eyes! The patch is but part of a disguise meant to get you past Vytellion's guards. As are these."

He accepted the forged letters of transit Glylina handed him and hiked the eye patch to feel beneath with two fingers. His exposed eye widened with surprise. He grinned again, "Ah, yes, you must remind me to tell you how I recovered my eye the next night. Only the master thief of Raemllyn could have accomplished such a daring feat."

"That or the greatest li—"

A knock at the cabin door cut the Challing short.

"Captain Glylina," a voice called. "Harwin is back aboard. He has horses waiting on the wharf."

"We'll be on deck in a moment." The Challing crossed the room to open a trunk pushed against the wall. She handed Davin the long oiled-leather bundle she pulled out. "This should serve you better than the poor Ohnuhnian sword you now carry."

"Vytellion's hounds ate my own blade." Davin untied the bundle and stared at the sword and sheath within. "But this is *my* sword! How did you retrieve it?"

Davin swallowed the rest of his questions when he saw the tears welling in Glylina's eyes. He now understood where she had got the sword and why it was so carefully stored in the chest.

She forced a weak smile. "It is only right that Davin Anane should wear the sword of Davin Anane."

"You honor me." He stood, unstrapped the stolen blade, and buckled on the new sword and sheath. How familiar the grip felt in his hand! Even without drawing steel, he knew the perfectly balanced blade would fit his hand.

"We've tarried here long enough. None in Ohnuhn knows me in this form and none will recognize you," she said. "It's time we were on the road to Gatinah."

"Past time." Davin's fingers crept to his chest and the violet ring beneath his clean white blouse.

On the deck of the *Windsong* where Glylina singled out Harwin to give sailing instructions for the voyage to Gatinah, the remaining two members of the Challing's youthful crew pressed to both sides of the Jyotian.

"Our captain is even more beautiful, if that is possible, when she dons her red wig, is she not?" the youth to the left asked.

"If that is possible," Davin agreed, suppressing a smile. The crew apparently knew nothing of Glylina's changeling abilities.

He stared at the woman. There was no denying her beauty. Dressed in doeskin breeches and vest over a white blouse, she appeared to be some huntress sent to the earth by the gods.

"There is none other like our captain in all of Raemllyn," said the youth to Davin's right. "It would be wise of the man who travels with her to Gatinah to see that no harm befalls her. Should that not be the case, that man would find three who will trail him more vigorously than Vytellion's hounds."

The threat surprised the Jyotian, but it did speak of the deep loyalty the three youths held for Glylina. No wonder she trusted them with the fortune hidden within the *Windsong*. "If harm befalls her, it will come only after I have died."

The two nodded, apparently satisfied by his answer. They beamed a smile when Glylina turned.

"Time for them to get under sail and us to begin our journey," the Challing said, motioning Davin down a rope ladder to the dinghy that bobbed in the water below.

From the wharf, Jyotian and Challing turned back to watch the vessel glide from the harbor to the open sea.

"Vytellion will not be so lax within the city," Glylina said. "When we face the guards who *will* approach us, simply show them your papers. Say nothing, friend Anane. Your Jyotian accent will give us away."

Davin offered no argument. Compared to Goran One-Eye, his counterpart seemed competent and able when it came to schemes of subterfuge. And, the Jyotian admitted, Glylina knew Ohnuhn and its ways far better than he. After all, she had organized and ruled the Fellowship for long months.

"Harwin was more than generous in seeing to our needs," Davin said when they approached the waiting horses. "Two pack animals laden with supplies as well as two mounts."

Glylina grinned. "Be not fooled by the packs. They hide saddles. When we are beyond Vytellion's patrols, we'll discard the bundles, keeping only the supplies needed for the journey. Two mounts each will carry us to Gatinah faster than one."

Guardsmen in pairs and patrols moved constantly along Ohnuhn's streets and avenues while the pair of adventurers rode leisurely toward the city's eastern gate. However, the soldiers never gave Davin more than a glance. Their eyes *did* hang on Glylina for more time than was polite. Yet there was no questioning in their lingering gazes, merely wistful wishing.

Only when the two reached the east gate did a guardsman halt them and demand their papers. While the officer in charge examined the artfully penned letters of transit, a fight broke out between two beggars who sat near the wall coaxing octens from passers-by. Within seconds, the fight spilled into the street. A ring of onlookers soon circled the two contestants, shouting out wagers on who would win the dispute.

Davin's right hand drifted to the hilt of his sword, but Glylina's soft fingertips were there to halt him. She shook her head as though tossing aside a stray strand of red from her eyes.

"You may pass," the officer said as he returned their papers. Attention diverted, he hastened them through the gate, then rushed to the fight, calling out, "A bist on the taller one!"

"Jajhana graces us with her smile," Davin said after releasing an overly held breath once they moved down the road. "The fight could not have been better timed if we planned it."

"Not a goddess, friend Anane." Glylina winked at him. "But two bists. I tossed them at the beggars as the officer read your papers. It seems little enough price to aid us."

Davin laughed. How unlike Goran was this Glylina. Goran's answer to any hesitancy on the part of the guardsmen at the gate would have resulted in a series of bashed skulls.

"It was but a small diversion unworthy of such mirth," she said.

The Jyotian explained the root of his laughter. This brought a complete transformation to his companion. The merry light in Glylina's eyes faded and her mouth drew into a tight, thin line.

"What's wrong?" Davin was not certain what he had said to upset her. "Did I offend you in some manner?"

She shook her head, her gaze focusing on the road ahead. "It is not you, but me. Whenever you mention the way I was in your world, it frightens me. This Goran One-Eye sounds as if he were no more than a wild animal – a beast."

Davin shrugged. "At times, I cannot deny that. But no better man ever walked Raemllyn."

"I do not doubt your words or love for that Goran. It's his wildness I find frightening."

Davin studied her before asking, "Or is it the wildness of your own Goran you find frightening?"

Glylina's head snapped around. Her mouth opened, then closed as she swallowed hard. "Damn you, Anane, your eyes see me as surely as Davin's did! How can that be?"

"Perhaps it is because we are one and the same," he said. Then Davin added, "With differences."

Again Glylina started to speak but held her words as though lost in a distant thought.

"Perhaps you have never had the chance to know Goran," Davin suggested. "If I prevented you from shape-shifting to Goran, you haven't worn his body long enough to know him."

She turned in the saddle and stared at him. "Do you want me to become Goran? I will if that is what you want, if it will be easier for you."

The question caught Davin off guard. He blinked as he gathered his thoughts and finally answered with a firm shake of his head. "No. To be honest, in less than the span of a day I have come to accept you as you are now. However, what I want is not the question. What do *you* want? You have the ability to take any shape you desire. It is your choice to select the body you want, when you want it."

His words shocked him. How many times had he admonished Goran One-Eye for his shape-shifting? He could not deny the changes his visit to A'bre had wrought within him. He had seen the Challing in its natural form, a beautiful mist sparkling with gemlike lights that shifted restlessly through the spectrum. No man who had seen that could ever wish to bind a Challing in shape or spirit.

"Then I will hold this form," Glylina said. "Goran is too savage in his hungers. He is insatiable in his desire to experience every sensation the human body permits. When I'm Goran, I feel there is no way to control what I do. Were he not stronger and a more fierce fighter, I would never consider shifting into his body."

Davin recalled Glylina saying how her own first experience of human sensation had frightened her. It made sense that Goran's unbridled hedonism would terrify her. Davin smiled. In truth, Goran's hunger scared him sometimes.

"We are beyond Vytellion's scrying spells and guards," Glylina said when they topped the rise from which Davin had first viewed Ohnuhn. "Time to discard the packs. And remove that ridiculous beard and earring so I can see your handsome face again."

Davin's head jerked around at that last pronouncement, and Glylina's cheeks blushed a rosy red when she realized what she had said. Had he not sensed how deeply embarrassed she was by the slip of the tongue, he would have gladly pursued the opening she gave him. Instead, he asked:

"Did I ever tell how I lost my eye to the fire maidens of Norgg?"

Despite tossing away the makeshift eye patch, he could not resist giving the Challing another taste of the tales Goran had barraged him with for years.

"No," Glylina answered as she removed packs to reveal a saddle with light supplies bundled behind it. "But if you persist in another ridiculous tale about your not-so-missing lost eye, I shall have to demonstrate how I once castrated a certain would-be assassin named Tuolouse-of-Tongue."

"Has anyone ever mentioned a lack of a sense of humor in a

certain Challing we both know?" Davin tossed away the last of the packs from his animal then swung back into the saddle.

"No," Glylina replied with a wink when she nudged her mount forward in an easy gallop. "And it would probably be better if no one ever did."

"Then I surmise, all that is left is Gatinah." He urged his own mount eastward toward the city of Lord Hormachi.

"To Gatinah!" Glylina cried out as the wind caught her long red tresses to spread them like a soft banner in the air.

16

"Gatinah," the pronouncement came from Davin's lips more as a murmured sigh of relief than a shout of victory.

"Ohnuhn presents a better face to the traveler," Glylina observed with a current of disdain barely hidden in her tone as she studied the dingy gray walls surrounding Gatinah. "But it's not beauty that brought us here, is it? It's a slumbering fire elemental that needs removal from your chest."

Two days, Davin mentally clicked off the time remaining before the violet ring ignited. Meals in the saddle, the non-stop ride, the horses stolen along the way to replace their spent mounts had been worth it. He still had two days before Hormachi's spell would again sear his flesh and brain.

Glylina pursed her lips and tilted her head to one side as though viewing the city-state from a different perspective. "I'm certain there are ample opportunities for thieves of limited resources to filch minor treasures here, but Ohnuhn offered a greater challenge and unlimited wealth."

"Come, we waste time sitting here when Gatinah is so close." Davin tapped his heels to a chestnut's flanks and reined toward the city, ignoring the Challing's verbal barbs.

In spite of the long nose down which Glylina viewed Davin's chosen profession, the changeling had delighted in detailing how she had entered Ohnuhn and within a matter of weeks established the Fellowship of thieves. Like her counterpart Goran-Glylina, the Challing obviously held herself superior to mere humans. She was, Davin admitted, far more subtle about voicing that opinion. Goran bragged of his conquests with the bellowing of a bull.

Or, Davin considered, was it that Glylina remained uncertain of the humanity rooted within her during her fifteen years on Raemllyn? He had seen a Challing in its natural form, a being nine parts mystical to one physical. Even after more than a decade in the body of a human, it must be difficult for an entity to accept itself as something – someone – it was not. Glylina might not boast but merely sought to convince herself she was indeed human.

The Jyotian caught himself. And what of Goran? He had never considered the same might have applied to that one-eyed giant. How strange to view his brother of the sword in this new light.

"Have you decided the approach we'll take with Hormachi?" Glylina asked. "We can't walk up to him and say, 'Here's the statue, remove your magicks.' "

Davin shook his head. "I know."

Throughout the ride he had pondered the best method of convincing the ruler-mage to remove the hex. The only thing he was certain of was that he could not rely on Hormachi's sense of mercy and fair play. The lord's deadly maze had taught the adventurer Hormachi had neither.

"We might prise loose the diamond and hold it back," suggested Glylina, apparently realizing her companion lacked a lever to move Hormachi. "Of course, when he examined the statue and realized the only thing of value had been taken . . ."

"You speak my thoughts," Davin said before she finished. "There has to be a way to beat Hormachi at his own game. Yet it eludes me! He has balanced the scales in his favor."

Glylina stared into the distance. "With a mage there is always his vanity. I have never met a human wizard who is not vain. They want to be seen as beneficent, omnipotent – even handsome. What is Hormachi's weakness?"

The Jyotian shook his head. "I met Hormachi but once. There is little opportunity to study a man when fighting desperately for life."

Handsome. Glylina's words danced in Davin's mind to awaken not an image of Hormachi but of Vytellion. He could not shake the feeling that he had seen Ohnuhn's ruler before the night Glylina and he invaded Vytellion's private chambers. He cursed the trick of mind that brought Vytellion back into his thoughts. The man was leagues behind him and no longer of consequence. He needed to focus on Hormachi.

"Perhaps we can use this Cal'Dreth," Glylina continued. "I'm certain his Brotherhood of Pliaton has open avenues to Hormachi. You could have saved yourself time and myriad bruises had you sought me in Ohnuhn when you first arrived."

"I would be dead if I had tried any harder to meet with you," Davin answered with a snort. "Your Fellowship thugs had little use for common hospitality."

The Challing shrugged as though it did not matter. Davin realized it no longer did. Gatinah and Hormachi were far more important.

Davin and Glylina entered the city through the wide open west gate without being questioned, although the ten guardsmen in their popinjay uniforms did eye them curiously.

Glylina hiked her eyebrows and glanced at the Jyotian. "It is strange for city soldiers to let anyone pass without demanding to see traveling papers."

"More unusual is the number of guards." Davin frowned when he glanced back over his shoulder. "Hormachi normally keeps no more than two men at each gate."

"What of those?" The redhead nodded to a four-man patrol that crossed the street ahead of them as another moved from one alley to another.

Davin's frown furrowed deeper. Each intersection they passed revealed another patrol of guardsmen. "Something has changed since I left."

Outside Aotesja's shop stood a full dozen soldiers, all in Hormachi's gaudy uniforms. The Challing noted the direction of his gaze and said, "It would not be wise to consider visiting the prosperous gem merchant this day."

"It doesn't make sense." Davin's frown remained. "Aotesja used private guards, not Hormachi's."

"We can ponder the changes later," Glylina said. "It's time we found a place to rest. There seem to be inns aplenty in this city."

Rather than a caravanserai, Davin led the Challing through the streets and back ways until he halted before the small house that had been home to him and his dogs. To his surprise and disappointment, the rooms remained empty – surprise because Gatinah overflowed with humanity, spare rooms commanding premium prices. His disappointment stemmed from the fact he saw no trace of his hounds. He did not expect to find his canine companions, yet he could not help but hope. It took only seconds for Davin to pick the simple lock used on the back door.

"Bring your horse inside," he said as he stepped into the

building. "The smell cannot get any worse than it already is."

The reek said the landlord had not bothered cleaning the place after the Jyotian's sudden departure. The undeniable odor of dog feces and urine had prevented the house from being rented.

"It's obvious you lived in the lap of luxury, Anane." Glylina spoke in a voice steeped in sarcasm when she took their mounts and led them into a side room to feed them the last of the grain in their supplies.

Meanwhile, Davin unrolled bundled blankets in a front room and stretched across his. Glylina joined him and did likewise. The gentle rhythm of her breathing as she slept eventually lulled him into dreams of his own.

"The mutton is better in Ohnuhn." Glylina delicately picked at roasted joint of lamb as they wandered through the bazaar. "And the bread isn't stale there either."

"It fills an empty stomach." Davin finished his portion of the meat and tossed the clean bone aside. "We were lucky to find such a talkative merchant. He never saw me stealing any of this from his stall."

"It wasn't my conversation that interested him. Didn't you see the way the swine leered at me?" Glylina tossed her half-eaten mutton after Davin's. "Besides, he wanted you to steal it. No one would buy such garbage and he was too lazy to feed it to the pigs."

Davin's gaze gradually worked around the marketplace. "The tension is so heavy I can almost see it. Everyone is expecting something to happen, something terrible from the dour expressions on all their faces."

"Or something has happened," Glylina offered. "Where is everybody? I've never seen a bazaar so empty."

"A question I've asked myself all day, milady." The answer came from a brass merchant who waved an arm over his table of goods. "Perhaps I might interest you in my wares? It costs nothing to look and little to buy."

Davin stopped, recognizing the man as a well-known gossip among the merchants. The Jyotian moved to the brass merchant's stall and dropped two gold coins onto the table. A leathery hand shot out and covered them. Davin leaned forward, his hand pressing the merchant's into the table to prevent him from spiriting away the money.

"A fine day, but one lacking in business," Davin said. "Why is that?"

"You do not know?" The merchant's eyes widened in surprise. "Are you newly arrived in Gatinah?"

"Yes," Davin said simply.

The man, small and furtive, looked from Davin to Glylina and back. "My wares are renowned throughout Raemllyn," he lied. "Your pick this day. Half my regular price."

"Shoddy workmanship." Glylina lifted a brass bowl and, with an enchanting smile on her face, crushed it in one hand. She dropped it back to the table. "I dislike everything shoddy."

The less than subtle hint of violence should the merchant lie was not lost on the man. He swallowed hard and paled.

"Tell me of Lord Hormachi," Davin said. He released the pressure on the merchant's hand, allowing the man to slide back the two coins. Idly dropping another coin onto the table kept the merchant's attention.

"What is there to tell? He is a mage and has ruled this fair city for more than a decade." The merchant lowered his voice as he added, "Few like him and all fear him. Cruel, he is. A tyrant."

"Aren't they all?" Glylina said with a displeased grunt. "There are those who say the same of High King Felrad or Vytellion in Ohnuhn."

"Hormachi's brother?" The merchant's head snapped up.

Davin and Glylina exchanged startled glances. Davin turned to the merchant. "Vytellion and Hormachi are blood brothers?"

"More," chuckled the small man, knowing he had their attention now. He took the third coin and slipped it into the folds of his clothing. He waited for Davin to toss a fourth before continuing. "They are twins."

Twins! The image of Vytellion that had popped into Davin's mind earlier appeared again. He silently cursed himself for not seeing the resemblance before as Hormachi's image appeared beside Vytellion. The two faces superimposed over each other, matching perfectly except that Vytellion lacked the neatly trimmed beard that fringed Hormachi's face.

"They have long fought, those two," the smallish merchant recounted. "No one knows the source of their hatred for each other, but it runs deep. Twice in the past decade have Ohnuhn and Gatinah gone to war. Assassins flit through both cities, one brother sending his killer after the other. And always it is the poor who suffer."

The merchant opened and closed his hand a few times to ensure a new flood of gold. Davin dropped three more coins into the callused palm.

"What more do you know?" Glylina picked up another bowl and threatened to crush it.

"It is said they each jealously guard an item given to them by their mother who was also well-versed in the arcane arts, fair lady." The brass merchant shrugged. "What that item is, I cannot say. But there are those who suspect Hormachi's and Vytellion's power flows from their mother's gifts. It is said each brother seeks to rob the other of his wellspring of strength so that he may destroy his sibling."

Again Davin and Glylina exchanged glances. These hasty looks bespoke a certain carved soapstone with a diamond embedded in its belly.

"Take with you what you desire most, my most favored patrons," the merchant suddenly changed subjects to indicate there was no more he could reveal. "You are my finest customers this day, the finest all week!"

Neither Davin nor Glylina bothered selecting from the base wares, walking quickly across the marketplace when a squad of Hormachi's soldiers approached. They wove through the sparse crowd and soon left behind the patrolling guards who now randomly stopped people and roughly questioned them.

"Hormachi fears his most recent attempt to steal the statue has failed," opined Glylina. "You have been gone longer than he expected and believes Vytellion has killed you."

"And now Vytellion sends assassins for Hormachi's head." Davin grinned as he patted the pouch dangling at his waist. "Is it not possible Hormachi has a statue similar to this one?"

"Or perhaps this is the only statue, and he seeks only to possess it for his own. A brotherly rivalry and nothing more," Glylina answered skeptically. "Remember how I felt scrying spells after you pinched the statue? Vytellion's power cannot originate in the figurine."

"Still, there might be twin statues," Davin said. "If there is another, it, too, can be stolen."

"You think to return this one, then force Hormachi to lift the curse from you before returning *his* statue?"

Davin nodded. "Correct, except I will see Hormachi dead when I return the second statue."

"Ah, yes, I had forgotten the mousy little thief you killed in Hormachi's maze." Glylina's voice carried a twinge of jealousy.

"Hormachi was responsible for Irisli's death," Davin corrected. "I promised her that he would pay with equal measure."

"Very noble," Glylina answered with heavy sarcasm. "But I see one problem. We don't know if Hormachi has a duplicate. Not to mention the obvious problem of stealing it, *if* there is one."

"Where would he keep his statue?" Davin thought aloud, ignoring the Challing. "If Vytellion kept his in his sleeping chamber, would a twin think any differently?"

"And steal it without him realizing it has been stolen," Glylina continued, staring at her companion. "A difficult plan to launch, Anane."

"It is the twin of this one," Davin assured her, thrusting aside his own doubt.

"*If* it exists," Glylina repeated.

"Hormachi's palace is an exact replica of Vytellion's." Glylina scrutinized the walled keep. "The only difference is the domed edifice there."

"His maze is under that dome," Davin answered with contempt.

In truth, he had never noticed the similarity of the two palaces. Now that the Challing mentioned it, he realized the two structures were alike. Davin grinned – he knew where Hormachi's bedchamber was and how to get to it. Once there, he would replace the ruler-mage's statue with the reproduction he had hired a local artisan to carve for him. So crude was the figurine, the task had been accomplished in the span of two hours, barely enough time to find a chunk of glass that resembled the diamond in the statue's belly.

"You lack your army of Ohnuhnian sewer rats to attack the marketplace and draw the guards away from the palace as you did with Vytellion," Glylina said. "Do you have any idea how we're going to sneak past the front gate?"

"Mayhap a bit of diversion," Davin answered.

"With so many guardsmen on patrol, it will have to be a riot to gain their attention."

"Maybe not. Wait here."

Davin hurried to a building down the street from the palace gates. It took ten minutes for him to break in and another ten to find enough dried rags to litter about the large vacant rooms of the abandoned building, but once in place the rags gave more than ample fuel for the fire he started. Davin was not content with this one building going up in a blaze. He carried a torch to the building next door. He kicked in the door, yelled "fire" and got out of the way as people inside scrambled to put out the conflagration he had visited upon them.

"Is it a fire bug I travel with?" Doubt lined Glylina's face when Davin returned. "First the mapmaker's shop and now this!"

"You forget what slumbers in here," Davin said, tapping his chest where Hormachi's fire elemental awaited the proper time to burst into fiery life. "As to the more obvious fires, they are just a matter of expediency in both cases," Davin answered with a shrug.

His ploy proved effective. A few guards gathered and pointed. Then another and still another pushed out from the palace courtyard and sounded the alarm. When the buildings began crackling with flame, the officer of the watch ordered his men down the street to douse the blaze. This gave Davin and Glylina the chance to fell a lone watchful sentry and slip into the palace grounds.

"The tower," Davin said, pointing. "Do you think he has a secret entry like Vytellion?"

"No," Glylina said, scanning the open area. "There isn't a secondary tower near it. We must go directly."

Davin walked more slowly than his friend, eyes fixed on the door into a corridor similar to Vytellion's hall of fears. Did voracious, gelatinous gray slugs slither about on patrol inside? He shivered at the thought. They needed a barrel of salt, if Hormachi employed the same magical guardians.

"The fire's spread," Glylina bellowed in a voice that belonged to Goran rather than herself. "Call out the entire guard! Save the town! All Gatinah is ablaze!"

Again, soldiers deserted their posts to answer the call. Davin took a deep breath and ran headlong up tne steps and into the tower containing Hormachi's sleeping chambers. Unlike Vytellion's tower, two staircases rose inside, pushing both left and right.

There was no time for hesitation. The guardsmen would soon have his little blaze under control. Davin pointed. "You take the left one. I'll go right."

Davin did not wait to see if Glylina obeyed. He took the steps three at a time, pain tugging at his chest as he ascended the tower. A full day remained before the violet ring ignited, yet the proximity to Hormachi's private keep made him abundantly aware of the pain and death painted on and embedded in his flesh.

Gasping for breath, Davin reached the top of the stairs before Glylina. He paused in front of the door into Hormachi's chambers, wondering if the lord of Gatinah lay asleep inside. A swift thrust of a dagger might prove as effective as anything else. Most spells died with the mage casting them. Did this one? It could prove Davin's death if it were not the case. He could not risk killing the only man able to remove the curse.

"Well?" Glylina demanded when she reached the top of the left staircase. "Is Hormachi within?"

Davin drew his sword and opened the door to reveal—
Nothing!
Hormachi was not inside. Nor was the statue!

17

"It *must* be here." Davin's temples pounded in a frantic race. "It must be here somewhere. The shape of the sleeping chamber is the same. But where's the table with the Qar-damned statue?"

"Calm yourself." Glylina casually strolled about the room, her fingertips exploring the walls for hidden compartments. "Hormachi might not share identical thoughts with his brother. Appearances alone do not ensure he is the same as his twin."

"Nothing!" Davin admitted defeat after a third search of the chamber.

"A twin statue apparently does not exist. The one you have is the only one, hence the battle that has raged over the years between Hormachi and Vytellion," Glylina pronounced with finality.

"What do I do now? Rational thought fled the Jyotian's mind. He had been certain a twin figurine existed. His thoughts fell together in a jumbled pile of jackstraws. The second statue was the key to saving himself from the death that slumbered in his breast. Without it Hormachi won and Davin lost his life.

"First, we leave." Glylina's voice of reason penetrated the chaotic muddle of Davin's panic-ridden brain. "We have a day before the violet ring ignites. There is still time to find a way to deal with Hormachi."

"His laboratory!" Davin's thought thrust through swirling flotsam. "There's still the grimoire. Another mage can lift the spell, no matter that Mairri cheated me."

"Ah, the Huata. They have such endearing traits," Glylina said coldly. "We dealt with them to aid Felrad. For such a scrawny lot, their women seemed fired by insatiable desire. There was one in particular who had an eye for Davin. Selene was her name."

"There isn't time for such reminiscence." Davin's tongue held a sharp edge he did not intend. Yet he had no patience for the Challing's jealousies.

Glylina's tone was honed equally when she snapped, "Nor is

there time for you to repeat a fool's game. You *know* Hormachi has ward spells protecting his tome of magicks. Would you alert him to our presence and risk losing this?''

She patted the pouch at her waist that held the genuine soapstone statue.

Davin slumped; she was right. Before he could answer, the Challing jumped lightly to Hormachi's bed and began pressing her fingers against the panels around the headboard. A small snap sounded. Glylina stepped from the bed when the wall opened to reveal a brass pole leading downward to the ground floor.

"In spite of my contention that one twin need not think like the other, some points of caution are obviously shared by Hormachi and Vytellion." The redhead jumped, caught the pole, and slid from sight.

Davin hesitated, unwilling to admit failure. If he could have wished the statue into existence, it would have popped into the air before his eyes. But wishes were not reality, and reality was that the statue was not here, nor was there any hint within the chamber that it existed. He grabbed the pole and slid below.

Before the Jyotian could utter a sound when he reached the ground, Glylina turned and pressed a finger to her lips. She motioned him toward the small door leading outside and pointed for him to peer through the crack she had opened.

Outside, Hormachi, surrounded by a score of bodyguards, stormed past. The ruler-mage's features burned an angry scarlet and his eyes were determined slits. The apprehension on the guards' faces bespoke their leader's foul mood.

"He must know I've returned and have not given him the statue," Davin whispered.

"Do you think he has no other worries? The lord of such a large city-state is deluged constantly with demands. I know. I ran the Fellowship for long weeks. Always someone egging you on, begging for this or beseeching you for that. It grows wearisome," the Challing answered.

"Nothing again will tire us unless we escape." Signaling Glylina to follow, Davin crouched low as he ran across the courtyard to find shelter behind a half-dozen horses that stood with flaring nostrils and lathered flanks.

When his Challing companion reached his side, they snatched

up the dangling reins and started for the stable. They took two steps when a voice called out:

"You, hold! Leave the horses. The scouts will head out again after conferring with Lord Hormachi."

"So soon?" The question pushed from Davin's lips before he realized what he did. He stood exposed before dozens of guardsmen, yet he drew attention to himself with a foolish question.

The response proved enlightening rather than delivering upon him a quick death.

"The Ohnuhnian swine march on us. We need constant reports if we are to defend the city."

"Aye, Captain," Davin said.

Glylina worked closer, slunk low to use the horses to shield her from the sentries.

"How do we get out of here?" asked the Challing, her sapphire eyes darting about. "I counted no fewer than a full company of men outside the gate."

Davin nodded. "Vytellion comes to reclaim the statue."

"And our heads!" Glylina shimmered for an instant, then regained her original form and spoke in distress. "By Yehseen's shriveled staff, I can't change shape! Conflicting magicks pull me this way and that. I had hoped Goran's additional strength might aid us."

"Make way for Lord Hormachi's scouts!" a voice called. "Bring their mounts and open the gate!"

"The gate opens! There's our way out!" Davin swung to the back of a dappled gray and slammed his heels into the animal.

With a snort, the horse bounded forward in a full run straight for the opening gate. The Jyotian risked a glance over a shoulder to see Glylina leap astride a bay and rein the horse after him. Using the reins like whips, he slapped leather to the gray, urging the mount to greater speed. Through the gate, past startled soldiers into Gatinah's streets he rode with Glylina only a length behind him.

Ten streets from the palace, Davin threw a leg over the animal's neck and pushed from the saddle. He hit the street in a run that carried him into the relative shelter of a narrow alley. Likewise, Glylina leaped from the bay and followed him, her red hair flowing like flames dancing in the wind.

"No pursuit," she said after taking a hasty glance over her shoulder. "We have tweaked Hormachi's nose in his own lair and he never realized it! It would be a fine jest if we had another statue to show for our efforts."

"Aye," was all Davin could manage. He could not escape the harsh reality that faced him. He either delivered the statue into Hormachi's hands by this time tomorrow night or the violet ring would burn into his flesh. The ruler of Gatinah's warning echoed within his head – only the strongest of men could survive the fire brought by the violet paint.

"There!" Goran of the two eyes roared with obvious delight. "I knew it was Vytellion's cursed statue that hindered my change! The strength in this body should serve us well!"

Davin stared at the familiar form of his old friend. The red-maned giant's muscular body strained every seam of the doeskins Glylina had worn, threatening to rip them wide if he moved so much as an inch.

"Hand me the statue," Goran said, "and we'll be on our way again."

Davin did as requested and immediately the mountain of muscle that was Goran quivered and quaked. In the space of three heartbeats, Glylina in all her sensuous voluptuousness again stood facing the Jyotian.

"Qar be damned!" The Challing stared at her feminine form. "There is something working here I don't understand. The magicks radiating from the statue are not that potent. Yet they seem to lock me in this body."

"Glylina will do quite nicely if the need arises," Davin said. "Remember, she and I have tangled before. I know her abilities."

The Challing smiled at his assurance. "Perhaps I should carry the fake statue. That way, my Goran shape might hold."

The Jyotian shook his head. "The only way we'll force Hormachi to remove his hex is to convince him that he must keep his part of the bargain before we deliver the real statue."

"It seems a weak plan," Glylina replied as they moved toward the palace.

Davin silently agreed, but within an hour the violet circle would flare alive with unbearable pain. Since fleeing the palace last night, he had been unable to think of anything else, except to face Hormachi and demand he unweave the spell.

"War drums." Glylina tilted her head to the side and listened. "It might be more difficult getting an audience with Hormachi than we anticipated. Vytellion's arrival sounds imminent."

"You underestimate the statue's power," Davin said, hearing the steady beat of the approaching drums now. "Hormachi risked a war to obtain it. He will see us."

"Mayhap it would be greater revenge if I were to return this ugly thing to Vytellion," Glylina suggested.

"No," Davin said firmly, with a determined shake of his head. "Hormachi will not play games. He will either agree to remove his magicks or kill me outright. If it's the latter, destroy the statue and save yourself. With the statue gone, you should be able to shape-shift to a night bird and take wing."

"Davin, there is the possibility Vytellion can unweave his brother's spell," the Challing continued. "If we returned the statue to him . . ."

"Destroy it," Davin repeated firmly, barely noticing Glylina used his first name. "Vytellion would have both our heads for stealing the statue. If I die this night, it will be with the satisfaction that you rob Hormachi of the thing he most desires in this world."

"I'll rob him of his life as well," Glylina said in a cold-blooded tone that left little doubt should Davin die this night so would Gatinah's ruler.

"No," Davin said again. "Just destroy the statue and then save yourself. My soul will be doubly tormented in the depths of Peyneeha if I should cause your death. There is still Aarrin who is in need. What is hap—"

Davin hastily retreated to avoid the point of a lance that poked at his gut. Two guardsmen, one with lance and the other with drawn sword stepped from a shadow-cloaked alley.

"What is the meaning of this outrage?" Glylina demanded with as much indignity as she could summon. "We are peaceable citizens performing lawful chores."

"You are out after Lord Hormachi's curfew," the soldier with the bared sword cut her short.

"Aye," the lancer agreed. "And there's a funny sound to your tongue. You're no citizen of Gatinah. You sound to me like spies for that pig Vytellion."

The soldier's logic left much to be desired, nor did he appear willing to be swayed from his conclusion, but Davin had to try. "Nay, that is not so. We are faithful subjects of Lord Hormachi. I was on my way to bring him his statue." He held up the sack containing the fake statue. "He sent me on a mission to Ohnuhn to retrieve it. It must go to him immediately."

"To the dungeons with ye," urged the guard with the sword. "We have no time, not with Vytellion's army at our gates."

"We heard the war drums. It is a shame you pass up the chance for easy victory," Glylina said, taking a tentative step toward the guardsmen.

"Easy victory? What are you getting at?" The lancer's eyes narrowed as he stared at the pouch hung at the Jyotian's hip.

"This statue," Davin took advantage of the opening. "Lord Hormachi needs the statue stolen from his brother, Lord Vytellion. It could well determine which army lives to see the coming dawn."

"What craziness is this?" The swordsman frowned and sucked at his teeth. "Fetch the lieutenant. This ain't a matter for the likes of us."

"The statue is one Hormachi desires above all else," Davin added when the lancer turned to go. "Ask any of his advisers and say that the dog thief has returned with the statue."

"Dog thief?" The swordsman's frown deepened.

"A code name, nothing more," Davin amended quickly. A sigh slipped past his lips when the lancer ran off to fetch a superior officer.

"Dog thief? What kind of name is that?" An impish gleam flashed in Glylina's blue eyes.

"Later," Davin said, nodding toward the mounted officer who rode toward them.

Halting beside the swordsman, the lieutenant astride his white courser peered at Davin for a moment, then pulled out a rolled parchment and examined it. "Your name, dog thief?"

"Anane, Davin Anane."

"This is the one Lord Hormachi desires. You have done well. A bonus for the both of you, corporal."

"What of the woman?" The lancer pointed at Glylina with a leer that brimmed with open lust.

"Bring her along, also."

"Keep it hidden," Davin whispered to Glylina as they were rushed along the streets.

Moments later, they entered the palace walls where the swordsman called out, "Captain Cahagnet, prisoners for Lord Hormachi."

"Why would he want to see prisoners? You know our standing orders. Take them to be questioned, then executed." An officer stepped from a guard station just inside the wall.

"The lieutenant said Lord Hormachi wanted his statue returned. I stole it from Vytellion." Davin pulled the fake statue from the sack and held it up for the officer to see.

The man paled. "It *is* the statue. This way. Now, Qar eat your souls, *now*!"

"Amazing how accommodating he became," Glylina said under her breath with a heavy portion of sarcasm.

She shifted the pouch with the statue farther back on her hip to make it less conspicuous as the soldier led them into the palace and a room where Hormachi sat with his generals. Davin noticed the Priest Cal'Dreth at the back of the room.

"There, bow before Lord Hormachi!"

When Davin and Glylina ignored the order, the lancer applied the shaft of his weapon behind their knees, dropping them to the floor. The darkly handsome lord of Gatinah looked up from a table littered with maps and started to curse the intrusion. Then he saw the statue in the captain's hands.

"The dog thief! He did steal it! I knew it, I knew it must be so. Vytellion would never launch such a massive assault against me otherwise." Hormachi grabbed the false statue from his officer's hands and swung back to the table.

"Wait!" cried Davin. "I stole the statue. Lift the curse on me."

"Lift it? Ha!" Hormachi turned, the statue clutched in his hands.

A shadow slid over his face. Anger burst like lightning from a thunderstorm when he rubbed the belly and found not a diamond but a chunk of worthless glass.

"Where is the true statue? Surely, you didn't expect to fool me with this pathetic fraud!'' Hormachi said angrily.

"Remove the curse, and the statue is yours, as we agreed."

"Dog boy, you have grown bold – and stupid. Tell me, dog thief. Tell me now!"

Before Davin muttered a syllable, Hormachi thrust out his right arm, forefinger stabbing at Davin's breast. Sparks traveled back and forth along the mage's hand, then leaped the gulf to Davin's chest. The Jyotian collapsed facedown on the floor as though beset by a fit. Try as he might, Davin could not stem the cries of pain that pushed from his throat when the spellbound fires ignited.

"I deliver this agony now, so you know the futility of lying to me, of trying to cheat me of what is rightfully mine."

Davin's world flowed with red-hot lava. He no longer controlled his body or voice. A thousand hot swords piercing his flesh could not have driven him to this level of pain.

"Tell me what you have done with the statue or I shall activate the white circle. Remember what I told you, dog thief? It will *kill* you. This is merely pain. The white circle will blossom with a thousandfold times the agony, and only when I desire it will you die."

Davin clutched at his body, but the unrelenting pain refused to go away. Through tear-blurred eyes he saw Glylina and read the horror on her face. Try as he did, Davin could not warn the Challing, could not beg her not to weaken.

"End his misery," Glylina spoke. "Stop this madness and I'll deliver the statue."

"No, Glylina, no," Davin's words came in sobs as the white-hot agony receded.

"Where is the statue? The truth or I will kill the dog boy, then begin on you." The ruler-mage turned to the Challing.

"Here." Glylina passed him the pouch.

Lord Hormachi extracted the statue and rubbed at the belly. A slow smile curled his lips. "The real one. The diamond is in this one's belly. The Jewel of Life!"

He cooed and cradled the statue to his breast, like a mother might caress a newborn babe. "Take them both away and let them savor my victory in the privacy of a dungeon cell!"

Strong hands dragged a trembling Davin across the floor.

Glylina rushed to his side. "I could not lose you. To see another Davin Anane die – your chest – I could not bear it."

Davin shook his head weakly. "There is no damage you can see. It is all magical. Where has Hormachi gone with the statue?"

"To a courtyard outside," Glylina said. "I could not see beyond that."

"No talking." As swordsman and lancer dragged Davin into the hallway, a captain of the guard approached with sword drawn.

When the officer poked at the Jyotian to emphasize that he was to remain silent, Davin reacted on instinct rather than intellect. He shifted to the side to let the captain's blade find the floor rather than his belly. At the same time, Davin threw up an arm and rammed two fingers into the officer's eyes to blind the man temporarily.

The captain's yowl of pain spun around both lancer and swordsman – to face Glylina. With a Challing's speed, she struck. Both arms shot out to grab each man by an ear and slam their heads together. There was a sharp crack, two groans and the men fell to the floor unconscious. The staggering captain joined them seconds later when Glylina's balled fist connected solidly with the man's chin.

"Hormachi," Davin gasped when the Challing pulled him to his feet. "We must find Hormachi."

Glylina shifted him around and pointed to an archway that led to the courtyard. "He disappeared through there."

Leaning heavily on his companion, the Jyotian could stand and take shaky steps. "The war drums are close. Listen."

"Outside the city's walls by the sound of them," Glylina agreed as she helped him toward the arch. "How long before the battering rams crack open the gates and Vytellion's armies flood into Gatinah?"

"What's this?" Davin blinked with uncertainty when they reached the arch and stared into the courtyard.

Hormachi stood at the center of the yard with his back to the adventurers, his actions hidden from their eyes. The courtyard itself was decorated with curiously hung strands of silver wire. The wires looped and soared above the ground, running from one wall to the other, forming a coarse metallic net overhead. A large metal pole driven into the middle of the courtyard held an iron cage the size and shape designed to hold a man.

"The statue," whispered Davin, puzzled even more when Hormachi opened the cage. "He put the statue inside the cage."

"And he securely locked it, as though it were a person slated for torture." The shake of Glylina's head said she no more understood what occurred than did Davin.

"Wait! Look!"

When Lord Hormachi moved, he revealed a marble pedestal. On it rested a duplicate statue of the one in the cage. As Hormachi began a low chant, Davin blinked. Green sparks danced along the silver wires above the iron cage and above the pedestal with its statue blazed vivid blue sparks.

"The belly, Anane, the belly! It has a ruby in its gut!"

As Hormachi's spell grew, the ruby in the second statue glowed with an incandescence that forced Davin to avert his head. His eyes fell on the imprisoned statue. The diamond in its belly also glowed, but with lesser intensity.

Glylina started forward, but Davin held his friend back. Both the Challing's eyes danced with the green sparks of witchfire.

Hormachi reached out and slightly turned the statue atop the marble pedestal. A ruby ray blasted from the gemstone in its belly. When the red beam crossed the white light that gleamed from the captive statue, heat erupted in waves that rolled across the courtyard.

"They grow," gasped Davin. "The statues are growing!"

"More, friend Anane," Glylina answered with awe brimming in her voice. "The statues *live!*"

18

Davin stared in disbelief. The statues lived! They swelled with life and transformed into grotesque mockeries of human beings. Above the courtyard the silver cabling crackled with blazing energy. Hormachi's voice rose and fell in a sing-song chant. The cables answered him, whining as power coursed through their weblike strands. Energy, raw and fierce, danced down and brushed the statues of animated soapstone.

The ruby-mounted statue received a jolt of mystical power, then it was the turn of the diamond-adorned one trapped within the iron cage. Over and over, waves of scintillant force shot down to bathe the statues. Lord Hormachi stood to one side, arms crossed on his chest, eyes closed as the magical light bathed him in eerie shadows.

"The statues – Vytellion and Hormachi – they are one and the same," Glylina said beside the Jyotian. "Each gem holds the life of the brother it represents. The diamond is Vytellion and the ruby Hormachi. I can feel it, Davin! I can feel it!"

The Jyotian did not question the Challing's ability to read spells. Glylina's interpretation of what played out before their eyes made sense. Hormachi sought to kill his twin, to end a lifetime of sibling rivalry.

"Stop him," Glylina urged. "We must stop him before his power grows too great!"

"Why?"

Davin failed to see how a feud between brothers was their concern. If Hormachi and Vytellion killed each other that was their affair. Besides, what man would be stupid enough to attempt to enter the nimbus of magicks rolling through the courtyard? Davin had seen similar ward spells cast. A thrust with a steel sword into that cloud would deliver death to the swordsman. A dagger was even worse. The merest touch of hand or body to the oscillating cloud of pure energy would sear beyond endurance.

His hand rose to his chest and the white circle beneath his tunic. Of more importance was removing the fire elemental slumbering within his body.

"Anane, don't you understand?" Glylina's gaze shot to him for an instant, then back to the roiling magicks within the courtyard. "Neither Vytellion nor Hormachi is complete. Each is but half of the other. Should either defeat his twin, the survivor will become a whole – a mage rivaling Zarek Yannis himself – and with a hunger to see the world at his feet. We have to stop Hormachi. He cannot be allowed to kill Vytellion!"

That Davin understood. He had not aided his half-brother Felrad to defeat the mage who had unleashed the Faceless Ones on Raemllyn, only to be the man who unleashed another power-mad wizard on the world.

"See how Vytellion's statue struggles to escape the cage!" Glylina pointed to the iron cage.

Huge muscles rippled and surged on the stony caricature of a human. Stone rang against iron bars and the cage swayed and rocked when the statue pounded hammerlike fists against its prison walls. Rocky fingers curled about the bars and bent them, but the cage held. Vytellion's statue, for all its strength and fury, remained securely imprisoned.

Davin's hand slipped the dirk on his hip from its sheath. Hormachi must be stopped without killing him. To end the Gatinahese lord's life would only give rise to a power-hungry Vytellion. A well-placed blade in shoulder or thigh should be enough to end Hormachi's chant and break the spell he wove.

The Jyotian's arm wrenched back, then shot forward. The dagger flew from his fingertips in a lazy spin straight for the ruler-mage's thigh. The tip embedded in the fog swirling around Hormachi – and stopped in its flight. Just inches from its target, the dagger hung in the air and began to quiver. Like a metal pole attracts lightning in a thunderstorm, the blade became a lodestone to the bolts of magical energy that coursed through the metal web stretched above the courtyard. A single spark arced to the dirk, then two, four and finally a torrent of energy rained down the silver wires to leap to the dagger.

It exploded in a cloud of burning steel and smoke.

Davin threw up his hands to protect his face. Molten metal

spattered him, burning his hands and setting his tunic to smoldering. He slapped out the spots before he ignited like a torch.

Hormachi continued his chant without so much as a blink of an eye to indicate he had noticed the attack.

"Fool!" A taunting voice cried out behind the pair of adventurers. "You cannot stop Hormachi now! Vytellion's power will be his soon! Then all Upper and Lower Raemllyn will bow to him. And I *will* share in that glory as no other priest before me has done!"

Davin whirled to see Cal'Dreth charge with sword raised high above his head as another man might wield a battle-axe. The Jyotian's hand dropped to his sword hilt.

There was no need to draw the weapon. Glylina's blade leaped from its sheath and struck in a wide arc. The priest of Gatinah's Brotherhood of Thieves died as his head flew from his shoulders amid a spray of fountaining crimson.

"Another advantage to this form," the Challing said as she bent to wipe her sword on the robes of the still quivering priest. "Human males refuse to view a female as a physical threat. It is a stupid trait."

"A deadly trait," Davin agreed as he turned back to the courtyard, feeling little regret that his companion had robbed him of the priest's life.

Hormachi's statue now crouched on the pedestal like a hunting cat. And like a feline it leaped from its perch. Flagstones shattered beneath its immense weight when it struck the ground. It balled stone fists and opened its mouth as though screaming dark fury into the face of a frightened world, but no sound issued from that gaping maw. Blind eyes turned toward Vytellion's statue that now kicked at the bars in a vain attempt to break free.

The ruby in the belly of Hormachi's statue radiated a brilliant light as it waddled ponderously toward the iron cage. The fury of Vytellion's statue redoubled as it twisted, turned and spun in what appeared an attempt to sever the cord of light binding it to the silver web. No matter how wildly it maneuvered, it could not break the unholy bond.

Umbilical cords! Davin could not escape the vision that filled his eyes. The statues were joined by umbilicals of light, one white and the other ruby red. The courtyard had become the womb for these twin demons of stone. No matter how it swung in the cage, Vytellion's statue could not tear itself free of the unholy bond at its belly.

Hormachi's statue halted before the cage. Again, its stone maw stretched wide, giving it the aspect of a tombstone above an open grave. It pounded fists the size of boulders against the iron cage. A ringing like a bell sounded throughout the palace. With the peal came the grinding of stone.

"The mere vibration of the attack has cracked Vytellion's arm!"

Davin did not correct the Challing. He, too, saw the animated monsters of rock as the personification of the two mages. Nor could he help but see the fracture that appeared near the left wrist of Vytellion's statue.

"Vytellion!" Glylina spun to face her companion. "Davin, we must find Vytellion. If there is one who can stop Hormachi, it will be the lord of Ohnuhn."

"And lose our heads in the process!" Davin shook his head. "We'd only jump from one dragon's mouth into another."

"This dragon's mouth means certain death. Better to try another!"

Her slender fingers closed around his right arm like a steel vice. Without warning, she ran from the palace, dragging the Jyotian behind her.

"Where do we go?" Glylina asked as she scanned the wall of the city that lay across the open avenue from the alley in which they huddled. "I see no portal leading out of Gatinah."

"Look at the street, not the wall." Davin's head twisted when the booming of a battering ram against the north gate resounded over the city. An instant later, the pounding echoed from the east and then the west. "Vytellion's commanders mount an assault on all of Gatinah's gates."

"Even if they breach the gates, they will not reach Hormachi before it is too late. Anane, I see . . ." She suddenly swallowed her words. "No, Anane. Not the manhole. You don't intend us to enter the sewer?"

Davin shrugged and smiled sheepishly. "All Gatinah's sewers join at that point. A single main tunnel then flows into the sea.

THE JEWELS OF LIFE

Whoever built these walls was wise. Only this tunnel undermines the wall. No invaders can enter. But we can exit."

Glylina wrinkled her nose in obvious disdain. "Why is it that you have such an affinity for city sewers? Perhaps in mankind's lost past the Anane line descended from sewer rats and you merely . . ."

The Challing's head jerked around and she stared at the Jyotian in horror. "Sea? You said sea, didn't you?"

Davin nodded.

"That means that we will . . ."

"Have to swim our way along the wall," the last son of the House of Anane completed her sentence.

"Anane, walking waist-deep in offal is bad enough, but plunging into a river of sh—"

Davin gave her no further opportunity to protest. He darted from the alley, ran to the manhole, and lifting the grating, edged it aside. He was halfway into the hole when the Challing ran to his side, cursing his name with every breath she took.

"Don't worry," Davin said as he moved down the ladder embedded in the wall of the tunnel, "this cannot go much— aiiieee!"

A rusted rung gave way beneath his hand. He fell, belly flopping into a slime pool afloat with the waste of a city. Twisting to his back, he gasped for air and called out, "Glylina, take care. The ladder is . . ."

Too late! The Challing tumbled from above, splashing into the ocean of muck. When her head bobbed to the surface, hatred glared in her sapphire eyes.

"Thank you for the timely warning, friend Anane." She twisted around in the pool in an attempt to get her bearings. "One day, I will repay your kindness in triple weight!"

"This way," the Jyotian said, ignoring her. "There is a light in the distance."

Refusing to give names to the dark things floating in the water around him, Davin employed a breaststroke to carry him beneath Gatinah's wall to an iron grating that covered the mouth of the sewer tunnel where it finally met the sea.

"I hadn't expected this." He turned to the Challing as she reached his side.

Glylina reached out, grasped the grating and wrenched. The iron bars tore away as though they were mere paper in her hand.

"The grating was as rusty as the ladder." She tore a wider hole and swam through.

Both Jyotian and Challing made good use of the fresh seawater beyond the flow of sewage to wash away the filth and stench left by their visit to subterranean Gatinah as they swam toward a rocky beach beyond the city's walled harbor.

"I suggest we move along the coast until we are far behind Vytellion's lines, then approach his forces from the rear," Glylina said, pulling herself from the water. "I don't think a frontal approach would gain us anything but a dozen arrows in the chest."

"Agreed." Davin reached a boulder and sought a handhold but found none. "Think you could help me from the water?"

"After this little swim, Anane, I should let you . . ."

The Challing's words drowned in a strangled gurgle!

Davin's head snapped up. Glylina's hands clawed at a dark line that encircled her slender neck.

The Jyotian's fingers found purchase on the slippery boulder. He heaved himself upward onto the stone. As he scrambled to his knees, his hand dropped to his sword.

Steel never slid free of sheath. Davin froze when a sword tip nipped at his throat.

"If you value your life, don't move," a man's voice coldly ordered.

19

As the seawater cleared from his eyes, Davin saw the voice's owner – and the three other men cloaked entirely in black.

"Hormachi's spies, if I ever saw any, Captain Mech'Alas," said a man behind the one with the sword to Davin's throat. "Came out of the sewer we was headed for, I'd bet."

"You'd lose your bet." Davin forced himself to reply. "Just as you'll lose your life if you don't release her very quickly."

As though to emphasize the Jyotian's words, Glylina's fingers wriggled beneath the garrote about her neck. With a single yank, the Challing snapped the cord. In the bat of an eye, she pivoted, grasped the man behind her by the neck, hoisted him into the air with her left hand while freeing her sword with her right. The woman's blade leveled at Captain Mech'Alas.

"We are spies, Captain," Glylina said without a quaver in her voice. "But we serve Vytellion, *not* Hormachi. We would be honored, if you and your men would escort us to our lord's tent. We have located the statue he seeks."

"Captain, if you desire a victory over Gatinah, you *must* take us to Lord Vytellion immediately." Davin edged the sword tip from his throat with the side of his hand.

"He has nightmares," the captain said obliquely. "He murmurs of a stolen statue."

"We were to enter Gatinah and kill Hormachi!" protested a soldier. "It'll be our heads if . . ."

"Vytellion will die if you do not take us to him. The statue, Captain, the statue is the key to the war," Glylina interrupted. "Without it, *he* will die. Without it, *all* of us will die!"

Mech'Alas lowered his sword. The man nodded. "Will you surrender your weapons?"

"In the middle of a war, we'd rather not," Davin answered, "but if that's what it takes to see Lord Vytellion, then take our blades."

Glylina shot him a glance meant to kill but said nothing. Her own sword returned to its sheath, and she carefully deposited the dangling soldier on the ground. When she began to unstrap the longsword, the captain shook his head and said:

"That you are willing is enough. Come, I'll lead you to Vytellion's camp."

Although the captain's words displayed trust, Davin noted that the three under his command remained at Glylina's and his back when they moved into the night. *Perhaps a bit too trusting*, Davin thought, *but Captain Mech'Alas is no fool.*

"Hail, Lord Vytellion!" cried the captain, closing his left hand and bringing it to his heart.

For a moment, Davin did not recognize the lord of Ohnuhn. He had seen him for only a few seconds and under less than ideal conditions, but there was no denying he was Hormachi's twin. In the space of four days Vytellion had aged as though decades had ravaged his body. His hair now flowed white and deep wrinkles creased his face. His hand, raised to dismiss his officer, shook with a palsy and when he moved it was with the hesitant step of an old man.

"The statue," he gasped. "Have you seen it?" Vytellion squinted as though his eyesight failed him.

If Ohnuhn's lord recognized him, Davin saw no indication of it in the ruler's face. He silently thanked Glylina for the close-cropped haircut given aboard the *Windsong*. "He holds it captive in an iron cage within his palace, while a statue with a ruby in its belly attacks it."

"Cracks develop in the diamond-bearing statue whenever Hormachi's stone champion strikes it," Glylina added. "The magicks permeating Hormachi's palace are extreme, disorienting, deadly. No ordinary man can penetrate them."

"You *have* seen it. You know what happens to it – to me! Don't you?" He paced nervously, bringing serving girls to quiet his agitation. Vytellion pushed them away. "Our mother did this to me. I never asked to be bound to the statue. Now Hormachi seeks to devour my power as he drains away my life!"

Had the tables been switched, Davin was certain Glylina and he would now be standing before Hormachi. What mattered was stopping Hormachi – and the canceling of the power of his white circle. "A favor for a favor, Lord Vytellion. I can lead you to Hormachi and the statues. In exchange, I need this removed."

Davin opened his shirt to display Hormachi's magic circle.

"You bargain with me?" Vytellion turned fiery eyes on Davin. His hand raised as if to throw a lightning bolt, but the shaking increased and the Ohnuhnian lord lowered it, suddenly powerless to continue his spell.

"I do bargain with you," Davin pressed his position. "You need to stop Hormachi. To do that, you must confront him inside his palace. I know the way inside."

"We can torture the information from you," Vytellion pointed out, taking some delight in the possibility.

"Before I reveal the path, you will be dead. How long can you survive? Do you weaken hourly? Minute by minute? I have seen the spells Hormachi casts and the way the two stone statues battle. The time cannot be long before yours crumbles beneath the assault."

"Describe what you have seen. Wait!" Vytellion cried. He then turned to Captain Mech'Alas. "Take the woman outside, out of hearing. Have they spoken of this to one another since you captured them?"

"No, Lord," confirmed the captain.

The officer herded Glylina from the tent while Davin described the dangling silver wires and the green and blue sparks jumping from them to each statue. When he described the umbilicals of light and how the red slowly pushed down the cord so that less and less of the diamond-white light showed, Vytellion shuddered as if taken with a fever.

"Enough. Be quiet. Turn from your friend. Move and you die on the spot." Vytellion ordered Glylina brought back. When the Challing's story confirmed all Davin had said, the rapidly aging lord of Ohnuhn dismissed his captain.

"But, sire, this is most dangerous. You cannot trust these two . . ."

"I can and will,' Vytellion said. Then turning to the Jyotian, "Now, give me directions to reach my brother. You have learned much."

Too much for your taste, Davin thought. He knew treachery lay within both brothers' breasts. For them, Glylina and he were merely coins to be spent as they saw fit.

"Hormachi's fire elemental," Davin pointed to his chest. "Remove it from my flesh."

"The spell is a complex one and I must have my statue back before I can unweave what my brother has created. As you can see, my strength fails me with each fleeing second. When the statue is again mine, my powers will return," Vytellion answered.

Before Davin could reply, Glylina spoke up, "A guarantee, milord, we need a guarantee. What reason is there to believe you will aid my friend in lifting the curse?"

"None," Vytellion said. "But remember, you came to me with this information. I reward those who help me. I punish those who oppose me." In a lower voice, he muttered, "Like my Qar-damned brother!"

"We must reach Hormachi before dawn," Davin said, estimating four hours of darkness remained before sunrise. "How many guardsmen will accompany us? The fewer who accompany us, the faster we can travel."

"I must come. And Captain Mech'Alas with two of his men. There is no need for more."

"Good," Davin answered, realizing the guardsmen would be needed to carry Vytellion before they reached the palace. "Captain, we must return to where you found us. The sewer tunnel is the only way back into the city."

Davin ignored the low growl that rumbled in Glylina's throat at the prospect of retracing their steps. The Jyotian silently cursed. He trusted Vytellion no more than Hormachi – and the deadly white circle still remained on his chest. He had to find some hold over Vytellion, no matter how tenuous.

Less than two hours before daybreak they came to the open palace gates. With Hormachi's forces manning the city walls, only two soldiers guarded the entrance. These sat with backs to wall, dozing.

Davin signaled Mech'Alas and pointed to the guards.

In the next instant, three deadly shadows fluttered across the broad street leading into the palace. Davin watched the captain and his two men quickly and quietly dispatch the unwary guardsmen. The job completed, they waved for the others to join them.

"Are you strong enough to face your brother?" Glylina asked as she half carried Vytellion to the gate.

"I will be," Vytellion wheezed.

Davin was not certain the Ohnuhnian was rational. In the short distance from the drainage pipe to the palace, Vytellion had aged another ten years. Hormachi's magical assault took its toll with each passing moment. Davin had seen corpses on funeral pyres that looked more alive than Vytellion.

No guard challenged them as they entered the palace and hastened toward the courtyard where Hormachi weaved his spells. The stillness of the hallways and rooms seeped into Davin to form a tight knot of dread.

Magicks, he realized, were the source of that sense of doom rather than the stillness. The very fabric of space filled with the potent spells and chants. An electric tension of magic filled every nook and cranny of the palace.

"There!" Davin pointed to the arch that opened onto the courtyard where Hormachi cast his spells.

A pale glow emanated from the entryway. Davin edged closer and peered at the silver cables aglow with blue and green sparks. A gut-churning hum constantly sang from the vibrating web of silver. Hormachi, his back to the arch, appeared oblivious to the energies coursing through the glowing strands.

"Yes, yes!" Vytellion pushed past the Jyotian. "Attend me, Captain. You have your instructions."

Vytellion boldly strode forward with a surprising display of strength. Glylina's and Davin's hands dropped to their sword hilts, expecting Mech'Alas and his men to attack. Instead, the captain and the two guards formed a wedge behind their leader when he entered the courtyard.

"He burns!" Davin exclaimed as glaring light exploded about Vytellion.

"Nay!" Glylina's eyes sparked with green witchfire. "He shields himself with a spell, as does Hormachi."

Davin saw that now. Both brothers bathed in light of constantly shifting hues. It was as if the radiance took shape and solidified into a cloud about each. Both men were cloaked in a morning mist, their forms but shadows in clouds.

"Your time has run its course, brother." Vytellion's voice rose above the hum of flowing energies. "I was always the better mage. Now I shall prove it!"

A ball of white-hot fire erupted from Vytellion's fingers and merged with the glowing nimbus surrounding Hormachi. The Gatinahese lord staggered forward, then whirled around.

"Vytellion, how?" Shock filled Hormachi's voice. He had been lost in watching the ruby-bellied statue destroy its diamond twin and had not noticed his brother's approach.

"You stole my life, Hormachi. You must die for this impertinence. We could have shared the power our mother bestowed on us, but you grew too greedy."

The silver net above the courtyard quaked then flared in exploding light. Molten silver rained from above. If magicks danced between the two cloud-enshrouded brothers, Davin could not discern them. He did see the mages grapple physically, arms circling each other.

Simultaneously, Mech'Alas and his men surged forward in an attempt to free the statue from the iron cage. Two of the men died as hammering fists of stone shattered their skulls like overripe melons. Hormachi's ruby statue stood defiantly before the iron prison, facing Captain Mech'Alas.

Sword in hand, the officer lunged. The tip of his blade skidded off stone in a shower of red sparks. He wrenched back and drove the sword at the ruby gemstone mounted in the belly of the living rock. Another shower of fat red sparks flared as the sword evaporated in a cloud of steam.

Then all Mech'Alas could do was scream. Those stone arms encircled him and crushed the life from his body. When the ruby statue released the mangled form that had once been a man, it turned and resumed pummeling the iron cage with its fists.

Neither Hormachi nor Vytellion noticed the three deaths. The twin mages now rolled on the ground, their magical clouds intermingling to form a black miasma about them.

"They are killing each other!" Glylina's gaze darted about as though seeking something – anything – to end the siblings' struggle.

As did Davin! Without the mages, there was no way to pluck the sleeping fire elemental from his body. There was nothing he could do but watch.

Hormachi and Vytellion were oblivious to all but their own private battle. Black vapors rose from the dark cloud surrounding them like tendrils of Qar's own breath. Whatever the blackness touched, dissolved. Like acid it ate into stone and metal!

"The gods be damned!"

Glylina charged into the courtyard, a war cry tearing from her throat. Three strides from Hormachi's statue, the ruby-bellied creature dealt Vytellion's statue the final blow. From stony lips hitherto silent came a shrill keening that rent the predawn morning.

And when that death cry ended, so did Vytellion's statue. Like sun-dried grains of a sandcastle, it disintegrated, crumbling into a pile of dust.

From the corner of his eye, Davin saw the statue's flesh and blood counterpart weaken. The dark cloud about him vanished, leaving the mage on his back, arms weakly flailing the air. Then the arms stopped and fell to the ground, never to move again.

Beside his dead brother, Hormachi pushed to his feet when the nimbus about him winked out. The mage's stance was hardly triumphant. The battle had cost him dearly. No longer young and handsome, he stood bent and crippled by the assault of countless years that had passed in the space of seconds.

Another war cry jerked Davin's head back to Glylina. With shoulder lowered, the Challing rammed full speed into Hormachi's statue. A grunt ripped from Glylina's lips when she rebounded off the living stone and took a shaky step away from the rocky monster.

Rather than retreat, Glylina charged again. She ducked beneath the rock arms that reached out to ensnare her and grasped the ruby embedded in the creature's belly. The Challing's face strained red as she wrenched at the gem with all her otherworldly strength.

The ruby popped free.

A new screeching filled the courtyard, this time from Hormachi's statue.

Davin rushed to the iron cage and reached inside to sift through the gray dust piled within. His fingers closed on the large diamond. He drew it from the cage.

"The figure cannot move without the ruby," Glylina called, waving him to her side.

The Challing snatched the diamond from Davin's hand and held them in her palms. The twin jewels pulsated with a life of their own.

"What have you done?' Hormachi forced himself to take a step forward, nearly tripping over his twin's withered corpse. "You are killing me. Give me the ruby. Give it to me! It must be returned to the statue!"

"Remove the curse," Glylina said without a blink of her witchfire burning eyes. "Lift the curse from Davin and the stones are yours!"

"I'll see you in Peyneeha first! Every one of Qar's demons will gnaw your body for all eternity. Your eyes will be plucked out! Your paps will be cut away to be used as money pouches by Yu-Vatruk. And the dog boy will die, that I promise you. He'll know the flames of hell before he knows an end to life!"

Spittle dripped from the corners of Hormachi's mouth with each word he uttered. Like a man weighted by passing years, his shoulders bent and shrank inward. His hands turned to skeletal twigs and flesh transformed to cracked leather across his body.

"The statue. My life was in that statue. I could never die, never, never. Our mother promised us that. It was her gift."

Lord Hormachi fell facedown on the courtyard. As fog swirls above a swamp so did his life essence withdraw from his body, leaving behind only a mummified corpse.

"Were they invincible as long as the jewels of life rode in their statues?" asked Davin.

Glylina had no answer. She lowered the pulsing jewels and stared at them.

Davin touched the deadly white circle that remained on his chest. "How do I escape the fire elemental now?"

To this Glylina had no answer either.

20

"Glylina," Davin whispered softly into the ear of his companion, "do you really think we can trust someone named Kobin the Slaag? Just look at him!"

The Challing did, her head tilting from side to side as she scrutinized the ancient wizard. Kobin the Slaag did not wear the cloak of prosperity one expected of mages who reached his obvious age – at least was expected of sorcerers competent in their craft. Kobin's robes were pieced together from rags discarded by Gatinah's most destitute beggars. So threadbare was his clothing, that when he walked before the single window in his one-room home, the scrawny shadow of his body was more than apparent beneath the robe.

Although Kobin retained both teeth and hair, the former were riddled with dark decay and the latter was dull white stained a dirty yellow from the fumes of virulent reagents. That hair was also in such tangle more than one bird might have built its nest there.

Glylina's gaze shifted from the wizard bent over the time-yellowed pages of a grimoire to the Jyotian, and shrugged. "It's either him or the fire elemental."

Like her counterpart, Goran One-Eye, the Challing's casual acceptance of the dangers that did not affect her was irritating, Davin thought. What she said was also infuriatingly correct. In the week since the deaths of Vytellion and Hormachi, the Jyotian had visited every mage, witch, wizard and sorcerer within Gatinah's walls seeking one with the power needed to remove the fire demon Hormachi had implanted in his flesh.

More than one of the magicians declared the removal of the fire elemental was a simple task. However, none could guarantee that the last son of the House of Anane would survive the extraction. In fact, most felt he would not.

"Yes!" Kobin cackled with delight, rubbed his hands together and did a little shuffling dance. "I thought I recognized

Faitita's work. Even after all these years, I can remember how beautiful she was. Stole my heart away she did, which is why I became her apprentice rather than studying under Ho'Gar the White."

"The man's lost his mind," Davin whispered, attempting to stem the tide of rising desperation that swelled within him. Mere hours remained before Hormachi's hex reached its final deadly stage.

"Son," Kobin said as he looked as Davin, "was it Vytellion or Hormachi who painted you like an archer's target?"

"Hormachi."

"It is as I thought. Never liked either of the bastards, both had a mean streak as wide as Diamond Street in them, you know. But Hormachi was always a mite nastier. Used to torment me with all sorts of tricks and pranks when I worked with his mother."

"Can you free the fire elemental, old one?" Glylina pressed. "Free it without killing Anane?"

Kobin the Slaag grinned widely to expose his rotting teeth. "Me? Not me. In all my years, I could never match the spells Faitita wove. The woman was magnificent! Her crowning achievement was creating the Jewels of Life. They were meant to give those two good-for-nothing sons of hers eternal life. Would have, too, if the useless mongrels hadn't been so jealous of one another."

"Then you can't help me?" Davin's last hope crashed down on him like a granite mountain.

"Didn't say that," Kobin answered, "but you and the pretty one have the answer in your pouches. Have had it all along. Felt the power the moment you walked through my door." Kobin paused and eyed Glylina carefully. He smiled. "Only seen three other Challings in all my days, but never one as beautiful as you, my dear. Have you ever considered an apprenticeship to an aging mage?"

"You recognize me as a Challing?" Glylina's head snapped back and her sapphire eyes went wide.

"Once you've seen a Challing, it's an easy thing to do." Kobin continued to grin. "Faitita brought the first one I ever saw from your world. He – she – it remained only a few hours before slipping back to its own world. But, oh, the marvelous shapes it assumed! Nothing as beautiful as your own, you understand, but quite marvelous. The second Challing . . ."

"You said Glylina can remove the fire elemental?" Davin pressed, unwilling to listen to the old wizard's senile reminiscences of the shape-shifters he had known.

"What? Oh!" Kobin blinked and looked at the Jyotian. "The Jewels of Life, my boy. Everything that was Vytellion and Hormachi Faitita wove into those two pieces of quartz. It's right there in her old grimoire." He cackled again. "What those two bastards would have given to get their hands on that tome. Never figured out it was me that stole it the night their mother died."

"The diamond and ruby?" Glylina asked. "The ones from Vytellion's and Hormachi's statues?"

"Ain't gems, my lovely, just chunks of worthless quartz. It's the power that's in 'em that makes them appear valuable," Kobin answered. "Faitita knew her sons. She sealed their powers in those rocks."

Glylina extracted the pulsating ruby from the leather pouch tied to her belt. "How do I use it?"

Kobin signaled for Davin to pull the diamond from his own pouch. "Give it to the pretty one, but don't let them touch. Now take off your tunic."

When Davin did, Kobin directed Glylina to place one stone atop the white circle and the other directly in line with it on his back.

"That's all there is to it?" Glylina asked as she did as he said.

"The Jewels hold all the magicks that were Hormachi and Vytellion," Kobin explained. "Faitita knew her sons well. She designed the Jewels so, should either Vytellion or Hormachi ever kill the other and gain his brother's stone, the two Jewels would eventually cancel each other."

"Ouch!" Davin yelped as he felt a needle prick begin at his back and shoot through his body.

A burning point of white light jumped from his chest, darted about the room like a firefly, then shot to the single window, burning a hole through the glass as it escaped.

Kobin cackled again. "Damn thing didn't want to be inside you any more than you wanted him there!"

"That's it?" Davin stared down as Glylina removed the stones. "But the white circle remains."

"Brush it off, son," Kobin ordered. "Ain't nothing but dried plant."

Davin did. Like dust, the white fell from his skin. A grin of pure relief mixed with amazement spread across his face. "It's gone. Hormachi's curse is gone! And I'm still alive!"

"What else did you expect?" Kobin shrugged as though the scene that had unfolded was no more important than an ale cart rolling by on the street outside.

"The stones – they've died." Glylina held out two pieces of dull quartz in her palms. Neither rock pulsed or glowed.

Again the wizard shrugged. "It's as Faitita planned. They canceled each other."

Davin could barely contain the rush of life that coursed through his body. He felt like a child who wanted nothing more than to run wildly down the street just to experience the sheer joy of running, breathing and living.

"Your price, old one?" Glylina asked. "You never mentioned a price for your help."

"Didn't do anything," Kobin replied with a shake of his head. "It was you that done all the work. But if I could have them rocks, I'd like to keep them. They remind me of Faitita. She really was a magnificent woman. If only I'd been her equal." He shook his unruly head in true sadness.

Glylina passed the two lifeless pieces of quartz to the mage, then leaned forward and kissed the single tear that trickled down his wrinkle-lined cheek. When she started to straighten, the wizard touched her shoulder and pressed his lips to her ear, whispering insistently.

"Thank you, old one," she said softly when Kobin eased away. She reached into a pocket to withdraw ten golden bists. Glylina placed the coins on a table. "It is as much as I suspected."

With that she turned and motioned to Davin. "Come, we have intruded on this good father long enough."

Davin bowed to the wizard, bade him thank you again, and trotted after the Challing as she left the small one-room house.

Outside, the Jyotian grabbed her by the shoulders, spun her about and planted a loud, smacking kiss on her lips.

Glylina's head jerked back in surprise, but a smile rode on her lips. "What was that for?"

"Because I'm still alive. Because it was you who saved me from two mad mages. *Because I'm alive!*" Davin looked down at his bare chest, then donned his tunic. "It is gone! It is really gone!"

For an instant Glylina's smile grew, then merely hung on her lips with a touch of sadness.

Davin stared at her in disbelief. "What is wrong? This eve is a time for celebration. Listen! Can you hear the trumpets? There must be a festival in the center of the city." Abruptly Davin fell silent. The Challing's thoughts wandered a distant path, far from the here and now. "Is it something the wizard said to you?"

Glylina nibbled thoughtfully at her lower lip. "He warned me that each day I walk Raemllyn's soil I grow more human, that with the passage of time I will eventually cease to be a Challing."

"Did he say when?" Davin could only guess at the conflict that now raged within his friend's mind.

Glylina shook her head.

"You said you chose to live in this world," Davin said. "Is the prospect of one day becoming human so abhorrent to you?"

Her head moved slowly from side to side. "I don't know. I have never desired to return to Gohwohn. But I have never considered being anything but what I am."

Davin said nothing as they idly strolled down Gatinah's avenues, moving toward the blare of the trumpets. He wanted to say something to comfort her, but the words that filled his mind were those of a human. How could they soothe one faced with losing all that she was?

"Kobin said more," Glylina eventually spoke. "He said I should follow my heart, that it was the only guide that would serve me true."

Davin reached out and rested a hand on her shoulder. "And where does your heart point?"

"To Kavindra," she said without hesitation. "The only thing I am certain of is that your son's – I mean Aarrin's – life is in danger, and I must save him."

"With me at your side," Davin assured her.

The smile returned to her face. "For now, that is enough, friend Anane. The harbor master announced this morning that ships awaiting port will be allowed to enter the harbor in the morn. When the *Windsong* docks, we shall load supplies and sail for Kavindra."

"Better than walking there," Davin answered with a grin. "And until the morning?"

Glylina extracted a handful of bists from a pocket. "I believe this should be enough to buy a feast and an ocean of wine to celebrate that you still live, Anane."

Davin's grin spread from ear to ear. "Glylina, you are a woman out to win my heart!"

The Jyotian did not have time to question the fleeting shadow of doubt he saw flicker across his companion's face. When they rounded a corner, they found themselves amid a flock of people lining a broad avenue.

"It seems we've found the festival," Davin said. "Or at least a parade."

"I believe procession would be a better term." Glylina nodded to the ranks and files of Gatinahese guardsmen marching with military precision down the avenue toward the palace.

"Another lord for the city? How many does this make so far?"

"Three coups," Glylina said, laughing. "Three rulers on the throne of Gatinah in less than a week – and now a fourth. 'Tis a pity Lady Ellea did not last longer than her coronation, though it is always nice seeing an adroit assassin at work."

Davin shivered. Glylina's cold-blooded remark said that she remained more Challing than human. "Gatinah's blue-bloods maneuver like vultures, each ready for the largest piece of the rotting meat."

"Not this time. See the carriage? A farmer rides inside," Glylina said. "The city guard has thrown their support to Harrel the Brown."

"A common-born man? A grower of carrots?" Davin shook his head. "It will never work. He'll awake within three days to find his throat slit from ear to ear."

"It is said Harrel alone convinced the Ohnuhnian armies to

withdraw from Gatinah's walls before a full war broke out,"
Glylina replied. "And who is to say a commoner can't rule with a
just hand? If he has the support of the people, what else does he
need?"

"Nonsense. The gods themselves ordained the royal houses."
Davin could not comprehend the possibility of a commoner at the
reins of a city-state. "Mark my words, this Harrel will last no
more than a week."

"Perhaps," Glylina agreed. "Still, what happens this day in
Gatinah is a novel idea, if nothing else."

"Few in Upper or Lower Raemllyn care much for novel . . ."
The Jyotian's sentence ended in a strangled sputtering.

"Anane? What is it?"

"The carriage!" Davin managed to choke out. His finger
stabbed toward the passing royal carriage in which Hormachi had
once ridden.

"Aye," Glylina said with a nod. "It's Harrel within, waving at
the people. Listen how they cheer him. I think his reign might be
longer than you expect, Anane."

Davin's head waggled from side to side. "Not the farmer! The
dogs!"

Glylina looked again and saw the six midnight black hounds
that rode in the carriage with Harrel the Brown. "His pets. So
what? There is nothing wrong with a man loving animals."

"Nothing wrong? You see nothing wrong!" Davin still sputtered, unable to believe his eyes. "Those are my pups, not his. *I*
trained those dogs. They belong to me. How could . . ."

Suddenly, Glylina threw back her head and roared with laughter. "Friend Anane, the Sitala cast their dice in mysterious ways.
It is all too apparent that your hounds – and the treasure they
carried – have found a new master!"

Davin stared, his head moving from side to side. He now
understood how this Harrel the Brown convinced the Ohnuhnian
forces to withdraw. The farmer had paid them off with jewels
taken from Aotesja's shop the night Hormachi had implanted in
the Jyotian thief a fire elemental.

"Come, Anane, there's no need to waste tears over what
cannot be changed." Glylina waved toward a nearby tavern. "It's
time to begin our celebration!"

"But I can't let him get away with this. Those gems are mine! He's nothing but a farmer. I worked long and hard for them. I can't . . ."

"But you can, friend Anane, you can!"

Glylina encircled Davin's waist with a graceful arm, nearly lifting him from his feet as she escorted him toward a promised feast and an ocean of wine.